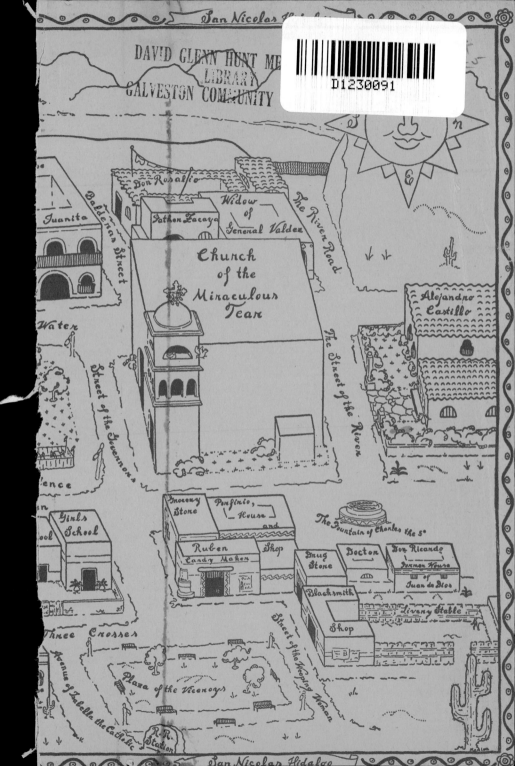

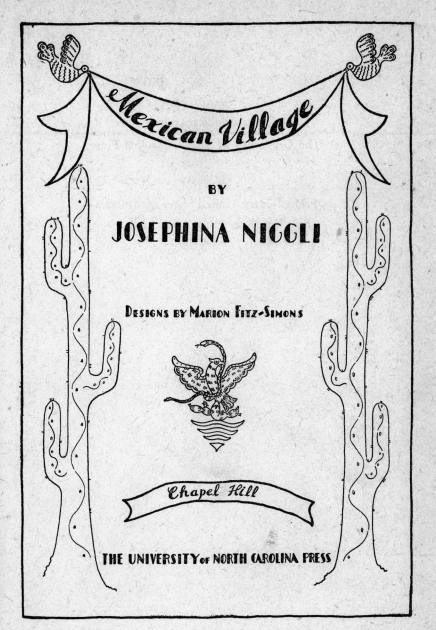

Mexican Village

BY

JOSEPHINA NIGGLI

DESIGNS BY MARION FITZ-SIMONS

Chapel Hill

THE UNIVERSITY OF NORTH CAROLINA PRESS

For

My Father and my Grandmother

CONTENTS

vii

CONTENTS

vii

THE CHARACTERS

THE PEOPLE OF HIDALGO

ALEJANDRO CASTILLO, youngest son of the valley's richest man

ALONSO, the orchestra leader

ALMA ORONA, the laundress. In love with PORFIRIO

ANDRES TREVIÑO, an owner of goats

ANITA O'MALLEY, the dancer

ANSELMO, the quarry foreman

CABALLO BLANCO, a bandit executed in 1873. Real name: DANIEL MENENDEZ

CANDELARIA of the quarry. Daughter of DON ANSELMO

CARLOS ORONA, father of ALMA

CHELA, the homeliest girl in the valley. Daughter of DON NACHO

DIADEMA, housekeeper to FATHER ZACAYA

DIONISIO, proprietor of the Saloon of the Devil's Laughter

DOROTEO LOZANO, a farmer from across the river

ERNESTO, the alcalde 2, who does all the work that DON NACHO, as alcalde 1, does not want to do

EVITA CANTU, wife of ALEJANDRO CASTILLO

FELA, great lady of the village

FIDENCIO, the blacksmith

FLORINDA, daughter of the civil judge. Engaged to XAVIER

ix

GENARO, the civil judge

GITANILLO, son of RUBEN

HILARIO CAMPOS, of the quarry. The father of four children

ISAAC, the grocer

JOAQUIN CASTILLO, who left the valley long ago

JUANITA PEREZ, the boardinghouse keeper

MARIA DE LAS GARZAS, the beautiful outcast of the River Road

MARILIRIA, wife of DON NACHO

MARTINIANO CANTU, father of EVITA

NACHO, mayor of Hidalgo, and father of CHELA

NENA SANTOS, engaged to ANDRES TREVIÑO

NIMFA, the herb woman and town witch

PABLO, the goatherd, feared by the valley

PEPE GONZALEZ, the wild boy of the village

PORFIRIO, the carver of wood

RICARDO, the one-armed policeman

ROMOLO BALDERAS, the Republic's greatest historian, who was born in Hidalgo and died in San Juan Iglesias

ROSALIO, one of the four rulers of Hidalgo

RUBEN, the maker of candy

SATURNINO CASTILLO, the richest man in the valley. Father of JOAQUIN and ALEJANDRO

SERAPIO, the town gardener. Uncle to XAVIER

TERESITA, the seamstress. Aunt to ROSAURA MALDONADO

TIA MAGDALENA, an eagle witch. Housekeeper to BOB WEBSTER

TIMOTEO GONZALEZ, the cheese maker. Father of Pepe

TRIUMFA, mother of ALMA ORONA

URSULO, who died in 1922

WIDOW VALDEZ, who began life in Hidalgo as ANITA O'MALLEY

XAVIER, the lover of horses

THE PEOPLE OF SAN JUAN IGLESIAS

MATIAS GALINDO, a fine horseman

ROMEO CALDERON, owner of the finest cocks on the frontier

SARITA, daughter of DON ROMEO

TIO DANIEL, the village wise man

THE OUTLANDERS

ABEL, the *arabe* trader, who supplies the two valleys with a movable drygoods store

BALTASAR, a soldier who rolls the eye at FLORINDA

BOB WEBSTER, the quarry master

CARDITO, the village invalid. Father of LOLA

FATHER ZACAYA, the village priest

GENERAL ELIZONDO, who comes to Hidalgo to catch a goat thief

JUAN O'MALLEY, the Irish father of ANITA O'MALLEY

LITTLE DOCTOR, a ruler of the valley

LOLITA, wife of RUBEN, the candy-maker

PORFIRIO DIAZ AAH, the school teacher from Michoacán

ROSAURA MALDONADO, from Monterrey. Niece of DOÑA TERESITA

RUBIO, a Revolutionary captain

SALVADOR SANCHEZ, a horseman from El Carmen

SAUCEDA, an itinerant photographer from Monterrey

VISITORS TO HIDALGO

PABLO GOMEZ, friend of ALEJANDRO CASTILLO from Monterrey

RICARDO MANCHACA
TOMAS BELEN } friends of ALEJANDRO CASTILLO

THE TOURING COMPANY

DECIMO CANALES, the actor-manager

SEÑORA CANALES, his wife and leading lady

CARMEN, the ingenue

FELIPE, the prompter

GREGORIO, the character actor

MANOLO DE FUENTES, the juvenal

THE PEOPLE BEYOND THE MOUNTAINS

ANTONIO DECA, a singer of popular songs

BERTA, cousin by marriage of RUBEN

GENERAL VALDEZ, husband of ANITA O'MALLEY

GITANILLO, the bullfighter

HARPER PASCHAL, superintendent of the Monterrey cement plant

HERMINA, chaperone to LOLA

OLALLA, gypsy mother of GITANILLO and LOLA

PEPE BOBO, a great Mexican clown

SOFIA, a night club singer

TRINA, friend of PEPE BOBO's and ex-mistress of GITANILLO

THE RULERS OF THE VALLEY

THE LITTLE DOCTOR: full name: Mariano López Martínez. Born: Jiménez, State of Chihuahua, 1869. Schooling under scholarship at the National University, Mexico City, and the National School of Medicine. Served internship at the Hospital de San Andrés, Mexico City. Practised medicine in various cities, State of Chihuahua. During Great Revolution served with Villa's forces. Met Don Rosalío in El Paso, Texas, and accepted invitation to visit Hidalgo. Never married.

DON NACHO, full name: Ignacio Villareal. Born: Hidalgo, State of Nuevo León, 1854. Village schooling. At twenty-one became Hidalgo's *Inspector de Policía*. Married Mariliria Govéa from the *Gallineros*, 1876. One child, Chela, born late in marriage. In Great Revolution served with Villa's men. Became alcalde 1 of Hidalgo, 1920. Retained that office until his death, 1935.

Don Rosalio, full name: Rosalío Lozano Torres. Born: Hidalgo, State of Nuevo León, 1862. Educated, National University, Mexico City, University of Salamanca, Spain. Married Ana María Sanchez in Spain, 1883. Wife died, 1886. Returned to Mexico, 1908. Served on Carranza's staff. Owned extensive orange groves in the Sabinas. Died, 1931.

Father Zacaya, full name: Manuel Leopoldo Zacaya Arrambide. Born, Mexico City, 1871, youngest son of the powerful Zacaya family. Educated, the Sorbonne, Paris, University of Dublin, Ireland. Strong tendency towards the religious vocation from childhood. Entered the priesthood, Mexico City, 1897. First parish, town of San Ignacio, State of Chihuahua. Met Don Rosalío during Great Revolution. Came to Hidalgo, 1920. Died, 1941.

MEXICAN VILLAGE

Rivers rise in flood and destroy,
Brooks water the land and sing.
—Mexican proverb

THE ENGINE SWUNG AROUND THE SHARP CURVE BETWEEN walls of packed yellow earth, travelled into open country long enough to free the rattling cars behind it, and then came to a jerking pause beside the tall wooden supports of the water tower.

A young man swung down from the last coach, his snap-brimmed felt hat pulled low over his eyes, the collar of his shabby tan raincoat standing up at the back. In one hand he held a heavy, battered suitcase that had seen hard wear in many countries. In the other was a cigarette caught between thumb and forefinger, the glowing tip protected by the cup of the narrow palm, an unconscious gesture, for there was no wind blowing.

He looked about him at the stretching fields hot under the clear yellow sun, bare of houses, with the line of mountains blue in the distance.

The conductor thrust his head through one of the open train windows and spoke jovially. "Do not be alarmed, friend. Under the slope of the hill lies the town of Hidalgo. I, personally, assure you of this."

The train, no longer thirsty, shook itself, tottered, gained speed, fled forward to meet another curve and so disappear. Its movements revealed another line of mountains, etched in gray against the dark blue sky, more cactus-studded fields, and, by the water tower, an old man standing between two saddled horses. He was slender, with a dirty blue shirt and gray trousers belted with rope. His broad-brimmed straw hat had a ragged edge, and a bushy gray mustache neatly bisected his brown face.

The stranger in the raincoat walked up to him. "Are you from the quarry?" he asked pleasantly in a deep, hard voice that clipped the words like scissors.

"As you say," the old man answered politely, but the black eyes were investigating the stranger without friendliness. "The letter that came yesterday by train, and it was read to me by Don Nacho, the alcalde, himself, said that you were a *Yanqui* with a most unpronounceable name. And yet you speak Spanish. I do not understand this. Pepe Gonzales, without doubt a boy of little worth, but with two years' schooling in Texas, taught me to say, 'Follow me, please.' It now appears that the lesson was of no necessity."

The stranger laughed, flicked his cigarette to the ground, stepped on it with the toe of his worn black shoe, grinding it to powder in the sand.

"It would also appear," continued the old man tranquilly, "that you were raised in the country, knowing well the danger of fire. That is a good thing."

"One learns."

"Yes. It is also possible that your grace knows how to mount a horse?"

"That also. Not so well, doubtless, as yourself, but that, too, can be learned. What does one do with the valise?"

The old man took the bag from him and placed it between the struts of the water tower. "Here it will be safe. You have papers in it?"

The stranger's mouth twitched in annoyance at this personal question. He answered stiffly, "No. My papers are in my pocket."

"That is good. Papers are better kept in safety. To me all papers are mysterious things, for I cannot read them, but my daughter Candelaria can read; she can also write. It is not good for a child to know more than the parent." He jerked the reins he held in his right hand. "The black horse is for you. It is one of the Castillo blacks, and the foreman of the Rancho Santo Tomás, may the good God take pity on his stupidity for he is in all things stupid save in the knowledge of horses, has assured me that it is of a complete gentleness. You understand," he added anxiously "that the letter did not state that you were learned in the matter of horses."

"I understand." The young man swung easily into the saddle, allowing his body to settle against its hardness, resting his arm across the broad pommel while the old man adjusted the stirrups.

"You are not so tall as we expected. Pepe Gonzales, who is truly a fool but has had two years' schooling in Austin, Texas, assured me that all *Yanquis* are tall, even as tall as Joaquín Castillo, may the saints watch over his soul in Paradise."

The stranger allowed the old man's chatter to flow over him like water. He reached up with a sudden gesture and pulled off his hat so that the soft, scented air could stir against his long square-chinned face. He thought, One year of this. Is it worth it for twelve God-forsaken months?

The old man had mounted the sorrel horse and was watching him, patiently waiting for the signal to move forward. But the stranger did not give it. He was looking up and down the narrow, mountain-walled valley, seeing the yellow sand broken by gray-green cactus, each leaf flaunting its crown of purple fruit, the small flowering thorn bushes covered with tiny yellow blossoms that distilled a too-sweet fragrance, and the tall *yuca* palms bent under the weight of long, purple-tipped white blossoms. Through this desolation ran the silver tracks, reflecting the sun in angry stabs of light, and curving indolently around a cement platform, which had originally been walled with red brick but was now a blackened ruin, obviously once gutted by fire. He pointed toward it.

"What was that?"

"The railroad station, and a fine building it was, presented to Hidalgo by that great good man Don Saturnino Castillo. But who is there to give buildings now that he is gone in exile from the valley? The Great Revolution was a grand thing. Don Nacho, who is alcalde, says so. Also Don Rosalío and the little Doctor, and even the priest, say so. They are all very wise. But me, I stayed safe from the battles in the hills, and now that the fighting is two years done, I say to them, 'Of what good is the Great Revolution save to hang people and to burn buildings? If it was so fine, why do they not bring people back to life and give us new buildings?' They answer me with pretty words that mean nothing. Your grace is ready?"

The stranger nodded and let the reins go lax against the silky arched neck of the black horse. With the old man in the lead, they trotted through the fields and found a trail that led them through still more fields to the line of eastern mountains. Then they came into a cañon, and the trail mounted upwards into air that grew sharper and colder. The vegetation changed, the cactus and flowering thorn disappeared, but the *yuca* remained, and lichens curved their feathery gray softness over the massive rocks. At last they reached a high mesa that hung out in space, the mountain supporting it like a placid woman carrying a tray.

In front of them was a tin-roofed wooden shack, the unpainted door fastened with a heavy chain and padlock. The old man found a key after much searching in his pockets, and with many requests for aid to various saints opened the lock and flung the door wide. "This," he said proudly, "is the office. Here much work can be done with papers."

But the stranger was paying him no attention. He had strolled to the mesa edge and was staring across the great cut in space that was the valley. The old man came to his shoulder and pointed with one gray-dirt hand toward the northeast. "There lies Monterrey.

You can see the smoke from the smelters. It is a very great city. Don
Nacho, who is the alcalde and should know, says it is the third
largest in all the Republic. This I do not believe. Monterrey is very
great. I believe it is the largest. No city could be larger. That is an
impossibility. Ay, the cloud has moved. That is a good omen. The
cloud wants you to see Saddle Mountain—the mountain of Monterrey. Do you not consider it beautiful?"

The young man nodded, looking at the distant purple smudge of
rock with the double peak that characterized it. For a moment he
was a little boy again, and a woman's voice was recounting softly
in Spanish, *"So the great god of winds, Hurikán, transformed his
horse into a mountain to guard his favorite valley. He smoothed
down the trembling limbs. The tail he smoothed down, the fine
arching neck and the proud head. But in his haste he forgot the
saddle . . ."* The stranger moved his shoulders under the shabby
raincoat. "Very beautiful," he agreed politely.

"And there," the old veined hand swept in a wide half circle
to the southwest, "is the Peak of the Prow. Like a ship it sails the
air, not so?"

"As you say. And the town at its base, that is Hidalgo?"

"No, señor, that is Mina. My daughter Candelaria, who has had,
you understand, a certain schooling, says that it was named for a
hero of the Revolution of 1810, one Ignacio Mina. This I do not
know for truth, but only as she says. We have five towns in the
Sabinas. It is a very rich valley. And there they are spread out
before you."

Like toys, thought the young man. Like toys a giant has thrown
down and forgotten.

The old man was saying, "Close to Saddle Mountain is Topo
Grande. There is no need for you to remember the name. A collection of mud huts, a small thing of no importance. But the next
town, the one with many houses and streets, that is El Carmen.
The people there raise cows and sell the milk in Monterrey. Don
Nacho says that many people there prefer the milk of cows to
the milk of the she-goats, but this is a matter of great amazement,
and I do not know it of my own knowledge."

The stranger nodded to the next town. "That one looks like a
seashell, one street spiraled around to a center."

"A curious thing," agreed the old man. "My daughter Candelaria says that it is named for another hero of 1810, one Abasolo.

A hero he may have been, but the name is stupid: the lonely bean!" For the first time the old man laughed, his face crinkling with mirth, like worn brown leather tortured into creases.

Another town stretched out far below them. It was oblong-shaped, with a church thrusting its belfry up from the center. The buildings were of all colors, and standing aloof was a single great house, the walls white, the roof of red tiles. This house seemed to rise out of a sea of glossy green trees, and beyond it were the sheer cliffs on which the town was built, swung out over a river that twisted through the entire length of the valley like a lazily curving shiny blue serpent. Across the river was a checkerboard of green and yellow, which the old man said were farms, and farther still was the wall of western mountains, small buildings tucked like colored dots into the folding flanks.

Looking at all this, the stranger raised his head slightly, his hazel eyes under the triangular brows filled with an almost passionate sadness. But the mouth, with the sharply cut corners jutting upwards, believed the eyes, as though the body wanted to laugh but the spirit refused the laughter. "So that's the hole I have to live in for a year," he said in English.

The old man grinned again, finding the incomprehensible sounds amusing. "If your grace will go into the office I can show you many papers. When the last *jefe* went away, he said to me, 'Anselmo'—for your grace understands that is my name, Anselmo Carvajal, your servant." He carefully wiped his palm on his trouser leg and extended it. When the stranger shook it without comment the old man seemed disappointed, as though he had expected words which had not been said. After a moment he continued, "The *jefe* said, 'Soon this Revolution will be over, and if I do not come back, another *jefe* will come, and he will want the papers; so guard them well.' That was in 1913. For seven years I have guarded the papers, and they are all in the office."

"That is a fine thing," said the young man. "I will now go and admire the papers."

Don Anselmo pattered after him into the shack. "Seven years is a long time. To God, of course, it is not even a moment, but to me, who am old, it is a long time. This office is even as the other *jefe* left it. He was a good *jefe*, not a *Yanqui* like your grace, but an Italian. He stayed here two years. He had a fine house in Hidalgo but he would not live in it. He slept on the office floor, sometimes alone but generally with one of the cave women. My woman was too old for him, and my daughter Candelaria, too young. She is, you understand, the child of my age. But many of the cave women rolled the eye at him, and then he would sleep with them. It was strange, for there were never any children. He had not in him the richness of seed. You are perhaps different, señor?"

The question was so politely put that it caught the stranger off guard. He was hardly listening to the interminable chatter while he surveyed the battered oak desk, a gaudy calendar showing a harshly colored picture of the cement plant in Monterrey, and the date, 1913, the scarred wooden filing cabinet, and the empty liquor bottles powdered with dust and linked together with strong cables of spider webs.

"How the hell should I know," he muttered with a curious sense of embarrassment.

"Precisely, señor. But then you are still young. You are perhaps twenty-four?"

The stranger's narrow face betrayed no hint of his resentment at this second invasion of his privacy. "Twenty-six," he said curtly. "Now that we have seen the office, where is the quarry?"

"But the papers, señor—all the beautiful papers in the cabinet. You do not wish to see the papers?"

To humor the old man, he pulled out a drawer of the filing case. For a moment his lips slid into a long sideways smile. The drawer was filled with French magazines devoted to displaying the beauty of nude women. "This Italian—what became of him?"

"It was a sad thing. The morning he chose to leave the safety of the mountains was the same morning that *El Rubio* captured Hidalgo and started to hang people. That blond one was very angry at not finding Don Saturnino Castillo. He would say, 'Where is Don Saturnino?' and if a man could not answer him, zas! he was hanged. Lucky for Hidalgo, all the good men were away fighting. This *Rubio* caught the Italian, and because he could not answer the question—for who was the Italian to know the secrets of such a great one as Don Saturnino—the *Rubio* hanged him. I personally went down and protested, but the *Rubio* paid me no more mind than if I had been the husband of an actress. It was a very sad thing."

The stranger shut the drawer with a quick gesture of finality. "And the quarry?"

"If your grace will follow me. It is around the slope of the mountain."

Once more in the clean open air, the young man took several deep breaths. I can't work in that place, he thought. I've got to change it. It's too small and it smells of filth. A year of this. Good God, a whole year!

He followed Don Anselmo around the curved slope, and then paused in speechless astonishment. The quarry was a deep, ugly wound in the mountain side, but above it, small ledges for walking having been carefully retained, was row after row of cave openings, so that the towering wall had a cynical resemblance to a New York apartment house sheered through the center.

People were wandering in and out of the caves, their quiet Indian poise ignoring the danger of the chasm below them, their laughter and high, shrill voices echoing in a constant flow of sound from the mountain sides. Children playing on the ledges were stepped over or pushed aside. Some of the men were squatting on their heels near a cave opening; others were stretched out at full length, their straw hats tilted over their faces, their bodies soaking up the welcome warmth of the sunlight. All of the women were working, some kneeling to pound corn into a thick white mash on porous gray-black stone, others weaving at ancient hand looms. A few were climbing the ledge, buckets of water balanced on their glossy black heads.

"This—you live in these caves?" the young man asked slowly after the scene had passed from his eyes into his mind.

"But yes, señor. The caves are very healthy. The other *jefes* wanted to build houses for us of the quarry rock, but it would not be the same. In the caves the rock still lives and gives us life. We do not sicken here as they do in the villages. Here we live to be very old, or we die from the clean stab of a knife. The living rock is very powerful."

The stranger cursed under his breath in English. Two of the children had seen him, and their shrill cries and pointing hands drew the attention of the people. They all looked at him with the blank eyes of the Indian, expecting nothing, giving nothing. He felt the blankness so strongly that he turned away, feeling as he had always felt, an outsider, a person to be tolerated but not accepted.

During the war in France, he thought, it had been different. Under the guns there are no strangers and yet there are no friends. Under the guns a man feels completely alone, completely shut off from all other men. But each man in his loneliness receives the comradeship of loneliness from those about him, so that he does not feel lost in a great void. But away from the guns and war, the people surrounding him withdrew into their private friendships, leaving him isolated, with only one friend to care for him.

When he was small he had accepted this loneliness as a part of his heritage, but later in Europe he had felt the lack to be a part of himself, and so he had come to Mexico, hoping that the nostalgia of the blood might be satisfied. Money being a necessity of living, he had posted a notice in the Foreign Club asking for a job, explaining that he was an expert with dynamite. Four years of war with the Engineers had taught him the uses of dynamite better than any school. Several offers had been made to him to work in the silver mines of Pachuca, but this northern cement quarry had attracted his fancy. He did not want the picturesque softness of the South. The blood that was in him demanded the serene austerity of the northern mountains, and although he had never seen Saddle Mountain until this morning, he could have described it minutely from stories told him in his childhood.

The blank Indian reception cut into him, for he had expected from these people the same easy response that the old man had given him, but even as he turned away he saw Don Anselmo's dark obsidian eyes hidden in the shadow of the hat brim, and he knew that the chattering tongue was only a result of politeness to a new *jefe*, and not an acceptance of him as a person.

He said quietly, "I think it is better to go into the town. I want a bath and some sleep. There was no pullman on the train, and I had to sit up all night."

"As your grace wishes."

They retraced their steps to the horses. As he started to mount the patiently waiting animal he remembered that he had left his hat in the office; so he turned and went into the shack again. The open door had freshened the dead air, but the narrow, dark room with the one small window oppressed him like a prison. He went

to the window and flung it open with a savage gesture, his eyes
seeing but not quickly reacting to the sight of the girl standing
in a small flower bed. The soft wind tossed her blue skirt around
her bare ankles. The plain white blouse was cut low and from
it rose the slender column of her throat. The oval face, with
arched brows and large black eyes, was proudly set. A closely
woven dark-red shawl flecked with green was draped over her
black hair, and in her arms was a large sheaf of pink dahlias. She
looked at him without shyness and yet without boldness, in a
serene confidence that he found her beautiful. Then she silently
turned and moved around a corner of the shack out of his line
of vision. He picked up his hat, pulled it down on his forehead,
and went outside. The girl was standing by the old man, who said
proudly, "This is my daughter Candelaria."

She extended her hand, murmuring, "Candelaria Carvajal, your
servant, señor."

He smiled at her, wondering why, like the old man, she also
seemed disappointed when he made no response. Then he was in
the saddle. They left her standing at the edge of the mesa staring
after them.

"Your daughter is very beautiful.'"

Don Anselmo shrugged. "Many men have found her so. Even
the worthless Pepe Gonzalez has climbed the mountain side to
see her. But he says, can you imagine, that the yellow-haired
María—that nameless wench from the River Road—is even more
beautiful. I have seen this María. She is all yellow like a grain of
corn and lacks the full ripe blood. That Pepe Gonzalez is a fool."

A clever warning, the young man thought with some amusement. Not to admire the daughter is to be a fool. But to admire
her too much, what then? Probably the edge of a knife. Other
subjects are safer with this old man. He bent forward and petted
the great black's arching neck.

"This is indeed a beautiful horse. Your sorrel is not so large,
but it seems also a fine animal."

"Indeed, señor, the sorrel is of all horses the best. If one says
to you, 'This morning I saw a horse flying through the air,' ask
him the color, and if he answers 'sorrel,' believe him."

"And the black horse?"

"If someone says to you that he saw a horse leap from a precipice without hurt, ask him the color, and if he says, 'black,'

believe him, for the black is the most energetic, the brown the most rapid, the piebald the gentlest, but the sorrel is the king of all."

The young man's mouth twisted into his slow sideways smile. His grandmother's voice sounded faintly, as though he were hearing her through water. *"Always he rode a white horse. They forgot his name, but the horse they remembered."* He said, "You have no words for the white horse?"

"Blessed Heaven!" Don Anselmo gasped. He hastily crossed himself and glanced fearfully about him. "In these mountains it is not good to mention the *Caballo Blanco*, for the witches, in their laughter, might fetch his spirit before you.'"

"But surely a white horse is not the property of witches."

"Ay, you mean a horse that is white. I thought you meant..."

"Yes? What did you think?"

"When I was small my father told me many stories, and they were true, for my father spoke the words. But there was once a man of my people the Huachichil, who rode through all these mountains, and many times he went into Monterrey, for he was without fear. His horse was white, and from the horse came the name *El Caballo Blanco*. He stole much gold and silver and many jewels, and he buried his treasure in the hills, and he guards this treasure very fiercely, so that all who try to find it go mad from seeing him ride toward them on his white horse."

"But he is dead?"

"Executed with bullets before I was born, and I am very old."

"How old are you?"

"I was born before the plague of locusts came."

"And when did the plague come?'

"Why, after I was born, señor. That is Hidalgo in front of us."

The trail opened into a crooked, dusty road, lined on one side by lime-washed varicolored houses of mud brick, and on the other by a cactus-enclosed pasture in which sat various little wooden shacks thatched with palm leaf. The stranger drew his raincoat collar closer about his face and pulled the hat lower on his nose, as though he shrank from seeing the poverty-stricken hovels. Dogs barked in mock fierceness at his horse's legs, and children peered at him through the cactus fence, but the man did not see their oriental faces as clearly as he saw the quick image in his mind of another shack and other children playing on the dirt floor, and a woman sobbing on a broken, white-painted iron bedstead.

"Is this all the town?" he asked harshly between clenched teeth. "From the mountain top it looked as though there were many houses and a church."

"So there are, señor. We call this the *Gallineros* in laughter that the poor should shut themselves off with cactus like a chicken coop. Let us turn here to the right. We are now on the Avenue of Illustrious Men."

The narrow street broadened after a block, and the stranger saw a square plaza, shaded with orange and lime trees, and a round bandstand in the center. Around the plaza ran a wide sidewalk dotted at intervals with massive cement benches. Beyond it reared the blue tower of a pink church. They turned into another street, passed the barber shop with its striped pole, a long green building with the word "Jail" written over the entrance arch, and finally stopped before a blue-painted wall, with an iron-barred window and a hand-carved door, behind which sat the dignity of the mayor of Hidalgo.

' Don Anselmo led the way through a narrow hall and into a small whitewashed office, which seemed filled to overflowing not by the desk but by the large-stomached man behind it. He sat very still, his black Stetson on his head, his upper chin resting on the soft fullness of the lower one so that he seemed to have a small face perpetually resting on a cushion of fat.

Don Anselmo went to the desk and carefully removed his straw hat, to hold it tight against him with both hands. "I give you good day, Don Nacho. The *Yanqui* is here."

The mayor's small eyes, cold as black glass beads, turned toward the stranger standing in the doorway. He saw a man of about five foot ten, with a slender body that could never grow stout. The straight black hair grew back at the temples, and was brushed neatly away from a side part. There were three wrinkle lines in the broad forehead, and the face was long, with well-set ears. The man was clean shaven, with no hint of beard under the skin as is common to most dark men. The wind- and sun-burned face was brown, with an undertone of red in it, and the eyes had green flecks in their hazel depths. Don Nacho's careful scrutiny did not miss the narrow, supple hands nor the shabby clothes. His penetrating glance returned to the sensitive mouth with the deep cleft in the center, the full lower lip, and the laughter-loving corners, then travelled upwards again to the somber eyes that were as unreadable as a forgotten language.

The quarry foreman spoke again, as though placidly showing off the good points of a horse. "He possesses Spanish. Some of the words are strange, and the accent is unfamiliar, but he speaks the language. I personally have heard him."

Don Nacho put his palms flat on the desk and pushed his large body upright. He held out his hand and spoke in formal tones. "Ignacio Villareal, at your orders."

As the young man moved forward to clasp the hand a vague wisp of memory returned to him in his grandmother's voice, *"When meeting strangers it is polite to speak your name."* He said self-consciously, "Bob Webster," and for the first time the name which he knew was rightfully his sounded strange and wrong to him.

The old quarry foreman sucked in his breath; then the tobacco-stained gray mustache rolled back in a grin from the jagged teeth. "He learns quickly. This morning he knew not the politeness."

"So," Don Nacho pursed his lips. "I welcome you to Hidalgo, señor Don Bobwebster. You are doubtless tired and wish to see your house." He took a large key from a nail and opened a side door into another street. In the block across the way, its side to them, was a narrow house. A young man with a flat Indian face lounged against the wall. His stocky body was clothed in a pink shirt, grease-stained gray trousers, and leather-thonged sandals. A straw hat with a curling brim was balanced on the back of his head. He was chewing on a toothpick, and he examined Bob Webster with frank interest while speaking to Don Nacho.

"Don Alonso wants an orchestra platform in the proposed Casino large enough to hold seven men."

"Did he ask the building committee?"

"Yes. They said it was a useless expense, but an orchestra platform would be a fine thing, and I would not charge much for it."

"You would charge as much as you think they would pay you, Porfirio. You are without shame."

The young man laughed and spat out the toothpick as they left him and went around the corner.

"That Porfirio," sighed the quarry foreman. "What he would not do to gain a peso."

when the quarry foreman would have launched into a long
anation, he added, "Time enough for you to learn of the feud
. The water in the well is still good. You have only to pull up
bucket. The town gardener tested it for you last night. We
leave you in the peace of God."

he old men bowed formally, shook hands with the ceremony
per for strangers, and went away. Bob carried his valise into
bedroom, started to unpack it, then looked at the dirt and the
dangling suits. He gathered up some towels and soap and
kly shut the case. After he had managed a fairly competent
nge bath, he scraped dry leaves away from one corner of the
io, spread out his raincoat, and lay down on it.

leep was heavy on him, but when he tried to sleep, it eluded
, and his mind filled with old memories which he thrust out
away from him. As he sought desperately for release, the
age of Candelaria as he had first glimpsed her that morning, the
lias a pink beauty in her arms, swam into his consciousness,
thinking of her he sank at last into the darkness of true sleep.

By the end of the first work day, the men at the quarry discov-
d that they had a new type of *jefe*, a type they had never
herto known. There had been many quarry masters in the ten
ars of the quarry's existence before 1913, when all work had
ased. There had been the martinet German, the casual Irishman,
e homesick Englishman, the excitable Frenchman, and, of
urse, the drunken Italian.

With each new master came the changes. For two weeks the
fe would ride the mountain trails; he would set up what they
lled *La Sistema*, the system. There would be much writing of
pers and many speeches to the quarry men, especially on the
bject of living in caves. But by the end of the two weeks the
ystem would dissolve into the endless procession of slow days
d nights. Speeches would be made to the women instead of the
en; and bottles of golden cognac or colorless tequila * would take
e place of the papers. And Don Anselmo, the foreman, would
e that the small red cars, fastened together by an endless chain,

* A drink distilled from the sap of the maguey (agave or century plant).
he sap, called "honey water," after fermentation becomes pulque. This is
istilled to mescal, which in turn is distilled to tequila. All three are much
rized as strong liquors.

"I like him," said Don Nacho, and the rebuke shut the quarry
foreman's half-opened mouth.

The mayor struggled to unfasten the door of the small house.
"It is not large, perhaps, but the walls are good adobe, and there
are five rooms."

Bob Webster looked without comment at the entrance hall,
with its dead rubber plant and dusty wicker settee. Fresh air came
to them from the patio, which had a cement floor save for three
dirt circles where two orange trees and a pomegranate bush were
planted. Somehow they had survived seven years of neglect.

Don Nacho showed off the rest of the house with an air of
quiet pride. The late Italian had obviously liked wicker furniture.
The narrow parlor was filled with it, and the chairs in the dining
room were also wicker, although the table was a cheap imitation
of American mission style. The kitchen lacked both stove and
sink, but there was a very large icebox.

"Every Monday and Thursday ice comes by train from the
brewery in Monterrey," said Don Anselmo. Bob Webster lifted
the box lid, and four dust-shrouded beer bottles brought a sudden
pathetic image of the hanged Italian. He gently closed the lid and
followed his guides into the patio so that they could show him
the two rooms on the opposite side of the house. The one in
front was a bedroom, with a rickety washstand, an iron cot with
a torn corn-husk mattress, and a pole stretched across a corner,
from which dangled on rusty hangers two suits of loudly checked
tweed. The three men looked at the suits, each with the uncomfortable feeling that he had invaded the privacy of the dead.

A knock on the front door came as a relief. They walked
quickly into the patio, and Don Nacho bellowed, "Enter!" Two
young men came in, the shorter with a head composed of circles,
the round face with round eyes and round stubby nose giving him
a cherubic air; the taller, handsome in a dark flashing manner,
the narrow line of his black mustache unable to hide his mischievous mouth. He wore a neat blue suit with a bandana knotted
around his neck in place of a tie. His hat was a worn gray felt.

He came forward with his hand outstretched, his black eyes
dancing with friendly laughter. "Pepe Gonzalez, your servant,"
he said formally in Spanish, and then in surprisingly good English,
"Now you say your name. It's an old Spanish custom."

"He speaks Spanish like an honest christian," the quarry foreman interrupted sharply. He looked at the shorter young man, who was standing in the hall arch clutching Bob's valise. His denim trousers and faded blue shirt, though of poor quality, were neat and clean. He wore thonged sandals on his bare feet, and a broad-brimmed straw hat like the foreman's.

"Andrés Treviño," he said in an agony of shyness, and quickly put down the suitcase. His brown eyes turned pleadingly to Don Nacho. "We found it beneath the water tower. Pepe said it belonged to the *Yanqui*, and that we should bring it to this house."

"Thank you," Bob mumbled, not certain whether he was supposed to tip the boy. Pepe Gonzalez winked at him.

"It is a fine thing that you can speak Spanish, for now there is no difficulty in making you a member of the Casino soon to be built behind this house. The dues are six pesos a year."

"Five," hissed Andrés Treviño.

"Porfirio said to ask for six. We need spittoons for the bar."

"Five," said Don Nacho firmly. He turned his head toward Bob. "That Porfirio, the carver of wood, watch out for him. If he can get a peso from you for nothing, he will do it."

"Porfirio is a good soul," protested the two young men in one voice. "With work he is generous, and with the spirit."

"But a peso is closer to his hand than the lines of his palm," snorted the mayor. "Pay them the five pesos so that they can leave us in peace."

Bob, who had no desire to be a member of the Casino or any other social organization in this Mexican town, but was afraid to say so for fear of giving offense, opened his overcoat and took out his worn leather wallet. From the coin compartment he extracted a ten-peso gold piece, and its shining beauty held everyone's attention for a long moment. Pepe looked at it with amusement, Andrés with longing, the quarry foreman with awe, Don Nacho with objective interest; then it dropped into Pepe's hand, and the dark young man counted out five silver pesos change.

"You have too much money for such a worthless one," Don Nacho snapped. "If I were your father, I would put you to work in the cheese factory."

Pepe grinned. "I don't like the smell of the vats."

"Such a scandal," Don Anselmo told him severely. "And your father the maker of the finest cheese on the frontier. Only yesterday I saw a goatherd from the Valley of the Three Marys . . ."

"On our side of the line?" the mayor asked

The foreman shrugged. "For lost goats th because he was of the Three Marys I cou Sabinas land without some punishment."

"Naturally," Andrés nodded with satisfacti

"So I made the forked sign against the evil christian . . ."

"And he was a goatherd," Pepe Gonzalez ch

"Continue, old one. What did you say to him

"Do not hurry me, do not hurry me. I said t like a taste of Don Timotéo's cheese?' And I it, very tempting, in my hand. You should hav the way his tongue touched his mouth with w

"He took it?" Don Nacho demanded, scanda

"No. He was a good son of his valley. But Marys unmentionables miss the good cheese And you, worthless one, are too proud to we factory."

Pepe shrugged. "I tell you I don't like the sm

Don Nacho patted Bob's arm. "Let me war Pepe Gonzalez, and that fool who calls himself and Porfirio, the carver of wood whom you sa talent for wickedness that is beyond belief. Bette away from them."

"He can't," grinned Pepe. "Is he not now a Casino, and that soon to be the finest social club l rey and Torreón?"

"Such talk," Don Anselmo said, "and this poor lack of sleep. Better we leave him to his rest."

"If you get lonesome," Pepe said mischievously the Devil's Laughter is on the next street. There w mittee meetings."

"Out of here," roared Don Nacho.

The two young men laughed, shook Bob's har departed, Andrés obviously glad to be free of the manding presence. Bob was sorry to watch ther friendliness seemed to be free of suspicion and dist himself to ask casually, "What is wrong with the Three Marys that it cannot eat cheese, and where i

"On the other side of the eastern mountains," sai

the rock-laden downward cars pulling up the empties, somehow reached the train tracks and that the rock was loaded on flatcars to be taken to the cement factory in Monterrey.

Sometimes the *jefes* would remember to tell Don Anselmo that he was a good foreman, and would present him with a small bottle of liquor. The Italian had even looked with soft eyes on the ripening beauty of Candelaria. On that day Don Anselmo had fastened a block of wood to a tree and had shown the Italian some tricks of knife-throwing, and after that the Italian showed no further interest in Candelaria. That Anselmo, said the Inditos,* was a wise one. Candelaria was worth more than a casual sleeping on an office floor. A man from the village might not be such a rich one, but he would be Candelaria's husband long after a *jefe* had forgotten the color of Hidalgo's mountains. And as for *La Sistema*, every master was entitled to his two weeks of amusement, but after that, well, the getting of stone from the quarry was a serious business and not to be entrusted to an outlander.

So the quarry men prepared themselves for the breaking in of the new *jefe*, who was, in himself, curious because he could speak Spanish, which no other quarry master had ever been able to do.

Their blank eyes hiding amusement, they watched Bob gallop up to the mesa the second morning after his arrival. He called the foreman to him.

"Good morning, Don Anselmo."

A ripple of movement passed over the waiting crowd. What manner of *jefe* was this that he should call Anselmo Carvajal "Don"? The other *jefes* in their arrogance had never bothered to bestow a title of respect on the Inditos, even though old age demanded it of politeness. New interest came to the men, and they pressed closer as Bob said, "You doubtless have a method for taking the rock to the train?"

"That is so, *jefe*."

"It is a good method?"

"There have been no complaints from the cement factory in Monterrey, señor."

"Continue it, then, in the old manner. I will watch it, and if I am not pleased we can make changes later. But now I will need five men to help me here."

* Indians, in the sense of the simple tribespeople, like those working in the quarry.

Don Anselmo, as curious as the rest, waved five men aside and took the others to the quarry; but during the day many, on one pretext or another, had to make little trips to the mesa, Don Anselmo with them, and what they saw amazed them. For the new *jefe* had ordered a fire, and the precious papers which had been so carefully guarded for seven years were tossed on the blazing wood.

The empty bottles were presented to the wide-eyed audience of children. And as for the women, well, that was the impossible thing. The new *jefe* gave them not so much as a passing glance as he went about his work. Nor did the audience seem to bother him. The other *jefes* had threatened all manner of punishment to keep children and old ones from the mesa—with the old ones they had been successful, never with the children. This new *jefe* accepted their attention without comment save to warn everyone to keep out of the working area. And once when a boy leaped forward with a shout to thrust his hand into the fire and show that even at nine years he was a man and not afraid of pain, the *jefe* had merely lifted him by the back of the neck and dropped him into the ditch that carried the irrigation water to Hidalgo. The child howled as the icy water flowed over him, and the *jefe* said mockingly, "You call yourself a man, and yet you scream at a drop of water."

All the old ones and the women laughed, and after that none of the children stepped across the line the *jefe* drew in the dirt.

When the sun was well overhead, the papers had been burned, the fire extinguished with water, and the furniture moved out of the shack. Then the *jefe* squatted on the ground like anyone else and drew from his pocket the package of food he had brought from the village.

For a long time the people rested in the shade of the mesquite trees, the men eating the food the women brought them, and the *jefe* listening quietly to the talk of the wise old ones, not once interrupting to show his superior wisdom, but listening with humility and silence as the young should listen to the old. There was talk of rain and crops, for the quarry people depended on the farms of Hidalgo for their food. And after a while there was talk of the Great Revolution and what it would mean to the Inditos, if it meant anything at all, which the old ones doubted; for, as the wisest said, through all the years there had been so many promises, and so many do-nothings. Now the Great Revolution was two years finished, and it, too, seemed to end in do-nothing.

Then at last the old ones were silent, and some of the younger men began to sing. At first the *jefe* listened to the songs, but when someone started the stirring song of Morelos to which many soldiers had marched in the far-off days of 1812, the *jefe* surprised everyone by singing also, knowing both words and tune. His deep voice gave a bass to their light tenors, and he sang without effort as men sing who have known a song from childhood:

> *For a corporal I'd give twenty cents,*
> *For a sergeant I might give fifty.*
> *But for General Morelos*
> *I'd gladly give all my heart.*

At the finish he went without pause into the song of *The Flea,* the children adding their voices to the merriment:

> *With all the fleas I am most angry,*
> *They bite me when I am in bed.*
> *Ay! How they jump! Ay! How they leap!*
> *Ay! How they jump! Those wicked little fleas.*
>
> *All these fleas fill me with terror*
> *For the holes they bore into my skin.*
> *Ay! How they jump! Ay! How they leap!*
> *Ay! How they jump! Those wicked little fleas.*

Candelaria, watching him sing, pulled her shawl closer over her head. She had never seen eyes so somberly tragic in a man's face, and it seemed to her as though, during the music, some of the sadness left him; but it seemed also as though he went away from her into another world where she could not follow. And into her mind came the clear and bitter knowledge that all of her happiness rested in the cup of his hand, but that to him she would never be anything more than a cloud's shadow on the mountain slope.

He rose, his arms lifted for a deep stretching of his body. "More work, friends. The hour of resting is over."

Earlier that morning the men had worked in silence, obedient to his orders, but curious. Now that he had sung with them they felt a greater ease. Secret laughter trembled among them, and words flowed from one to another. One man put the large desk chair on its side and showed how he could leap over it ten times without pause. Expressionless eyes swiveled to the *jefe's* face. Bob took a deep breath.

"After this, enough of games," he told them. Keeping his feet close together, he made twelve leaps back and forth across the chair, and there was no panting in his chest as he finished. The children mischievously sang the applause music,* and the women and the old ones obediently clapped.

Bob knew that the men were now ready to accept him on trial. He was their *jefe*. In all things he must be better than they were. This chair jumping was but the beginning of tests that would grow more difficult until they were satisfied that he was competent to lead them. His grandmother's wisdom flowed into his memory. *"And always the patrón, the master, must ride with the least fear, throw the longest rope, climb the highest mountain. For is he not the patrón?"* Bob's mouth lifted in the slow sideways smile, and he waved his hand towards the shack. "Amuse yourself, my children. Storm this castle with fortitude. Make it as though it had never been. The glass from the window and the tin from the roof we will keep. But the boards can be broken up and put in the cooking fires."

The men looked at each other with little curious glances. The laughter passed out of them for the *jefe* had became a stranger again. To destroy this office was a terrible thing. Was it not the symbol of authority? Surely the mind of a *jefe* was a matter not understood by common christians.

Bob felt the change in them. His fingers trembled with anger as he unfastened the door staples. Supposing they did want to keep the shack. He was the one who had to spend most of the day in it. What difference did it make what they did or did not want? He was the *jefe*, he was the outlander, he was the stranger. For a year he would be a stranger, and then he would go away and forget them. Two hundred and fifty American dollars a month in salary. He could easily live on fifty. That left two hundred clear. Twelve times two hundred was twenty-four hundred. The letter

* The last eight bars of the *Jarabe Tapatío*, known in the United States as the "Mexican Hat Dance." This music, called the "Diana," is always played in recognition of an outstanding feat, whether it be bull-fighting, a great speech, or anything else of value.

from Tommy Eaton was very plain: "I tell you we could clean up in South America. With your Spanish and the way you understand these Latins it would be a cinch. And the whole world's going air-conscious. With me to fly the planes and you to manage the business on the ground, we'll be set. Of course we have to have capital to start with. But this flying circus I'm with now isn't bad. Besides what I can borrow, I should have about four thousand saved up by the end of the year if I can keep the wings sewn on my crate. Do you think you could swing at least two thousand by that time?"

Yes, the letter was plain, and Tommy Eaton would make a good partner. A little stupid, but the knowledge of airplanes was in his blood and his bones. And a year wasn't a long time to wait. Twelve months—three hundred and sixty-five days. Oh God, three hundred and sixty-five days of living in these mountains, of constantly proving that he was better than any quarry man, of seeing that endless cars of rocks were turned over to the care of the railroad. He'd be damned if he'd spend those days in a two-by-four shack that shut out the opalescent air and the blue arched sky. The door came loose from the jamb, and he let it fall to the ground. By evening the only reminder of the shack was a patch of hard-packed earth that marked the floor.

Don Anselmo, careful to make no reference to the desecration of the office, rode back to the village with him.

"It is in my mind," he told Bob, "that you would do well to purchase that horse. Don Fidencio, who keeps the blacksmith shop, has certain nags for hire, but they are of little value." He used the word *rocinante* for nag, and Bob looked at him curiously.

"Is it possible that Don Quixote has come to these mountains?" he asked.

"Don Quixote, señor? I do not know him. He is perhaps of Monterrey?"

"No matter. But Rocinante was the name of his horse."

"Indeed, señor. Now that is a strange thing. The horse of the young Castillo, Joaquín, you comprehend, not Alejandro, was also named Rocinante. Every day he rode it along the mountain trails. How he could ride, that one! And his horse was the finest of the Castillo blacks. He called it Rocinante for a little joke. And on Sunday mornings, for the sweetheart mass at twelve o'clock, he would ride that horse to the door and make it kneel in honor of the Blessed Virgin. Ay, he took much laughter with him when he left this valley."

"Where is he now?" Bob asked idly, not really curious.

"Dead, señor." The thin lips under the gray mustache closed tightly, as though afraid of giving away too much information. This, more than the words, attracted Bob's attention. What a strange place Hidalgo was, with its minor mysteries, and its feud with the neighboring valley. Well, it was no concern of Bob Webster's. But a horse was. He really needed a horse, and perhaps it would be better to buy one. The money problem was an item, but he could always sell it, and if he took good care of it, he might make a little profit. And besides, there should be some compensation for this twelve months' exile. He had always wanted to own a horse . . . ever since he had been old enough to comprehend what such an animal was. And his grandmother's voice came into him again: "*It was white, with tail and mane of cream. And when its hoofs struck the ground, sparks flew. I tell you such an animal has never been seen before or since.*"

Bob said lightly, "As you say, this is a fine animal. But it is in my mind to buy a white horse."

"Ay, no, señor!" Don Anselmo hastily blessed himself. "To bring a white horse into these mountains is not wise. *El Caballo Blanco* would not like it."

"*El Caballo Blanco* is dead. You yourself said this yesterday."

"Dead he may be in body, but the goatherds often see him on the trails in the moonlight, his hand on his gun, his hat on the back of his head, and his white horse between his knees."

"Have you ever seen him?"

"With my own eyes, no. But it would take a very brave soul to face his jealous anger. The men like you, señor. They think you will make a good *jefe*. They would not want to see you with your mind emptied of reason and foolish laughter on your mouth."

"A brave soul," Bob repeated thoughtfully. Perhaps a white horse would solve his difficulties with the men. If they saw him riding one without harm they would set no further tests for him, for they would know he was indeed the *jefe*, afraid not even of ghosts.

But his skeptical mind could not prevent the cold touch of fear within him that was a part of his heritage. "Eh, grandmother," he whispered, "shall I buy a white horse?" And the answer came out of his memory. "*When you are grown, young one, you, too, shall own a fine white horse, and the knowledge will console him in purgatory.*"

"Tomorrow I have business in Monterrey," Bob told the foreman. "See that the men do their work well, and clear me good blocks of stone for a new office. I will draw you a picture of what I have in mind."

Three afternoons later he sat in his dismal parlor and counted over his money with a grimace. At this rate it would take him longer than twelve months to clear that two thousand dollars, although the horse trader in Monterrey had agreed to buy back the animal within the year. In Bob's original calculations he had forgotten to count in the saddle, and the dignity of a *jefe* could not, of course, be lessened by an ordinary saddle. Luckily the harness maker had a real beauty which had been ordered by a general, and, after the manner of generals, casually forgotten.

It was resting on the back of the settee beside him now, and he ran his hand lovingly over it, for he liked the feel of good leather. In the darkened room its burnished red-brown seemed to gleam with an added golden light. The skirts and pommel were decorated with crossbars of stamping, and he was admiring the plain design when a voice said behind him, "A very beautiful thing."

He rose hurriedly and turned around. A delicate slender man was standing in the door, his round collar and black clothes revealing his profession. The finely chiselled face under thick silky white hair was like a cameo flushed with life.

"The door was open," the priest said tranquilly, his tenor voice clear and resonant. "I knocked but you did not hear me." He glanced about him, nodding his head. "You have swept well. The Huachichil said that you were very clean. Being dirty, they are great admirers of cleanliness." He sat in an armchair and crossed his knees so that one foot in its thick-soled black shoe swung in answer to some inner rhythm. "Before the Conquest most of the Indian tribes were clean. It was a part of their religion. And because it was pagan, the Christian conquerors did not allow them to bathe. Europe had not yet learned the necessity of the bath." He smiled easily, the warmth beginning in his serene blue eyes and spreading to the thin lips. "But I have disturbed you at your work. That was not polite. And in politeness I should have introduced myself. My name is Zacaya. I am the priest of this valley."

Bob Webster repeated his own name and sat down on the edge of the settee, very upright, so that his back did not touch it at any spot. He had not spoken to a priest since 1913 in that narrow rock cell where he had listened to a deep voice genially explaining that to die for Ireland was a worthy death, and that hanging was not so terrible, for the English were very clever at it. But the voice had not been able to bring Ned Kelley back to life, nor prove to Bob's nineteen years that death should be accepted with patience.

"You think it strange that I should come here?" this Mexican priest was asking, and the rich Irish baritone was lost in the clear tenor. "You are not, perhaps, Catholic?"

"I'm not anything," Bob said frankly, feeling suddenly oppressed in the small room, with the bare walls that had once been white and were now streaked with long, jagged, brown stains. He crossed to the window and flung open the wooden shutters as release from the feeling of being still in the Irish prison waiting for morning and the hangman's rope. But he had escaped from there with the help of some Irish patriots, and he would in time escape from here with two thousand dollars, and he would be free in South America, really free, although they had priests there, too, to remind him of the Dublin jail. He said aloud, "If you don't mind, Father, let's go into the patio. I don't like being shut up in rooms."

The sun was hot, but the orange and lemon trees threw purple shadows on the cement, and Bob pulled two black wicker chairs into their shelter.

"You were not at mass this morning," the priest said amiably, resting his forehead against his hand so as to shield his eyes from the glare. "I said to myself, perhaps he is Protestant. But I also said, perhaps in the excitement of his arrival, he has forgotten the day."

Bob tapped his pipe against his boot-heel. "The day? But it is Friday, not Sunday. Oh, yes, of course. First Friday."

"Ah," Father Zacaya contentedly expelled the syllable. "So, you were Catholic reared. When Pepe Gonzalez told me you spoke Spanish like a Tejano* I did not think you would be Protestant. But then one can never be sure."

* A person of Mexican blood born in Texas.

Bob laughed, showing his white even teeth. "I haven't been to mass in years, Father, and I'm not thinking of starting again now. I'm sorry, but I like thinking that my life is my own, to do with as I choose."

The priest shook his head. "Not in a Mexican village, my son. Already I know that you are a Tejano with perhaps a little of the blood, for it shows in your skin and hair in spite of the *Yanqui* name; that you understand the mind of the Inditos; that you like eggs with chili sauce for breakfast; that you were reared in the church and for some lamentable reason have left it; and that you are not afraid of superstitions."

The last word attracted Bob's attention. "Why do you say that about superstitions?"

"You bought a white horse in Monterrey."

Bob slapped his palm against his chair arm. "How the devil— pardon me, Father—how did you know that? I told no one of the purchase, and the horse is not due to arrive until late this afternoon."

"The man from whom you bought it has a wife who has a sister who has a friend who is related to the aunt of Andrés Treviño. It is very simple. Also, Anselmo Carvajal from the quarry told me that you showed much interest in white horses, which did not seem strange to me as they are much favored in Ireland."

"Ireland!" Bob rose and paced up and down the square-enclosed openness, his body etched in black by the sunlight. "Did a minor miracle change you into a mind reader?"

The priest chuckled softly. "I amuse myself with these small details. I was standing on the plaza when Don Nacho brought you to this house. I saw the ulster you were wearing and recognized the goods and workmanship. They make very fine coats in Ireland. I went to the University of Dublin and bought such a coat myself many years ago. But tell me, is the city greatly changed?"

Bob smiled wryly. "I was there only a week and—much occupied."

"Yes, I understand." The priest took a large watch from his pocket and gazed at it intently. "Almost night. You eat at Doña Juanita Perez' house?"

"For the present. I'm hoping to find a woman who will come

every morning and cook my breakfast and dinner. At night it is not necessary. I prefer to do for myself."

"There is a woman in the *Gallineros* who, I understand, once worked in the House Castillo. She has the training. I will speak to her and perhaps she—" a small and almost secret smile touched his lips. "She is rather—difficult but, I understand, competent. Unfortunately she does not approve of—foreigners."

Bob frowned with irritation. He did not like this constant interruption of strangers in his own affairs. "Do not bother. I will find someone."

"But no bother. Like yourself I am an outlander, for I came to this parish but a year ago. And we who are strangers should help each other."

His handclasp was firm and strong for so delicate a man. "My residence is across the street from the church. You must come some evening soon and we will talk of the world beyond the mountains. After nine o'clock, for earlier I play dominoes with the doctor, the mayor, and Don Rosalío. You will come?" He gazed so intently at Bob that the young man suddenly realized that this priest was lonely with a loneliness for the companionship of minds, and so he mumbled that it would be a pleasure.

After the priest was gone and Bob was cleansing himself before going to eat, he began to see this town and the people in it in a new perspective, and himself also. After Ned Kelley was hanged in Ireland, and he himself had fled to Morocco, he had found the sun-dried African city interesting and the French types amusing. His job as croupier at a gambling casino had kept him among people and yet aloof from them. He had watched their feverish intentness upon the small white ball that bounced ceaselessly around the whirling wheel, and he had felt contempt for their avid eyes, and their hands that clenched and unclenched, as though they could physically force the ball to grant them the wealth they craved. Because he despised them, he could seek no friendship among them, and during his leisure hours he would walk alone down the narrow sun-bleached streets, listening to the rhythmic chants of the street-vendors, and smelling the spiced sour odor that was compounded of unwashed bodies, of onions and garlic drying on long strings, of fermenting beer and other nameless things he remembered not so much with his mind as with his nostrils and his pores. To his senses, the painted sun-brick houses, the shrill voices, and the milling people were strange and exotic, but to his memory the scene was familiar with that awareness that comes not from knowledge but from the inherited recognition of the spirit. He had found a history of Spain in a bookvendor's stall, and as he read it he amused himself with wondering which of his own ancestors had walked down these same streets or similar streets in the days when the Alhambra was a Moorish palace.

He took the book to the Casino with him, and a woman who played every afternoon at his table commented upon it. She was a Frenchwoman, and her eyes were black and tear-washed in her narrow white face. She did not particularly attract him, and he answered her curtly, but when his hours at the table were finished, she was waiting for him in the bar. Because he was lonely he took her home and discovered that her name was Yvonne, that she was married to a Dutch importer who bored her, that she hated Morocco and wanted to return to France. That was why she gambled in the afternoons, in the hope that the money would, as she said, gather itself together to pay her passage home. Bob was still young and the woman found him easy to control. By the end of the week she was a wine in his blood, and he adjusted the wheel so that she won nearly five thousand francs. They managed to get passage on a Spanish boat bound for Marseilles just in time to escape an angry husband and an even angrier Casino proprietor. Once in Paris, Yvonne was kind to Bob as long as the money lasted; then she found a richer lover and Bob was alone again. The night she dismissed him, his set expressionless face frightened her, and she screamed "Indian!" at him. To her he was an American, and the few films she had seen had convinced her that all Americans were savages with feathers in their hair. But he did not know this, and the word conjured a scene in his memory where a very blond man stiffened in an office chair and said bitingly, "Are you suggesting that I admit an Indian is a son of mine? Damn it, I'm a white man!"

So Bob had walked away from Yvonne's apartment in a daze of hatred and pain, convinced that his blood had betrayed him as it would always betray him. He spent the few francs Yvonne had left him on cheap brandy, and the only thing that kept him from starving to death was the declaration of war. He joined the French army because he was hungry, and wanted three meals a day. They put him in the engineer corps and he learned how to use dynamite. He found that he was very clever at it, and he enjoyed working with explosives because the capped danger fascinated him. He liked the sense of power the small sticks gave him. With them in his hand he was the master, not the despised outsider, and he moved with a swift and silent efficiency about his work that he did not realize was calling attention to himself until he was offered the chance to be flown into Germany to do some work behind enemy lines. The pilot on that first flight was an exuberant young man named Tommy Eaton, who had joined the Lafayette Escadril because he loved flying and here was opportunity for the greatest flying in the world.

The two of them managed the job so well that they were sent back several times on other similar missions, and when the States entered the war and both were transferred to the American army, their teamwork was recognized and they were kept together. And between them there evolved a friendship that was both dependent and independent. Their difference in rank separated them on the ground, for Tommy was a captain and Bob a sergeant, but out on mission Bob acquired the leadership and Tommy followed him with a blind confidence that did not seem strange to either. Bob could move through the dangerous darkness with a quietness and a controlled movement that the taller and heavier Tommy could not hope to imitate, and this erected in Tommy's mind an awe and a deep admiration for his slighter comrade. When Bob taught Tommy to swear in Spanish, the idea for a commercial airfield in South America was born in Tommy's mind. So Bob had come to Mexico and was now bound to a year's service in this mountain-enclosed valley—a valley chosen deliberately because it lay west of Saddle Mountain, the mountain which he had been taught in childhood to regard as the symbol of his heritage.

Five days ago when he stepped from the train he had not been conscious of any feeling save weariness, nor of any thought for the single year ahead, but only for the years to follow. Now the present flicked across his consciousness. He was no longer moving in an isolated cloud. The village was flowing towards him like a wave, and its first softness had already touched him. He shut his eyes and sweat was cold and heavy on his face. His grandmother's voice stirred faintly in his memory, *"Once, to every man, comes a vision of the future...."* For a moment it seemed that he could see his life spread out before him, with the mountains barring his exit on either side, and in front of him Saddle Mountain refusing him passage to the outer world. As quickly as it came the feeling dissipated, but it left him trembling although he laughed softly at his own stupidity. As he thought back over that momentary vision he muttered to himself in English, "Stay here until you die? You're crazy. One year from today you'll be on the train, headed for South America. You forgot to eat lunch. You're hungry. Shake yourself over to Doña Juanita's and get yourself some supper."

As he stepped into the street a shrill woman's voice screamed at him from the plaza, "Stop that chicken!"

He stumbled backwards as a scrawny feathered creature skittered past him. His hand shot out automatically and his fingers grazed the outspread wings. A clenched fist punched his back.

"After it!" snapped the voice, so like his grandmother's that he instinctively obeyed.

The chicken had swerved around the corner of the sugar-mill and was loping towards the cliff edge. As Bob ran, he was vaguely conscious of someone following him but he did not turn. Time had played another of its tricks and he was an eight-year-old child chasing a chicken through the littered yards of tumbledown huts in San Antonio's Mexican section. With a forward swoop his curved hands closed around the feathered body and he was aware of a momentary surprise that he was not afraid of stabbing beak and raking claws. Then time settled once more into its proper perspective, and when he turned he was the grown Bob Webster politely extending the captured hen towards the old woman standing some distance away from him.

She was very thin and very small. Her head did not reach the level of his shoulder. And she was very old with the age that comes from the spirit rather than the body, so that she might have been forty or sixty or a hundred. Her gray hair was platted into two neat wisps of braids, and gold earrings dangled against the thin corded neck. A blue wool shawl was pulled taut across her shoulders, and her blue striped skirt and white blouse were so stiffly starched that she seemed encased in a machine of clothes. On her bare feet were scuffed and broken men's shoes, obviously too large, and on her wrists were numerous brass bracelets that tinkled when she moved her arms. Her face was covered with a net of wrinkles through which emerged, as through a veil, a strong straight nose, a mouth almost empty of teeth, and a pair of glittering black eyes.

She examined Bob with the blank scrutiny of her kind, then took off her three-cornered shawl and made a sack of it, into which Bob dropped the chicken. With a flick of her wrist the shawl closed and was once more folded around her shoulders so that she appeared to have a wriggling hump on her back.

"The hen will smother," Bob protested horrified.

Her lips slid away from her toothless gums in a broad smile. "Impossible. I have just had it blessed by the priest, for it is, you understand, a poor layer of eggs. The good saints will keep it alive for me. You are the *Yanqui* who wants a servant?" The lips returned from the smile and hardened into a tight line. She walked around Bob, examining him as frankly as though she were thinking of buying him. He jerked in angry embarrassment and started to speak, when her question startled him into silence. "You are afraid of witches? Not the stupid witches of the town like that fool of a Nimfa, but a true witch who has eaten the hot liver of the freshly dead eagle?"

"Witches?" he repeated blankly, and his heritage frightened him while his mind laughed at the question. "What have they to do with me, señora?"

She shrugged careless shoulders. "I am of the eagle clan and well versed in magic, green, red, and white." Her voice sank into contemplative softness. "Also at times black, although that seldom." She stepped closer and tilted her head so that she could better examine his face. "Your teeth are good. My son—it was Severo, the one killed in the Great Revolution—did not have good teeth. But Adán, the one who fell to his death from a mountain crag—his teeth were very good. White, like yours. He ate many cocoanuts. Perhaps that accounted for it. I have not studied the reason." One veined hand touched Bob's cheek. "About you there is a look of Gregorio. He was my youngest—who died from the kick of a horse. My youngest, and sometimes I think my best beloved. Perhaps because I cannot remember what his father looked like. Yes, the little Gregorio was all mine, with no memories attached to him. The father of Severo was a drunkard, and the father of Adán was a soldier. But Gregorio's father, no—I cannot remember. No matter. He is dead. They are all dead, my lovely sons. You live in the Italian's house?"

Bob, caught in the spell of her thin voice, nodded dumbly.

"That is a very dirty house. The Italian was very dirty. Before him was the Frenchman and all the rest, the men of little worth. They were all dirty. I do not like dirty men."

Bob, feeling vaguely that this statement demanded comment, opened his mouth, wondering what words would flow out of it. He heard himself say, "The Italian's suits are still hanging in the bedroom. I do not like to touch them. . . ."

"Naturally. They have the smell of death on them. Not for you to touch them.—Me, I am different. I am a witch—an eagle witch. Remember that. I do not belong to the stupid clan of town witches. In me there is power, not simple spells to win a lover or kill an unwanted husband." She jerked her shoulders in irritation. "This fool of a chicken is scratching my back. Tomorrow morning I will give the Italian's suits to the quarry men. Why not? One of them might have been his father-in-law, or perhaps all of them. It is impolite to inquire into such matters. What is your name?"

When he told her she said, "A stupid name, but for that you are not responsible. I am the Tía Magdalena. I have another name also, but my father forgot to tell my mother what it was. All the world calls me Tía, but that is a little joke, for I am not aunt to all the world. It is a matter of no importance. Tell Doña Juanita that I said to give you a good supper." She stepped away from him and narrowed her eyes, the better to see his face through the deepening purple of the twilight. "No, I will tell her myself. You lack the proper firmness of manner. Come."

As she walked away from him, the chicken on her back bobbing in protest against the smooth glide of her movements, Bob followed her with the dazed realization that through some process not clear to himself he had acquired an eagle witch as a housekeeper—an eagle witch who bore a disturbing resemblance to his grandmother, not in appearance but in manner, so that the tyrannical training of his childhood made him defenseless now against this newer tyrant.

He said in a hope of establishing some sort of authority however slight, "You are the woman of whom Father Zacaya told me? You have served in the House Castillo?"

Her right shoulder rose in a gesture of indifference. "The good

priest told me you wanted a servant for the mornings only. I was
not interested." The left shoulder also rose and implied what she
had not put in words: that she was not interested in foreigners. "I
did not know then that you looked like my son Gregorio, may
the saints be kind to his pains in hell, for he was a worthless creature, like his father perhaps, whom I do not remember."

"I was thinking," said Bob, hoping his voice sounded assured,
"that the arrangement would be satisfactory to both of us. I can
cook my own supper or eat at Doña Juanita's—" The sentence
stopped as she turned and looked at him, her face quiet and without expression. What he wanted was of no importance, said that
blank face. He was a child and without judgment. He was eight
years old and his grandmother was rejecting his desires. Then he
was grown again, watching Tía Magdalena walk into Doña
Juanita's house, where she led the placid, fat boardinghouse keeper
into the kitchen.

There were no other paying guests tonight. He sat at the dining
table alone, the blue-white dishes with their green Greek-key
pattern spread in front of him. In the distance he could hear the
faint murmur of voices. He thought in English, It's my house and
I'll run it the way I damn please even if she is an eagle witch.

Then Tía came into the room and set a dish of fried rice covered with strips of red pimento and slices of bananas in front of
him. When he started to eat she tapped him on the shoulder with
one stubby finger.

"Are you completely stupid?" she demanded sharply. "Supposing you dropped dead in the middle of a bite? What would
happen to your soul? I will tell you, it would go straight to Purgatory and Grandfather Devil would shake his tail in your face."

Bob shut his eyes and inhaled deeply. Far in the distance he
heard the lonely whistle of the train. Against the curtain of his
closed lids he could see it grind to a stop beside the water trestle
before it plunged east to Monterrey. If he pushed back his chair
now and ran, he could catch it. In two hours he would be safe
in the shadow of Saddle Mountain. Then, even as his muscles
tensed against his rising, the old woman's hand came to rest on
his shoulder. It had no weight at all, and yet it was heavier than
the largest slab of quarry rock. "Come now," said her voice as to
a sulky child, "speak the proper words and eat your supper."

He slowly opened his eyes and murmured the grace in Spanish

and began to eat. He was hungry. The rice was very good. He did not hear the whistle of the train as it travelled east to Monterrey.

As Bob finished his supper, Pepe Gonzalez, followed by his shadow, Andrés Treviño, came quickly into the dining room, both of them moving with that assured grace common to men who walk the mountain trails.

Pepe grinned impudently at Tía Magdalena, standing like a small bronze statue beside Bob's chair, before he said to Bob, "Your horse has arrived. All the world is at the blacksmith shop."

"It is truly a white horse," Andrés murmured in awed tones.

Bob, frowning, went with them into the deserted street. This avid interest in his affairs was distasteful to his reticent mind, although he had realized from the beginning that a white horse would make him a subject of common gossip throughout the Sabinas Valley.

The two young men on either side of him were chattering excitedly about the animal, comparing it to Don Anselmo's sorrel, to the Rocinante of the now long vanished Joaquín Castillo, and to other horses in the five towns. But Bob heard them as from a whispering distance. This was the first time he had walked through the village at night. The moon had not yet risen, but the stars were fixed points of diamond hardness in the sky's black ceiling. The houses with their lighted rectangles of windows and doors seemed to belong to a ghost world. Water, sprinkled at sundown on the dusty streets, gave the earth the pleasant fragrance of growing things. From potted plants and the plaza flowers came a sweet and nostalgic aroma that recalled to him the perfumed hedges of Ireland. In many ways this Mexican village had an Irish quality: the same quickness to laughter and anger, the same concern with death instead of life, the same easy friendliness and courtesy which stood strong as a stone wall between the stranger and true intimacy.

Then he heard the distant crowd voices, and the air seemed to break about him like the quick chirping of hungry birds: those little undulations of sound almost vanishing before they reached him.

The glow of various lanterns moving like giant fireflies on the small Plaza of the Viceroys ahead of him made him quicken his steps. "Lord," he thought, "the whole village. They'll destroy that horse."

He started to run, Pepe and Andrés pounding after him. They passed into the crowd of bodies moving restlessly in the darkness. Bob pushed against them, but they were as resilient as soft rubber, moving away from him and then returning to place. Pepe, behind him, shouted, "It's Don Bob," and a lane to the stable opened for him.

Someone caught and held his arm. He looked down into the excited face of a twelve-year-old boy.

"It is a magnificent animal, Don Bob. I, Xavier, say it."

The crowd murmured, "Xavier says it," like a Greek chorus in the background. There was friendly laughter and the gentle warmth of voices. Bob could see the people dimly against the shadowed lantern light—men, women, and children, all of them interested and eager in this grand event.

"You must never race him," the boy said, pulling Bob through the crowd like a knife through butter. "White horses never win races. They have the heart but not the speed."

"Xavier says not to race it," chanted the crowd.

Bob wanted to ask Pepe who the child was that his advice on horses should be so respected, but the young Xavier was guiding him through the arched door of the blacksmith shop, where small groups of men were discussing horses with much argument and waving of arms. And then they were in the corral of the livery stable in the presence of the horse itself.

In the yellow lantern glow its whiteness was tinged with cream, and the silky mane and tail were of gold thread. The long curved body, the legs, dainty and slender, the arched proud neck betrayed an Arab strain. He paced slowly, his small hoofs flicking the dust, and with a casual and almost bored unconcern, allowed Porfirio, the carver of wood, to walk him up and down in front of five men, two of whom Bob Webster recognized as Don Nacho, the alcalde, and the cameo-faced priest.

Father Zacaya came up to him and shook his hand. "It is a fine animal and much admired. Eh, do you know our doctor and Don Rosalío?" His hand gestured toward a short plump man with heavy eyebrows, and a tall thin one with a luxuriant white beard, who murmured their own names in voices too low for Bob to understand them. The priest put his hand on the fifth man's shoulder. Bob knew from the swelling muscles and heavy thighs that this must be Don Fidencio, the blacksmith and livery stable owner.

"Eh," said Don Fidencio to the young Xavier. "What do you think?"

The boy ran his hand over the glossy coat and down one trembling leg. He hummed soothing cadences without words, which seemed to quiet the delicately boned animal, then lifted a hoof and examined it. He glanced up at Bob. "I say it again. You have bought well."

The white-bearded man nodded rapidly. "Xavier knows. He was born speaking the language of horses." He smiled at the boy. "Take the royal creature out and show him to the crowd. But do not let them frighten him. He has nerves, this one."

Bob, feeling like an onlooker rather than an owner, started to protest, but Don Nacho's trumpeting voice boomed through the corral.

"We must now name the animal."

"Not here," said Father Zacaya, with a quick glance at the white-bearded man, who nodded in answer to some unspoken question. "We could go perhaps to the Residence..."

"Too far," said the short fat man. "My house is only around the corner." He locked his arm through Bob's and smiled engagingly up at him. "You are very brave. As a doctor and a man of science I do not, of course, believe in ghosts, but I would not ride a white horse in this valley."

Bob looked over his shoulder. "Pepe Gonzales and Andrés Treviño were with me. I seem to have lost them." He was absurdly frightened to be without them. They had a pleasant friendliness that these older, dignified men lacked.

"Those two are doubtless admiring the horse," said the white-bearded man, who must, Bob decided, be Don Rosalío if the small fat man were the doctor.

They went through a back gate and around the corner, and it was not until they were entering the small, bare house that Bob realized the blacksmith was not with them. He felt like a child thrust suddenly into an entirely adult world as the four elderly men led him into a narrow room filled with overstuffed furniture upholstered in purple velour. There were no curtains at the deeply recessed window, nor rugs on the bare cement floor. In one corner was a white enameled case of surgical instruments, and in another a rolltop desk so covered with books and papers that it was impossible to close it. On one of the yellow plaster walls hung a calendar showing two handsome Chinese lovers and the printed message that the Quong Lee grocery in Monterrey was the finest in the Republic. Bob looked steadily at it to reassure himself that the year was really 1920, the month was March, and he must be, without doubt, twenty-six years old.

He took his eyes away from the calendar and examined a large framed photograph of a fat man, who wore a Stetson hat and carried a tennis racket. The face had the vague familiarity one associates with pictures of celebrities, but it was not until he was leaving that Bob realized the man was Pancho Villa.

The room had about it an air of emptiness as though the person who owned it lived somewhere else. The little Doctor tugged at his heavy brows. His full name was Mariano López Martínez, but no one ever used it. Like the cameo-faced Father Zacaya, he was an outlander, having come originally from Chihuahua. During the Great Revolution he had ridden with Villa's Golden Men. When the years of peace came, he visited Hidalgo, intending to spend no more than a night. Instead, he rented a house, opened his office, and became the medical adviser for the five towns in the Sabinas Valley.

"This is my office," he said to Bob. "Sometimes in the evening it is a little lonely. You are more fortunate."

Bob looked at him, not understanding. Don Rosalío explained that Tía Magdalena was the only woman in the *Gallineros* who could live unchaperoned in a man's house without gossip. "The town is too afraid of her spells to start any rumors about her," he said.

"For a year I have been trying to get Tía to work for me," the little Doctor said. "And Don Rosalío longer than that. Tía is an excellent servant, trained in the House Castillo in the old days before the Revolution, when, I understand, the House Castillo represented the culture and wealth of the northern frontier."

"From all over the world," Don Nacho said, "people of importance came to visit the House Castillo." He sighed for past glories and blew his nose on a large, red bandana handkerchief.

"So naturally," continued the little Doctor, "with such a background Tía is much to be prized as a servant. But she is a woman of strong whims, and unfortunately Don Rosalío and I do not appeal to her—shall I say, sympathies?"

Don Rosalío waved a graceful hand. "Father Zacaya is lucky. His housekeeper is sister to the cook of Don Juan O'Malley. The two women share a room in the Residence. But the little Doctor and I, our homes lack the woman's touch."

Bob shook his head in bewilderment. "But how did you know—about Tía working for me? She only just arranged—I mean I only—just before supper—the arrangements—there's been no time to know!" he finished desperately.

The men smiled at each other and then at him. The priest explained patiently that no one had ever been able to explain how news circulated so quickly in a Mexican village. "Any village," he said, "all over the Republic. They are all the same. And as for keeping a secret—Blessed Saints, why attempt the impossible?"

"Unless they are like Chela," Don Nacho said suddenly. He explained to Bob that Chela was his daughter. "Although a woman, she has a tongue as silent as death. I do not understand her." He shook his head and sighed. The little Doctor whispered in Bob's ear that poor Chela had been born homely and would die an old maid without doubt. "It is a great sadness on Don Nacho."

Don Rosalío patted his chair arm with his palm and said they were not assembled to speak of Chela or Mexican gossip but to choose a name for a fine animal.

Bob explained that he had thought of calling the horse *El Blanco*, the white one.

"Why?" asked Don Rosalío kindly.

Bob bit his lip and said that after all the horse was white. He saw no reason to add that his grandmother had often told him, *"He called the horse El Blanco. Ay, what a fine beast he was!"*

The priest commented mildly that perhaps the name lacked a certain vigor. The little Doctor thought that the horse had the white purity of the moon. Perhaps Diana. . . ? Don Nacho pointed out coldly that Diana was a woman's name and the horse was not female. Don Rosalío suggested *El Negrito*, the little black one. "He is so white, you understand. It would be an amusing jest."

Bob felt anger mounting through him. He looked at the four men and thought in English, What the hell! It's my horse. He said aloud in clipped Spanish, "Forgive me, señores, but it is my horse and I like *El Blanco*."

No one answered him. Against the imperturbability of these four old men he felt his own desires to be like a stream resisted by a narrow passage, so that they ran round to an eddy and were pushed back with more swiftness than he could bring them forward. The first day he came their eyes had been blank against him, and now, because he had bought a white horse, they were taking a strange new interest in him which he could not understand. Surely a childish ghost story would not attract the attention of these four men. Don Nacho, it was true, was peasant bred, but Don Rosalío and the little Doctor were obviously men of certain learning, and the priest had admitted to schooling in Dublin University. Why, then, would they take such an interest in his private affairs unless ...

A sensation of helplessness flowed through him. Like Tía Magdalena, they saw him as a child, without judgment. But he was a man. He was *jefe* at the quarry. Did not the whole cement plant in Monterrey depend on his sending the proper amount of limestone to them at the stated time? What was more, he had been a sergeant in the A.E.F. An American army sergeant had an established reputation as a man who definitely knew his own mind. He would tell these four remote and fatherly men that important fact. He would say boldly: You do not understand. I know my own mind. I can prove it. In the World War I was a sergeant. Sergeant Bob Webster ... Bob Webster ... Bob Webster ... Like an automatic recording machine his memory clicked a record into place, and he heard a blond man's voice say with cruel clarity, *"You have the impudence to call yourself Bob Webster? Do you think I'd admit an Indian is a son of mine? Damn it, I'm a white man!"*

The moment passed, and Bob relaxed against the sofa, the velour pricking his back through his thin shirt. He knew that his closed face would not betray the cold sickness that enveloped him, but his hands were trembling so violently that he had to thrust them into hidden safety in his pockets.

Don Rosalío was speaking to him. "You do not understand. There was once a famous bandit who came from these hills. His name was Daniel Menéndez. In 1871 the roads to Monterrey were heavy with rich traffic. Riding always a fine white horse, so that he gained the name of *El Caballo Blanco*, this Menéndez stole much gold and jewels ..."

"He was a kind man," rumbled Don Nacho suddenly. "He never killed anyone. Only knocked them down and robbed them."

"The soldiers," continued Don Rosalío after a gracious bow to Don Nacho, "nearly captured this bandit several times. At last he had to escape to Texas. A woman betrayed him to the authorities. He was returned to Monterrey for execution."

"She was jealous," Bob said under his breath. "She didn't know they would shoot him."

"You spoke?" Father Zacaya asked politely.

Bob bit down on his lower lip. "I said, that seems a heavy penalty for nothing but robbery."

Don Rosalío nodded, his white beard gleaming in the lamplight. "In those days money was taken seriously, even as now. But the stupid ones shot him too quickly. He never revealed where his treasure was hidden. There are stories that he left a map, but only the wind has claimed ownership to it. And through the years the legend of Daniel Menéndez and his white horse has grown, until now people are afraid to hunt for the treasure for fear he will appear before them in ghostly wrath and drive them into insanity."

"I do not approve of ghosts," the priest said gravely, "but that legend has kept many a foolish boy from getting lost in a mountain cave or falling to his death from a cliff."

"The point is," said Don Rosalío ponderously, "he called his famous horse *El Blanco*. Now do you understand why it would not be a wise name for your animal?"

Don Nacho settled his large body more comfortably in the big chair. "The people would be terrified if a real white horse named *El Blanco* should travel the mountain trails again. They would expect Daniel Menéndez to return. A valley shaken with terror is not an agreeable Eden. It is, you comprehend, a matter of importance. The people are our responsibility."

Bob realized with a flash of understanding that these four men were the actual rulers of the village. He had been brought here, not as a friend, but as a supplicant before a Board of Regents.

"It occurred to me," Don Rosalío told him, "when I first saw the animal that you would want to call him *El Blanco*. The name is obvious—he is so very white. And so I spoke to my friends..."

A crisp knocking at the door interrupted him. He frowned at the little Doctor, who shrugged. "I can't understand it. No babies are imminent, and no other sickness would cause an interruption at this time."

Of course not, thought Bob, watching the short fat man go to the door. The whole damn village knows I'm being told what to name my own horse.

His surprise at sight of the visitor brought him to his feet. The other men did not move, but they smiled at him in approval before they greeted Tía Magdalena.

"Well," said the old woman, her arms folded across her sunken chest. "Do you know the hour? And he has to rise at dawn to reach the quarry in time."

"I'm not a child!" Bob protested furiously. "I'll go to bed when I please!"

She shook her head in reproof. "Look at him," she ordered the four old men. "Like a ghost he looks, his eyes sunken in his head. He's been sleeping in a hammock in the patio."

"A habit much enjoyed in Yucatán," the priest suggested helpfully.

"Not in Hidalgo," retorted Tía Magdalena. "I borrowed a bed from the boardinghouse. Come to bed now," she added soothingly to Bob. "A good bed with a fine straw mattress."

"The horse . . ." Don Nacho began, with a glance of appeal at his friends.

"I have thought about the horse," she said quickly. "And I have thought of a fine name for him. Don Bob, because he bought the horse, is obviously not afraid of ghosts. It is good for the people to witness bravery. Through the sight they acquire bravery as a child acquires strength from the sun. And surely only a very brave man would ride a white horse in this valley—especially a horse named . . ." She produced the final phrase with a triumphant sniff, "*El Blanco*. So," she added to Bob across the silence, "the matter is settled and you can come to bed."

He picked up his hat and meekly followed her from the house. There were, he decided, certain advantages in having an eagle witch for a housekeeper.

Years later he liked to recall his entrance to the Indian-crowded mesa, riding on the white horse, its glossy coat whiter still beneath the red-brown beauty of the saddle. Where there had been chattering and laughter there was silence. Frightened eyes concentrated on animal and rider. A few hands surreptitiously lifted in the quick gesture of the evil eye. Others blessed their owners with rapidity. Bob sat on the horse and looked down at them, feeling the muscles of the animal quivering beneath his thighs. His long fingers stroked the creamy mane and his mouth slid into the habitual sidelong smile. Then a woman started screaming. "It is *El Caballo Blanco* come to take us all to Hell. Saints preserve us. Blessed Virgin, keep . . ."

The thin high thread of sound broke as a competent palm snapped across her cheek. Candelaria said coolly, "The more fool you. It is only the *patrón*. A good day to you, *patrón*."

"And to thee, Candelaria." Not until the words were spoken did he realize he had used the familiar pronoun, but there was no offended dignity in her eyes.

"As you say, *patrón*," she murmured formally.

As always he felt afraid of her dark beauty. Since Yvonne, he had accepted women lightly, allowing himself no feeling beyond the pleasure of the moment. But Candelaria, ripe and beautiful as a pomegranate in full flavor, was to him as intoxicating as an opium dream distilled from poppies. He wanted not to look at her, but he looked at her with eyes as blank and somber as the eyes of the Inditos who surrounded them.

He shifted his attention to Don Anselmo. The old quarry foreman was staring at him with the interest of a bird watching a new animal.

"If your grace will descend," he murmured. And then, "It is a noble horse."

"And if a horse is white, what then, Don Anselmo? You never told me the proverb."

"If someone tells you he saw a horse ridden by a king, ask him the color of the horse, and if he says 'white,' believe him."

"So? And does that make me a king, Don Anselmo?"

The secret glances passed across the crowd like wind rippling a field of barley. Don Anselmo shrugged. "Are you not the *patrón*?" It was not a question but a statement. And Bob Webster knew with inner exultation that he was now, in truth, *jefe* of the quarry.

But in his house in Hidalgo, Tía Magdalena ruled. She took for her own the small room at the back of the patio near the kitchen.

Her nostrils pinched in a supercilious line when she first saw the dead rubber plant, the jumbled wicker furniture with cushions torn and exposing their cotton stuffing. Federal soldiers and Revolutionists had both been quartered here after the Italian's death, and the Brussels carpets and flower-stenciled window curtains had large squares cut from them for use as saddle blankets or shirt material. In the patio the roses and potted plants had long since decayed into rotting wood and yellow leaf. Bob had hung a hammock between the orange and lemon trees, and his pyjamas were flung over the pomegranate bush.

Porfirio, the carver of wood, the dark, laughing Pepe Gonzalez, and the small, round Andrés Treviño had been ordered to bring Tía's clothes from the *Gallineros* under threat of a bad-luck spell. They trotted after her from room to room as she carried smoking incense of crushed laurel leaf, garlic, and cloves through the house to cleanse it of evil spirits, and added their voices to hers as she chanted the exorcism:

> *House of Jerusalem,*
> *When Jesus entered*
> *Evil departed as Good appeared.*
> *I, also, ask of Thee,*
> *Sweet Jesus,*
> *That Evil leave this house,*
> *And Thy goodness cover it*
> *In the smoke of this incense. Amen*

When this ceremony ended, Pepe Gonzalez recognized the thoughtful expression in her eyes and quickly remembered an errand from his father to the priest, but Andrés and Porfirio, less astute, were caught in her witch's net and found themselves drawing water from the well and scrubbing floors.

When Bob came home that night he discovered a clean house with nothing to remind him of the Italian save the wicker furniture and the jagged cracks in the plaster walls, exposing the gray adobe brick beneath.

Tía waited until the food was warm in his stomach and he was smoking his pipe in the patio before she approached him. He was stretched out in the hammock, his arms locked under his head, one foot dangling over the side so that he could now and then give himself a slight push. In his mind he was on a boat gliding across the phosphorescent water of the Gulf toward South America, the moon a silver radiance about him. But Tía Magdalena knew nothing of South America as she came to stand beside him, her arms folded across her flat chest.

"It is necessary," she said coolly, "to purchase certain things. I have made a list." She pulled a grimy sheet of paper from her pocket and held it close to the lantern in order to read it. "I am," she said with formal pride, "a person of education. I can write words. I can also read them. And the mystery of numbers is not unknown to me."

"Magnificent," murmured Bob, his foot pushing against the floor so that the hammock swung in a wider arc. He was still riding in his boat, and her words had not yet left his ear to enter his mind.

"A new door at the entrance of the house. This thin wooden thing is of small account. Porfirio will carve one for a reasonable price. I shall see to that. And new furniture. And curtains for the windows. And a stove that cooks with wood instead of charcoal. In the House Castillo there is such a stove. It is very grand with a base of tiles. For you it is not necessary to have the tiles. And the walls must be painted. Those on the outside green with blue, I think. I have given the matter consideration. Green is cool to the sight, and around the windows and doors a design of blue for dignity . . ."

"One moment!" He sat up and stared at her. "What are you saying?"

She carefully repeated everything that she had said with one part of her mind, while the other part was concerned with his stupidity. Something, she thought, will have to be done about that. I shall work a spell upon him to give him wisdom. But her tongue curved smoothly around her speech with no hint of her inner plans.

Bob shook his head three times, and then once more for emphasis. The money for the horse and saddle and now this—and only a year in which to save two thousand dollars. Impossible. He said it aloud, "Impossible. That will cost much money and for nothing."

"So? And you intend to live in a hut for pigs?"

"No, Tía, it is only that . . . you see, I . . . Well, I'm to be in this house only a year. After that I'm going away."

"Is it possible?" She folded her slip of paper and returned it to her pocket. "You do not like Hidalgo?"

"Yes, very much." He brushed his hair back from his face with an impatient hand. "It's just that . . ." By a trick of moonlight her face was in shadow, and he saw her as a silhouette against the lantern glow, so that she was no longer Tía Magdalena but his grandmother, cold and imperious. Because of this he told her more than he wanted to tell. He told her of Tommy Eaton, and the plans for the commercial airfield in South America.

"This friend, he flies through the air?" The disbelief in her voice was so strong that it made him smile.

"Yes, in what is called an airplane."

"You yourself have seen this?"

"I've flown with him."

"In the air?"

"Higher than these mountain peaks."

"Hm!" She said nothing more but left him to go to her room. He lay back in the hammock with a sigh of contentment. She no longer had him locked in a cage. He had won an argument from her, had shown her that he was the master of his own house. Why, he was even stronger than those four old men who ruled Hidalgo. They had not won an argument from Tía Magdalena. His foot pushed happily against the patio floor, and he was again in his boat bound for South America.

But Tía was not so easily vanquished. She lighted a candle and pulled a small box of books from under her bed, books whose ownership she had never confessed to the priest nor to anyone else. Years before, the young Joaquín Castillo had brought them to her as a present from his voyaging into the world beyond the mountains, and had patiently taught her to read and write so that she could decipher the mysterious pages. All were bound in paper, with strange pictures on the front. One showed a masked man clutching a dagger, with a crimson-robed woman bending over him. Another had a clock's face framed by a red-eyed owl and a greenly glowing candle. The book she opened portrayed a naked woman bathed in flames, a blue serpent coiled around her, and in her upthrust arm a golden apple.

Tía's thin, claw-like fingers ruffled the pages until she found the heading she sought: "Instructions for Flying Through the Air." She read avidly, skipping remembered formula as a lawyer skips familiar legal phrases, until she found the important sentence: "To a glass of strong wine add a cup of English whiskey and drink it in three mouthfuls. If it is the wish of the lords of darkness, you will then feel yourself rise into the air."

Tía sniffed in disdain. "So, airplane he calls it. Flying he calls it. Does he think I am a creature of delicate sensibilities that he cannot say honestly, 'I am saving my money in order to become a drunkard?' "

She pulled thoughtfully at her ear and considered her responsibility in the matter. Obviously he was not meant to be a drunkard or the Blessed Saints would not have sent him to Hidalgo, nor herself into his house. Therefore her duty was clear. She must save him, and to do so she must first devise methods to make him spend all his money, to keep him healthy so that illness would not demand liquor, to keep him too busy to think of such nonsense, and finally, to keep him happy. These achievements, she realized, were all of an extreme simplicity for an eagle witch. While making her plans she knew that she would need help, and finally decided on Pepe Gonzalez, Pepe who thought himself so clever in escaping work. It would be good for him.

But first things first. Don Bob had to be kept healthy. And that was why Bob complained about his eggs at breakfast. "They taste strange, Tía. What did you put in the chile sauce?"

"Nothing. They are the same as always."

"They taste strange," he repeated, but he ate them. Tía fondly smiled at him, pleased that he liked chile, because chile deadens the taste of anything else and he was only vaguely aware of the nine grains of juniper, the powdered pecan meat, and the mashed dry fig which she had added to the usual sauce, a mixture which all her magic books assured her would keep anyone healthy until one presumably disintegrated from old age.

After Bob rode off on his white horse, Tía put on her shawl and paid a visit to Doña Nimfa, the town witch, referred to in the valley as the "herb woman," who lived near the *Gallineros*. Doña Nimfa occupied the peculiar position of being Tía's best friend and bitterest enemy. Both being witches, Tía, who was smarter, lorded it over her lesser rival. Both being women, Doña Nimfa, who was softer and more pliable, was far more popular in the five villages. The Sabinas Valley was frankly afraid of Tía Magdalena, as were the quarry Inditos, and although Bob did not realize it, the fact that she had become his housekeeper had as much to do with his overlordship as the white horse. More, really, because a man of certain will power might control the jealous spirit of *El Caballo Blanco*, but only a great and forceful man could hope to control an eagle witch. That the eagle witch controlled him was a secret which Bob kept out of pride, and Tía out of policy, but Tía was well satisfied with her hidden power as she approached the door above which was fastened the stuffed lizard that advertized the herb woman's calling.

The one small room with its rough, windowless walls of woven cane, and its roof thatched with maguey leaf, was a squalid darkness, from which furniture began to emerge as the eyes lost their sun-blindness. To one side was pushed the battered wooden bed with its thin corn-shuck mattress and pink crocheted spread. There were various chests kept level on the uneven dirt floor with stone slabs, a small table covered with cheap lithographs of the saints, and a stone brazier in which charcoal redly gleamed.

And everywhere, piled against the walls, upon the chests, and under the bed, were stacks of herbs, weighting the air with their spicy perfume. Here a sufferer could find powdered rice for fevers; eucalyptus for heart trouble; ant weed for appendicitis; flowers of magnolia for nervousness; mint to augment mother's milk; rosemary for thin blood; flower of the wicked woman for gonorrhea (when placed under the bed it also killed bedbugs); and hundreds of others for as many sicknesses or ailments. Besides this fragrant wealth there were bottles filled with such things as swallow's eyes—when placed under the pillow, a husband would remain asleep through any disturbance; dove's hearts—to bring back an errant lover; dried frogs—when rubbed on the stomach would destroy a tumor; rattlesnakes preserved in wine—when devoured by a man using the proper spells, all women must instantly love him, regardless of his age; pulverized coral to show a man his future wife; and many others.

Since Doña Nimfa was a business woman who believed in aiding the saints as well as the Devil, there were also stacks of small slips of paper printed with prayers against enchantments, for preservation from evil spirits, against being inducted into the army, and to gain luck in the lottery.

Such a display of mysteries caused most of Doña Nimfa's customers to stay in safety outside the door, but Tía Magdalena, who was not only an eagle witch, but the daughter and granddaughter of eagle witches, had no such uneasy qualms of the spirit. It was true that Doña Nimfa was superior in reading hidden writing and the lines of the palm, but in magic spells and incantations, Tía was supreme in the valley.

She looked at the younger woman with hard, bright eyes. "I want the heart and right foot of an owl. And don't tell me you haven't any because I know you have."

Doña Nimfa hastily wrapped the purchase in a cone of white paper, protesting that such a thought was not in her head. Tía tossed her some copper coins which brought a wail of anguish from the herb woman.

"Wicked names of five devils, owls are rare birds in these parts. Goatherds must bring them to me from the other side of the mountains. Surely they are worth more than ..."

"Silence!" snapped Tía Magdalena, stalking through the door into the clear air and brilliant sunshine. "This is no day to anger me. I am engaged in making plans."

Doña Nimfa hastily put both fat hands over her mouth to keep her tongue from betraying her, but the moment Tía was out of sight she muttered three curses for bad luck.

Tía, hurrying home, her too large shoes slapping the dust in little spurts, automatically muttered three counter-spells—for she understood Doña Nimfa's cunning habits—and then forgot the herb woman in her impatience for the arrival of night.

At last it came, and Bob perversely sat for long hours in the patio, smoking his pipe, his mind, as usual, intent on South America. Tía, watching him from the seclusion of her bedroom window, was aware of a tingling excitement in her blood. The owl charm was very potent. What would it reveal to her? She could only wait in nervous impatience. These *Yanquis!* Did they not know that nights were made for sleeping? Under ordinary circumstances she would have informed him that his bed was waiting for him, but she had already observed that motherly advice irritated him, and she wanted, at the moment, not the slightest disturbance of his placidity.

Finally he yawned hugely, tapped out his pipe on the heel of his shoe, and went into his bedroom. After his candle was blown out, Tía waited another hour to make certain he was asleep. Then, clutching the cone of paper, she slid noiselessly across the patio and listened at his door. She could hear his deep, even breathing. Satisfied, she entered and crept cautiously to the bed. With slow care she laid the owl's heart and right claw on his chest. Then she knelt beside him and murmured softly over and over, "Speak your secrets, speak your secrets, speak your secrets."

His head twisted deeper into the pillow, but he did not waken. Tía whispered the words again, monotonously, but there was no reaction. The owl charm, which all her books assured her would make any sleeper reveal the most reticent mystery of the enigmatic soul, had failed. In sudden anger, she snatched up the heart and claw, and started into the patio, but as she reached the door he spoke. "Sofía," he muttered drowsily. "You've cut your hair, Sofía." Then he turned over and the speaking was finished.

Tía was much puzzled. The only Sofía in Hidalgo was eighty-five years old. The Sofía at the quarry was aged seven months. Neither of them had enough hair to merit cutting. Don Bob's Sofía obviously lived beyond the mountains. Doubtless she also wanted him to save his money so that he could become a drunkard. Were not the eyes and ears of drunkards sealed by drink so that a woman could live her life as it pleased her? From this logic Tía came to the conclusion that Sofía was a woman of little worth, and without morals. How fortunate that she lived far from Hidalgo. Of what use to a man was a distant woman? And in Hidalgo were there not two women of great beauty: the golden María of the River Road, and the dusky Candelaria of the quarry? Undoubtedly María was the more beautiful, but she was also the more independent. And Tía liked independence only in herself. It will have to be Candelaria, she decided. Tomorrow she would go to the quarry.

This settled, she had one more task before she went to bed. Using some paper yellowed with age that she had stolen from Don Nacho, and adding water to the ink so that it would look pale and old, she carefully began to draw. A cross indicated north and south. In the northeast corner she sketched a fairly creditable saddle. In the southwest, a ship appeared. Between these two she drew a giant lizard. By this time her nose was very close to the paper, her snaggle teeth closed tight on her outthrust tongue. Finished, she cocked her head and examined her work. But it did not altogether please her. She felt that it was still too vague. After a long period of brooding, she took up the pen again and added to the design a very small turtle, its head pointing toward the lizard, and below it four quick strokes of the pen to form an oblong. Satisfied, she left the ink to dry of itself and went to bed. That will give Don Bob and Pepe Gonzalez pleasure for at least three years, she thought happily to herself, and by that time I will have spent so much of Don Bob's money he will not have enough to buy a ticket to Monterrey, much less to join the wicked Sofía and the wicked Tommy Eaton who would teach him to die a drunkard.

After her household chores were finished the next morning, she went to Doña Nimfa's, and handed the softly fat woman the drawing.

"Perhaps," she murmured, "if you are clever, you might sell this to the young Pepe Gonzalez."

"Indeed," snorted Doña Nimfa, "and since when have you become so generous?"

Tía permitted herself the luxury of a shrug. "Do you question me, little one, and I an eagle witch?"

"No, no, Tía, but ..."

"You might say when you show it to Pepe that a man riding a white horse would undoubtedly bring added luck."

"The only man on a white horse in all the valley ..."

Tía finished a sigh with a bored yawn. "Pepe might pay you a peso for the paper, although I cannot see that it is worth more than fifty centavos." As she rose to leave she added with casual unconcern, "If he asks you where you got it, say it came to you in a dream. The arch-demon Astarot, grand duke of Hell, appeared to you and left the map in your hand. But I would not like you to mention my name. No, I would not like that at all."

She said no more, but Doña Nimfa's round eyes showed clearly that she understood what would happen in case she disobeyed. Tía smiled to herself, automatically murmured her three charms against Doña Nimfa's maledictions, and set off on the long, slow climb to the quarry.

Arriving at the mesa, she was pleased to see that the new office of rough stone was completed. It was much closer to the rim than the old one, and a single great window gave a sweeping view of the valley and the western mountains. Someone had planted flowers all around the small building, and Tía, seeing this, sniffed in comprehension. Obviously some woman was already rolling the eye at Don Bob. Well, bad luck to her, unless she was, of course, Candelaria.

Carefully skirting the building so that Bob would not notice her, Tía went into the quarry and climbed one of the ledges until she reached the cave where Candelaria lived with her father.

"Tía Magdalena!" Candelaria came forward to greet her, the oval face flushed with heat from the cooking fire. "You do us honor."

Tía smiled, and squatted on the floor, her knees drawn up close to her chin. From behind her right ear she took a corn-shuck cigarette, which Candelaria lighted for her. Not until it was puffing to her satisfaction did she begin the long business of courtesy greeting, Candelaria standing meekly in front of her, the lovely eyes lowered in modesty as became a young woman in the presence of an older and wiser one. Tía passed at length to the subject of flowers and painlessly extracted the information that it had indeed been Candelaria who had planted the beds near the office. "Don Bob said one day that he liked flowers."

"Also such flowers as you, little one?"

In the dusk of the cave it was difficult to see the blood surging beneath Candelaria's soft bronze skin, but Tía was aware of the blush and smiled gently at her. "Eh, he admires you, little one. And only this morning," she lied glibly, "I read in the cards that there was such a woman as you in his life."

"Ay, Tía," the soft young voice stumbled over the words. "Such happiness. Not for me, Tía."

"And why not? Are you not a pretty creature? Not so pretty, of course, as María of the River Road, but very pretty as women go?"

"Thank you, Tía."

"Why? Because God made you pretty? I had nothing to do with it. Give me a lock of your hair."

"Ay, Tía." Candelaria began to tremble as with a chill. "For me you would—but I have no money to pay you—I, please, Tía . . ."

"Stop your chattering and give me a lock of your hair."

The girl's fingers so trembled with nervousness that Tía, impatient, cut out the glossy lock herself and thrust it into her pocket.

After the hair had been steeped all afternoon in Bob's cherished bottle of French cognac. Tía added the liquor to some fried bananas buttered with thick cream.

Bob, eating the dessert, smiled at her. "You are spoiling me, Tía. You wouldn't want to go to South America with me, would you?"

"And ride in an airplane?" she demanded, scandalized.

"Naturally. You might even meet one of your friends, the eagles. Who knows?"

The thought of herself as a drunkard made her shudder. "I'd meet more than an eagle," she told him tartly, and went to open the door to the loud knocking of Pepe Gonzalez, Andrés Treviño, and Porfirio, the carver of wood.

"Bob," Pepe yelled in English. "I've got something to show you."

Bob came curiously into the patio, smiled at the three young men, shook hands with them, and examined the yellowed sheet of paper Pepe thrust into his fingers.

Andrés said, "It is a matter of great excitement."

"Perhaps," whispered Porfirio, his eyes rolling in excitement, "there is a million pesos all in gold pieces."

Pepe reverted to Spanish. "Jewels, too. Pearls, rubies, sapphires, diamonds . . ."

"The shining gold pieces," sighed Porfirio. "What a beautiful thought. What a delicious thought."

"Do you think anyone else has found it?" asked Andrés anxiously. His two friends stared at him with pity and then turned their eyes to Bob.

"We need you to find it," Pepe explained. "The person from whom I obtained it said a man riding on a white horse would bring us great luck."

Bob bent closer to the lantern, his long face and square chin thrown into bold relief. Pepe drew in an audible breath. "*Chispas!* For a moment you looked like a Huachichil!"

Bob jerked erect and Porfirio grinned. "You are too much with those Inditos. You should join with the village more."

"Only this morning," chirped Andrés, "Father Zacaya was asking what you did in the evenings. This house is not all the space in the world."

"It would be good for you to join us," insisted Pepe. "Think of it: amethysts, topaz, pearls—the gleaming frosted pearls."

"The gold," sighed Porfirio. "The shining heaps of gold."

Bob shook his head in bewilderment and again leaned forward to examine the paper. "What kind of a drawing is this? A saddle, a ship, a lizard, a turtle, and—what's that—an oblong?"

"Saddle Mountain," Porfirio explained rapidly. "The ship is of course the Peak of the Prow. The lizard is the western range of mountains. That's what the country people call them, because of the shape that the peaks take."

Andrés shifted his weight from one sandaled foot to the other. "The turtle, anyone knows what the turtle means. And the box— well, that is obvious."

"Not to me," Bob told him. "I can't understand . . ."

"The turtle," Pepe explained kindly, "means buried treasure. And the oblong shows that the treasure is buried in a box."

"Treasure?" Bob repeated blankly.

"But, naturally," cried Porfirio with excitement. "You hold in your hand the lost map of *El Caballo Blanco*."

Bob sank into the hammock and started to shake his head. A blast of sound greeted the gesture. Tía, eating her supper in the kitchen, smiled as she heard it. "I must perform a kindness for Pepe Gonzalez," she told herself benevolently. "Such a silver tongue he has. Who can resist his arguments? Ah, well, with me to spend Don Bob's money, the morning potion to keep him healthy, Candelaria to bring him happiness, and treasure hunting to keep him busy—no drunkard's life for this one, eh, pretty saints?"

But Tía had forgotten to include in her plans the person of one Dorotéo Lozano. This Dorotéo had a small farm across the river, where he grew orange trees. The Sabinas Valley contended that the saints loved him, for his crop was always a good one. The enemy Valley of the Three Marys said Grandfather Devil pitied him, as such a good disciple had to have some compensation. But both valleys were for once agreed on two things: Dorotéo Lozano was not only the laziest man on the whole northern frontier, but he could stay drunk longer than any other man west of Saddle Mountain. It was whispered from Topo Grande to Mina that in his mouth his mother's milk had turned into tequila, and no man could boast of ever having seen Dorotéo sober.

News travels fast in a Mexican valley, and Dorotéo soon

learned that Pepe Gonzalez, with the aid of Andrés Treviño, Porfirio, the carver of wood, and the *Yanqui* quarry master were hunting for treasure; that it was undoubtedly the treasure which *El Caballo Blanco* himself had buried many years before anyone now alive was born; and that the *Yanqui*, who was not afraid of Grandfather Devil's fiery breath (did he not ride a white horse called *El Blanco* and have Tía Magdalena as housekeeper?) had himself defeated the spirit of *El Caballo Blanco* in ghostly battle, and when the treasure was found, as surely it would be found with Don Bob hunting for it, everyone in the Sabinas would be wearing silk, and the people of the Three Marys would be cutting their own throats in envy, and not even the archbishop would be able to bury them in sainted ground because of their blasphemy at taking their own lives.

Dorotéo examined the news and found it good. He also decided that it might be many years before the treasure was found, but that in the meantime there was no reason why he should not profit from the excitement; and also it would do no harm to visit Don Dionisio, that distinguished owner of the Saloon of the Devil's Laughter in Hidalgo.

When he reached the saloon he was pleased to see the young men he sought sitting around a small table, the treasure map as well as a rough map of the eastern range of mountains spread out before them, the latter drawn by Bob with advice from the other three.

"The difficulty is," Bob was saying impatiently, "the turtle isn't pointing to any particular spot. It's simply pointing. We could search all our lives and never find anything if that turtle's the guide."

Dorotéo smiled happily as he heard these words. He had made no plans, depending on blessed San Martín, patron of drunkards, to aid him when the time came. It was now evident to him that San Martín was very powerful indeed, and worth at least one small candle in the church, which he promised with solemnity as he draped his fat body across the back of Bob's chair.

Pepe was saying, "We could divide the map into sections and then search each section."

"With seven years' effort to each section?" Bob drummed on the table with his fingers. "Even if there were a treasure, we would be too old to enjoy our find."

"You can say that?" squeaked Porfirio. "And all that lovely gold waiting for our hands? You can say . . ."

Dorotéo Lozano smacked his lips so loudly that the four young men jerked as from the explosion of a bullet. Ignoring the inhospitable glances, he pulled a chair from a near-by table, elbowed Andrés out of his way, and drew the treasure map toward him. "As I thought," he said gravely. "Indeed it is as I thought." He finished this profound statement by draining Pepe's half-filled glass, making a grimace at discovering the liquid was beer instead of mescal.

"Who the devil are you?" Bob demanded sharply, realizing that his three friends were too stupefied to say anything.

"Permit me, señor. I am Dorotéo Lozano. My *ranchito* is across the river. You are doubtless Don Bob," a wave of his hand dismissed the unpronounceable *Yanqui* name. "Eh, but these three little ones are friends of my youth."

"You're drunk," Andrés accused with obvious accuracy.

"I am not sober," Dorotéo admitted after grave reflection, "but I am not completely drunk. When I am completely drunk, I snore. At the moment I am not snoring."

"This is a matter of business," Porfirio said flatly, "and no concern of yours."

Dorotéo sighed. "Friends, you pain me."

Pepe Gonzalez had held his temper as long as he could. He now slapped the table with his open palm. "Friend, this will pain you even more. Remove yourself from this table."

"Ay, but that is indeed a sad thing. And me, señor," Dorotéo turned with heavy courtesy to Bob, "I am a lazy man. All the world will tell you that I am a lazy man. Yet I ride here to Hidalgo from the comfort of my *ranchito* to bring these friends of my youth a great gift—and to you, also, señor, who will be, I trust, a friend of my age—and with what am I greeted? A kindly smile? A small glass of warming cheer? No. Nothing but coldness and the request to remove myself." He clutched at his breast and sighed deeply.

Pepe pushed back his chair and laid his hand on Dorotéo's shoulder. His voice was liquid and soft. "With my hand I will help you, friend—so!" He thrust forward and Dorotéo, caught off balance, tumbled sideways into Andrés Treviño's lap, who, with the anguished expression of a cherub with the toothache, sat holding the fat body.

The more practical Porfirio jerked Dorotéo back into place. "One moment, friends. This friend speaks of a gift. We are always glad to hear of gifts."

Andrés asked excitedly, "What type of gift, Dorotéo?"

"Shh," Dorotéo glanced cautiously around at the men playing dominoes near by and the other men lounging against the bar. He leaned forward to the center of the table so that the others were forced to lean forward also to hear his words. "My father told it to me, and he had it of his father. You can see for yourself on this treasure map that the story is true."

"What story?" This came in chorus from four interested throats.

Dorotéo beamed at them. "Why, naturally, even as the map says."

"Porfirio," Pepe said urgently. "I am going to slit this one's throat two minutes from now. Warn him that I shall use a dull knife, and draw the blade very slowly . . ."

"Now, now, friend Pepe, contain yourself." Dorotéo swayed his head from side to side. "I am a lazy man. You are the four with energy. To you digging is an amusement. To me it is a burden invented by the stepbrother of Grandfather Devil on his mother's side."

"Just a moment." Bob put out his narrow hand and hit Dorotéo's shoulder with the palm. "Are you trying to tell us something about the treasure?"

"But naturally. Are the words not clear in my mouth?"

"No!" flared Porfirio. "And if Pepe cannot find a knife dull enough, I myself will find one. Speak! Throw the words out of your mouth, one, two, three."

"Me, I wait with patience," Andrés said humbly. The rancher smiled at the round-faced boy.

"To you I will tell the truth. My father has said many times that the treasure of *El Caballo Blanco* was hidden on our *ranchito*, but it was necessary to dig for it. The thought of digging helped me to think the story false, but this treasure map shows that he spoke true words."

"How does the map show that?" asked the practical Porfirio.

"Behold it yourself. You followed the line of the head, and where does the head point? Towards the eastern mountains. But the head is oval and flat. Should you draw a line from the nose, from the right eye, the left eye? On the map those three lines leave a little space between my fingers, but in the mountains, ay, those spaces broaden to kilometers."

"That's what I've been saying," Bob muttered.

"*El Caballo Blanco* was very clever," Dorotéo said. "If he lost the map, naturally every treasure seeker would follow the stupid lines of the head. But no one would ever think to follow the single, the pretty, the sweet little line of the tail."

"The tail!" Four pairs of eyes concentrated on the drawing of the turtle. Four pairs of eyes noticed the short, straight stroke that was the tail. Four pairs of eyes returned to Dorotéo's bland face. The rancher said smoothly, "The head might point anywhere, but the tail points to but one place, and that is to the *ranchito* of Dorotéo Lozano."

A flurry of voices greeted this pronouncement, over which Bob's harder and more clipped voice rose triumphant. "How do you figure that? There's no western line of mountains on the map."

"The beauty of it," sighed Dorotéo. "Why should *El Caballo Blanco* indicate the obvious?"

"Well..." said Pepe doubtfully.

"Well..." echoed Andrés Treviño.

"I don't know..." said Bob.

"We could try it," said Porfirio. "We have to dig somewhere, and ay, the pretty little stacks of shining gold!"

The following Sunday the four young men appeared at the *ranchito* of Dorotéo Lozano.

"Welcome, friends, welcome," he cried grandly. "See, I have spades for you, and even a pick. And I can show you the spot—the very spot in which to dig.

Bob looked at him suspiciously. "You mean you know the exact spot where the treasure is buried?"

"But naturally not," Dorotéo protested. "Only the locality. Here among my fruit trees." He led them to a section of the irrigation ditch in the orchard where no trees were planted. "So sad that the water is flowing. You will get a little muddy."

"For such a treasure," Porfirio assured him, "I find the mud of no consequence."

"Precisely. This is the location. You will have to dig up and down the ditch. That is all I can tell you. And now, forgive me, friends. I am a lazy man. Even to watch labor—you comprehend." He went back to his house and sat in the shade of a weeping willow tree. From a water-filled bucket close at hand he would now and then take a bottle of beer. But most of the time he gazed placidly down the gentle slope of the hill and contemplated the peaceful scene of distant river and more distant town, with the blue line of mountains beyond. "Blessed San Martín," he said tranquilly, "you and I together, we are very clever fellows."

By sundown the perspiring young men had dug twenty deep holes and found nothing. Bob put down his spade and mopped his face with a grimy handkerchief. "Personally," he said grimly, "I think our friend Dorotéo has not been honest with us."

"But the tail..." began Andrés.

Pepe snapped at him with irritation. "Do not mention that tail to me. Twenty holes—look at them. And my hands covered with blisters, my back aching with muscle pains. And for what? Twenty empty holes!"

Porfirio's voice was a melodious murmur, "How nice that our good friend Dorotéo is a lazy man."

Bob suddenly began to grin. "True words, friend Porfirio."

"What a pity," continued Porfirio on the breath of a sigh, "if we forget to fill in the holes. These deep, deep holes."

For a moment there was silence. Then they all shook hands, made their way to the ranch house, where they courteously bade their host goodnight with the gently expressed hope that he would let them return to dig again, and rode home through the lavender dusk. It was not until Bob was going to bed that the thought occurred to him that Dorotéo's actions had been tinged with mystery. All we gave him, he thought, was one small glass of mescal. And he came to Hidalgo especially to find us and tell us that story. But why? He fell asleep before he had found an answer.

All the next day in his office he puzzled over the problem. "I'll ask Pepe tonight," he decided finally. "Pepe knows the fellow. He'll be able to figure out the reason."

Bob was placidly happy in the sudden knowledge that these

weeks of treasure hunting had not been entirely fruitless. The nimble-witted Pepe Gonzalez, the obvious-minded Andrés Treviño, and even the penurious Porfirio had given Bob a sense of security he had not known since his mother's death two days before his sixteenth birthday.

It was true that the long-dead Ned Kelley, and the airplane-mad Tommy Eaton had given him friendship. But these three Mexican young men gave him a feeling of comradeship that grew, not so much from a meeting of minds as from a relationship of blood. *I understand how they think,* Bob summed it up finally for himself, *and what actions will follow the lines of their thought. And that's because,* he added with a slight feeling of surprise, *I think and act the same way. We have no need to explain ourselves to each other.*

He was so pleased with this logic that he decided to ride down to the village, and treat the three young men to a drink. As he started out the door, Candelaria darted away from it. She was obviously trying to hide something behind her back.

As always his sharp awareness of her warm beauty embarrassed him, but he forced himself to smile at her. "What is it, Candelaria?"

To his surprise the red blood gushed in quick flood across her face and throat. He took a step toward her and his voice sharpened. "Candelaria, what is wrong?"

"Nothing, Don Bob. Believe me—I had nothing to do with it."

"What are you talking about?"

"Oh, Don Bob!" she crumpled to her knees and began to cry, her face unshielded, as a child cries.

For a moment panic shook him at sight of her tears. Then he was kneeling beside her, his arm across her shoulders. "What has happened, little one? Who has hurt you? Tell me. What is it?"

She dumbly extended her hand, her fingers crushing a sheet of paper. He took it from her and smoothed it out. "But this is only a drawing—a drawing of a line of trees. How could this make you cry?"

"When my father finds the evil creature who pinned it to your door for a jest, I personally will kill him." Her voice sank away in a wail of sound.

"But why would anyone pin such a drawing to my door? What does it mean? I have nothing to do with trees."

"Yesterday you dug some holes—for that worthless Dorotéo Lozano."

"Well?"

"He—he—oh, Don Bob . . ."

Bob gave her his handkerchief and she pressed it against her eyes. "He is such a—a lazy one. Some new trees he had to set out—and—and he didn't want to dig the holes, and . . ."

For a moment there was a black silence. The morning of his interview with his own father he had been angry. The evening Yvonne had casually dismissed him, he had been angry. But never in his life had he been so angry as now, for those other moments had been solemn and dignified, but this was tinged with ridicule. The men at the quarry, the people in the village . . . wherever he walked or rode, faces would turn to him veiled with secret laughter. Bob's body stiffened. His hazel eyes, always somber, took on a murky greenness.

"Pepe, Andrés, and Porfirio," moaned Candelaria, "are like wild men. They are waiting at the *ranchito* now—waiting for Dorotéo to come back from wherever he is hiding. They want you to join them. They want you to bring some oil to boil him in."

"Pepe," repeated Bob. "And Andrés, Porfirio." Why, he was not alone in this. Between us, Bob thought, we will figure out a beautiful revenge. Dorotéo Lozano will remember with sorrow the day he got us to dig his tree holes. And suddenly the idea of himself and his three friends holding solemn conferences over the proper punishment for a rancher too lazy to plant his own orange trees struck Bob as ridiculous, although he knew that, ridiculous or not, the four of them would pass many unfruitful but satisfying hours planning such a revenge.

He began to chuckle softly, and his arm tightened across Candelaria's shoulders. Although it was still daylight on the high mesa, in the valley below darkness had come and lights were appearing in the toy houses. Let the people laugh and have their little joke. It was not against Bob Webster, stranger, but against Bob Webster, member of the community, who had gone treasure hunting with more fervor than good sense. He was no longer an outlander to be ignored, but a comrade of Pepe Gonzalez, of Andrés Treviño, of Porfirio, the carver of wood.

His chuckle deepened into laughter. The mountains caught the sound and tossed it back to him, so that he seemed to be laughing in chorus with himself.

Candelaria stared at him with bewilderment. "You—you are not angry? All the world points with ridicule and you are not angry?"

He put his slender hand on her hair and felt the softness of it against his skin. "You are not pointing with ridicule, little one."

"Ay, no, Don Bob. How could I—at you?"

His hand moved down the side of her face and cupped the chin in the palm. The natural perfume of her skin, sweet as night blooming jasmine, made his heart beat faster and his bones feel flaccid and without substance. He said irrelevantly. "The first night I was in Hidalgo, I dreamed of you. Did you know that, Candelaria?"

"The first night—but you didn't know Tía the first night."

"I dreamed of you, pretty one, not of Tía Magdalena."

"But—without the charm—how could . . . ay," she put both hands over her mouth and stared at him with wide eyes. Surely, her mind told her, Tía must be indeed a powerful witch if her lover's spells could work backward through time.

Bob, serenely unaware of Tía's magic, put his hands under the girl's elbows, and as he rose lifted her to her feet. "You are so beautiful, Candelaria," he whispered unsteadily. "So very beautiful."

She stepped closer to him. He could feel the heat of her body against him. "I dreamed, too, the first night, Don Bob."

He kissed her deeply, then rested his cheek against her hair. His white horse was tethered a little to the left of them, and a rock shadow gave the illusion of a ghostly figure standing near it. Bob smiled and wondered briefly if it might really be the ghost of *El Caballo Blanco*. His grandmother's voice spoke in his memory. *"It is necessary to be polite to all things . . . even to animals."* Surely such a statement included ghosts, even ghosts of famous bandits.

Bob put his hands over Candelaria's ears. Then he looked at the shadow and spoke with all the politeness at his command. "Good evening, Grandfather."

The Street of the Three Crosses

Porfirio

April, 1921

He who eats with his nose, pays with his mouth.
—Mexican proverb

THE MOON HUNG LIKE A SILVER CRESCENT BEHIND THE BLUE belfry of the pink church, and the sky was night indigo with a silver sheen. At the four corners of the Plaza of Independence hung oil lanterns, throwing their small circles of yellow light on the broad cement walk.

Beyond this walk, in the center of the plaza, the bitter orange trees were heavy with fruit; the limes were in blossom, and their sweet perfume drenched the music-filled air—for the orchestra was playing in the bandstand.

Clusters of women moved counter-clockwise on the street side; the men clockwise on the orchestra side. Some of the older people sat on benches, or on straight chairs hired from the "Sunday Evening Plaza Chair Association," a concern owned by Porfirio, the carver of wood, Pepe Gonzalez, and Andrés Treviño.

Although the orchestra conductor was urging his men to play as loudly as possible, the shrill voices of the plaza crowd were louder still. Above the noise rose the high tones of the candy maker, calling his wares: "Almond paste, nut cheese, candies of burnt milk, of sweet potato, of cactus heart. Who will buy my candies? Almond paste! Nut cheese!" And when he paused, the town gardener would take up the refrain with, "Carnations, roses, gardenias! Buy flowers for your mother, your sister, your sweetheart, your wife! Carnations for her mouth, roses for her heart, gardenias for her hair!"

As the gardener wandered through the crowd, his white trousers flapping around his thin brown legs and his straw hat set well back on his head to show he was an honest man, Porfirio stopped him.

"Eh, Don Serapio, give me a small gift of flowers."

The old man chuckled, tipping his head to one side. "A gift, is it? Wood is your trade, flowers mine. Let me see the color of your money."

"Now, Don Serapio," Porfirio protested, "you know I am a poor soul. I have not the wealth of Pepe Gonzalez, that son of a cheese factory. One little gift of flowers is not much to ask."

Don Serapio rolled his eyes toward heaven and ran his tongue over his teeth. His tray needed mending, and he had intended to take it to Porfirio the next day. That job would cost about fifty centavos. A bouquet of flowers cost ten centavos. . . .

He beamed and said, "Listen to me, Porfirio. Every man knows the worth of his own blanket. This tray of mine needs mending.

In exchange for such labor I will give you a bouquet of flowers. Is it agreed?"

Porfirio answered eagerly. "But naturally, Don Serapio. Bring your tray tomorrow. And now I want your most beautiful gardenia—one with a very loud smell."

For forty centavos profit, the gardener handed over a waxen white flower. As Porfirio hurried across one of the cement paths, Don Serapio chuckled and fell into step with Don Nacho. It was whispered in the town that because of his great stomach, the mayor had not seen his own feet for the past ten years.

"That Porfirio," said Don Serapio, and recounted the little episode. He finished with, "Someday he will learn that his fine deals always lose him money. Much cheaper to pay out the coins and be done with it. Forty centavos that ten-centavo flower cost him, but Porfirio thinks he got it for nothing. What a magnificent intellect."

"Flowers," said Don Nacho thoughtfully. "So Porfirio makes deals for flowers, does he? And for whom were the flowers?"

Don Serapio's mouth dropped open. "I never thought to ask him!" He slapped his palm against his forehead. "San Benedito, is it possible that Porfirio, that tight-fisted man, is rolling the eye at some girl?"

When Don Nacho laughed, his stomach quivered in sympathy. "And you the finest gossip in Hidalgo. Every man knows the worth of his own blanket, you said!" Still laughing, he passed on with the crowd.

Porfirio found his friend Andrés Treviño walking with Nena Santos and Alma Orona. He knew that to join them was impossible. Two boys and two girls walking together would create a scandal. But sitting in a chair beside her mother was Don Nacho's homely daughter, Chela. He hurried to her and whispered. She nodded, and a moment later joined the promenade. Porfirio sat impatiently beside Doña Mariliria, waiting for the group of three girls and a boy to encircle the plaza and return to where he was sitting, so that no gossip could connect his name with Chela's.

He sat very straight on one of his own chairs, the gardenia tightly gripped in his hot palm.

"That is a pretty flower," said Don Nacho's fragile wife.

Porfirio smiled weakly at her. If she continued to admire it, he, of politeness, must offer it to her, and he knew enough of women to know she would not refuse.

"It is a poor thing," he said quickly. "Already it is wilting."

"Do you like gardenias?" she asked with a mischievous gleam in her eye. She wondered what excuse he would make to keep from giving it to her. Porfirio's love of money was famous not only in Hidalgo, but through all the five villages strung along the banks of the Sabinas River.

"The little Doctor," he said hastily, "tells me that gardenia perfume is very good for weakness of the chest."

"Have you a weakness of the chest?"

Porfirio squirmed on the hard straight chair. "No, not exactly. But I might have. Better to prevent sickness than to pay doctor's bills."

"Indeed, yes," said Doña Mariliria, hiding a smile behind her large black net fan and winking at Pepe Gonzalez, who came up to them.

"Eh, Porfirio, have you paid for that chair?"

"Why should I pay for it? I own it."

"Not that chair," said Pepe, with a sly glance at Doña Mariliria. "That one belongs to me. Your chairs are on the other side of the plaza."

"Come now, Pepe, is this a kind thing? Do not you and Andrés and I own all the chairs? Besides, the money would go to the Association. Why should I pay money to myself?"

"And steal the rightful share that belongs to Andrés and myself?" Pepe flung up his hands in a scandalized gesture. "I ask you, Doña Mariliria, is that fair, is that honest? Every Sunday night we divide the profits between us in three equal sections. Is it right that one should have more than the other two?"

"But I don't have more than you," Porfirio snapped. "If the money is not there at all, how can I have more nothing than you do? That is foolish."

Doña Mariliria tapped him on the arm with her fan. "But if you were not sitting in the chair someone else would sit on it, paying ten centavos for the privilege. In that way you deprive your partners of three and one half centavos each."

"A small amount, true," said Pepe. "But if all of us sat in our chairs, how could we make a profit?"

Porfirio sprang to his feet. "There is your chair," he cried. "It is cheaper to stand. Soon you will be charging me for the air I breathe!"

At this moment he saw his group coming toward him, and with a curt bow to Doña Mariliria, he hurried to join them. With careful management, he contrived to walk between Chela and Alma Orona. To his prejudiced eyes, Chela's homeliness, her large nose, heavy black brows, and wide, full-lipped mouth, pointed up the serene prettiness of Alma, with her large clear eyes, her heavy black hair worn in a crown of braids, and her skin warmed by the sun to a dark gold.

The gardenia slipped from his fingers to Alma's. She gave him a quick sideways glance, and he said with careful innocence, "Don Nacho says the moon will be late tonight."

Andrés Treviño said, "Pablo, the goatherd, told me that a late moon gives the goats moon-madness."

There was a gasp of protest from Nena Santos. "Andrés Treviño! And you a good christian talking to Pablo, the goatherd! Have you no care for your soul, and he the son of Grandfather Devil?"

While Andrés was trying to explain to Nena that it was impossible to be a goat owner without having traffic with goatherds, Porfirio asked Alma if she would be at her window later in the evening.

"If you come with musicians," she whispered wickedly.

"Ay, but Alma, musicians cost money."

"So! Am I so worthless then?" With a toss of her head she separated herself from the group and walked away with Chela. Nena gave a little scream at finding herself alone with two men and darted after them. Andrés and Porfirio stared moodily at each other.

"That Nena Santos," Andrés mourned. "Why is it given to a man to be afflicted by a stubborn woman?"

"To your own troubles," retorted Porfirio, moving toward the bandstand. "I have enough of my own."

But Don Alonso, the orchestra leader, who knew Porfirio's bargaining ways, was adamant. To play the rooster cost five pesos. It had always cost five pesos, and he did not see why it should be cheaper for the wood-carver.

"But five pesos," Porfirio wailed, "is a lot of money for thirty minutes' work. And when the music is done, what do I have left?"

"The smiles of a woman," said Don Alonso promptly, who had often parried this argument. "That should be enough for any man."

"Five pesos," mourned Porfirio. "Ay me, that is a fortune—a very fortune."

"For two pesos," said Don Alonso, "I could give you a guitar and a violin. But a proper rooster is played with five men. Of course if you want your girl to think herself worth only two pesos..."

Porfirio shuddered. Alma Orona was as proud as the mountains. If she thought he put her value so low, she would never speak to him again. And he loved Alma Orona. He really loved her. He loved her more than the two hundred pesos he had saved to buy her trousseau and rebuild a house and shop for their married life. But during the time he had saved those two hundred pesos he had not counted upon all the extra money it seemed a courtship needed. For example, these five pesos, thrown, as it were, on a musical wind.

"I can't pay five pesos," he cried desperately. "I can't, Don Alonso."

Don Alonso looked over his shoulder at his musicians and winked. As one man they winked back at him.

"In the new Casino they are building," said Don Alonso smoothly, "it would be a nice thing to have an orchestra-stand at the far end of the patio, as I have told you many times."

"But the committee says it would be a useless extravagance."

"The committee lacks a musical soul. Should you erect such a platform..."

"But that would take lumber!"

"Of course," said Don Alonso, shrugging his unconcern, "if you prefer to pay us five silver pesos cash, we will be glad to play..."

"One moment," said Porfirio, wrinkling his forehead in a desperate endeavor to think. "One little moment. I have some lumber left over from the making of two coffins. It might be possible—it might be just possible."

"A stand," said Don Alonso, "to seat seven men, and sufficient room for me to walk about."

"At the southern end of the patio ... yes," said Porfirio, "it is possible. And you will play for me?"

"In return for a really fine stand," said the harp player, "perhaps we could excel ourselves and give you all of us tonight."

"All of you," Porfirio breathed happily, looking around at the seven faces—eight, with Don Alonso. "Including the drum?"

"Including," said Don Alonso grandly, "the saxophone."

It seemed to Porfirio that time moved slowly forward to the hour of the serenade. The free benches were occupied, and he was afraid to sit in one of his own chairs for fear Pepe Gonzalez or Andrés Treviño would demand payment of him. His legs ached from standing, and he was thankful when Bob Webster invited him to his house for a glass of wine.

"To the ending of a year," Bob said in toast, and Porfirio echoed him.

"So you are leaving Hidalgo, Don Bob?"

"At this hour next month I will be on the blue Gulf."

"Ay, that will be a grand thing. But the valley will miss you."

Bob said with an air of surprise, "And I will miss the valley. Sometimes I almost wish I didn't have to leave."

Neither man noticed Tía Magdalena standing in the shadow of the pomegranate bush. She slid into her room on quiet feet, poised for a moment beside her bed, then knelt and drew out the box of books. Her hands hesitated above the volumes, and finally selected one with a plain cover on which was printed in scarlet letters, "Black Magic." She flicked the pages to the section marked, "Wishes of Importance," and settled herself to read.

In the patio Bob poured another glass of sherry for Porfirio.

"Enough, enough," murmured the young man. "Already my brain clouds, and I will have no words to speak to Alma Orona. Wine makes me stupid and sleepy."

"A *tequilito*, perhaps?"

"Thank you, Don Bob, but—well, a little one. This is my first playing of the rooster. I shake with nerves."

Bob laughed and gave him a small glass of tequila. Porfirio poured some salt on his palm, licked it, tossed the tequila down his throat, and ended by sucking a lemon. "Wine is for women," he said firmly, "but tequila puts heart in a man."

He rose and solemnly embraced Bob. "My good friend, when you leave Hidalgo, I will light a candle for you. I will even weep a little." With a formal bow, he walked steadily out of the house to meet Don Alonso and the orchestra members.

The men grouped themselves near the house of Alma Orona on the Street of the Three Crosses. Pepe Gonzalez had come along to offer his advice.

"Now, Porfirio, you stand there beneath the window. Don Alonso, the musicians, and I will stand across the street."

Porfirio looked at his friend suspiciously. "But that window belongs to the house of old Don Ursulo. Alma Orona's is there."

"Nonsense! How can you tell the difference?"

"By the color. Alma's house is pink and green. Don Ursulo's is blue and red."

" 'By the color,' he says." Pepe turned to the musicians. "At night he thinks he can tell the difference in color. Has he not remarkable eyes? And only today I was reading in a book that under moonlight nothing has color—nothing."

"I don't care," said Porfirio stubbornly. "I'm not going to play the rooster in front of the wrong house."

Don Alonso said gravely, his eyes twinkling behind his thick-lensed glasses, "There is a true way to distinguish the houses. Only this afternoon Don Ursulo said that of all pieces, his favorite was the North American jazz piece, "Yes, We Have No Bananas." If we play it, it will bring him purring to the door. Then we will know to whom the window belongs."

"A most excellent idea," said Pepe, who had heard Don Ursulo on the subject of bananas.

Porfirio, his head buzzing from the effects of the tequila and wine, rolled his eyes from Pepe's face to Don Alonso's. Although Pepe was his very good friend, Porfirio never quite trusted him. But at last he nodded his head. "Very well. Play the jazz. We will see what happens."

"But first," said Pepe quickly, "you are too far from the window. Stand closer so that you can hear Alma's sighs. Remember, she is too shy a maiden to open the window immediately. Oh, and take off your hat, Porfirio. You are serenading a young lady, not drinking beer in the saloon."

When Porfirio was placed to Pepe's satisfaction, the cheese-maker's son hastily retired to the safety of the musician's group.

At a nod from Don Alonso, the violins released a wailing note of warning; then the harp added its rippling sound, the drums and flutes joined in; and finally the precious saxophone, ordered from a North American mail order house and entrusted to Don Alonso's fifteen-year-old son, took up the melody. "Yes, We Have No Bananas" ricocheted down the narrow Street of the Three Crosses.

Suddenly the window was flung open. Old Don Ursulo, in lavender nightgown and bright pink nightcap, swung up a pail of water and flung it with full force over Porfirio's head. The wood-carver, his mouth open ready to voice lover's phrases, stood immobile in surprise, the water running down his face and dripping from his shoulders. The music came to a jerking pause.

As Porfirio slowly turned around, musicians, Don Alonso and Pepe Gonzalez whirled and ran up the street, stumbling and pushing against each other, harp, guitars, and violins clutched for safety against their owners' stomachs. They did not pause for breath until they were safely crouching behind the bar in the Saloon of the Devil's Laughter. Then Pepe emitted a choked snort, and they pounded each other's backs and laughed until the tears came.

But Porfirio, left alone, water dripping in a pool about his feet, was not laughing. He slowly put on his hat and trudged home, his heels dragging in the dirt. He realized with mournful certainty that his playing of the rooster for Alma Orona had entered the pages of Hidalgo's history.

Although the villagers laughed at him, it was sympathetic laughter, for more than one had felt the barbs of Pepe Gonzalez's sharp wit. Even Andrés Treviño, Pepe's faithful slave, was cold towards his friend. And so, at the conclusion of mass on the next Sunday morning, Pepe rose from his knees and in a loud voice asked Alma Orona to forgive him. "For," he said, "if it had not been for my joking, you would have been honored with the finest playing of the rooster in the history of the Sabinas."

Alma smiled shyly at him, and did not glance over her shoulder at Porfirio, who was standing at the back of the building, but everyone knew that her blushes were for him, and that Don Carlos Orona would soon be sending out invitations to witness the marriage proposal.

After Pepe and Porfirio had gravely embraced in the church-yard and gone off to seal their peace with a glass of beer in the saloon, Andrés Treviño trotting like a shadow at their heels, Tía Magdalena hurried home to tell Bob the news.

She found him, still in his pyjamas, swinging in the hammock and reading the Mexican version of "Bringing Up Father," called in Spanish, "Educating Papa."

"Eh," she said tartly, "if you went to church like an honest christian, you would know more of the village."

He grinned at her. "Now, Tía, leave my religion alone. And what were you doing stealing into the house at four o'clock this morning?"

To his surprise she flushed, backed away from him, and then, without answering, whirled and ran into the kitchen. He sat up and stared after her. Good Lord, he thought, what's she been up to? Surely not a lover at her age. He bit his lips. Tales of Tía's powers as an eagle witch, heard from the quarry foreman, from Candelaria, and the villagers, began to filter through his mind. He suddenly jumped to his feet and went to the kitchen door.

"Tía, have you been playing with black magic?"

Her back to him, she bent over the brasier of glowing coals, blowing them to a brighter ruddiness.

"Tía, you hear me? As long as you stay in this house, you leave black magic alone." All the superstitions of his inheritance found utterance in the urgency of his voice. As an intellectual, he considered black magic pure nonsense, but as a grandson of the bandit Daniel Menéndez, his Indian blood foamed in terror at the thought. He had learned in childhood that black magic was distilled from the Devil's breath, and that even to think of it meant centuries of agony in hell.

The old woman straightened and faced him, her arms folded across her chest. "I am an eagle witch, and the daughter of an eagle witch, and I..."

"I know all that! But black magic has no place in the Sabinas. If you don't stop it, I'll tell Father Zacaya."

"Now, little one," she said conciliatingly, "and me a poor woman with no one but you to love since Joaquín Castillo, bless his sweet spirit, rode away to the Revolution. Do you think I would harm you with black magic?"

He ran impatient fingers through his hair. "You're up to some mischief. I know you, old woman." He asked quickly, "Did you receive communion this morning?"

"No, but..."

"Ha! I thought not. Evil was too heavy on your conscience. My grandmother used to say, 'Black magic is the love song of Lucifer.'"

"You think, then," Tía snapped, "that the old gods sleep forever? Sometimes they wake from their dreams. And when that happens someone must guard the world from their eyes."

"Then let another be the guardian." He rested his long, narrow hand on her shoulder. "Old woman, I shall soon be gone from this valley. If I could take you with me, I would..."

"There is no life for me beyond the mountains."

"A truth that you know and I know. And so I ask you, Tía, as a present of farewell, to leave the old gods to their dreaming."

She refused to look at him. Both realized that such a promise meant the end of her witchhood, for the eagle witches gloried in their secret rituals to the ancient gods.

She whispered at last. "I cannot make such a promise."

"But, Tía..."

"Hear me." Her hand brushed his in a pleading gesture. "Don Nacho says that soon the exile of the House Castillo will be lifted and Don Saturnino will return here to live, bringing with him his youngest son, Alejandro. Between Don Saturnino and myself there has been enmity for many years."

"Why, Tía?"

"No matter. If you leave the valley, the knowledge will not concern you. If you stay..." She paused for a moment, and turned her eyes away from him. She repeated firmly, "If you stay, then, with the years, you will learn there are many great secrets in Hidalgo."

"In this town," he scoffed, "where the grocer has your purchase wrapped before you make up your mind what to buy?"

"All towns," she told him slowly, "have their secret lives. Do you think the golden María lives alone on the River Road from choice? Have you never wondered why Joaquín Castillo vanished in the fire of Revolution? And as for Don Saturnino and myself, we have not spoken since the day his blessed wife put her head against my shoulder and died. He would have sent me from the valley long ago, but the people fear my anger. When he returns and finds I've lost my witchhood, he'll set every mouth to mocking me. Thrown sticks and rocks will drive me out of the Sabinas. I am old, Don Bob, so old that at times I forget the span of my years. My bones ache for the peace of Hidalgo earth..." She raised her palms and dropped them flat against her sides.

He nodded slowly. "I understand, Tía. I ask no promise of you."

A knock came at the front door before she could answer. Instantly she was transformed from a small and tragic figure into her usual snappish self. "That door! One more good knock and it will be a heap of splinters on the street."

"Stop hinting for a new door, Tía, and answer the knocking."

She scurried across the patio and returned in a moment with a large square envelope. "It's an invitation from Don Carlos Orona to attend the proposal of Porfirio to Alma. What's the hour?"

"Four o'clock this afternoon." He grinned at her. "At least, Tía, I am a man who can have no secrets in Hidalgo."

She did not answer, but she was thinking, No? And who then is Sofía? Is she the woman whose picture you cut from the newspaper and keep hidden in that box in the wardrobe? And poor Candelaria sick with jealousy because you whisper "Sofía" in your sleep.

While Tía was mixing the bitter chocolate sauce for the dish of fried young goat, she peered out at Bob now and then as he swung in the hammock. "Let this Sofía call you," she snorted, "for you'll not leave this valley while I have knees to pray in the church, and strength to climb the mountain trails and sacrifice hot blood to the old gods. I will concern myself with your future. You need think only of Porfirio's marriage proposal."

Alma's father and mother greeted their guests with much ceremony that afternoon. Doña Juanita Perez, the boardinghouse keeper, came early, secretly elated at having Bob Webster for escort. The little Doctor, Don Nacho, Father Zacaya, and Don Rosalío arrived in a body as befitted the dignity of the four rulers of Hidalgo.

They sat in the narrow oblong living room on stiff cane chairs, Doña Juanita Perez enthroned in a rocker, and Alma's parents side by side on the settee. Above their heads, a large mirror framed in gold reflected the tan lace curtains at the window, the oval photograph of Don Carlos and Doña Triumfa in their wedding clothes, and the round table, covered with an embroidered cloth, which supported an oil lamp of hand-painted china displaying purple morning glories and dark red pansies.

Don Carlos served the men small glasses of very sweet wine, while the women drank cups of steaming hot chocolate flavored with cinnamon sent in by Alma from the kitchen, for Alma, as a modest girl, was not permitted to be present.

Finally, from the hall, came the sound of muted voices. The little Doctor tiptoed forward and cautiously opened the door. They could hear Andrés Treviño say plaintively, "My feet hurt. Your shoes are too small for me, Pepe." And Pepe's lofty answer, "Your mind should be on the sufferings of Porfirio, not on your feet."

The little Doctor slid the door against the jamb and turned around. His eyes were dancing with devilish delight. "How long shall we make them wait?" he whispered.

Don Rosalío lifted his white beard with one hand, and with the other drew a large gold watch from his vest pocket. "Do you think fifteen minutes would be too long?"

"Andrés is perspiring. Pepe is very pale," warned the little Doctor.

Doña Juanita Perez smothered a laugh with a large green handkerchief. "My father made my first husband's petitioners wait over an hour."

Doña Triumfa tossed her head with disdain. "Your father, who was also mine, Juanita, was a man of wicked humor. But wicked!"

"He was that," said Don Carlos gloomily. "He kept my friends waiting nearly that long. I never forgave him for it."

"Eh," rumbled Don Nacho, "but what use to be old if we cannot have amusement at the expense of youth? What say you, Don Bob?"

Bob grinned. "I feel sorry for Porfirio, but Pepe Gonzalez needs a good dose of humility."

Once more the wine and chocolate were passed around. The liquid slid down throats with careful slowness.

Doña Juanita's curiosity could stand the suspense no longer. "Look at the poor innocents again, little Doctor," she ordered.

The door opened for the space of an inch, and Pepe's voice

said, "This black suit is too hot. I should have worn my white one. I am sweating like a mule."

"But black is more dignified than white," answered Andrés' clear tenor.

"A theory. A mere theory."

"They bury you in black," said Andrés, "and what could be more dignified than being buried?"

The door closed quickly, and the little Doctor leaned against it, shaking with merriment.

"Haven't we punished them enough?" quavered Doña Triumfa, wiping the laughter tears from her eyes.

The men had stuffed their handkerchiefs in their mouths to deaden the sound of their mirth. Doña Juanita Perez had both hands clasped tightly across her lips, and her rocker was shaking under her heaving body.

Don Rosalío examined his watch again. "We've kept them twenty minutes. Let them in, little Doctor."

Handkerchiefs were quickly returned to pockets, and the assembly was very dignified as the two young men supported each other into the room, each trying to hide behind the other. Their stiff collars were obviously too tight, and on both foreheads there were beads of perspiration. The little Doctor returned to his chair, and the various eyes seemed, in Pepe's imagination, to swim together and form one great lidless eye, as hypnotic as a coiled snake's. He cleared his throat and glassily fixed his gaze on Don Carlos Orona's face.

"We are here..." he squeaked. He paused, swallowed an Adam's apple that seemed to have enlarged to twice its normal size, and began again at a more natural pitch. "We are here in the name of our good friend Porfirio Rodriguez, known to Hidalgo as the carver of wood. This fine friend is famous for his—for his..." he paused with an agonized glance at Andrés Treviño.

Andrés smiled vacantly, shrugged with a helpless gesture, and then suddenly realizing what was wanted of him, he pulled a much folded paper from his hatband. With his tongue caught between his teeth, he carefully unfolded it and skimmed his eyes over the penciled words, smudged from constant handling. "Famous for his sobriety, steadiness of character, lack of vices and..."

"I know the rest of it," Pepe said with irritation. He looked again at Don Carlos Orona. "This fine friend is famous for his steadiness of character, lack of vices, and his great honesty. It is true knowledge that his worldly goods are few, but his parsimony..."

"Care of money!" hissed Andrés.

"Care of money," said Pepe meekly into a chorus of sudden coughs, "identifies him as being a man well able to face the future free of monetary difficulties. With an established sum of two hundred pesos, he proposes to rebuild and furnish a house one block north of the Plaza of Independence on the street known as the Avenue of Illustrious Men. This house will face the back of the Church of Our Lady of the Miraculous Tear..."

"Why that's just down the street from me," said the little Doctor cheerfully. "When Alma has her babies I have only to run..."

The concerted stare of everyone, including Pepe and Andrés, stopped the sentence. The little Doctor twitched his bushy eyebrows, coughed, and hastily examined the heavy watch-chain that hung suspended across the lower part of his chest.

Pepe looked at Andrés again, who prompted, "This house will face..."

Pepe said, "This house will face the back of the Church of Our Lady of the Miraculous Tear, and will consist of four rooms, a patio, and a workshop at the back. Also from the two hundred pesos Porfirio proposes to buy a fine satin dress with wax orange blossoms, a pair of white kid shoes, and a long net veil, as well as a wedding bouquet of appropriate dimensions. With these offerings, our friend Porfirio Rodriguez..."

Andrés said quickly with a strangled gasp, "You forget the two down pillows for kneeling at the church, two tall candles for the altar, and the marriage sums to Father Zacaya for the church ceremony, and to Don Genaro for the civil wedding."

"Those matters can be taken for granted," said Pepe, who was growing irritated by the interruptions. He continued, "With these offerings, our friend Porfirio Rodriguez, the carver of wood, humbly asks in marriage the hand of the gracious and beautiful Señorita Alma Orona, the first banns for this wedding to be sung in the church on Sunday morning next."

The words ended on a long sigh of relief. Pepe stepped backward until he was in line with Andrés. Both young men bowed from the waist, clapped their hats to their heads, and managed to walk backward through the door without falling over each other. They then turned and ran to the Saloon of the Devil's Laughter, where Porfirio, that young man famous for sobriety, steadiness of character, and lack of vices, was imbibing five-cent glasses of beer to aid his waiting. Pepe ordered two ten-cent glasses and glared at his friend. "It's over!" he said harshly. "Twenty minutes they made us wait—twenty minutes! An hour of my life disappeared with each minute."

"He kept wanting to leave," said Andrés, lifting his face from the glass, a line of foam marking his upper lip. "He said when it came your turn to ask for him, he hoped they kept you waiting five hours. Who are you going to ask for?" he added, turning to Pepe.

"Oh, I don't know," said Pepe lightly. "Probably some girl from the Valley of the Three Marys."

"The Valley of the Three Marys!" shrieked Andrés. When he saw the other customers and Don Dionisio, the saloonkeeper, looking at him, he hastily lowered his voice to a loud whisper. "The Three Marys' men would kill you. Wouldn't they kill him, Porfirio?"

"I hope they do," said Porfirio, mournfully ordering another glass of beer. "Death is better than all this waiting."

"You've had enough beer," said Don Dionisio. "Soon you will be too drunk to go to the plaza tonight. Besides, you owe me thirty centavos."

"Thirty centavos!" gasped Porfirio. "How can you do this to me, to me—your good friend? Did I not repair your shelves when that fool Dorotéo Lozano thought he was a ball and bounced against them?"

"For which I paid you two fine silver pesos," said Don Dionisio firmly.

"But the perfection of the job—the fine precision with which I swung the hammer on each nail head . . . is such artistry to cost but a mere two pesos? And now you want to charge me thirty centavos . . .

"Seventy centavos," said Pepe.

"Seventy?" whispered Porfirio. "He said thirty! I heard him say thirty!"

"But Andrés and I each had a glass," Pepe pointed out. "At ten cents a glass. That's seventy centavos, isn't it, Don Dionisio?"

"And five centavos extra for washing the glasses," said Don Dionisio, promptly. "Those large glasses take extra labor for the washing. After all, they are twice as large as the small ones. That makes the full sum seventy-five centavos."

"Seventy-five centavos!" Porfirio clutched the bar's edge and shut his eyes. He stood there a moment, his jaw clenched in silent agony. Then he shrieked, whirled, and rushed out of the saloon, a wave of laughter tumbling after him. Don Dionisio drew two more foaming glasses and set them in front of Pepe and Andrés. Then he drew another for himself. They lifted the glasses in toast. "To marriage," sighed Don Dionisio. "The poor fool should have guessed I would charge him nothing. I remember when I was waiting for my own proposal to be accepted. Such agony should not come to any man."

"That Porfirio and his money," said Andrés solemnly. "Someday someone will take five pesos from him, and they will not be joking. And that will be a sad day."

"True words," said Don Dionisio. "I wonder when that day will come?"

The men shrugged and drank their beer.

That night on the plaza, Porfirio arrived before Don Alonso and the orchestra were settled. They argued amiably over whether Porfirio still owed the orchestra platform. Porfirio contended no, because the rooster was never played. Don Alonso said yes, because the intention was good, and it was not his fault that Porfirio had stood under the wrong window. They finally settled the matter by Don Alonso's agreeing to play for nothing at the wedding feast, provided the family Orona agreed to take Porfirio as a son-in-law.

During this argument the plaza filled with people. News of Porfirio's request for Alma's hand had spread through the town, and good-luck wishes were called to him. No matter how much they teased him, the villagers were fond of the wood-carver and knew him to be excellent husband timber. Not so wealthy, of course, as the wild Pepe Gonzalez, heir to the cheese factory, which seemed to curd gold as well as milk. Don Timotéo Gonzalez contended that once Pepe settled down any woman would be proud to call him husband, but Pepe's quick wit and mischievous humor had been felt by too many fathers to make him a favorite bachelor. It was rumored that many a parent's daily prayer ended with, "and please do not give me Pepe Gonzalez for a son-in-law." And as for Andrés Treviño—well, Andrés had loved Nena Santos for many years.

Yes, Porfirio had been the mother's hope of Hidalgo, and now he had chosen Alma Orona. Well, Alma was a good girl. And a good worker. Did she not wash the clothes for Don Rosalío, yes, and for Bob Webster? There were many who felt that perhaps Porfirio was not quite good enough for her. He had not yet encountered that moment of testing of the soul when his true value would be stamped upon him. But in spite of village doubt, tonight Alma's and Porfirio's fates were to be solved.

The family Orona appeared on the plaza in a compact group. Porfirio, with much clearing of the throat, went up to them. Don Carlos spoke about the weather. Doña Triumfa expressed the hope that the spring rains would be heavy enough to help Don Rosalío's orange trees. Alma sat on the end of the bench, her eyes staring fixedly at the ground, saying nothing. At last Doña Triumfa said, lazily fanning herself, "Why do you two young people not walk around the plaza? Leave conversation to the old ones."

The ordeal was over. Porfirio gave a grin of relief and extended his arm to Alma. With a shy smile, she laid her fingers on his pink sleeve. As she rose and turned to walk with him, Don Alonso, in a fine burst of friendship, ordered the orchestra to play the beautiful "Song of Dolores Guerrero" which came out of Durango in 1840:

> *To you, girl of the beautiful black hair,*
> *Of the amber skin,*
> *Of the great eyes and ardent gaze,*
> *Of the proud head and sweet voice—*
> *To you will I offer my love,*
> *And to no other.*

Scattered voices over the plaza took up the song. Soon the whole plaza was singing as Porfirio and Alma, proud as two children, walked around the great square three times, and thus

formally announced their engagement to the village and the Sabinas Valley.

Three times they passed a slender, bronze-haired girl, standing
near one of the lampposts, who looked after them with thoughtful green eyes. She spoke to her aunt, Doña Teresita, the seamstress, whom she had that day come to visit from Monterrey.
"And you say this man brings two hundred pesos to the wedding?"

"It is a fine sum," said Doña Teresita with an envious little
sigh. "That Alma Orona is a lucky one."

"Yes," said Rosaura with a twist of her full red mouth. "I
should like to have two hundred pesos. I should like it very much
indeed." And the green eyes continued to follow the promenading couple.

Rosaura Maldonado had come to Hidalgo from Monterrey on
what she called a short vacation. The real reason was that a wife
of a neighbor had threatened to slit her throat if she stayed
another day. So Rosaura thought it better to visit her aunt in
Hidalgo until the neighbor's wife recovered from her fit of
jealousy. Considering that Rosaura had merely persuaded the
neighbor to use his wife's egg money to buy a silk dress with lace
at the throat and sleeves, Rosaura considered the neighbor's wife
had acted most childishly. Nevertheless she had a high opinion
of the neighbor's wife's right arm. So here she was in Hidalgo,
and almost immediately, as reward for all she had suffered, two
hundred pesos had strolled past her. She put herself to sleep that
night dreaming of the clothes that two hundred pesos could buy.

The next morning, after a late breakfast, she put on her silk
dress, knowing that its brilliant yellow made her bronze hair
shine like sunlight and heightened the fire in her green eyes.
As she passed the Saloon of the Devil's Laughter, the men in the
doorway politely murmured little phrases after her, such as, "Ay,
what a queen," or, "A beautiful child," or, "I kiss your hands
and feet." She pretended not to hear, but there was a pleased
curve to her lips as she sauntered past the building site of the
Casino. For a moment she paused in natural curiosity and surveyed the half-erected structure. Then, letting her curiosity carry
her forward, she entered the gaping door hole and smiled at the
workmen lent by Bob Webster from the quarry.

The men put down their tools and came forward to meet her out of their natural politeness, for she was a stranger in Hidalgo. They showed her the long room where the bar and card tables were to be set up. They showed her the lady's parlor at the north end of the oblong, where chaperones could sit in gossiping comfort and yet keep a strict eye on their charges. And finally they took her into the patio, where Porfirio was erecting the musician's platform. At the moment, with his tongue clenched between his teeth, he was sawing a plank laid across two saw-horses. One of the men called out to him, and he paused in his work long enough to look up and see Rosaura. As he stared at her, she put out a small pink tongue and moistened her full red lips. Porfirio felt his heart leap up and then skid down toward his stomach where it began to pump with wild alacrity.

She graciously smiled at him and said softly, "It has come to my ears that you are a carver of wood."

"Yes, señora," he muttered.

"Señorita," she corrected him gently. She stretched out her small hands with the shining nails. "I would like you to make a chest for me—no larger than that. I would pay—well for it." The slight hiatus before the adverb carried its own meaning. The workmen grinned, nodded to each other, and went back to their labor, leaving Porfirio alone with Rosaura.

He made a forward motion as though he would follow them, but she was between him and his only exit. To leave he would have to brush past her. In politeness, he had to stay where he was. As she moved closer to him, he backed until he could feel the patio wall against his shoulderblades.

"I have much work," he stammered. "I am afraid that I . . ."

"Please," she murmured, opening the green eyes very wide and then shutting them so that the long black lashes brushed her soft pink cheeks.

Porfirio inhaled audibly. He really loved Alma Orona, but he had never seen such a woman as this. His heart was pounding so hard he wondered in amazement that she could not hear it. Her hand brushed his, and the brief contact burned his skin. She said softly, "You are busy now. But come to my aunt's house this evening and I will tell you how I want the chest made." She gave him a gracious nod and went away, but Porfirio stayed close to the wall. His knees trembled slightly and there was a hollow feeling in his stomach. He forced himself to go back to work, but the laughter of the workmen enraged him. He knew what they were saying—what jokes were causing their laughter. In ordinary circumstances he would have laughed with them, but not now. Just now he wanted to dash past them and follow Rosaura. He realized that she had not told him her aunt's name. It did not matter. He would find out. He would have to find out. No, he did not! He would borrow a horse from the blacksmith, and ride up into the mountains—stay there with Pablo, the goatherd, until this soft-bodied woman left town.

He put down his saw and hurried to the Plaza of the Viceroys. "Don Fidencio, I want to rent a horse."

Before the surprised blacksmith could answer, Porfirio flung a silver peso on the anvil, saddled a horse for himself, and rode at full gallop toward the cañon. Don Fidencio, the peso on his limp palm, stared after him. "And not one effort to argue me out of payment," he muttered. "Porfirio must be sick!"

Unfortunately for Porfirio, the goatherd was on one of the higher crests with his goats. Although Pablo, by virtue of being a goatherd, was a child of Grandfather Devil's and no fit companion for decent christian folk, he had, even at twenty-one, a level-headed wisdom that was admired by most of Hidalgo's men. In difficulties of the heart they went to the young Pablo as naturally as they went to the older Father Zacaya with difficulties of the spirit. Porfirio sat in the hut all afternoon, but when Pablo had not returned by sunset, Porfirio, realizing the laughing-eyed goatherd might be gone for weeks, rode dejectedly back towards the village. He dared not wait until after dark, or the hill witches would haunt him for intruding on their domain. Pablo knew how to keep them at bay, but Porfirio lacked such wicked knowledge; so he thought it best to put as much distance between himself and the witches as possible.

But the long afternoon in the mountain air had cleared his mind. He was going back to the village, return the horse to Don Fidencio, try to argue the blacksmith out of the peso that had been too recklessly flung down, and after a good supper he would go and play the bear to Alma Orona. She was engaged to him. He had the engaged man's right to talk to her through her iron-barred window. And he would forget all about Rosaura.

Feeling much better, he allowed the horse to follow the trail close to the ditch where the irrigation water ran from mountain spring to the village. The ditch curved through the cañon like a great, twisting snake, the water here and there falling over banked stones to form moss-lined pools. At one curve in the trail, the horse danced back from something brightly yellow showing behind some bushes. Frowning, Porfirio swung to the ground and brushed the bushes aside to reveal one of the pools. A yellow silk dress was draped across a small *yuca*. And in the pool, Rosaura Maldonado, wearing nothing at all, was allowing the cold water of the falls to ripple over her body. In the thickening twilight, with her bronze hair and green eyes, she seemed to be one of the witches who had put on a young girl's form.

The blood suffused Porfirio's face, and he would have stumbled back towards his horse, but Rosaura chose that moment to laugh.

By the end of the week all Hidalgo was talking of Porfirio's infatuation for Rosaura Maldonado. When Pepe tried to talk to him, Porfirio knocked him down. Don Carlos Orona wanted to send for him, but Alma burst into tears and refused to speak to her father if he did. When Alma walked the streets, her head was high, and there was a gleam in the black eyes that forbade any comment.

Don Nacho, Don Rosalío, Father Zacaya, and the little Doctor discussed the problem night after night over the domino table. If they sent Rosaura out of Hidalgo, they knew that Porfirio would follow her. They tried to talk to the wood-carver, but he told them curtly to attend to their own affairs. And always, in the background, was Alma. She had been hurt enough. They must do nothing to harm Alma.

They even called in Don Juan O'Malley, that strange, whiskey-loving Irishman, who had married an Hidalgo girl, and through the years had become more Mexican than Irish. But he could contribute nothing. "When a wild woman like that gets her claws in a man, there's nothing anyone can do but stand by with a bottle of strong liquor to help him afterwards."

At Bob Webster's suggestion, they appealed to Tía Magdalena to see what she could do. She agreed to help, and went off to interview Rosaura's aunt, Doña Teresita, the seamstress.

Doña Teresita had a high temper that matched Tía Magdalena's. The heat wave that had enveloped the valley during the past week added to their irritation, and the argument ended at a point where nothing but a fight could satisfy honor.

"When you accuse my niece of wickedness, me you also accuse," Doña Teresita said.

Tía thoughtfully measured her short height against the heavy frame of the seamstress. "Me, I am too old and too little. You will accept Doña Nimfa as my proxy?"

"As you choose." Doña Teresita shrugged indifferent shoulders. "But no witch spells."

"Naturally," Tía sniffed. "Do you think I would stoop so low as to bring magic into an affair of this kind?"

She hurried to the herb woman, who at first flatly refused to fight. "It's too hot. Also, my body is soft and tender, and the argument is yours."

"Listen to me, Nimfa, am I not an eagle witch? How can she even touch you?"

"You mean to cast a spell on her?"

Tía pursed her lips in a tantalizing smile. "Do you think I would stoop so low as to allow a friend of mine to be hurt in battle for me?"

And so the fight was arranged. Since Tía worked for Bob Webster, and was therefore a woman of importance, it was decided to stage the affair in the churchyard on Sunday after mass.

When the hour came, the herb woman tucked her skirts into her belt and slapped out at Doña Teresita with one fat palm, which was slick with sweat. Doña Teresita easily parried the feeble blow, and thrust a powerful fist into Doña Nimfa's flaccid stomach. The herb woman doubled up on the ground, squealing that she was dying. Doña Teresita kicked a well padded hip, and then leaped into the air, coming down with her full weight on Doña Nimfa's back. The squeals crescendoed to a loud shriek.

A few people had stayed to watch the fight, but now, realizing that it was a matter of little interest, wandered away, fanning themselves and yawning, exhausted from watching such exertion in the oppressive heat. The one-armed policeman, who had remained in the background until the first fury was over, as he was terrified of fighting women, came forward to arrest the herb woman for starting the brawl.

Tía Magdalena, who had stood in the church door throughout the fight, her eyebrows lifted in objective superiority, touched the policeman on the shoulder. "I will pay the fine, Don Ricardo. This one," she indicated the sobbing Doña Nimfa, "was my proxy in this affair."

The policeman scratched his head, shrugged, and pointed out that it was Sunday and the churchyard. "You know what that means," he warned.

"Am I not Don Bob's housekeeper? Should a fight for my honor be carried out on a week day? What am I, a common woman from the *Gallineros?*"

"Ay, no, Tía..."

"Do not forget, Don Ricardo, that I am an eagle witch, and can make you see spiders in your sleep. Spiders with hair on their legs."

"As you say, Tía, as you say," blessing himself hastily to make certain that she could not harm him.

She helped Doña Teresita to her feet, and mopped her perspiring face with a handkerchief. "Are you satisfied, giant one?"

"I am satisfied."

"I am dying," wailed Doña Nimfa.

"A night in jail will cure you," said Tía coldly. "You should not have lost the fight."

"But you promised me she couldn't hurt me. You said you would cast a spell."

"To make you fight, pretty one. Do you think I would use magic against my good friend, Doña Teresita?"

With a broad smile for Tía Magdalena, the seamstress pulled the herb woman to her feet. "Come, let there be no ill feelings between us," she soothed. "The argument was Tía's and mine, not yours. I will aid your steps to the jail, and tonight I will pay you a visit. I will even teach you a new stitch in crochet, one that I invented myself and have revealed to no other soul."

With the single-armed policeman on one side, and Doña Teresita on the other, the herb woman tottered off to the sanctuary of the jail, her soft body trailing the acrid odor of sweat, while Tía Magdalena went home to consult her books of magic. She reread the spell for winning a fight and shook her head in perplexity. "I can't understand it," she muttered to herself. "I'm certain I worked that spell correctly, and yet Doña Teresita won. Perhaps she was still enveloped in sanctity from the mass. That is the only explanation."

The next evening she went into the patio where Bob was trying to relax over a glass of beer and the Monterrey newspaper. The air was so heavy that it seemed to ripple over the skin, and breathing was difficult. Don Nacho had told Bob that these heat waves sometimes came to the mountains. "But this is the worst," he said, fanning himself with his battered felt hat, "that Hidalgo has known in fifty years. Soon it will break. When the thunder and the water comes, then it will be cool again."

That was five days ago, and the rains had not yet come. Bob wondered if the shower bath he had just taken had been wasted effort. His white shirt was already plastered to his back, and his freshly starched white duck trousers clung limply to his legs.

He looked up at Tía Magdalena. "You are an eagle witch," he said plaintively. "You have ridden the lightning and played games with the thunder. Make it rain, Tía. Surely an eagle witch can make it rain."

Tía shrugged her thin shoulders and casually ignored his words. "Tomorrow is your early day at the quarry. The little Doctor told me you haven't been getting enough sleep at nights. So go to bed. Yes, and give me ten pesos."

"Ten pesos now? But today is Monday. I gave you some money this morning . . ."

"This is to pay a jail fine for Doña Nimfa, the herb woman."

Bob sighed and counted ten pieces of silver into her work-hardened palm.

"I thought you said Doña Nimfa was a town witch and not fit to associate with decent christians."

"And so she is," snapped Tía Magdalena. "But Teresita the seamstress and I became involved in an argument. As I am too old to fight for my honor, Doña Nimfa agreed to fight for me. Yesterday they exchanged blows. Naturally, I must pay the fine."

Bob's mouth opened slightly in surprise. "And since when has Don Nacho felt that women must pay fines to fight for their honor? I saw a good fight up at the caves not three weeks ago, and Don Nacho made no effort to arrest or fine anyone. This Doña Nimfa is playing you for a fool, Tía."

"Ha!" said the old woman, "it is Sundays and feast days that cost money. Women can fight any day in the week, but on Sundays and holy days Don Nacho says we must keep the peace.

It is a good law." She nodded her approval. "Of course, as your housekeeper, a Sunday fine means nothing to me." She dropped the money into a capacious pocket and trotted out of the patio.

Unfortunately the fight accomplished nothing, beyond involving Bob and the little Doctor in an argument over his bill for taking care of Doña Nimfa's injuries. When Bob found out that Sunday street fighting would have cost only five pesos, but fighting in the churchyard had lifted the fine to ten, he went up to the quarry and stayed three days with the cave-dwelling workmen without coming down at all. He was not sulking. He had merely learned through bitter experience that the only way to punish Tía Magdalena was to remove himself from her domination.

She had to go up to the quarry to get him, and she scolded him soundly all the way back to town. "Those cave dwellers," she snorted, riding sidesaddle on the white horse while Bob led it. "They might have killed you with their dirt."

"But they are healthy people, Tía. They say their health comes from the earth. And you know they never die from anything but knife fights and old age."

"That may be," said the old woman, "but you come home to clean dirt and leave their dirt alone. Besides, it's too hot for me to carry your meals to the quarry every day."

"Now, Tía, I never asked you to ..."

"How you turn a woman's words in her mouth. Did I say you asked me to? Did I?"

"No, Tía, but ..."

"Ha! How you ever lived to grow up alive is more than I can understand. It is a good thing you came to Hidalgo. If I hadn't got hands on you, you would be in your grave and you know it. But are you grateful? No! You sulk in the quarries for three days with dirt."

Although Bob did not know it, this high temper was the result of a guilty conscience, for Tía was concealing a letter which she believed was from Tommy Eaton.

While Bob was gone to stable his horse, the old woman took the letter from her pocket, still undecided whether to give it to him or not. She remembered with aching pain Doña Nimfa's revelation of its contents. After the herb woman had tossed aromatic spices on a small fire, and breathed in the smoke, she had said, "There is news, great news, hidden in the writing."

What kind of news? The answer was more than a mere summons to South America for Bob. From the first moment that she had seen him standing on the cliff's edge, the squawking chicken in his hands, she had adopted him as her own. With her sons dead, and her beloved Joaquín Castillo long gone from the valley, she had lavished on Bob that fierce maternal love that only a woman past childbearing can have for a young man. All that stood between herself and complete possession of his affections was his decision to go to South America.

As the time for his departure came closer, she spent many hours in the church praying to Santa Mónica, the widow, patron of parents with disobedient children, and had burned many candles; but it was well known that the saints frown on selfish prayers, and so for many nights Tía had climbed into the mountains to sacrifice young kids and gray doves to the sleeping gods.

Through prayer and enchantment she hoped to wipe all thoughts of the strange world beyond the mountains from Bob's mind, but now the letter had come to tempt him even as Santa Mónica's son Augustine was tempted by the Devil. Could it be possible, Tía thought, that after so many prayers and sacrifices, the blessed saint and the sleeping gods would allow the wicked Tommy Eaton to draw Bob away from the safety of Hidalgo into a life of drunken dissipation? Or had the letter been sent as a test of her own faith as a good christian and her power as an eagle witch?

She remembered how the spell to protect Doña Nimfa from battle injuries had failed. Was she then no longer a beloved disciple of the ancient magic? Did her christian prayers count for nothing? The answer was in this letter.

Better to let Bob open it. Better to know the truth, however disastrous, than to live suspended between knowledge and doubt. She put the envelope on the patio table, her fingers trembling with fear weakness.

From the kitchen she heard him stamp into the house, shouting, "Tía, the miracle has happened. Don Fidencio says Porfirio paid him two pesos horse rent to take Rosaura riding." Then, his voice changing slightly, "Why here's a letter from... That's funny. It's from Tommy Eaton's boss. I wonder what..." She could hear the crackle of paper as he ripped the envelope open. Her ears were so attuned to sound that the mockingbird singing in its wooden cage near the well cut her ears like a shrill whistle. But from Bob there was silence.

At last she could bear it no longer. She went into the patio and found him sitting at the table, his head buried in his arms.

"What is it?" she whispered, touching his crisp dark hair with shaking fingers.

He said dully in a muffled voice. "Tom's dead. His plane crashed with him. And we were leaving next month."

So, she thought, the wicked one had drunk himself to death. She blessed herself and murmured a quick prayer to Santa Mónica. "Tomorrow," she whispered, "I will light you a candle as long as my arm. And for you old gods, tonight I will steal a fine rooster from Don Rosalío, and pour out the warm blood for your drinking."

Bob was muttering, "I can't get it through my mind that Tom's dead. He was my only friend, and now he's dead."

"Your only friend! Was he now? And what of Porfirio, and Andrés Treviño, and Pepe Gonzalez? Are they not your friends?"

"You don't understand, Tía. These three are fine companions, but Tommy was—well, he was like a brother."

"I see. He was your *compadre*,* eh? Well, I have found that when one *compadre* dies, there is always another waiting to take his place. To cure the pain in your heart, I am going to get Pepe Gonzalez and three bottles of brandy."

After Pepe and Bob had drunk themselves into a stupor, and she had put them to bed, she captured a cock with practiced ease from Don Rosalío's chicken house and hurried along the Street of the Cañon into the Cañon Road. She followed this for two hours until she reached a spot where the trail and the irrigation ditch met so that they formed a cross. Here was placed a great flat stone with ugly red-brown markings on it.

Securely tying the cock to a bush, Tía Magdalena knelt and pulled from behind the stone a broom made of mountain grass tied to a stick, a small paper filled with white chalk, and a skirt painted with crossbones. Slipping out of her own clothes, she fastened the skirt around her thin hips, leaving the upper part

* Untranslatable. Literally, co-father. A term used between very intimate friends. The feminine is *comadre*.

of her body bare, the thin dry breasts hanging in limp folds almost to her waist. Then she thickly powdered her face with the chalk, drawing a butterfly-shaped space round her mouth. From the pocket of her discarded dress she took a wooden-handled flint knife and a flat dish woven from plaited corn-husks, over which she arranged two long, thin threads of dried corn silk. These she laid on the flat stone. Then, holding the squawking, fighting cock by its neck in one hand, and the knife in her other, she began to dance around the stone, keeping her feet together and retreating and advancing by means of small jumps.

There was no dank odor of the jungle here. No red fires gleaming, nor the muffled pounding of drums. The moon swung full in the clear night sky, and the jagged mountain rocks were gray with misty light. Black shadows fell sharp on the ground from sage bush and *yuca* tree, and the jerking shadow of the woman was black also. As she swayed and dipped and turned, her feet made no noise on the moss-grown trail. There was silence everywhere—in the sky, in the mountains, at the crossing of earth and water.

Then a whisper of sound came from the woman, so faint, so nebulous, that it was no sound at all. But the awareness of sound was there, and the sound became a word, a word in the language the Spaniards thought they had destroyed with the death of the last Malicheño Indians in the closing years of the seventeenth century.

The mountains remembered the word, and echoes tossed it back to the woman, so that her voice rose and other words came, and the old names: Juquialán, Pitale, Corianúa.

The chant grew wilder and higher in pitch. The dancing jumps came faster and faster. There was a sudden swing of the right hand towards the cock's throat and red blood spattered on the corn threads in the dish—the corn threads along which traveled as on a highway the desires of the worshipper to the minds of the sleeping gods.

With a wild cry, the old woman flung herself across the stone, so that the sacrificial blood stained her breasts. Then she caught up the broom, dipped it in the blood, and began to sweep the ground in front of the stone, for this was the broom that symbolized death and she was brushing it away from her and all that was hers. As she swept, the broom pointed toward some of the gray sage bushes that lined the trail. There was a sudden high scream, and Rosaura leaped forward, trying to evade its pointing. Her escape was cut off by a great marble slab that had fallen years before from the mountainside. She whirled, with her palms flat against it, and stood poised. In the moonlight her slanting eyes were large and dark.

"Eh," said Tía softly, "you come to watch the witch dance of thanksgiving for answered prayers. Perhaps it is true what they say in the village. Perhaps you are a witch yourself."

"I am not," sobbed Rosaura, cold with fear, crossing herself again and again. "I am a good christian girl. I will not burn in hell like you."

"Then how did you know the broom pointing towards you meant death?"

Rosaura took a deep breath. "Doña Nimfa—she told me."

"And what have you to do with Doña Nimfa?"

"She has been casting a spell for me."

"So, Doña Nimfa fights for my honor in the daytime and casts spells for you at night, does she? What kind of spells?" She moved closer to the girl. "What kind of spells? Answer me!"

Rosaura moaned with fear. She thought this terrible painted creature with the death butterfly outlined around her mouth, was one of the mountain witches, and to conceal her knowledge from a witch would bring the punishment of stealing the soul. She said wildly, "Love spells on Porfirio, the carver of wood. He has money. Two hundred pesos, he has. I want them, but he won't give them to me. His hands close on the silver as though it were a part of his bone. Doña Nimfa told me if I spent the night near this rock, and in the morning brought her flakes of dried blood from it, she could make me such a charm as would force him to give me the money."

"Do you love Porfirio?"

"Love that close-fisted fool?" cried Rosaura proudly. "Of course not. This Rosaura is for richer men than a carver of wood."

"Alma Orona loves him," said the old woman.

Rosaura shrugged. "The more fool she. Will you let me take the blood flakes and go?"

Tía nodded and laughed softly, for an idea had come into her mind. "Take them if you like. The charm will be worthless, for Doña Nimfa is no true witch. Useful for reading of secret writings, but that is all. If you want true success tell Porfirio to get you a shawl—the same kind of shawl that Alma Orona crocheted for her mother. When he brings it to you, wear it to mass every morning for seven days—remember that—seven days."

"To mass?" whispered Rosaura. "But a mass is christian. How can a witch use the mass..."

"What a fool you are," snapped Tía Magdalena. "Did not God make everything including Grandfather Devil? Do not witches therefore belong to God?"

Rosaura took a step toward her. "And you vow that if I wear this shawl as you say, Porforio's money will be mine?"

"I swear that Porfirio will pay a high price for you," said Tía with a cackling laugh. She lifted the broom and pointed it at the girl. "Now off with you, or I will take you riding on an eagle's back, and that will be the end of Rosaura Maldonado."

The girl gave a tight little scream, darted past Tía Magdalena, and ran off down the trail. When she was out of sight, the old woman sank to the ground and rested her forehead against the broomstick held upright in front of her. She was suddenly very tired, and her many years were heavy on her shoulders.

When Rosaura told Porfirio what she wanted, he protested that obtaining such a shawl was impossible. "Alma invented that pattern in crochet. She told me she did. Where could I find another such?"

"Get it from Alma for all I care," said Rosaura, "but I'll not speak to you again until you fetch it to me. Pepe Gonzalez could get it for me if I asked him."

Porfirio threatened to knife Pepe if she so much as looked at him. Rosaura pouted her full red lips. She refused even to look at Porfirio; so he went off down the dusty Avenue of Illustrious Men in a rage.

The next afternoon, Abel, the *árabe* * tradesman, came through Hidalgo with his mule cart loaded with woman's goods. When Porfirio asked him about buying such a shawl, Abel shrugged his fat shoulders. "I might be able to find you one, but it would cost money."

"How much?" Porfirio asked fearfully.

"At least thirty pesos," said Abel, his small black eyes gleaming

* A term used indiscriminately for Assyrians and Arabians, many of whom own small drygoods stores along the frontier, or are itinerant pedlars.

with mischievous laughter. He had known Porfirio for years, and he also knew that such a shawl could not be found anywhere. "Perhaps more than thirty. Perhaps fifty."

"Thirty pesos!" Porfirio gasped. "Perhaps fifty! For a shawl?"

"Why not?" Abel wiped the sweat from his greasy face. "You have heat in these mountains, friend. What need have you for a shawl in such heat?"

Porfirio turned dejectedly away. As he crossed the Plaza of Independence, he saw Alma sitting in front of the church waiting for rosary to begin, her fingers busy with her crochet needle. He walked hesitantly toward her, the thought of the thirty pesos urging him forward.

"Good afternoon, Alma."

The eyes she raised to him were clear and dark. "Good afternoon, Porfirio."

"I thought you might not wish to speak to me," he said miserably.

"The priest is still singing the banns in church. Next Sunday is the last time." Her steel crochet hook flashed in and out along the twisted thread.

Porfirio squatted beside her, and took a corn-shuck cigarette from behind his ear. As he lit it, he said, "You crochet very fast, Alma."

"Fast enough," she answered amiably. "I have set our wedding date for the fifteenth of May. Does that please you, Porfirio?"

"You are too good for me, Alma. Anyone in Hidalgo will tell you that."

Her fingers were busy with the crochet hook as she looked past his shoulders and across the Plaza of Independence and the low-roofed houses to the pale violet shadow of the Mountain of the Prow, which reared its height in the far distance beyond the town of Mina.

"There are thoughts in my head, Porfirio, but the speaking of them is difficult. We have known each other for many years. Between us there is no hiding of faults or of virtues. Your mind and my mind are as one mind, like two rivers flowing in one bed."

He drooped his head toward her, listening to her. "You speak truly, Alma, for I love you, you know that. But this woman, she is a sickness in my blood. She is a fever that mounts and recedes and mounts again." He spread his hands in a wide, palm-down gesture. "I tell you she is a sickness, and a man cannot control a sickness."

"But naturally, Porfirio. You and I are to be married. The sickness will go, but you and I will be left. What good is a wife who deserts her husband when the sickness is on him? If you were hungry, would I not feed you? If you killed and robbed, would I not protect you? Why should I desert you now? No, Porfirio, I have chosen you. I am satisfied."

The crochet needle flashed in and out, the late afternoon sun shining on it in little points of light. Porfirio felt humble before the goodness of Alma, and, because he was a man, he despised the humbleness, and tried to evade it by counting the needle sparks, but they seemed to merge together to form little figures—first thirty and then fifty. A clear voice kept repeating in his ears, "Pepe Gonzalez could get it for me. Pepe Gonzalez could get it for me." At the thought of Rosaura in Pepe's arms, Porfirio's humbleness dissolved. After all, he was a man, and Alma would understand. Even if he lied to her a little, she would understand.

"Alma, would you make a shawl for me?"

"A shawl, Porfirio?" She stopped crocheting and stared at him. "What would you do with a shawl?" Her tone said: for that creature Rosaura?

He reddened and muttered, "My mother has a saint's day on Sunday . . . she admired that shawl you made for your mother . . . I thought . . ." His throat dried and refused to pass any more words. With a quick gesture he tossed his cigarette away, then reached for it, blew off the dust, and stuck it behind his ear again.

Alma looked at him for a long moment. "Yes, Porfirio. I'll make you the shawl. I have enough wool left over at home. Does it matter if it is the same color as my mother's?"

He mutely shook his head. She gathered her work together and stood up as the bell began tolling for Rosary. With a calm nod she passed into the church.

Porfirio stood very still for a moment, then crossed the street and walked to the new house and shop he was building against his marriage. Safe inside with the door shut he sat down on the floor and scuffed his feet against the wall. Alma was so good. He loved her so much. When he was with her, he hated himself. But that Rosaura—how could a man live without Rosaura? Her silky brown hair, her slanted green eyes.... Women with those eyes could play the devil with a man's happiness. And Rosaura's soft white body ... Porfirio lowered his chin against his chest. How could he give her up? But she was so wicked, so wicked, and Alma so good, so good. He sighed, and his eyes closed. The heat made his black hair curl against his forehead. There was a line of perspiration around his mouth, but he did not know it. Porfirio was fast asleep.

The following Saturday afternoon, Alma brought the shawl to the house that would soon be hers. When Porfirio took it from her, his hand trembled slightly.

"I saw your mother this morning," Alma said, "but I didn't mention the shawl. I thought you might want to surprise her."

"Yes," he muttered. How he would explain to Alma tomorrow about Rosaura and the shawl he did not know. But that was tomorrow's trouble. And this was today. He had not seen Rosaura since Tuesday. She had refused to let him come near her until he brought her the shawl. Now, as he held the soft length of blue wool, edged with a long heavy fringe, he could think of nothing but holding Rosaura once more in his arms.

"It is a pity," said Alma, touching the shawl, "that it's too hot to wear. It would smother her in this weather."

"Yes," he said dumbly, not noticing that the combination of heat and grief had put dark circles under Alma's eyes, and sharpened the cheek and chin lines until they stood out like a caricature of her former prettiness.

After supper that night Porfirio ran all the way to Doña Teresita's house. He thrust the shawl into Rosaura's arms, and then caught her to him. "My beautiful," he muttered, his face hidden in her silky hair.

She slid away from him. "It's too hot for hugging," she protested, her nose wrinkling fastidiously against the heavy damp smell of him. "Talk to me, Porfirio."

"But I don't want to talk to you," said Porfirio. "I want to kiss you."

"Not now." Rosaura gently stroked the shawl. "It's too hot. Much too hot."

The next morning being Sunday, Porfirio, after a wretched,

sleepless night, went to five o'clock mass because that was the freshest moment of the day.

All night the heat lightning had silently split the darkness with glaring flashes, and only that hour before dawn was cool.

Bob Webster, who had tried to sleep in a hammock in the patio, gave up the battle at four-thirty and tried to find relief under a cold shower. He came to mass with Tía Magdalena because the church's lofty dark interior possessed the illusion of coolness.

Most of Hidalgo's young people, who usually attended "sweetheart's mass" at twelve o'clock, were there. Heat had so clamped itself about the village that any exertion after nine in the morning drained energy of mind and body.

When Father Zacaya looked out over the packed church, he smiled to himself and murmured, "A cool church in a heat wave makes more than one man religious." He did not notice the stir at the back of the church where the men stood. But Tía Magdalena did. She punched Bob with her elbow, and he turned around to see Rosaura, a heavy blue wool shawl over her head and the perspiration beading her face, coming down the aisle. She passed the Orona family and knelt beside her aunt. By the time the people rose for the reading of the gospel, she was almost fainting from the heat, for although the windows were open, the closely packed bodies of the worshippers gave forth a heat of their own. She swayed slightly, and Tía shocked Bob by giggling.

"She'll never stand seven days of that shawl in this heat," she whispered delightedly. "And when she gives up the shawl, she gives up two hundred pesos."

Bob, who could not hear her, muttered "Quiet," as Father Zacaya came down from the altar and mounted the steps to the high carved pulpit. While he settled his robes about his shoulders, Rosaura suddenly pushed her way into the aisle and hurried toward the door. Alma Orona turned and followed her. The congregation looked at each other, at the open door, at Father Zacaya, then as one person pushed toward the outside. Father Zacaya sighed, came down from his pulpit and followed them.

Alma, hands buckled on her hips, was staring at a fainting Rosaura, who stood with her head pressed against the church's pink-washed stone wall.

"That shawl is pure wool," said Alma's clear voice. "I should know. I made it myself."

"Alma, please," Porfirio started forward, but Doña Juanita Perez drew him back.

"Leave them alone," she ordered. "This is woman's business."

Rosaura allowed the shawl to slide from her shoulders to the ground. "You were a fool for making it," she said, opening her mouth the better to breathe the thick heavy air. From behind the western mountains came the distant roll of thunder.

"I wanted you to wear it," said Alma. "I knew it was for you. Porfirio came and asked me. 'Will you make me a shawl for Rosaura?' he said. 'She wants one like your mother's.'"

Porfirio gasped and stared at Alma as though he had never seen her before. There was a small murmur of excitement from the crowd as they edged nearer the two women. Rosaura laughed weakly.

"The more fool you for making it."

Alma shrugged. "Why not? Why should I not be kind? It is me he is marrying on the fifteenth of May."

"Do you think I want to marry him?" asked Rosaura contemptuously.

Porfirio could not see the pain in Alma's eyes. She did not want to hurt him, but she wanted him to see this woman with clear understanding. "In Monterrey, it is true, he would not be so grand, but in Hidalgo he has position and worth."

"Who wants to live in Hidalgo?" Rosaura raised her voice above the nearing thunder. "Not I. And as for marrying your Porfirio . . ." She raised her open hands and let them drop. "All I wanted was his two hundred pesos."

"Indeed," said Alma. "And his house nearly finished, and my wedding clothes hanging in my closet? Let me ask you, what two hundred pesos?"

There was a shout of laughter from the crowd. Rosaura whirled on her aunt. "You told me he had two hundred pesos—you!"

Doña Teresita backed away from her. "Now, Rosaura, he did when I told you. Can I help it if he spent it?"

"And I dying from the heat in this thing!" Rosaura's foot kicked the shawl to one side. Her angry hand descended in a resounding slap on her aunt's face. Doña Teresita gave a shriek of rage and struck back. The next moment they were a tumbling, kicking mass on the ground. Porfirio darted forward to separate them, but after a well-placed kick in his thigh he was glad to rejoin the crowd of laughing, cheering spectators.

The thunder, which had been growling louder and louder, now slapped its great palms together. The sky, unable to endure such punishment, opened its trap door, and the rain fell in great sheets of water. The people of Hidalgo tried to push their way back into the church without taking their eyes off the fighting women. It was as though the battle between water and sound, and the battle between woman and woman, were the same battle.

It was Doña Fela, the town matriarch, who finally stalked through the heavy curtain of rain and caught each woman firmly by the back of the neck, in the way a child holds two fighting puppies.

"To the jail with this Rosaura Maldonado," she said firmly to Don Nacho, who meekly nodded and signaled Don Ricardo, the one-armed policeman, to take the prisoner in charge. But Don Ricardo pretended not to see, and fled into the church for safety. So Doña Fela herself marched Rosaura off to jail.

As Bob was smoking his after-luncheon cigarette, he grinned at Tía Magdalena's carefully edited story of the night on the mountain.

"Did you think it would end in a fight, Tía?"

"I hoped it would. But that Alma—she is too calm."

"Alma is a great lady," said Bob wickedly. "She has no need of fights to protect her honor."

Tía choked with rage over this, but Bob pretended not to see her. "By the way, even though you started it, I refuse to pay out another ten pesos fine. That's right, isn't it? Five pesos for the fight, and five for the churchyard?"

"No matter," said Tía contentedly. And then, with—for her—a strange shyness, "I gave Porfirio the order for a new door for this house now that you are going to stay in Hidalgo. You are going to stay?"

He rolled the burning cigarette between his fingers, too embarrassed to look at her pleading eyes. "Yes, Tía, I'm going to stay."

She shut her lids tightly to keep the happiness tears from overflowing. To avoid betraying her feelings, she said quickly, "Porfirio paid the fine. I saw him do it with these two eyes. He dropped the money peso by peso into Rosaura Maldonado's hand. And," she added with some amazement, "he never argued once about the price. But the way he did it ... *Vaya*, he took the skin off her back, he did."

"Poor Alma. First the shawl and now the fine. That girl has paid a high price for Porfirio."

"Oh, she punished him well. The worst punishment a woman can give a man, I say."

"What's that?" Bob looked curiously up at her.

Tía winked her right eye at him. "She forgave him," said Tía Magdalena.

The Chicken Coop

Andres Treviño

November, 1921

God gave me bread so I wouldn't long for cake.
—Mexican proverb

MAY THIS HAND WITHER ON MY ARM BEFORE I SIGN THE marriage contract!" shrieked Nena Santos, her back tense against the door of her house.

The November moonlight spilled a silver mist over the two young people. Andrés Treviño flung out his hand in helpless gesture, his round face darkly creased between the brows. "But the house has been built, Nena. The finest house in the *Gallineros*. All the world says so."

Nena tossed her head. "You build a fine house for the world to admire, but one little request from me, and it is a closing of the hand. That Porfirio has drugged your senses with love of money."

"That is a wicked untruth!" Andrés took a step toward her and pushed one clenched hand against the shack's wooden wall. "Twenty pesos I paid for your wedding gown. Of fine white satin it is, with waxen orange blossoms for your hair. With twenty pesos I could have bought a young goat, but did you hear a complaint from my mouth? I ask you!"

"A wedding dress!" Nena snapped her fingers. "Every girl in the *Gallineros* comes to her husband with a white satin gown. But when I ask you for one little thing—one little grander thing—you wail of money and the need to buy goats, while my heart —mine—the heart of your intended bride—breaks with longing for a thing of little size, a small thing, a thing no larger than your hand." Her eyes suddenly shone with tears, and the firm chin began to tremble.

"But, Nena," wailed Andrés, "of what good to you is a pair of shoes? You've never worn a pair in your life. You'll never wear them again. You say yourself they cost ten pesos—the same price as this lovely little goat I want to give you. And besides, a married man must be a man of property. Two stomachs hold more food than one stomach."

"Speak not to me of goats and stomachs and property. You yourself were at the wedding of Alma Orona. Are you less than Porfirio, the carver of wood? He bought her a pair of shoes. Shall all the world say that Alma Orona's wedding was grander than Nena Santos'?"

"In ten years," Andrés said stubbornly, "who will remember which wedding was the grander?"

"Indeed!" Nena buckled her hands on her hips and abandoned tears. "If I were as beautiful as María de las Garzas, you'd buy me a pair of shoes quickly enough."

"I'll hear no more of such stupidity," snapped Andrés. He, like all the men in the village, had learned from bitter experience that when María's name entered the conversation it was time to beat a hasty retreat. The fact that María lived alone in her house on the River Road and would have nothing to do with any individual from the five villages was of little importance. She was much too beautiful for the female population of the valley complacently to ignore.

Nena was not motivated by jealousy. She had merely introduced María's name as a flank attack. Now she struck straight to the center. Pulling her *rebozo* * over her head, she opened the door of her house. "Hear my words, Andrés Treviño. No shoes to wear at my wedding, no wedding! My mouth has spoken!" Before the boy could answer, she retreated hastily into the house, slamming the door for emphasis.

Andrés pulled his straw hat over his eyes and stalked down the Avenue of Illustrious Men toward the Plaza of Independence. As he walked, his bare toes, strapped into flat brown sandals, scuffed at the powdery dust. Here he had been doing without sandals he really needed in order to buy that goat while Nena calmly ordered shoes she would wear but once in her life. Perhaps he would be lucky and sell a young kid to the man from the shoe factory in Monterrey. In that case he could buy a pair of sandals from Abel, the next time the *árabe* trader passed through Hidalgo. Andrés lifted one foot and glared at it, then stamped it on the ground in punishment. His feet were so large, and Abel demanded two pesos for such a size in spite of fine bargaining. Porfirio was lucky. His feet were small. He had to pay only a peso and a half for his sandals. But then Porfirio was a wise man. He had chosen for himself a wife who knew the difference between a peso and a peso.

Perhaps the best thing to do was to go into the church and pray to the Blessed Lady for a miracle. Women understood women. The Sainted Mother might be able to convince Nena that shoes were of little importance where the buying of goats was concerned.

Andrés crossed the plaza and was just entering the church-yard when he saw Pablo, the goatherd, emerge from the pink-washed adobe temple. The round-faced boy frowned slightly

* A long shawl, fringed at two ends. Used by lower-class women.

and paused. Goatherds were necessary, of course, but Pablo had no right to come down from the hills and desecrate the church. A goatherd was the beloved of Grandfather Devil, and had no place in the churches of honest christians.

Pablo waved his hand. "Eh, Andrés Treviño," he called, "Don Saturnino tells me your herd of goats increases by the month. Soon you will need a fine herder to care for them in the hills."

"That is true," said Andrés soberly. "I feed them along the river banks now, but the hot months will make them sicken for the hills."

"Add them to my flocks," said Pablo generously. "Don Timotéo won't mind. As for me, it is no trouble to watch yours as well as his."

"And the price?" asked Andrés suspiciously. One never knew when these lovers of the black-robed mountain witches would pull a fine trick on one.

Pablo rolled a corn-shuck cigarette between brown fingers. "The great ones are even now playing dominoes at Father Zacaya's. We could go to the priest's house and ask their opinion in the matter."

Andrés swung on one heel and started off towards the Residence. As a good christian, it never occurred to him to allow this outcast to walk beside him. The wild men from the hills were cursed with a madness the townfolk could not understand. Father Zacaya said it was loneliness and pitied the herders, but the townfolk knew that the witches stole their souls for Grandfather Devil, and in exchange taught them the language of the goats.

There was, of course, a great social distinction between being an owner of goats and a herder. Fat complacent Timotéo Gonzalez, father to Pepe, the wild one, owned hundreds of goats. Andrés owned a very small flock that someday, he hoped, would develop into the finest herd between the Peak of the Ship's Prow and Saddle Mountain. But these men lived in the town, as proper christians should. When Father Zacaya argued with the villagers about their attitudes toward the herders, they would merely shrug their shoulders and remind him of poor, insane John of God, the goatherd, whose soul the witches had stolen by forcing his blind sweetheart to fall over the river cliffs to her death.

But Andrés was not thinking of these things as he opened the Residence door and passed into the parlor with Pablo following at his heels like a brown shadow.

Seated around a small square table playing dominoes were the "great ones," the four rulers of Hidalgo. With his back toward the door sat Don Nacho, the mayor, his great stomach resting on his knees. To his right was Don Rosalío, his long, silky white beard flowing down over his narrow chest, and a sprig of orange blossoms from his beloved trees fastened on his lapel. Across from Don Rosalío sat the little Doctor, and the fourth man at the table was the white-haired Father Zacaya, spiritual head of the Sabinas Valley. He often said that the Devil had cursed him with a sense of humor. Lucky for him he possessed such a curse, or he could never have survived the eddying pool of village life.

These were the four men playing dominoes: science, the village government, the church, and the landed interest—absolute rulers of a town of one thousand inhabitants. With the exception of Don Nacho, they were not a part of the town's duly elected board of *regidores*, or administrators. Of these Don Nacho was the *alcalde primero*, that is, the municipal president. Meek little Don Ernesto, much bullied by Don Nacho, was the *alcalde segundo*, or secretary. The treasury was headed by Don Martiniano Cantú, whom no one liked very much, but he could add a column of figures without difficulty, and that was the important thing. Don Genaro was the civil judge. He had held this office for years, dealing out impartial but wise justice. He also performed all the civil marriages, for Mexican couples must be married twice: once according to the laws of the Republic, and once according to the laws of the church. Don Genaro had a full, rich voice, and he loved to read the marriage service, being careful to affect a lisping "z" and a rolled double "l" in the best Castilian tradition, so that the ceremony acquired a grandiloquent effect. The final member of the *regidores* was one-armed Don Ricardo, *inspector de policía*, a title in which he took much pride.

But these men were cold and aloof in their dignity of office. Only Don Nacho had been able to bridge the gap between the municipality and the individual. For he knew that a town has problems which the impersonal law can neither understand nor solve. And so it was arranged long ago that the administration should answer the needs of the state, but the four men around the domino table answered the need of the people.

Here was not so much a capitalistic system as a patriarchy. When any villager was in trouble—from the dancing young Anita O'Malley to John of God, the goatherd—he came to one or all of these four men, perfectly confident that the problem would be taken off of his shoulders and solved to complete satisfaction. The only one who never came was María de las Garzas—the beautiful golden María of the River Road. But she was a lost wild creature whom not even these four wise men could save.

It was Father Zacaya who first noticed Andrés standing shyly just inside the room, his broad-brimmed straw hat clutched tightly between his hot, nervous hands.

"Eh, Andrés, how goes the world with you?"

"Sadly, Father, sadly."

"Are those proper words for an intended bridegroom to speak?" boomed Don Nacho, his great voice bounding back from the low-ceilinged walls.

"Who's that standing behind you?" demanded the little Doctor sharply. Then, recognizing Pablo, he smiled. Like Father Zacaya he had no fear of goatherds. "Come in, Pablo. Even a Devil's disciple can enter a priest's house, eh, Father?"

"Of course, Pablo. I didn't see you standing out there." Father Zacaya smiled gently at the two boys, thinking how much loneliness could age a man. Pablo was two years younger than Andrés, but he appeared at least five years older.

Pablo slipped past Andrés and paused at Don Rosalío's shoulder. "Good evening, my ancient ones. This young rooster has many goats. I thought I might take them up to the hills with Don Timotéo's herd in the spring, as this friend is a poor one and without money to hire a private herder."

The little Doctor looked gravely across the tops of his glasses at the round-faced boy. "Come into the circle of lamplight, Andrés. I do not like to speak with shadows."

Andrés moved slowly toward the table, his feet sliding reluctantly across the blue tiled floor. Sensing the boy's shyness, Father Zacaya poured a glass of wine from the decanter at his elbow and pushed it across the table.

"A bit of sherry will chase the November moonlight from your brain, my son."

"Thank you, Father." Andrés drank the wine and wiped his mouth politely on his sleeve. "This idea of the goats was Pablo's, not mine."

"And a good idea it is," Don Nacho boomed loudly. "Timotéo Gonzalez, that worthless man of many lies and magnificent cheeses, was telling me you are buying a goat from him every month now. He says you were looking at a fine new kid this morning."

"I was," acknowledged Andrés miserably, "but..." He paused and gravely replaced the wine glass on the table.

"But," prompted Don Rosalío, "the price was too high, eh?"

"That Timotéo Gonzalez is a robber," said the little Doctor sharply. "The mayor of El Carmen was telling me just today that Abel, the *árabe*, has more of a conscience than this same Timotéo Gonzalez."

"Oh, no, little Doctor," protested Andrés. "Don Timotéo asked a fair price—just ten pesos for a fine kid."

"A good price," agreed Don Rosalío, blowing out his full lips and sucking them in again. "What then is the difficulty in the sale?"

Thankful for an opportunity to recite his woes, Andrés poured forth the story of Nena and the shoes. "Women are strange creatures," he finished sadly. "She's never owned a pair of shoes. Why should she want them now? And shoes are items of expense. And the little goat of Don Timotéo...such a pretty creature." He sighed and rocked back on his heels. "It was in my mind to present it to Nena for her very own. But now— I am only a man. Who am I to understand the mind of a woman?"

For a moment after the question there was silence in the room. Into each man's mind sprang suddenly an individual image. Father Zacaya thought of the red-haired Anita O'Malley. What strange inheritance from Irish father and Mexican mother set her feet to dancing and her spirit to rebellion against all authority?

Don Nacho thought of his homely daughter Chela and her gift of seeing beyond the actions of men to the minds that controlled them. It would need a man of many mysteries to hold Chela's interest for very long. And Chela was too homely to attract many men.

Don Rosalío thought of his dead wife and the strange thing she had said to him just before she died: "Leave this Spain and return to your Mexican village. Hidalgo is your true wife." She was right, of course. But how had she understood the love of a Mexican for his land, and she Spanish born and bred? Of course, the death sight had been on her eyes. . . .

The little Doctor thought of María de las Garzas, María of the River Road. Why did she stay in the valley? With her blond beauty she could command the Republic. Instead, she lived in the cliff caves and watched the people of the five villages travel back and forth—watched them not with the humility of an outcast, which she was, but with the arrogance of the great lady of the village, which she was not.

Pablo, the goatherd, the man from the hills, thought not of one woman but of all the village girls. He thought of the patient Alma Orona; of Chela, Don Nacho's homely daughter; of the plump, stubborn Nena Santos. He thought briefly of the red-haired, Irish-eyed Anita O'Malley, and all the rest of them, with their narrow, proscribed lives. Which one had hidden in her that love of wild freedom which would carry her out of the safety of the village to the thin, cool wind of the hills? None of them? All of them? Even Alma Orona had slanted a glance toward him from beneath demurely lowered lashes. Women were strange creatures, indeed, he thought, preferring the safety of the pen, yet peering always between the bars toward the dangerous open fields.

It was Father Zacaya who broke the silence. "Andrés, your problem involves its difficulties. On one side is a wedding plus ten pesos spent for foolishness. On the other is no wedding plus a goat."

"The question is," added Don Rosalío gravely, "which is most important: Nena or the goat?"

"But they are both important, Don Rosalío," insisted Andrés. "Surely you can understand my difficulty, Don Nacho."

"I understand this," said Don Nacho firmly. "I speak as a man possessed of both a wife and a daughter. If you give in to her now, there will be no stopping her. She will rule you into the narrow width of your coffin."

"But Nena is a stubborn one," said the little Doctor. "I once tried to vaccinate her. After she broke three needles, her mother had to tie her to a chair before I could apply the serum. If Nena says, 'No shoes, no wedding,' she means, 'No shoes, no wedding.' "

"If women were only creatures of logic," sighed Father Zacaya, recalling some of Anita O'Malley's comments when he was trying to teach her her catechism.

"That is the true difficulty," agreed Don Nacho, thinking of his daughter Chela.

"If you want to marry Nena," said Don Rosalío, passing his hand delicately down the length of his white beard, "you'll have to plan on buying the goat some other time."

"But ten pesos is a good price for a goat," protested Andrés. "Maybe two years will pass or three before I can buy another at such a price. And Don Timotéo is a man of business. If he can't sell it to me, he will offer it to the mayor of El Carmen, or the mayor of Mina."

"Wait a moment." Pablo bent forward, his broad shoulders heavy in the shadowy light. "To whom do you sell your goats to make your profit?"

"To the butcher."

"But the little ones—the kids?"

"To the shoe factory in Monterrey," answered Andrés, puzzled by the question. The four seated men turned their heads silently toward the wind-tanned, wiry goatherd.

"Precisely," said Pablo. "You say you want to buy a goat. Nena wants a pair of shoes. To buy her the shoes would be unmanly, for all the world would know that this Nena Santos could command you at her pleasure."

"True words," agreed Andrés. "But I love Nena. I want to marry her."

"Then buy her the shoes."

"But . . ." began Andrés.

"Not as shoes," said Pablo quickly, "but as a goat."

"What's that?" snorted Don Nacho. And Don Rosalío and Father Zacaya hastily covered their grinning mouths with their hands.

The little Doctor frowned in perplexity. Andrés' mouth opened slightly and his head dipped to one side as he tried to understand Pablo's words.

The goatherd pushed closer to the table as he warmed to his argument. "Don't you understand? Shoes are made out of kidskin. Therefore when you buy the shoes you are really buying a goat—a dead goat, that is true—but still a goat."

"Magnificent," breathed Don Nacho. The little Doctor abruptly turned in his chair and hid his face against his palm.

"Of what good," demanded Andrés angrily, "is a dead goat to me, and I am owner of live ones?"

"You want to marry Nena, don't you?"

"Naturally."

"Yet you want to appear a man in the eyes of the world?"

"Very true."

"Buy her the shoes, call them two dead goats, you will marry Nena, and all the world will applaud your cleverness." Pablo, having settled the question, squatted down against the wall.

Andrés thrust out his chin. "But the live goat of Timotéo Gonzalez—what about it?"

"A man fool enough to marry," said Pablo, the goatherd, "can not expect to own the world."

"Buy the shoes, Andrés," said Don Rosalío. "You are a boy of ambition. Foolish now and then, but the village is proud of you. We are all proud of you. And as for the goat—the little Doctor will give you this same one for a wedding present."

"I," sputtered the little Doctor. "I—ten pesos—a goat—I?"

"Certainly. Andrés will pay you enough in childbirths to make it up to you."

The men laughed loudly as the lamplight intensified the crimson of Andrés' face.

"Abel, the *árabe*, will be pleased to make such a fine sale of a pair of shoes," rumbled Don Nacho.

"Abel, the *árabe*, has gone to Torreón," said Pablo. "He told me this morning he would be gone a month."

"And my wedding ten days off!" gasped Andrés. "If he is gone—where can I buy the shoes?"

"In Monterrey," suggested Father Zacaya.

"And shoes from Monterrey would be a grand thing in Nena's eyes," slyly agreed Don Nacho.

"But Monterrey is a day's journey by horse. And a train ticket costs a peso." Andrés drew in a deep sobbing breath. "Is there no end to this spending of money?"

"Father Zacaya goes in to Monterrey on Wednesday," said the little Doctor softly.

As though pulled by one string, four faces swung around toward the white-haired priest. Father Zacaya hastily pushed back his chair and stood up. "One moment, my little ones. I have never bought a pair of woman's shoes in my life. I . . ."

"No arguments," rumbled Don Nacho. "All you have to do is tell the clerk the size you want and put down the money. It is of a sweet simplicity."

"The problem is finished," said Don Rosalío firmly. "Pablo, take Andrés away from here and arrange about the summer herding. I, myself, will speak with Timotéo Gonzalez about the inclusion of Andrés herd with his."

"The price," began Andrés.

"The price will be two pesos. This also I will arrange."

Both knew that the two pesos meant nothing to Don Timotéo, but to Andrés they represented his position as a man of business.

"Now leave us," said the little Doctor. "We four are concerned with the importance of dominoes."

Pablo obediently put his hand under Andrés' elbow and guided the boy from the room. As they emerged from the house into the quiet starlit street, a girl hurried toward them down the Street of the Hidden Water and with a murmured greeting to the two boys, slipped through the dark entrance of the O'Malley house next door.

Andrés looked after her and shook his head in disapproval. "My Nena is trouble enough. I thank the Blessed Saints I'm not to marry Anita O'Malley—and she out alone at this hour of the night."

"Anita O'Malley," said Pablo thoughtfully. "The name makes a rhythm on the tongue."

"What's that you say?" Andrés peered suspiciously at him through the silvered darkness.

Pablo shrugged his shoulders. "Nothing," he said easily, "and a good night to you, Andrés Treviño. I will see you at your wedding." He had learned long ago that goatherds were not permitted to make comments about the town girls. Hooking his hands in his pockets, Pablo walked swiftly across the plaza and up the Avenue of Illustrious Men to the Street of the Cañon. In his own mind he repeated the name of Anita O'Malley. He was right. It did make a rhythm on the tongue.

On Wednesday morning Andrés hurried to the railroad station, a converted freight car near the blackened skeleton that was all the Revolution had left of Hidalgo's fine brick train platform. Near it was the water tank where the thirsty engines drank their fill before chugging southwest to Torreón in the evenings, or northeast to Monterrey in the mornings.

The passage of the slow-moving train was a social event. Girls with their hair rigidly set in water-wave combs, boys lounging loose-limbed on the saddles of restive horses, old men placidly chewing broom straws, old women balancing trays of chicken smothered in chili sauce, which they sold to the train's passengers, would begin to congregate at the first puff of approaching smoke in the distance. The single pullman car was the focus of all attention. Eyes would peer curiously up at the wealthy tourists, who would as curiously stare back at the villagers. Most of the tourists were unaware of the first, second, and third class coaches between the pullman and the freight cars.

It was in the third class coach that Father Zacaya thought, in all humility, he should ride. But Hidalgo, as the richest of the five valley towns, demanded that he should ride in elegance in the first class to uphold the village dignity. After much argument, the priest and the town compromised on second, and it was into this car that the white-haired man of God was climbing as Andrés caught up with him.

The usual village audience gaped like an audience in a theatre as they watched Andrés, his hands moving in quick gesture, tell something to the priest. The train whistle was blowing too lustily for anyone to overhear the conversation, but Andrés' graphic hands and body were acting out the pantomime of buying something that was small. By afternoon the entire village knew of the meeting. Several friends had made a point of informing Nena about the morning's encounter. She smiled in secret satisfaction and went happily about the preparations for her wedding. When Nena met other girls from the *Gallineros* she would hold her head high with pride. She knew that she would be the only girl in the poor man's section to walk to her marriage in shoes. No girls from the wealthier districts—not even Evita Cantú or Anita O'Malley would be any grander at their weddings than Nena Santos at hers in her white satin gown and her new white shoes.

And then an event occurred which drove all thought of Andrés Treviño's wedding and Nena Santos' shoes from the village mind. A telegram arrived at the railroad station which sent Don Nacho scurrying to Don Rosalío's. The two old friends read the words and both sat down to cry a little.

"After all these years," sighed Don Nacho. "Home again. Is it possible?"

"Candles in the church," said Don Rosalío. "Firecrackers on the plaza. And someone to open and air the great house."

"Tía Magdalena?"

"We could ask her."

They put on their hats and walked with slow dignity to Bob Webster's house, although their feet wanted to run. They found Bob standing in the street admiring his new door, which Porfirio had hung in place that morning. "Look," he said happily, "roses and lilies and intertwined vine leaves. Is it not a magnificent carving job? Porfirio has talent."

"Who cares for Porfirio?" Don Nacho boomed. "Friend Bob, we have news, great news. Where is Tía Magdalena?"

"Making sweet tamales and *atole* * to celebrate the new door. What has happened?"

Instead of answering him, the old men pushed their way into the house. Tía was in the kitchen, punching raisins into a dough of mashed cornmeal, and expertly wrapping small chunks of the dough in corn-shucks. When she saw who her visitors were, she slid to her feet, and wiped her hands on her apron before folding them over her chest.

Don Nacho looked at Don Rosalío, who shrugged and stepped back. "You're the mayor. You ask her."

"But your tongue is smoother than mine, friend Rosalío."

"Nevertheless, you are the mayor."

Then, with one accord, their heads turned towards Bob. Each caught him by an arm and pulled him to the far side of the patio, while Tía watched them, her forehead creased in a frown. Their voices were only an indistinct mutter, but she saw Bob suddenly shake his head and try to pull away, while Don Rosalío and Don Nacho gripped him more firmly by the arms. Then Don Nacho made a sweeping gesture toward the southwest, and she suddenly realized what they wanted.

* A hot drink made of thin corn gruel flavored with sugar, cinnamon, and sometimes chocolate. Sweet tamales and *atole* are generally feast-day dishes, being especially popular at Christmas.

"So," she called out, "that black devil, Don Saturnino Castillo returns to Hidalgo. Is that what you want to tell me?"

The men came toward her in relief.

"Precisely, Tía." Don Nacho mopped his forehead with a large red bandana. "And we thought—I mean Don Rosalío thought . . ."

"It was your idea, too," said the white-bearded man quickly. They both looked so pleadingly at Bob that he grinned.

"They want you to air out the house and see that there are servants and food waiting."

Tía's mouth shut in a straight line. Before she could answer, Don Rosalío said quickly, "The young Alejandro comes with him, grown now to man's size."

"Doña Elvira died in the birthing of Alejandro," said Tía slowly.

"Is that Alejandro's fault?" Don Nacho asked. "And Joaquín loved Alejandro."

"Yes," Tía said. "Joaquín loved him." She tapped her foot thoughtfully against the cement. "It is for Joaquín that I do this, you understand."

Don Nacho blew his nose with satisfaction. Bob promised to send women from the quarry to help clean, and by nightfall the news had spread from Mina to Topo Grande that Don Saturnino Castillo was coming home after eight years of exile.

On the morning of the arrival, people streamed into Hidalgo from River Road and Mina Road, some in carts, some riding on donkeys, on mules, on horses, and many on foot. Stands for eating were set up on the plaza, and Don Alonso's musicians played old melodies from the days before the Great Revolution, such as "Over the Waves," and "The Song of the Ripe Peach," and the ever beautiful "The River Lures Me."

When they heard this song, the people began to sing, the words seeming to shimmer in the air:

> *Shadow of our lord St. Peter,*
> *The river lures me, the river lures me.*
> *And thus does your great love*
> *My love allure, my love allure.*

Faintly in the distance came the sound of the train whistle, but no one moved towards the station. Eyes looked at eyes and turned away in delicacy. Don Saturnino was coming home, with Alejandro but without Joaquín. Better to let the proud old man weep in secret with sorrow for his lost oldest son, and with joy at being home again.

Don Nacho and Don Rosalío had gone to the great white house to welcome their old friend, whom Don Nacho, a good Revolutionist, had helped to escape the fury of Revolutionary soldiers.

Bob Webster, drawn to the plaza late that afternoon by the music and the crowd, found himself standing near Don Nacho's daughter Chela, who had mounted one of the benches and was looking about her with an intent air.

"Can I help you, Chela? Are you hunting your mother?"

She looked down at him. He was suddenly aware of her green eyes, startling under the thick black brows. She's not beautiful, he thought, but she has a strange, bone-drawn distinction. I wonder why I ever saw her as homely.

"Thank you, Don Bob," she murmured, jumping lightly to the ground. "I was hunting María of the River Road. I thought she might like to stand with me. She has few friends."

"You know," he said idly, "I've never seen María. Think of it. I'll have been here two years next March, and I've never seen the most beautiful woman in the Sabinas. I've even ridden past her house on the River Road, but I think she hides away in the cliff caves."

Chela shrugged. "She's very shy."

"What makes you think she'll be here today?"

"During the days of the Great Revolution she hid Don Saturnino and the young Alejandro, who was then, you understand, but thirteen years of age, on the Rancho Santo Tomás, until my father could make arrangements to pass them safely across the Río Bravo.* I thought that in honor of this fiesta, she would come to the plaza, but..." She shrugged and laughed.

The little Doctor, pushing his way through the crowd, tapped Bob on the shoulder. "The speaker's platform has been set up in front of the Boy's School. Come, friend Bob, let us take our places."

"But I'm not going to speak."

"Nor am I, thank the blessed saints. But we are important citizens." With a bow to Chela, he firmly led Bob across the plaza. "I want to ask you... As you know, I've bought a little goat for

* "Fierce River." Name used in Mexico for the Río Grande.

Andrés Treviño as a wedding present. Could you keep it in your patio until the wedding?"

"Me? Keep a goat?"

"I thought perhaps—I mean the village says—well, the village contends that it will not smell so bad if it stays near an eagle witch. Ay, don't laugh, friend Bob. As a man of science, I recognize your laughter. But as a man of the village, you comprehend, the goat does smell."

Bob bit down on his lower lip to control his merriment. "If Tía Magdalena can guarantee the lack of odor . . ."

"Good. I will speak to her this very . . ." He broke off and yelled, "Hurry, friend priest. Hurry! From the movement of the crowd, the procession must have started."

Father Zacaya collapsed on a platform chair, his black robes fluttering about his thin legs. "Such a morning," he groaned. "All the world wants to start cooking-fires inside the church. I've put Porfirio at the door to bar the entrance, and now he is furious with me because he wants to be in the procession. Why do people have to cook inside the church? Why can't they cook in the yard?"

"I don't know," the little Doctor answered moodily. "I've even seen them cooking inside the sainted Guadalupe Shrine outside the City.* Don't ask me why village people do what they do."

Bob stood up. "Here they come."

The orchestra began to play the *Golondrina*.† The crowd turned like a single entity to stare up the Street of the Forgotten Angel. Small boys in the churchyard set off strings of fire-crackers that snapped into gray doughnuts of smoke.

First came Don Nacho, walking in stately dignity, the tall staff of his office in his left hand. Behind him, riding abreast, were Don Rosalío and Don Genaro, the civil judge. After them followed on foot a group of village men, Rubén, the candy-maker leading them as a general leads an army. Last of all was the Castillo victoria, the Castillo coat of arms on low curving doors, drawn by the proud Castillo blacks.

Bob stood on tiptoe, but even from the eminence of the plat-

* Mexico City. Since the country is generally referred to as the Republic, Mexico City is called the City, or the Capital, or simply Mexico.

† This song, composed by an unknown musician, came into Mexico in 1840, and is the Republic's "Home, Sweet Home."

form it was difficult to see the carriage occupants because of the pressing crowd, which was shouting, "Long live the Castillos! Long live Hidalgo! Long live the Revolution! Long live the Republic!"

"I like that," sighed the little Doctor in Bob's ear. "The Castillos represent everything that the Revolution sought to destroy; so the people couple them in one long Hurrah! How wonderful is Mexico." The phrase came from his heart, and Bob smiled at him in sympathy.

The procession was coming down the Avenue of Independence. Small boys were clambering over the victoria's sides, and the candy-maker's regiment had dropped back to brush them off like flies.

Don Nacho climbed up on the platform, and bowed to the three men, and then turned and bowed to the people, who loudly applauded him. Don Rosalío and Don Genaro dismounted from their horses with a flourish, and also came up on the platform. Then the candy-maker's men linked arms to hold back the forward rushing people as the victoria swung around the corner and came to a stop in front of the Boy's School.

Bob looked at the two occupants with curiosity. He realized that he was prejudiced against them by Tía Magdalena, and he tried to free his mind of resentment as he examined the courtly old man, with the closely clipped white hair and the delicate, finely chiseled features.

As Don Saturnino stepped to the platform and shook hands with all of them, Bob was surprised to notice that he and this Spanish gentleman had the same type of hand: narrow, flexible, with the little finger almost as long as the ring finger. He murmured his own name as the great man reached him, and once again, as on that morning when he first met Don Nacho, he had a feeling that the name of Webster, which he knew was his by right, should not be spoken in this clear Mexican air.

Then Don Saturnino was past him, and he found himself looking at Alejandro, who, since his older brother's disappearance, was now the young Castillo, and heir to all the valley lands. Bob had to look up at him, for Alejandro was tall, well over six feet, with the broad shoulders and narrow hips of a man who has lived much in the open. But his clear white skin lacked sun-warmth. His black hair, brushed back from a center part, had a soft wave in it, his eyes were a clear brown, and his Spanish nose was thin and finely cut. He, too, had the long narrow hands, and his grip on Bob's fingers was strong, lacking the loose Mexican formality.

His voice was rough and hoarse, but it had an oddly gentle timbre, as he said, "I hear that Tía Magdalena is your housekeeper." At Bob's nod, he smiled, and a light shone behind his eyes. "You will permit me to call upon her? I am very fond of her."

"Of course," Bob answered with surprise at this formality.

Don Saturnino's cold, remote tones sounded over his shoulders. "Be seated, Alejandro," and the young man sat down so quickly that Bob realized the reason for the request. Unspoken between them were the words: My father and Tía are enemies. Are you, too, an enemy of the House Castillo?

Don Nacho opened the ceremony with a long speech on the glories of the Great Revolution which he had made so often that when he paused for breath the people prompted him in a loud chant.

Then Don Genaro, the civil judge, stepped forward, and in his pure Castilian diction, harnessed to a Mexican accent, welcomed the great family home again.

As Don Saturnino advanced to the edge of the platform with many small bows, there was a shout of delight from the crowd. Chela, homely and awkward, but conscious of her dignity as daughter of the mayor, presented him with a large bouquet of white roses. The orchestra loudly played the applause music. Don Saturnino bowed again, but he was still not permitted to speak, for down the Avenue of Illustrious Men came the young Xavier riding on Bob's white horse.

Bob half rose from his chair in surprise, then shrugged and relaxed. Alejandro jumped to his feet. "A white horse! In this valley?"

A ripple of surprise passed over Don Saturnino's coldly perfect features. "A white horse," he murmured. "Is it possible?"

Don Nacho began a quick explanation, with many gestures towards Bob, but no one was paying him any attention. All eyes were focused on the young Xavier.

The boy raised his arm in signal, and the music swung into the greatest of Mexican waltzes, "Over the Waves." The horse lifted one dainty forefoot, replaced it delicately in the dust, and then began a rhythmic dance, advancing and retreating, swinging now to the right and now to the left.

The crowd yelled with pleasure, and Don Saturnino nodded his appreciation.

"I'll have that boy's ears," Bob muttered to the little Doctor. "Where did he get the courage to ride *El Blanco?*"

"He'd ride anything, even Satan's smoke-crowned dragon. There's horse's blood in that boy's veins, I'm sure of it."

The music came to a melodic close, and Xavier brought the horse to its knees in a deep curtsey. Don Saturnino gently applauded, and Alejandro bent forward to shake the boy's hand.

"They know how to honor the valley," Bob whispered. "Their technique is very interesting."

The little Doctor shrugged. "They should know how. They have three hundred years of training in their bones."

Don Rosalío leaned forward and tapped Bob's shoulder. "If Joaquín were here, he would show the young Xavier how to really ride a horse."

"You mean he was better than that boy?"

"Xavier has horse's blood in his veins, but Joaquín! ... He grew out of a horse like a tree from the ground. And let me warn you. Never mention Joaquín to Don Saturnino. The loss of the oldest son, ay, that is always a sword in the heart."

As Don Rosalío sat back, Bob noticed that Xavier had dismounted and was proudly standing at the base of the platform, while Don Saturnino, his palm resting on Alejandro's arm, began to speak. The clear voice floated across the heads of the quiet crowd, and was returned to them in a faint echo from the western mountains.

After a moment, Bob was lulled into sleepiness by the monotonous tones. He realized that it was a perfection of oratory, delivered in the finest Spanish tradition, but the words meant nothing to him.

He glanced up and saw that Alejandro had turned his head, so that his profile was etched against the deep blue November sky. One hand was plucking nervously at his throat as though he were trying to loosen something inside of it. He was frowning slightly, and he seemed to Bob to be a strangely solitary figure, a part of this valley, and yet not a part of it. He had been gone

since he was thirteen, and now he was—Bob made swift calculations in his head—he must be twenty-one. But he looked older
than that. He lacked the coltish youngness of his years, and
had about him an aura of maturity, as though he had already
completed a major part of his allotted span of life.

Bob caught a glimpse of Pablo, the goatherd, perched on the
roof of the bandstand. Pablo, too, was just twenty-one, and he,
too, had this quality of isolation. But Pablo's maturity was bred
from loneliness, whereas Alejandro's ...

But of course, Bob thought in quick sympathy, the boy is
lonely. He's been snatched out of a glittering, sophisticated
world, and plunged into this isolated valley, and he's too young
to make a spiritual adjustment by himself. He needs help, and
he needs it badly. It must have taken a good deal of courage
for him to ask me that question about Tía Magdalena. I wonder
if he would come home to supper with me?

After the ceremonies were over, Alejandro accepted the invitation with delight. "Don Rosalío is giving my father a little
dinner. There will be many speeches, and much talk of days I
can't remember. This will be a relief for them, and for me too."

He arrived at Bob's house with punctual courtesy, a long
wooden box under his arm for Tía Magdalena. "All the way
from Paris I brought it," he assured her, and was too excited
to allow her to open it for herself, but tore at the wrappings
with his nervous fingers.

The open box revealed a dress of green satin. Tía stared down
at the fragrant softness with eyes that were misted with tears.

"For me?" she whispered, her hands hovering above the material and afraid to touch it.

"Put it on, Tía," Alejandro urged. "Show us how beautiful
you are."

"Ay," she whispered, "if only Joaquín could know this, how
pleased he would be."

She snatched up the box and fled with it to her room.

At mention of his brother's name, Alejandro's sensitive mouth
trembled slightly. He looked quickly about him. "I remember
when the Italian lived here. What a pigpen!" He patted the
pomegranate bush, pulled an orange from its tree, and inhaled
the skin's spicy perfume. "Now it is a house. Have you changed
it inside?"

"No, not much. Tía complains about the furniture, but I'm too lazy to change it."

Alejandro nodded, and strolled to the dining room door. "The table is too big. If it were sawn in half and painted . . ." He stopped abruptly and color stained his too white skin. "I like to work with my hands," he said shyly. "My father tells me I have the mind of a carpenter."

"If it would interest you to play tricks with this furniture, you're welcome to the job." Bob began filling his pipe from a leather tobacco pouch stamped with his initials.

"Thank you," Alejandro said formally. "It would interest me very much." He looked at the pouch. "R.W. I did not hear your name on the platform."

"Bob Webster. Robert to my enemies."

"So? There is a family Webster in San Antonio. You are perhaps related?"

Bob could feel his face closing into Indian immobility. "There are many Websters," he said coolly. "It's a common name."

"Of course. And you are dark. This family I mentioned are all blond." He was talking quickly to prevent Bob's thinking him too curious of personal affairs.

An anguished yelp from the patio sent them running to Tía Magdalena, who was stretched out full length on her face, the dress a green wave about her. As Bob set her on her feet, she wailed, "I took a step, and zas! I was on the ground."

Alejandro began to howl with laughter, and Bob, after a desperate effort to control himself, laughed too. Tía had put the dress on backwards, so that the train spread out like a pheasant's tail in front of her.

"You laugh at me! Ay, Alejandro, such grandeur is not for an old woman."

When Alejandro managed to explain what had happened, she looked down the length of green satin and shook her head. "But how else could I button it, save down the front? Am I a creature with rubber arms, that I can reach to the back?"

With their help, the dress was reversed and fastened correctly, Alejandro managing the buttons with many grunts while she moaned that he was cutting her breath into two sections. Then they stepped back to admire her.

The dress was cut low in front, and even lower in back, so for modesty's sake she had put on one of her long-sleeved pink blouses. From the tight basque waist, the skirt fell away in soft folds, and from ankle to knee large pansies of purple velvet were appliquéd, with trailing stems embroidered in gold.

"I remembered how small you were," Alejandro told her, "and I said to them, 'Make a dress for a child of twelve, who is really a hundred years old ...'"

"You!" shrieked Tía with flashing anger. "A hundred years indeed! Is it in my grave you are putting me?" As she advanced toward him, her hand outstretched for a quick slap, there came a loud pounding at the door.

"I am now a lady," she snapped at Bob. "Go yourself."

Still convulsed with mirth, he opened the door. A white something flashed between his legs, catapulting him forward into the arms of the little Doctor, who yelled at him, "I've lost the goat. Don't let it get away!"

Both men jumped inside and slammed the door shut. In the patio there was pandemonium. The goat, attracted by the perfume of the dress, had dashed straight toward Tía, who leaped with agility to the top of the well. Alejandro was trying to drag the animal backwards, while the little creature, a section of the train in its mouth, was kicking its four tiny legs in an effort to free itself.

Bob's hand closed on the small black muzzle. By cutting off its wind, he forced the goat to open its mouth, but Tía was not prepared for this sudden release of tension. Trying to protect her dress, she had been pulling backwards, and now, with a high, shrill scream, she tumbled into the well.

It took the combined efforts of Bob and Alejandro, with the little Doctor clutching the goat and yelling instructions, to get her out.

They finally set her upright on the patio cement, her four feet eleven inches trembling with wrath. Water plastered her wispy gray hair to her face. The pink blouse clung to her bony shoulders, and the dress was now a lank twist of material, with the velvet spreading its purple dye over the green satin.

"That goat!" she shrieked, as soon as she had sputtered the water out of her mouth. "May it die in agony. May its feet sink uicksand. May it cause tears and lamentations to its owner..."

Ay, Tía," howled the little Doctor, "it is a wedding present for Andrés Treviño."

"The more fool he for wanting a goat as a wedding present. Look at me. Look at me!"

Bob had rushed into his bedroom for a blanket, and now he wrapped it around her, so that she was a small cocoon of striped wool, shading from dark brown to bright orange and back to brown again.

The little Doctor said firmly, "Light a fire some place," and while Alejandro started a blaze in the living room, Bob carried Tía in and settled her in a wicker rocker.

"Tell that little man to take his Devil's beast out of here!"

"Of course, Tía, at once," Bob said soothingly.

The little Doctor, still clutching the struggling goat, hovered in the doorway. "Such a pretty animal," he murmured temptingly. "Behold it, Tía. Its eyes are like two dark pools of innocence."

"Ha!" Tía glared at him. "For the first time in my life I have a magnificent dress, and what happens? That goat—that goat..."

"Yes, Tía, but look at it." He approached her cautiously, holding the goat upside down by its small hooves. "All white, with a little black moon on its forehead. Is it not a dainty thing?"

"Goats are the sons of Grandfather Devil..."

"But this is such a jewel of a creature." He swung it tantalizingly in front of her. The little animal began to baa piteously, and Tía's mouth softened.

"Well," she said grudgingly, "after all a goat is a goat..."

"Precisely. And with intelligence. Immediately it recognized the beauty of your dress. And with a goat, beauty is something to be eaten."

As he approached her, Bob and Alejandro drew closer together, admiration for him in their eyes.

Tía wriggled her shoulders inside the blanket, the wool scratching her through her thin clothes. "As you say, the entire world is an object for a goat's stomach."

"And if you could keep it for a few days—just until after the wedding, Andrés Treviño will bless you in his prayers, and I will bless you in my prayers."

Her lips covered her sparsely toothed gums, the chin rising to meet the nose. "The animal has a certain, a certain..."

"Personality," suggested the little Doctor.

"Ummm," said Tía. She opened the blanket and stretched out an arm to caress the small head. And then her eyes saw her dress. The pink blouse and green satin had absorbed the browns, yellows, and orange of the wool. Her mouth opened, and for a moment there was silence. Then a bursting shriek made Alejandro and Bob snap their hands over their ears, and tightly shut their eyes against the vision of the little Doctor being flayed alive. But hearing nothing more beyond that whip of sound, they cautiously opened their lids. Where the little Doctor had been was empty space. In the quiet they could hear the front door slam and the rapid patter of departing feet on the sidewalk outside. Then they looked at Tía, who was contemplating them with scorn.

"In this house," she said firmly, "no more of goats!" She stalked through the patio to her own room, and that door also slammed.

Bob and Alejandro, choked with laughter, got their own supper. They timidly tried to persuade Tía to eat something, but silence was their only answer.

"Perhaps tomorrow I had better go to Monterrey and buy another dress," Alejandro suggested anxiously.

"Perhaps we'd better both go," Bob said gloomily. "I don't think Tía's really angry with either you or me, but I have a feeling that no man will be very popular in this house for the next few days."

"Men," said Alejandro, "and goats."

They stared at each other, and the memory of the goat eating Tía's train rose in their minds. They had to run out of the house to keep the old woman from hearing their mirth.

The days passed quickly, and on the evening of Andrés Treviño's wedding, the November moon rose brightly clear and full above the black jagged peaks of the western mountains. The village streets were dark and deserted, for most of the people were pressing through the wide gates that separated the cactus-enclosed *Gallineros* (the "chicken coop") from the rest of the town. Why the poorest people of Hidalgo had chosen to enclose themselves within a cactus wall, no one knew. It was the same in Mina, in El Carmen, in Abasolo, in Topo Grande.

Tonight, Andrés and his good friends Porfirio and Pepe Gonzalez were in the patio of Nena's home, staring into the well where the wedding bouquet was being kept to preserve its freshness. Through the door of the house came a low hum as of angry bees around a hive. The guests, from the sound, were screaming at each other above the tuning of the orchestra. There would be no dancing, of course, until after Don Genaro, the civil judge, had married the young couple according to the laws of the state. Then the dancing would begin, lasting through the night until five in the morning, when the whole party would march through the town in the false dawn light to the pink-washed temple of Our Lady of the Miraculous Tear, there to attend the second wedding by Father Zacaya according to the laws of the church.

"Think of it," said Pepe Gonzalez, thrusting one long arm into the well and poking at the tightly bound bouquet of gardenias and tuberoses. "In the Republic a man must buy a house, furnish it, purchase the bride's trousseau, pay for the wedding festival, and provide the bouquet; but in the States all a man needs is two dollars and the girl."

"Me," said Porfirio, remembering with bitterness a certain ten-peso fine, "I should have been married in the States."

"You are a stingy man," said Andrés, hoping that the cold terror of the approaching ceremony was not apparent in his voice. "Me, I am generous. And what happens? Nena wears shoes and the little Doctor gives me a goat."

"It's a fine goat," said Pepe Gonzalez. "I raised it with these two hands from the day it slipped from its mother's womb . . ."

"You never did anything but get Andrés and me into trouble in all the years of your life," snorted Porfirio. "If it hadn't been for you, Andrés and I might have passed many a terror-filled night in sweet peace and comfort."

"Did I ask you to follow my lead?" retorted Pepe sharply. "But when I ring the bell, who is it comes running?"

Porfirio thrust out his chin. "Are you calling me a two-legged sheep?"

"Your nose grows flatter to your face every day!"

Andrés slipped quickly between the two quarreling men.

"There'll be no fight at my wedding. There has been enough trouble what with goats and shoes without fights being added. May St. Andrew of the Crooked Cross protect me from any more difficulties."

Nena's shrill voice rose above the conversation hum in a clear, decisive scream of anger.

"Blessed Saints," gasped Andrés. "What has happened now?"

At that moment Doña Fela, the town's great lady, surged through the door, something white and dainty clasped tightly between her hands.

"You, Andrés Treviño! Were you born entirely without brains?"

"What is wrong, auntie?" asked Pepe in as soothing a voice as he could muster. His mother was Doña Fela's sister, and he and Anita O'Malley were supposed to be the only two beings who were not secretly afraid of the old lady's anger.

"What is wrong, indeed, and this fool of an Andrés standing there as innocent as a bird freshly cracked from the egg."

"Why was Nena screaming?" Andrés stepped toward Doña Fela. "Was she hurt? Did someone wound her feelings?"

"Something wounded her feet!" snapped the old lady, and suddenly thrust what she was holding under Andrés' nose. By this time the patio was filled with people, and even Pablo the goatherd (invited as a gesture of good will toward Grandfather Devil), was listening wth avid interest.

Slowly Andrés reached out and took the white slippers from Doña Fela. The brilliant green-silver moonlight threw their whiteness into strong relief against his dark hands. Those close enough to see the slippers caught their breath in admiration. These were not fashioned for a human being but for a delicate lady of fantasy. From heel to toe their length was no greater than a man's palm. They were dainty bits of leather belonging to the dancing useless feet of a fragile city girl, not the sturdy broad soles of a girl from the *Gallineros*.

"Nena thought them beautiful when I brought them to her this evening," said Andrés with a puzzled helplessness in his eyes. "What made her change her mind?"

"And what made you buy such trifles?" snorted Doña Fela. "Do you think a normal-sized woman can get her feet in those shoes?"

"Holy Mother of God, she can't get them on!" said Pepe Gonzalez with sudden illumination.

"Ah," breathed Doña Fela with heavy sarcasm. "A man of wisdom is amongst us. You are correct, my pretty nephew. Nena can't get even one toe inside of them. And as for you, my wise buyer of woman's goods..." her head snapped back to Andrés, "what evil devil suggested that you purchase these toys?"

"To save money," muttered Andrés, so low he could scarcely be heard.

"To save money?" shrieked the old woman. "Do you think women's shoes, then, are bought like your sandals, by the size?"

"But naturally. I went down to the station and asked Father Zacaya to purchase the smallest pair he could find. I never thought Nena's feet would be too large to wear them."

"Oh, didn't you!" There was a pushing aside of people as Nena advanced, her plump body sheathed in white satin, and her bare feet silvered bronze in the moonlight. "Are you saying now that I have the feet of a giantess?"

The low curve of the well prevented Andrés from retreating. "I swear such a thought was not in my mind."

"I told you, Andrés Treviño, with my own mouth I said it— that I would wear shoes at my wedding or there would be no wedding. And these shoes I cannot wear!"

As her voice died away into silence, the whole patio tensed, every eye on Andrés. The boy looked beseechingly at Porfirio, at Pepe Gonzalez, even at Pablo the goatherd for aid. But these three could offer him nothing. Over the heads of the quiet guests he could see Father Zacaya, Don Rosalío, Don Nacho, the little Doctor. But they, too, for once in their lives, had no advice to give him. Then, through the silence, came the soft baaing of a goat, the little Doctor's wedding present. Andrés felt bitterness flood through his entire body. He had heard that Tía Magdalena had cursed the goat, and she was an eagle witch. His hand went up to the small silver pin shaped in the figure of St. Peter, called the "Shadow of St. Peter," which was fastened under his coat lapel.

"A candle as long as my arm to break the curse," he whispered. If there was no wedding, the goat—in all honor—must be returned. It was bad enough to lose Nena, but to lose her and the goat, too, was not to be endured. He turned his back on the crowd and peered intently into the well to hide his misery from their curious eyes.

Suddenly his back stiffened, his head lifted with new authority. He swung on his sandaled heel and faced the silent group. His voice rang clear and strong in the narrow patio.

"Tell the musicians to start the music. Nena, return to the kitchen. This wedding will be now. I have spoken."

"But the shoes," began Nena rebelliously.

"You will have your shoes. That, too, I have spoken."

At a nod from him, Pepe Gonzalez and Porfirio began to push the guests back into the house. Andrés, his mouth set in a straight, thin line, reached out and grasped Nena's arm firmly just above the elbow. In spite of her tugging and kicking out at him, he half carried, half led her into the kitchen where he shut the door with a bang, an inch from Doña Fela's startled nose.

A few moments later the long, narrow parlor, softly yellow in the glow of the hot, rancid oil lanterns, had a cleared space down the center from kitchen door to the far end, with the black cane sofa and the table behind which waited Don Genaro in all the dignity of his office as civil judge. To his right stood Don Rosalío, Don Nacho, and the little Doctor, ready to sign the book as witnesses for the groom. To his left stood Doña Fela, Doña Mariliria, and Doña Juanita Perez. They, too, would sign the book as witnesses for the bride.

There was tense expectancy in the crowd. What was Andrés saying to Nena behind that firmly shut kitchen door? Every head was turned at a polite angle toward that door. Tía Magdalena, encased in a new dress of bright red satin, clutched Bob's arm with one excited hand, and Alejandro's with the other. Like everyone else, their conversation was carried on automatically and in as low tones as possible, so that curiosity would not be too apparent, and yet in the hope that even a fragment of momentous dialogue could be heard. Once Nena's voice rose in a shrill, "No!" followed by something that sounded like the crashing of a chair. Again, Andrés gave a howling shout of rage, which quickly sank to a low, undistinguishable murmur.

The little Doctor whispered to Don Nacho. "I have a feeling that Nena is discovering Andrés intends to be master in his own house."

Suddenly Don Alonso's orchestra, at a signal from Pepe Gonzalez through the iron-barred patio window, began to play that favorite song of all northern frontier weddings: Tosti's "Goodbye Forever." The kitchen door opened and the bridal party marched in. First entered Nena's mother with Andrés' father; then Andrés' mother with Nena's father. Next, in couples, came Alma Orona, Pepe Gonzalez, Anita O'Malley, and Porfirio. And finally, Andrés and Nena.

Necks craned for a better view. People in the back stood on tiptoe. Softly at first, then gaining in volume, came the laughter. There was loud clapping in abrupt appreciation. The orchestra, catching the spirit of the occasion, swung out of the doleful Italian melody into the gay, jerky rhythm of the applause music. Nena, clutching Andrés' arm, bowed proudly to right and left. Had ever girl from the *Gallineros*, from the whole Sabinas Valley for that matter, had such a wedding as this? Alma Orona had worn shoes at her wedding, true, but she had worn them on her feet. And as Andrés said when he broke the chair on the kitchen floor for emphasis, "You said you wanted to wear a pair of shoes. But you never mentioned wearing them on the feet. That was not in the bargain. Any fool can wear them on the feet. But the wife of Andrés Treviño is not a common bride. Why, then, should she wear elegance in a common manner? I said you would wear shoes and you shall—like gloves on your hands in place of a wedding bouquet!"

Street of the Hidden Water

Anita O'Malley

November, 1921—June, 1925

When bread is lacking, crumbs are good...
—Mexican proverb

A T THE LOWER END OF THE STREET OF THE HIDDEN WATER stood a house whose great wooden shutters were always closed.

The woman who lived there never left her house save to go to church. No one ever called on her, not even Father Zacaya. A few superstitious souls, when passing the green-washed walls, would cross themselves and mutter to each other that it was as though this woman were already dead and in the tomb with her husband. She was truly a person set apart.

Even her name was different from other women's, for they kept their maiden names regardless of how many times they had been married. There was Doña Juanita Perez, for instance. Three times she had been married, and three husbands she had put in the cemetery. But Juanita Perez she had been born, and Juanita Perez she would die, whereas this cloistered woman was never referred to as Anita O'Malley. That name was hidden behind the more somber title of The Widow of General Valdez.

Hidalgo had known her as a high-spirited girl, and now knew her as a broken woman, but the five years between had not belonged to the village. When she returned to Hidalgo from exile, the town accepted her mourning and respected it. After a while even those who had known her best in the old days forgot that she had ever been the red-headed daughter of that worthless Irishman Don Juan O'Malley, who had run off with her to Mexico City because of his fight with Pablo, the herder of goats.

The years between had belonged to that strange world beyond the mountains which the valley tolerated but did not recognize. Indeed, the five villages would have been very much surprised to learn that Anita O'Malley was known in Mexico City as the Great O'Malley, the woman without a soul, an automaton whose only awareness of life came when she was dancing on the stage under the management of that great Spanish clown, Pepe Bobo. No, Hidalgo did not know that it was the fashion to drop into the theatre to see the O'Malley. Diplomatic breasts, covered with medals and red ribbons, were seen in the boxes. The best of the Republic's society willingly lent its spirit, that Anita O'Malley might come alive for a little space of time. If she could dance only to an audience, no one knew. What she did when she was alone ... but then, she was never alone. A maid went with her everywhere, dressed her in the morning, put her to bed at night. Her father was never far from her, even when he was drunk, which he usually was. Pepe Bobo, who had been afraid of her.

became enchanted with her, and finally followed her around like a faithful dog. He worshipped her. Most men did. She had a peculiar power over them. It was the eternal song of Lilith... the savage spirit demanding the savage response. Flowers from would-be lovers filled her dressing room. Men boasted of receiving a smile, a special sideways glance. They were lying, and everyone knew they were lying, but the boasts continued. Mejía, one of the lesser romantic poets, shot himself (being careful to avoid a vital spot), and during the wave of publicity following his recovery wrote a poem comparing the O'Malley to Rosario for whose beauty the poet Manuel Acuña committed suicide in 1873. Although the Mejía was a very bad poet, his poem made him a famous man, which, after all, was what he wanted.

This and other stories General Valdez heard when, having resigned from the army, he came to the City from Sonora. He was curious to see her, of course, and he felt the common bond which those who come from the frontier states feel for each other.

He was a giant of a man, with an egg-shaped head totally bald, and had been famous in the army because his ugliness was so fascinating to women. He was forty-five and had never married, because, he said, he had never found a woman difficult enough to make courtship interesting. It was his boast that no woman could resist him; that he would never marry until he found one who could.

The O'Malley stories fascinated him. He considered all of them fiction, and thought that a woman clever enough to build up such a reputation was worth meeting. Everyone claimed to know her, but when the General sought an introduction, he was put off with the protests that she didn't like strangers, and refused to meet new people.

The General grew tired of this evasiveness, and one night out of pure curiosity went alone to the theatre to see her. Musical shows bored him, and he almost fell asleep waiting for Anita's appearance. He knew that she could not possibly be as good as people said; that, after all, she was just a fad, but he was curious. She always came on at the end of the show, and the house remained half empty for a greater part of the performance. Then people began slowly to trickle in, until, just before Anita was to appear, the house was packed.

The performer who preceded her was Antonio Deca, a singer of popular songs who accompanied himself with a guitar. The audiences liked him, and after his first number it was the custom to call out songs for him to sing.

Tonight, as he stood there in the spotlight, one foot resting on the seat of a straight chair, his black leather *charro* costume making him look like a splinter of pencil lead, and his black felt hat, embroidered with silver, cocked over one eye, he seemed a dashing, jaunty figure from the pages of that great Mexican romance, *Los Bandidos del Río Frío*. Because of this the women liked him, and a feminine voice called out, " 'The Stars, the Sun and the Moon.' Sing 'The Stars, the Sun and the Moon.' "

With a graceful wave of his hand, he settled the guitar more comfortably on his upraised knee, rolled two or three chords with a supple finger, and began to sing in his mellow voice:

The stars, the sun and the moon
Are witnesses that I have loved you ...

If he had known, of course ... But he did not know. No one knew, not even Don Juan O'Malley. As the lyric tenor cascaded across the back of the stage, Anita O'Malley, sitting quietly on the sofa in her dressing room, raised her head. Her maid was darning a small hole in a long black silk stocking. Don Juan was seated by the dressing table, reading over the script of a new musical comedy. Neither one noticed Anita. They were so used to her immobility that the idea that she might act alone never entered their minds.

The singing voice swept on through the cloyingly sweet music, repeating again and again the refrain:

But I return to find you married ...
Ay, what a sad fate is mine ...

For a brief moment Anita imagined herself once more beneath the orange trees in Hidalgo. Pablo's fingers were on her wrist, and he was saying, "You will never belong to another man. Swear it to me, Anita."

Slowly the girl rose to her feet, walked out of the room. Neither the maid nor Don Juan saw her going, she moved so silently. The electrician by the light-board stared at her as she passed him, his mouth opening slightly with surprise. He said afterwards he was too startled to try and stop her. She walked through the wings and out onto the stage. Antonio Deca, concerned with his song, did not notice her until she was almost upon him. The audience saw her, of course. The General saw her and realized at once who she was by the sudden burst of applause all around him.

But she did not see the audience. Her red head flung back, her long slim body moving forward in an effortless glide, she saw the guitar. It is possible that the long neck of the guitar reminded her of the gun. Perhaps the black-clad singer sharply outlined by the spotlight brought back with too clear vividness that moment when Pablo had entered the dim hall with the sun streaming around his body. Whatever it was, she gave a single piercing scream and jumped at Deca. Jerking the guitar from him with such force that the sustaining yellow silk cord around his neck snapped like a piece of dry grass, she threw the instrument to the floor and jumped on it. Then with another cry, a name this time, "Pablo!" she fell in a heap across the splintered wood and began to cry.

The audience was on its feet trying to see what was happening. The General's superior height gave him a good view of the stage. Then the curtains rippled shut.

Back stage there was a fever of excitement. Not until Anita was actually on the stage did Don Juan look up and see the empty sofa. He darted into the passageway, and was caught by the electrician with his wild tale of Anita stalking past him. Pepe Bobo, hearing the loud voices, came out of his dressing room, one half of his face made up like an American tourist, the other half plastered with cold cream. He was furious at the noise, and was saying so in loud tones when they heard the crash of the smashed guitar. The stage manager had sense enough to close the curtains without being told, and Pepe ran onto the stage and gathered Anita into his arms. She turned and fought against him, but his long, thin arms, trained to acrobatics, were too strong for her. She was crying terribly. Mascara and grease-paint were smeared on her face. She kept sobbing, "Pablo, Pablo," over and over again. When Don Juan bent over her, she screamed so that he had to draw back out of her line of vision. Anita's maid sent an usher out front to get a doctor. Then she bent over Anita and gave her a resounding slap on either cheek. Anita stopped screaming, but she kept on crying, and fastened both arms around the maid's fat neck.

Reminded by the stage manager that the audience was still out front, Pepe Bobo hastily wiped his face on the skirt of his dressing robe, and stepped between the curtains onto the apron to make his announcement. The people did not want to leave. They hissed and yelled at him, but he made no answer, simply stood there with his head bowed, his attention focused to the exclusion of all else on the problem of Anita. Had her thin hold on sanity broken at last? Would she ever dance again? Was this the end of Anita O'Malley, of his Anita, whom he worshipped as a man worships the last of the pagan blood in his body?

Finally he raised his arms and said loudly above the storm of the crowd, "Believe me, our Anita is very ill." This quieted the people. They began to leave the building in a breeze of secret voices, as men leave a house of the dead. General Valdez went with them, but where, before, he had been merely curious about Anita, now he was consumed with a fire of interest. He had heard her cry of "Pablo" and he fitted that against the story, many times repeated, of the dead goatherd. For the first time he began to wonder if some of the tales he had heard might have more truth in them than he imagined. A woman who could grieve like that for a dead lover! he thought. God, what a woman she must be! What would it be like to breathe life into her again, to make her realize that the living were more important than the dead? There was a wife for a man to have...a wife who had literally to be torn...not from the arms of a living rival, but from the memory of a dead one.

General Valdez did not belong to the usual run of officers, pushed into prominence by the Great Revolution. His family, although not of the best in Sonora, belonged to the comfortable middle class, and as a boy he had been sent to receive his military training at San Jacinto, Mexico's West Point.

Not long after he was graduated, and had stepped into all the glory of a lieutenanthood, the Great Revolution of 1910 thundered across the Mexican horizon. He fought at first in the Federal army, but the assassination of Madero, the green-eyed spiritualist, was more than he could stomach; so he made his way north and offered his services to the Revolutionary party. It never entered his mind that he was a deserter. He could not, in honesty, serve men he despised. Luckily for him, the Revolutionary party won, else he would have been court-martialed and shot. Instead, he was created a general, and became famous through the North as a strategist. He had the ability to see beyond and around a problem and to calculate the reaction of the opposing forces.

This same talent now came into play. He knew the person to see was not Anita but Don Juan, and he knew Don Juan's weak point, the one point that had escaped even Pepe Bobo.

There was no need to hunt for Anita's house. The morning papers told him that she had been placed in a hospital, and exactly which hospital. He drove out there, parked the car, and settled himself to wait. After a while he saw Pepe Bobo and Antonio Deca come out. Bobo's arm was across Deca's shoulder and they were both crying. He heard Bobo say, "It wasn't your fault. How did you know that song would bring everything back to her? Nobody knew."

Finally a small stocky Irishman dragged himself through the door. The General had never seen O'Malley, but his friends had painted a vivid description of the Irishman with his shock of white hair and his red face. The General walked over to the little man and gentled his booming voice as much as possible. "*Hola, compadre*, it is a sad world, this one."

Don Juan shrugged but made no answer. The General fell into step beside him. Neither man spoke for almost a block; then O'Malley looked at him curiously. "Have we met, friend?"

They were close to a saloon, and the General jerked his head towards it. "Let a bottle of cognac introduce us. That should be good enough for any man."

"I shouldn't," said O'Malley, pausing and looking about him. Then he shrugged and pushed his way into the saloon, with the General at his heels. It was a small saloon, deserted except for the bartender, with a mechanical piano beating out a sad version of the American song, "My Blue Heaven." The General ordered a bottle of cognac and two glasses.

"I am of the frontier," contributed the General. "From Sonora." The Irishman nodded. "I fought there. I was with Villa."

"So? And I with Carranza."

O'Malley gulped down the glass of cognac. "If I were a Mexican, I suppose I should have to kill you for having fought with Carranza." He watched the General refill the glass and shrugged. "Instead, I drink to them. To Villa and Carranza. To the soldier and the hypocrite. May God rest their souls in hell."

"Amen," said the General, watching Don Juan put down his empty glass and wipe his mouth with his sleeve. He wondered how many glasses of straight cognac were needed before Don Juan got really drunk.

"Eh, Sonora. I don't like Sonora."

"I don't like Nuevo León," said the General promptly.

O'Malley half raised the newly filled glass to his lips and then put it back down on the table. "How did you know I was from Nuevo León?"

The General smiled and lit a cigarette, flicking the wax match in a wide arc across the room. "Does not all the world know Don Juan O'Malley?"

"Oh, so that's it!" O'Malley pushed back his chair and jumped to his feet. "You want to meet my daughter, eh? Well, no blue-eyed sand frog from Sonora can buy an introduction to my Anita with a bottle of cognac. This is how I answer you!" He snatched up the bottle and flung it to the floor with his full strength. It broke on the gray cement, and the golden liquid gushed out to form a dark brown pool.

The General did not seem at all startled by this display. He merely signaled the bartender to bring another bottle, and sat back in his chair amiably watching O'Malley. "You jump to conclusions, friend. Your daughter may be named Anita, or Carmen, or María Fulana. That does not concern me. My world is a small one. It knows nothing of matters social . . . only of matters military."

"You said all the world knew of Don Juan O'Malley," said the Irishman accusingly.

He's drunk, thought the General. He's really drunk, only he doesn't show it. He said aloud, "Did you think the fame of Colonel O'Malley was confined to Villa's Golden Men? Carranza and Villa may have hated each other like goats and sheep, but they grazed in the same field."

"Speak not of goats to me," muttered O'Malley, pouring himself another drink, and gulping it quickly, as though he were afraid it would evaporate before it reached his stomach. "What's your name?"

"I am General Mario Valdez, at your orders, sir."

"Valdez?" O'Malley's blue eyes raked the man's face. "I've heard of you." After a moment he grumbled in half apology, "You were too good for Carranza."

"And you for Villa."

This snapped up O'Malley's head. "Villa was the greatest, the finest . . ."

"Yes, yes," interrupted the General, recognizing the extraordinary loyalty which the yellow-eyed general, who could barely read and write, had instilled in all his followers. "Villa was the genius of the Revolution, without doubt. Another cognac, friend colonel?"

"I want a tequila with a beer chaser," said O'Malley, still only half appeased.

The General, undisturbed, called the order across the narrow saloon. The bartender brought the tequila, some salt, a slice of lemon and the beer. He stood beside the General watching O'Malley lick the salt from his palm, down the tequila, suck the lemon and drink the beer. Both men were professionally curious as to what would happen to the red faced little man when tequila, beer and cognac met in his stomach. To their surprise nothing seemed to happen, except a slight thickening of the voice when O'Malley demanded that the player-piano be turned off. The bartender obediently pulled out the electric cord and came over to watch O'Malley pick up his empty cognac glass and fling it on the floor. "The trouble with your glasses," he said with dangerous sweetness, "is that they are always empty. You should fill them once in a while." He pushed back the table and pulled himself to his feet.

"The two of you! What do you care for the troubles of a man? My daughter goes mad in front of two thousand people, and you feed me cognac. The doctor says she may die, and you pour beer for me. And that damn piano plays without a conscience while my heart breaks in me!" He took a step toward the silent piano, veered off to aim a punch at the bartender's chin, missed by a half a foot, and fell forward onto his face.

The bartender let out a deep breath. "By the sacred ribs of

Christ, that is a man, that one. The liquor had to wait five minutes to knife his brain! Eh, you cannot leave him here, señor."

The General tossed a twenty-peso bill on the table and slung O'Malley over one broad shoulder. "Buy your wife a new red dress and drink the rest of the cognac in memory of a great drinker," he said pleasantly. The bartender grinned and ran forward to open the door for him, then watched the tall man stride down the street and dump O'Malley into his parked car. "I thank you, San Pedro, for sending me a drinking fool and a generous man. This evening I will burn a candle for you in the church." This off his conscience, he cleaned up the spilled liquor and wondered when his patron saint would send him another lucky day.

After O'Malley was put to bed in the General's hotel room, the General returned to the hospital. Explaining to the doctor that Don Juan had been taken suddenly ill, he asked for news of Anita.

"It is a strange case," sighed the doctor. "She eats, she sleeps, but if anyone speaks to her, she begins to cry. That so many tears could be in one thin body is amazing."

"She has waited a long time to cry," said the General gravely. "Perhaps it is best for her."

"Who knows, señor? There are some sicknesses where medicine is useless. Do you know a man named Pablo?"

The General hesitated a moment. After all, he was only guessing. "I believe he is dead," he said at last.

"What a pity. This Pablo could help her. She calls for him so much. If one believed in God, señor—I, myself, do not—but if one did . . . well, prayers cost nothing," and the doctor hurried away in answer to a nurse's call.

The General telephoned the hotel, but Don Juan was still unconscious. Wondering why he had allowed himself to become involved in this affair, the General made himself comfortable on a wooden bench and prepared to wait. After all, he had seen Anita for only a brief moment. The curtains had closed too quickly. But he had sensed her, as an animal senses his female, and with the help of God and Juan O'Malley, he would marry her before the month was out.

By two that afternoon, Anita's condition had not changed.

Pepe Bobo came in and threw a tantrum when he found the General waiting.

The General did not lose his temper. He merely shrugged and said indifferently, "Except for that moment in the theatre, I never saw the girl. Her father and I were in the Great Revolution together." His statement was entirely true, and Pepe's jealousy turned into gratitude for the great General's kindness to an old friend. The great General's conscience writhed a little under this halo, but his face remained gently impassive. Pepe Bobo, taking a good look at the man, felt more secure. In case this sickness cured Anita of her impassivity, how could she even look at this bald-headed elephant, when she could have his own handsome person for the asking? Antonio Deca was the rival to watch, not this mountain with an egg for a head.

He went away to rehearsal quite satisfied, and so missed the next episode. The doctor came quickly down the hall, hunting for Juan O'Malley. Unfortunately, the General told him, the Irishman was still sleeping off as beautiful a drunk as a man could experience. "Perhaps you'll do," said the doctor to the General with a worried frown.

"What do you want me to do?"

"Just sit by the bed and hold her hand."

"Is that all?" The General was surprised.

"I don't know." The doctor flung out his hands. "These cases are so strange. Sometimes only a little thing is necessary. She is the Great O'Malley. It is a pity. Yes. Just sit there and hold her hand. We can try it. Yes."

The General was taken to the darkened room. He felt monstrously out of place as he sat beside the bed and lifted her long dry hand in his own huge palm.

"The nurse and I will be just outside the door. If you get any reaction, call me," whispered the doctor. "I don't think it will work," he added pessimistically, "but something is better than nothing."

He and the nurse went out then, and the General slowly began to rub one finger across the back of Anita's hand, tracing the blue veins through the transparent skin. He did not look at her face. To do so, he felt would be to peer into a book he had no right to read.

At last he stopped the rubbing and dropped his hand in his lap.

As startling to his ear as a thunder clap came the husky whisper from the bed. "Don't stop. Keep rubbing, please."

Hunching his chair around, he rubbed Anita's hand with such violence that she moaned, "That hurts."

"I'm sorry," he muttered. "I didn't mean..."

"I know. Who are you?"

"General Mario Valdez. Your servant, señorita."

She did not answer for a long time, and now he felt he could look at her face. How thin her face was under the cloud of red hair. The cheekbones were so very high, and the eyes were so black...no, they were blue, a dark, vivid blue. To his surprise the pale lips curved upward in a faint smile.

"Have you never seen a woman before, General?"

"I have never really seen you before," he answered frankly. "Perhaps I had better call the doctor."

"Why? He is a stupid fool. They are all stupid. I like you, General. Do you think I am touched by God?"

"We are all touched by God, señorita. It makes the world more interesting."

She frowned and moved her body slightly in the narrow bed. "Pick me up and take me to the window. I want to see the sun."

He lifted her, bedclothes and all, and she chuckled suddenly, deep in her throat. When he threw back the curtains he saw for the first time how white her skin was. It was an unhealthy white —the white of too little blood. She looked up at him and chuckled again. "You are the ugliest man I ever saw. And the biggest."

"I am too big," he said morosely, "for this little room."

"You belong to the mountains, just as I belong to them, and..." she paused, and he knew she had almost spoken another name. With a quickening of the blood he realized that now was the time to say it...now was the moment to know whether she was going back into insanity or forward into reason. He had never been so frightened in his life, but he said it quickly, for fear he would not say it at all:

"You and Pablo?"

He felt her tense in his arms. She was as rigid as a splinter of stone. "What do you know of Pablo?" she whispered, and there was terror in her voice.

"Nothing," he answered honestly. "I heard you call out the name in the theatre."

"If you are lying to me . . . if you and my father have planned this . . ."

"I'll never lie to you, Anita," he said quietly. She relaxed then, and her body was as heavy as though it were twice her weight.

"Put me back on the bed," she commanded huskily.

He did so and expertly tucked the covers about her. She did not take her eyes away from him. "Where did you learn to make a bed?" she asked abruptly.

"In the army."

"You fought in the army?"

"Yes."

"You killed men?"

"Yes."

"In cold blood? When they stood in front of you without a weapon, did you shoot them down?"

He felt that he was treading on dangerous ground, but he dared not lie to her. She would have smelt the lie in his mouth. "Many times," he said calmly. "Generals command execution squads. It is part of our duty."

"Execution," she said. "Duty," and turned her face away from him. He wondered if she had started to cry again. The doctor came noiselessly into the room, bent over her, but when the General waved him back, he nodded and slipped out again. She said, from very far away, "Thank you. If that little fool had touched me . . ." her voice trailed off into silence.

The General leaned toward her. There was a question he had to ask. "Tell me, Anita. During these past years, since Pablo died . . . have you really been insane?"

She waited a long time to answer, so long that he wondered if she had heard him. Then she began to talk, as one talks who has been starved for speaking. She told the whole story of Don Juan O'Malley, Anita, his daughter, and Pablo, a herder of goats.

Don Juan was one of those Irish rovers who wander until they are sucked into strange pockets of the world. He was a man of violent temper who loved to drink and fight, and he found Hidalgo a paradise where no obstacles were put in the way of his doing either. He married an Hidalgo girl, and when she died at Anita's birth, the O'Malley wept loudly, mourned openly, felt very sorry for himself and became gloriously drunk.

Because this business of self-pity took so much of his time,

Anita grew up as best she could. Her hair was the purple red of polished mahogany, her skin was pale olive with the blood showing through on the curve of the high cheekbones, and some Irish ancestress had presented her with a pair of eyes that seemed black until one realized they were darkly blue. Anita O'Malley was not beautiful, but the fire burning in her thin body was pagan instead of christian, and she had the fascination of a wild creature trapped in a cage.

There was only one thing she liked to do—really liked to do—and that was dance. Whether she had an audience or not did not concern her. She danced as she breathed or talked; no one was ever able to mold her into stillness. She danced through childhood and adolescence. When her long legs swung her body about, and her full skirts swirled in a circle from her hips, she spoke to the pagan recesses in every man's heart, and frightened the women with a glimpse of something from which they shrank with all the terror of Eve flying down the hill from a mocking Lilith.

Pablo, the goatherd, was one of the tribe of Lilith. Goats are sons of Grandfather Devil, and the herder must make his pact with the Devil before the goats will obey him. When he was a small boy, the silent goat laughter had drawn Pablo away from christian folk. The day he signed himself to Don Timotéo Gonzalez as a herder, the town went to mourn with his mother for his dead soul. What matter that Father Zacaya insisted Pablo still had the right to come to church? The priest was born a city man and knew nothing of the Devil's power in goats.

When the herders took the goats into the hills for the long summer months, which lasted in the valley from March until December, was it not a true thing that many times the Devil came and snatched their souls, leaving their bodies to wander around in darkness? Father Zacaya might read in his books that this was a result of loneliness, but the village knew better. What did writers of books know of witches riding on eagles' backs, and of Grandfather Devil stamping his cloven feet in the rocks of the hill trails?

Pablo knew all this, but Pablo laughed at the Devil and his witch wives. Pablo said he liked to drink great mouthfuls of the thin, sweet air of the hilltops. He said that the mountains towering beyond the hills were the walls of his house, and that it was finer sport to fight the enemy eagle for possession of a kid than to fight the little Doctor over a checkerboard. Sometimes he had to come into the village to consult with Don Timotéo. In the evenings, if there were a dance, he would show himself, lounging in the doorway and making eyes at decent christian girls. No woman would dance with him, but he would stand there just the same, boldly watching the whirling couples. No man dared to fight him because of the Devil's curse. And, in a way, his presence meant good luck. For Pablo could give or withhold the Devil's curse at his own pleasure.

One night—it was at the wedding of Nena Santos to Andrés Treviño—Anita and Pablo really met for the first time. They had seen each other about the village since they were children. They knew each other's names. He knew she loved to dance. She knew he was a herder of goats. But there is another kind of meeting . . . the meeting of eye and eye, and spirit and spirit.

They were both pagans. Perhaps that accounted for it. Perhaps it was like calling to like. No one can be certain of these things.

She was sitting beside Doña Fela, who, for love of the girl's dead mother, had been trying for eighteen years to make a proper lady of Anita. The civil wedding was over. The married couple were enthroned on the black cane sofa under the long mirror at the end of the room. Women and girls sat primly on the straight chairs lining the lamp-lighted walls, and the men were standing in the patio drinking glasses of mescal and waiting for the music to begin for the next dance.

Pablo, his short, muscular body neatly clad in a plain black suit, strolled into the patio, and, holding a glass of mescal in his hand, wandered over to the door to his usual vantage point. No one paid him any attention. He merely lounged against the door and looked around. Anita, tired of waiting for the music to begin, glanced toward the door. Their eyes met. It was as simple as that. Neither one had ever heard of Olympus. They knew nothing of nymph and faun. But they knew, somehow, that this was not the same as the love of the bride and groom sitting so proudly on the sofa. Here was fire calling to fire, flame answering flame.

He started toward her, then drew back into the shadow of the doorway. Above his head an oil lantern, rancid and hot, stirred in the brief breeze from the patio. Pablo felt an electric current pass through his body, sharpening his senses. The heavy odor of the burning oil was strong and rank to his nostrils. Everyone in the crowded room had taken on a sharper outline, as when a painter draws a heavy black line around his figures. As the music began, and the men pushed past him to hunt for partners, the mournful sweet notes of flute and violin cut his ears like a knife:

> *Farewell, my little girl,*
> *Do not weep for your Pancho*
> *Who goes from the ranch,*
> *But will soon return to you.*

That was the song they were playing, very slowly, very sadly, as the couples joined the thickening promenade.

Anita was refusing partner after partner. She did not bother to be polite, to murmur the accustomed, "This dance is promised." She knew why Pablo had not come for her. The christians in the room would not have allowed them to dance together; yet she could not tolerate the feel of another man's arm around her waist while Pablo stood there in the doorway, watching her.

With a muttered excuse to Doña Fela, Anita slipped through the promenading couples and reached the kitchen door just as the music ended its slow wailing and jumped into the gay measures where the adventuring lover promises to bring back some ribbons for the hair of his future mother-in-law. As though a spring had released them, the couples began whirling around the long narrow room, but Anita was not concerned with them. It was only a step from the kitchen to the patio. She stood in the shadows by the well, light from the living room door splashing across the hem of her full white skirt. Pablo did not need to be told where she was. He felt her presence as a throbbing wound feels the approach of a knife. The empty mescal glass in his hand fell with a tinkle to the flagstone under his feet, but only the two in the patio, so sensitive to sound, could hear the tiny note above the glittering tones of violin and flute.

The tinkling glass released them from immobility. She turned and ran across the patio and into the orchard at the back of the house. It was late November, and the orange trees were heavy with ghostly white blossoms. Their perfume was like incense burning to the moon-goddess. Anita ran noiselessly, swiftly, but Pablo's wiry body was swifter. His hand touched her shoulder, and she turned like a swooping falcon into his arms. They clutched each other so tightly that it seemed as though they were trying to sheathe themselves in each other's flesh, and his mouth against hers was so hard that the inside of her lips were cut by her own sharp teeth.

He released her at last, and they sat on the ground together, her back against a tree, his arms about her waist, his head on her shoulder. They did not speak. There was no need. This was no meeting of mind and mind but something far more primeval. This was the meeting of earth and sky, or wind and water.

After a few moments she said harshly, "I have to go in. When the dance ends they will miss me and start hunting for me."

"Only a minute more," he whispered. "The musicians haven't started playing the second piece yet."

They knew that this was a dance of *dos paradas* where the couples dance, then promenade, then dance again before they separate to find new partners. The night air softened the shrill tones of the second piece as the musicians began to play that rollicking song of a lover's tragedy:

> *The stars, the sun and the moon,*
> *Are witnesses that I have loved you.*
> *But I return to find you married ...*
> *Ay, what a sad fate is mine.*

As though the words had released a thought in Pablo's mind, he clamped her wrist between his long thin fingers. "You will never belong to another man. Swear it to me, Anita."

"I swear it," she repeated faithfully. "No other man will ever own this Anita O'Malley."

"Anita!" called Doña Fela from the patio. "Anita! Where are you?"

With a single fluid movement the girl rose to her feet. "I am coming, Doña Fela. Wait for me. I am coming," she answered quickly, then looked down at Pablo who was kneelir on the ground beside her, his hands buckled on her hips.

"Tomorrow night the moon rises late."

"I will wait for you in my father's patio when the moon is full," she whispered. She cupped her palms about his face. She felt rather than saw the sharp-boned contour, for the moon shadow was on him. She dipped toward him, and their mouths closed against each other, draining the breath from their bodies and leaving them fluid and shaken. Then she was gone, her white dress gleaming ghost-like against the dark slender trunks of the orange trees.

The next morning Anita draped her black lace prayer shawl over her dark red hair and went across the churchyard to the pink-washed church. The cool gloom of the old adobe building was a welcome respite after the yellow glare of the November sun, and several women were sitting inside the door, crocheting and busily discussing the last night's wedding.

While she was lighting a candle before the lithograph of the Miracle Virgin of Guadalupe, Father Zacaya came down the aisle toward her. She knew that she was his favorite child in the parish, and she smiled at him.

"The world goes well with you this morning, eh, Anita?"

"It is a beautiful world, Father. Beautiful."

"It is most certainly religious," he teased her. "Even Pablo, the goatherd, came in this morning to light a candle to the Guadalupe."

She turned her head away so quickly that he frowned. "Come, Anita. Do not believe this foolishness that goatherds are sons of the Devil."

"I don't believe it," she answered in a low voice, still not looking at him. She took a step toward the small altar and laid her hand on it. "Father, will you hear a vow?"

"A great vow, daughter?"

"The greatest in my life. May my hand wither on its wrist if I ever light another candle to the Guadalupe save to thank her for one great miracle."

The intensity of her speech amazed him, and he bent toward her a little. "Take care, Anita. Do not put a miracle of life in place of a miracle of God."

"This was a miracle of God. Believe me, Father, I know."

"We are not in the confessional, child. But let me give you a word of advice. Never love a man more than you love God. Tragedy lies that way."

Her eyes were startled as she jerked her head toward him. "How did you know I was in love?"

His laugh aroused the curiosity of the crochet workers by the door. "There are only two great miracles in a woman's life, and you carry no child in your body." His hand shot out suddenly and he clutched her arm. "You have done nothing foolish, Anita?"

"No, Father," she answered steadily.

He nodded and released her. "Be a good child, Anita. That is all God asks."

She bowed her head for a moment, then slipped to her knees. "Bless me, Father."

He made the sign of the cross above her heavy, dark-red hair, then stretched out his hand to her. As she kissed it, a fifteen-year-old girl came down the aisle toward them. It was Evita Cantú, daughter of the village treasurer. She broke the intimate spell between the priest and Anita. As she rose to go, she heard Evita ask hesitantly, "Father, is it true that the spirit of the dead sweetheart of Juan de Diós haunts the River Road?"

Anita did not wait to hear Father Zacaya's answer. She hurried out of the church into the sunshine, passing the curious old women by the door. They gave her disapproving glances. Any woman who made a priest laugh out loud in a church should be ashamed of herself. But Anita paid them no attention. Evita's reference to the insane goatherd's dead sweetheart had caught her fancy. Perhaps the dead girl walked the River Road so as to comfort her lonely lover. Anita wondered if, when she died, Pablo would die for love of her. That was what Juan de Diós had done. His spirit had died with his sweetheart... what was her name? Luz, that was it. Luz, meaning "Light." But Luz had been the light in poor Juan's mind, and when she died, he had died, too, although his body still walked the mountain trails. Anita felt a cold prickle of fear run through her. How terrible to think of death when she and Pablo were so gloriously alive.

She found her father yelling at their one old servant.

"Daughter of a thousand donkeys, is there no food for me in this house? You Anita, where have you been?"

"To the church, father."

"Eh, did you hear the news? Pablo, the goatherd, lighted a candle there this morning."

Anita pulled her scarf down over her face as she murmured that she had heard it. There had never been companionship between herself and her father. Both were of too violent temper for that. And it never occurred to her to tell him of what had happened to her the night before. Now she followed him into the small, ugly dining room.

"What a fuss about a goatherd," he was muttering savagely. "This Hidalgo with its small gossip is making my soul sick."

Since this was an old complaint, Anita did not bother to answer him. She played with her food until he bent across the table, asking her abruptly, "How would you like to go to the City?"

"To Mexico, the Capital?"

"Of course to the Capital. You can dance there. You'd like that, eh?"

To Mexico? Away from Pablo? "Oh, no, father!" Her voice was a thin high cry.

He said nothing for a moment, merely staring at her frightened face. Then he rose and, coming around the table, grasped her shoulders between his hands. "I thought so. There was a look on your face at breakfast. I've seen women with that look before."

"What are you trying to say?"

"You're in love."

She jerked away from him and came to her feet. Dark blue eyes looked into lighter blue eyes with a glare that was almost enmity. "What if I am? I have a right to be in love. Any woman has a right to it."

"Not you. Not in Hidalgo."

"Why not?"

"Hidalgo isn't good enough for the daughter of Juan O'Malley. You're going to marry a man who can put jewels in your ears and silk on your body."

"I've found a man. He's all I want."

"He's not what I want."

"This is my life. Father Zacaya says . . ."

"Blast Father Zacaya to the seven rings of Hell!"

Anita darted forward and sank her teeth in her father's shoulder. O'Malley, yelling with rage, hit her with his arm. She fell back against the table, pulling cloth and dishes in a loud crash to the floor with her.

In the kitchen the old cook heard this rage and ran out of the house, screaming that Grandfather Devil himself had entered the house O'Malley.

"I won't go! You can't make me go!" shrieked Anita from the floor. "I'll kill you before I go."

He picked her up, biting and scratching at him, and flung her over one shoulder. "You'll go," he panted, "if I have to walk you across your lover's dead body."

At her bedroom door he dumped her unceremoniously inside. "The train for Mexico leaves in two hours. You've heard me speak. Prepare yourself!" Then he slammed the door, and she heard him lock it on the outside.

For a few minutes she was too exhausted to move. She lay there, dry angry sobs choking her. At last she pulled herself to her feet, her mouth creased in a thin, straight line. No man would force her away from Pablo. The mountains were filled with strange and distant caves, the trails were deceiving, to be read only by the few who knew them well. She would run away with Pablo into the mountains, and her father could never find her there.

Her plan for escape was simple. She would trick Don Juan into opening the door. After that, she could push him out of the way and be gone from the house before he had caught his breath. And if she went to the mountains, Pablo would find her, would take her to his own stone hut. Pablo would never let anyone steal her from him. They would be safe and happy in the mountains.

Even as she thought this, she began pounding on the door. Soon she heard footsteps coming down the hall. "What do you want, Anita O'Malley?" called her father's voice.

"Let me out," she sobbed. "Let me out. I'll do anything you want, only let me out."

There was silence in the hallway. Then she heard the click of the turning key, and the heavy, hand-carved door swung open.

Now, now! She tensed herself to dash past him. Her body tightened for the forward spring, but at that moment her father flung his hunting rifle horizontally across the door.

"Oh, no you don't, my pretty girl!" The tones were thickened, and she sickly realized that he had been drinking. "I knew you were Mexican enough to try and trick me, and Irish enough to damn the consequences. But you'll not get away from me as easy as that."

She caught hold of the gun in a gust of passion and tried to pull it toward her, but it was longer than the width of the door and she could not move it. O'Malley laughed at her impotent rage, and he yelled, "Do you think I would let an O'Malley go to some village scum? You're going to be a great lady, do you hear? Great enough for me to take back to Ireland and throw in their black-browed faces."

"I won't go! I won't go!"

"You'll dance to the tune I play for you. You're my daughter, and you'll make the O'Malleys rich again. I was born in a great stone house, and, by God, I'll die in one."

She flung herself toward him, scratching and kicking, but he merely stepped back, laughing at her, being careful not to move the gun.

Suddenly the door at the end of the passageway was flung open and Pablo stepped from the brilliant afternoon sunshine into the blindness of the cool dark hall. His compact, wiry body was silhouetted against the brilliant light as he peered through the darkness.

"Anita, I heard your servant screaming. Anita, what has your father done to you?"

"Pablo," gasped Anita. And even as she said it, she felt her father's hand tense on the gun's trigger. Her fingers, rigid with terror, fumbled for his, tried to push his hand aside. But the gun was a very fine weapon, and the trigger very delicate. Two shaking hands pushed and pulled against the trigger. There was a roar of sound, a belch of smoke from the gun barrel, an acrid odor in the air.

For a moment no one moved. Pablo slowly clutched at that spot between the lungs and just above the stomach where the heart is. Then he sank to his knees and forward to the floor, and the sun covered him with golden light.

General Valdez leaned toward the bed. "That is enough, Anita," he said gently.

Anita moved slightly with irritation. "It is not enough. Don't you understand? I can't remember. After that, I can't remember. There is a long time that I can't remember. My father knew that although the village believed that goatherds have no souls, it was also true that goatherds were men, and to kill a man, an unarmed man, was murder. And Pablo, in his way, had been popular in the village. The young men liked him. They would take their little problems to him, for Pablo was very wise. He was only twenty-one, but he was very wise. And they would not look with kindness upon his murderer. My father knew this, and somehow he got me away from Hidalgo, and on the train to Mexico City. Once we had crossed the state line, only the governor could order his return. This governor had fought in the Great Revolution with my father. They were both of Villa's Golden Men. This governor would not bother to bring him back and hang him to avenge a dead goatherd."

"And after that, Anita? After you reached the City?"

She turned her head away from him, with her eyes toward the bare hospital wall, but she did not see the wall. She saw instead that first dark bitter year.

O'Malley took her to various teachers to learn the technique of dancing. Later, many teachers claimed her. Some even wrote her name into their advertising signs: *Señora Fulana de Tal, Mistress of Dancing, Teacher of Anita O'Malley*. But she remembered none of them. She never looked at their faces. She listened to their voices and learned what they taught her, and in the hours between the lessons she practiced.

O'Malley rented an old bare house, installed a table, a few chairs, two beds, and a battered piano. The rest of their money was spent on a small amount of food and a large amount of liquor. Early in the morning he would sit at the piano and play for her. Hour after hour the piano beat out its tinny notes. Toward evening, the wrong notes were more numerous than the right ones, because the whiskey imbibed during the day forced his stubby fingers to wander over strange keys.

This did not affect Anita. She had the endurance of a young centaur, and she never really heard the piano except as a motivating force. The music to which she danced sang in her mind. It was the music of mountain crags, and wind-swept valleys, and the shadow of an eagle's wing on gray bare rock.

The moment Don Juan stopped playing, Anita stopped dancing. She would relax in a chair while he rubbed his aching hands and took another deep drink of liquor.

She made no effort to speak to him, to listen to him. Indeed, his voice was far away, as though he were murmuring in a distant room. Their lives leveled into a routine. The clothes he put out for her, she wore. The food he placed in front of her, she ate. When he played, she danced. But beyond this terrible docility, he could not reach her.

After she had apparently learned as much as the teachers could show her, he told her that the time had come for her first public appearance. He chose the company of Pepe Bobo with fine Irish simplicity. In the Republic, all theatrical enterprises are under the command of an actor-manager. This particular Pepe Bobo was a minor genius in his way, and his shows usually made a profit. Since Pepe Bobo was admittedly the best that Mexico had to offer, it never occurred to O'Malley to take Anita to anyone else.

The theatre, built in the days of the Spanish viceroys, was cold and dismal. A single electric light burned on the bare, splintery stage, and Bobo was sitting under it, frowning over some costume material. Various members of the cast were sprawled around on the floor, some of them eating and drinking, some smoking, most of them merely resting and gossiping. A gaunt, henna-haired woman was standing beside Bobo, the harsh light making the rouge stand out on her cheeks in orange patches. She did not like the costume material, and her voice was husky with anger.

She saw the little Irishman with the tall, white-faced girl behind him. Her hand touched Bobo's shoulder, and the clown glanced up with irritation. O'Malley found a rickety straight chair for Anita, and she sat there while he went over to talk to Bobo and the woman. From time to time they would turn and look at her, but she paid them no attention. The odor of the building fascinated her. It was a compound of damp stone, mustiness, tired, unwashed bodies, cheap perfume, and grease paint. She took a deep breath of it, testing it, trying to decide whether she liked it or not. It was very different from the clean, sweet mountain air, and yet it reminded her forcibly of Pablo. Once more she was in the crowded narrow parlor of Nena Santos' house. The acrid scent of oil lanterns, the rich fragrance of water on hard earth, the heavy aroma of closely packed powdered bodies, was very close to this new odor. She took another deep breath. Yes, she liked it. She must have it. It was a sharing with Pablo, and he was no longer dead.

She was dimly conscious of Don Juan telling her to dance. Someone began to play a piano. The music of the Spanish *zar-*

*zuela** La Paloma de la Verbena* rippled across the stage in that
famous duet beginning:

> *Where do you go with mantón of Manila?*
> *Where do you go with your gay flowered dress?*

Anita glided into the light, her head bowed, listening to Pablo's
voice calling to her through the music. One heel began to stamp
an answer against the floor. The other took up the odd broken
rhythm. Her hands fluttered against an invisible wind, then
reached into the bodies of those who watched her and drew
forth their spirits so that they danced with her. As her body
swirled and dipped and turned, the stage was peopled with the
dancing ghosts of her audience. When they surged against her,
she thrust them away from her, then tantalizingly led them on to
an ever deepening awareness of beauty and power. She poised
on bent toes, joyously, vibrantly alive as the Spanish music came
to its crashing close. Then she released her hold, and the people
who were watching her sank back, exhausted with the experience.
There was silence. She returned to her chair to sink once more
into impassivity. Then the applause came. Even the stagehands
and the doorman were applauding. But she did not notice it. She
did not understand that these stage people were paying her their
highest compliment. Jealousy is a bitter thing in the theatre,
especially the Mexican theatre, where existence is precarious for
even the greatest artists. She knew only that she liked this shadowed building; that here Pablo was so close to her that she
could hear him whispering in her ear.

When Don Juan put his hand on her shoulder and told her
gently that she was to start rehearsals immediately, something that
had been cold within her began to melt. She even tried to smile
at him, but the smile vanished before it reached her lips. Two
years' habit of hard withdrawal could not so easily be broken.
But she gave as much of herself as she could. She listened to new
music; she learned new steps; she stood for hours while costumes
were fitted. Beyond that she could not go. When Pepe Bobo, or
Antonio Deca, or the hard-faced, henna-haired woman the others

---

* A type of musical drama which may be either comic or tragic. The
Paloma is extremely popular with Mexican audiences, and has been in the
repertory of every opera company since it was first introduced into the
Republic in the last years of the nineteenth century.

called Trina spoke to her of life outside the theatre, she gazed blankly at them. She felt that they were in league against her, were trying to steal her away from Pablo, and she would shrink into herself and shut her spirit against them so that they could not harm her.

One afternoon, not long before the show opened, a compact, wiry figure walked lightly across the stage. Anita was resting on a chair near the back wall, and as the man neared the piano a spotlight hit his head and shoulders. Anita, her body singing with excited delight, ran forward and caught his arms with her strong fingers. She looked deep into his eyes. But the eyes were not black. They were a clear ice blue. They were not Pablo's eyes. Her hands relaxed, and her own eyes filled with grief and disappointment.

Trina darted forward from the shadows, whirled her around, slapped her across the mouth. "So! You not only steal my place in the theatre. Now you try to steal my man! If it needs a bullfighter to change you from a ghost to a woman, I will teach you how to fight bulls!" Her hand snatched for Anita's hair.

The man lifted Trina backward, kicking and screaming. Pepe Bobo and Don Juan O'Malley, attracted by the noise, hurried on to the stage. Don Juan ordered Anita to return to her dressing room. But Anita did not want to leave this man who reminded her so forcibly of Pablo.

Then the bullfighter spoke, and his frigid voice destroyed Anita's illusion. As in a dream she heard him say, "This ghostwoman is your daughter, señor? I do not know her. She seems to think she knows me. I have never seen her. But she has seen me, perhaps? I am Gitanillo, the bullfighter."

"She's never seen a bullfight," said Don Juan harshly. "I don't understand this. I don't understand it at all."

"Then let me explain," said Trina viciously. "You are very clever, you and your daughter. Already the publicity of a woman without a soul is making her famous. That is all right for the public, yes? But here in the theatre it is nothing but stupidity."

"Trina speaks true words," snapped Pepe Bobo. "I, myself, am a little tired of this masquerade. There is no doubt that Anita is a fine dancer. But she is not yet a star. She has not proved herself. The temperament must be left to those who have arrived."

"Before she came," cried Trina, "I was the star. Now she plans to steal my public from me. But the public loves me. I am the great Trina. The public will not desert me."

"Don't be a fool, Trina," said Gitanillo. "The public is a great sheep. It follows the loudest bell. That is true here and in the bull-ring. If this ghost creature is better than you, then you are a lost soul."

"So! You, too, desert me. You say you adore me, but when she tosses her head, you, too, become a sheep."

"This episode does not amuse me," said Gitanillo flatly. He turned slightly toward Don Juan. "Your daughter lacks a certain fire. I do not think I should care to become her lover." He bowed with a certain cynical grace and moved away on his bullfighter's feet, his body merging with the shadows.

Anita felt her father's hand clamp down on her arm. His voice shook with anger as he cursed in Spanish and English. "My daughter is a genius. What has she to do with bullfighters and harlots?"

"Watch your tongue, old fool," ordered Trina dangerously. "If this ghost of yours has cost me Gitanillo, I will not soon forget it."

But Don Juan was paying her no attention. He released Anita's arm and bent forward to stare intently into her eyes. "Listen to me, Anita. When this bullfighter walked away from us, I saw the resemblance. You thought he was Pablo, didn't you?"

At the sound of the name, Anita shrank away from him. She lifted her arm to protect herself from the word as she had not tried to protect herself from Trina's blows.

"I thought so." Don Juan's voice was suddenly very gentle. He pushed her toward the dressing rooms. "Go and rest, my daughter. Soon the rehearsal must start. Go and rest."

As she moved away she heard Pepe Bobo ask irritably. "Pablo! Who the devil is Pablo?"

And she heard Don Juan dully telling the story as she closed the dressing room door.

As the rehearsals continued she noticed vaguely that Trina was no longer in the company. And Pepe Bobo as well as the entire cast treated her with a new gentleness. She liked Pepe Bobo. He followed her about with a fierce protectiveness, and flared like an angry puppy at anyone who tried to annoy her. He told her story everywhere. He realized that her tragedy possessed a dark, romantic glow which appealed to the Mexican spirit, and by the night of the opening performance Anita was already famous. She had only to confirm the story with her dancing.

The first show was at four in the afternoon, the second at seven, the third at nine. By nine o'clock every seat was sold, and people were standing in the aisles. The next morning Anita was the Great O'Malley. Don Juan moved her into a nice apartment, although she did not notice the difference between the silk-hung bedroom of the present, and the bare, half-furnished room of the past.

Anita's voice slipped into silence.

The General said gently, "I think you were a little mad, Anita."

"I suppose so. When I danced, I was dancing for Pablo. I felt him standing and watching me, and liking my dancing. Do you like my dancing?"

"I've never seen you dance."

"You haven't?" She was amazed. "Then why do you like me? Pablo was the only one who ever liked me without seeing me dance first. And then," she added honestly, "I don't think they really liked me. They just wanted to see if they could tame me. Even Father Zacaya felt that way, and I loved Father Zacaya. I really did."

"Is all that time past for you? Are all those people dead to you?" The General was fascinated by the finality in her voice.

She tried to shrug her thin shoulders. "I don't know. In the last years I couldn't think about them very much. I had to think of Pablo."

The General, aware that she was very tired, lifted her long fingers to his lips. "But you will get well now, eh, and come back to the people who love you."

"No one loves me," she said flatly. "My dancing is something else, but no one loves me . . . except Pablo."

"I love you," said the General. "And I have never seen you dance. Remember that."

She turned her head on the pillow and tried to smile at him, but the effort was too great, and the lids quivered down over the deep blue eyes. Gently replacing her hand on the white cover, the large man tiptoed as quietly as possible from the room. He found the doctor and nurse anxiously awaiting him.

"You were there so long," protested the doctor. "You must have tired her. She spoke, yes? I heard voices."

"She spoke," said the General. And with certainty, "She will get well."

"Eh, one cannot be sure of these things. There have been telephone calls. Her father is tearing up the hotel. They think he is very crazy."

"Only a little crazy," grinned the General, and went away to tend to his prospective father-in-law.

He found Don Juan sitting cross-legged in the middle of the bed, a bottle of cognac at his elbow, and singing Spanish curses at the top of his lungs. The hotelkeeper, a Swiss, was helpless with rage. The great General Valdez could surely understand? The other customers were complaining...

The great General Valdez nodded pleasantly. The annoyance would instantly cease. The Swiss hotelkeeper went downstairs with a sigh of relief. The tales about the great General Valdez were true. He never lost his temper, he was always reasonable, he believed in the rights of other people. Incredible, but true.

The General sat down and inspected the little Irishman. When O'Malley tilted up the cognac bottle for another long drink, the General reached out his arm and removed the bottle. Don Juan began to splutter.

"That is my bottle. Give it back to me."

"Not until we have talked a bit."

"I am not in the mood for stories of the Revolution."

"Neither am I," said the General. And then, "I want to marry your daughter."

O'Malley opened his mouth, shut it again, then opened it to say, "That is ridiculous."

"Why? I have money. I have position. The wife of General Mario Valdez would be a very different person from Anita O'Malley, dancer," and into the word "dancer" went all the contempt which the well-born Mexican holds for stage mummers.

O'Malley glared at him. "Anita is different. She is a genius..."

"She must never dance again, except at her own pleasure."

This blow knocked Don Juan back among the pillows. His face turned as white as the linen beneath his head. "Has the doctor said that? I don't believe it. I'll get another opinion. I'll take her to the States...to Europe..."

"Don't be a fool. I forbid it, not the doctors."

"She is not going to marry you. I forbid that."

"You forbade another marriage," said the General brutally.

O'Malley raised trembling fingers to his mouth. "This is different. She doesn't love you."

"She will," said the General placidly. "Already she likes me. I think she likes me even better than Pepe Bobo. Certainly more than she likes you."

"I am her father. She depends upon me. Ask anyone in the theatre. They will tell you ..."

"That is over and done with. She talked to me for hours this afternoon ..."

"That is a lie. She is a body without a soul. She can't ..."

"Ask the doctor and the nurse. They heard her talking."

O'Malley pulled a pillow down over his face. Except for the twitching of his shoulders and the rhythm of the General's arm as it raised a cigarette to his mouth and dropped again, there was no movement in the room. After a while O'Malley pushed the pillow aside.

"Do you know what it has been like? Do you think she hasn't punished me? It was like living with a doll, a helpless dancing doll. And I did that to her. I killed Pablo, but I didn't know ... How could I know? But she is my daughter. I love her. I didn't think it was possible for a man to love his own child so much. There are so many women in the world. Why do you want my Anita?"

"I don't know," answered the General honestly. "I have known many women, but this Anita ... she holds magic for me."

"I won't let her go."

"You must," came the quiet answer.

"Why? Because you have ordered it? This is not the army, my general."

Valdez leaned forward and carefully extinguished the cigarette. "How many bottles of cognac do you drink a day? And tequila and beer? And the rest of it?"

"What has that to do with it?"

"Already you are only half a man. You can't begin to think until cognac has opened your mind. If you hadn't been drunk in Hidalgo, you wouldn't have shot Pablo."

"She told you I was drunk?"

"She told me more than you know of the story or anyone else. She told me of how you've drunk yourself into long periods of unconsciousness. Who took care of you during those periods in the poor years? And you thought Anita a body without a soul! You must have been completely the fool."

O'Malley pulled himself to the far side of the bed. "She was without a soul. These are lies from your mind."

"You know they are not lies. Already you are sick with drink. This is Mexico City. You are seven thousand feet above the sea. The air is thin in your lungs. Your heart beats too fast from the liquor you drink. Some day your heart will grow weary of its labor. When you are dead, who will take care of Anita?"

"You are only trying to frighten me."

The General came to his feet with a great laugh. "Go see a doctor. Hear what a doctor has to say to you."

"Pepe Bobo will take care of her. He loves her," O'Malley said.

"If you believe that, then you wear donkey's ears. He'll take care of her only so long as she is useful to him. Who else is there? Antonio Deca, perhaps? Do you think he wants a sick woman on his hands? Bah! I am going to marry Anita in the church, and you will give her to me. That is the end of it."

When Anita heard of his plans she merely shrugged. She was too tired to battle this large man, and also she liked him. She felt safe with him, as a child feels safe with a large shaggy dog. She said, "You know I don't love you—that I have promised to belong to no one but Pablo."

He merely smiled. "I know," he said, but he knew that in time his own vital aliveness would win over the dead Pablo.

Their marriage was so quiet that the papers did not know about it until after it was over. When Pepe Bobo heard the news, he threw periodic tantrums, and made elaborate plans to kill the General. He met Juan O'Malley on the street one morning and flew at him like a fighting cock. The police put them both in jail, but the fight had been too great a strain for O'Malley's heart. Not long after the General got them both out of custody, O'Malley climbed the stairs too quickly to his room, a great pain tore his chest, a blackness closed down over his eyes, and he tumbled to the floor. When his landlady found him, he was dead.

About two days after the funeral, Anita went to her husband in great perplexity. "Do you think it is wrong that I do not grieve for him, Mario?"

"How do you feel about it?" asked the General curiously.

"I don't know," she admitted, after a moment's thought. "It's just that I don't feel anything at all. It's as though I never knew him, and I was trying to grieve for a stranger. Is that a sin, Mario?"

"I don't think so, Anita. This is a matter for your own conscience."

"I'm not glad he's dead." Anita laced her fingers together, and then pulled them apart. "But I'm not sorry, either. Perhaps I should have a mass said for his soul."

"That would be nice," agreed the General, trying to hide the amusement in his eyes. He watched her as she wrapped her head in a shawl and trotted off like a good child to the church. Like a good child. That was the difficulty. Anita was married to him, but she was a child playing house, not a woman who came warm and expectant to her husband's arms. She would rest her hand on his shoulder, lean against his strength, kiss his cheek with soft lips, but beyond that she would not go, for Pablo would not like it.

Pablo had a real existence in the house. Anita talked about him as simply as though he lived around the corner. Her highest praise was, "Pablo likes it." "Likes," never "Liked." Never the past tense. Not any more. Some way in her mind she had connected Pablo with the General. Pablo was there because the General was there. Valdez could not understand her line of reasoning, and Anita was never able to make it quite clear to him. One day when he caught a cold Anita became nearly sick with worry that the cold would turn into pneumonia; then the General would die, and with his death Pablo, too, would die again. The General had fought many battles, but this fighting with a ghost was fast becoming a lost cause. He was frantic for fear that Anita should become so concerned with Pablo that she would really lose her mind. Something had to be done, but what?

The day that mass was sung for the soul of Don Juan O'Malley, the General went back to the church to hunt for Anita's missal, which she had laid down on the seat beside her and forgotten. A friend of his was just coming out from lighting a candle to St. Joseph, the patron saint of men whose wives have proven unfaithful to them.

"Why are you lighting a candle to St. Joseph?" asked the General. "You're not married."

"I'm lighting it as thanks offering for a friend of mine," said the man with a broad grin. "His wife was rolling the eye at a young rooster down the street; so my friend came and lighted a candle to St. Joseph."

"Did it work?" asked the General curiously.

"Beautifully. That night his wife found a note from my friend's mistress. There was such a fight that the mistress had to go to the hospital. Then his wife forgave my friend, forgot the young rooster down the street, and they are now very happy. St. Joseph is indeed powerful!" The man laughed out loud, shook hands, and went on his way, but the General turned back into the church and sat down in one of the back pews. Anita was so certain of him, so sure. If he could make her jealous, she would have no time to think of Pablo. After a while Pablo's memory would fade into nothingness, and Anita would become the true wife of Mario Valdez.

The General tiptoed down the aisle and lit his own candle to the placid-faced saint, standing cool and aloof in his red satin robe with the lily branch across one arm and the Infant in the other. If ever a man needed heavenly aid against a rival, the General felt that he was the one. In common with most Mexicans, it never occurred to him to question the existence of God and the army of saints. He accepted the teachings of the church as he accepted the bread that he ate and the air that he breathed. He knew, of course, that other churches existed, and other manners of thought, but that he himself should explore them was outside his realm of vision.

So the General lit his candle to St. Joseph, and then went out to find himself a mistress. He found one. He found several. His name shot into prominence in Mexican gossip. Men discreetly admired him. Women shook their heads in condemnation, and even as they consoled Anita (being careful to give her all the latest details) they thought, "*Ay, que hombre*," Ay, what a man!

Anita was puzzled at first by his strange behavior. She was worried for fear she had displeased him in some manner. Then, one night at dinner, she smiled at him. "There is gossip about you, Mario."

"Does it worry you?" he asked eagerly.

She shook her head. "At first, yes, but I have thought it out. I must not be selfish. After all, I have Pablo. Sometimes I feel him so close that I can reach out and touch him with my hand. It is not right that you should be lonely."

"But Anita, I am not . . ." he protested, but she waved his words aside.

"There is gossip, but you are fortunate. You are a man. You can step over gossip. Amuse yourself, Mario. Amuse yourself. That is right."

The General, sick with disappointment, took himself off to the church. Standing in front of St. Joseph, he lit a candle and then blew it out. "That is what I think of your help," he said grimly. "On your day—on the nineteenth of March—I shall bring you nothing . . . not one flower, not one candle." Having cleared his mind he turned to leave when someone called him.

"Eh, my General. Have you a word for Pepe Bobo?"

He peered into the shadows, and saw the clown resting one hip against the carved upright of a pew.

"So? Pepe Bobo? I give you good evening."

"I'd like a word with you, my general."

"How did you know where to find me?" asked Valdez suspiciously. He had never liked Pepe Bobo. He liked him even less now.

"All the world knows of the General's devotion to St. Joseph. I waited and you came. It was of a simplicity."

"What do you want with me?"

"Not here," said Pepe Bobo, trying to smile by pulling back his too red lips over his pointed teeth. "If you will come with me, I have something that I think will interest you. It concerns Anita."

The General started to refuse, then shrugged and followed the slender man into the street. Pepe Bobo had been with Anita for fifteen months. Don Juan might have given the actor-manager a piece of Anita's jewelry. If the man were honest enough to return it, the General should be courteous enough to receive it. Valdez disliked anything connected with the stage, but that need not keep him from being polite.

They walked in silence to a squat apartment house on a street two blocks off the Alameda.

"I didn't know you lived here," said the General as they went into the small, barren patio and started to climb the steep stairs. "When did you move? Weren't you in one of the *Colonias?*"

"I still live there," answered Pepe Bobo, going out on the balcony that overhung the patio and unlocking a door. "In the *Colonia Roma*. A friend of mine lives here." He stepped aside and allowed the General to pass him into a tiny hall that opened into a living room. The ceiling was low, and the General felt cramped in the small room. A bird was singing in a cheap cage, and against one wall was a wooden stand of ferns. Portieres of colored glass beads and shells cut the room off from the rest of the apartment, and a cheap incense was heavy in the air. The furniture was upholstered in vivid purple plush, and a black Spanish shawl embroidered with large red roses was draped across the long sofa.

The only light came from a lamp with a shade of yellow silk. In a chair near the iron-barred windows was sitting a woman. Her body was too thin, and there were gaunt hollows in her cheeks. The skin was coarse, and brilliant orange rouge stood out against her sallow complexion. The hennaed hair showed very black at the roots and gave a hard gloss to the heavy, sullen face. The General thought, "She must starve herself. Her body wants to be fat, that one."

Pepe Bobo waved his hand toward the woman. "This is my friend. We call her Trina. She sings badly. Her dancing is worse, but the audiences like her."

The woman laughed and spoke in a husky, elemental voice. "Give the General a drink, Pepe."

As Pepe Bobo went across the room for a cognac bottle and three fairly clean glasses, the General glanced about him again. He did not like the room. He did not like the people. He said, "Give me what belongs to Anita, and then I will go."

The woman laughed again. "Not so fast, my General. Sit down. The sofa will hold your weight."

Pepe thrust a glass into his fingers, snickering a little. "You'll not find the cognac so fine as your own, but we theatre people are poor. We cannot afford the best, as generals can."

The General put the liquor, untasted, down on a cheap, rickety table, already overloaded with messy sheets of manuscript weighted with a *baile* knife, one of those long, folding knives with a narrow curved blade. "What do you have that belongs to Anita?"

"Nothing," said the woman.

"But you said . . ." began the General, puzzled, to Pepe.

Pepe shrugged fatalistic shoulders. "I said I had something that concerned Anita." He tossed the *baile* knife aside and gathered up the sheaf of manuscripts. "Trina and I thought you might like to read this."

The General, smelling blackmail in the air, frowned as he fitted a pair of glasses on his nose and began to read the single-spaced typewritten sheets. If these two fools thought they could black-mail General Valdez, then they were worse than fools . . . they were stupid.

When he finished reading the papers, his hands trembled slightly as he replaced them in order. It was a brief theatrical sketch, cruel and vivid in its satire, concerning a dead goatherd, a dancer, and a soldier. "I come in on stilts with my body much padded," explained Pepe Bobo silkily. "I am the soldier, of course. Trina will burlesque the dancer. Antonio Deca will be an excellent ghost of a goatherd, eh, my general?"

The woman's voice was almost a baritone as she said, "All the City will enjoy the sketch. It will be quite a triumph."

"I could kill you," said the General pleasantly. He had rolled up the manuscript and was twisting it over and over between his hands. "Had you thought of that?"

"Of course," said the woman. "We are not fools. But the reputation of the great General Valdez is well known. A calm man who never loses his temper. Besides, would you like such publicity, General? And a hanged general will be fine meat for people's mouths."

The General looked down at the twisted manuscript, and then tossed it on to the table. Pepe Bobo chuckled. "Do not be concerned with the paper. It is only a copy. We have others."

"Five copies more," said the woman. "They are expensive. The work of writing them . . . the typing. You understand."

"How much dost thou want?" asked the General heavily, and he used the familiar tense as though he were speaking to a servant.

Pepe Bobo flushed and came up out of his chair. "We were going to ask five. I think ten thousand is a better price."

"For the five copies?"

"For each one," said the woman, and bent forward to strike a match on the sole of her cheap red shoe.

The General laughed. The laughter seemed to start in his legs and bubble up through his body like lava escaping the mouth of a volcano. "I wouldn't pay you ten centavos for the lot."

Pepe Bobo bent forward and thrust his face close to the General's. His eyes were blazing. "I loved Anita. You stole her away from me. If you think I won't make you pay, you're a fool."

The General pushed him back with one hand, and came to his feet. "Put on your little sketch. Let all the Capital roar with laughter. Anita will never hear it. I do not concern myself with you."

Pepe Bobo pushed forward one foot as though he longed to kick out at the General, but lacked just the right amount of courage. The General noticed in a detached way that the foot was shod with a black patent leather shoe that had a lavender cloth top. "You have bad taste, friend," said the General quietly. "I don't like your clothes, I don't like this room, I don't like your woman, I don't like you. Stand away from the door."

"There is another sketch," whispered Pepe Bobo in a voice like dry leaves crackling. "A more intimate sketch. One you haven't read. The soldier comes home from a long war and finds very amusing things. Perhaps you prefer to read that one."

The woman said harshly, "You will pay. I am a bad enemy. I do not forget. This Great O'Malley. She stole my place in the theatre. And she took my finest lover. Eh, he said he found me no longer amusing. I have not forgotten. He was the great Gitanillo, the bullfighter. He spent money on me. I wanted him. But after he saw her he found me no longer amusing."

Pepe Bobo's voice took up the thread of sound. The General suddenly felt very tired. How did these two fools imagine his mind worked? Did they think he would crawl toward them, begging for mercy? He would take Anita to Sonora, to the mountains where few white men had ever walked. She would love their rocky faces, and the stocky Indians who lived in the shadows of the crags. A sketch on a Mexican stage would mean nothing to her nor to him. Let Mexico City rock with laughter. Her happiness was all that mattered. But he could not crawl to buy it. Anita would not want that. Her honesty and courage were equal to his. He knew in that moment how much he really loved Anita. And also, in an odd way, how much she loved him, depended on him. If he were necessary to her, that was enough. He had fought his battle with Pablo and had lost, but in a way he had won. Pablo was only a dream, but he was flesh and blood, and Anita's need of him was too strong for this Pepe Bobo to stand in the way.

This reasoning, which was more feeling than reasoning, passed through his mind so quickly that Pepe Bobo had hardly finished speaking before the General, with a contemptuous shrug, pushed him out of his path, pushed him so hard that the clown fell on the sofa clutching out at the small table for support. Bobo's fingers closed, by accident, on the *baile* knife. As though its presence in his hand thought for him, he pushed the release spring, the curved blade snapped into place, and he sprang at the General with a cat-like cry. The General flung one long arm about his body, caught his wrist with the other hand. Feeling that his wrist bone was being crushed, Pepe Bobo screamed and released the knife.

Here was action. The General ceased to think like a human being. He was seldom angry, but he loved a fight, and the savage blood danced in his mind, making him forget everything but that he had an enemy in his hands. Giving Bobo's slight body a twist, he rested his foot on the sofa and began to bend the comedian backward across his knee. The pain in the clown's back, and the terror as he saw the calm, mask-like face above him, made Pepe Bobo moan like an animal in pure fear. Both men had forgotten the woman crouched, terrified, in the chair. As she heard Pepe's gurgling sobs she acted almost automatically. Picking up the knife from the floor she struck with her full strength into the General's back and then twisted the curved blade. That was what the curve was for.

Very slowly the General released Pepe, who fell to the sofa, then wriggled away from him. As a tree straightens against the blast, the General pulled himself to his full height, looked down at the two frightened people below him; then, as a tree falls, pitched forward on to his face. Although the two watching him did not know it, he died very much as Pablo had died on that long-ago morning in Hidalgo. Both had died in silence. Both had died by violence. Both had died because of Anita.

Pepe Bobo and the woman stared at each other, frightened, across the dead body. The woman started to whimper, but Pepe gave her a violent push. "Shut your mouth around your teeth!" he whispered savagely. Gathering up the manuscripts, he thrust them into her hands. "Burn them. Burn all of them."

"But what . . ." said the woman.

Pepe's cat-like mind had leaped to the only solution. "We will tell the police he was your lover. He came and found me here. He tried to kill you. I had to kill him to save your life. The police will believe that. After all, he was famous for his women."

The police did believe it. So did all the City. Anita, too, believed it. After his funeral, she went to see the image of St. Joseph and lit a candle for the soul of Mario Valdez. "He loved you," she murmured as she knelt before the image. "He was kind to me, and he brought Pablo back to me. That is all a woman could ask. I am glad he did not love me too much. That would have been a sad thing, for Pablo has all my heart."

The next day she returned to Hidalgo. She lives alone in her father's house on the Street of the Hidden Water, and the front door through which Pablo walked that far-off day is never opened. Every morning in the winter months when the herders drive the goats along the Street of the Hidden Water to the River Road and so to the river to crop the lush, rank river grass, she leaves her house and walks among the goats, allowing them to nuzzle her black skirts and white hands. In the early, clear morning light she talks to the goats and they answer her. Then they go on to the river, and she goes back to the pink church and lights a candle to Our Lady of Guadalupe, because Pablo once lighted a candle there. But every year on the nineteenth of March she lights a candle to St. Joseph. The General, too, had loved her in his fashion.

To the best cook goes the whole tomato.
—Mexican proverb

IT WAS MAY, THE FLOWERING THORN WAS SWEET IN THE AIR, AND the village of San Juan Iglesias in the Valley of the Three Marys, was celebrating. The long dark streets were empty because all of the people, from the lowest paid cowboy to the mayor, were helping Don Roméo Calderón celebrate his daughter's eighteenth birthday.

On the other side of the town, where the Cañon Road led across the mountains to the Sabinas Valley, a tall slender man, a package clutched tightly against his side, slipped from shadow to shadow. Once a dog barked, and the man's black suit merged into the blackness of a wall. But no voice called out, and after a moment he slid into the narrow, dirt-packed street again.

The moonlight touched his shoulder and spilled across his narrow hips. He was young, no more than twenty-five, and his black curly head was bare. He walked swiftly along, heading always for the distant sound of guitar and flute. If he met anyone now, who could say from which direction he had come? He might be a trader from Monterrey, or a buyer of cow's milk from farther north in the Valley of the Three Marys. Who would guess that an Hidalgo man dared to walk alone in the moonlit streets of San Juan Iglesias?

Carefully adjusting his flat package so that it was not too prominent, he squared his shoulders and walked jauntily across the street to the laughter-filled house. Little boys packed in the doorway made way for him, smiling and nodding to him. The long, narrow room with the orchestra at one end was filled with whirling dancers. Rigid-backed chaperons were gossiping together, seated in their straight chairs against the plaster walls. Over the scene was the yellow glow of kerosene lanterns, and the air was hot with the too sweet perfume of gardenias, tuberoses, and the pungent scent of close-packed humanity.

The man in the doorway, while trying to appear at ease, was carefully examining every smiling face. If just one person recognized him, the room would turn on him like a den of snarling mountain-cats, but so far all the laughter-dancing eyes were friendly.

Suddenly a plump, officious little man, his round cheeks glistening with perspiration, pushed his way through the crowd. His voice, many times too large for his small body, boomed at the man in the doorway. "Welcome, stranger, welcome to your house." Thrusting his arm through the stranger's, and almost dislodging the package, he started to lead the way through the maze of dancers. "Come and drink a toast to my daughter—to my beautiful Sarita. She is eighteen this night."

In the square patio the gentle breeze ruffled the pink and white oleander bushes. A long table set up on saw-horses held loaves of flaky crusted French bread, stacks of thin, delicate *tortillas*, plates of barbecued beef, and long red rolls of spicy sausages. But most of all there were cheeses, for the Three Marys was a cheese-eating valley. There were yellow cheese and white cheese and curded cheese from cow's milk. There was even a flat white cake of goat cheese from distant Linares, a delicacy too expensive for any but feast days.

To set off this feast were bottles of beer floating in ice-filled tin tubs, and another table was covered with bottles of mescal, of tequila, of maguey wine.

Don Roméo Calderón thrust a glass of tequila into the stranger's hand. "Drink, friend, to the prettiest girl in San Juan. As pretty as my fine fighting cocks, she is. On her wedding day she takes to her man, and by the Blessed Ribs may she find him soon, the best fighter in my flock. Drink deep, friend. Even the rivers flow with wine."

The Hidalgo man laughed and raised his glass high. "May the earth be always fertile beneath her feet."

Someone called to Don Roméo that more guests were arriving, and with a final delighted pat on the stranger's shoulder, the little man scurried away. As the young fellow smiled after his retreating host, his eyes caught and held another pair of eyes—laughing black eyes set in a young girl's face. The last time he had seen that face it had been white and tense with rage, and the lips clenched tight to prevent an outgushing stream of angry words. That had been in February and she had worn a white lace shawl over her hair. Now it was May, and a gardenia was a splash of white in the glossy dark braids. The moonlight had mottled his face that February night, and he knew that she did not recognize him. He grinned impudently back at her, and her eyes widened, then slid sideways to one of the chaperones. The fan in her small hand snapped shut. She tapped its parchment tip against her mouth and slipped away to join the dancing couples in the front room. The gestures of a fan translate into a coded language on the frontier. The stranger raised one eyebrow as he interpreted the signal.

But he did not move towards her at once. Instead, he inched slowly back against the table. No one was behind him, and his hands quickly unfastened the package he had been guarding so long. Then he nonchalantly walked into the front room.

The girl was sitting close to a chaperone. As he came up to her he swerved slightly toward the bushy-browed old lady.

"Your servant, señora. I kiss your hands and feet."

The chaperone stared at him in astonishment. Such fine manners were not common to the town of San Juan Iglesias.

"Eh, you're a stranger," she said. "I thought so."

"But a stranger no longer, señora, now that I have met you." He bent over her, so close she could smell the faint fragrance of talcum on his freshly shaven cheek. "Will you dance the *parada* with me?"

This request startled her eyes into popping open beneath the heavy brows. "So, my young rooster, would you flirt with me, and I old enough to be your grandmother?"

"Can you show me a prettier woman to flirt with in the Valley of the Three Marys?" he asked audaciously.

She grinned at him and turned toward the girl at her side. "This young fool wants to meet you, my child."

The girl blushed to the roots of her hair and shyly lowered her white lids. The old woman laughed aloud.

"Go out and dance, the two of you. A man clever enough to pat the sheep has a right to play with the lamb."

The next moment they had joined the circle of dancers and Sarita was trying to control her laughter.

"She is the worst dragon in San Juan. And how easily you won her!"

"What is a dragon," he asked imperiously, "when I longed to dance with you?"

"Ay," she retorted, "you have a quick tongue. I think you are a dangerous man."

In answer he drew her closer to him, and turned her towards the orchestra. As he reached the chief violinist he called out, "Play the *Virgencita*, 'The Shy Young Maiden.' "

The violinist's mouth opened in soundless surprise. The girl in his arms said sharply, "You heard him, the *Borachita*, 'The Little Drunken Girl.' "

With a relieved grin, the violinist tapped his music stand with

his bow, and the music swung into the sad farewell of a man to
his sweetheart:

> *Farewell, my little drunken one,*
> *I must go to the capital*
> *To serve the master*
> *Who makes me weep for my return.*

The stranger frowned down at her. "Is this a joke, señorita?"
he asked coldly.

"No," she whispered, looking about her quickly to see if the
incident had been observed. "But the *Virgencita* is the favorite
song of Hidalgo, a village on the other side of the mountains in
the next valley. The people of Hidalgo and San Juan Iglesias do
not speak."

"That is a stupid thing," said the man from Hidalgo as he swung
her around in a large turn. "Is not music free as air? Why should
one town own the rights to a song?"

The girl shuddered slightly. "Those people from Hidalgo—they
are wicked monsters. Can you guess what they did not six months
since?"

The man started to point out that the space of time from February to May was three months, but he thought it better not to
appear too wise. "Did these Hidalgo monsters frighten you,
señorita? If they did, I personally will kill them all."

She moved closer against him and tilted her face until her
mouth was close to his ear. "They attempted to steal the bones of
Don Rómolo Balderas."

"Is it possible?" He made his eyes grow round and his lips
purse up in disdain. "Surely not that! Why, all the world knows
that Don Rómolo Balderas was the greatest historian in the entire
Republic. Every school child reads his books. Wise men from
Quintana Roo to the Río Bravo bow their heads in admiration
to his name. What a wicked thing to do!" He hoped his virtuous
tone was not too virtuous for plausibility, but she did not seem
to notice.

"It is true! In the night they came. Three devils!"

"Young devils, I hope."

"Young or old, who cares? They were devils. The blacksmith
surprised them even as they were opening the grave. He raised

such a shout that all of San Juan rushed to his aid, for they were fighting, I can tell you. Especially one of them—their leader."

"And who was he?"

"You have heard of him doubtless. A proper wild one named Pepe Gonzalez."

"And what happened to them?"

"They had horses and got away, but one, I think, was hurt."

The Hidalgo man twisted his mouth remembering how Rubén the candy-maker had ridden across the whitewashed line high on the cañon trail that marked the division between the Three Marys' and the Sabinas' sides of the mountains, and then had fallen in a faint from his saddle because his left arm was broken. There was no candy in Hidalgo for six weeks, and the entire Sabinas Valley resented that broken arm as fiercely as did Rubén.

The stranger tightened his arm in reflexed anger about Sarita's waist as she said, "All the world knows that the men of Hidalgo are sons of the mountain witches."

"But even devils are shy of disturbing the honored dead," he said gravely.

" 'Don Rómolo was born in our village,' Hidalgo says. 'His bones belong to us.' Well, anyone in the valley can tell you he died in San Juan Iglesias, and here his bones will stay! Is that not proper? Is that not right?"

To keep from answering, he guided her through an intricate dance pattern that led them past the patio door. Over her head he could see two men and a woman staring with amazement at the open package on the table.

His eyes on the patio, he asked blandly, "You say the leader was one Pepe Gonzalez? The name seems to have a familiar sound."

"But naturally. He has a talent." She tossed her head and stepped away from him as the music stopped. It was a dance of two *paradas*. He slipped his hand through her arm and guided her into place in the large oval of parading couples. Twice around the room and the orchestra would play again.

"A talent?" he prompted.

"For doing the impossible. When all the world says a thing cannot be done, he does it to prove the world wrong. Why, he climbed to the top of the Prow, and not even the long vanished Joaquín Castillo had ever climbed that mountain before. And this same Pepe caught a mountain lion with nothing to aid him but a rope and his two bare hands."

"He doesn't sound such a bad friend," protested the stranger, slipping his arm around her waist as the music began to play the merry song of the soap bubbles:

> *Pretty bubbles of a thousand colors*
> *That ride on the wind*
> *And break as swiftly*
> *As a lover's heart.*

The events in the patio were claiming his attention. Little by little he edged her closer to the door. The group at the table had considerably enlarged. There was a low murmur of excitement from the crowd.

"What has happened?" asked Sarita, attracted by the noise.

"There seems to be something wrong at the table," he answered, while trying to peer over the heads of the people in front of him. Realizing that this might be the last moment of peace he would have that evening, he bent toward her.

"If I come back on Sunday, will you walk around the plaza with me?"

She was startled into exclaiming, "Ay, no!"

"Please. Just once around."

"And you think I'd walk more than once with you, señor, even if you were no stranger? In San Juan Iglesias, to walk around the plaza with a girl means a wedding."

"Ha, and you think that is common to San Juan alone? Even the devils of Hidalgo respect that law." He added hastily at her puzzled upward glance. "And so they do in all the villages." To cover his lapse he said softly, "I don't even know your name."

A mischievous grin crinkled the corners of her eyes. "Nor do I know yours, señor. Strangers do not often walk the streets of San Juan."

Before he could answer, the chattering in the patio swelled to louder proportions. Don Roméo's voice lay on top, like thick cream on milk. "I tell you it is a jewel of a cheese. Such flavor, such texture, such whiteness. It is a jewel of a cheese."

"What has happened?" Sarita asked of a woman at her elbow.

"A fine goat's cheese appeared as if by magic on the table. No one knows where it came from."

"Probably an extra one from Linares," snorted a fat bald man on the right.

"Linares never made such a cheese as this," said the woman decisively.

"Silence!" roared Don Roméo. "Old Tío Daniel would speak a word to us."

A great hand of silence closed down over the mouths of the people. The girl was standing on tiptoe trying vainly to see what was happening. She was hardly aware of the stranger's whispering voice although she remembered the words that he said. "Sunday night—once around the plaza."

She did not realize that he had moved away, leaving a gap that was quickly filled by the blacksmith.

Old Tío Daniel's voice was a shrill squeak, and his thin, stringy neck jutted forth from his body like a turtle's from its shell. "This is no cheese from Linares," he said with authority, his mouth sucking in over his toothless gums between his sentences. "Years ago, when the great Don Rómolo Balderas was still alive, we had such cheese as this—ay, in those days we had it. But after he died and was buried in our own sainted ground, as was right and proper . . ."

"Yes, yes," muttered voices in the crowd. He glared at the interruption. As soon as there was silence again, he continued:

"After he died, we had it no more. Shall I tell you why?"

"Tell us, Tío Daniel," said the voices humbly.

"Because it is made in Hidalgo!"

The sound of a waterfall, the sound of a wind in a narrow cañon, and the sound of an angry crowd are much the same. There were no distinct words, but the sound was enough.

"Are you certain, Tío?" boomed Don Roméo.

"As certain as I am that a donkey has long ears. The people of Hidalgo have been famous for generations for making cheese like this—especially that wicked one, that owner of a cheese factory, Timotéo Gonzalez, father to Pepe, the wild one, whom we have good cause to remember."

"We do, we do," came the sigh of assurance.

"But on the whole northern frontier there are no vats like his to produce so fine a product. Ask the people of Chihuahua, of Sonora. Ask the man on the bridge at Laredo, or the man in his boat at Tampico, '*Hola*, friend, who makes the finest goat cheese?'

And the answer will always be the same, 'Don Timotéo of Hidalgo.' "

It was the blacksmith who asked the great question. "Then where did that cheese come from, and we haters of Hidalgo these ten long years?"

No voice said, "The stranger," but with one fluid movement every head in the patio turned toward the girl in the doorway. She also turned, her eyes wide with something that she realized to her own amazement was more apprehension than anger.

But the stranger was not in the room. When the angry, muttering men pushed through to the street, the stranger was not on the plaza. He was not anywhere in sight. A few of the more religious crossed themselves for fear that the Devil had walked in their midst. "Who was he?" one voice asked another. But Sarita, who was meekly listening to a lecture from Don Roméo on the propriety of dancing with strangers, did not have to ask. She had a strong suspicion that she had danced that night within the circling arm of Pepe Gonzalez.

That was on Wednesday. By the following Sunday night the story of the stranger and his magnificent cheese had swept through the valley, gaining intensity with every telling. "He was a giant, two meters tall," said one story. "He was so tiny," said another, "that he came but to a girl's shoulder." "He was blond as the yellow corn silk"; "he was as black as the cave of the seven witches"; "he was handsome as Blessed Michael, Archangel"; "he was hideous as Satan's youngest son."

On the plaza no one had words for anything else—not even of Don Roméo's wonderful roosters, who were so vicious they had to be taught to respect each other. The village of San Juan Iglesias loved its cockfights, but it loved cheese even more; and a nibble at the fine cheese of Hidalgo, after ten years' abstinence, was enough to make any mouth water with longing.

But the young girls of San Juan were interested in something else than cheese. The stranger occupied their thoughts. And Sarita was looked upon with awe because she had actually danced with him. As she walked around the plaza counter-clockwise, two girls on either side of her, their arms intertwined, she felt as superior as her father's cocks must feel to all the other cocks on the wide frontier.

"What was he like, Sarita? Was he nice?" demanded one girl excitedly.

"Hmm," said Sarita in thoughtful judgment, "I would say—yes, I would say he was nice."

"Could you see his horns?" asked the little girl on the right.

"Naturally not. He was no devil but a man."

"A devil can take on the shape of a man," said the tall, homely girl on Sarita's left, "with no difficulty at all."

Sarita was tempted to say, "You can see for yourself—tonight." But she held her tongue. Surely even Pepe Gonzalez would not attempt to walk around the plaza with her after such a scandal. Little shivers of excitement ran up and down her spine at the thought that Pepe Gonzalez might really be a devil—and all the world knows that a devil will try anything.

The boys walking clockwise in the inner circle called gaily out to her, "Take care, Sarita, a devil doesn't snatch you from your house," and, "How does it feel to dance with an Hidalgo man, eh, Sarita?"

She would laugh and tell them that they should be ashamed of themselves to let an Hidalgo man play such a joke on them. If they became too boisterous she would insist that she was much more interested in listening to the orchestra playing in the center of the plaza than to their silly talk.

The orchestra was really outplaying itself tonight. They had a new song called *La Norteña*, "The Northern Girl"—the first song in years to eulogize the frontier girls in place of the more languorous beauties of the south. The words swept rapidly around the plaza. In a little while everyone was singing:

> *Her eyes are as green as the mountain slopes,*
> *The northern girl I love.*
> *When you look into her eyes*
> *You can see a thousand stars*
> *Colorful as precious stones.*

The great bass drum—added to the orchestra for the occasion—boomed out the rhythm, and the shrill voices, singing in thirds, floated like smoke on the clear air. With a final great roll of the drum, the piece came to a close, and the orchestra leader shouted for attention.

"We are proud we have so many *Norteñas*," he called out, and was answered by lusty applause. "To honor the beautiful sex of San Juan Iglesias, the orchestra will march around the plaza, each member escorting one of our most exquisite ladies. Because the bass drum is the loudest instrument, it will lead the procession with Sarita Calderón."

Again there was loud applause and much chattering and laughter, as the people congregated in front of the bandstand. The bass drummer, looking like a pouter pigeon with his drum thrust up high in front of him so that his face was hidden behind the upper curve, started off with a grand flourish of the sticks. Sarita had to trip along, three steps to his one long stride. In a few moments they had outdistanced the crowd.

"I—I can't walk so fast," she protested breathlessly.

The man stopped banging the drum long enough for the music to be heard. "Your eyes are as green as the skirts of the mountains," sang the violins. "As green as emeralds," insisted the flutes. The guitars tinkled the plea, "Your eyes are like a garden of flowers, and when you weep it seems that they will fade. Do not cry, my beautiful."

"That song should be about a woman with black eyes," said the man behind the drum's rim.

Sarita gave a gasp and hastily looked about her. "Are you a fool? What are you doing here?"

"I told you I would walk around the plaza with you on Sunday night."

"But to come back here—so soon. The men will be furious. Already San Juan has lost face in the valley because of Wednesday. This would have the whole frontier laughing."

"Eh, there is terror in your voice. Are you afraid for me, *Norteña?*"

She shrugged, but there was no disdain in her eyes. "You are a fool. You are only one man and here are a hundred men."

They were nearing the grandstand and he spoke quickly. "It is true that I am one man. It is also true that you are one woman. I will be under your window tonight when the moon has slipped behind the mountains."

She caught her breath in a gasp of alarm. "Now you are twice a fool. Do you think I would talk to you?"

"You said you wouldn't walk once around the plaza with me—but you have."

"Eh, you tricked me—you and your great drum."

The bandstand was in front of them. They paused on the lower step and the rest of the procession was rapidly nearing them. The people were singing the last verse of the song:

> *I don't know what I see in your eyes.*
> *Is it the light of love?*
> *But I know that if you weep*
> *Your eyes will wilt like flowers.*
> *Please, my beautiful, do not cry.*

He said quietly, "If you do not talk to me from your window I will call to all the world that I am Pepe Gonzalez. I will tell that it was I who brought Hidalgo men to steal the bones of Don Rómolo Balderas. Will you wait at your window for me?"

"I can't. It would be a great scandal."

"Who would know? When the moon is behind the mountains I will be at your window."

"You are a great stupid fool," she repeated desperately.

"Where do you live?"

"You don't even know my name," she wailed. "Why do you do this?"

"I saw you that night in the cemetery. For three months I've remembered your face. The other night at the dance I recognized you—where do you live?"

"I'm Sarita Calderón. Where the dance was—there I live."

The procession had reached the steps. People were laughing and turning their faces up to the moonlight. Pepe industriously swung his sticks against the sides of the protecting drum.

"My window," said Sarita between the strokes, "is at the back of the house, on the right corner as you face the door." Then she walked swiftly forward while Pepe went up to the grandstand.

Three hours later the moon was half hidden by the jutting peaks of the mountains that divided the two enemy valleys. Pepe, seated on the cañon trail, stretched his weary body and rose to his feet. He thrust his hands in his empty pockets and grimaced at the memory of the heavy bribe he had had to pay the orchestra director to let him beat the drum. (The orchestra director was lately come to the valley from Torreón, and had no patriotic feeling for the feud.) The *Norteña* procession had cost Pepe five pesos more. Don Timotéo, the cheese-maker, would howl with rage when he discovered that his son had spent ten pesos on a girl—and a San Juan girl at that. Pepe, as he walked through the sleepy streets could almost hear his father's voice ringing in his ears: "There are plenty of fine girls in Hidalgo, and ten pesos would shower them with gifts for a year. What devil in you makes you walk the dangerous paths?" The answer was not a single answer, but a mosaic of many things: The feud between the two valleys because of a man ten years dead. A girl's face glimpsed in the moonlight, angry and yet beautiful. A parchment fan signalling its coded message. All of these things were answers, and yet there was still another, a greater one, for Pepe, the wild one, had been born out of his time. He belonged to the days of the viceroys, when perfume-scented ladies, silk fabrics sheathing their soft white bodies, rode these same mountain trails in lumbering carriages bound for the regal, glittering court of the Count of Monterrey, protected by troops of armor-clad soldiers, swords naked and ready in their hands, eyes constantly watching the cactus-studded landscape, alert for any shadow out of place that might warn them of Indian attack. And when the attack came the Spaniards often won through. But sometimes searching parties found armor, flat and bone-filled, on the trail, the coaches empty of their delicate cargo. And high in the mountains some women would leap to their death from a rocky precipice, while others would shrug fatalistic shoulders and learn the bitter business of bearing children with the Moorish eyes of Spain and the lank, dark hair of Mexico. These children, in turn, bore other children, who came down from the mountains to the valleys and learned to live in small civilized groups. But once in a while such groups produced atavistic spirits who roamed the trails with the sound of clashing armor always in their ears ... a sound whose source was divided from them by a space of three hundred years. And Pepe Gonzalez possessed one of these spirits, trapped in the body of a cheese-maker's son. But this knowledge was not clear to him. He was only certain that Sarita was his girl and twice his girl because he had to walk through danger to reach her. He knew perfectly well that if the San Juan men caught him, he would be lucky to escape as had Rubén, the candy-maker, with nothing more than broken bones. And all because of that great historian, Don Rómolo Balderas, who had been born in Hidalgo and died in San Juan Iglesias. "Why couldn't he have died in Mexico City?" Pepe muttered to himself, and yet, he honestly admitted, if there had been no feud he might never have met Sarita—or, if he had, she would probably have remained nothing more than a pair of laughing black eyes above a parchment fan at a dance.

The blue-stained walls of Don Roméo's house were a dusty gray in the starlight. Unlike most Mexican houses, it was set back in a little garden. The heavy fragrance of night-blooming jasmine and gardenias was very strong, and the honeysuckle intertwined with bougainvillea was a sweet-scented shadow against the house.

Pepe found Sarita's window with no difficulty. She had lighted a small oil lamp and placed it beside her on the wide cement window-ledge.

"Sarita," he whispered. As she opened her mouth, he laughed softly. "I know. I am a great stupid fool."

"Well, you are. What do you want here?"

"To see how the black braids curve over your head like a crown. To watch your eyes crinkle at the corners with laughter. To wonder if your mouth tastes like honey."

"*Ay Diós!* The man is quite mad!" And then shrewdly, "If you think I'll help you steal the bones of Don Rómolo Balderas, you wear donkey's ears."

"Should we talk of a dead man's bones on such a night as this?" He rested his hands on the window's iron bars. She immediately withdrew hers and folded them primly in her lap.

"Am I to sit here and listen to you make love, then? Let me tell you, my fine young rooster, that I could choose any man in the Valley of the Three Marys. Why should I roll the eye at a fool from Hidalgo?"

He moved closer to the bars. "Because you love me."

"Do I now? And who told you such a great secret?"

"Then why did you ask me to dance with you last Wednesday night?"

She slipped from the ledge and stood up, her eyes snapping with anger. "What lies spout from your mouth!"

"Your fan spoke. You closed your fan against your mouth. You looked straight at me and closed your fan. Remember?"

Sarita bit down on her lower lip and refused to look at him. "How was I to know you could read fan language? The men of San Juan are not so clever." One small pointed finger traced the joining of two iron bars. His hand moved down and closed over hers.

"Why should a dead man keep us from seeing each other, Sarita?"

"A dead man?"

"As long as Don Rómolo Balderas rests in the sainted ground of San Juan instead of Hidalgo..."

"I thought so!" she blazed, jerking her fingers away. "It was bad enough to try and steal his bones. But to make love to me so as to get them—that is to be expected of an Hidalgo man. I give you good night!" She stepped back and started to swing the long shutters closed. He moved in to the bars and pressed his face against them.

"Please, Sarita, you don't understand. That was not in my mind. Please!"

One shutter snapped into place. As she reached for the other he whispered hoarsely, "For all of me, Don Rómolo can sleep in San Juan until judgment day. I swear it!" The second shutter was slowly swinging shut, and his tense words tumbled out of his mouth. "I swear it by the five wounds of God!"

At the sound of that most desperate of oaths, the second shutter paused its forward swing, hesitated, and then, very slowly, began to move backwards into the room. Her small, pointed face slid around its edge.

"And the tears of the weeping Mother?"

"And the breaking heart of St. Mary Magdalen," he finished quickly. "Will you listen to me, Sarita?"

"Well," she said uncertainly, and coming around the shutter she rested one knee on the window ledge. "Let the words make sense in your mouth."

"Do you know who I am, Sarita?"

"You are Pepe Gonzalez. All the world knows that."

"But do you know also that my father is Don Timotéo Gonzalez?"

She smiled with superior knowledge. "You mean the Don

Timotéo who deals in goats—who makes, so they say, the finest cheese on the frontier?"

"The same!" Pepe peered at her curiously, trying to see the expression of mouth and eye in the glimmering darkness. "And why does a San Juan girl have such interest in an Hidalgo man?"

"Why . . ." Sarita paused and again her finger traced the twisted iron bars. "I thought you knew."

"Eh, secrets you are keeping."

"So!" she tossed her head. "And I know more of your father than you do of mine. Is not Don Roméo Calderón the raiser of the finest fighting cocks from Matamoros to Tijuana? And in their young days your father and mine matched many a bird in the pit."

"So that was it," said Pepe moodily. "He has not allowed a mention of cockfighting in the house for the past ten years."

"Ah, Pepe," Sarita said dismally, "we are a foolish two. Better for you to go back to Hidalgo and forget the Valley of the Three Marys and this Sarita Calderón. It is more practical, that."

"And you think I am not practical! Do you know why I came the other night?"

"To make a fool of San Juan Iglesias. Which you did!" She moved backward again. Pepe was afraid that she would snap the shutters closed in a sudden change from amiability to anger.

He caught her wrist with his hand. "You heard what that old man said at the dance. 'Ask the man from Chihuahua,' he said, 'Ask the man from Sonora. The man from Tampico in his boat.' And he was right. We do make the finest of goat cheese. And it is a sad thing that the valley of San Juan—just across the mountains—should have none of it."

"The cheese is very grand," she admitted.

"Precisely. And my father is angry with me. He says I am good for nothing but climbing mountains and deeds that are of little worth. He told me Wednesday morning that if I were a proper son I'd win the San Juan trade back to Hidalgo."

"So that's why you came."

"Yes. I thought if once the people of San Juan tasted the cheese their appetite would be greater than the feud. Why should a man ten years dead still be so powerful?"

"You know," she said with the air of making a great discovery, "that is true. Do you remember Don Rómolo?"

"I saw him once when he came to visit my father. I was twelve, and he looked very tall on his great sorrel horse."

"He died when I was eight. And you know, Pepe . . ." she drew closer to the window so that her sacrilege could be heard no farther than his ear. "It makes no difference to me whether he is buried in San Juan Iglesias or Hidalgo, and that is the truth."

"Nor to me," said Pepe firmly. "Nor to any of the other young people. And why should the old ones say, 'Hate each other because of our pride in this great man'?"

"Precisely. If we could stop this feud then everyone would be happy. Hidalgo could sell us its cheese, and—and—we could eat the cheese—and—"

"And you could marry me," said Pepe with a mischievous grin.

"I didn't say that," protested Sarita. "How dare you put words —ay!" She broke off with a startled exclamation, her eyes fastened on a great swooping darkness that was passing above the chicken houses.

"It is an eagle!" exclaimed Pepe.

"He's after one of my father's cocks. You stay here!" she whispered excitedly.

She disappeared from the window. Pepe ran toward the chicken pen. He snatched up a stick of kindling and began flailing it over his head. The great bird darted toward him, but, frightened by the sharp jerking of the stick and the loud crowing of the roosters, glided away as a boat retreats over waves.

A light appeared in Don Roméo's room. His booming voice called out, "What is it? Are you there, Sarita?"

Pepe crouched by the chicken yard fence as he heard Sarita, just behind him, answer her father. "It is nothing. An eagle after the cocks, but he's been frightened away."

"Are you sure?"

"Yes, father." The girl put out her hand, and Pepe touched it with his to let her know where he was.

"I thought I heard a man's voice," protested Don Roméo.

"Ay, father, what would a man be doing here—and at this hour?"

Grumbling a little at having been disturbed in his sleep, Don Roméo extinguished his light. In the stillness Pepe could hear the shutters snap closed to prevent the dreaded sickness of "catching the night air."

"Why didn't you hide?" gasped Sarita as soon as it was safe to speak.

"If I had," retorted Pepe, "your father would have lost a fine cock."

"Better that than to have him find you here."

As Pepe rose, she began retreating hastily toward the house. "Now, Pepe Gonzalez, it is time for you to go home."

"But I am possessed of a magnificent idea."

She had reached the back door. She put her hand on the latch. "Magnificent or not, get you back to Hidalgo and leave this poor girl in peace." The door was open and the next moment she would be through. He caught her arm. "Let me go."

"Please, Sarita . . ."

"Let me go or I will scream."

"Scream, then," he said roughly, "but hear me speak first."

She opened her mouth, took a deep breath, and then noiselessly relaxed on the foot-worn stone step. "How wicked you are. You knew I wouldn't scream. Ay, the priest will give me ten days' penance at confessional for this."

He sat beside her and imprisoned her hand again in his. She pretended not to notice when his other arm slipped behind her waist.

"Supposing," he said excitedly, "there was a cockfight . . ."

"Eh . . ." she began.

"One moment. And these were the stakes: the fine cheese of Hidalgo against the bones of Don Rómolo Balderas."

Sarita stared at him with widened eyes. "Now I know you are mad."

"But don't you see? That would settle the feud. If San Juan wins, it cannot with dignity refuse to speak to the men from whom it buys its cheese. And if Hidalgo wins, well—Don Rómolo will return at last to his birthplace and the reason for the feud will be gone."

"You wear donkey's ears. Let me ask you—where in the whole Sabinas Valley, or even in Monterrey, would you find a cock to match against one of my father's?"

He released her hand and propped up his chin with his fist. "Now that is a difficulty." Suddenly he snapped his fingers. "But wait! Supposing that I had not been here tonight, and the eagle had stolen one of your father's cocks . . ."

"But you were here, and he didn't steal it."

"But if I hadn't been, and he had stolen it—the cock would be gone, wouldn't it?"

"Yes."

"Then, as I see it, your father owes me a cock."

"Dear saints in Heaven, protect me from this man!" She sprang to her feet. "First you convince me that the feud is not a proper thing. And now you want one of my father's cocks!"

"But, Sarita . . ."

"I'll have you know," stormed Sarita, "that I am a good daughter. I am not one to give away my father's property to just any stranger who winks at the stars outside my window!"

"But, Sarita . . ." said Pepe again, and this time he openly put his arm about her waist.

In Hidalgo the next morning, Pepe, with the little Doctor and Andrés Treviño in tow, stopped in front of the house of Porfirio, the carver of wood. "Eh, Alma!" he called to the girl sweeping dust from the front stoop. "Is your good man at home?"

"In the back, in the shop," said Alma, resting her arm on her broom and thoughtfully surveying the trio, "and I'll not have you get him into mischief."

"And we the most solid of citizens," protested the little Doctor.

"Better for you to stay with your pills, and Andrés to stay with his goats, for when Pepe Gonzalez leads the way, you'll come home riding a horse backward."

"Stay out of men's affairs, Alma Orona," said her husband from the house. He came out on the street. "You wanted me?"

"In silence we want you," said Pepe, with a gay bow to Alma. "As you said, this is a man's affair."

Alma shrugged, letting her hands rise and fall in fatalistic acceptance of the inevitable, and watched them walk away, Pepe leading them across the churchyard in spite of Porfirio's protests that it was bad luck to walk through the yard without entering the church. When they reached the rooming house of Doña Juanita Perez, they could hear the gentle voice of Rubén, the maker of candy, trying to sell some of his almond paste and fruit cheese to the thin-faced old woman. Porfirio whistled through the iron-barred window, and Rubén came out to join them in the small corral at the back. As long as any of the boys could remember, Doña Juanita, who had never had children of her own though three times married, had kept their secrets. It was only natural that Pepe Gonzalez should bring his fine cock to her for hiding until the psychological moment to show it to the village.

The cock was in a wooden box Pepe had hammered together. Through one slotted side they watched him pacing royally back and forth. The five men silently squatted on their heels, their hats pulled forward over their faces, for this was secret business.

The little Doctor lighted a cigarette and pronounced grave judgment. "A fine cock. There is no doubt. The finest on the frontier."

Five pairs of eyes minutely examined the proud bird. His black feathers had a greenish sheen, and his small vicious eyes glittered back at them.

"I should say he weighs two kilos," said the little Doctor.

"Better than two kilos," pronounced Rubén thoughtfully.

"But not so much as three," agreed the little Doctor. "Two kilos is a better weight. He must be trained down. And the comb needs cutting. It offers too good a mark."

"There is a man in Abasolo," said Porfirio. "You know him, Pepe, the brother-in-law of Don Serapio, the gardener, who has a talent for the trimming of cocks. The tail feathers need shortening by a third their length, and the hackles and rump feathers must be trimmed."

"The wings must be cut out at a slope," contributed Rubén, the candy-maker. "Has this brother-in-law of Don Serapio the proper experience for such delicate work?"

"I know that man," said Andrés. "The people of Piedras Negras send for him to trim their birds, and the betting for their fights runs as high as two thousand pesos.

"This fine bird looks like a Dominique. Is he a Dominique?" the little Doctor asked Pepe.

The young man pursed his mouth silently for a moment. He sank back on his heels and looked upward, away from their faces. "He is from the flock of Don Roméo Calderón."

The men did not exclaim. They looked at the cock and knew that such a fine bird could have its origin in only one place. This was no common fighter but a very king of fighters. Here was no usual death challenge but a viciousness bred in the hollow bones. What prevented Don Roméo's cocks from tearing each other to pieces in the home corral was a secret known only to Don Roméo. Once in the pit a red haze seemed to enfold them. They might die, but they were never vanquished.

The men were too polite to ask Pepe how he had acquired the bird. If he did not offer to tell them, that was his affair. They were interested only in what he planned to do with the cock now that he had it.

"I will tell you," said Pepe Gonzalez.

At first they would not listen to him. Porfirio and Andrés reminded him of the ill-fated February expedition. Rubén shook the arm that had once been broken and said that he would never walk in peace with San Juan men—truce or no truce. The excited voices grew so loud that they drew Doña Juanita to the door with a stern admonition for quiet, or Father Zacaya across the narrow street would hear them. "And you know what he'd say if he found you planning a cockfight!"

Pepe smiled with secret satisfaction. Even Father Zacaya could not stop this fight. There would be the crowing of cocks instead of the clashing of swords; the shrill placing of bets instead of the death rattle in steel-sheathed throats; but the results would be the same. Pepe Gonzalez would win, and as reward he would lift Sarita Calderón to his saddlebow.

"Eh, Pepe," cried the little Doctor at last, "win Don Nacho and the other mayors of the Sabinas towns to your scheme, and I'll supply the fine white bread for the feeding of this beauty. By the five wounds I swear it."

"There is a difficulty," said the cautious Andrés. "This is a very famous cock. I have heard Abel, the *árabe* trader, speak of him. The green sheen on the black feathers—that is the great Satan, the very pride of Don Roméo's fighters. When we show him in the pit, Don Roméo will recognize him. In honor he can refuse to meet us, saying we stole his fighter. What then, Pepe?"

Pepe's eyes hooded with disappointment. "There must be some solution," he said fretfully.

The little Doctor grinned mischievously. "Father Zacaya knows the secret of dyeing birds. If you could win Father Zacaya..."

"I will win him," said Pepe confidently.

"Remember," warned Rubén, "if we lose this cockfight, Hidalgo men can never again walk in honor. You know that."

"Do we walk in honor now," retorted Pepe, "with Don Rómolo buried in the ground of San Juan?"

"Don't listen to this high-prancing fool," cried Porfirio, covering his ears with his flat palms. "I know how his tongue can argue. And to reach here he led us across the churchyard. You know what that means! Grandfather Devil was breathing down my neck. I could feel his breath tickling the ends of my hair. Doesn't the Devil roost in churchyards to steal the sanctified souls of purified sinners? And his black feet followed us here. He's sitting on that cock's back this very minute!"

Five pairs of eyes stared at the cock. Five pairs of eyes saw the ruff at the neck fluff outward in full battle challenge. Five left hands surreptitiously thrust up forefinger and little finger in the horned sign to ward off the evil eye. But almost immediately Pepe Gonzalez curled all of his fingers and clenched his fist hard enough for the nails to pierce the palm. Under his breath he whispered a prayer to Blessed Michael, Archangel. No devil riding on a cock was going to dissolve the fine schemes of Pepe Gonzalez.

The month of May and part of June passed in a male whisper. Father Zacaya was worried. For the first time his good friends Don Nacho, Don Rosalío, the little Doctor, and even Bob Webster, were keeping a secret from him. All of the village men were keeping secrets. There was a notable lack of attendance at the Friday confessional, and at Sunday mass only the older women came forward to take communion. Father Zacaya knew from bitter experience that secrets too often lead men to dance on the Devil's tail. But no matter how cautiously he probed, he encountered nothing but a blank wall of silence. Every day men rode down the Street of the River and turned their horses north on the River Road. Father Zacaya even went up that road himself as far as the cave in the cliffs where María de las Garzas lived to ask her if she knew anything.

The tall blond girl rested her hands on her hips and shrugged her shoulders. "What does it matter to me where the men of Hidalgo ride?" she demanded in her voice like a golden gong.

"They call out to you, María. Surely you know where they are going."

"Abasolo, if that's any good to you."

Father Zacaya thanked her and returned to his house. The

next day he borrowed a mule from Doña Juanita Perez and went to the town that spiraled like a seashell around its one street. There was no priest to consult, for the four valley towns came to Hidalgo for mass. Father Zacaya went to the mayor, a thin, shriveled black bean of a man, who dry-washed his hands and protested that he had noticed nothing unusual. But all the time he was protesting, his eyes were sliding secretively about the room. Recognizing the symptoms, Father Zacaya sighed, shrugged his shoulders, and turned his mule's head toward Hidalgo. As on so many other occasions he wished that Pablo the goatherd were still alive.

As Father Zacaya's mule trotted past the cave of María de las Garzas, the girl called out to him, "So, little Father, try the road to San Juan Iglesias," and then flung her laughter against the hard dirt walls of the cliff.

Father Zacaya, protected from the feud by his vocation, rode into San Juan Iglesias just before sunset. The church bells were calling the people to rosary, and the mountains tossed the jangling music back and forth. The wind was sweet with flowering thorn, and the air was golden with the powdered light of the dying sun.

The priest at the church of the Three Marys was pleasant but reserved. No, he had noticed no secrets among the men of San Juan. But, his tone implied, the men of San Juan were peaceable folk and not given to mischief as certain other folk were. He offered a glass of wine to Father Zacaya. Father Zacaya tasted it in courtesy but did not drink it. The priest, with many polite protestations, begged to be excused as he was needed in church. Father Zacaya bowed and mounted his mule once more, humanly exasperated with María de las Garzas for sending him on a useless errand.

He turned the mule's head toward the Cañon Road and allowed the little animal to amble along at its own slow trot. He was frankly worried. The people of the Sabinas Valley were his children, and when children keep secrets from their parents, they are up to mischief—bad mischief.

As he reached the turn in the road that led past the cemetery, a girl stepped from behind the tall iron gates. "What a pretty child," he thought to himself as she called out, "Tell me, are you not the priest from Hidalgo?"

When he nodded, she came up to him and caught the mule's bridle in her left hand. "I saw you come into the town," she said breathlessly. "I've been waiting for you to come back."

"You want something, child?"

"Yes, Father. I want you to buy something for me."

"Buy something?" Father Zacaya tipped his head to one side and frowned. "But surely..."

"Please, Father, this is important. I can't ask anyone else."

"Yes, but..."

"Look." She held up her right hand and he saw some gold coins. "Here are fifty pesos. For ten years I've saved this money from the selling of eggs. Ever since I was a little girl I've saved it against my wedding day. But now..."

"But now your wedding day is no longer important?"

"Oh, yes it is, Father." The color rose in a red film from throat to hairline. When he smiled at her, she lowered her white lids as a curtain between them. He could hardly hear her as she mumbled, "But this is more important."

"So. And what do you want me to buy with your fifty pesos?"

She swallowed tightly and turned her head away in embarrassment. "A statue, Father."

"Saints in Heaven!" He tossed his head back and laughed for the first time in three weeks. "What do you want with a statue? A statue of what?"

"A man."

"What man?"

"Don Rómolo Balderas."

Although the valley feud had started before Father Zacaya came to Hidalgo, he felt a prickle of anger run across his nerves. "San Juan Iglesias has his bones. Is that not enough for you? Must you have a statue, also?"

"You don't understand, Father. It's because of the fight."

"What fight?"

"Surely Pepe Gonzalez has told you about..." She stopped her mouth with quick fingers, and her large black eyes were frightened. The priest sighed. Here was the secretive gesture, the fear of revealing too much that he had found in his own valley. And it centered, of course, in that mischievous young fool, Pepe Gonzalez. The girl was saying desperately, over and over, "I must have the statue, Father. I must..."

"And where do you think I may find a statue of Don Rómolo Balderas for fifty pesos?"

"A friend of mine in Monterrey knows a man who owns a statue of Julius Caesar. She says he'll sell it for forty pesos. And for ten pesos a stonecutter could take off the name of Caesar and put on the name of Don Rómolo. That is simple enough, eh, Father?"

The church bells began to toll their second call to rosary, and the girl glanced anxiously toward the town. "I must go now, or people will ask questions. The name of the Monterrey man is Tomás Acuña. He lives on Calle Washington, 16, West. Here is the money. Tell Pepe Gonzalez that . . ." She paused. Snatching at Father Zacaya's hand, she pressed the coins into it, pulled her white lace shawl over her black hair, and ran off down the road toward the village.

He started to call to her, but relaxed in his saddle with a weary sigh. Secrets in Hidalgo and secrets in San Juan! Was the whole frontier turning into a mighty bin of secrets? And Pepe Gonzalez in the middle of it as usual. For a moment the priest longed with nostalgic fervor for the days with Villa's men in Chihuahua. Those Golden Men had fought like maniacs and killed with casual ease, but there was nothing dark and hidden behind their placid, childlike eyes.

Father Zacaya kicked the little mule with his heels and this time reached the cañon trail before meeting anyone else. He pulled the mule to one side to make room for the light spring buckboard of Abel, the *árabe* trader. Usually Abel, who was a good Mohammedan, had a cheery greeting for the priest, but today he only mumbled something and pretended to be in such a hurry that he had no time for stopping to pass the time of day.

Father Zacaya called out, "Abel, where are you going?"

"To San Juan Iglesias, Father. Please forgive me. I have a big order waiting for me."

Father Zacaya edged his mule closer to the wagon and saw some large sheets of cardboard piled on the seat beside the trader. He would not have noticed them had Abel not been awkwardly trying to sit on them. "What have you there, Abel?"

The trader wriggled the cardboard farther under him. "I—the seat—it's broken. I brought these boards to sit on."

"Abel, what kind of mischief are you up to?"

"Why, nothing, Father, and I as innocent as a child." Abel raised his placid round face and blinked his lids quickly over his small black eyes.

Father Zacaya sighed and reined back his mule. "I see. A good afternoon to you, Abel."

"And to you, Father." Abel flicked his horse's rump with the long braided whip, and the wagon careened around the turn on two wheels. He patted himself on the left shoulder with secret satisfaction. He had really emerged from the encounter very well. If the priest had ever seen what was written on those cardboards, the entire Sabinas Valley would have received a spiritual spanking, and would have taken out its anger on Abel, the *árabe* trader. So far Abel had managed to stay free of the valley feud. In the Three Marys he implied that the men of Sabinas were rogues and thieves. In the Sabinas he let it be known that he thought the men of the Three Marys were no better than crawling worms. This attitude had worked very well for the seven years that he had been hawking his wares through the mountain district. But this afternoon Bob Webster and Don Nacho had presented him with the posters, and the troubles of Abel, the *árabe* trader, had begun. "You will post them on all the plazas throughout the Three Marys."

"But, Don Bob," Abel had wailed, "what will happen to me if they catch me? You know well enough that the men of that valley hit first and ask questions afterwards."

"You have the slyness of your race," said Don Nacho, firmly. "You can do it well enough."

Abel, after reading the posters, was terrified, but his guiding principle in life was never to allow anything to interfere with trade. He knew well enough that if he refused this commission he could sell nothing more in the Sabinas Valley; so, with a sigh of resignation, he piled the posters on the wagon seat. "And," said Bob Webster as a final admonition, "keep them from the eyes of Father Zacaya. What that good man of God does not see cannot bother his conscience."

"By the mighty horse Rakhsh," Abel muttered to himself, "the first man I meet is Father Zacaya. This living among christians has put a curse upon my days. If I come out of this without a broken head it will be by the grace of Allah (all honor to His name), and the smile of Mohammed, His prophet."

But that night, in the dark of the moon, Abel rode through the villages of the Three Marys tacking up his posters.

The next noonday found the Valley of the Three Marys as nervously excited as in the early days of the Great Revolution, when half the men left to follow the Federal flag, and half to ride with Villa and Obregón. In San Juan Iglesias, old Tío Daniél, Don Roméo, and the fat, perspiring mayor sat in the jail' corridor and glared angrily at one of the offending posters. Its wording was simple:

> *Men of San Juan, do you lack courage?*
> *Are you afraid to match the bones of*
> *Don Rómolo Balderas against the cheese*
> *trade of Hidalgo?*
> *The men of Hidalgo challenge you to a*
>
> ### COCKFIGHT
>
> *One main only, two cocks to fight. The*
> *place: the boundary line at the center of*
> *the cañon. The time: two weeks follow-*
> *ing St. John's Day.*
> *Men of San Juan! Do you lack courage?*

"I smell a trick," said Don Roméo dismally. "Those thieves, those men without conscience. I smell a trick."

"How can the men of Hidalgo hope to win over one of your cocks?" demanded Tío Daniel, puzzled.

"Ever since the eagle stole my little Satan, my lovely bird, I have felt the salt of disaster. And now the tragedy is here. I smell a trick."

"We cannot in pride refuse," said the mayor, mopping his damp face. " 'Men of San Juan, do you lack courage?' The insolence of them!"

"Thieves," chanted Don Roméo, "robbers, grandsons of Grandfather Devil."

"No time for mourning," said Tío Daniel. "This is the time for the training of a cock. And remember, Roméo, your birds have never been vanquished."

"If I but had my little Satan. My green-shining black little Satan," mourned Don Roméo.

"No time for mourning," repeated Tío Daniel. "Satan is food

in the eagle's belly, but this fight is two weeks from tomorrow. Go home and train the finest cock you have."

"And," added the mayor, "tell Sarita to practice the dance of the Spur. There will be blood in the pit—blood to be stamped into the ground."

"And you," said Don Roméo, rousing himself from his weeping, "gather together the men of the valley and order them to the church. Tell them to pray to Blessed Michael, Archangel. And to Brother Raphael, too. We'll need the legions of Heaven to conquer these devils of earth."

Father Zacaya was puzzled to find a full church on the morning of St. John's day. Long boughs of pomegranate, heavy with the fruit sacred to the mighty prophet of God, rested on the altar. The faces of the young men were gravely pious as they came forward to lift the saints from their niches and carry them to the river for their yearly purification by running water. He thought guiltily of the statue of Julius Caesar (now renamed Don Rómolo Balderas) standing in his Residence, and wondered if the men of San Juan Iglesias were being equally pious on this day. The only link between the statue and Hidalgo's secret mischief was that girl's breathless reference to Pepe Gonzalez, but Father Zacaya had learned long ago to solve mysteries from just such small details. Now there was no time for wondering, as the people were waiting to make the river pilgrimage.

The fifteen-year-old Xavier, nephew to Don Serapio, the gardener, headed the procession in his long scarlet cassock and white lace surplice, swinging the golden censor back and forth in steady rhythm. Father Zacaya followed him robed in red, for Blessed John the Baptist was a martyred saint. Then came the men carrying litters on which rode the images of the Blessed Mother, of Christ her Son, of St. Joseph carrying the lily, and of the Prophet with a purple velvet mantle over his rough brown cassock. The women walked behind the images, their heads veiled in their long black shawls. And as they walked, the people chanted the ancient chants of the church.

At the river's edge, the litters were carefully lowered to the ground. The women came forward to take the embroidered robes from the images. Father Zacaya cupped river water in his palm and allowed it to flow across the foreheads of the sacred figures.

Then they were reclothed in clean vestments and replaced on the litters. The people knelt on the rocks and sand, Xavier swung out the pungent smoke of incense, and Father Zacaya prayed to the saint who had baptized Jesus as a Child.

The moment the prayer was finished and the Amens echoed from the cliff walls, the people jumped up with low squeals of enjoyment and, pulling off their shoes, waded into the water, the young girls shrieking that, as it was not yet noon, the boys had best beware; for all the world knew that a girl who bathed on the morning of St. John's day would surely marry within the year.

Father Zacaya sat on a broad flat rock and smiled as he watched the villagers playfully splashing water on each other. Perhaps he had merely imagined the nervous tension of the past month. What he needed was a bit of rest or, better still, a liver prescription from the little Doctor. But in the back of his mind was the memory of the statue of Julius Caesar—pardon, the statue of Don Rómolo Balderas.

The priest turned his head slightly as Don Saturnino Castillo limped painfully across the stones and sat down beside him to wipe his feet and put on shoes and socks.

"I like this ceremony," said Don Saturnino, "but my feet object."

"The flesh and the spirit," smiled Father Zacaya. "You know the proverb."

Bob Webster came toward them, grinning. "I have to keep an eye on Tía Magdalena. If she wades in that water very long, she'll catch a cold. Have you heard from Alejandro lately, Don Saturnino?"

"I had a letter this morning. He sent you his greetings and said he had shipped you some furniture from Paris: a sofa and some chairs, rosewood upholstered in green satin, very elegant."

"It sounds terrible," Bob groaned, "but I suppose the pieces are really very beautiful. Alejandro has good taste."

"Very. He is a true connoisseur of the beautiful. What a pity he had to miss this lovely ceremony." Father Zacaya shielded his eyes from the dancing diamonds of sunlight on the rippling water. "He always loved it."

Bob pulled off his broad-brimmed Stetson and ran his hand through his crisp black hair. "He told me the heart of the village was Sunday night on the plaza, but the soul is St. John's Day on the river."

"I sometimes wonder," mused Don Saturnino, "if these frequent trips to Europe are really necessary to keep a man contented in a village."

"Where is he now?" asked the priest.

"Venice. Floating down the canals. Feeling romantic."

Father Zacaya waved his hand toward Pepe Gonzalez, who had just tripped Andrés Treviño full length into the water and was struggling to keep Andrés from dragging him down, too.

"There is the real romantic of Hidalgo. That boy was born out of his time. He should have lived in the days of the viceroys. Who knows? His escapades might have carried him to that shining, wicked court."

"Or to the faggots of the Inquisition's fire," said Don Saturnino moodily.

"Not that boy," insisted Bob Webster. "He'd have argued himself free in five minutes."

"Doubtless," agreed Don Saturnino. "That boy could argue his soul out of the Devil's palm."

After a moment Father Zacaya said softly, "What mischief has he argued this village into now?"

Bob's face closed as a box closes. He lifted himself to his feet and dusted sand from his rough riding trousers. "I think Tía has been in long enough. That old woman's supposed to take care of me, and what happens? I spend all my time rushing around pulling her out of trouble. Good afternoon to you." He moved quickly away, his shoulders squared, proud of his easy escape.

But Don Saturnino remained beside the priest, a part and yet not a part of the festival. The *grand seigneur*, thought the priest, come to mingle with his people, and yet aloof from them as the mountains are aloof from the valley. And for a moment the priest fought bitterness, because obviously Don Saturnino had been taken into the village confidence, while he, their spiritual parent, was left out. When he spoke, his voice was unintentionally cold, "I repeat. What mischief has Pepe Gonzalez argued the village into now?"

"Not the village," sighed Don Saturnino, "but the entire valley. Every night I swear I'll not have it, and every morning that boy convinces me again. I can't understand what devil is driving him on."

For a moment Father Zacaya saw the image of a black-haired girl with a blush staining her skin from throat to forehead. "I think I can imagine the spirit," he said dryly. "I don't suppose there is any use my asking the nature of this mystery?"

"No, my friend, no."

"I have a feeling I'm going to disapprove of it—enough to give the entire valley ten days' penance."

Don Saturnino rose to his feet. "If we win, the ten days won't matter. If we lose—ten days won't be nearly enough."

"How much, then, if you lose?"

"I couldn't say. I shall be sixty-eight next month. There are not enough days left in my life. Young Pepe Gonzalez might be able to span the penance. But I doubt it. Men like Pepe live fast and die young. It's the only way quiet sober folk like us have a chance to keep a sane world." With a smile and a nod the elegant old man strolled away.

"Ay, me," sighed Father Zacaya to himself. "It's much worse than I thought. And all I can do is guard a statue and wait."

He waited two weeks, during which time he saw the valley men come to the church every day. Candles were lit in front of all the saints and there was much praying. There was always someone kneeling at the rail staring up at the patron of the valley —the Blessed Lady of the Miraculous Tear, where she stood enthroned in her niche above the center of the altar. The men seemed to be praying to her in relays of one hour each, day and night. Even Pepe Gonzalez, who attended mass to wink at the girls rather than for his soul's salvation, faithfully served his turn.

Father Zacaya was pleased by this devotion until he received a note from the priest of San Juan Iglesias saying that his parish had suddenly turned pious, with a special affection for the Archangels Michael and Raphael. From that moment Father Zacaya worried in earnest. The girl in San Juan had mentioned a fight. What was the valley planning . . . a miniature frontier war? Surely Don Saturnino would not approve. And yet, he would not really interfere. He never interfered in anything. Don Rosalío said he used to be different. While Joaquín was home, Don Saturnino knew the troubles of every soul in the valley. Then Joaquín disappeared, and Don Saturnino changed. He wrapped his entire interest around his youngest child, Alejandro. And since Alejandro was safely away from the valley, Don Saturnino would not interfere with valley affairs.

Of course there was always Bob Webster. He might do something. But Pepe Gonzalez was a good friend of Bob's. And Pepe had a silver tongue. He could argue any man into anything.

Father Zacaya stood in front of the statue of Don Rómolo Balderas—once Julius Caesar—and asked the dead historian what deviltry was being committed in his name. But the placid brow below the laurel wreath did not wrinkle in answer.

"That Pepe Gonzalez is here," said his housekeeper from the doorway. "Do you want to see him in the dining room?"

Father Zacaya hurried into the room with the great fireplace, decorated with tiles that formed a mosaic of the life of that most noble knight of Mancha, Don Quixote.

"So, Pepe, you've come to tell me your secret at last."

The young man's eyes opened wide in limpid innocence. "I have few secrets from the world, Father."

"Perhaps," snorted the priest, sitting in a hand-carved chair, "but even the world keeps secrets these days."

Pepe shrugged. "To that I couldn't say, Father, but I come on an errand of curiosity."

"So?"

"The little Doctor says that you are skilled in dyeing the plumage of birds."

"It is my small hobby," agreed Father Zacaya, wondering what Pepe Gonzalez, who could not tell the difference between an oriole and a crow, wanted with such knowledge. "If you cared to see the canaries in the patio, I'd be glad to show them to you. With a canary, green is the most successful shade. Blue is a good color, too, but not purple. Birds do not look well in purple."

"What of a bird that is black—black with a greenish sheen? Could you change his color?"

Father Zacaya made a pyramid of his hands. A black bird with a greenish sheen. Where had he heard of such before? In San Juan Iglesias, Don Roméo Calderón had a . . . Father Zacaya put his tongue in his cheek. "It is possible," he admitted cautiously. "What color are you seeking?"

Pepe smiled blissfully over the vision in his mind. "Red, Father. A brilliant warrior's red."

"Hmmm," the priest leaned back in his chair and slowly crossed his knees. The relief from fear of a valley war made him slightly nauseated. "The bird in question—tell me. Is it about the length of a man's forearm?"

Pepe hesitated. Andrés Treviño had always insisted that Father Zacaya could read a man's mind, but Pepe had never believed it. Now he was doubting his cynicism. "Yes, Father."

"And weight about two kilos—a little more, perhaps?"

Pepe's eyes were everywhere in the room save on the priest's cameo face. "Yes, Father."

"So. A cockfight! After ten years of humane sport we descend again to the cockfight! Pepe, you know I don't approve. The entire valley knows—," he broke off and stared unseeingly through the long window to the tree-shaded patio with its tall cages of singing varihued canaries. His hand slapped the surface of the table. "Why, Pepe?"

Pepe Gonzalez, who would have laughed in the palm of Grandfather Devil, was frankly afraid of a priest's anger ever since that Sunday years ago when, in the midst of a sermon, Father Zacaya's predecessor had descended from the pulpit, abstracted Pepe's bean-shooter from his grimy, hot little hand, turned him across one knee, and soundly spanked him. So once more the story came tumbling forth, with firm deletions in the sections dealing with Sarita Calderón.

When he finished, the priest rose and began pacing slowly up and down the green-tiled floor. "And the girl?" he asked at last.

"What girl?" demanded Pepe quickly. No cynicism now. Andrés Treviño was right. Father Zacaya was truly gifted with the reading of minds.

"The girl with the white shawl—the girl in San Juan Iglesias. What about her?"

Pepe sighed and repeated his story, adding everything he had left out. There was no doubt, the strength of God was stronger than the strength of the Devil. The witches in the hills could speak the language of goats and coyotes, but they could not read the minds of men. Yet now this priest, with no difficulty at all, saw straight through Pepe's eyes to the face of Sarita Calderón.

Father Zacaya sat down again at the table. "What do you know, Pepe, of a statue of—of Julius Caesar?"

"I know nothing of statues, Father, except the new one in your hall. And you keep the base of it covered with paper so that none can read the name of the saint it represents."

"Julius Caesar was no saint, Pepe."

"I know that, Father. Did I not have two years of schooling at Austin, Texas? I was only repeating the story of Doña Diadema. Your housekeeper has a long tongue that swings constantly from right to left like a pendulum on a clock."

"Doña Diadema is a fine soul with no ambitions to disturb the bones of men buried in consecrated ground."

"Yes, Father."

"I'll remember this conversation at your next confession. Ten days' penance will be hardly enough to cover the range of your sins."

"No, Father."

"You should have told me about this cockfight at once."

"Yes, Father."

"Cockfights are wicked and terrible things."

"They are indeed, Father." Pepe looked virtuously at a fireplace tile showing Don Quixote tilting with a windmill. "But this is for a good cause. The settling of a feud is a fine thing."

"A feud is a wicked and terrible thing."

"Precisely, Father." Pepe beamed at the white-haired priest. "There have been holy feuds, Father. Perhaps there can be holy cockfights?" He left the suggestion dangling in the air. The moment of decision had arrived. They looked at each other, Pepe impishly, the priest with resignation. "Pepe, Pepe," thought the priest. "Pepe of the silver tongue." He said aloud, "I don't approve, but I am only a man. Perhaps the thought behind this deed is better than the deed itself. It is a noble thing to settle a feud between two valleys."

"It is indeed, Father."

"Of course your noble motive is rather on the selfish side. But it needed a Judith to conquer Holofernes, and I suppose it needs a Sarita Calderón to settle the bones of a man who never harmed anyone until he made the mistake of dying on the wrong side of the mountains."

"Yes, Father," muttered Pepe helplessly. He was not quite sure what Judith had to do with Sarita, but Father Zacaya was given to strange parallels.

"Why are you standing there, stupid as the brothers in front of Joseph? Go out and get the rooster. It takes a week to properly change the color of a bird's feathers, and if this bird is truly vicious, the work must be slow and cautious. Go and get him!"

"Yes, Father!" Pepe ran out of the room and through the hall, passing the statue of Julius Caesar without even a flickering smile for the sternly carved features that were now labeled "Don Rómolo Balderas."

A cockpit with an earth-packed floor was laid out by Don Serapio of Hidalgo and Don Roméo of San Juan Iglesias. Each man worked efficiently on his own side of the lime-washed line that marked the division, high in the mountains, between the two valleys. Ten years before, Don Timotéo Gonzalez had drawn that line and then sat on his own side, eating one of his famous cheeses and muttering curses on the Valley of the Three Marys between bites, while across from him sat Don Roméo, hunched up like one of his own cocks and muttering little sounds very close to the crowing of a bird as it prepares to attack the enemy. Twice a year since then, the line had been repainted: in January by Hidalgo men, in June by the men of San Juan Iglesias.

The line was clear and white today, and Don Serapio and Don Roméo were very careful to put not so much as a toe across it. The new ropes enclosing the pit were dipped in water and then looped around four giant *yuca* trees. When the sun came out, the ropes would dry and pull firm and tight. A space was cleared on Don Roméo's side for the orchestra that would play the music for Sarita's dancing when the fight was done. The red blood in the pit had to be pounded into the earth by the stamping feet of a virgin so that the crops would be fertile and rich at the November harvesting.

At four that afternoon the people of the two valleys began the slow climb over mountain trails to the meeting place. Some walked, some rode on horses, some on the rumps of little donkeys. A few of the more courageous sprawled up the stone-broken slopes that rose straight from the narrow cañon floor.

And as the people came, they sang. They sang of Pancho who went off to market to buy a shawl for his sweetheart. They sang of the deer who came shyly down to drink from the streams by day, and to court his sweetheart by night. They sang of the palm trees and the flowing rivers and the roses of the Blessed Virgin.

They sang sad tales of false love in merry rhythms, and dolefully referred to a certain Doña Clara, who, if she were not dead, was living still. The mountains caught the words and tunes and tossed them back again, so that there was no melody anywhere, but clashing sound.

The moment the people of the two valleys caught sight of each other the singing ceased and the insults began.

"Men of Hidalgo," shouted the blacksmith from San Juan Iglesias, "where did you ever find a cock to match one of Don Roméo's birds?"

"We had him as a gift from the mountain eagles," retorted Rubén, the maker of candy.

"Our bird has won five mains," came from the Three Marys side.

"Ours has vanquished birds from Matamoros to Mazatlán," called out the little Doctor, and there was a roar of laughter from the Sabinas Valley men.

This laughter worried the Three Marys' crowd. The good humor that enveloped their enemy was a sign of trickery, for the Sabinas people were true devils, as all the world knew, and given to villainous acts, as witness their efforts to steal the bones of Don Rómolo Balderas from sanctified ground. No one but grandsons of the hill witches would contemplate such an abomination. These and other things the people of the Three Marys muttered among themselves as Father Zacaya stepped into the cockpit. When the last echoing murmur died away, he raised his hand and implored the Beautiful Mother to enfold the two valleys in Her blue robe and store them away for safe-keeping in the Sacred Ribs of Her Son. Then he retreated to the Sabinas Valley side, and Don Nacho, flanked by Don Rosalío and Bob Webster, came forward. In his booming voice, which resounded in echoing spirals down the length of the cañon, he repeated Hidalgo's challenge to the men of San Juan Iglesias. Their fat mayor, perspiring more than ever, accepted the challenge. Don Nacho suggested Abel, the *árabe* trader, as the master of the fight —the one man in the past ten years who had known the freedom of both valleys. Abel, the *árabe*, having been accepted by San Juan Iglesias, now entered the pit as the other men retired.

"Hear me, my friends," he yelled, shaking his clasped hands over his head. "This fight shall consist of a single cocking-main between two noble birds: Satan, the brother of Satan, from the corrals of San Juan Iglesias, and ..." Abel paused and frowned in sudden bewilderment. "Eh, Pepe," he called, "you forgot to tell me the name of your bird."

In one voice the people of the Sabinas Valley answered him, "The Conqueror of the World."

Abel sighed and turned back to his task of announcing. It was such incidents as these that hurt his pride. For seven years he had served the valleys faithfully and well, but to them he was an outlander and not to be trusted with important matters unless he was peculiarly gifted for the job, as in the case of tacking up the challenge posters.

"Very good!" he shouted. "The Conqueror of the World from the corrals of Hidalgo. Are you ready, San Juan Iglesias?"

"We are ready," came the answer in loud chorus.

"Are you ready, Hidalgo?"

"We are ready," chanted the second chorus.

"Men of San Juan, name your setter-to."

The crowd to the east of the dividing line opened a path, and Don Roméo Calderón came to the pit, carrying a basket filled with softly stirring hay.

"I am the setter-to," he announced, placing the basket on the ground between his feet.

"Men of Hidalgo, name your setter-to."

The crowd to the west of the dividing line opened a path, and Pepe Gonzalez came to the pit. He, also, was carrying a basket. "I am the setter-to."

"Very good. Both of you know the rules. The birds may not be touched after being set down in the pit. If one bird refuses the challenge, he may be set breast to breast with his adversary in the pit's center. If he still refuses to fight, he will be regarded as defeated."

"My bird will fight," said Pepe confidently.

"And mine," growled Don Roméo.

"This main will be fought to the death. On the spurs of the survivor will ride one of two things: the fine cheese of Hidalgo, or the bones of Don Rómolo Balderas. It is agreed?"

"Agreed," said Pepe quickly.

After a moment's hesitation, Don Roméo muttered, "Agreed."

"Is the virgin ready for the stamping of the blood?"

"I am ready," called Sarita Calderón. She pushed her way forward, her small feet in green velvet slippers sliding on the rocks of the trail. Abel lifted her over the ropes into the pit, and stepped back so that everyone could see her. Her white blouse was heavy with brilliant embroidery. Her red flannel skirt hung in heavy folds under the weight of metal sequins that cascaded in glittering design from the green satin sash to the white lace hem. To each slender heel was fastened a tiny silver spur that tinkled like bells at her every movement.

With a graceful swoop she lifted her skirts in a wide arc, the orchestra played the applause music, and the sun glinted on her black braids fastened to the top of her head with red, white, and green striped ribbon. Abel locked both hands at her waist and, raising her above his head, carried her around the pit while the crowds on both sides shouted and whistled and clapped enthusiastically. Then he deposited her gently in the orchestra's cleared space, where she would be ready to enter the pit the moment the fight was finished. He held up his hands for silence. The heavy breathing of the spectators was the only sound.

"Don Roméo Calderón, show your bird."

Slowly and gently Don Roméo slid his hands into the hay of the basket and drew out a bronze cock with a short, red comb and long, sharp spurs. The wind of breath sharpened to a whistle. Here was a mighty bird, a king of killers, a vital viciousness. The pride of Don Roméo flowed through his hands to the cock. There was a fluffing of the neck ruff, a spreading of the wings. Satan, Brother of Satan, was crowing his challenge to the enemy.

The young Xavier put his fingers to his mouth and gave a shrill whistle. "What bird is this?" he cried in his clear treble. "Is this fight of so little account that you leave your best bird safe with your flock?"

"This is my best bird," snapped Don Roméo, quieting the jerking cock with gentle movements of his hands.

Bob Webster and the young Xavier put their heads close together in muttered conversation, and then Bob made a trumpet of his hands and called defiantly, "Then what of the black-feathered Satan, the same that you call the Conqueror of the North? The same that is famous in Monterrey and in Laredo? The black bird with the green shining wings? Where is the great Satan?" As his voice rose to a climax the Sabinas men suddenly burst into loud guffaws, and slapped each other on the back. Don

Rosalío, alone of all that crowd, recognized the importance of that speech. For the first time since Bob had come to the valley, he spoke with a Mexican, not a North American, mind. In that moment Bob Webster truly became a part of the valley.

But Don Roméo Calderón was unaware of this as he thrust out his lower lip, his eyes gleaming with hatred. "You know well enough that Satan, my lovely bird, was stolen by the eagles."

"The same eagles that gave us our cock?" taunted Rubén, the candy-maker. Again the people around him laughed.

Don Roméo looked perplexedly at his own adherents, who were moving jerkily with worry. "Enough of this," muttered Sarita's father. "If you have a bird, show him. This bird of mine will vanquish any you have to offer."

"Pepe Gonzalez, show your bird," chanted Abel.

Pepe bent over so that his body hid his bird until his arms lifted it above his head. Beak and comb and feet and spurs, shortened tail and sloped wings, throat and back and puffing breast were all the same shade—a brilliant, eye-filling crimson.

An angry shout rose from the men of the Three Marys. "What trick is this? The bird is dyed."

"Shall the Conqueror of the World show his wounds?" Pepe yelled above the shouting. "If he must die, he would die in the fullness of his blood. If he triumphs, he would triumph in the fullness of his perfection."

"Our bird will leave yours redder than any crimson," snorted the blacksmith of San Juan.

Pepe honored him with an amused bow and glanced with a sidewise grin at Sarita, but the girl, her eyes fixed on the dyed splendor in his hands, was obviously worried. She seemed almost on the verge of tears. Pepe, for the first time, felt apprehension. Could Don Roméo's bird actually be good enough to conquer the far-famed Satan? After all, Don Roméo was the finest trainer of fighting cocks on the entire frontier.

But he had little time for worry. Abel, who had been nervously eyeing one of the tall *yucas* and wondering if it would give him shelter in case trouble started, loosened the collar at his neck and came forward again.

"Bronze bird and red bird, prepare yourselves. Setters-to, are you ready?"

"We are ready," answered Don Roméo and Pepe Gonzalez almost in unison.

Abel vaulted over the ropes beside Sarita and glared sternly around at the whispering crowds, who quieted down in expectant silence. "Set your birds!"

Filling their mouths with water, the two men blew a fine spray under the wings of their cocks. Then Don Roméo carefully lowered his bronze beauty to the floor of the pit. His hand covered the beak, pointing it gently towards Pepe who was doing the same for his scarlet masterpiece. For a moment the men remained in position, secretly muttering their private prayers: Don Roméo to Blessed Michael, Archangel; Pepe to the Blessed Lady of the Miraculous Tear. Defeat in this battle meant more than the loss of the cheese trade or a dead man's bones. It meant facing the mocking laughter of the whole frontier.

The two men relaxed and stepped out of the pit. The birds shook their plumage, and with little circling detours, approached each other. Neck feathers rose in a high ruff. Three-toed feet lifted in prancing jumps, heads stretched out with small black eyes evilly glittering. The wings spread wide, the feathers stiff and tense. They were too wary. Something was obviously wrong. The vicious forward jump, the snap of breast against breast, the spur-tearing leap into the air, were absent. Satan, the Brother of Satan, seemed dazzled by the crimson splendor of his adversary, and the Conqueror of the World appeared to be waiting for something. Pepe glanced again at Sarita. Her eyes had widened and her lips were parted with apprehension. Pepe felt a hard lump forming in his throat which made swallowing difficult. These were surely the two greatest fighting birds in the Republic. What had happened to them?

The two crowds were beginning to mutter. Finally the cries came thick and fast. "Abel, give them the warning. We came here to see a fight, not a round dance."

At a nod from Abel, Pepe and Don Roméo climbed into the pit and snatched up their birds with practiced quickness. Once more fingers probed gently into soft feathers while hands covered the beaks. Then the cocks were set breast to breast and the two men hurriedly retreated to their places outside the ropes.

There was a plumping of plumage, a shaking of trained bodies.

Then, from the Conqueror of the World's scarlet beak came a gentle crow, while from Satan, the Brother of Satan, came a jerky cooing sound. Beaks rubbed affectionately against arched necks. As far as the two cocks were concerned, they were simply two brothers meeting after a long separation.

A wail of rage went up from the startled, staring crowd. Don Roméo caught up the crimson bird. For a long moment he glared at an astonished Pepe and then, with slow deliberation, he pulled a tail feather from the Conqueror of the World. Where the red dye ended there was a streak of black tinged with green. "Satan," he whispered, "my little beauty." Then, conscious of the feather's significance, he flung back his head. "Mine!" he shrieked. "Mine! From my own corral! You, Pepe Gonzalez— thief, robber, stealer of helpless birds!"

Dropping the cock, he flung himself on Pepe, his small body leaping into the air like the launched attack of one of his own birds. He beat against Pepe's shoulders and chest with clenched fists. Pepe staggered backwards under the blows, but his hands, clenched at his sides, did not come up to defend himself. No one else moved. Too stupefied with surprise, the people of the two valleys were silent as the little man struck again and again at the tall slender boy. Then Sarita, with a mewing scream, scrambled through the ropes and snatched at her father's back. "Stop it. Stop it!"

"Let go of me!" Don Roméo slapped at her, but Sarita dodged the blow, and tightened her fingers on her father's coat. She dragged it down so that his arms were locked in the folds of the sleeves.

"How can he defend himself, and you my father?"

"What has that to do with it?" roared Don Roméo, his face scarlet with fury.

Free of his tormentor, Pepe Gonzalez, white to the lips, automatically straightened his tie and pushed his pulled-out shirt into his trousers.

"I gave him the cock." Sarita's chin went up and she stared defiantly at her father.

"You gave it to him!" Don Roméo smacked his open palm against his forehead. "By all the saints who walk the streets of Heaven, why?"

"You told me to."

"I—I—I told you—" Don Roméo's voice was visible in a spray of fine mist.

"You certainly did. 'When she goes to her marriage,' you've said with your own mouth many a time, 'my Sarita will take to her man the finest cock in my corral.'"

"Marriage," whispered Don Roméo.

"Marriage," gasped the crowd from the Three Marys.

"Marriage," yelled the crowd from Sabinas.

"Yes," cried Sarita's clear voice above the uproar. "On Sunday the first banns will be read in the church. And three weeks from this day, book and candle will bless my womb at the marriage altar."

"You will stand on my dead body." Don Roméo was almost voiceless with rage.

"Your own hand will give me to him," said Sarita Calderón.

"May I never be buried in consecrated ground, may the eagles eat from my skull, may the seven fiends of Hell dance on my soul before..."

"One moment," said Pepe sharply, "I've taken your words and I've taken your blows, and now I'll take your daughter. By the five wounds of God, I swear it!"

When he had drawn sufficient breath to speak, Don Roméo thrust out his chin in caricature of his daughter Sarita. "You'll have to climb a convent wall to reach her."

"People of Sabinas," cried Pepe, "I ask you. Have I the right to this woman or not?"

"Yes!" yelled the people of Sabinas.

"No!" howled the people of the Three Marys.

"I am the bride," said Sarita, "and I have the right to say."

"You are a woman," called out old Tío Daniel, "and the words should be dry in your throat."

"Dry it for me," snapped Sarita, "and hear my words. Either I marry Pepe or no man."

"Just a moment," said Father Zacaya, pushing his way into the pit. The sight of his black robes brought an uneasy silence, for the wrath of a priest could be a terrible thing. But he was not angry, only curious. He went to Sarita, and tilted her head back so that he could look into her eyes. "There is a certain statue that stands in my house, my daughter. What has it to do with today's affairs?"

"Ay!" Sarita's hand flew to her mouth. "The statue!" Suddenly her large black eyes brimmed with tears and she sank to her knees, her wide skirt billowing around her in a glittering thick red cloud.

"Sarita!" Pepe pushed past the two men and bent over her. "Do not cry, my little dove."

"The beautiful statue," wailed Sarita. "And all that money—fifty pesos."

"The gardens in your eyes," crooned Pepe, stroking her glossy black braids. "All the flowers in your eyes will wilt with the tears. Do not cry, my *Norteña.*"

"Fifty pesos?" snapped Don Roméo. "A statue? What nonsense is this?"

Sarita caught Pepe's wrist in both her hands and looked imploringly up at him. "Forgive me, Pepe. Please forgive me."

Pepe and Father Zacaya looked at each other with the expressions of men who have never understood women. "Forgive you for what, my beautiful?"

"My father's roosters. They are trained to love each other. It has been on my conscience like a black mountain storm. Please, Pepe..." Her voice sank as she saw his rising anger.

"You knew? From the beginning you knew...Sarita! You knew, and you let me...In the eyes of the world I am a fool, Hidalgo is a fool, the whole Sabinas Valley..." He jerked away from her and stood up. His face was whiter than it had been when Don Roméo was beating at him. He walked in frozen anger to the pit ropes. Sarita came to her feet in a single movement and ran after him. She flung her arms around him from the back, clung to him. His body went rigid, and the muscles under her cheek were hard and unyielding.

"Please, Pepe. Listen to me."

He did not answer, but merely stood there waiting for her to release him. Weariness flooded through him. The excitement of the past two months was gone, and he felt tired and empty.

"The roosters must be taught to love each other, or the flock would destroy itself. My father has to separate them and teach them to hate each other before they can be matched in the pit."

When he said nothing, she continued desperately, "I didn't mean to betray you, Pepe, I swear it. Please turn around. Please look at me."

Pepe's voice crackled like dry paper. "Why do you hold me? Why don't you go back to your house and laugh at the poor fools of Hidalgo with all your friends? You have won. The bones of Don Rómolo are safe in your sainted ground. No Sabinas man can ever again claim them with honor. Isn't that enough?"

"No! When you told me your plan—when you said you were going to dye the bird—I thought they would fight. And they were kept apart so long. I thought they would fight. You—you didn't give me time that night to really think about it, but afterwards I was afraid. You must believe me, Pepe. I was afraid my father had a secret way of training them—something I didn't know. That's why I bought the statue. Don't you see, Pepe, that—"

"I have heard enough," interrupted Pepe wearily. "What do words count for now?" As he started to crawl through the ropes, Father Zacaya stopped him.

"One moment, my son. Let us hear more of this statue. I, at least, would like to know the reason for it."

"I said to myself," sobbed Sarita, " 'What difference does it make where Don Rómolo is buried? The man is dead. The bones are not the man.' "

A low murmur of anger came from the two crowds at this blasphemy, but it died away at Father Zacaya's upraised hand.

"Continue, Sarita."

"My father took me for a visit to Monterrey. There on the plaza I saw the statue of Father Hidalgo. That great man is buried in the South, but the people of Monterrey do not care. They have his statue to remind them of the days when he preached in San Fernando Cathedral. And I thought that if money from San Juan Iglesias bought a statue and gave it to the village of Hidalgo, it wouldn't matter if the cocks didn't fight. But I was wrong!" Her voice cracked with tears. Her head drooped into her hands.

"Don Roméo," snapped Tío Daniel, "you should lock this girl safe in a convent to save the world from women's brains."

Sarita paid him no attention. She was looking imploringly at Pepe, her eyes begging him to understand. "Please, Pepe. Don't you see? If Hidalgo has a statue, what difference does it make if San Juan has the bones? Why can't he belong to both of us?"

Pepe could feel it as he had felt it so many times before in arguments. This was the moment. From it events would flow in one direction or another. He knew that everyone was watching him: the people of Sabinas, the people of the Three Marys. And even as he knew this, a certainty came to him, and he realized that he was no longer Pepe, the wild one, but a man grown. Life flowed into his face again and he spread his arms in a wide gesture that commanded attention from the muttering crowds. "Listen to me, you people. The feud between the two valleys is a stupid thing. This cockfight was not enough. I realize that now. Suppose we had won—or the men of San Juan Iglesias. The anger would still be there, worse even on the part of the loser."

"True words!" called out Don Timotéo in sudden defense of his son.

"And it would be a stupid anger," continued Pepe, caught in the surge of his thinking, "because Don Rómolo doesn't belong to Hidalgo."

"What's that?" gasped the Sabinas men. The people of the Three Marys were open mouthed in astonishment.

"Nor," said Pepe flatly, "does he belong to San Juan Iglesias. He's bigger than the towns or the valleys. He's bigger than the whole frontier. Don Rómolo belongs to the Republic." They were coming now, the silver words. Pepe felt secure again. He could argue Grandfather Devil out of an eon in Hell. All the world said so. This was the true way for him to settle the feud: with fighting words, not fighting cocks. And for the first time he felt a strength in himself that came from his own belief in what he was saying. "Don Rómolo belongs to the people of the southern states: to Jalisco, and Aguas Calientes and—Michoacán, yes, and to Yucatán and Vera Cruz just as much as to our Nuevo León. What right have we in our littleness to say, 'This man is ours!' Of course he is ours. But he is the Republic's, too. All these ten years while he has been sitting up there in Heaven with Father Hidalgo and Don Benito Juarez and the great Cuauhtemoc, how ashamed he must have been of us while he looked down on our petty little feud. How do we know but that he entered into these cocks, forcing them to remember each other and teach us a lesson in—in brotherly love."

"Oh, Pepe," breathed Sarita, gazing up at him with misty adoration. "How wonderful you are."

His smile brought her answering smile. "And, Pepe, you do forgive me?"

"Naturally," snapped Don Timotéo, crawling through the ropes. "You thought of the statue, didn't you? I think I can safely speak for the Sabinas Valley." He carefully took a large red handkerchief liberally sprinkled with yellow polka-dots from his pocket and carefully unfolded it. The eyes of the two crowds followed his actions with hypnotic attention. "At least I can speak for myself, and I the maker of the finest goat cheese on the frontier. Give us the statue and you can have the cheese trade." He took a deep breath and then violently blew his nose.

"On two conditions," snapped Don Roméo, stalking forward on his short legs. "First, the statue must be paid for by the entire Valley of the Three Marys . . ."

"Agreed," shouted his own people.

"And secondly," said Don Roméo firmly, "I want to learn the secret of dyeing birds. This crimson joy, my sweet Satan, now has a color to match his courage. And," he added in a half mutter, "my cocks are all that are left to me now that I have lost my daughter."

Sarita gave a half sob and flung her arms about her father's neck. Pepe grinned and patted Don Roméo on the shoulder. Don Timotéo blew his nose again. All the people were laughing and shouting pleasant phrases across the stretched ropes of the cockpit. Then Father Zacaya pulled his rosary from his pocket.

"On your knees, men of the Three Marys. And you, men of Sabinas, on your knees. Today is a great day in our history, and this is a time for prayer."

One by one at first, and then in little groups, the people knelt on the hard rocks of the trails. The priest lifted a handful of dust and sprinkled it over the white line that divided the two valleys. "Tomorrow," he said firmly, "Don Serapio can blot out this line. There is no more need of it." He fingered his rosary and lifted his face to the white and blue striped awning of cloud and sky. The mountains caught his voice and tossed it through the cañon. "Hail, Mary, full of grace," said Father Zacaya. "Full of grace," echoed the mountains. Far away the notes of a conch shell, calling the goats to home corrals from the twilight chill floated toward them. There was peace once more in the valleys.

Plaza of the Viceroys

December, 1891—February, 1923

The greatest danger is the danger a man fears least.
                                    —Mexican proverb

HIDALGO WAS A TOWN THAT LOVED GOSSIP. IN THE AFTER-noons the women would sit on straight chairs in front of the church doors, skirts spread about them, their prayer shawls easy on their shoulders, crochet hooks flashing in their fingers, and talk. In the evenings, men would gather in little groups on the plaza, or sit in chairs tilted back against house walls, and they, too, would talk. The little Doctor said in disgust one day that the village was nothing but one big mouth. But the little Doctor, too, liked his glass of wine, his domino game, and the gossip of his three cronies.

No one was safe from the chattering lips. Don Saturnino Castillo in his grandeur, Doña Nimfa, the herb woman from the *Gallineros*, even the priest—the rich, the poor, the religious, were dissected every day. There were certain ones of course who were natural subjects for gossip. María of the River Road, the wild young Pepe Gonzalez (tamed now by marriage), the secretive Widow Valdez, Bob Webster, Porfirio, the lover of money, these were the most often discussed. At one time or another every soul in Hidalgo was the subject of speculative conversation.

But one pair of names which were rarely mentioned were Rubén's and Lolita's. The candy-maker and his wife seldom joined in the town's activities. He was generally busy in the kitchen making his wares, and his wife had to take care of their young son Gitanillo, and of her father Don Cardito, who was an invalid. Lolita and her father Don Cardito were not, strictly speaking, of Hidalgo. They were Tejanos, people of Mexican ancestry born in Texas. But the great San Antonio flood of 1921 had left them homeless and penniless, and they had been forced to return to Monterrey to the niece of Don Cardito. This niece was married to Rubén's cousin. Through him Rubén had met Lolita, married her, and brought her and her father to Hidalgo in 1923.

The town's people had at first enjoyed listening to Don Cardito's terror-filled story of the flood that had inundated the largest city in Texas. But with the passing years, the stories grew a bit monotonous. They were always so completely the same.

"It's remarkable," Bob Webster told Alejandro Castillo. "The old man never varies. Even repeats the same words, have you noticed?"

"He's told them so much," Alejandro said lightly, "that the stories have ceased to be true to him and have become inventions."

Alejandro was wrong. Don Cardito had told inventions so much that they had become true to him. Because the truth was that

Don Cardito on the morning of September 10, 1921, the day the San Antonio River rose in flood, had never heard of San Antonio. It was Rubén's cousin who suggested the flood story, and Rubén who devised a plausible tale for his father-in-law to tell. Through those terrible days Lolita sat quietly, her eyes fixed on Rubén, allowing him to think for her, to do all that was necessary to take her out of one life and place her in another. And not once, then or later, did it ever occur to any of them: to Don Cardito, nor Rubén, nor Lolita herself, that Lolita might be considered Rubén's mistress. She was his wife in the sight of God, if not in the eyes of the church, and when her baby was born, Father Zacaya baptized it with no thought of illegitimacy in his mind. He did think it strange that the child was named Gitanillo, which is a way of saying Gypsy, but the priest was used to such names as Pío Nono, Santito, and Nimfa, which slide into natural speech as Pious the Ninth, little saint, and nymph; so to call a child Gypsy was not indicative of anything strange.

Thus the greatest mystery in Hidalgo continued its placid course, and the chattering tongues were kind to Lolita and her Rubén. If Tía Magdalena knew that once a year Lolita went into the mountains to dance the witch's dance, Tía kept the information to herself, since those who deal with witches must walk carefully in christian towns. And if Bob Webster or Alejandro Castillo noticed anything strange about Lolita's appearance, they never mentioned it, for they were not the type of men who discuss women. And even if they had spoken of it, their knowledge of gypsies was far too slight to allow them to place the strange race strain they sensed in her.

For Lolita's mother had been a gypsy woman from one of those wandering tribes that sometimes can be seen on the frontier roads in December. She was a stocky, full-bosomed creature with the straight black hair, velvet eyes, and long hands of her race. Don Cardito saw her near the bull ring in Monterrey, standing with that proud aloofness so typical of gypsies. Her contempt for the arena crowd from whom she was begging money was so apparent that it both amused and attracted him. His work in the ring with the *banderillas** was very bad that afternoon, and the matador cursed him roundly when the *corrida* was over, but Don

* Darts with steel points which are stuck by the *banderillero* (also called *peón*) in the bull's back near the shoulder blades.

Cardito, who, like most *peones* (*banderilleros*) was badly paid, merely shrugged and went off to find the gypsy girl.

He found her in the *Café de los Toros*, a small, dingy eating house patronized almost exclusively by bullfighters and their women during the fighting season of November and December in Monterrey. She was standing near the badly tuned piano, singing a song of the arena in her hoarse, throaty voice:

> *When my lover takes the sword in his hand*
> *I want to die.*
> *All the women throw him flowers.*
> *I want to kill the women.*
> *What do they know of the torment in my heart?*
> *I watch my lover face the black bull of death,*
> *And death enters my heart.*

The room was small and hot, and the air was heavy with smoke, the dank sweat of humanity, and the full, rich flavor of food and wine. The only light came from candles stuck in bottles on the rough wooden tables. Cardito went to her, his eyes on her flat-cheekboned face. He knew that she was a gypsy, but it made no difference to him. Bullfighters take love where they find it, for what man can say when the sharp horns will rip out stomach or lungs?

He lit a cigarette for her and told her he was a *peón* in the retinue of the great Chato. She listened to him in silence while he spoke of the ring. He knew nothing else. He came from a family of fighters. None of them had true genius, but someday a genius would appear—perhaps Cardito's own son, for he would have a son. All the men in his family had sired many sons, legitimately and otherwise. Her red mouth curved in a faint smile, and she allowed the smoke to ooze from her nostrils, and still she said nothing.

"It is true I am nothing but a *peón*, always under orders," said Cardito, "but I have a certain talent with the *banderillas*, and I know bulls. I lack the wrists for a true matador. You can see, they are thick and slow." He thrust them out, but her eyes stayed on his face. He had a delicate, high-nosed face, with black hair that grew down in a peak on his forehead. She liked his face, so different from the sullen-browed, heavy faces of the gypsies.

For the first time Olalla spoke. "How long are you to stay in the North?"

"Three weeks with one week in Laredo. El Chato has good contracts."

She nodded slowly, already making plans. Three days later Cardito married her. Not in the church, since Olalla was a gypsy, but before the civil judge. Cardito, like most fighters, was very religious, and he considered this no marriage at all. And since there had been no gypsy ceremony, Olalla, too, felt free. But she had a legal hold on him and that was all she wanted. When he left her to go south again she gave him no tears, but promised to meet him in Vera Cruz when he returned in the fall from the spring and summer season in Spain.

When he arrived in Vera Cruz the following October he had almost forgotten her. He was sick with the bullfighter's greatest ailment, tuberculosis, and the doctors ordered him to a dry, warm climate. This, of course, was impossible. Cardito was a *peón* with no money save his small salary, which was paid only when his matador had a contract. He had to fight to keep from starving.

One November night when, half drunk, he staggered home to his small, bare room, he found a very old gypsy woman waiting for him. She held a small squirming bundle in her arms. She told him flatly that Olalla was dead, and the bundle was his child. The death of Olalla meant nothing to him, but the child... with a shout of joy he caught the crying creature in his arms. A son! Perhaps the genius his family had awaited so long.

The old woman showed toothless gums in a soundless laugh. "She has fine lungs, that one."

"She?" whispered Cardito. He tore at the rags and stared at the thin naked body. He cried in rage, "She is not mine! I refuse her. From my seed come sons!"

The woman hobbled closer to him, and pointed to the baby's head with a withered, dirty finger. "Look for yourself. You cannot deny her." On the small round head the black hair grew to a peak on the forehead.

Still clutching the child, Cardito sank into a chair. The old woman said, "Olalla was no fool. She married you in front of the judge. Everything that she has is yours. Gypsies want nothing from women who marry outside the race. The boy is in the patio. You can have him, too."

This was better, much better. It was only a gypsy joke to give him news of twins. Cardito rushed into the patio. There was no tiny baby anywhere, but playing by the fountain was a four-year-old boy, obviously a pure gypsy. When Cardito returned to his room, he found the old woman gone. He cursed steadily in three Spanish dialects, but a fit of blood-flecked coughing calmed him. So these gypsies thought they could palm off this bastard on him, did they? He'd take the brats, yes, both of them, to the nuns. He was a sick man with hardly enough money to keep himself alive. Why should he concern himself with gypsy offspring?

With the baby on his arm, and the boy's hand in his, they walked along the narrow street. The boy had Olalla's proud aloofness and her silence. The tiny fist was hot and soft in the man's hand. Cardito took long steps, and the little feet trotted unprotestingly beside him. As they passed the *Plaza de Toros* the child suddenly darted towards the entrance. When Cardito ran after him, the small body swerved so that Cardito missed him. The child laughed joyously. "Bull," he cried. "Bull! Bull!" Again Cardito lunged for him, and again he slid aside with beautiful precision and timing. Cardito paused and stared at him, really seeing him for the first time. Then he sat on the sidewalk, his chin propped on his hand, not speaking, not moving. When he rose he held out his hand, saying simply, "Come. We must go to bed early tonight. There is much to do tomorrow."

That night terminated Cardito's career in the ring. The next day he offered his services to the Rancho Santa Clara as a tester of their fighting bulls, provided the child could gain experience with the yearlings. Cardito was well known in the Republic to have a sound knowledge of bulls, and the ranch overseer was glad to hire him. And the child from the first showed what is called "genius" for the ring. The herdsmen enjoyed his sullen aloofness, and because Cardito had never made any effort to name him, they called him Gitanillo since he was so obviously a gypsy. The ranch women took care of Lolita until she was old enough to stumble after Gitanillo on small fat legs. When he was not with the bulls, he washed her and fed her and clothed her. It pleased his young arrogance to have so willing a slave, for Cardito, intent on the son who was not his son, paid little attention to her.

By the time Gitanillo was eight, he was a complete matador, well rounded and skillful. The herdsmen collected a purse among themselves and launched him on his ring career in Mexico City. The critics were more than kind. Child bullfighters are popular in the Republic, and Gitanillo was soon attracting the crowds, with contracts for Torreón and Monterrey. Cardito watched him carefully, ironing out faults almost before they appeared. The boy was that rarest of combinations: a born killer who could handle the cape like an artist. And Cardito had seen to it that his work with the *banderillas* was excellent. Very few matadors could use the *banderillas*. Even the great Spaniard, Juan Belmonte, hired a *peón* to place the darts. But in spite of this lack, Belmonte of the twisted deformed body was the very king of bullfighters. To train under him was a privilege any fighter might envy. And Belmonte was introducing a new technique with the cape that was threatening to upset all the older rules.*

"The moment of truth was in the death, now it is in the cape," said Cardito's friends, shaking their heads over the sweet days that were past. So Lolita, Cardito, and Gitanillo went to Spain.

Cardito wanted to apprentice Gitanillo to Belmonte as a *banderillero*, but Gitanillo was proud, and this stepping aside from the limelight as a matador irked him. Cardito ordered Lolita to try her influence.

Gitanillo adored Lolita. The delicate girl with the widow's peak growing low on her forehead was his only passion outside of the bull ring. He tolerated Cardito for a precise knowledge of bulls. But Lolita belonged to him. One winter she contracted Spanish influenza, and for that season he was no good in the ring.

"A man cannot have his mind in two places," Cardito shouted at him. "When you are in the ring, think of the bull, and the bull only! What difference if Lolita is sick? She will get well again."

Lolita recovered, but only because Gitanillo's money, which the ordinary matador spent on women and food, was paid to good doctors to cure her. The men in his train thought this a foolish expenditure. A bullfighter's life was too short to concentrate on anything but the pleasure of the moment. They could not understand the binding power of gypsy blood. Gitanillo was all gypsy, and Lolita only half, but that half came from the same mother. Naturally he was wildly jealous of her. He half killed one of his *peones* because the man mentioned her name in a café. He

* Juan Belmonte killed his first bull as an apprentice fighter July 24, 1910, but for the purpose of this story he has been placed earlier.

hired an old woman, one Doña Hermina, to chaperone her. Lolita led a life as secluded as any girl in a convent. But as far as material things were concerned, she had merely to express a wish for something to have it granted. Her closets were filled with expensive dresses. Her heavily embroidered *mantones* and sheer lace *mantillas* were the finest Spain could produce. Once she asked for peaches out of season, and a box was rushed from France by fast express. But she was never allowed to speak to any man save himself and Cardito. And she had to sit in the *barreras* * whenever he fought. He never dedicated a bull to her, he never glanced toward her, but he knew she was there.

That this was sheer torture for her never occurred to him. Bullfighters' women are rarely delicate, emotional creatures. Bullfighters want vital women with flashing white teeth and pliable bodies, who are interested only in the moment, not the outcome of tomorrow's fight. But once in a while they attach themselves to women who love them, and then their days as great fighters are finished. Either they must leave the ring, or the continued tears and pleading at home turn them into cowards, so that their feet dance away from the bull, and the crowd turns vicious, whistling in derision, throwing cushions and empty wine bottles that often fracture skulls. But gentle, clinging women were not for Gitanillo. He wanted women who could laugh with him, fight him, and bite at life with wild enthusiasm. Pleading and tears were not for him.

Lolita understood this and never wept in front of Gitanillo. She never pleaded with him. She, too, had the gypsy pride. Not even Doña Hermina was aware of the long hours the girl spent on her knees praying for Gitanillo's life, nor of the secret tears in the night. When she attended the fights, her face was as white and still as Gitanillo's own, and she had about her that same quality of death-awareness that only matadors have, for the matadors enter the ring never knowing whether they will emerge crippled for life, or perhaps dead. Even the greatest and most skilled have died on the sharp-pointed horns.

Up to the time when he went to fight in Spain at eighteen, Gitanillo was lucky. He had been tossed several times by bulls,

* The boxes closest to the presidential box. The most expensive seats in the ring. Also the name of the low wall in the arena behind which the matadors await their turns at the bulls.

but had never received a true *cornada* or horn wound. The critics were therefore inclined to be cynical about him, for a genius is never truly known until after he has been badly gored. Many an apparent genius turns into a coward after his first *cornada*, his feet taking him away from the horns in spite of his desperate determination to be brave. And no matter how intellectually brave he may be, the coward cannot maintain the constant artistic perfection demanded of the true genius. So Gitanillo was still on trial when he went to Spain.

And he considered Cardito's fears for him stupid. "I am a matador. I have been one since I was eight. Can you deny that I am an expert with the cape? Can you deny that I know bulls?"

"I deny nothing," said Cardito. "But you have fought small bulls—easy to handle. These large beasts are strange to you. And the new rules of the cape—they are strange, too. Serve this season with Belmonte. Next season, you can . . ."

"Belmonte!" interrupted Gitanillo. "The man's body is bent. Certainly he had to change the rules. He is too twisted to use the cape as it should be used. I am the greatest matador in Mexico . . ."

"A great matador in Mexico," said Cardito dryly, "is not a great matador in Madrid. Even Gaona * had to fight here before he was truly acclaimed. And as for you, remember, you have not stood the test of the *cornada*."

"Do you want me to fling myself on the bull, then? Should I gore myself so that all the world can say, 'Here is a brave man'? I am brave enough, I can tell you, *cornada* or no *cornada*."

"Who denies your bravery? But no matter how famous you are in Mexico, Spain has never heard of you. Luckily, Mexico has a great reputation for *banderilleros*. And Belmonte has no knowledge of the *banderillos*. He is anxious to have you in his following."

"I refuse!" snapped Gitanillo. "Nothing can change my mind. Nothing."

So Cardito went to Lolita. He explained the situation and she listened to him with her still, white face. After he left she sat by the window for a long time. To be a *banderillero* was dangerous. The *peones* needed strong legs and light feet to place the long wooden shafts with the steel points close together on the very

---

* Rodolfo Gaona, generally accepted as Mexico's greatest bullfighter. He was particularly talented with the cape.

top of the withers so that the prongs caught just under the skin. A *banderilla* that was thrust in too deeply so that the shaft stood upright, or one that was placed too far back, could injure the bull so that the matador had no chance to make a perfect kill. To place it properly, the *peón* stood with feet close together, body stretched high, and arms up and out. As the bull charged him head on, he thrust in the points and swayed to one side, allowing the animal to pass him. To be a good *banderillero* a man needed courage, grace, and complete body control. But the matadors were always there with the capes to take the bull away if need be. Whereas the matador went in alone to the kill. All of this was in Lolita's mind as she waited for Gitanillo.

When he entered, he was wearing his street cape, and carrying the high-crowned Spanish hat in his hands. His flat high-cheekboned face looked very brown from his hours in the sun, and his straight black hair was brushed back to end in the pigtail that was the caste mark of his profession. As he walked toward her, she looked at his fine body, wide at the shoulders, narrow at the hips, with the muscular legs and the easy grace of him, and her breath caught in her throat. She said with effort, "Gitanillo, when do you fight again?"

"I am waiting for Cardito to sign the contracts." He flung himself into a chair with his legs thrust awkwardly forward. Chairs were not made for him. He was built for action.

"Cardito says he wants you to join the followers of Belmonte."

Gitanillo stroked his strongly curved nose. "Cardito is a fool. I'm a matador, not a *peón*."

She clenched her fists in her silken lap, but her face was expressionless as she said, "To be a *banderillero* is a fine thing."

"Doubtless. But leave the *banderillas* to men who lack the wrists. I have good wrists," he added complacently, admiring them and the long supple fingers. When his ice-blue eyes looked up again, he saw her black eyes with the terror in them.

"Eh, Lolita," he bent forward and reached out to touch her, then drew back. She was always so fragile to him that it seemed as though a too rough touch would injure her. "What is it, little one? What do I read in your face?"

Her lips closed convulsively. She was making a desperate effort not to cry, but the tears betrayed her and slid over the lids down her cheeks.

The sight horrified him. He had never seen her tears before. "Lolita! By the grace of God!" He flung himself on his knees beside her. "What is it, my little one? Who has hurt you?"

She rested her hand on his thick black hair. "No one, Gitanillo. No one."

"But you are weeping. What do you want? Name it! Anything! Anything! But do not weep!"

"Anything, Gitanillo?" Her hand slid over his hair and touched the pigtail. "Anything?"

"Yes, Lolita. I cannot bear the tears in your eyes."

To her imagination it seemed that the moment was suspended between them. The pigtail curled in her palm like a living thing. She knew that she had only to ask him, and he would never re-enter the bull ring. And she knew that if she asked it, he would die. He loved her with his heart, but his soul belonged to the blood-drenched sand and shining horns. Slowly her palm fell away from his hair.

"Gitanillo, it isn't enough to be a good matador. I want you to be a great one. Belmonte is the greatest in Madrid, which means the world. He has so much to offer you. Go with him for a year, and then people will say, 'Who is Belmonte? If you want great fighting, Gitanillo is the man.' Is that not worth a year?"

"It means so much to you—my going with Belmonte?"

For a vivid moment she saw him as the matador leaning in for the kill across the top of the horns. She saw the horns come up, his body rise high in the air to come down broken and still in the arena. To banish the vision she shut her lids tightly. "Yes, it means so much."

"Very well, little sister. If that is what you want." He bent his head over her lap, and in a gesture rare for him, kissed her fingers. "But you will not weep any more?"

"No, Gitanillo. I will not weep any more."

So the Mexican boy entered the retinue of Belmonte. He watched the master's technique carefully—the slow-moving veronica, that graceful half turn with the cape caught firmly in both hands as St. Veronica holds the napkin of Christ in the sacred pictures; the *paso de rodillas,* where the fighter goes down on his knees and passes the bull with the short cape on the wooden sword, called the *muleta;* the use of the *muleta* itself to draw the bull out, step by step, until that perfect moment for the kill. He studied the man's sinister grace until he knew his technique better than Belmonte himself. And when the season was over, Gitanillo took Lolita to the town of Ronda before they started on the long trip to Mexico.

Ronda was built for lovers. The scenery is not scenery but a background for the people who walk through it. Mountains encircle it, and a great gorge cuts through the town to end in a high cliff that drops sheer to the river. Beauty is everywhere and lovers come to it naturally. But Gitanillo did not think of the lovers when he took Lolita there. He wanted to see it because it was the cradle of bullfighting, and the highest tribute a critic could pay a fighter was to say "He comes from Ronda."

They stayed at a fine hotel, and in the lavender dusk they wandered through the town that still celebrates the triumph of Ferdinand and Isabella the Catholics over the Moors in 1490. Lolita, white lace *mantilla* over her hair, walked beside him, and her hand resting easily on his arm.

"It is all so beautiful, so old," she whispered.

"Not so old as Mexico City," he said coldly.

She glanced sideways at him and laughed. "How Mexican you are, Gitanillo."

"No," he said slowly after a pause. "No, you are wrong, Lolita. You and I—we are gypsies."

"Mexican gypsies."

He shook his head. "Like the Jews, we have no country. But the Jews can go in and become a part of the country they choose. Not gypsies. We never belong to any country. We are the true wanderers."

"There are many Spanish gypsies," she protested.

"Yes. And when I am with them, I feel at home. And when I am gone from them..."

He paused so long that she prompted gently, "Yes?"

"I feel at home, too." He laughed suddenly, and she smiled in response. As though to echo them, a passing young couple laughed. She looked after them wistfully.

"How happy they are. Doña Hermina told me this morning that they came here on their honeymoon."

"Doña Hermina had no right to speak of such things to you!" He was so vehement that he startled her.

"Why, Gitanillo, what is wrong? Is it not natural to marry?"

"For them, perhaps. Not for you!"

"But, why, Gitanillo?"

He drew her to a bench and sat down beside her. He bent forward so that his face was half hidden by the turn of his shoulder. "I don't want you to ever marry."

His harsh tone filled her with a vague uneasiness. "As you wish, Gitanillo."

"No." He half turned his head toward her. "It is easy for you to speak now. You are not in love. Later, it will not be so easy."

"Please, Gitanillo. You frighten me when you speak like that . . ."

"I want to frighten you!" He turned quickly so that he half knocked against her. She drew back from him, surprise flooding her face. "Yes, it is necessary. I told you we are gypsies. You'll never find happiness except with a gypsy. And I forbid you to marry one. I forbid you."

Her question came on a breath of sound. "Why?"

He shrugged and looked at the ground again. "Gypsies are poor husbands. They are brutal and cruel. They will destroy you."

"I am only half a gypsy, Gitanillo."

"Yes, half. But you are all mine. And I won't share you with anyone. If a man touched you, I'd kill him."

"Gitanillo!"

"It's true." This time he stared straight into her eyes. His own blue eyes were wide and intent, and the nostrils flared with passion. "You are the only thing that I own. What difference does it make to you if I am Gitanillo, the fighter, or Gitanillo, the shoeblack? You are my security. Let the rest of the world whisper their little praises. If I died in the ring tomorrow, the world would not weep. But you would weep, Lolita, because you are mine. Mine! No one shall ever take you from me. Swear to me that you will never marry. Swear it!"

She started to flare out against him, and then the agony in him flowed from his body into hers. From her earliest days she had worshipped her brother with that blind devotion the weak have for the strong. All their lives the gifts had come from Gitanillo to Lolita. She could not refuse him the first request he had ever made of her. She caught her lower lip between her teeth and bit down on it until a drop of blood appeared. "If you wish," she said faintly.

He caught her wrist and pulled her upright. He looked down the street until he saw a church, and then he hurried her toward it. Once inside the purple gloom, he led her to the shrine of St. Veronica. He lighted a candle and thrust it into her hands, then forced her to kneel on the *prie-dieu.* "Swear it by the blessed napkin that wiped the face of our Lord."

"I swear it," she said through dry lips.

He relaxed then, and drew a long quivering breath of relief. "That is right, little one." He placed the candle on the shrine and helped her to her feet. She swayed, half fainting with emotion, and he drew her hand through his arm to help her from the church. "You know so little of men—of their brutality, their cowardice, their vileness. There is no such thing as a gentle man..."

"Fernando on the ranch in Mexico..."

"A coward, that one. Afraid of his wife save when he was drunk, and then he beat her. You can remember her screaming, Lolita. Surely you remember that?"

"Yes, I remember."

"I want you to be safe, protected from harm. I want that so very much."

She lowered her head so that he could not see her face. For the first time in her life she was frightened of him. She had never realized how violent he could be. She had always been able to bend him to her will, but in this, she knew, she could never change him. And, in a way, it gave her an odd feeling of pride that she could be worth so much. Now, truly, she felt herself on a level with his love of fighting. And she knew that she was necessary to him, and this gave her a feeling of contentment. It is not an easy thing to love a man who plays with death every afternoon. Her life was chopped in little segments from dusk to the following midday. Then from one to six she waited, as all women of the condemned must wait, for the reprieve, and when it came there was another little segment of life until the next noon.

But now a new security came to her. Always before she had been in doubt. If he had to choose between herself and the bull ring, which would he take? That question had haunted her from childhood. But lately the question was beginning to answer itself. When she asked him to be one of Belmonte's *peones,* she thought she had been sure of her power over him, but not as she was now sure. Now she knew that in time she could win him from the ring. Other fighters had retired. He, too, could retire. Let him have his hour of triumph in his own country. She could not deny him that. But at the end of the Christmas season in Mexico City she would ask him to leave the ring. They could buy a ranch outside of the City, import a fighting strain of bulls from Salamanca or Andalucía, and breed a new line of Mexican fighting bulls. With his knowledge of bulls and of what fighters wanted, it would be easy, so easy ...

But she had not counted on the Great Revolution. Two weeks before they were to take ship for Mexico, Porfirio Díaz fled to Paris. There was no time for bullfighting in the Republic. Men were fighting each other instead.

So they stayed in Spain. Gitanillo's apprentice season as a matador was not very successful. The larger bulls worried him. Cardito got him contracts in the provinces, and he did fairly well, but not well enough. Cardito was worried about the Madrid performance. No matter how good a man may be in the provinces, it is Madrid that counts. Madrid is the center of the bull-fighting world. It is to the matador what the Metropolitan Opera House is to the singer. How would the twenty-two-year-old Gitanillo rank against the far more experienced Belmonte, El Gallo, the Mexican Gaona?

The afternoon of Gitanillo's graduation fight, Lolita trembled so much as she dressed that Doña Hermina had to help her. "Do not worry, little one. That brother of yours has the genius. You will see."

But Doña Hermina had not spent her entire life with bull-fighters. And she was not a gypsy. She did not know the symptoms of fever in the air, of salt on the tongue, as Lolita did. Suddenly Lolita broke one of her life-long rules and hurried to the room where her brother was dressing. On a table a vigilance candle was burning before a lithograph of the Blessed Virgin of Guadalupe. Gitanillo dropped his rosary in front of it as she entered. He had on his short gold-embroidered rose satin trousers, and the long-sleeved white linen shirt, with the tie already fixed. She lifted his heavy padded jacket, and waited until he had tested his shirt sleeves to be certain that they would slide easily on his arms, then held the jacket while he put it on. He flexed his shoulders to adjust the fit and smiled at her in the mirror.

"There is a wind," she said suddenly. "It is not bad, but still ... why must there be wind today?"

He shrugged, but his face was already settling in the still, remote lines that all matadors have when they go into the ring. She felt that in a few moments he would no longer smile, that he would be remote from her, from Cardito, from all of them. Silently she put the dress cape on his left shoulder and watched him fold it around his arm. Then she went out of the room. There was nothing to say. There was never anything to say.

When she reached her seat in the *barrera*, Doña Hermina flung the great *mantón*, white with red roses and green leaves embroidered on it, over the railing in front of her. Lolita was late. The President had already entered his box, and the musicians were playing. The sun was very hot, the light dancing on the white sand of the arena. Directly facing her were the entrance gates. A bugle blew, and the gates were flung open. Lolita thrust her hand into her bag and clutched her rosary, a beautiful one of filigreed gold that Gitanillo had presented to her on the day of her first communion. She did not tell the beads. She simply clutched the rosary, repeating, "Blessed Mary, Mother," over and over in her mind.

The two mounted bailiffs in their Phillip II costume galloped across the ring, doffed their hats and bowed to the President. He waved his handkerchief, and they galloped off to their separate places. The musicians began the entry march. First came the three matadors, Gitanillo, the apprentice, in the center, their elongated hats straight with the eyes, their dress capes furled over their left arms, their right arms swinging in unison as they walked lightly forward in their soft leather pumps. Following each matador came his train of *peones* and picadors, the latter mounted on horses. They marched forward to the President's box, took off their hats, and bowed with proper respect. Then the procession broke up, and the matadors with their followers retired behind the low *barrera* wall that encircled the arena. For a moment the ring was empty. Then the arena servants pulled back a low dark door, and a bull rushed into the ring.

Because Gitanillo was the youngest, he was to kill the last two bulls. The other two matadors were competent but not brilliant. The man just before Gitanillo, who was to graduate him, was called *El Halcón*, the falcon, and he was a coward. He had been gored badly, and this was his first fight since coming from the hospital. His feet betrayed him. They carried him away from the bull before he could get himself well into place, and he was too slow. A bull learns quickly. For a fight to last longer than fifteen minutes is disastrous. The bull knows enough then to follow the man and not the moving cape. And this bull had early found for himself a place of refuge, a terrain where he felt safe, with his back to the *barrera*, and placed so that his small eyes could watch warily from every direction. *El Halcón* should never have allowed him to enter this spot, but the damage was done now, and the man had to prepare for the kill, knowing that the bull would get him. And *El Halcón* was not a killer. His hand was not sure on the sword. Step by step he edged closer, the *muleta* lowered and swaying to keep the bull's head down. The bull's ears were twitching slowly, blood and foam on his half-open jaws. Then he charged. The right horn caught *El Halcón's* jacket and ripped it. A *peón* ran forward, a cape grasped in both hands. As he flared it out the bull swung away from *El Halcón* and returned to his place of refuge. The moment of death, which the arena calls the moment of truth, had come.

El Halcón, flushed and worrying his lower lips with his teeth, walked toward Gitanillo. As senior bullfighter it was his privilege to "graduate" the novice by presenting him with his own *muleta* and sword, and allowing him to make the kill.

The ring was very quiet. All eyes were fixed on Gitanillo's expressionless flat-boned face. *El Halcón* removed his hat, pressed it against his body under his armpit. He watched Gitanillo anxiously. Why did the young fool keep his hat on? Surely he knew the customs of graduation. When Gitanillo made no move, *El Halcón* extended his cape and sword. Gitanillo looked at them, shrugged, turned on one heel, and returned to the *barrera* wall for his own *muleta* and sword.

At this gesture of contempt, the crowd went wild. Whistles and yells filled the wind-stirred air. *El Halcón* had to run to escape the pillows and bottles that were thrown at him.

The bull nervously pawed the ground. The excitement worried him. He wanted something to charge, to conquer with his thousand pounds of iron sinew and muscle. And that something was coming toward him at last—a man with a fluttering cape that tempted him, step by step, to leave his refuge.

There was a feeling in the air which the bull sensed but could not understand. But Gitanillo understood it. It was a demand from the crowd to bolster his arrogance with proof that he could really fight.

Unfortunately, this was not the bull to prove his worth. This bull was already ruined by *El Halcón's* cowardice. Gitanillo killed him coldly and with little artistic effect. He wanted his own bull, broken to his own style. Let the crowd mutter and catcall. He was Gitanillo. He would not be hurried.

After the kill he retired to the *barrera*, indifferent to the crowd's antagonism, and stolidly watched the arena servants run out to smooth down the sand with water. The wind was growing stronger, and they were obviously worried by it. Then the next bull came in. He was fairly large, roan-colored, with a shining pelt and small sharp horns. The crowd liked him. He was a good bull. Lolita gripped the rosary so hard her fingers were numb.

Gitanillo lifted his dress cape and looked about the ring. He hesitated as though he were wondering to whom he would send it. Then he caught sight of Juan Noyola, the great critic, and with a cynical shrug of his shoulders, ordered a *peón* to carry the cape to Noyola. As the critic spread the cape on the railing in front of him, he bowed and Gitanillo returned the bow. It was all very amusing, for Gitanillo was quite certain that regardless of how good his performance, Noyola would call him a Mexican amateur.

His preliminary cape work was adequate but lacked brilliance. Cardito was frankly worried. What was the matter with the young fool? He had given much better performances than this on the Mexican ranch. Now he seemed no better than an ordinary novice. Only Lolita recognized the grim humor that was keeping Gitanillo from revealing his genius until the moment of death—the moment when *El Halcón*, the senior fighter, had failed.

The members of Gitanillo's troupe unknowingly supported his cynicism. The picadores did fairly well, but they were tired with waiting so long, and their horses were too small for the bull. Then came the second five minutes of the *banderilleros*. When the *peón* lifted the gaudy wooden shafts he glanced toward Gitanillo, who merely shrugged. So the *peón* went out to place the *banderillas*, which he did with competence but little showmanship.

Finally the last five minutes came. Gitanillo lifted the great cape and held it tightly grasped in his two hands. He walked toward the bull with that insolence of courage which was so much his. It was a good bull, who charged straight—the kind that every fighter prays for and so seldom gets. Gitanillo's *veronicas* were low and slow and sure. All of his true genius was concentrated in the controlled wrists. The bull charged and whirled and charged again. With his feet together, his body swaying slightly from side to side, Gitanillo played with the animal until the small head was well lowered. Then he draped the cape around his shoulders and strolled away, the bull remaining as though hypnotized in position.

The crowd was very quiet. Here was a superlative performance charged with true emotion. They avidly watched Gitanillo put down the cape and lift the *muleta* and sword. Holding them lightly in one hand, he faced the President's box and raised his hat. His voice was full and rich and steady. "I dedicate this bull to the beautiful women of Spain, to the music of Spain, and to the wine of Spain!"

This dedication from a Mexican caught the crowd's fancy. There was a loud shout of approbation. Gitanillo bowed again, and returned to the bull. He knelt in front of it, his head forward, his arms thrust back. The bull was slow to start, but the man made no effort to force the charge. Both had an intolerable patience. Suddenly the curly head lowered, and the heavy body dashed forward. But Gitanillo's angle of calculation was exact. The *muleta* passed easily across the horns, without the fighter's having to spring out of the way or to sway back. The crowd went mad, shrieking and screaming. Even the critic Noyola bent forward with a show of interest. Only Lolita sat rigid and quiet.

Gitanillo came up from his knees, and began a series of passes with the *muleta* that brought the horns so close to his chest they ripped the embroidery from his jacket. Finally, he was ready. Feet firmly together, he brought the *muleta* slowly down with his left hand, and went in over the horns with the sword held in his right. It found the exact spot of entry, and he followed the right arm with his body—then came out and away from the bull. It tossed its horns at him in a last gesture of defiance, collapsed and rolled over on its back. It was dead.

While the crowd howled and cheered, Lolita sank half fainting into her chair. As she shut her eyes she could feel the cooling breeze blowing against her face. In the tenseness of the moment, she had forgotten the wind. And the wind is the deadliest enemy of the fighters, deadlier even than the bull. It blows the sand, but, what is far more dangerous, it blows the cape.

For the first minutes of the second bull, she kept her eyes closed in an agony of praying. She could hear the sharp, whistling breath of the crowd as it followed Gitanillo's magnificent cape work. In the second five minutes a yell from the crowd brought her upright. This bull was large and fierce, far more difficult to handle than the first one. He had gored the picador's horse, and was now nudging the fallen pic' with his head, in an effort to thrust in the horns, while Gitanillo and the other cape men were endeavoring to distract his attention. They took him away at last, while the pic' scrambled to safety behind the low wall, unhurt but badly bruised. When the moment for the putting of the *banderillas* arrived, Gitanillo, because he felt in this bull the same wild strain that was in himself, took the shafts from the *peón* and cited the bull for the placing of the first pair. The crowd grew very still. The bull was temperamental, with a fancy for the right side, and he hooked to the right as he charged. But Gitanillo was ready for him. He poised lightly on his toes, his body stretched and arched slightly forward at the waist. His arms were very high, and the horns brushed his belt as the steel points hooked into place. The crowd was motionless as he chose two more *banderillas* and cited the bull again. The charge came, suddenly and without warning, but the slender shafts dangled at the correct angle. Even the critic Noyola applauded.

When Gitanillo cited the bull for the third time, the cries of "No, no, no!" resounded from the arena walls. But Gitanillo was alone with the bull. He heard nothing but the panting of the animal, saw nothing but that hump of muscle that was to receive the barbs. The bull came in, the head so low that the right horn scraped Gitanillo's leg, but the *banderillas* were perfectly placed. In that moment, the crowd took Gitanillo to its heart. Lolita could feel the love for him heavy in the air, but she could also feel the breeze.

So, obviously, could Gitanillo. When he came for the *muleta*, he bowed in his insolent way to the President. "This bull," he shouted, "I dedicate to my dearest friend, the wind of Spain!" It was a challenge that was more than a challenge. It turned the arena into a contest for man and bull and fast moving air. The crowd tensed, opera glasses fixed in trembling, excited hands. Lolita sat rigid, her eyes on the red cape fastened around the slender wooden sword. She no longer saw Gitanillo as a whole, but only as an outgrowth of the *muleta*.

When he addressed the bull a fit of trembling seized her. She watched the beautiful performance through glazed eyes. She saw the bull's head droop lower and lower. She saw Gitanillo go in over the horn for the kill . . .

And then the wind, the treacherous wind, whipped the *muleta* cape away from the bull's eyes into Gitanillo's face. Thrown off balance, he staggered backward. As he did this the dying bull, in a last mighty effort, charged forward, his horn penetrating the gold embroidered jacket and entering the left armpit. For a moment, Gitanillo dangled like a woman's loosely held glove in the air, but the bull had exhausted his last strength. He crashed to the ground and Gitanillo was flung clear.

His men rushed him to the infirmary, and the doctors allowed Cardito to see him for a few minutes before he was wheeled into the operating room. Then Cardito came out to find Lolita waiting, wide eyed and white faced, at the door. "I'm to take you home," he said gruffly. "He doesn't want you here with all these men." Then something about her frozen misery made him add gently, "It was a bad *cornada*, there is no denying, but he won't die from it. A few weeks in the hospital, and he will be fighting again. You'll see."

So she went home. She read the critics' paeans of praise in the next morning's papers with bitter eyes. It was Noyola's comment that interested her the most. "Gitanillo has the genius, there is no doubt. But today he suffers from his first bad wound. His next fight will mark him as a man condemned to the ring, or as a fighter with salt in his blood."

His next fight. She sat tense, with the paper crushed in her lap. Would his proud arrogance be gone? Would he be another *Halcón* with feet that carried him away from the bull? Her

Gitanillo who had always been so brave? Saints in Heaven, he
had to fight again, to prove that he did, in truth, have salt in
the blood.

Lolita was not permitted to visit the men-filled hospital, and
she did not know and Cardito did not tell her that Gitanillo had
decided to fight again at the end of three weeks with the wound
still unhealed. The doctors had protested; even the promoter had
been doubtful, but Gitanillo was determined. "If I wait longer
the crowd will forget me. And I must prove that I can still fight."
He did not add that he had to prove it to himself. He had gone
unscathed for so many years—the knowledge that a bull could
harm him as it did other men frightened him. He could not wait.
He had to know.

When Cardito came to take Lolita to the ring, she refused to
believe him. "Not so soon," she whispered. "No. I must tell him.
Not so soon."

"You will tell him nothing!" said Cardito sharply. "You will
smile at him from the *barrera* and he will fight. I have made a
genius of him. Today he will prove it."

"What do you care about him?" she cried. "All you want is a
genius in the arena. No one would think you were his father."

"I am not," said Cardito brutally. "Don't forget that. It is the
fighter who is my son. Gitanillo himself is a gypsy—a bastard
gypsy."

"And I?" she asked in a low voice. "What am I to you,
Cardito?"

The man shrugged his thin shoulders. "You are a woman," he
said indifferently. "Does it matter? Be ready to leave for the ring
within half an hour."

When she reached the *barrera*, there was such misery in her
that Doña Hermina touched her hand in sympathy. Lolita tried
to smile, but the muscles of her face would not respond. Although
she did not realize it, she was entering the second phase of her
existence. Up to this moment, her agony in the ring had been
solely for Gitanillo. But now it began to take a more personal
turn. She was only half gypsy, but the gypsy self-pride was
strong in her veins—the gypsy demand for self-preservation. "If
he dies, Blessed Mother, what am I to do? Where am I to go?
Oh, Blessed Mother, what is to become of me?" The unspoken

question received no answer, and her eyes were dull as she watched the entrance.

Gitanillo made his bows to the cheering crowd as though there were no pain in his body. The critic Noyola wrote on his block of paper, "The man is outside of pain. His will is stronger than his body. The wound must trouble him, but he refuses to notice it." And, in the florid Spanish manner, he added, "Nothing but death can conquer his will."

This afternoon Gitanillo again had to wait for the third lot of two bulls. The waiting was hard for him. He was impatient, and when it finally came his turn with the cape he went in too fast so that it bothered the bull and made him difficult to handle. But Gitanillo had been born with the smell of the arena in his nostrils. The *peón* placed the *banderillas* for him. Then Gitanillo again lifted the cape. As he walked toward the bull he had a sudden vision of *El Halcón's* feet dancing away in fear. He looked objectively down at his own feet. They were moving in easy rhythm, seemingly of their own volition. But towards the bull, inevitably towards the bull. An elation seized him. It was all right! They would not betray him—those wonderful sure-moving feet had found their own tempo. They would not betray him! His blood pounded in his veins. His bones were flexible wires. His skin tingled with a new certainty of power. There was surely wine in the air. Wine and sunshine and golden sand, and the brilliant color of the shawls draped over the *barrera* boxes, and the beautiful women with their avid eyes and their small pink tongues caught between white teeth in emotion for the kill, and the whistled breathing of the men, and all of this centered in him as the water swirls around the pointed cone of an eddy, and he was Gitanillo—he was the gypsy death walking forward, forever walking forward—forever a part of the pulsing rhythm of the arena, never again to leave it—for this was power, this was certainty, this was the true arrogance.

He extended his wrists. They were loose and easy. He held the cape so low, he turned so slowly, that the passes were rituals of beauty. He finished his series of *veronicas* with a turn that sent the cape billowing around him like a flamenca dancer's skirt, and the bull turned so short that the animal came to its knees.

This time there was no flamboyant dedication. After he took the *muleta* he merely waved his right hand at the crowd and they knew that the bull was theirs and they loved him for it. He started with a chest pass, and his feet stayed in place, the right foot slightly back, his body balanced on his toes, his chest arched as the bull, in passing, left blood from his shoulder on Gitanillo's blue satin trousers. The moment of killing, of truth, the moment which above all others Gitanillo had feared, was performed with such ease that it made a tourist exclaim, "Why, there's nothing to it!"

Lolita, hearing the exclamation, smiled bitterly. No, she thought, nothing but years of arduous training, nothing but a brave, proud heart, nothing but a knowledge of bulls so profound that the bull and the man become a single thinking machine, nothing but a genius for living that tilts without regret against the black bull of pain in the arena.

Noyola wrote in his paper the next morning, "Yesterday, Gitanillo proved himself a man from Ronda." It was the accolade. Gitanillo had reached the height of his profession. Crowds followed him when he appeared on the street. Women bombarded him with flowers. Critics and bullfight fans came to watch him dress for the ring. And some women gave him more than flowers.

He saw little of Lolita during the next few years. Sometimes weeks would pass, and the only times she saw him were in the ring. She was desperately lonely, and thinking he no longer needed her, she stayed at home one afternoon. A disheveled Cardito came rushing into the house five minutes after the fight was scheduled to begin, for in a country where to be on time is to be unique, the bullfight always begins exactly on the stated hour.

"What is wrong with you? What are you doing, moping in the house?"

She shrugged slightly. "I am tired. If I want to rest what difference does it make?"

"Difference?" Cardito shouted. "He marched into the ring, and when he saw you were absent, he marched straight out again. Madrid is wild with excitement. They want to know what is wrong! And if you aren't there, he won't fight. You know how he is. He can afford to be temperamental now."

"Yes," she said, her face lighting with joy. "I know how he is."

When she entered the *barrera* even the President stared at her through his opera glasses. She was in an agony of shyness, but her gypsy poise came to her aid. As she sat there, proud and aloof, she became a part of the Gitanillo legend. She became known as "Gitanillo's luck." And for the first time the *peón* threw Gitanillo's dress cape over the heavy fringed silk *mantón* on the railing in front of her.

The fight was one of the greatest of Gitanillo's career. The bulls were magnificent. The air was still. And the slow-moving *veronicas* were as liquid and flowing as water in a quiet pool.

Noyola wrote the next day that Gitanillo was the greatest genius that Mexico had ever produced, and was certainly one of the greatest geniuses in the history of bullfighting. When they met at a café one night, Belmonte of the delicate twisted body toasted him as a great rival. Gitanillo returned the toast, but his eyes lacked sparkle. It was true that he had reached the top, but for a man of Gitanillo's temperament, that was tragedy. He could perfect what he already possessed, but he could climb no higher. There were no further heights to scale. Madrid had acclaimed him. Beyond Madrid was nothing. So he fought on, inventing new uses of the cape, which were so difficult that no other fighter could copy them, and constantly improving the style that Belmonte had invented but Gitanillo had lifted beyond the scope of the inventor. He longed for but one thing: to fight in the arena at Mexico City.

At last the Great Revolution was over. Gitanillo was thirty-two. For ten years he had held his own in Spain. But now he was going home. When he drove to the boat, he sat on the back of the car, and the cheering crowd bombarded him with roses and carnations. Lolita rode with him, and from time to time she had to shake the flowers from her hat. A man leaped on the car to be closer to his idol, and he clutched at her shoulder to save himself from falling. Gitanillo's hand shot out and down in a vicious cut to the man's forearm. The man screamed and fell backwards to the sidewalk, and the swift-moving car soon left him behind.

Lolita said quietly, "That was not necessary, Gitanillo. The man meant no harm."

"He touched you," said Gitanillo, as though that were explanation enough for anything. Cardito looked thoughtfully at Lolita but said nothing. Gitanillo was his god. If Gitanillo wanted to assassinate a dozen men for no reason but his own pleasure, that was his affair. Lolita looked at the cheering crowd that passed her eyes in a blur of faces. She remembered the oath she had made in the church ten years ago. Ten years. Was it possible? And she was still necessary to him. Her position was assured. It was enough for her. She was content.

The Christmas season in Mexico City was a personal triumph for Gitanillo. His name was everywhere. He was as famous as Zapata, or Obregón, or Pancho Villa. A woman with one of the greatest names in Mexico became his mistress. She had heard of the Lolita legend; so she stayed away from the ring one day to test him. He did not even know she was not there. That night she tried to stab him, and he nearly broke her arm for her. Then he walked out of her house and never returned. She sent him presents and begging letters. But a dancer named Trina Olivares, who worked in the Revue of Pepe Bobo, had attracted his attention; so he returned the presents and tore up the letters without bothering to read them. He was with Trina the night the woman killed herself. The next morning the City was afire with the scandal. And that afternoon the ring was packed to capacity. Would he refuse to fight? And if he fought, would he be off tempo, distracted, give a poor performance?

He marched into the ring with the loose-hipped stride that bullfighters have, and Lolita knew that the remote expression on his face had nothing to do with the dead woman who had brought disgrace to her family for love of him. His performance was flawless. The Mexican bulls, small and short-horned, were easy for him after the great bulls of Spain. He seemed to read their minds as easily as though they were human and could talk to him. After the fight, the Mexico City public carried him from the ring on excited shoulders. Mexico loved the streak of cruelty in him that gave him a dangerous, sinister glamour. Contracts poured in from all over the Republic. But Gitanillo refused them. He liked the City. He preferred to stay there for the season instead of wandering about the country. To Spain for the spring and summer, to the City for the winter. That was the history of the next three years.

Then, one night in December, 1922, he came home and told Cardito to pick up some northern contracts. He had broken with Trina Olivares and he was afraid of her. "She'll come after me with a knife. And she is no easy silken thing. She'll put the knife in me no matter how strongly I fight her."

This was not the truth. He was not afraid of Trina, who had simply ceased to amuse him. At Trina's rehearsal that afternoon he had met a tall, white-faced woman with red hair whom he wanted to forget as quickly as possible. If he stayed in the City he would go back to see her again and again. He might even fall in love with her. He might even want to marry her. And marriage was not included in Gitanillo's scheme of life. That red-headed woman was no bullfighter's woman. Her shadowed, grief-filled eyes were more dangerous than any breeze in the arena. Let stupid little fighters fall in love. Gitanillo belonged to the blood-drenched sand.

So Cardito, knowing nothing of Gitanillo's meeting with Anita O'Malley, chose Monterrey and Laredo because they offered the best money. He had almost forgotten his first meeting with Olalla in Monterrey. Indeed, he had almost forgotten Olalla. He would not have recognized her picture if anyone had shown it to him. His entire life was wrapped up in Gitanillo's ring career, and the doctors who marveled over his ability to fight the tuberculosis in his lungs maintained that it was his interest in Gitanillo that kept him alive. Cardito was one of those tragic men who are born with ambition but without ability. Through the medium of Gitanillo he projected himself into performance. The fact that Gitanillo was his wife's child meant nothing to him. Gitanillo might have been the child of any strange creature that Cardito had never seen. There was no affection in him for anyone. But there was a burning passion for beautiful performance in the arena. Gitanillo never swirled the cape or stilled his feet that Cardito did not feel the motion pulling at his own muscles. It was as though Cardito had a second body capable of performing exploits his first body could not attempt. And so Gitanillo's relationship to Olalla was of minor importance. And Olalla's ghost walked no streets of Monterrey for Cardito.

They arrived in Monterrey on the sixth day of January, the Day of the Magi. The town was in fete, and people from all the surrounding country had come to celebrate the day of the giving of gifts. Hucksters sold their wares in high shrill voices, calling out water of pineapple, water of sweet lime, candy of almond paste, of burnt sugar, of pecan cheese, and roses, carnations, tuberoses, gardenias.

Rubén, in his late thirties and still a bachelor, had come from Hidalgo to visit his cousin, who owned a small ice-cream stand near the bull ring just outside of town on the road to Caydereta. Knowing that Rubén was an *aficionado*, a man who loved bull-fights, the cousin secured one of the candy-selling concessions for him.

The morning of the fight, Doña Berta, the cousin's wife, brought in several girls from the neighborhood to help her pre-pare dinner, and paraded them before Rubén with all the earnest-ness of a man parading sheep before a possible buyer. The cousin thought this a great joke, and slapped Rubén on the back. "Eh, she thinks you will soon grow too old for marriage. And it is true. It is time you took yourself a wife."

"A candy vendor has little time for women," said Rubén. "Besides, women are always in the kitchen. They think they can mix my candy better than I can. I am better off without them."

"You are a wiser man than I," said his cousin, with a quick glance around to make sure Doña Berta was not within earshot. "But if you do marry, do not choose a Tejana as I did."

"Never fear," said Rubén. "Doña Nimfa, the witch woman of Hidalgo, told my fortune for me. She said that I would meet a woman and in that moment I would love her. She said I would be to this woman a refuge."

"A refuge!" shrieked his cousin. "This Berta of mine was a refugee from the flood in San Antonio. I took pity on her. And what happened? She married me!"

Rubén grinned. "She has made you a good wife."

"And, by the saints I swear it, a bossy one. These Tejanas! They have no proper modesty. They think a house is a place where women rule. You had better leave quickly, or she will invent some fine task to keep you from seeing the fight, just to prove that she can boss you, too, as well as me."

Rubén took his cousin's advice and reached the ring early. He passed up and down the rows of seats, figuring the best places to stand, so that he could see the arena and at the same time be ready to answer any uplifted hand that might signal to him. He especially did not want to miss Gitanillo's performance, and, being well acquainted with the Gitanillo legend, he found himself

a place near the *barreras* where he could get a good view of
Lolita. He had heard that Gitanillo kept her as cloistered as any
nun, that her only public appearances were in the arena, that no
man save her father and her brother had ever spoken to her. "Not
even a candy vendor?" thought Rubén impishly and grinned to
himself.

The idea of a cloistered sister was not strange to Rubén. It was
a common occurrence in Mexico for brothers jealously to guard
their sisters. Why, in Abasolo there were two old maids, now in
their nineties, whose brothers had never permitted them to marry
or to attend any public gathering save mass. So Rubén was not
interested in the cloistering but only in the fact that Lolita was
Gitanillo's luck.

The fight was scheduled to begin at three o'clock. At two
forty-five precisely, the six queens arrived in horse-drawn victorias, three wearing the high combs and *mantones* of Spain, three
in the sequined red flannel of Mexico, with the white blouses
and the long green shawls tucked around their waists. At five
minutes of three, the governor, acting as the ring president,
arrived with the mayor and other notable politicians. And at three
o'clock, Lolita, followed by the slow-moving Doña Hermina,
walked down the steps to the *barrera*. Rubén, staring at her, forgot to move out of the way, so that she was forced to pause. She
lifted her proud black eyes to his long thin face, and he was
the first man, outside of her own family, ever to look straight
down into them. "Saints in Heaven!" he exclaimed under his
breath, "but there are tears in you!" Her white cheeks flushed
slightly with anger, and with a muttered apology he stepped
aside so that she could go to her chair. Doña Hermina passed
him without even a curious glance. After all, he was only a candy
vendor with the manners of a stupid mule. She had not heard
his words.

That evening when his cousin asked him how Gitanillo fought,
Rubén looked at him stupidly. "I didn't notice," he answered,
and hurried away from the ice-cream stand before the surprised
cousin could ask anything more.

Gitanillo's party was staying at a famous hotel on the Plaza
Hidalgo. Rubén waited near the entrance, and every time Lolita
passed in and out of the door, he came forward with his tray.

Once Gitanillo stopped and chose a piece for her. When he started to pay for it, Rubén shook his head. "It is a gift. A poor one, that is true, but it is all I have." He was looking straight at Gitanillo, but Lolita heard the words, and the blood rose to her cheeks again. She knew, but she could not have explained how she knew, that the words were meant for her, not for her brother. For a dizzy moment she remembered Gitanillo's vicious downward swing on the arm of the man who had leaped on their automobile. He would not hesitate to half strangle this officious candy vendor.

She looked at Rubén from the corner of her eyes, and that night she dreamed of his long thin face with the thick black hair combed back from a side part. His clothes were patched but very clean, and one had the impression that the candy was very clean, each piece wrapped in white tissue paper. He was not handsome. He was obviously very poor. But there was something restful about him, a security about him that Lolita had never before encountered.

She turned over on the bed and pushed her cheek deeper into the soft pillow. How lucky his wife was to have such a husband. Surely, at his age, he had a wife. But if he had a wife, would he watch her, Lolita, as he did? No, not that man. He would never look at any woman that way except his wife. There was a gentleness in his eyes. Gitanillo said there was no such thing as a gentle man. But this candy vendor looked at her with gentleness. But why did he look at her—at Lolita, the sister of Gitanillo, the great bullfighter? At Lolita who spent more on her stockings than he made in a year? At Lolita, the daughter of a gypsy who had probably never even owned a pair of shoes? A fit of hysterical laughter shook her, and she had to stuff the pillow in her mouth to keep Doña Hermina from hearing her. But Doña Hermina could not hear her. The long years of soft eating and heavy fat had finally closed on her heart. She died quietly in her sleep without even knowing that she was passing out of sleep into death.

Since by Mexican law the dead must be buried within twenty-four hours, Doña Hermina was laid to rest in the cemetery at Monterrey. Because Gitanillo attended the funeral, with a bored Cardito beside him, so did half the men in the city. But Lolita stayed in the hotel, as was proper, in a darkened room, wearing a black dress.

A shy knock at the door attracted her attention. She knew before she opened it that the candy vendor would be standing there.

He said hesitantly, extending his tray, "It is said that candy is very healing for tears."

She backed into the room. Her fingers locked themselves together and her head was high as she said, "Again you speak to me of tears. Do you think I am forever weeping?"

"No," he said slowly. "I think it would be better for you if you were."

She meant to take another backward step. Instead, she found herself moving forward. "You like me," she said. "You really like me."

He tilted his head to one side and frowned in concentration. "I think I love you," he said finally, and then, at her little gasp, "Please, señorita, do not concern yourself. I am sure that many men have loved you. One among so many. It does not matter."

"It matters to me," she said fiercely. "It matters to me!" And then she burst into tears. When his arms folded about her she clung to him, her fingers digging into his shoulders with fierce strength. He lifted her as though she were a child, sat in a chair and rocked her back and forth without saying anything. To have her here in his arms was almost beyond his comprehension. Her soft perfumed body, so fragile and delicate, with the flesh so finely drawn over the bones, had no weight. She might have been carved from cork.

Her sobs turned into long easy breathing. She was asleep. He looked at her and saw the black lashes silky and tangled from tears, resting against the white cheeks. He saw the flat bones of the face, which betrayed her gypsy blood, and the high-arched nose with the proud flaring nostrils, and the pale lips.

She is too black and white, he thought, brushing the heavy black hair away from her white forehead, his finger tracing the widow's peak. She needs more color. He knew that it was time for him to leave, but he wanted to keep on sitting here, holding her warm body against him. At last he rose and laid her on the bed, covering her with the quilt. Then he tiptoed from the room.

He did not return to the hotel the next day. He thought perhaps she would be ashamed that she had allowed a stranger to
touch her, and not only a stranger but a candy vendor, a man
without position or estate. He knew that he should return to
Hidalgo. The city streets were not for him. But as long as she
was in Monterrey, he could not leave. So the third day he returned to the hotel, to discover that she had gone that morning
with Gitanillo to Nuevo Laredo for a week.

Rubén had made several pesos with his candy at the bull ring,
and after an hour of intense figuring, which included plans for
eating but one meal a day for the next two weeks, he bought a
third-class ticket on the evening train to Laredo.

Ducks and chickens and squalling babies surrounded him. A
young kid was tethered in a box at the end of the car, and it
squealed loudly when the train swung around a curve and one
of the benches crashed into its cage. Rubén, who always travelled
third class from Hidalgo to Monterrey, preferred the floor to the
benches, for those who sat on the benches eventually landed
on the floor anyway. He exchanged some candy with a very fat
woman for a rolled *tortilla* filled with fried beans; and the father
of three young children, all of whom seemed to prefer Rubén's
lap to his, gave him half a bottle of sour red wine. Around mid-
night a boy with a guitar started to sing and everyone joined in.
The melancholy love songs pleased Rubén. They seemed to express the very beating of his heart. He added his baritone to the
lovely old song that is called *Lagrimas del Corazón*, "Tears of
the Heart":

> *Of what value is living in the world*
> *If I cannot be your lover,*
> *If I cannot stay at your side?*
>
> *Just heaven! Why do I love you so much?*
> *Why do I love you with such blindness?*
> *If this is martyrdom*
> *Then fate has condemned us both.*

It was a very fine journey.

The train arrived early in the morning, but it took Rubén until
noon to arrange for one of the bull-ring candy concessions. Luckily the soft-drink vendor had fought with Rubén in the Great

Revolution, and his influence swung the decision of the arena manager. Rubén stayed in the background until after Lolita, in her black dress of mourning, entered the *barrera*. When he bent over her to show his tray of candy he said softly, "Be careful. People are staring at you through their glasses."

"I know it," she answered bitterly, pretending to finger his wares. "I am used to it. But how did you come here?"

"A week," he said. "You are to be here a week. How could I stay away?"

As she chose a piece she looked up at him. "I knew you would be here," she said simply.

He gazed straight down into her eyes. "The tears are still there. Will they never be gone?"

She made no answer and opened her purse. He shook his head and backed away from her with a little bow. The crowd applauded his small gift, and he resented the applause. But he forced himself to bow to them, and because of what they thought was a generous gesture to Lolita, the people soon emptied his tray, watching the fight between bites.

Today Gitanillo was fighting third, from choice. It amused him to think of himself as the climax of the afternoon, and he fought very well, but not as well as usual. He and Lolita were involved in an argument over a new chaperone. She did not want one, and he was determined that she should have one. He refused to let her eat in the public dining room, or to go shopping alone across the river in Laredo, Texas. Cardito, furious at being what he called a nurse-maid, had brought her to the ring in a closed car. But there is an old Mexican proverb: "The greatest danger is the danger we fear the least." And it never occurred to Gitanillo that his deadliest enemy was a long-faced, stoop-shouldered candy vendor, so poor that he had to save for months in order to buy a pair of shoes.

And in all justice to Lolita, she did not realize that she was in love with Rubén. To her he was a man who liked her, not because she was a part of the Gitanillo legend, but because she was herself. To Gitanillo she was a possession, just as his great talent was his possession. To Cardito she was a strange creature who brought Gitanillo good luck, and good luck is important to a bullfighter. But to Rubén she was an individual, an entity. And she who had lived with violence all her life found his gentleness almost overpowering. She could not have expressed her emotions to anyone, not even to herself. She only knew that when this candy vendor was near her he gave her a happiness that she had never experienced, and she wanted him near her always, where she could see him and touch him.

After the fight, as she passed him on the steps, she dropped her purse. He picked it up for her and she bent for it at the same moment. She whispered so quickly he almost missed the words, "Come to my hotel at ten tomorrow morning with your tray."

At nine o'clock he was outside the hotel, his tray set up on its three-legged stand. At nine-thirty, Gitanillo came out with Cardito. They were going to the corrals to examine the new lot of bulls for the afternoon fight. Gitanillo was one of the few matadors who went to the corrals in person. Most matadors sent their most trusted *peón*, but Gitanillo had lived with bulls since his fourth year. He knew what he wanted better even than Cardito. When he passed Rubén, the candy vendor heard him say, "I've never known her to be so stubborn. Does she think I will let her wander around by herself like a common whore?"

"Perhaps she still mourns for Doña Hermina," said Cardito. His voice, dying against the walls, added, "Women are strange creatures when it comes to mourning. Leave her alone for a few days, Gitanillo."

Then the two men turned the corner. Rubén waited another five minutes, in case one of them returned for a forgotten object, but at the end of that time he lifted his tray and went into the hotel. The clerk hastily ordered him out, but he explained that the señorita Lolita had sent for him. "She is very fond of candy," he said.

The clerk thought this over and then condescended to speak to Lolita on the telephone. Receiving his orders, he called a bell-boy and had Rubén led around to the back stairs. The boy, fascinated at this chance of seeing Gitanillo's Luck, knocked and then entered with Rubén, standing by while Lolita nervously chose candy she did not want. She started to dismiss the boy, but realized that he would think it strange that she desired to be alone with a candy vendor.

"Wait here," she said, then went into the bedroom and shut the door. When she returned she carried some money and a slip of paper. She said to Rubén, "I like your candy. This pass will admit you to the bull ring this afternoon. Bring me some there."

"Thank you, señorita." As Rubén lifted his tray, Gitanillo, nervous at leaving Lolita so long alone, entered the room. His face darkened with anger, until he saw the bellboy. Then he stepped aside and jerked his head for the two to leave. As Rubén passed him, the eyes of the two men met for a moment. In Rubén, the peasant, was the calm certainty of fertile fields and immutable mountains; in Gitanillo, the gypsy, was a sudden sense of terror . . . the sense that gypsies call the "smell of death."

Gitanillo slammed the door and said furiously, "What were those two doing here?"

"I wanted some candy," said Lolita steadily. "You won't let me go out; so the man had to come here."

He flushed and bit his lip. "Now, Lolita," he began, "if you had a chaperone . . ." The argument had started again.

As soon as Rubén freed himself from the bellboy, he opened the slip of paper. The writing, in a round childish hand, was brief. "I will try to meet you at the back entrance of the hotel tonight at eleven."

At the bull ring that afternoon he thought it better not to go near her. But he could watch her, and she knew he was there. The meeting that morning with Gitanillo disturbed him. The fighter's blue eyes had flamed with anger, and Rubén realized that only the bellboy's presence had saved him from a beating. The man was a maniac. Lolita was not safe with him. And yet, in his own queer way, Gitanillo was kind to her. Perhaps she was actually safer with him than away from him. For where could a poor candy vendor hide her that Gitanillo, with all his great power, and he was certainly one of the most powerful men in the Republic, could not find her?

When he waited by the hotel's back entrance that night, Rubén was glad that only the stars were shining. The northern moon would have revealed him as clearly as daylight. But with the stars it was just light enough to show Lolita passing through the door. "I am here," he whispered, and she came like a blind person toward his voice. He caught her arms and drew her into the deeper shadow of an oleander bush.

"Tell me," he said harshly, "is he cruel to you?"

"Cruel? Oh, no. Only jealous."

"I know," he said, and laughed briefly. "I think I am a little jealous, too."

She sat down on the hard-packed ground and clung to his hands. "Tell me about yourself. Who are you? Why do you sell candy?"

So he told her about Hidalgo, and the people who lived in it. Of how his father had sold candy and his grandfather and his great-grandfather. And he told her something about himself, of his childhood and his dreams of making the finest candy in the Republic. "I make good candy," he said proudly. "Everyone who buys it says so."

"Yes," she said eagerly, "it is good. I like it. I ate all you gave me."

"But naturally. Doña Nimfa put a spell on our house. My father did her a kindness once, and so she put a spell on us."

"A spell? What do you mean?" He could feel her turn toward him in the glimmering darkness.

"Doña Nimfa is a witch who lives in my village. Sometimes she can be very kind, and sometimes very cruel. But to me she has been kind. She told me about you."

"About me?"

"Yes." His finger traced the shape of her hand. "She also said that there was danger, and a mystery...something she could not understand."

"Ay, she must be indeed a true witch," said the girl, her gypsy blood flowing faster at the word. "Are there many witches in the north of Mexico?"

"Oh, yes. One lives just down the street from here. It is easy to recognize their houses. The cross beside their door, the black cross to keep the lightning off, is always painted upside down."

"And they can put spells on people...make them do what they want?"

"So it is said. I don't know. Witches—good witches—demand a high price for their services. And I have no money to spend on them. You see, I—I am very poor. And you are very rich. You don't know what it is to go hungry to bed."

"Yes, I do," said Lolita abruptly. "Do you think we have always had money? My mother was a gypsy, a wanderer. She owned one dress and that one on her back. She died when I was born, but Gitanillo remembers her a little, and sometimes he will talk about her." She added candidly, "She was not a good woman. Cardito says she had many lovers, and sometimes he wonders why he married her. There was no need, really. It was only an accident that I am legitimate. Gitanillo is a bastard. Who that father was..." She shrugged. "I am not a fine lady at all. If I were I would not be here in the dark talking to you like any common street cat. I don't even know your name. Do you know mine?"

This amazing speech was delivered in a strange, childlike voice that gave the words an overtone of unreality. Rubén was silent for so long that she touched his arm. "Do you still like me?" she asked, and her voice trembled slightly.

For answer he gathered her into his arms. He kissed her fiercely as though to prove his right to kiss her, and then he lifted his head. "My name is Rubén," he said, and kissed her again. Her arms went around his neck and he could feel her shaking against him. As soon as she could speak, she whispered, "Mine is Lolita."

"I told you I was poor, Lolita. You have seen my shirt, how ragged it is. I have nothing to give you. Nothing but a heart that aches for love of you. Will you marry me, Lolita?"

She twisted away from him and rose to her feet. "No," she said slowly, "No, Rubén. I can't marry you."

He rose also and took her hand in his. "It is not too terrible being poor, Lolita."

"It's not the poverty. That isn't the reason. There is something else. I—I want to know—the witch women, can they force someone to—to change a vow?"

"What kind of vow?"

"Does that make any difference? Just a vow!"

"I suppose they could. But what have vows to do with you and me, Lolita? I want to marry you. I think you want to marry me..."

"I do. I do want to marry you."

"Then who can stop us? Gitanillo may object at first, but he cannot expect to keep you cloistered all your life. And if he knows that you love me..."

"No!" The word was wrenched from her with passionate intensity. How could she hope to make Rubén understand the emotion of that hour in Ronda? There were no words in her to explain why she had accepted the vow. Better not to try to explain. "There is something you don't understand. I can't explain it to you."

"But there is nothing that concerns you that I can't understand."

"Yes, there is. You don't understand Gitanillo. You never will. You are too gentle, too kind—and he is violent, as violent as death." The words tumbled out of her mouth so rapidly that he could hardly understand them. "He does not comprehend your kind of gentleness. He thinks all men are like himself, heartless and brutal and cruel. A woman killed herself because of him in Mexico City. Did you know that?"

"I heard," he began, but her voice swept over his.

"All she wanted was kindness, but he had none to give. She came to see me, and she cried like a mad creature, and I had nothing with which to comfort her. I wanted to comfort her, but what could I do, how could I explain? He is a gyspy . . . pure gypsy. The gypsy blood is wild blood. I know. It is in me, too. And what we want, we want at any cost. Even if we have to steal for it or kill for it. Tell me you still want me. In spite of my wickedness, you still want me. Tell me."

He held her safe in his arms. "You are not wicked. You are only frightened. And I'll want you all my life."

"Then be patient. Let me go to the witch woman. Perhaps she can help us. Will you be patient with me?"

"When do you want to go?"

"Now. I want to go now."

He took her arm and led her down the narrow street. The witch woman's house was small and dirty, with a door so low they had to bend over to enter it. There were red coals glowing in the high brasier. The bed was a rickety brass with a blue crocheted cover thrown over it. There was a rough deal table with some three-legged stools. A very old woman, with dirty, stringy gray hair, was crouched on the hard-packed dirt floor. There were bundles of aromatic herbs stacked everywhere, and a large toad hopped out of a bundle and into her lap. Lolita shrank closer to Rubén and the old woman laughed wheezily.

"He won't hurt the pretty child," she said in a thin, high, nasal whine. "He loves the pretty ladies, don't you, my little dear?" She lifted the toad and rubbed it against her brown, wrinkled cheek.

"The night is dark," said Rubén formally, "and the path is a long path."

"So?" She took some steel-framed spectacles from her pocket and fitted them on her nose. Then she peered at them through the darkness. "Come here, gentleman." As Rubén approached her, she pulled her lips back from toothless gums. "Who taught you the witch greeting?"

"I am not of Nuevo Laredo. My valley is to the south. There are witches who fly in the mountains, and witches who live in the villages."

"The eagle witches are more powerful than I. What do you want with me?"

"This lady would ask you a question," said Rubén steadily with a gesture toward Lolita. "Will you answer her?"

"And if I do, what will she give me?"

Rubén looked around at Lolita, and she came to his side and slipped her hand in his. "What do you want, auntie?"

At the sound of Lolita's voice, the old woman fumbled in her clothes and pulled out a candle stump. She lighted this and held it high so that she could see Lolita.

"Eh, a gypsy. I know the signs. Go back to your own kind. They can help you more than I."

Rubén put his arm around Lolita, drawing her closer to him. "I am not a gypsy," he said. "Will you help her because I ask it, auntie?"

Lolita took off a pearl brooch and put it on the table. "Will that serve?"

The old woman examined the pin. She held it close to her eyes, sniffed at it, and finally bit down on the gold mounting. "Yes, it will serve." She fastened it to her dress, her eyes fixed on the young couple. "Wait outside," she told Rubén. "This pretty child is safe with me. I won't frighten her."

Rubén nodded and left the room. Outside he squatted in the shadows to smoke and wait. Lolita sat on one of the low stools. She was terribly afraid, but her pride kept her head high and her feet still. The old woman listened silently while Lolita told her of her brother and the vow in the church at Ronda. "Can you soften his heart? Can you make him change the vow?"

"To do this you must pay a great price."

"I can pay. I have gold, jewels . . ."

"That is not the price I meant." The old woman came closer to Lolita. The girl shrank away from her, and the old woman laughed. "I won't hurt you. Give me your hand."

She bent over the soft palm, and brought the candle closer to it so that she could see the lines. "If you go with your poor man you will lose these pretty hands. You will work like any common woman in the fields."

"I am not afraid."

"What you win with witchcraft is not easy to keep. Every year you must go to the mountains and dance the witch dance. Alone, you must go, in the still hours of the night, and sacrifice the cock with corn silk and corn leaf so that the ancient gods will be appeased."

"I can do that."

The old woman dropped her hand and crouched again on the floor. The light from the brasier threw a red glow over her body, leaving her face in shadow. "The price will be very heavy. There is always a price for happiness."

"I told you," cried Lolita, "I will pay you all I have. I am a gypsy. What I want I want. The price is of no consequence."

"The first payment will be heavy. But the second will be heavier still."

Lolita shook her head with irritation. The old woman sighed. "Very well, then. Bring me a cutting from your brother's hair, and a bit of his shirt that is stained with his sweat. Bring me also a fine black rooster with a good red comb, and the poison sac of a rattlesnake. And bring me a black candle, one that is used in mourning for the dead. Bring me these things tomorrow night."

Lolita waited a few moments longer, but as the old woman said nothing more, she went out to join Rubén. He promised to bring the rooster, the candle and the poison sac the next night. "But, Lolita, the price. What do you think she meant by the price?"

Lolita kept her head lowered. "I don't know. I love my brother very much. Perhaps she means that I must go away and never see him again. Or perhaps that his love for me would turn to hate. I could not bear for him to hate me. Do you think she meant that, Rubén?"

He frowned in thought. "I don't know, my beautiful. The words of witches are strange words. Are you sure you want to return to her?"

"What else can I do?" she asked plaintively. "Who else can help us?"

Rubén had no answer for this, but he was badly worried as he told her good night. The next evening they returned to the witch's house, carrying the things she had asked for. Again Rubén waited outside, while the old woman killed the cock and mixed the blood and the rattlesnake venom with the candle wax. This she kneaded until the wax began to take the shape of a man. On the head of the tiny figure she fastened the clippings of black hair, and around its waist she tied the strip of sweat-dried cloth.

"Give me a pin. One you have been wearing."

Lolita slowly unfastened a gold safety-pin from her belt and extended it. The old woman straightened it until the shaft and the pin made one straight piece. Then she threw some herbs on the brasier, and as the aromatic white smoke billowed up, she held the little figure over it and plunged the pin into the left breast. As she did this, she chanted strange old words that possessed a strong rhythm of clicking consonants. She flung the figurine on the coals and turned to Lola.

"Go home. I have done all that I can."

"But—but when will I know the answer?"

"At this hour tomorrow night. What more can I say? And the payment will be hard—hard. Quickly. Quickly! I am tired."

Lolita ran out of the house. She was suddenly terribly afraid, and trembling so much that Rubén had almost to carry her back to the hotel. She kept repeating over and over, "Tomorrow afternoon. I will ask him after the bullfight tomorrow afternoon. And he will hate me. I know it. That is the price. He will hate me. But he will let me go. Wait for me after the bullfight, Rubén. Because he will let me go."

"I will wait for you," Rubén promised, and kissed her good night.

The next afternoon was very fine. The blue and white canopy of sky and cloud shone like clean-washed linen in the brilliant sunlight. The bull ring was packed with people: tourists from the States, travellers from other sections of the Republic, and the Nuevo Laredo people themselves. As one man said, there was salt in the air, and everyone had the feeling that Gitanillo was going to give them his best.

Lolita waited impatiently for Cardito to come and get her. He grumbled because he had to wait until she put on her hat. "Gitanillo is even now with the priest in the chapel. You are late, the entrance will be late, and that is a sweet crowd. Sweet but impatient."

"See, Cardito, I am ready now. Let us go, Cardito."

"If you had a chaperone I would not have to return for you," he said querulously, and then had to pause for a coughing fit. She brought him a clean handkerchief and hovered over him until he relaxed, gasping for breath.

"Ay, Cardito, this life is not good for you. Better that you should go to the mountains, and the dry clean air."

"Twenty years ago the doctors said I would die in six months, and I am still alive. I am smarter than the doctors, me! And why are you standing there? Gitanillo is waiting. Get out of here!"

They hurried to the taxi. If Cardito had been an observant man, he would have noticed that Lolita was not her usual remote white self. Instead there was color on her flat, high cheek-bones, and even her lips, usually pale, were tinged with pink.

After he placed her in the *barrera* seat, he hurried around to the entrance patio, nearly knocking into Rubén as he passed.

Lolita signalled for the candy-maker to bring her his tray, and as he bent over her, she murmured. "How can you be so calm? Gitanillo fights last this afternoon. I am so nervous I feel that this chair is covered with needles."

"Patience, my little one."

"I know. But if he has a good fight, it will be easier to talk to him. He is always kind after a good fight. Pray that he has a good fight, Rubén."

The trumpet drowned his answer. He nodded to her and went off to sell his wares, as the gates opened and the bailiff galloped across the arena.

The first two fighters were competent, but the crowd wanted Gitanillo. They yelled his name at every opportunity, and he smiled faintly as he stood behind the low wall that separated him from the sanded ring. The crowd's voice sounded distant and far away, as though he heard it through a thick wall. He was remembering what the priest had said to him in the confessional, "Danger is too sweet a bread in your mouth." It was true. He loved this feeling of arrogance, this knowledge that he was wiser and stronger than death. Since that first terrible wound, years ago, he had this same feeling whenever he entered the arena. He had been wounded several times since then. When he moved his hand across his body he could feel the pitted scars. But it was the first *cornada* that had released him into a world of blood and power so great that he felt he had only to glance at the bull and it would stagger and fall from the authority in his eyes.

When it was time for him to lift the cape, he went as a king goes to the people he has conquered. The tempos of bull and man matched perfectly. It was not a fight but a ballet. The cape swung in the low controlled circles of the *veronicas*, and the bull swung with it. Gitanillo finished with a half-*veronica*, the cape gathered close to his body so that the bull curved around him like a dancing partner and stopped in place so perfectly that Gitanillo could fling the cape over his shoulder and walk away from the animal without even a contemptuous backward glance. The crowd shrieked and howled, but he did not hear them. He and the bull were in a separate world of strength, and cunning, and courage, where one or the other must triumph or die. He lifted the *muleta* and went back for the kill, so entranced with the emotion of the moment that he forgot to dedicate the animal. The crowd, sensing his absorption, bent forward like a great animal crouching.

As Gitanillo passed the sharp horns across his chest, the bull's blood staining his belly, the crowd grew still. It realized that it was seeing the greatest fight that had ever been shown in the Nuevo Laredo arena. Even Lolita and Rubén forgot their mutual interest long enough to stare without movement at Gitanillo. And no one, not even the ever-sensitive Lolita, noticed the little vagrant wind that came sweeping down over the flat-roofed houses and the high top of the back rows of seats.

Gitanillo was now thrusting his sword into one serge fold of the *muleta* in order that steel sword and wooden sword could spread it like a great flat fan. His feet still, his body straight, he swerved to neither right nor left, but allowed the red serge to guide the bull in a high pass across the horns. Then with ease and grace he brought the *muleta* around and under so that the bull was forced to turn in a space shorter than its own length. The animal was obviously tiring and the moment of the kill, the great moment of truth, had arrived. With slow control, the *muleta* in the left hand went down. The right hand rose, wrist poised for the strike. Gitanillo peered down the length of the sword, guiding the point precisely toward that vital spot on the spine, as clear to him as though it were marked with chalk. And the wind came in . . .

It caught the heavy serge of the *muleta* and flung it straight across his face, blinding him. He tried to claw it away, but the bull had lost the *muleta* and seen the man. The horn went straight into the left side, crushing the rib case and piercing the heart. When Cardito lifted Gitanillo's broken body from the arena, he was already dead.

Lolita made no outcry. No one noticed her as she turned and ran up the steps to the exit, with Rubén at her heels. He stopped her on the small deserted platform outside. "There is nothing you can do, Lolita."

"Nothing," she whispered. "Nothing."

"And there is nothing I can do, except to go away. Do you want me to go away, Lolita?"

She turned her head slowly towards him. And he saw her eyes, the black gypsy eyes. And as though written there he saw that twenty years of sunny afternoons of waiting for this afternoon were finished. "Why," he said in wonder, "the tears are gone." He caught her as she fell toward him.

He took her to the hotel. He collected a broken, weeping Cardito. He arranged for the funeral. As Rubén looked down at the dead face before the box was closed he thought that at last the fierce gypsy spirit was quiet. Gitanillo had found the thing beyond success that he had waited for so long.

Then Rubén returned to the hotel. Lolita was as dependent on him as a child. He wanted to marry her before they left Nuevo Laredo, but this she would not do. And for the first time she told him of the vow in the Ronda church. He tried to convince her that Gitanillo's death broke the vow, but this she would not believe. "He never broke his word to me. I cannot break mine to him. And it is the only thing he ever asked of me. In all the years, the only thing!"

Cardito could not argue with her. He was a very sick old man. And it was Gitanillo's confidential *peón* who told Rubén about the money.

"There is none left. Gitanillo made three fortunes, but he spent four. What is to become of them, I don't know. Me, I will stay with the ring. There is always work for a good *peón*. But Cardito, Lolita—they are helpless, and a *peón* makes little money. I can hardly support myself on what I make."

So Rubén went in to talk to Cardito. "I swear that she will be my wife. I will think of her only as my wife. The words that are spoken in a church are nothing. It is the words in the heart that matter."

Cardito agreed. He was too sick to argue. He was not even curious to know who Rubén was. This strange man in the ragged shirt with the gentle face had an authority about him that Cardito could only obey.

When they arrived in Monterrey, Rubén's cousin, who had grown up in Hidalgo, suggested the story of the San Antonio flood. "It will stop gossip. I know Hidalgo. And what is one more little lie? Besides, it will give Cardito something to think about."

Doña Berta was added to the conference. She loved to talk about her experiences in the flood, and she retold them now, fully and at great length. A story was carefully evolved and as carefully taught to Cardito. Then the beautiful clothes, the great closets stocked with magnificent bullfighter's costumes, were sold. The money paid debts and the hotel fare, with enough left over for three third-class tickets to Hidalgo.

They arrived in the village at night. Rubén lived on the Plaza of the Viceroys so that they did not have to pass through the town, and no one in Hidalgo knew they were there until the next morning. And Rubén, who had theories about fathers-in-law, saw to it that Cardito, an invalid now and elevated to the dignity of the title "Don," lived across the street. "Two masters in one house," said Rubén, "is a stupid business."

Lolita quickly recovered from the loss of Gitanillo. She had cushioned herself against it for so long that his death came as a relief. And the new freedom: the right to walk down town alone if she liked, even to go into Monterrey alone, thrilled her as a new toy would thrill a child. And if her gypsy blood told her that she had killed Gitanillo as the price of this freedom, her gypsy blood also reminded her that what a gypsy wants, a gypsy takes, even with death as the price. But once a year she went into the mountains to sacrifice the cock and dance the witch's dance, for there was still the second price to pay—the price the witch had warned her would be even heavier than the first.

Neither Rubén nor old Don Cardito had the courage to tell her that on his fourth birthday her son, the young Gitanillo, had run into his grandfather's house shouting, "Outside there is a bull, a bull, a bull!"

A clipping from the column of the Mexican critic, Villamelón, "Gold, Silk, Blood and Sun," February, 1938:

"Pepe Moros proved himself a great prophet when he said, 'When there are bulls, there are no fighters . . . when there are fighters, there are no bulls!'

"Yesterday there was a fighter in the ring, but 'there were no bulls!' If there had been, we might have seen a fight of genius. As it was, this young man who calls himself 'The Second Gitanillo' brought to the arena an effortless ease in which he seemed to make no movement save the slow turning of the wrists. He is very young and has much to learn before going on to Spain, but he already possesses the old Gitanillo's arrogance . . . the arrogance so necessary to a really great fighter. What a pity that he could not have been matched with a bull worthy of his talent."

Plaza of Independence

Love is action, not kisses and hugs.
—Mexican proverb

DON NACHO WAS SITTING AT HIS DESK IN THE SMALL OFFICE next door to the jail, his hands folded on his big stomach, placidly looking through the long iron-barred windows at the people of Hidalgo as they wandered through the Plaza of Independence, or stopped to exchange small bits of gossip.

It was a beautiful summer morning. The air had an opalescent quality; the breeze that ruffled the glossy foliage of the orange and lime trees was not too warm for comfort; the church's blue belfry was sharply outlined against the darker blue of the sky; and Don Nacho felt very content with his small world.

Now and then a man would pause at the window and call a greeting, to which Don Nacho would reply with a pleased little grunt. He felt himself a very lucky man. No difficulties to disturb him, and the *kermés* * only a week away.

This *kermés* was a yearly event with Hidalgo. People from all the neighboring villages and even as far as Monterrey and San Juan Iglesias came to win the prizes at the gambling stands, to dance at night on the plaza, to hold reunions of old friends. But the chief attraction was the final Sunday afternoon horse race. The track for this race was the Avenue of Illustrious Men, beginning at the Avenue of Independence and ending at the Street of the Governors, exactly one block long. Only very fine riders dared attempt it, for it demanded complete co-ordination of hand and eye and perfect horsemanship. The custom was to set up two poles, ten feet tall, one on each side of the street, across which was stretched a wire. From this wire dangled varicolored ribbons, with two-inch rings attached to each fluttering bit of satin. One rider at a time, armed with a stick, would thunder down the stretch at full gallop. As he reached the wire, he would stand up in the stirrups and try to pierce a ring with the stick, pulling it from the wire as the horse loped forward. The man who won the most rings had the right to walk once around the plaza with any girl of his choice, and on Sunday night the privilege of opening the dance that officially closed the *kermés*.

Most of the young men in the two valleys entered the race, but few of them had the fine co-ordination needed to capture even one of the rings. Hidalgo was very proud that the champion for

*A carnival, very different from *Carnival* held the week before Lent. A *kermés* has no religious significance, and its primary object is to make money for the town sponsoring it.

the past two years was an Hidalgo man, Don Serapio's nephew, the young Xavier.

Betting on the race was heavy, and Don Nacho was thinking of this year's bets. The mayor had long had his heart set on fixing a pool with flowing water where animals could drink. The Fountain of Charles V, at the intersection of the Avenue of Illustrious Men and the Street of the River was perfect for the purpose if Hidalgo could just get together money enough to put water in it. A present to Hidalgo of the "Sunday Night Plaza Chair Association," it was very pretty with its tiled sides, but it was dry. The Chair Association could afford only the fountain, not the piping to bring in water. Don Nacho had carefully set aside a few pesos from municipal funds for this purpose, and the betting would complete the sum.

Hidalgo would, of course, put its money on Xavier, but San Juan Iglesias had a man named Matías Galindo, who was pretty good. And El Carmen, farther up the Sabinas Valley toward Monterrey, also seemed to have a good contestant. Don Nacho picked up a notice from El Carmen which had to do with the reports of some goat thefts. Across the bottom of it El Carmen's alcalde had scrawled, "We have a new horseman named Salvador Sánchez. If you would be a fool, put your money on another man to win the race." Don Nacho had heard of Salvador Sánchez. He and Galindo both were men with horse blood in their veins. But Xavier—ah, Xavier, so slender, so graceful, so long of arm and leg, with an eye as keen as an eagle in flight... Yes, there was no doubt of it, Xavier would triumph again this year as he had last year and the year before that, and Hidalgo would have a practical fountain at last.

Don Ricardo, the one-armed policeman, thrust his head through the patio door. "Don Nacho, there is a general here to see you."

"A big general or a little one?" asked Don Nacho comfortably. On such a fine day as this, not even generals could disturb his tranquillity.

Don Ricardo's head disappeared for a moment, then again came into view. "He has red hair," said Don Ricardo doubtfully.

Don Nacho lifted off his hat and carefully placed it on the desk to indicate that he was not impressed by his visitor's importance. "Show him in."

As the one-armed policeman had said, General Aristéo Elizondo had flaming red hair. But Don Ricardo had forgotten to mention that the General also had cold blue eyes and a selfish, narrow-lipped mouth. Following at his heels was a stout sergeant, with a bushy mustache, eyes that saw everything and an arrogance of manner that matched his superior's.

Don Nacho decided that he did not like these soldiers, but he rose heavily to his feet and bowed politely as he gestured toward a cane-bottomed chair with one fat hand. "Hidalgo is honored by your visit, my General. How can I serve you?"

The General flushed angrily as he saw the mayor's hat on the desk. He knew these small town mayors, and he also knew what the hat on the desk meant. The sergeant saw it, too, and turned hastily to the window in an effort to hide the half smile on his face.

Conscious of his soldier's action, the General's tones were brusque as he said, "I am come to hunt for goat thieves in this district."

Don Nacho looked bewildered. "But we have no goat thieves, my General."

"Not in the town, no. But we have reason to believe that some of these thieves are hiding in your mountains. I want provisions made for the quartering of my men while we search your hills."

"Ah..." Don Nacho took a long breath, preparing for the eternal conflict between the arrogance of the army and the treasury of Hidalgo. "And who will pay for the men's quarters?"

"Pay?" The General's eyes narrowed. Although he was on an expense account, any money saved from the account became his personal property. "We are on important business. It is the town's duty to give us food and lodging."

"No, my General. I did not send for you. No goats have been stolen here. My people are poor. Pay us a fair amount and we will be glad to take care of you. Otherwise I am sorry, but no." Perhaps, thought Don Nacho slyly, this would anger the General enough to make him move on to the next town of Mina.

Before the General could answer the soldier by the window spoke up. "I read a poster as we rode through the town. There will be a *kermés* in one week ... And a contest for the jumping of horses."

"A *kermés*?" The General's voice was silky. "But we poor soldiers see so few *kermeses*. And a riding contest as well. It is permitted that one of my poor soldiers should enter the contest?"

Don Nacho felt his heart drop into his stomach. The men of the two valleys were excellent horsemen, but soldiers were especially trained to the saddle. Still, the contest was open to all. He could not refuse the request.

"It is permitted," he muttered.

The General seemed to beam on him, although the blue eyes were still narrow and cold. "Excellent. We will stay in this village."

"We must be paid for your lodging," insisted Don Nacho.

"Very well. Your money will arrive from Monterrey. And I shall enter this fine soldier in the race. You will win, eh, little sergeant?"

"I will win," said the soldier stolidly, looking through the window at a girl walking across the plaza. "Look, my General, there is beauty in Hidalgo."

Don Nacho snorted. "That is Florinda Farías, the promised bride of the best rider in this village."

"Not now," said the sergeant softly, "for I am here, and I am the best rider on all the frontier. Is that not right, my General?"

At this calm statement, Don Nacho lost his temper. "You may be what you say, but it will take more than fine riding to win our contest."

"So?" asked the general. "Why?"

"This is not merely a race for the jumping of horses. It is a contest for the pulling of rings. That is not an easy thing to do. It calls for a good eye and a steady hand..." His voice dwindled into silence as the two soldiers began to laugh. The laughter bothered him. Don Nacho did not trust generals, especially red-headed ones. Pancho Villa, as he had learned to his sorrow during the Great Revolution, was a red-headed man. He inhaled sharply. He was so angry that he spoke without thinking. "Do you conceive that you will win so easily? Let me tell you that in this very village there is a champion who can destroy you with ease."

"But our sergeant," purred the General, "is also a champion. In the great race between Monterrey and Saltillo, this same sergeant won with a beautiful precision." He kissed his fingers. "You behold before you none other than Baltasar Quiroga!"

Don Nacho felt numb. He had heard many tales of Baltasar Quiroga's horsemanship. But his pride in Hidalgo won over his reason. "Our Xavier has not the reputation, for he is a modest man little given to travelling. But he and his horse are as one animal."

"Our soldiers can collect among themselves the sum of two hundred pesos," said the General. "Of course if Hidalgo cannot meet the bet..."

Too late Don Nacho saw the pit that had been dug for him. He could make the soldiers pay for their lodging, but if Hidalgo lost the race, the soldiers would take with them far more than they paid out (and no water in the Fountain of Charles V). No wonder the General had agreed so easily to his terms. For from this challenge there was no honorable retreat. "We will meet the bet," said Don Nacho tonelessly.

The two soldiers bowed. Don Nacho bowed. The sergeant asked, "Will this Florinda Farías be one of the queens at the races?"

Don Nacho silently nodded and the two men left, the soldier slightly behind the General. The moment they were out of the room the mayor sank back in his chair and mopped his wide face with a corner of the red bandana knotted about his thick neck.

"You, Don Ricardo," he shouted. "Come in here."

As the one-armed policeman shuffled across the room, he said brusquely, "Go find me the young Xavier."

"I can't," said the policeman sadly.

Don Nacho felt a quiver run up his spine, a quiver that was always there whenever he was about to hear bad news. "What do you mean, you can't find him?"

"His uncle will tell you. Old Don Serapio is waiting to see you now." The policeman jerked his thumb toward the patio.

Don Nacho hardly waited for the gesture. He lumbered from the room and found Don Serapio, the town gardener, sitting disconsolately on the edge of the patio fountain.

"What is this mystery about your fool of a nephew?" Don Nacho roared. "Why can't he be found?"

Don Serapio gave a private sigh. Could Xavier be in more trouble? That orphaned boy whom he had reared as a fond parent was both the delight and despair of his heart. He said aloud, "He's in jail in Mina."

"By the ears of St. Joseph, why?"

"He stole some hens."

"Could he find no hens in Hidalgo? Did he have to go to Mina to steal them?"

Don Serapio shrugged fatalistic shoulders. "He said he wanted to sell the hens in Hidalgo to make enough money to buy a present for the saint's day of Florinda, daughter of Don Genaro, the civil judge."

Don Nacho rested his folded arms on his stomach and began to pace thoughtfully up and down the sun-drenched patio. He had often secretly thought that Pepe Gonzalez in his wildest days had never compared to the untamed Xavier. Now he was sure of it. "How long," he asked, pursing his lips, "must he stay in the Mina jail?"

"He stole seven hens," said Dona Serapio plaintively, "so that makes seven days. You know the law in Mina... one day for every hen."

"And he has served how many?"

"One," said Don Serapio. "It was yesterday morning that he was arrested. He has six days left."

Six days! Don Nacho saw all chances of winning the contest fluttering away in the distance. Six days. A man cannot practice riding a horse in jail, and Xavier needed practice to win from such a great champion as Baltasar Quiroga. "We could pay his fine," he suggested.

"No," said Don Serapio firmly, wondering what compulsion would force Don Nacho to pay out good township money for Xavier's fine. "If we did that he would only try to steal more hens. You know Xavier."

Yes, Don Nacho knew Xavier. He remembered taking the boy as a baby for a ride on his broad shoulders. Xavier was always trying to ride something. First a broom handle, then a baby donkey, and finally a horse. Xavier was always to be seen either on a horse or near one. He loved fine animals as much as the long vanished Joaquín Castillo. Xavier, the genius of horses. Xavier, his white teeth showing in a fine grin, riding around the Plaza of Independence at full gallop, his head flung back, his voice ringing in a shout of pure enjoyment. And now this same Xavier, this willow-wand of laughter, had to steal seven hens just when Hidalgo needed him the most.

"There is but one solution," said Don Nacho heavily. "Is not your brother-in-law a good friend of the alcalde of Mina?"

"They are as brothers."

"I will lend you my horse. Ride to Mina this afternoon and ask your brother-in-law to borrow Xavier for a week ... no, make it ten days. By that time the *kermés* will be finished and Xavier will have won the contest. He must win it," he added grimly. In a few words he sketched the tale of the two-hundred-peso bet.

"But that is a great fortune," cried Don Serapio. "How can Hidalgo pay if Xavier loses?"

"It can't pay, for we have not the money. So he will be riding for the honor of Hidalgo. He must not lose."

Don Serapio nodded and trotted out of the patio.

Feeling that this burden was more than he could bear alone, Don Nacho went searching for his friends the priest, the little Doctor, and Don Rosalío. He would explain the situation to them, so that they could place their bets on Xavier against the soldier. Of course Father Zacaya could not put up any money, but he could lend moral support, which, at the moment, Don Nacho desperately needed.

As the fat troubled man reached the center of the plaza, he met Florinda returning from church. There was no doubt of it— she was a beautiful girl. Her hair was as black as a widow's shawl, and her large black eyes were shadowed behind thick long lashes. Her skin was velvety brown, and her cheeks and mouth were a vivid red. Alejandro Castillo said she looked like a mountain poppy, and he often teased her by saying that, like the flower, she had no heart. But she would merely smile a little secret smile and flutter her long lashes as she fluttered them at every man, young and old. She was fluttering them now as she called to Don Nacho in her tinkling voice, "Is it true that there are soldiers in the town?"

"Hunters of goat thieves," muttered the old man. "And one of them wants to enter the horse race." Again he told his story, his stubby-fingered hands moving in quick gestures. "But Xavier will win," he finished, more to assure himself than to flatter Florinda's sweetheart.

"Will he?" murmured the girl diffidently. "Is this soldier the one who was standing in the jail door? The tall, stout one with the fine mustaches? He seemed a very handsome man."

Don Nacho was scandalized. "Such a statement. And from a promised bride!"

"Promised, perhaps, but not a bride," said Florinda with a toss of her head. "Also, does Xavier refuse to look at every pretty girl he sees? Why should I not look at handsome men?"

"Xavier is a man," said Don Nacho flatly, disturbed by this new turn of events.

"Ay, and so is this soldier. A very nice man. What is his name, Don Nacho?"

"Why should I tell it to you—and you a most immodest girl?"

"If you don't tell me, I'll ask someone else. And if I ask someone else, within an hour the news will be all around Hidalgo: 'Florinda, the daughter of Don Genaro, the civil judge, is rolling the eye at the handsome soldier.'"

No one knew the truth of this statement better than old Don Nacho. He glared at her, but he told her. "His name is Baltasar Quiroga. And if Xavier finds out your interest in this sergeant, there will be a fine fight in Hidalgo."

"How nice!" said Florinda. Her eyes narrowed thoughtfully. "Baltasar Quiroga, the fine horseman? But how nice!" A faint smile curved the red lips. "Xavier and Baltasar Quiroga racing against each other. And I a queen. I wonder with which one I shall walk around the plaza?"

Before Don Nacho could sputter an answer, she gave his arm another pat and strolled across the plaza to her house on the Boulevard of the Fifth of May.

It was a very worried Don Nacho who went into the priest's Residence. Bad enough to have the complication of the race without the added complication of Florinda's flirtatious nature. He transferred his burden to the shoulders of his three friends, but their only solution was the same as his own: the honor of Hidalgo—and Hidalgo's women—rested on Xavier's horsemanship. The little Doctor shocked Father Zacaya by quoting a refrain of the Great Revolution, "By noon there are no honorable women or repentant soldiers." There was no doubt. Xavier had to win.

The next day, which was Sunday, found the town in a turmoil of excitement. At mass, when Florinda followed her mother through the great hand-carved doors, the soldier Quiroga dared to salute her. What a scandal! And poor Xavier in jail in Mina. That afternoon the soldier Quiroga actually promenaded up and down in front of Don Genaro's house on the Boulevard of the Fifth of May, pausing now and then to peer through the iron-barred windows. When reproached for allowing this, Florinda very sensibly asked what she could do about it? The sidewalk was free, and if the soldier Quiroga chose to walk there, could she deny him the privilege? Then, via Doña Teresita, the dress-maker, who lived across the street, the news filtered through the town that the soldier Quiroga had actually asked for lodging in Don Genaro's house. This had not been permitted, of course. After all, Don Genaro was the civil judge and no host to common soldiers, but nevertheless, the soldier Quiroga had plainly shown interest in Florinda. After rosary late that afternoon, little groups of women gathered to discuss the situation. Everyone except Florinda and the mustached sergeant was worried about Xavier's reaction. These two, the two most concerned, apparently gave the matter no thought at all.

The real scandal broke that evening, when the whole town turned out for the Sunday plaza promenade. Florinda was walking with her friend, Don Nacho's much older and homelier daughter Chela. Some people were unkind enough to say that Florinda had fostered this friendship because Chela's stocky body, yellow skin, and slanted green eyes made such an excellent contrast to Florinda's dark brilliance. If Chela had heard this, her honest, kind nature had never allowed it to dampen her affection for Florinda.

As Chela said afterwards in quick defense of her friend, there they were, the two of them, walking slowly around, paying attention to their own affairs, when the soldier Quiroga left the men's circle and fell into step beside them. When Florinda saw the sergeant she stopped walking so suddenly that the line behind her was forced to stand still. Almost immediately she regained her composure, and coolly started to walk again. Poor Chela, who abominated gossip, did not know what to do. She could not desert her friend. Florinda was so stubborn that she would continue walking, even though she were alone with the man. And that would proclaim that she was seriously considering this sergeant as a suitor, which would never do. So the unhappy

Chela trotted along, and Florinda and the soldier strolled peacefully side by side while the plaza stared and gaped. In a minute a little wave of sound began rippling across the lime-sweet air . . . a wave that soon began to hum like a hive of frightened bees. Gossip, thought the frightened Chela. Gossip, thought Florinda, a bit frightened also, but larded with pride at the knowledge that her beauty had tumbled her into this situation. Gossip, thought the sergeant, and grinned to himself. Gossip was of small account to soldiers.

"Baltasar Quiroga, your servant," he said to Florinda as the opening gambit.

"Florinda Farías," murmured the girl. "And this is my good friend."

"Chela Villareal," choked the homely girl, still unwed in her twenty-eighth year.

"Hidalgo is famous through all the valley for its beautiful women. A man finds comfort in the thought that such glory is based on fact."

"The women in the other towns must be very homely," said Florinda promptly. This was the correct statement and response. Obviously this soldier knew the rules of courtship.

"I've seen the other villages. The women are beautiful enough . . . but not so modest."

"Modesty is more valuable than beauty," said Chela quickly. The soldier winked at her, and she jerked her head to one side so that he could not see her blush. She knew he was laughing at her, and she had never felt the tragedy of her homeliness so keenly as at that moment.

"You are right, señorita. Modesty is a rare virtue," said Baltasar Quiroga.

"All virtues are rare," said Xavier's voice. Then he stepped out of the shadow of an orange tree to Chela's side. Chela instantly halted, and the line behind her obediently halted also. The sound of humming had ceased, but she knew that it would begin again in a moment with heightened fervor.

"You are no sweet friend of mine, Xavier," she said icily. "Your place is beside Florinda, not me. If the three of you care to continue walking, do so, by all means. I'm going home!" With that she turned and started running toward the Avenue of Illustrious Men. She passed the professor of the Boy's School without even a nod of greeting, although she had secretly admired the slender, delicate little man since his arrival in Hidalgo two years before. She knew that by noon tomorrow every woman in town would find some excuse to call at her house. That night she begged Don Nacho to let her visit her aunt on the Mina Road. By sun-up she was safe from prying gossip.

But Florinda was not made of the stuff that runs away. She grinned wickedly at Xavier and murmured, "Well, so they let you out of jail. How nice." Then she calmly continued to promenade. As she knew he would, the soldier paced slowly at her side, thus forcing Xavier to trot along beside them.

"We two are engaged," said Xavier frigidly to the sergeant, "and I would speak with Florinda."

"Of course." Quiroga bowed just in time to mask his grin.

"But I would not speak to Xavier," said Florinda promptly. "If you leave I will be forced to go home, and the night is too beautiful for such a sacrifice."

"In that case..." Quiroga shrugged, flung out his hands to show that he was a gallant man who could not disobey a lady, and kept on walking.

"You are engaged to me," Xavier muttered in Florinda's ear. "I have some rights."

"Because I am engaged to you, my young rooster, is no sign that I am actually going to marry you. Besides, the banns have not yet been read in the church; so I can change my mind as much as I like."

"Then there is still hope for me," said Quiroga with a wide smile. He knew, and he knew that she knew, that this was only a courtesy speech and meant nothing.

"What would a soldier do with a wife?" snapped Xavier. "Will you upset our whole lives, Florinda, for a man who will stay here only a week? And after he is gone he will forget you soon enough, I can tell you."

"Can you now?" she retorted angrily. She turned the full magic of her velvety eyes on Quiroga. "Will you forget me in a week, soldier?"

"I shall remember you when I am roasting in purgatory," said the soldier promptly.

Xavier swung around to face him. "You have no right to speak such words to my promised wife."

"And who are you to stop me?" demanded Quiroga, drawing himself up to his full height.

The promenading lines had halted again, every eye and ear intent on the two men and the girl.

"I can teach you soon enough." Xavier was so furious that he was pale, and his long slender body was shaking as with a chill.

Florinda stepped between them. "There will be no fighting over me. Do you think I am a girl from the *Gallineros* that I want two men clawing at each other's throats? If you keep this up, I won't marry either one of you!"

At the word "marry" the sergeant's head jerked around. Marriage was not in his bargain. What idea was the little fool getting into her head? Yet his pride as a soldier would not let him withdraw gracefully now.

"This affair must be settled," stormed Xavier, "one way or another. I will not have . . ."

"Stop ordering me about!" snapped Florinda furiously. "I can settle everything very easily."

"Settle it by sending this man about his business." Xavier was sullen.

"I have a right to walk where I please," retorted Quiroga, his eyes narrowing angrily.

"Next Sunday afternoon you both ride in a contest at which I shall be queen. Until then I am a free woman, free to talk to whom I please. After the contest I shall give the winner my answer."

"I won't have it," said Xavier. "Do you think I want to win my wife like . . . a . . . a . . . prize in the lottery?"

Quiroga was insulted. "And who says you will win? Am I not the finest rider in the army?"

"I do not give a one, two, three for your riding," Xavier flashed. "I will match you horse for horse and arm for arm any place you say, but not in the contest."

"So I mean so little to you that you will not ride down a street to prove your love for me," said Florinda between clenched teeth. "Find yourself another bride, then. I'll have none of you." With that she whirled and ran down the street to her own house.

Xavier stood on the plaza sidewalk yelling after her. "I tell you I will not ride in the contest . . . not for you nor any other woman under such conditions!" And he, too, rushed away from the plaza.

The next morning the entire Sabinas Valley was in an uproar. Xavier's noble stand was not appreciated. After all, two hundred pesos were at stake—and water for the Fountain of Charles V. Don Nacho, Don Rosalío, the priest, and the little Doctor sent for Bob Webster and Professor Porfirio Diaz Aah.

"It has come to our ears," said Don Rosalío, stroking his white beard with nervous fingers, "that the young Xavier has returned to Mina to finish his jail sentence. Now you two men are out-landers. He must, through courtesy, listen to you. Promise him anything, but bring him back, and what is more, bring him back ready to ride in the contest."

When the two men arrived in Mina they found Xavier standing on the outside of the jail loudly demanding entrance. The alcalde of Mina was on the inside with the door locked.

"Certainly you cannot enter," the alcalde was saying. "I am a man of my word. I promised to lend you to Hidalgo for ten days."

"But I don't want to go to Hidalgo," shouted Xavier. "I want to serve out my sentence now."

"Impossible. Come back in ten days and I will let you in! But until then this jail is locked to you."

"As a man of honor I cannot return to Hidalgo until after the race," protested Xavier. "If you don't put me in jail, where shall I go? Where shall I eat or sleep?"

"That is your problem," answered the alcalde coldly. "Sleep in the street and eat with the dogs, but do not come whining to this jail. I, too, am a man of honor. And I gave my word to the alcalde of Hidalgo."

Xavier turned dejectedly away. When he saw Bob and the Professor watching him, he shied like an unbroken colt, and tried to evade them, but they caught up with him. With a firm grasp on each arm they led him into a corner saloon and began to argue with him. His mouth shut tightly, he listened to them with politeness but without agreement.

"Two hundred pesos," said the Professor, "has been bet on you. Conceive the vastness of the amount. In all your life you have never seen two hundred pesos. But if you do not ride, and win, Hidalgo must pay out such a sum to those pigs of soldiers."

"There are other horsemen in Hidalgo," said Xavier. "Let Alejandro Castillo or Pepe Gonzalez ride."

"They are fine horsemen," agreed Bob Webster, "but they lack your co-ordination of arm and eye. Everyone in the valley is betting on you, boy. You can't let them down."

"In the two valleys!" said the Professor, his fragile hands flailing the air in his excitement. "San Juan Iglesias is equally concerned in this. Pepe Gonzalez told me that his wife Sarita told him that her father Don Roméo told her that the Valley of the Three Marys was supporting their Matías Galindo, but the serious money was being placed on you."

"You see?" said Bob.

The Professor leaned across the table. "Believe me, Xavier, this is no race of man against man but the honor of the people against the army. Are you going to be selfish and allow the army to win without even one little effort? Have you no feeling for the honor of the people?"

"How about my honor?" demanded Xavier. "Shall it be said that I won my wife with the swiftness of my hand instead of my nobility of spirit? I tell you I will not enter the race." His mouth closed tighter than ever, and he folded his arms on his chest as though he were protecting his body against their onslaughts.

Bob sighed, and for a flashing moment longed for the old days when Pablo, the goatherd, his eyes bright with merriment, had an answer for every argument. If Pablo were here now, he would have Xavier panting with an eagerness for racing. But Pablo was dead, and the duty of persuasion felt heavy on Bob's shoulders. He ordered another round of beer. Perhaps, if they could get Xavier drunk enough, he might give his consent. But the beer merely made Xavier more stubborn. At last Bob and the Professor retired to a secluded corner for a conference.

"You read a lot of books," whispered Bob. "Can't you remember anything that would help us now?"

The Professor wrinkled his thin face in an obvious effort at thinking. At last he regretfully shook his head, and flung out his narrow hands in despair. "Nothing. Not one little idea."

Bob pulled at his ear. If Pablo had been alive, what would he have suggested? Surely there was some answer. In his mind's eye he could see Pablo's compact wiry body, his twinkling eyes, his mouth that was always so ready for laughter. He could see Pablo standing near a lamppost on the Plaza of Independence watching the Sunday evening parade with a mocking grin for christian folk. He could hear Pablo's merry voice saying, "God has been kind to Hidalgo. He has given us so many beautiful women...so very many..." The voice died away, but Bob clutched the Professor's arm with delight. "I've got it!" he yelled, and then he dashed back to Xavier's table, with a startled Professor stumbling after him.

Bob flung himself into a chair and bent across the table, pushing the beer glasses out of the way. "Listen to me, Xavier. You have an argument and a good one, but don't forget that women are strange creatures. If you don't enter the race, Florinda is going to have her pride hurt, and wounded women are dangerous."

"I, too, have pride," said Xavier.

"Yes, but do you know what Florinda will say about you? She will say that you were too much of a coward to even enter the race."

The little Professor picked up his cue with professional ease. "Naturally, she will say that the very reputation of Baltasar Quiroga defeated you."

"All the world will know that is a lie," muttered Xavier. "I am a brave man—me."

"All the world will be glad to believe anything," said the little Professor, "when it has to pay two hundred pesos to the army. Why, Xavier, women will spit in the street when you pass, and men will hide their eyes from you in shame."

"Can they do less if I win a bride as a man wins a bet at cards? If I do not ride, the world will despise me. If I do ride, the world will despise me. So—I do not ride."

Bob started to remind him that there was always a possibility of his losing. After all, Quiroga was a great champion. But he was afraid to destroy the gossamer argument which still floated on the tip of his tongue.

"There is a solution," he said carefully. "Suppose that you do ride—and win—," he held up his hand to prevent Xavier's interruption, "but choose another girl to walk around the plaza with you."

"What?" gasped Xavier. "But Florinda is promised to me. Alejandro Castillo and you yourself presented my case before her family and it was accepted. Because she is a wicked one, should I forget my obligations?"

"It is because she is a wicked one," answered the Professor gravely. "All the village spoils her. She thinks she has only to raise her hand and the world will follow her bidding."

Xavier pulled at his lower lip. "It would be a terrible scandal."

"You will have to choose," said Bob, "between a scandal and a wife. Because if you don't ride, she certainly won't marry you. She's much too proud to marry a coward. But if you do ride, and honor another girl, then she'll marry you quickly to prove her right to you."

The Professor caught up his glass in a toast to Bob. "A speech of rare wisdom. I congratulate you."

"I learned it," said Bob modestly, "from Pablo, the goatherd."

The Professor had never met Pablo (who had died before his arrival in Hidalgo), but Xavier remembered him. So they drank another toast to his memory and then rode back to Hidalgo.

When Bob told Don Nacho that Xavier had agreed to ride, the mayor of Hidalgo sighed with relief. "I have a terrible confession," he admitted, "which, of course, you will keep to yourself. You see, Don Bob, the village does not possess two hundred pesos. If Xavier does not win, we will have to borrow the money from Don Saturnino, and of that I do not approve. Every town in both valleys will know that Hidalgo is a thing of poverty. Even Topo Grande, that collection of mud huts, will have the right to feel superior to us. And that cannot be."

"But, Don Nacho, why did you take on the bet if you knew you couldn't pay?"

Don Nacho spread his hands in a flat palm-down gesture. "How could I refuse in honor? That red-headed General—he is a devil. When he offered the bet, I was too angry for a cunning answer. All I could do was accept."

"Give me leave," asked Bob, "to speak of this to Alejandro Castillo. Between us we should be able to develop some sort of training for Xavier."

The permission was granted and Bob went to Alejandro's beautiful house on the Street of the River, where he found Alejandro in the narrow, low-ceilinged library, the walls of which were lined with books in English, French and Spanish and with the framed moulding of photographs, for Alejandro was an expert photographer. The young Castillo was sprawled in a heavily upholstered red leather chair, one leg hooked over the arm. His right hand was nursing a pipe, his left holding a much thumbed Shakespeare. He waved his pipe at Bob and spoke in English. "I've just found another line to admire in Shakespeare. Listen, 'Of Nature's gifts thou mayst with lilies boast, and with the half-blown rose.' *King John* is a queer sort of play. The more I read it the better I like it."

"Never mind *King John*," Bob told him. "Listen to the fix Hidalgo's in."

Alejandro listened in frowning silence and then he said, reverting to Spanish, "Of course, the most necessary object is the horse. In my father's corrals there should be one that will do."

He tossed the book aside and stood up, his body long and beautifully balanced in his well-worn English riding clothes, the shirt open at his throat, which he had a habit of nursing with his hand. "Let's find Xavier."

They took Xavier to the corrals. The great blacks romped easily around the enclosure, kicking up their heels and jerking their fine heads to show their royalty. Xavier examined them closely, and then cut out three which suited him. He rode them in turn and finally decided on two. "One or the other. They seem to be of equal worth."

Alejandro carefully examined both animals, their mouths, their eyes, their slender legs.

"This one," he said at last, putting his hand on the shining flank. "A bit too nervous, perhaps, but he has the temperament, I think."

The three of them went to Alejandro's ranch across the Sabinas River for the training. Alejandro's men had orders to keep the soldiers away from the front gates. "There is no need for spies here," he said curtly. As he gave orders for the erection of two posts with stretched wire and ribboned rings, Bob watched him curiously. In Hidalgo, Alejandro had a lazy complacency, but here on the farm, he took on an air of efficiency that stiffened him and made him, somehow, more adult. Bob knew that he had owned the Rancho Santo Tomás since he was thirteen, and it furnished him with an income that was more than proof of his business ability. He was exerting this executive force now on Xavier, who was given the traditional long flexible stick and started on his many hours of practice. By the end of the morning, Xavier had pulled down several of the rings, but not enough.

"You miss too often," Bob said miserably over lunch. "The hand and eye need more control."

"Am I a genius then?" Xavier's easy anger flared. "No man can pull down a ring every time. That is impossible."

Alejandro extended a package of cigarettes. "You have practised enough for today," he said abruptly. "There is no virtue in getting too tired at the beginning. Stay with the men this afternoon and amuse yourself. Don Bob and I have words to speak to each other."

Xavier went sulkily away. Bob pushed his chair back from the table and crossed his knees. "Well, Alejandro, what do you think?"

"I don't know. He is temperamental, that one. And this sergeant has a cool brain. I saw him in the contest at Saltillo. As a puller of rings, he is far superior to our young Xavier."

"You think he will win?"

"I am sure of it, unless a miracle occurs. And I do not believe in miracles."

"Poor Don Nacho and his two hundred pesos," sighed Bob.

Alejandro bent toward him, his voice very low. "Perhaps, I am not sure you understand, but perhaps I know someone who might give us advice."

"Then for the love of God produce him!" Bob lifted his glass to take a long drink of the sour red wine, his eyes straying, as they always did, to the large painting of María of the River Road, which hung over the sideboard. Don Saturnino had ordered it put there because of services she had done the Family Castillo during the Great Revolution.

Alejandro drew little figures on the table with his forefinger. "You and I are good friends, eh, Bob? Friends in confidence? What we call in Mexico *compadres?*"

Bob looked shyly at the Mexican over the top of the glass. He wanted to tell Alejandro how he felt, but there were no words, not in English, or in Spanish. And then he was no longer in the raftered dining room. His body was there, sitting on the red chair with the painted yellow and blue flowers, but his mind was in San Antonio, and Ned Kelley was saying in his rich Irish voice, "So the Websters are too damned proud to take you into the family, are they? What the hell! We're buddies, ain't we? How about jumping a boat to Ireland with me, and fighting the English off the green shore?" And then time shifted and he was in France, and Tommy Eaton's Harvard accent was saying, "Some more German hedge-hopping for us tonight, pal."

That's all, thought Bob, just a Harvard accent and an Irish voice. In thirty-three years that has been all, and you sit there and call me *compadre*. What do you want me to say? *Compadre*? Pal? We're buddies ain't we? But the words won't come. Not in Spanish or English, because they're deep inside of me and I can't get at them. He took another drink of the wine. He said aloud in Spanish, slowly, carefully, "As far as I'm concerned we're friends."

Alejandro busied himself with drawing an intricate geometrical design. Bob saw the arch of the fine neck and the thinly chiseled Spanish nose and chin. And as he watched, he saw a glow come into Alejandro that made him shine with an inner light. When he spoke at last, his hoarse voice deepened, caressing the words.

"Do you know María of the River Road?"

Bob looked up at the painting. "I spoke to her once. It was right after the beauty contest. She was walking through the town, and laughing at all the women who scurried away from her as though she were a plague-ridden creature. And of course I've caught glimpses of her when I've ridden past her house under the cliffs."

"You think she is beautiful?"

"I didn't know a woman could be so beautiful," admitted Bob, "and that's the truth. There's a 'Sleeping Venus' by Giorgione in the Art Gallery at Dresden. When I first saw it, I fell in love with it. The delicate flesh tones, the sensual lovely body, the exquisite pure oval face. But I always thought it was just a dream—a perfection of the occidental Venus, until I saw María. But as far as I'm concerned, María is that picture brought to life."

Alejandro quoted softly, " 'Of Nature's gifts thou mayst with lilies boast, and with the half-blown rose.' The minute I read them, I said, 'Those are the only words to describe my beautiful María.' You see . . ." he was still intent on his geometrical designs, "María is my wife."

Bob stiffened in surprise. "Are you crazy? You're married to Evita Cantú!"

"Yes. I'm married to Evita. But María is truly my wife. Not in the church, you understand, but in the heart. And has been for many years."

"I never thought anything could surprise me so much. Why, the story in Hidalgo is that María won't look at any man. Not that enough men haven't tried or wanted to make her, including me," Bob added honestly.

"The point now is," said Alejandro, "that María is very wise. I take all my problems to her. Perhaps she can solve this one of the young Xavier."

Bob was on his feet. "What we need now, friend, is an idea. If María can solve it, by all means go to María."

Alejandro laughed and strolled lazily to the door. "Come with me. María told me that she wanted to meet my friend."

Bob knew then why he had been taken into Alejandro's confidence. It was at María's request. And in this strange "marriage," as in most Latin marriages, the man was the head of the house, but the woman was the señora doña, the strength and the guiding will.

They found María in the small garden at the back of her house beneath the cliffs on the River Road. She was on her knees tending some flowers, and when she lifted her head and saw Alejandro, Bob caught his breath at her radiant beauty.

Alejandro sat down with his back against a tree and took out his pipe. "This is my friend," he said simply, filling the pipe from an oilskin pouch.

María came to her feet in an easy, graceful movement. "My house is honored, Don Bob. That stool is comfortable, I think."

Bob sat on the stool and she went to stand by Alejandro, her hand on his shoulder. He glanced up at her and smiled. Then he flicked his lighter into flame and applied it carefully to the filled pipe bowl. "We have a problem, María," he said, after he had taken a deep lungful of the smoke. He told her what was wrong in short clear sentences while Bob watched them. Bob thought, this is the caste system, right enough. The *grand seigneur* and the girl from the river bank. But they've managed to pull something pretty fine out of it. She is his true wife. It shows all over them. Poor Evita. She will pay a heavy price for this.

Bob did not like Evita. He thought her too imperious and

selfish. But he was suddenly very sorry for her. It was not her fault, but neither was it Alejandro's and María's. It was the fault of their inheritance. Alejandro came from the carefully-tended pure blood and the proud challenge of a handful of conquerors who had subdued an empire with cruelty and in the fierce knowledge that they were the chosen warriors of God. María, this full-bosomed long-limbed woman, was as much a part of the earth as though she had grown from it.

She locked her hands on her hips and began to pace up and down the small, cliff-shadowed garden. Her bare feet in stiff leather sandals moved lightly between the rows of heavy-headed pink poppies and purple iris, and her ankle-long skirts swirled gracefully around her.

Watching her, Bob was vividly aware of her golden quality. It was not the hardness of gold metal, of nuggets found in streams and dug from mines, but rather of all soft and gleaming things that are gold: the wedge of moonlight on black water, late afternoon clouds, sunflowers, globes of oranges against green leaves. Even her voice had golden overtones, not brassy as cymbals, but golden as gongs, and the full notes of trumpets and horns.

Against María's radiance, Candelaria's dusky beauty faded into shadow. To turn from Candelaria to María was to turn from the darkness of a cave to the brilliance of light, but it was the cave that blinded, and the light that was kind to the eyes.

Bob knew that Candelaria would never again hold magic for him, and that all of his dreams of fair women were summed up in this one glowing woman. And she belonged to Alejandro, who was his friend.

He shut his eyes against her, and forced himself to forget the melodic enchantment of her voice, and listen only to her words.

"I have seen these contests. Don Nacho is kind, and permits me to sit on the roof of his house where no one can see me."

Alejandro's hand that held the pipe bowl jerked slightly but he made no comment. She did not notice the movement as she continued placidly, "I think the difficulty is with the stick the rider holds. It appears to be too long and too flexible. I know that when I want to lift something down from a high shelf my arms and hands go rigid."

"Of course," cried Bob. "That's it! You need a flexible stick for strength—as in fishing. But Xavier doesn't need strength to pull down those rings. If we chop the stick in half and give him the sturdier end, I believe he can do it."

Alejandro gazed at María with pride in his eyes. "Always the solution. She never fails me, this María."

María turned her head toward him with a joyous gesture. "I am glad."

As the two men rose to go, Alejandro suddenly dropped his pipe and caught at his throat with both hands. He seemed to be choking for breath. María was instantly beside him, her strong arms half supporting him, with such terror on her face that Bob found himself frozen with panic. Then the dreadful moment ended, and Alejandro relaxed against her, his head cradled on her shoulder, taking deep gasping breaths.

"Good Lord!" cried Bob, catching at his friend's arm. "What happened to you, Alejandro?"

"It is nothing," María said through lips that hardly moved. "Only a tightening of the throat."

"Hadn't we better go to the little Doctor? He..."

"No!" Alejandro straightened with an effort, and shook his head as though to clear it. "It is nothing and is to be forgotten."

Bob flushed and bit his lip at the peremptory tone, but Alejandro dismissed the subject with a shrug and turning to María, kissed her passionately. "I will see you soon, my beautiful," he murmured.

When the two men rode away, Bob looked back over his shoulder. María was standing in front of the door gazing after them with such intensity that Bob had the feeling that she did not expect to see Alejandro again.

He said slowly, "Listen, Alejandro, it's none of my business, but hadn't you better go to the States and see some big specialist about your throat?"

"I have seen them," said Alejandro curtly. "Also in Paris and Vienna."

"Well, what do they say it is?"

"They say—it is a sore throat." The finality of Alejandro's voice closed the subject permanently. Bob exhaled a little puff of air in irritation. Alejandro was so used to the royal manner that there were times when he was excessively trying to his friends. But this same royalty made him oddly vulnerable, and Bob did not want to hurt him. Certainly Alejandro had troubles enough without having his friend add nagging complications. So Bob began talking about the young Xavier.

They tried Xavier with the shorter stick, and the improvement was amazing. Xavier was delighted with the new technique, and for the first time showed any enthusiasm for the race.

That night Bob stayed awake in his room for a long time, reading a new book. Then he went into Alejandro's room to borrow an aspirin for a slight headache. But the room was empty. Alejandro had slipped away to María so quietly that no one had noticed his going. On the chest was a large framed photograph of Evita. Bob, furious at his own sick jealousy, lifted the photograph and closely examined the narrow, selfish mouth, the hard, shallow eyes, the thin, proud nose. He thought, "Alejandro had better be careful of you, little one. You've got a devil in you." Then he hunted for the aspirin and went to bed.

In the meantime, Hidalgo was having its *kermés*. Porfirio had built a line of booths along the school side, where ice-cream of goat's milk, and soft drinks could be bought. The lotto booth took up a large section, as did the marriage booth. A girl presided over the latter, and other girls, provided with large flowered hoops, captured giggling couples and brought them to the booth to go through a mock marriage. The "groom" had to pay one peso for the ceremony, and to the "bride" was given a slip of paper on which was scrawled the young man's name. A girl's popularity was measured by the number of slips she had at the end of the evening, and it was said that the girl with the most slips would be the first to make true marriage vows. Naturally, it was an extremely popular booth, and Florinda was put in charge of it, since she was engaged and therefore ineligible to stand in front of it.

As soon as Don Alonzo could be persuaded to leave his late supper and lead the orchestra, the dance that formally opened the *kermés* began. The side of the plaza across the street from the church was used for this purpose. The "Sunday Evening Plaza Chair Association," gallantly offered free chairs for the chaperones. All men paid ten centavos for admission to the roped enclosure. The beautiful sex, as usual, was admitted free. Confetti was bought by the bagful, and many a black head was sprinkled with gayly colored disks of paper.

The moon was kind to *kermés* week. It shone with its own peculiar brilliance, so that the corner oil lanterns with their hot rancid odor, were really unnecessary. Laughter and high shrill voices drowned out the music, but the dancers did not care. They needed no music for dancing. The gay rhythm within their own bodies was melody enough.

Don Nacho sat by the admission booth dolefully counting the money, most of which was in coppers. Even a full week could not possibly produce two hundred pesos. The peso stake at the marriage booth was his high hope. Every once in a while he would lumber over to it, and dip into Florinda's cash box.

"Now, Don Nacho, it is only two pesos more than the last time you counted it."

"Money is a necessary thing, Florinda. You will discover that after you are married to Xavier."

Florinda tossed her head and rolled her eyes provocatively at the sergeant who was lounging against one corner of the booth. "And is it written in black and white that I shall marry Xavier?"

"You know it is," gasped Don Nacho, scandalized.

She shrugged her shoulders. "Then perhaps I shall destroy the writing. If he really loved me, he would not leave me alone for the whole of *kermés* week."

Don Nacho wagged a finger under her nose. "He is training for the wire-pulling contest. He recognizes his obligation to Hidalgo, and you should honor him for it instead of playing the bear with soldiers."

"Am I playing the bear?" she asked so innocently that the sergeant laughed.

"Eh, Don Nacho, there is no value in arguing with a woman."

"You should know!" snapped the mayor of Hidalgo. He added slyly, "Are you so fine a rider, then, that you do not need to train for the great race?"

The sergeant complacently stroked his fine mustaches. "I am a champion of champions. These country competitions are of little worth." He leaned towards Florinda. "It is only the prize that interests me."

Florinda blushed and provocatively lowered her lids, not in coquetry as the men imagined, but to hide a sudden flash of mischief. She had her own ideas about the outcome of the race, which she was revealing to no one. And she revelled in the sense of her own importance. What girl in all the Sabinas Valley had ever had two men fight such a duel for her pleasure as this daughter of a civil judge? She preened herself like a small, complacent bird, and Don Nacho walked away, muttering angrily to himself.

On the Saturday before the race, he sent a message to Alejandro's farm. "The *kermés* money lacks eighty pesos of the betting sum. Is there good hope?"

Xavier sent the reply. "There is indeed good hope."

The next day dawned clear and beautiful, with much sun, full white clouds, and no wind. After the poles were erected and the wire stretched, with the ribboned rings fluttering in place, the sergeant rode down the street at full gallop. There were nine rings, and nine times he sent his horse down the short track. At the end of that time, he held six rings in his palm. As he dismounted, he tossed the rings with a royal gesture to Porfirio, who was responsible for pinning them in place. "Six rings," he said, "in nine tries. Is your champion better than I?"

The little Professor, who had witnessed the performance from the school window, sniffed audibly and came out on the sidewalk. He held the rings while Porfirio silently lowered the wire in order to replace them. "That creature and his mustaches," said the Professor bitterly. "These soldiers think they own the world."

Porfirio fastened the wire end to the side of the pole, and then gave the lead strand to the top of the pole a strong pull. This caused the wire that spanned the street to jerk higher so that the rings dangling from the colored ribbons danced in the air. "I suppose that is tight enough. And Florinda had best be careful that Xavier does not give her a fine beating. Look at the sergeant gossiping to her through the window. It is a stain on the honor of Hidalgo, that's what it is."

"You are too hard on young people," protested the Professor, who had not come to the village until several years after Porfirio was married.

Porfirio carefully spat in the gutter. "Do you think the young can not be wicked then? Ten pesos it cost me to learn that lesson, and I will not quickly forget it."

But Florinda was not thinking of Porfirio and his hard-bought lesson. She was listening with satisfaction while the sergeant insisted that he would fetch her the moon if she so desired it.

At precisely two o'clock the crowds began to line the narrow sidewalks. Some of the horsemen had already arrived, including Matías Galindo from San Juan Iglesias and Salvador Sánchez from El Carmen. When Xavier, mounted on his fine black horse, rode into view, followed by Bob and Alejandro, the village cheered lustily. Xavier bowed and smiled, but Bob noticed that Alejandro was looking at the roof of Don Nacho's house. Bob glanced up in time to see a flash of sunlight on gold hair before María crouched down behind the shielding rail of the wall elevation.

"Whether we win or lose," Alejandro muttered under his breath, "Don Nacho shall have his fountain. He shall have a thousand fountains if he wants them."

"A fountain where the animals can drink is a very humanitarian thing," said Bob cheerfully. "And stop looking at Don Nacho's house or the entire village will wonder if you want to buy it."

Alejandro grinned and turned his attention to Xavier. While he helped the boy examine the stirrups and saddle girth, the queens arrived. The orchestra loudly played the applause music. Two tiers of seats had been erected for them directly in front of the Boy's School. There were girls from each of the five villages and one girl from San Juan Iglesias. Florinda represented Hidalgo. It was their duty to fasten the captured rings to the sleeves of each contestant, and they were shaking with excitement.

The race was to begin at two-thirty. Don Nacho was timekeeper, and he was frowning at his large watch. "It lacks but three minutes of the time," he told Bob, "and the soldiers have not yet arrived. Should I hold up the race for them, considering the size of the bet?"

"For five minutes," Bob told him, "but no more. Just because they are soldiers doesn't mean they are entitled to all the privileges in the world."

"My opinion precisely," pronounced Don Nacho with finality. At two-thirty-three, General Elizondo and a group of his men strode up to the riders.

"You, Xavier of the fine horse, where is my sergeant?" The General was so angry his blue eyes were flecks of clear ice.

"Your sergeant?" Xavier gazed around in perplexity at the other riders. "What should I know of him?"

"He has been missing since noon. And you know very well that he is a greater champion than yourself. If you have harmed him, I, myself, shall hang you on the spot."

As one man the other riders closed in behind Xavier. Matías Galindo and Salvador Sánchez turned sideways to the General, ready to catch his guns. But Xavier moved away from them and drew himself to his full height. His voice was as icy as the General's eyes.

"I am a man of honor. This race was not of my choosing, but since it is necessary, I ride to the rings. Your sergeant is your affair, not mine. Do you question my honor in this matter?"

The General glanced around at the silently watchful people. He had his soldiers behind him, but Xavier had all of the civilian population. And honor cannot be lightly challenged in the Republic. With a shrug he backed away and consulted Don Nacho.

"I cannot understand his disappearance. There can be no doubt that he intends to race. And no doubt, of course, but that he will win."

"Of course," said Don Nacho with heavy sarcasm.

The General snorted angrily. "You will hold up the race until he appears."

"I will hold it up," said Don Nacho, "precisely five minutes, no more."

When the five minutes were finished, the sergeant had still not appeared. Don Nacho, with punctilious courtesy, borrowed the General's gun and shot it into the air.

Each man rode nine times, corresponding to the nine rings. Then the wire was lowered, the rings were replaced, and the next man came thundering down the narrow street. Since Xavier represented Hidalgo, he rode last. Salvador Sánchez, from El Carmen, that being the most distant town (for poor little Topo Grande of the mud huts had no representative), rode first. He gathered five rings, and the musicians played lustily for him when he went to the queen from El Carmen to have the rings fastened to his sleeve. Matías Galindo, of San Juan Iglesias won four rings. Some of the riders won none at all, the rest not more than two.

The sun was already lowering behind the western rim of mountains when Xavier rode up to the starting post, his short sturdy stick firmly held in his right hand. The General quickly protested the stick, which was not the usual type, and both Bob and Alejandro held their breath in suspense until the little Professor pointed out that the sergeant had made a practice run that same morning with a short stick. The General shrugged and gave way, leaving Alejandro and Bob to look at each other with relief.

"The little Professor," Alejandro muttered, "is a surprising man. When he first came here, he had the courage of a mouse. Now he beards this lion of a general."

"Maybe he's in love," grinned Bob. "I saw him talking through the window to Don Nacho's daughter Chela the other day."

Alejandro puffed his cheeks with air. "That poor homely child give a man courage? She has not enough for herself."

At that moment Don Nacho fired the gun. Xavier's horse reared and then shot forward in the easy lope that Xavier had taught him.

The boy stood up in the stirrups, his body stiff and steady. His right hand rose and fell, and a ring dangled from the stick. The crowd applauded delightedly as he trotted back to place. Again he rode, and again a ring swung on the stick's end. But the third time as he lifted from the saddle, his stick poised for the lunge, the wire seemed to dance up out of his reach, and the horse carried him on without the prize. He shook his head in bewilderment and tried once more. The same thing happened again. He rubbed his hands across his eyes, thinking that the slanting light was betraying him, when he heard a loud argument on the sidewalk.

Looking like a small bantam rooster, the little Professor was shouting at the General. "What right have you to touch the wire? Is this a pulling of baskets above the heads of children?"

"Do you accuse me of dishonesty," yelled the General, "and my fine sergeant kidnapped as by witchcraft?"

"Then go to the witches to find him," retorted the Professor. "But you stand on the other side of the street. I, myself, will guard this wire. Return to the race, Xavier."

The General crossed the street with poor grace. He did not like having a little man who barely reached his shoulder order him about. But he could afford to have no trouble. These people had doubtless kidnapped Baltasar, and therefore could hold him as hostage against any act of the General's. But they would pay the two-hundred-peso bet. To kidnap Baltasar was to admit that he was the better rider. Therefore the two hundred pesos belonged to the soldiers.

But the General grudgingly had to admit that Xavier was a magnificent rider. The rest of the rings dropped on his stick as easily as though he had lifted them from a pile. When he swung off his horse to approach the queens, the orchestra played the applause music so violently that the violin and guitar were two measures ahead of the rest of the instruments. But no one listened to the music. Everyone was watching Xavier. His attitude about the race was well known. Would he dare to hand the rings to some other girl than Florinda?

No one had counted on the spoiled Florinda. Before he could reach the queens, she stepped forward and snatched the rings from his hands. "I will pin them on," she said with firm emphasis, and counted as she pinned them: "One, two, three, four, five, six and seven."

"Xavier of Hidalgo is clearly champion," Don Nacho announced in a pleased roar.

"But," said the General, stepping forward. "The two hundred pesos belong to me."

"How so?" snapped the little Professor, thrusting his head around Don Nacho's great bulk.

"My sergeant has been kidnapped..."

"Do you accuse..." began Don Nacho wrathfully.

The General held up his hand. "Not the town, no. But doubtless some committee of patriotic young men have thought it expedient to remove this danger." He stared first at the Professor, then at Pepe Gonzalez, Alejandro Castillo, and Bob Webster. "Which proves that Baltasar Quiroga would undoubtedly have won."

Don Nacho sighed and passed his red bandana across his forehead. He knew that Pepe Gonzalez was perfectly capable of thinking up such an exploit, and Alejandro and Bob of carrying it out. The little Professor pushed his way forward.

"Baltasar Quiroga lost the race, and this morning."

At his firm tones the murmuring people became very quiet. The General tossed his head in amazement. "What words are you speaking?"

"It is true. He ran the nine lengths and pulled only six rings.

For witness I have Porfirio, the carver of wood, and Florinda, daughter of Don Genaro, the civil judge. Do I speak true words, señorita?"

Eyes swung towards the girl's face. Xavier lifted his hand as though to touch her arm, and then let it drop. Bob kept punching his elbow in Alejandro's ribs. "Look at Xavier," he whispered excitedly. "He's so pale you could write a letter on him with white ink."

Then Florinda gave her head a defiant toss. "I saw it with my own eyes. And when he was finished he called the rings. 'Six rings,' he said. 'Can any man do better?'"

"With these ears I heard him," Porfirio affirmed loudly.

The color rushed back into Xavier's face, and a soft breeze of laughter floated across the people.

Florinda took a step toward the General and fluttered her long lashes. "Xavier did better. Or are seven rings not better than six?"

"And he would have won all nine," the little Professor added with unblinking faith, "if you had not pulled the wire. We win our victories with skill, not cunning. Use cunning on your goat thieves, who are doubtless waiting for you in the hills beyond Mina."

There was a loud round of applause to greet this speech. The General looked at the derisive faces; then he nodded to his soldiers and they strode to their horses. As they were about to mount, the little Professor called out, "One moment!" He walked toward them, and dignity touched him so that he was no longer a delicate nonentity, but a man of worth and assurance. "You have forgotten the little matter of two hundred pesos which you owe to the town of Hidalgo."

Everyone was very still. Don Nacho bit down on his lip in an agony of worry. Better for the town to lose the money than for the red-headed General to lose his temper. But the General was actually smiling. "You have courage, little man. If you ever serve in the army, I hope you serve under me. Give him the money."

A soldier unfastened a money bag from the saddle and counted twenty ten-pesos gold pieces into the Professor's hands. There was a loud shout of, "Long live the Professor! Long live the General! Long live the Revolution!" from the people. The soldiers mounted, waved their hats. Their horses reared and broke into a sudden gallop. There were more shouts. The orchestra played the applause music. The soldiers were gone from Hidalgo.

Don Nacho clapped the little Professor on the back. "Well done, friend. You have a fine head on your shoulders. Fine enough, do you think, to play dominoes at the priest's house this evening?" It was the ultimate triumph. The little Professor had been admitted into the sacred circle of Hidalgo's rulers. And no one saw the quick smile of delight that he flashed at Don Nacho's homely daughter Chela.

The musicians had started to play again. It was time to begin the triumphal procession around the plaza. Florinda had such a firm grip on Xavier's arm that he had no choice but to fall into step beside her. The other riders and queens paired off behind them, and then came the rest of the people.

Xavier had a worried line between his brows. "This business of Baltasar Quiroga I do not like. Do you think that Pepe Gonzalez really had him kidnapped?"

A shadow of a smile flickered across Florinda's mouth. "I must admit the truth. I sent the clever Baltasar to Mina to bring me a gift of fourteen hens from my Uncle Odilón."

Xavier stopped walking so abruptly that the parade behind them was forced to a standstill. Everyone heard him exclaim, "But your Uncle Odilón lives in Abasolo."

"As doubtless the alcalde of Mina informed the fine sergeant when he put him in jail."

"Fourteen hens," Xavier said blissfully.

"Fourteen days," corrected Florinda placidly. "Did you think, you fool, that I would allow any man but you to win this race?"

A loud gasp swept the plaza when Xavier suddenly pulled Florinda to him and kissed her. But Florinda was contemptuous of Hidalgo's shocked surprise. Was she not the daughter of Don Genaro, the civil judge? Was she not queen of the *kermés?* She put her arms around Xavier's neck and soundly returned his kiss.

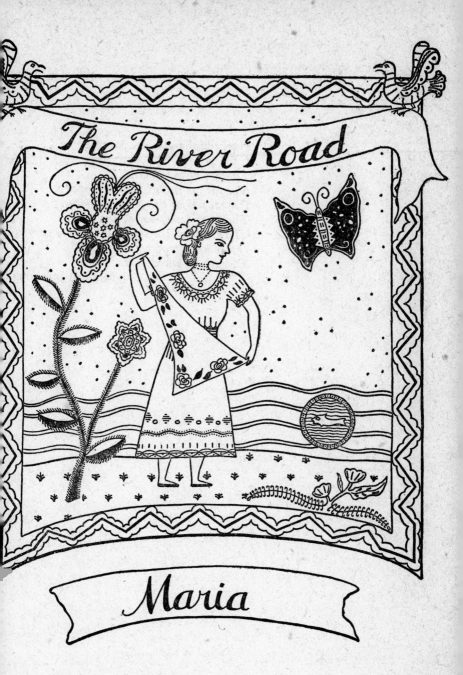

The River Road

Maria

Ungrateful and cruel fortune,
I, for my sorrows, have come
To gaze on the cactus.
Not for me its red fruit of honey,
But for me its sharp ivory thorns.
The merry may eat of the fruit,
The weeping are stabbed with the thorns.
I, for my sorrows, have come
To gaze on the cactus.

—Mexican folk song

I T WAS DURING THE BEAUTY CONTEST THAT THE MYSTERY OCCURRED.
Don Ricardo, the one-armed policeman, saw it first. He was
supposed to guard the exhibit, and was wandering past the
photographs that hung on the Casino wall, thoughtfully examining them at his leisure while the rest of Hidalgo ate its
noonday meal. Friend Sauceda has taken good pictures, he
thought, chewing on a *tortilla* filled with fried beans. Doña
Fela's youngest daughter is not really as pretty as that. But Nena
Santos' sister, now she is a true pretty one. Evita Cantú—he shook
his head. Sauceda should have tried harder with Evita, and she
engaged to be married to the young Castillo. Her face looked
like a mask, cold and hard, with disdain in the eyes, while in life
her eyes were like black flowers drenched with rain, lips that
were small and proud, and skin that was sweet scented and soft.
Not so soft as María of the River Road's, of course, but still soft.
Ay, that María! Now she was the beautiful one. What a pity
that her picture could not be in the contest.

And then he saw it, hanging in the center of the wall, in the
very best position. It showed her kneeling by a flat porous rock
piled with moist corn meal. Between her hands was a long,
rounded grinding stone. Her head was thrown back and she was
laughing into the camera so that she seemed to be laughing at
Don Ricardo.

The one-armed policeman choked on a bite of *tortilla* and
thrust his head closer. Unlike the other photographs of heavy
gray cardboard decorated with flying doves, it was printed on a
thin, rough paper. Underneath was the entry blank: María de las
Garzas; Age: twenty-six; Height: five feet, six inches; Weight:
65 kilos; Hair: gold; Eyes: blue; Skin: color of honey.

Don Ricardo drew a deep breath. Who had put this picture
here? Was he not on duty every minute, so that no mischievous
soul could play tricks with the pictures? (As one mischievous
soul obviously had.) Why, he had not left the exhibit this morning save to carry that little love note from Alejandro Castillo to
Evita Cantú, and Alejandro himself had been in the room during
that time.

The policeman took off his broad-brimmed straw hat and
scratched his head. Seeing the young Xavier lounging on a plaza
bench, Don Ricardo put him to guard the sacred door, and then
hurried up the Street of the Forgotten Angel to the great Castillo house, where he waited in the back patio while a servant
went to fetch Alejandro from his lunch. Surely this was a cata-

clysmic enough occurrence to merit disturbing Alejandro at his food. In all the history of Hidalgo such a thing had never happened. To think of a picture of María de las Garzas . . . that outcast girl from the river bank . . . entered in the great beauty contest along with pictures of decent girls from the town! No, the idea was not to be tolerated for a moment.

Don Ricardo sat on a low turquoise-painted bench and rested his chin on his hand, while his slow-thinking mind remembered the events of the past few days. *El Porvenir,* Monterrey's largest newspaper, was sponsoring a beauty contest for the neighboring valley towns, the winner in each district to be brought to Monterrey to act as queen at the bullfight. Oh, it would be a magnificent event, with the queens real queens of beauty and not chosen simply because of their social position.

Every girl in every village shook with ecstasy at the idea. Hidalgo belonged to the Sabinas Valley district and had to compete with the neighboring towns that were strung along the Sabinas River like dusty brown beads: Mina, Hidalgo, Abasolo, El Carmen, Topo Grande. Five towns, with a girl in every house. Hidalgo was confident that its entrant would represent the Sabinas, for the other towns lacked the delicacy, the soft warm grace of Hidalgo girls.

Their fame for beauty was great enough to bring an itinerant photographer, one Amadéo Sauceda, from Monterrey. He could take a picture and produce a print in five minutes, and he was clever. He arranged with Don Nacho to keep all other photographers out of the village, and so made enough money going from house to house to buy a whole ticket on the sixteenth of September lottery. He did not win the grand prize, but he won enough to open a studio in Monterrey, and finally became the great Sauceda, with the reputation of being the finest photographer of women on the frontier.

Even with his meagre equipment his talent was sensitive enough to produce flattering portraits of his models. With one exception . . . Evita Cantú. Sauceda had been told many times that Evita was considered the beauty of the valley (always with the exception, of course, of María de las Garzas, who did not count), and that she was engaged to the young Castillo. It would be a marriage of families, true, but it was a well known fact that Alejandro had worshipped her for years. He had never played the bear to any other girl, and as for her, when she looked at him with those soft black eyes, ay, sweet saints, it made even old hearts beat faster. A true romance, of that there could be no doubt. But Sauceda, the artist, saw that the soft black eyes were shallow, the head was held too proudly, and the small red mouth was narrow and tight with selfishness. He tried to show her as Hidalgo imagined her. But his talent betrayed him. He took three pictures. They were all the same, cold, hard, mask-like. "I am sorry," he said at last. "I give you the picture for nothing. Some women have faces too delicate to photograph." So the too revealing portrait was entered in the contest.

Poor Alejandro, thought Don Ricardo waiting in the patio. What will he do about this great scandal, and the photograph of his adored Evita on the wall next to María's?

Alejandro came through the arched doorway. "Eh, Don Ricardo, what is this terrible thing that has happened?"

Don Ricardo told him in long, involved sentences. "It is a wicked impudence, Alejandro. Who put the picture there? You were guarding the room while I was gone."

Alejandro turned his head slightly so that the policeman could not see the merriment dancing in his eyes. "Not all the time, Don Ricardo. There was trouble with the liquor bill, and I went to the Saloon of the Devil's Laughter to straighten the account. Anyone could have entered, filled out the blank, put up the picture."

"You had better come and take it down before anyone sees it, Alejandro."

Alejandro's hoarse voice took on a rougher note, his nervous fingers touching his throat. "Why? The picture was properly entered."

"You mean to leave it there?"

"Certainly. Admit to yourself, Don Ricardo. Is not this María a truly beautiful creature?"

"Even as the angels, Alejandro, but the women won't like it. María is an outcast, a poor creature from the river bank. The women will be very angry."

Don Ricardo was right. The women shook with anger. Even Doña Fela, the town's matriarch, wanted Alejandro to take it down.

"How can I, Doña Fela? The contest is open to all. Only a photograph and the proper filling out of the entrance blank are necessary."

"But this woman," fumed Doña Fela, her three chins quivering in righteous indignation, "is a creature without even a name. Only the saints know where she gets money enough to keep clothes on her body. From the boys in the town, I expect."

Alejandro's long-fingered hands tightened over the knobs of the uncomfortable Victorian chair until the knuckles turned white. His husky voice, however, kept its pleasant, even tone. "Her morals have nothing to do with the contest, Doña Fela."

"Certainly they have. Supposing she wins. How can Hidalgo send this creature to Monterrey to be a queen at the bullfight, along with decent girls from other villages? It would be an impossible situation."

"Even if she wins in Hidalgo, she might not win over the other girls in the valley district . . ."

"An Hidalgo girl is certain to win in the valley," said Doña Fela with cold pride. "It could not be otherwise. But this shameful creature is impossible. She . . ."

"Doña Fela," he leaned forward tensely, "have you certain knowledge that she is any less good than the town girls?"

"I do not discuss morals with young men," said Doña Fela primly. "Also, as the promised bridegroom of Evita Cantú, you have no right to keep their pictures on the same wall."

Alejandro stood up. He seemed to tower in this room, which was darkened against the noonday sun. "I am sorry, Doña Fela. Her picture was properly entered. I have no right to take it down."

Doña Fela snorted daintily into a lace-trimmed handkerchief. "If Pepe Gonzalez were not two years decently married, I might believe—Alejandro, do you think Bob Webster could have put that picture there?"

"I doubt it. He was saying this morning that he has never more than glimpsed her on the River Road."

"Ha! An easy statement. And it might appeal to his *Yanqui* sense of humor to help this creature win the contest."

"Ay, but Doña Fela, we know who will win the contest, don't we?"

Doña Fela missed the tinge of sarcasm as she smiled at him.

"My blessings on you and Evita both. It will be a fine day for Hidalgo when you two are married. And your father so happy over it. I have not seen him so happy since the days when your brother was still here. It is a magnificent wedding, Alejandro. A magnificent wedding."

Out on the street, Alejandro paused for a moment to wipe the palms of his hands with his handkerchief. Be careful, he muttered to himself. They will drive you to the wall someday, and then such a scandal will thunder as will shake the very mountains.

He strode quickly along the Street of the Cañon to the Casino.

"Eh, Alejandro," called the little Doctor, emerging from the Saloon of the Devil's laughter. "How is the throat?"

"It does very well. And I would rather not talk about it." Alejandro shrugged. "After all, it is my affair."

"It will soon be Evita's," warned the little Doctor. "You should tell her the truth, boy."

"Why?" Alejandro flung back his head so that the sun illumined his thin Spanish face. "She would only worry. And there is nothing she can do about it."

"Have you felt any pain?"

"Nothing but the choking. The doctor in Canada said I would not feel any for perhaps three years. Then will come the pain and . . ." He snapped his fingers. "I try not to think about it. And you shouldn't. It is our secret. It is better that way." With a graceful nod, he crossed the Street of the Hidden Water to the Casino.

The little Doctor shook his head helplessly and then re-entered the saloon to sit down at the table with Don Nacho.

"Does Alejandro know any more about the picture?"

"He didn't say," mumbled the little Doctor, gulping down a glass of beer.

The fat mayor sighed heavily. "Personally, I think it is the work of Bob Webster. I think I shall have a little talk with that young man."

But when Bob was called to Father Zacaya's house, he protested his innocence. "I don't even own a camera. How could I take her picture?"

"You might have borrowed one of Alejandro's cameras," suggested Don Rosalío, playing nervously with his white beard.

Bob laughed curtly. "Alejandro thinks more of those cameras

than he does of his right eye. If you think he'd let me—or any-
body else—borrow one, you're crazy."

"But you are Alejandro's *compadre*," persisted Don Nacho.
"If you wanted the camera he would lend it to you."

"Perhaps Alejandro took the picture," suggested the little
Doctor with a broad grin for his own joke.

In the midst of laughter, Father Zacaya said, "Alejandro's eyes
are blank, save when resting on Evita Cantú. At least we can be
certain of Alejandro's innocence."

"Understand that we are not angry with you," said Don Nacho
placatingly. "We merely want you to solve this mystery for us,
Don Bob."

"But I can't," said Bob stubbornly. "I don't know anything
about it."

And there the matter rested, although the four rulers of
Hidalgo and the town itself were certain of Bob's guilt.

Amadéo Sauceda was the only one in the village who was more
interested in the model than in the photographer. He looked at
the picture for a long time. A woman like that was not to be
seen every day. He had found the selfishness in Evita's face. In
María's he saw the ability to *gozar la vida*, enjoy and fulfill life.
On impulse he snatched up his cumbersome camera and hurried
down the Street of the Hidden Water to the River Road.

He found María by her little house in the cliff's shadow as
though she had never stopped grinding corn since the snapshot
was made. Her fine large body with the full pointed breasts reminded Sauceda of pictures he had seen of island women walking
down sun-bleached coral roads. María's bone structure was almost perfect, and he discovered after a moment's scrutiny that
the secret of her peculiar attractiveness lay in the combination
of Nordic coloring with the high cheekbones, blunted chin, and
slanting eyes of the Latin.

At this time María was at the height of her beauty. Her hair,
gold with a green glint to it, was thick and long, parted in the
center and twisted into a loose knot on the back of her neck.
This hair had the luster of raw silk, and curled in soft tendrils on
the broad low forehead. Her nose was straight and chiseled, the
eyes blue as dark sapphires set under narrow black brows that
flared at the outer corners like wings. The mouth was wide and
full, very red, with a sensual lower lip. Her skin was soft and

clear, tanned by the sun until it resembled honey fresh from the comb. She was tall for a Mexican woman, and her body, narrow of shoulder, heavy of hip, with long arms and legs, moved slowly in harmony with a languorous inner rhythm.

When Sauceda asked to be allowed to take her picture, she put her hands on her fine hips and laughed at him. But at last she said indifferently, "Take as many as you like."

Instead of striking some awkward pose, her features freezing into self-conscious stolidity, she turned back to the grinding of the corn, humming under her breath:

> *Sweetheart of the fields, red poppy,*
> *Floating in your jade green sea...*
> *Flaming poppy of the valley,*
> *Would you care to marry me?*

He thought, she knows how to pose, this one. She's been photographed many times, and by a man who knows his business. That picture he took of her showed good work. I wonder who he is? But the slanting afternoon sun would not wait for curious questions. The mountains were already turning purple in the evening air. Sauceda grimly set himself to the task of photographing her as best he could with his limited equipment. When he was finished, he showed her the prints. She looked at them without curiosity, as though they portrayed a chance acquaintance. One of them, showing her bending over the flat stone to get corn from the tin pail, amused her. "Do I look like that," she asked, "all arms and legs like a spider?" This was the photograph she chose to keep although he tried to get her to accept another pose.

"*Vaya* friend! The others are very beautiful, but this one is María de las Garzas. I keep this one."

He went away after that. As the road turned out of sight, he waved to her, but she paid him no attention. It was as though he had left no impression on her. He shrugged and went up the road, stepping aside to allow Alejandro, on one of the great Castillo blacks, to gallop past him.

At the bend of the road, Alejandro pulled his horse to a standstill and waited until Sauceda was out of sight. Then he whistled softly three times. The whistle was answered, and he hurried to the sheltered garden at the back of María's house. She rubbed the back of her hand across her mouth, and lifted her face for his kiss. "Eh, mischievous one. I hear my picture is entered in the contest."

Alejandro sat on the ground with his body resting against a huisache tree, and lighted his pipe. "It is a magnificent scandal," he said contentedly.

María wrinkled her nose at him. "You have the devil in you, Alejandro. Why did you enter it?"

He looked at her through narrowed lids, the blue smoke from the pipe curling about his face. "Did anyone ever tell you, María, that you are the most beautiful woman in the world?"

She snapped her fingers at him. "Answer me, foolish one. Why did you enter it?"

"Why?" He touched his hands to his throat. "How can I answer you? Because the devil was in me. Because I looked at all those pictures, and Evita's like a mask, and I said to myself, my María is more beautiful than any of these. I said, all the valley must say that my María is the most beautiful. I said, she will be my María for only one month more, and then..." His harsh voice was silent. He put his face against his hand. "María, I can't marry Evita. It is impossible! My father would understand. Surely my father would understand!"

He felt her kneel beside him, take him in her arms. "Quiet, my own. It is difficult, yes. It tears the heart, yes. But it can be done."

"María." He put his hands on her arms, pressed his fingers down until she bit her lips with the pain. "I love you so much. What am I to do?"

She said softly, teasingly, "You and your five names... Alejandro Gregorio Mauricio Castillo Buentello and I with my one name, María. Would they not look stupid together in the marriage book?"

He drew her to him, kissed her. "They would be written in gold, María."

"Not in the eyes of the world, Alejandro. Not in the eyes of your father."

"María, after I am married, why not... why can't we..."

She shook her head and gently drew away from him. "No, Alejandro. For myself, your marriage makes no difference. But for you, it is a difference. It is right that you should be her true husband, have a son by her. That is what your father really wants, for you to have a son to carry on the Castillo name. The Castillos have been lords of this valley for a long time. How long, Alejandro?"

"More than three hundred years."

"Imagine. Three hundred years. And now it is coming to an end, if you have no son."

He turned away from her, put his hands on the trunk of the huisache tree. He did not notice the sweet fragrance of its feathery yellow flowers. "I don't want her son. It is your son I want."

"What use to want now, Alejandro? One thing or the other, it is all the same. And you must take to her son all of your strength and your virility. No, the night you marry, the story of Alejandro and María will be finished."

"It has been a long story, María."

"Very long. So much to remember. That is good, to have so much to remember. Look, Alejandro. The sun is behind the mountain peaks. The train from Monterrey with the men to judge the contest will be coming soon. You must go to meet it."

He nodded without saying anything, turned and pulled her to him, kissing her eyes, her forehead. He rested his cheek against her forehead. She was very quiet in his arms. Finally he kissed her mouth, gently and without passion, and went away.

The judging of the pictures was handled in an easy manner. Anyone who cared to vote could do so, writing his preference on a slip of paper and pushing it into a locked ballot box. Don Nacho put Don Ricardo to guard the box so that there could be no ballot stuffing. All the town's men voted, first examining each picture as minutely as though it were the quality of the camera work and not the beauty of the sitter that impressed them. None lingered for more than a minute in front of María's portrait. They scurried past it as though they expected their wives' long arms to dart forth and pluck them home by the ear. The voting was laborious, requiring much wetting of lead pencils and scratching of ears, but finally the last ballot had been thrust into the box, and it remained for the committee to sort and count them. To keep from showing any hint of favoritism, Alejandro had invited three of his Monterrey friends to make up the committee.

They all gathered in the bar for a last drink before the grim business of finding the winners began. "I give you a toast," said Alejandro, lifting his glass high in the lamplit room. "To the most beautiful girl in Hidalgo, whoever she may be." The toast was drunk with loud shouts, and as a final gallant gesture, the glasses were shattered on the cement floor. They all knew to whom Alejandro was drinking. Evita Cantú would surely win, in spite of the odd, mask-like portrait.

While the votes were being counted Alejandro walked around the plaza, bowing to his well chaperoned fiancée, who, along with three quarters of the town, was sitting on the plaza waiting for the contest results. Suddenly Don Ricardo was seen running toward him across the plaza. Alejandro hurried to the Casino, while a buzz of conversation turned the plaza into a giant beehive. Something had happened, but what? Who was winning? The policeman flung up his single arm, refused to answer questions, and trotted after Alejandro.

Inside the Casino one of Alejandro's friends, Ricardo Manchaca, was striding up and down, his eyes shining. "But it is magnificent," he cried as the tall young man appeared in the doorway. "I have never seen such perfect taste in a small town."

"What do you mean?" Alejandro's sharp voice whirled Manchaca around in a flurry of apology.

"I'm sorry, Alejandro. I shouldn't have said that. You see..."

His voice died away helplessly and Pablo Gomez, the second judge, took up the sentence. "You see... Evita hasn't won."

"Not won? You mean..." He paused and stared at his three friends who stared gravely back at him.

It was Tomás Belén, the third judge, who answered him. "This María... this river girl won by a great majority. There were three hundred votes cast, and she won two hundred and ninety-three of them."

"Evita won the other seven," added Manchaca consolingly. "The others didn't win any."

To their surprise Alejandro began to laugh. He straddled a chair and laughed until Manchaca pushed a glass of raw whisky into his fingers. He stopped abruptly and held the glass between his face and a smoking lamp chimney. "And I drank to the most beautiful girl in Hidalgo. With your permission, gentlemen, I drink to her again." He drained the glass and set it carefully down on the table.

Manchaca said with a worried frown, "This is, of course, an impossible situation."

"What are we to do?" asked Pablo Gomez.

"Why not give the decision to Evita?" put in Tomás Belén. "After all, she did get some votes which is more than can be said for the rest of them."

"No," said Alejandro thickly. "This María won the contest. Her name shall be declared as the winner in Hidalgo. The counting of the votes will be kept secret."

"You are a little drunk, friend," said Pablo Gómez brutally, "or you wouldn't make such a suggestion."

Alejandro looked sullenly at him, his nervous fingers worrying his throat. "It isn't a suggestion. You were asked to count the votes and that was all. I am chairman of the committee. We shall simply anounce that María won by a majority of votes."

That was the way it was done. María's picture also won in the finals at El Carmen, but the chairman of that committee was a married man; so no girl of Hidalgo was sent to Monterrey. The Sabinas Valley mocked Hidalgo for allowing a common river girl to triumph over a town full of beauties. The result was that the town turned on the girl. When she walked the streets, the children booed her and women would step hastily inside the most convenient doorway in order to let her pass. María found this enmity amusing. The day she drove Doña Fela into the Saloon of the Devil's Laughter, her own great laughter resounded from the pink walls.

The town hated her, but the more it hated her, the more it amused her, and finally it was forced to ignore her. She came and went in her usual manner, speaking to no one, expecting no one to speak to her. Some of the town's wilder boys made a great show of calling out to her, but she looked straight through them as though they were shadows on a wall. At last Hidalgo left her alone, and the months slipped along without noticeable friction.

Strangely enough, none of this enmity was turned against Bob Webster. His housekeeper, Tía Magdalena, championed his innocence (although she was privately convinced of his guilt) and she was too powerful a friend of the eagle witches to be lightly ignored. So Bob was again admitted to the village confidence, but he could still feel an undercurrent of resentment.

One day, as he and Pepe Gonzalez were crossing the Plaza they saw María strolling along the Street of the Governors. Catching Pepe's arm, Bob ran after her, stopping her in front of the grocery store. Don Isaác, the grocer, avid for gossip, joined the little group.

"María," cried Bob, "tell these men the truth."

"About what, señor?"

"Who took the contest photograph of you?" demanded Pepe Gonzalez.

Her blue eyes veiled with mischief. "Perhaps you did," she said, and entered the grocery store.

Pepe's mouth fell open with surprise. Don Isaác punched him in the ribs. "What will your wife Sarita say to that, friend Pepe?"

"But I didn't!" gasped Pepe. "I never took a picture in all my days..."

"Now you know how I feel," said Bob.

"But this is serious," Pepe protested. "Sarita will have my ears!"

Afraid to enter the store, thus shutting them off from the chaperoning gaze of the village, the three men pleaded with her from the doorway. "Tell us the truth, María. Please tell us the truth."

María, after helping herself to the groceries she needed, flung the money on the counter and came out to them, her basket balanced on her head. She carefully surveyed each one and then said loudly, "Do you stupid fools think that only Hidalgo men are skilled in the art of taking pictures? After all, I live on the River Road. Men from Abasolo, El Carmen, even from Topo Grande, pass my door. Look to them for your answer, my little ones. For you'll never have one from me." Her laughter drenched them with its golden tones, and she strode away, leaving three dazed but satisfied men.

Hidalgo stormed with anger that someone not an Hidalgo man should have dared to play such a joke on the town's dignity. But no feuds were started. The memory of the San Juan Iglesias feud was still too fresh. Also, all the other towns hotly protested the accusations. So Hidalgo, the martyr, held her head high with magnificent disdain, and life returned once more to normal in the Sabinas Valley.

In due course Alejandro and Evita were married. The town was swollen with guests from Monterrey, Saltillo, and even as far as Torreón, for the Castillo name was well known beyond the mountains.

Evita, in white satin, was as beautiful as a pale candle. Alejandro, correct in tails, made such a handsome groom that more than one girl wept, not in friendship but in pure envy. After the civil wedding in the Cantú house on the Street of the Three Crosses, low-swung victorias, drawn by the Castillo blacks, transported the guests to the Casino, where the bride cut her wedding cake with the sword that the first Castillo brought from Spain in 1566 when he came with Don Luís Carvajal y de las Cuevas to establish the most royal new kingdom of León.

Evita had wanted Alejandro to import a fine orchestra from Monterrey, but Alejandro refused to hurt Don Alonso's feelings. So Hidalgo instruments, including the saxaphone, played for the dancers.

Bob Webster, as best man, was everywhere at once, introducing strangers, seeing that the tiled floor was kept waxed, keeping children under seven out of the way of whirling couples. By three in the morning he was exhausted. He went into the bar to get a drink, and while he was standing there, Ricardo Manchaca tapped him on the shoulder. "Eh, friend, where is Alejandro? I want to toast him in good French cognac, but I cannot find him anywhere."

Bob sighed and began the hunt for Alejandro. But the groom was not in the Casino. He was not on the plaza. He was not in the Castillo house. Manchaca and Bob finally came together again in the bar. They whispered in English so as not to start a public scandal.

"What do you think we should do?" Manchaca mopped his forehead with a white silk handkerchief. "We must find him before five o'clock for the church ceremony."

"I don't know," said Bob helplessly. "I've looked in every damn hole I can think of."

"Maybe he left a message for us with someone."

"With whom? What do we do—go around asking people if Alejandro left a message for us?"

"I don't know," sighed Manchaca. Then with a fatalistic shrug, "Better to wait than to start a scandal. If he returns by five, all will be well. If he doesn't, nothing we can do now will help matters."

"Where's that French cognac of yours, Manchaca? Right now I need some. And when Alejandro does come back, I hope I'm too drunk to wring his neck."

A few minutes before three, Alejandro had felt the dreaded tightening in his throat. Glancing swiftly around to make certain that no one was noticing him, he slipped through a side door to the Street of the Sad Young Poet. He hastily unfastened his white tie and stiff collar, and rested his hot forehead against the cool yellow-washed adobe wall of the Casino. The moon had set long ago, but the stars glimmered brightly in the night sky, and the June air was soft and sweet with flowering thorn, night-blooming jasmine and honeysuckle. A dog howled mournfully at the end of the deserted street. The thick mud bricks muffled Don Alonso's music so that it sounded very far away.

The dreadful two minutes of blood-flecked choking passed, but he did not re-enter the Casino patio. It was his wedding night and it was the unhappiest night of his life. With a sudden tightening of his lips, he walked down the Street of the Hidden Water to the River Road. There he turned and descended the narrow, cliff-walled road to the Sabinas River. Here the night odors changed. The fragrance of flowers was gone, and in its place was the fresh smell of the river combined with a peculiar aroma of wet satine that came from the rank river grass. Alejandro followed a narrow trail, stones bruising his feet through the thin soles of his patent leather dancing pumps. He reached the small unpainted adobe house set far back in a recess under the over-hanging cliffs. The heavy wooden door was fastened with a complicated modern lock. Alejandro took a key from his breast pocket, weighed it in his palm for a moment. He thought, strange, I can't remember putting this in my pocket...he quietly opened the door.

There was only one room in the house. Facing him was a waist-high brasier in which banked coals gleamed redly. Above it hung an open cupboard filled with red and brown clay dishes. To his left was an open window, and below it a rough pine table and a three-legged stool.

He shut the door and moved through the darkness to the table, with the ease that comes from knowing a room well. His groping hand found a candle wedged in the top of a bottle. He lighted it, and holding it above his head, turned around. The soft yellow light sent dancing shadows across the room and touched the edge of a narrow cot. On the wall above it hung a lithograph of Our Lady of Perpetual Help, but the vigilance lamp, a wick floating in a ruby glass of oil, was not burning. Alejandro frowned, and for a moment his dark eyes were filled with fear.

The woman on the cot spoke softly. "I blew it out. After to-night, what use for prayers? After tonight?"

The resonant tones quivered and were silent. Alejandro, with a jerk of anger, thrust the candle forward and touched the flame to the wick. The sacred lithograph glowed once more with its red and gold Russian beauty. Then he blew out his candle, put it on the floor, and sat beside the woman. His hand touched her hair, her cheek.

"Are those tears I feel, María?"

She caught his hand and turned her face against it. "Women are stupid things," she said dully. "And tears are easy."

He slid his arm behind her, lifted her up against him. "María, María, what difference are words in a church? You are my wife. Our Blessed Lady knows that. We have argued this so often."

María rested her head against his shoulder. "I know that. But Evita is very beautiful..."

Alejandro put his fingers beneath her chin, and tilted her face backward. He took a match from his pocket, lighted it, and held it so that the tiny flame illumined her blue eyes, her straight nose, her red and passionate mouth. He flicked the match toward the brasier, chuckling softly. "By all the saints, María, you are right. Women are stupid things. For you to be jealous of beauty in another woman..." Then his arms closed convulsively about her. They sank against the pillow, their mouths trembling and tight against each other.

The first faint glow of day, when the night is no longer dark and is not yet light, warned him that it was time to leave. María's face was expressionless as her stubby peasant fingers fastened his stiff collar. He said, "No more stupidity?"

"No," she whispered.

"María, if it were not for this," he touched his throat, "I would have taken you away long ago."

"I know," she said gently, and even as she said it, they both knew that it was not the throat alone, but also his duty toward his father which he felt so keenly and which his older brother had not felt at all . . . his duty toward the remote, sorrowful Don Saturnino, who loved his oldest son, and whose youngest son loved him. But María and Alejandro did not speak of these hidden things to each other because in their respective blood, Indian and Spanish, there was a fatalism which recognized and accepted the events binding them to action.

María said, "Be a good husband to Evita."

"I will try, María."

She said suddenly, violently. "When we meet on the street, you must not look at me, I must not look at you. You must not pass my house nor I yours. It must be as though we had never been born, I for you or you for me."

"Yes," said Alejandro, "that is how it must be."

María covered her eyes with cupped palms. "Leave me, Alejandro. Leave quickly. I do not want to see you go."

He stretched out his hand toward her, drew it back, dropped it, open and empty, at his side. He turned on his heel and walked quickly out of the house, not realizing that the door key had been replaced automatically in his pocket. He went along the silent River Road, but when he reached the Street of the Hidden Water, he did not turn toward the Casino. To hear the music, to see the laughing faces, to see Evita, proud and cold in white satin, was beyond his endurance. Instead, he went into the church and knelt at the altar rail, his head pillowed on his arms, not praying, his body heavy with emotion, his mind thick with memories . . .

He curled his small body into a more comfortable position on the broad window ledge. Tomorrow he would be ten years old, and Joaquín could no longer refer to him as a creature without substance, having but a single number to his years. Tomorrow there would be two numbers, and all the rest of his life.

He sighed happily and peered through the window at the quiet pool below, where swans were floating in the moonlight. He loved the swans. He had made himself a rope ladder, for he liked doing things with his hands, and often, when his father and brother were asleep, he would go down the ladder to the pool and talk to the swans. There were three and they were named for his favored historical friends: Don Benito Juarez, Don Abrán Lincoln, Don Simón Bolívar. Now he opened the window and called softly, "Good evening, friends. I shall be ten years old tomorrow."

"Will you indeed?" answered one of the swans in a sweet thin treble. "And is the world to end because of it?"

Alejandro gulped and clutched at the window-ledge to keep from tumbling out in sheer astonishment. Don Nacho often said that animals and birds talked among themselves, but no man heard them ever until it came his time to die. And Alejandro was not ready to die—not yet with his tenth birthday so near.

He took the ladder from its hiding place and climbed down it, his white nightgown billowing around him. (After tomorrow he could sleep with his body naked between the sheets like Joaquín. That was one of the birthday presents.) His bare feet touched the tiled edge of the pool, and he knelt to call the birds to him. "Don Benito, Don Abrán, Don Simón, which of you spoke to me?"

"Ay," said the treble voice, behind him this time, "and birds also speak on tenth birthdays?"

Alejandro twisted around quickly. A girl, several inches taller than himself, was watching him. In the moonlight, her hair was a silver cloud around her thin pinched face, and she moved awkwardly because her legs were much too long for her small torso. But Alejandro, in his relief that he was not to die before tomorrow, did not notice these things.

"Who are you?" he whispered fiercely. "What are you doing on Castillo land?"

"I often come to look at the swans. Why not? The *Gallineros* is but a short distance down the road."

His arrogance flamed between them. "People from the *Gallineros* have no business here. Go, and come here no more."

"Can you make me leave, little boy in a white dress?"

He lashed out at her with his hand, caught his feet in the folds of the gown, and tumbled forward on his face. Her soft laughter mocked at him as he struggled upright. "What a fine small gentleman to kneel before a lady!"

Scarlet with rage and humiliation, he grasped the folds of the gown in one hand and plunged toward her. She instantly turned away from him, bent forward until her palms touched the ground, and kicked up with one bare heel. It snapped against his chin and sent him staggering backwards into the pool. She started to run away, and then, realizing that something was wrong, knelt and watched him. The blow had knocked him into unconsciousness, and the heavy folds of the gown, weighted with water, were dragging him to the tiled bottom. The swans, hissing angrily at this invasion of their kingdom, had retreated to the colonnade that sheltered the upper end of the pool. The girl paid them no attention. Frightened, she slid into the water. It came to the level of her chin. She waded forward, locked his head in the curve of her elbow, and managed, with much tugging and grunting, to pull him out on the ledge. She knew nothing else to do for him; so she sat beside him until his lids fluttered slightly. Then she slapped his face.

"Eh, you cannot fight, you cannot swim. Of what good are you, and you ten years old?"

Alejandro sat up, shaking his head to clear it. "You...you from the *Gallineros*..."

"I have a name," the girl interrupted coldly. "I am called María."

"María of what?"

"Of nothing," she said with surprise. "It is necessary to have more than one name?"

"I have five," said Alejandro haughtily.

"Indeed, and you know them all?"

"Naturally. Alejandro Gregorio Mauricio Castillo Buentello."

"Is it possible?" she whispered with mock amazement. "So many names, and you only ten tomorrow?"

He was silent for a long moment, his hands busily wringing water from his wet gown. There was a great humiliation in him that a girl could so easily vanquish him. If news of this reached the ears of the town, all the men would laugh at him. Even Joaquín would mock such weakness, for Joaquín was strong and tall, and in all things perfect, and no girl from the *Gallineros* had ever put a shame on him. But perhaps this girl would say nothing to the town. Perhaps he could persuade her not to talk. "Tell me, María, if I say nothing about your being here, will you say nothing about pushing me into the pool?"

"I didn't push you," said María coldly. "Can I help it if you are such a small stupid that you do not know how to fight?"

"But I can fight," insisted Alejandro. "Every day my brother Joaquín teaches me to box."

"Fine fighting, and you so easy to knock into the pool."

"Will you teach me your tricks of fighting? Will you, María?"

"In return, can I watch the swans?"

"I will introduce you myself, personally. But be careful of Don Abrán Lincoln. He is a wild one, like all *Yanquis*."

Alejandro shifted his weight from one knee to the other, and rubbed his cheek against the altar rail. Memory continued to toss images across the screen of his closed lids. He remembered Joaquín's anger when he was knocked down in the boxing lessons by a small, well placed heel.

"You, beastly one, where did you learn such a trick?"

"Is it not a fine one, Joaquín?"

"No!" Joaquín sat on the tiled floor and pulled his younger brother down beside him. "That is fighting for the *Gallineros* and not for gentlemen. Such tricks are not for you, little one. For you, only kindliness and wisdom, and love for our father. For me . . ." his voice sank into silence.

"For you, my brother?" prompted the young Alejandro.

"For me the wildness. Now, teach me the trick. For me it is a good one to know. I think I will need it soon."

Even then, thought the older Alejandro, Joaquín must have realized that he would soon be gone from the valley, gone into silence, Joaquín the wild one. Joaquín. Alejandro, remembering, compressed his lips. It had been reported long ago that Joaquín was dead, killed in one of the battles of the Great Revolution, but Joaquín could not be dead. Even now, after twelve years of silence, his image was still vivid, riding the narrow Hidalgo streets at full gallop on one of the black Castillo horses, Alejandro's small excited body in front of him on the saddle. He remembered how Joaquín had pulled the horse to a halt, tossed Alejandro to the ground, and lifted Don Nacho's Chela to the saddle bow. "Eh, green eyes, do you want to ride with the wind in your hair?" And surely Joaquín must have ridden with the wind in his hair when he left that sorrowful night to fight with Obregón. Alejandro clenched his nails against his palms. If he had only known that he would never see his laughing brother again when Don Saturnino sent him away to Connecticut to school. But he had not known. He was too concerned with saying good-bye to María, to María who was taller and stronger than he, to María who was his secret even then.

"But why must you go away to learn things in books, Alejandro? Me, behold, I am taller than you. By five fingers I am taller than you. And I know nothing of books. Books are silent, stupid things."

"So that I can be wise, María."

"What need of wisdom in this valley?"

"I must take care of my father. Joaquín says I must always take care of my father."

"The great Don Saturnino? And you but twelve years old?" María laughed her golden laughter. Later, she did not laugh. Later she helped Alejandro take care of Don Saturnino—one year later, when Alejandro made his great journey that ended in a tightening of the throat that no doctor could cure.

Alejandro touched nervous fingers to his throat, the throat that was making him marry Evita, the throat that was cutting him away from María, the throat that was cutting him away from life.

He thought of the first time that it had betrayed him. The night was as silent and as quiet as this one. He was thirteen. For three years the Great Revolution had swept across Mexico. The fighting was everywhere: in the green jungles of Michoacán, the great haciendas of Tabasco, the gray rocks of Sonora, and finally in the peaceful valley of the Sabinas. A letter came to him in his school in Connecticut, from Joaquín, words scrawled in pencil on a piece of cheap tablet paper: "I have quarreled with our father. Is it not true that I was always a wild one? He wants me to fight with the Federals. Not for me the pretty uniforms covered with gold braid. For me a gun and the hills with Obregón. You must take care of our father now, my little wise one."

That night Alejandro ran away from the school. He stole rides in the backs of trucks. He rode in boxcars and on tops of trains. And finally he reached the Rio Grande near Laredo. He swam the river in the night and went on foot, hiding in the hills, living on berries and a piece of stale bread he had stolen in San Antonio. It took him ten days to come in sight of Saddle Mountain with Monterrey nestling at its base. Then he turned into the familiar paths of the Sabinas Valley. He skirted the mud huts of Topo Grande, the adobe houses of El Carmen, the spiraling street of Abasolo. And that was two more days. At last he recognized the Hidalgo cliffs. It was night, and his feet made little whispering sounds as he crept between the tall rushes of the river bed. A hand snapped out and caught his ankle. Another hand covered his mouth. A voice whispered close to his ear, "And where are you going, my young rooster?"

Alejandro twisted and pulled to free himself, but the hands were tight and strong. He was lifted and carried over a broad shoulder into one of the cliff caves where men, wrapped in dirty wool blankets, were sleeping. His captor kicked at the still bodies until they woke to grumbling and curses.

"I've caught us a pretty Federal spy. They use children now," said the man. Voices asked excited questions out of the darkness. Someone stirred up the fire until there was a flickering light against the curving sandy walls.

"Eh," said someone, "look at the dirt on him and the town clothes. But there's no beard on the face. Who is he?"

"Who are you?"

Alejandro bit down on his lips. He looked around him at the dirty, ragged men, with their hard, cold eyes. These men knew no distinction between rich landholders and the hated Federals. "I am called Alejandro," he muttered.

"Alejandro? What else?"

María's voice came into his ears and he answered in her words, "Is it necessary to have more than one name?"

"Where were you going when the *Rubio* caught you?"

"To Hidalgo."

"To take sweet words to the Federals, eh?"

"I told you he was a Federal spy," said the *Rubio* proudly, rubbing his hand across the blond hair that gave him his nickname.

Alejandro breathed deeply. "Are there many Federals in Hidalgo?"

"Enough men to fill the town, burning and looting everywhere. As though you didn't know," snapped one of the men.

The *Rubio* was rubbing his palms together. "His hands are the soft hands of the rich. I tell you he is a Federal spy. Let us amuse ourselves with the little bastard."

He reached for Alejandro, but the boy, remembering a hard-learned lesson, whirled, dropped his palms to the ground, and kicked up with his heels. He felt it crash against jaw bone, and he turned, hesitant, to see what he had done. That was his moment to escape, but his hesitation lost it for him. The *Rubio* was sprawled on the ground, his mouth sodden with blood, his gray eyes small and red with hate. He caught Alejandro around the knees, toppled him forward, then reached for the throat and pressed his fingers together.

The pain tore through Alejandro, and there was a roaring darkness. He seemed to be running towards a place that was light and beautiful, with music sounding, and he knew that the place was death. The light was coming nearer, the music sounding louder; then a great wave of water dashed over him, knocking him down into quiet blackness. In the far distance were voices. They came closer and receded from him, and then came closer again. Feeling returned to his body. Under his hands was the feel of earth, and against his face. A voice—a familiar voice—said, "Wake up, Alejandro. Wake up, boy."

Alejandro opened his lids. Rubén, the candy-maker, was bending over him, holding water to his lips, pressing the gourd against his mouth. He said rapidly, "I was on sentry duty. The cave noises brought me back. I told them you were my cousin. Can you hear me, Alejandro? I told them that you were my cousin, come back to protect our family in Hidalgo. Alejandro, can you hear me?"

The effort to speak tore new pain from Alejandro's throat, but he whispered, "I hear you—cousin."

Rubén stood away from him, turned to the *Rubio*. "You are always too ready to kill. This one's brother fights with Obregón."

The *Rubio* said sulkily, "How was I to know? He has the face of a rich one. And his hands are soft, like a woman's."

"Naturally. He is to follow my own trade of candy-making.

Not all poor ones have hard hands." He bent over Alejandro again. "Come, my cousin. I will guide you past the other sentries into Hidalgo."

He pulled the boy to his feet, and the two went out of the cave. Alejandro massaged his throat with his fingers. "Thank you, Rubén." He forced the words.

"No thanks," Rubén answered gruffly. "Lucky for you I was with this group."

Alejandro put his hand on Rubén's sleeve. "Tell me, Rubén, is there to be a battle?"

Rubén jerked free of him. "Should I tell you secrets so that you can betray us to the Federals, you and your father? I saved you tonight. Tomorrow you must take care of yourself."

They walked past the cliffs, Rubén whistling now and then to warn the sentries, until Alejandro paused at a deep cut in the dirt walls.

"There is a ladder here. I built it for a plaything. It ends at the back of the house." He did not add that he had built it so that he and María could descend to the river to play after darkness had sent the people of Hidalgo to their beds.

Rubén touched Alejandro's shoulder. "I don't know whether to let you climb up or not. There are Federal officers living in your house. If you tell them we are camped here by the river, they will kill us all. It will be a fine victory for them. Can I trust you, Alejandro?"

Alejandro put his two hands on Rubén's breast over the heart. "By the blue robe of the Blessed Virgin, by the five sacred wounds, by the tears of the Magdalen, by the Castillo name, I swear that you can trust me."

They were both silent. The moon, a great orange disk, was rising behind the western rim of mountains. The soft breeze stirred the rank grass of the river bed. High in the hills there was a point of light from a goatherd's fire.

After a long time Rubén said remotely, "Tomorrow there will be a great battle. Your father loves the Federals. If we take the town..." He paused. He said, "The *Rubio* is our captain. He is a cruel man, very cruel. With justice, you understand, but cruel."

Alejandro said, "My father made me a present of the Rancho Santo Tomás for my birthday. If I could take him out of the town tonight I could hide him there..."

"There!" Rubén laughed softly. "A young witch from the *Gallineros* who calls herself María has taken possession of your ranch. She stole a gun from the Federals. When anyone comes near a door or window, she shoots. And good shooting, I can tell you!"

I taught her, thought Alejandro with pride. He said, "María! At the ranch?"

"You know her?"

"A little. I think I can persuade her to take us in. Do you think we will be safe there?"

"There, yes. That María is a mountain cat, all claws and teeth. But your father is a stubborn man. How will you take him out of Hidalgo this night?"

"I have a plan," said Alejandro confidently. He whispered the plan, and in his excitement, the pain in his throat lessened. Rubén finally agreed to his words. The two of them climbed the narrow iron ladder, waiting in silence until the Federal sentry passed them. Then, two black shadows in deeper shadow, they raced across the narrow strip of ground to the back of the Castillo house. Rubén, by mounting Alejandro's shoulders, opened a window, slid inside a darkened room, and pulled the boy up. With Alejandro in the lead, they stole across the tile floor and into the hallway. They could hear men talking in the library. Alejandro peered through the large keyhole but could not see his father. They climbed the stairs and crept down the hall, past doors that sheltered laughing, drunken Federal officers, to Don Saturnino's own door. Alejandro gently pushed it open. Don Saturnino was seated by a table, reading. He lifted his head in annoyance, his near-sighted eyes blinking at them.

"The entire house is at your disposal. There is no need for you to come in here."

At a nudge from Alejandro, Rubén said pompously. "You are my prisoner, Don Saturnino."

The tall old man rose, his face calm and remote. "I know you. You are Rubén, a maker of candy. Who is that with you?"

"Alejandro, father."

Don Saturnino put his hand on the table for support. "Impossible! You are too tall."

Alejandro went to him, put his arms around him, kissed him

on the cheek. "It is true, father. I have grown a little, that is all."

"What are you doing here? You should be in school in Connecticut. I did not give you permission . . ."

"No time for speeches," said Rubén urgently. He pressed against the door, listened to distant voices singing drunken songs. "You must come with me, Don Saturnino."

Don Saturnino took off his reading glasses, put them in his pocket, calmly and without hurry. "This is my home. Here I stay. Because you belong to this valley, I give you five minutes to leave this place."

Rubén and Alejandro looked silently at each other. They had expected this attitude. It was time to put into effect Alejandro's plan. He said, "You don't understand, father. We are Rubén's prisoners."

"I have only to call out . . ." Don Saturnino's words were cut off as Rubén stepped behind Alejandro, laid the flat of his knife against the boy's throat. For a moment the three stood there, poised in silence. Alejandro held his breath. The blade felt cool and good against his aching throat. He said softly, "There is no choice, father. Please come quickly."

Don Saturnino said bitterly, "The jest does not amuse me. Like your brother you have turned to the Revolutionists. Rubén will not kill you. You are his friend. He is your friend. This is all very melodramatic, very amusing."

"Enough of clever words," said Rubén roughly. "There is shelter at the Rancho Santo Tomás. There you will be safe."

Alejandro stretched out his hands. "Father, please. I ask it of you, please." His voice was hoarse from the pain in his throat. Don Saturnino heard the hoarseness. Years afterwards, retelling the story, he would say proudly, "Thirteen, can you imagine? And a voice deep and rough as a man's. And such a hurt in the eyes. The voice of a man and the eyes of a child. Not like Joaquín, the wild one, sharp as glass. But tender and humid. The voice begged but the eyes commanded. Children do not know how to beg. Only men beg. Children command. I had to obey the eyes. If I had not, they would have turned into a man's eyes. They, too, would have begged. Always, through life, they would beg. What could I do? I had to obey the eyes."

But Don Saturnino did not speak these words that night. He lifted his hat and glanced at Rubén, who in turn looked at Alejandro. The boy, accepting the leadership, nodded, and the three of them descended the high stairs that led from Don Saturnino's room on the outside of the house. They went down the iron ladder and across the river. There Alejandro left them and went ahead to the ranch. He whistled three times in a familiar code, and María opened the door.

"Alejandro!" she cried joyfully. And then, "But, Alejandro, you are taller than I!"

Alejandro pressed his palms against the coolness of the altar rail. For a moment the memory of the Battle of Hidalgo was vivid to him. The Revolutionists won, and many houses were burned, including the new railroad station Don Saturnino had presented to the town. The Castillo house was saved because the *Rubio* wanted to make it his headquarters. And there were many hangings, for, as Rubén had said, the *Rubio* was a cruel man. He was pallid with anger because Don Saturnino had escaped him. But the Federals could tell him nothing. No one could tell him anything. And on the Rancho Santo Tomás, Don Saturnino sat in the sun and listened to Alejandro teaching María how to read and write.

"So that is an 'a.' How wonderful that you should know that is an 'a.' "

"Now you know it, too, María. And this is a 'b.' "

"Ay, Alejandro, but that is a true marvel. Imagine, the 'a' and the 'b,' so beautiful. Like little twisted snakes."

Sometimes Don Saturnino would speak to them bitterly, recounting how Joaquín had gone away like a coyote in the night to join the men who were destroying the great Spanish tradition, who were building a new Republic that had no need for the Castillos with their three hundred years of harvesting valley land.

The children would sit on the ground, listening to him, watching the Castillo pride twist in him at the thought that he was a fugitive on his own ground with a nameless girl from the *Gallineros* as a protecting shield between himself and the cruel hands of the *Rubio*. They saw him turn from a grand proud man to a bent old one, and at night they could hear him sleeping heavily, drugged with his own sorrow.

Because of this it was not he but María who went stumbling to Alejandro's door.

"What is it, Alejandro? Why are you gasping like that? Answer, me Alejandro!"

But Alejandro could not answer her. He could only clutch his throat, and stare at her with terrified eyes, as he fought desperately for breath. María put her arms around him, pressed his face against her warm young body. "It is only a catching of the air. Tell me that is what it is. Speak to me, Alejandro."

The seizure passed. Alejandro relaxed weakly against the pillow. "There was a tightness in the throat. I couldn't breathe, María."

"I will call your father."

"No!" He caught her arm, held her still. "No need to worry him. You see, it is past."

"But, Alejandro, this is not good. He should know . . ."

"Why? Has he not enough to worry him? He is a proud man, and to hide in the hills is a cross on his spirit. And Joaquín gone . . . my brother Joaquín, whom he loved. No, María, this little tightening of the throat . . . It is a matter of no importance."

Nor was it, then. Doctors in the United States, and later in Europe, explained it with scientific words. They called it a laryngeal spasm, brought about by a highly sensitive nervous system being subjected to extreme tension. A psychoanalyst would have said it was the throat nerves remembering the pressure of the *Rubio's* fingers. But Alejandro did not go to a psychoanalyst. He went from medical doctor to medical doctor, always alone (Don Saturnino had a high contempt for nerves in a man) and the verdict was always the same, "There is nothing we can do. No treatment has yet been invented to cure laryngeal spasm."

Sometimes the attacks came close together. At other times, as much as six months would pass without one. In the first days at the ranch they came nearly every night. And María always heard him, came in to hold him safe in her arms until the two or three minutes of agony were over. This wove a closer bond between them, which Don Saturnino commented upon. "I understand, Alejandro, that you two are but children. Nevertheless, you are of the great Castillo family, and María is a girl without a name."

"I will find one for her," answered Alejandro.

He and María went through book after book, hunting a name for her. One day she saw the picture of a crane. Its small body and long thin legs amused her. She twisted her own long-legged young torso. "Behold me, I, too, am like a crane. María de las Garzas ... María of the Cranes. Is it not true perfection?"

Don Saturnino, watching her, laughed, but soon after that, with Don Nacho's aid, he took Alejandro to the States. When they left, he offered María money, but she refused it. "What good is money to me? If I want clothes, I steal them. If I want food, well, I can steal that, too."

Alejandro saw the hurt in her eyes, and he pushed against his father, so that they went quickly through the sunlight to the horses Don Nacho was holding for them.

Don Saturnino kept Alejandro in the States and in Europe for the next six years. Alejandro changed from a sensitive, quiet boy into a laughing, eager young man, handsome in the steel-blade Spanish fashion, with a delight in taking photographs of every city they visited. "Behold, Father," he would say, "here is Europe captured on these slips of paper." He had a good mind and he learned rapidly, but in one way he disappointed his father. He stayed aloof from women.

"It is not good," Don Saturnino would say crossly. "You are handsome. You have money. These are your bright hours. Make them shine, Alejandro. Later, when you have a wife, you will sigh for these lost days, believe me."

But Alejandro would only smile and touch his throat in that quick nervous gesture that had grown on him with the years. Away from his father, he would read and reread a small package of letters that were written in carefully formed, misspelled words, which began, always, "My beloved Alejandro," and ended, "Thy María."

At last Don Saturnino, thinking Alejandro had completely forgotten María, returned to the valley, his exile as a Federal sympathizer having been lifted through the efforts of Don Nacho and Don Rosalío. When they arrived in Hidalgo the two old men were waiting for them in the library, a bottle of cherished French brandy on a table. The three friends were so happy to see each other, so rich with gossip, that they did not notice Alejandro slip away. He climbed down the rusted iron steps of

the cliff and found the small unpainted adobe house the priest
had ordered built for María. When he whistled the familiar code,
she flung the door wide. They looked at each other with the bold
eyes of children. He stepped into the house. The door was
fastened with a heavy wooden bolt. To cover his shyness, he
said, "This bolt is not good. When you leave the house there
is no way to lock it. I will order a fine mechanical lock from
the States . . . one with two keys. A key for you, and . . ."

He paused. She filled out the sentence. "And one for you."

"And one for me." He took her in his arms, then, and kissed
her. He had come home.

The years passed quietly. The village recovered from the
wounds of the Revolution, and there were many marriages. Andrés Treviño bought a pair of woman's shoes. Pablo, the goatherd,
was killed because of Anita O'Malley. The wild young Pepe Gonzalez ended a valley feud.

But for Alejandro there was no marriage. He made no effort
to play the bear at any girl's window. Once in a while he would
go away on long trips to the States or to Europe. Letters, mailed
by arrangement, were sent to his father from New York, Lon-
don, Paris, and the watery beauty of Venice. But Alejandro was
in none of these places. He would hear of a good throat man in
California, Brussels, The Hague. The answer was always the
same. "It is a disorder of the nerves. Nothing can cure laryngeal
spasm. No, it's not dangerous. It's simply uncomfortable. We
are sorry, but there is nothing we can do."

So Alejandro came back to the valley to stay. He no longer
bothered with doctors. The Rancho Santo Tomás fascinated him.
It amused him to make it pay. He said to Bob Webster, "If I
really needed money, that ground would yield nothing but rocks
and sand. As it is, the fields are rich with grain." He lighted his
pipe, his eyes cynical and amused through the blue smoke.

Bob shook his head, "You're smoking too much, Alejandro.
Your voice gets hoarser every day."

Alejandro touched his throat with light fingers. "It is nothing.
Since I was thirteen my voice has been hoarse and rough."

"It's getting hoarser," repeated Bob obstinately. "You'd better
do something about it."

A few nights later, when Alejandro was with María, the spasm came again. Only this time there was blood in his mouth. María was terrified. "You must go to the doctor."

"It is no use, María. You know that. The doctors say it is no use."

"But there has never been blood before. Alejandro, I am afraid." She began to cry. They argued, as they always argued, for they were too unlike ever to agree easily; but in the end she won as she always won, for of the two she was made of the stronger fiber.

The little Doctor, sworn to secrecy, examined Alejandro's throat. Finished, he paced about his small office, kicking at the purple velour chairs. "I don't want to give you an opinion. I think you should go to the States to a great specialist."

Alejandro sighed and fastened his collar. "Why, little Doctor? They all say the same thing. There is nothing they can do."

"For the laryngeal spasm, no. But for the tumor..." The little Doctor shrugged.

"Tumor?" Alejandro stopped his hands in surprise. "What are you talking about?"

"I can't tell. My equipment is too poor. But I would say you have a malignant tumor on the bilateral vocal folds."

"That is—dangerous?"

The little Doctor spread out his hands, palms down. "I tell you my opinion is worthless. Go to the States, Alejandro. Get a true examination."

"On one condition. That you never mention this to anyone."

"But Alejandro, your father..."

"To anyone," said Alejandro firmly. He knew how his father grieved for the lost Joaquín. And Joaquín had left a duty on Alejandro. It was his place to care for his father. If the little Doctor was mistaken, better not to frighten the old one. If he were not mistaken, then for Don Saturnino to worry would be of no help to Alejandro. "To anyone," he repeated.

The little Doctor sighed. "You have always been a queer one, the tongue secret in your mouth." But he promised to say nothing.

Alejandro went to Canada. There was a French doctor there, famous for throat surgery. He said, "It is a malignant tumor. Usually, I would not say this, I am not the good God. I make mistakes, like any stupid man. But you have come a long way to see me. You should have come long ago, but the spasms, of course, prevented you from knowing. Now it is too late."

"You can do nothing?"

"Certainly I can do something. I can operate. But if I do..." The doctor lifted his eyebrows. "You will die on the table. Quick. Like that!" He snapped his fingers.

"And if you don't operate ... how long, doctor?"

"One year. Two. Three. I am not God. How should I know these things? Go to other doctors. Ask them. Me, I am only a stupid fool."

But Alejandro did not go to other doctors. He had seen the truth in this man's eyes. So that night he wrote a long letter to his father. It said, "I have known for some time that it is your great desire that I marry Evita Cantú. Will you ask Bob Webster and Ricardo Manchaca to speak to her father for me, please?" He put down his pen and stared at the words. How cold and businesslike they sounded. How could he write the truth? How could he write, "My Father, my brother Joaquín left a duty upon me. He said that I was to care for you and make you happy. And this marriage is close to your heart. There is so little time left for me. It means the giving up of my beautiful María, but we love each other enough for that, and you are my father, and I love you, and there is a duty on me." He sighed and pulled another sheet of paper toward him. He wrote, "My adored María." In that letter he wrote the words he could not write his father.

The church was cold and still. The light was the color of a gray pearl. Dawn was very near. Bob Webster and Ricardo Manchaca, despairing of finding Alejandro anywhere, came to the church as a last resort. They saw him kneeling in front of the candle-studded altar and sighed with relief.

"Alejandro," Manchaca called softly, "it is time for the procession."

Alejandro did not answer them. But he rose and came toward them down the aisle. When he reached them, he put his hands on their shoulders. "Yes," he said, "it is time."

He took Evita to Mexico City for the wedding trip. They arrived in the City in the morning. On the train he had stayed away from her. "A train is no place for a Castillo to take a woman to wife," he said. And Evita fluttered her black lashes with pleasure that she was now a part of the Castillo tradition.

The hotel was small, expensive, close to the Zócalo. Tourists seldom found their way there. Its Swiss manager catered exclusively to the great Mexican families, some of them, like the Castillos, with a royal title. The Marqués de Guadalupe, his slender body clad in the gray *charro* costume which he affected, the broad-brimmed gray felt hat trimmed with heavy silver embroidery dangling from one hand, came up to them as Alejandro signed the register. "Ah," he said, "the young Castillo. And how is your good father?"

Alejandro answered politely, introduced Evita, giving her the formal title of Vizcondesa,* for the Marqués delighted in such things. The Marqués kissed her small gloved fingers. There was an invitation made and accepted for sherry before lunch, and the two were shown to their suite of two bedrooms and a parlor.

The moment they were alone, Evita turned to Alejandro, her face glowing. "It is true, Alejandro? I am a Vizcondesa?"

Alejandro answered her absently, taking a camera from its case and carefully examining it. "Naturally. Father is *el Duque de Huachichil*. It is a very old Mexican title."

"And me? I am the Vizcondesa de Castillo?"

"No. Castillo is the family name. You are the Vizcondesa Mogollón. What difference does it make, Evita? The sun is good and I want to take some pictures. Let us go out now."

"You are more interested in the camera than in me," she pouted, lifting her head in an invitation to be kissed, too obvious to be ignored.

He brushed her cheek with his lips. "The sun, Evita."

"The sun! Always the sun!" She walked with a high angry head through the door. He shrugged, picked up the camera case and followed her. He thought, I must take many pictures to show María. Then he remembered that he would never again show an excited María photographs of the world beyond the mountains, and the pain in him was so intense that he had to pause and take deep breaths to shut it out.

Evita paid him no attention. She was sulking. She tried to sulk

* Viscountess. Many of the old Mexican families hold titles granted by the Kings of Spain during viceregal days.

all day, but by night the beauty of Mexico City, the glamorous idea of being a Viscountess, the exciting anticipation of her marriage bed, changed her into a softly glowing woman.

As she sat at her dressing table, she could hear Alejandro moving about in his room, getting undressed, preparing to come to her. Then she heard something else. It was a half strangled gasp, a sound of choking. Terrified, she ran to the door, opened it. Alejandro was sitting in a chair, his hands at his throat, fighting for breath.

"Alejandro! What has happened?"

As she spoke, the spasm passed. He turned his head with a slow, exhausted movement, touching his handkerchief to his lips to hide the blood from her. He said, "It is nothing. Leave me alone, Evita."

"But, Alejandro . . ."

"Leave me alone!"

She retreated into her own room and shut the door, her eyes puzzled and hurt. What was wrong with Alejandro? Before their marriage he had been so courteous, so much the shy, reserved lover. Now he was cold and aloof, not wanting her near him. She went to bed, pulling the sheets up to her chin. When he came in, she would ask him. Tears filled her black eyes. How could he be so cruel to her? Was she not his wife? True, the Cantú name lacked the historical luster of the Castillo's, but the Cantús were a proud family also. She could meet his pride with pride. She would show him that she was not to be so politely ignored. Then she heard the key turn in Alejandro's door. She sat up, clutching the sheets about her. Was it possible? Could he be locking her out, and she his lawful wife?

She thrust her feet into dainty, feathery slippers, stumbled across the room, and banged on the door with clenched fists.

Alejandro said, "Stop that pounding, Evita!"

"Alejandro, open this door. I want to speak to you."

He unlocked it, opened it. His face was very white. "What do you want?"

"Are you going to sleep in there tonight?"

"Yes." He touched his throat with his nervous fingers. "I don't feel well, Evita."

"But I am your wife. If you are sick, you should share your sickness with me."

"Listen to me, Evita. Sometimes I have a little choking in the throat. It is nothing. You should pay no attention. Now go to bed, please."

"But, Alejandro . . ."

"Please go to bed, Evita!"

He shut the door, locked it, leaned weakly against it. She knocked again, but he ignored it. After a moment the knocking stopped. He could hear her crying. Frowning with pain he crossed to the window, stared at the distant towers of the largest cathedral in the three Americas, built on the foundations of a temple to one of the bloodiest gods in the history of man's religion. But he did not see the towers. He saw instead a heavy wooden door, fastened with a complicated modern lock to which he had the key, held it even now in his hand. While he was unpacking the key had dropped from the pocket of his dress clothes, and the shock of seeing it, combined with the knowledge that Evita was waiting for him, had brought on the fit of choking.

He pulled a chair to the window and sat gazing at nothingness for a long time. Slowly his thinking began to take on a more ordered pattern. He had brought happiness to his father. He had married Evita, he had given up María, but he had forgotten his treacherous throat. He was certain that if he went to Evita now he would have another spasm. If he went to any woman save María, the spasm would come. María was his safety, his refuge. One year more, perhaps two, and there would be nothing for him but the long dreamless sleep. María belonged to him and he to her. No firm decision to stay apart, never to speak together again, would do any good. He relaxed in the chair. He knew what he would say to Evita in the morning.

A bellboy brought up the breakfast tray, smirked at seeing Alejandro's tired eyes, arranged the food on a table in the parlor, closed his palm over the generous tip, and bowed himself out. Alejandro called Evita, and she entered, a sea-green negligee trimmed with white feathers pulled around her. Her skin was pale and lifeless against the green chiffon, and her eyes were heavy with sullen anger.

They played at their food in silence. Finally Alejandro pushed back a fragile Louis XV chair, began to pace the narrow, high-ceilinged, pink-walled room. "I'm sorry, Evita." He touched his

throat in his usual nervous manner. "I came to this marriage prepared to be a good husband to you, but there are reasons which
I can't explain to you, to prevent this. If you want a divorce..."

"A divorce!" Her lips worked stiffly. "You know what it is
to be a divorced woman in the Republic. You must truly hate me
to suggest such a thing."

"I don't hate you!" His voice was hoarse and deep. "It is only
that I do not love you... cannot love you. I thought it would
be easier for you if I went away."

"So that all the world can whisper that I failed you as a wife?"

"What difference do the whispers of the world make?"

"To me, a great deal. True, I am of the family Cantú, a person
of little value in the eyes of the fine titled Castillos..."

"Evita, you know that isn't..."

"Let me finish, please. You married me before the civil judge
and in the church. I am your wife. You owe me certain obligations..."

"You mean you want to stay married to me? But why, Evita?
I don't love you. And somehow I don't think you love me,
really."

"I don't!" For the first time in her narrow, sheltered, selfish
life, her eyes opened with honest intensity. "I never have. I don't
love anyone."

"Then why did you marry me?"

"Because I wanted the Castillo money. I like money and the
things it can buy. I also wanted the Castillo name. I didn't know
about the title. Your father never mentions it. But now I want
that, too. I like being called the Vizcondesa de Mogollón. I have
all those things. You may be sure that I shall not give them up
easily."

"You want to return to Hidalgo as my wife, knowing I will
never touch you, never come near you?"

"I want to keep what I have with pride." She sat very stiffly
in her chair, not looking at Alejandro. "I will never release you,
Alejandro. You made your mistake when you married me. Your
father wanted me as a daughter-in-law. But if it is happiness you
want, you should have ignored his wishes. You should have
married her, instead."

Alejandro dizzily stretched his hand out for the back of a
chair. Surely Evita could not know about María. No one knew

about María, not even Don Saturnino. He said carefully, "What makes you think there is another woman?"

"Chela, the daughter of Don Nacho, is very wise in reading the ways of people. She said to me, 'Alejandro will make you a gentle husband. He needs a woman's strength to lean against.' I believe her. Somewhere in Hidalgo there is a woman who provides you with that strength—who is your mistress. I shall find her. And when I do, I shall not be kind."

"You would break a scandal to satisfy your own pride?"

She pleated the green chiffon on her knee. "No scandal. The Castillo name is now mine also. There are other ways to deal with such a creature besides scandal."

Alejandro smiled bitterly. "You will never find her, Evita. Not in time. After that, it won't matter."

"What do you mean—not in time?"

He picked up his camera, gestured toward the window. "The sun is very beautiful today, and there are many places to visit. Shall we go now?"

She came to her feet, her hands clenched. "I asked you a question."

"And I answered it, for the true answer is one you could not understand. I am glad we had this little talk, Evita. I understand you so much better now. I see you so much more clearly. And remember this, what I have I keep. Because for me, there is no time. It is, I suppose, the only advantage I have...not to own time."

"You speak in secrets."

"Why not? All my life has been a secret. One more costs very little. If the pretence of a happy marriage is what you want, you shall have it. I owe you that debt for marrying you. But between us there shall be no intimacy and no questions. After this hour, no questions at all."

Evita lowered her lids, the heavy lashes resting on the white cheeks like black thorns on ivory. "There shall be no questions."

So they finished their days in Mexico City. Because they were intelligent people, they achieved a basis of conduct fashioned out of good manners. During the day Evita helped Alejandro photograph the bleak grandeur of the pyramids at Teotihuacán, the floating islands of Xochimilco, the stately beauty of the shrine of Guadalupe, when she would have much preferred to spend

Castillo money in the French and Chinese stores. In the evening Alejandro, who hated night clubs, took her dancing at the famous Abél's, across from the leafy green beauty of the Alameda; at Bach's, with its cubicles of leather benches; at small German and Hungarian restaurants that appeared and disappeared in the changing rhythms of the City life. They appeared briefly at Embassy receptions, where Evita used her broken English and listened to Alejandro casually chat in French and German. They attended a banquet in the cold, formal dining room of Chapultepec Castle, where the ghosts of Maximilian's silver court and Porfirio Diaz's golden one, fluttered about them. They did all the things they were supposed to do, very cool, very correct, very polite. And finally they returned to Hidalgo, to the rambling white house with the red-tiled roof that Don Saturnino had built for them on the Street of the River. And with them they brought the extreme politeness that enchanted the servants: the gardener, the maid, the cook, the laundress. "They treat each other like shy young lovers," the women would tell in the town, with many sighs for husbands who had not treated them with politeness.

The fact that they used two bedrooms caused much raising of the eyebrows, but Evita explained to her mother that this was fashionable among people of wealth and position. She reminded her mother that she was now a Viscountess, and so the story of the two bedrooms became a part of Hidalgo tradition.

The afternoon of their return Alejandro went down the iron steps of the cliffs to the house on the river bank. María, hearing his whistle, opened the door quickly, her eyes filled with anxiety. "Alejandro, she didn't find out?"

"No, María, not that. But in all our fine plans, we forgot my throat." He put an arm around her, pressed a hand against her silky hair. "Oh, María," he whispered joyously, "we forgot my stupid, nervous throat."

Evita had no one with whom she could share the weight of her jealousy. She was aware that many men, many respectable married men, kept mistresses. It was whispered that even Don Rosalío had a son or two in the *Gallineros*. But she knew that Alejandro was too fastidious for any casual affair. She also realized that in his eyes, he was satisfying his bargain with her. She had far more money than she could spend. When she wanted to go to Monterrey to a concert, or the theatre, or a dance at the Great Casino with its glittering crystal lights and wide marble stairway, he took her without protest, and with a gentle courtesy that set her apart from other women, so that even her Monterrey friends envied her. His apparent devotion to her had created a proverb that was already spreading through the Sabinas Valley, "That young rooster is almost as faithful as Alejandro Castillo."

Every time she heard the words, her mouth would tighten with bitterness. Alejandro Castillo was faithful in truth, but not to his wife. And Evita's selfishness was too great to accept the situation easily. She was sick with the knowledge that some other woman owned what rightfully belonged to her...that some other woman laughed in secret at the proud head of Evita Cantú.

She set little traps for him. For three nights she hid in the garden so that she might follow him. But he rarely left the house in the evening, and then only with Bob Webster, Pepe Gonzalez, or perhaps Rubén, the candy-maker, whom he laughingly referred to as "cousin" by reason of some stupid joke of his childhood. He spent most of his days at the Rancho Santo Tomás, to which she could not go unaccompanied, as there were too many men there, and Alejandro might be gone when she arrived. But one day she ordered the Castillo victoria and rode out there, taking with her Pepe Gonzalez' wife, Sarita Calderón.

Alejandro was not there; so she prowled through the house, hunting for a clue to the woman. Surely in this place, which was Alejandro's own, he would keep some trifle, some memory of the creature. There was nothing in the wide, pine-raftered living room, with its chairs of leather stretched on polished steer horns. Nothing in the bedrooms. In the dining room, its furniture brilliant in the Mexican manner with blue and yellow and crimson roses, she found a painting of the outcast girl from the River Road, María de las Garzas. It had obviously been done by a very fine artist, showing a sun-drenched corner of the ranch patio, María standing with her head high, her feet wide apart and firm on the earth, her left hand on her hip, her right gripping the barrel of a long rifle. Evita stared at it for a long time. Surely not María. The river creature was beautiful, true, but a Castillo was too proud for nameless wenches. Also, Alejandro would never be so stupid as to blatantly exhibit her portrait to the gossiping tongues of the men, and the stern eyes of his father, who often came to the ranch. But what was her portrait doing here? What was her connection with the family Castillo?

When Alejandro rode up to the house, she said nothing about the portrait. He greeted Sarita and kissed Evita's hand with casual grace, but his eyes were laughing at her, and she knew that he knew why she had come.

She said curtly, "The ranch is amusing, but too barbaric for my tastes. It is time for us to return to Hidalgo, Sarita."

As he helped them into the carriage he said gravely, "When you come again, let me know. I will have the men do some trick riding and roping to amuse you. I am sure this hour of waiting has bored you."

She wanted to slap his face. Instead, she nodded gracefully to him and ordered the coachman to drive on.

"What a magnificent husband," sighed Sarita. "So gallant. You are very lucky, Evita."

She raised her brows, but said nothing. Sarita was a stupid fool. They were all stupid, all the people in the village. She wanted to get away from Hidalgo, away from the valley, away where she could think and plan. She said, "Next week I go to San Antonio to buy clothes. I am tired of my wedding dresses."

Sarita said again, "How lucky you are, Evita."

On Thursday nights it was customary for Alejandro and Evita to go to the great Castillo house for dinner. Alejandro and Don Saturnino wore the formal black *charro* dress clothes: the tight black trousers fitting closely over square-toed, high-heeled black boots, the soft white shirt with flowing black bow tie, the black cummerbund, and short jacket with its embroidery of silver vines and flowers. Don Saturnino preferred Evita in color, and on this Thursday she wore crimson velvet, straight and full from shoulder to hip, with a wide girdle, and a skirt that ended just below her knees. Gold beads were braided into the thick black hair, and a large gold flower was fastened to one narrow shoulder strap.

Don Saturnino bent over her hand. "You are very beautiful tonight, Evita."

She smiled at him with her lips, and drifted towards the fireplace as Alejandro kissed his father's hand. "I went to the ranch two days ago. Did Alejandro tell you?"

"It was the first time?" Don Saturnino poured a glass of sherry and handed it to her, then poured two more for himself and his son.

"Yes. I was interested in the portrait in the dining room." She looked sideways at Alejandro from under lowered lids.

There was no strain in his manner as he lit her cigarette (for now that she was a married woman she could smoke with propriety). He said lightly, "Father is thinking of bringing the portrait here to the house. It seems that the artist has gained a reputation in the world."

"It is not that at all," protested Don Saturnino. "But I have thought for some time that it is too fine a thing to keep at the ranch where any hands might take it away." He turned courteously to Evita. "I had it painted after Alejandro and I returned from exile. The family Castillo owes María a great debt." He told her of María's protection during the days of the Great Revolution as they ate dinner, and while he talked, Evita watched Alejandro. He seemed politely bored by the story, as though tired of hearing it so often retold. She thought, whoever the woman is, she is not María. At least it is no girl from the river bank, and she felt tired with the relief of that certainty, and yet at the same time more angry that it was some woman in Hidalgo, someone she knew, perhaps saw every day; someone with whom, doubtless, she laughed and talked. And she knew that she had to leave Hidalgo, or her bottled anger would make her scream out the story before she was ready to use it to her best advantage. She said quickly, "I would like to go to San Antonio, please."

The two men glanced at each other with raised brows. Alejandro said, "As you please, Evita. We can go whenever you like."

"I want to go alone."

Don Saturnino frowned. "To travel alone to the States? Impossible."

"Please." She clasped her hands and rested them on the edge of the table. "It is often done now. Many of my friends from Monterrey go up alone."

"They are not of the family Castillo."

Alejandro lifted his wine glass, the Castillo crest engraved on its shining crystal. "Doña Perfecta, mother to Ricardo Manchaca, allows her daughter to make the trip alone, and you know her strictness. Also, Hidalgo is very small, very dull. Life is monotonous. Let Evita go and see strange sights and strange people. New things are good for the spirit."

Evita relaxed, listening to Alejandro's hoarse voice flowing smoothly on, convincing his father that traditions changed, even for the family Castillo. How clever he is, she thought. His father thinks him so generous to my little whims. And all the time he is glad that I am going, glad to be rid of me. How I hate you, my clever Alejandro.

Two days later she went alone to San Antonio, Texas. In a large store for women on Houston Street she found the answer to her problem of identification, in the form of a three-cornered scarf, a delicate affair of thin white wool, with small roses woven into it. When she bought it there was such a gleam of triumph in her shallow black eyes that the salesgirl stared at her curiously. But she did not notice the stare. She was planning exactly what she would do with the scarf, and what she would do afterwards slid into her mind also.

In Monterrey, while waiting for the train to Hidalgo, she visited the *Mercado del Norte*, which spreads its white bulk over a large area of land near the station. This market belongs to the wholesale dealers and the poorer people. None of Evita's friends ever went there. But it was a good market, and in it she found what she had been hunting: a small, pearl-handled dagger, not much longer than her hand, but with a sharp blade of German steel.

On the train the wheels clicked a little song to her: Viscondesa de Mogollón, Vizcondesa de Mogollón, Vizcondesa de Mogollón. And for a Viscountess there was no law, nor any penalty for breaking one. The creature would be removed, very quietly, very simply, and after the removal there would be no one left to laugh at Evita, to point the finger and whisper, "I own the man of Evita Cantú."

Alejandro met her at the station. Because it was February and cold, the crowd was much smaller than usual. Rubén, the candymaker came toward them, his tray slung by cords from his neck, his small son Gitanillo clutching his finger. The child slid shyly past Evita, and flung his arms around Alejandro's leg.

"Eh, Alejandro, there are actors coming. Will they have a bull with them?"

Alejandro flung him high in the air. "No, my brave matador, no bulls with the actors. But come out to the Rancho Santo Tomás and you can play with as many bulls as you like."

Rubén shook his head. "Better to keep him at home. He is too young for bulls."

"The great Gitanillo started when he was only four. And this one will soon be five."

Rubén's face closed into stillness. "Doubtless. But Lolita, my wife, does not like the bulls." He turned to Evita with easy familiarity. "Perhaps your son will be a brave killer in the arena. That would be a fine joke, eh? A proud Castillo killing bulls in the arena?"

Evita's eyes dulled with anger. "It would be very amusing," she answered coldly.

Alejandro helped her into the victoria and then stepped in himself, bringing Gitanillo with him. "I will leave him at your house for you, cousin."

"I thank you, cousin," Rubén answered, and both men laughed as the coachman flicked the reins.

Gitanillo crawled over Alejandro, gravely examined the contents of his pockets, found the square of sugar he knew would be there, and nibbled at it contentedly. As the coach swung around a corner, Evita's sleeve brushed his face. He slapped it away and thrust his head inside of Alejandro's coat. Evita said nothing, her face very pale. People on the street waved to her, calling out little greetings of welcome, but she did not answer them. Alejandro, contentedly playing with the child, noticed nothing, but she was sick with anger. As long as the woman lived, Evita would never have a son. She would have to endure such scenes as this, with Hidalgo whispering that she was already four years married and no sign . . . that she was perhaps barren. New whispers added to the laughter of a creature whose face she did not know, but whom she would find, and soon. Her fingers gripped her bag. She could feel the outline of the knife through the soft leather. Soon now, very soon. The scarf would identify the woman. The knife would play its part, and then . . . Evita shut her eyes and visualized a scene in the future: Don Saturnino dead these many years—she and Alejandro living in the great house on the Mina Road, their oldest son with his wife and children living in the house on the Street of the River, their other sons away at school or playing in the shady patio. And she herself, Doña Evita, Vizcondesa de . . . no, Don Saturnino's death would make her la Duquesa de Huachichil. Men with famous names would visit them and kiss her hand. When she spoke, they would listen, for they would whisper that she was the strength of the Family Castillo.

The stopping of the victoria at the house of Rubén on the Street of the Three Crosses jolted her free of her dreams. Lolita, her black hair pulled back from the widow's peak on her forehead, came to the door, wiping her hands on her apron.

"Ay, Alejandro, that Gitanillo. What mischief has he been in now?" She lifted her son to the ground, slapped at him lovingly, and brushed him through the door.

"No mischief," Alejandro grinned. "Rubén was tired of him and sent him home."

Lolita laughed. "That Rubén. He may speak such words with the mouth, but not with the eyes." She was very serious. "Rubén is such a good man, Alejandro. So good."

"Very good," Alejandro said gravely. "I have reason to know."

She stepped forward and put her hand on the carriage's low door. "Did he tell you what I saw in the cards last night?" When Alejandro shook his head, she added, "I was running them in the gypsy manner. Next to your card was a dark woman, and across her the ace of swords. Be careful, Alejandro, be very careful. She is dangerous to you. The ace of swords means death. It frightened me."

"Cards are small magic, Lolita."

"But magic can kill," she said passionately. "I know, Alejandro. Believe me. Magic can kill."

Alejandro kissed her work-hardened fingers, and the carriage creaked as the coachman turned it around and headed it toward the Street of the River.

Evita spoke very low so that the coachman could not hear her. "Such familiarity. And with the family of a candy vendor."

"Rubén is a fine soul," Alejandro protested quickly.

Evita shrugged her shoulders. "It is not becoming to call him cousin."

"He called me cousin once and saved my life. I've not forgotten it."

"You have a long memory, Alejandro."

"I find it useful."

I have a long memory, too, she whispered to herself. Very long. Afterwards, when the woman was gone, there would be no more easy familiarity with the Rubéns, and Porfirios, and Pepes of Hidalgo. The family Castillo would have friends from beyond the mountains, friends of importance, not stupid village folk. And the Castillo name would shine again in the Republic, as it had shone in the days of the viceroys. Perhaps it would be better if they went to live in the City, keeping the Hidalgo houses for the dull summer months. Yes, the City would be better, with its European atmosphere, its music, its theatres. As they passed the Plaza of Independence, a poster announcing the coming of a company of actors caught her eye. Her lips curled as she remembered the days before her marriage, when such an announcement would have filled her with delight. A stupid, crude little show, with actors who were of no importance. They were good enough for the old Evita Cantú, but not for the Vizcondesa de Mogollón...the Duquesa de Huachichil. She could hear the soft whispers as she appeared in the Castillo box at the marble *Palacio de Bellas Artes* with its great glass curtain. "Who is the beautiful woman? But of course, the Duquesa. And with her her oldest son. So young to have a son so tall and handsome."

Alejandro said, "Welcome home, Evita."

"Ay!" She started and lifted a gloved hand to her forehead. "I was dreaming. So stupid of me."

She went into the low-ceilinged living room, gave her coat and hat to the maid. "Your apron lacks freshness, Beca. Change it."

"Yes, *madama*," Beca was afraid of her, and she scurried out of the room, with a warm glance for Alejandro, whom she adored as all the servants adored him.

Alejandro sat on one of the blue velvet chairs and watched her as she warmed her fingers at the fireplace. "You amused yourself in San Antonio?"

"All women amuse themselves at shopping. I brought you a present."

"How kind of you." He played with his pipe, then remembered she did not like it in the living room, put it away and took out a cigarette case. He lighted two cigarettes and handed her one. "I am flattered that you thought of me while you were gone."

She rang the bell for the maid as she said, "You are my husband. Naturally I thought of you. Ay, Beca, bring me the package wrapped in tissue paper from the large black bag." And when the maid was gone, "You found excitement in Hidalgo?"

"Nothing of importance." He twisted uncomfortably on the chair that was too low for his long legs. He hated this room, preferring the red leather comfort of the library, but Evita loved it. The blue furniture, the white and blue tiled floor, the white velvet drapes at the windows made a cool background for her dark paleness. "Bob Webster stayed with me while Tía Magdalena visited her sister in Mina. She was to be gone a week. She stayed three days, and came home, she said, because of the mischief she was afraid we would get into. She treats Bob as though he were no older than Gitanillo."

"How stupid." Evita took the package from the maid, her fingers clenching tightly around it. It had no weight at all, and yet it represented so much: her whole future, her entire happiness.

"Oh, he likes it. He's never said very much, but I think he must have had a lonely childhood. Tía has become a mother to him."

Evita was not interested in Bob Webster, whom she intensely disliked, because she felt that he could see through her shell of pride to her ambition, and found it amusing that an Hidalgo girl could possess such dreams. She shrugged the thought of Bob away from her, and extended the gift.

Alejandro's fingers were clumsy with the wrappings. Evita watched him, wanting to tear the paper herself, to rush him into action. But she held herself rigid as he unfolded the feminine trifle no man would wear.

His head was tilted so low that she could not read his face. "It's a very pretty scarf, Evita. Thank you."

"I noticed that you wore one knotted about your throat at the ranch...a common red handkerchief. I thought that this one was better for you."

He thanked her again and took it into his bedroom. Had he guessed why she bought it? She held her breath. What would he do with it? Put it in a drawer, forget it? Or would he use the pretty thing as she hoped he would use it? So much depended on it, and it was very pretty. Her heart was beating as fast as though she had been running. Tomorrow she would look in the drawer. Tomorrow she would know.

The moment he rode out of sight down the River Road the next morning she hurried into his bedroom, pulled open the dresser drawer. The clean red handkerchiefs were there, but the white scarf was missing. To make certain, she looked in the other drawers. She found nothing but piles of shirts and underclothes. She smiled at herself in the mirror. The daintily fragile scarf had truly been beautiful enough. He had taken it to the woman. And what woman in Hidalgo could resist wearing it? Evita's smile broadened. Even if she did not see it with her own eyes, someone in the town would. And Hidalgo loved gossip. No detail was too small for comment. In all the Sabinas Valley there was not another such scarf. For the first time in days, she found herself breathing normally. More days of waiting, but soon, soon, she would discover the truth at last.

Time passed in a slow, dull rhythm. She invented a careful little story: Alejandro had given her a scarf with three corners. She had lost it. Had anyone seen it? She went to the station the afternoon the actors arrived, because most of the village was congregated there. She asked Don Nacho, and the little Professor, for men would notice the scarf as quickly as women. But no one had seen it. Never mind, there was time. She had waited so long . . . to wait longer was not difficult.

A week passed. Another week. A month. But still no news of the scarf. Never, anywhere, from anyone, any news of the scarf. Evita's face took on a pinched and bitter look. New lines etched themselves from nostril to mouth. People, passing her on the street, wondered how they could ever have thought her pretty enough to win a beauty contest. Her voice took on a sharper edge, and Don Saturnino at the Thursday night dinners, watched her from behind veiled eyes. She worried him. He had expected her to be a soft docile creature in marriage, blindly adoring Alejandro. Instead she was cold and shrewish, with a tongue like a whiplash that curled itself around Alejandro with increasing bitterness. Don Saturnino looked at his son. He had never recognized his true character until now. Joaquín, the wild one, would

have beaten this woman into submission. But Alejandro, the gentle
one, had about him a shell of contentment that her gibes could
not pierce.

Don Saturnino began to wonder about his youngest son. He had
always accepted Alejandro too casually. He faced the truth that
Alejandro was a stranger to him. The old man sat for hours in
the sun and pieced together all he knew about the secretive
Alejandro. And in his amazed mind a new portrait emerged,
entirely different from his former conception. Joaquín had been
like a great breeze blowing. He was as transparent in actions as
a shallow pool. Not so Alejandro. He moved quietly, saying
nothing, revealing nothing. Even as a child his mouth had been
firmly shut, the deed apparent only after its accomplishment.
For example that strange friendship with Rubén, strong enough
even in the days of the Revolution for Rubén to protect them
from the wrath of his companions. Joaquín, like all the Castillos,
never mingled with village folk. But Alejandro was a part of the
village, sharing in all its customs and simple pleasures. Don
Saturnino, as lord of the valley, was required to know every
soul within its boundaries. And he felt a deep personal friendship for many of them, especially Don Rosalío and Don Nacho.
But as a young man, he, like Joaquín, had ridden the trails with
no interest for the people who walked along them. His knowledge of the village had come with his later, settled years, as it
would have come to Joaquín had he not shrugged off Castillo
duty, preferring the world beyond the mountains. Joaquín, Don
Saturnino could understand. Joaquín was himself reproduced. It
was Alejandro who was the mystery. For a more loving or dutiful son a father could not ask. A more remote and secretive son,
a father could not seek to comprehend.

As Don Saturnino sat in the sun, his cane tracing the spiraling
designs of the mosaic walk, he discovered the depths of his own
selfishness. The weeks of hiding at the Rancho Santo Tomás had
been his opportunity to return Alejandro's devotion with a full
measure. Instead, he had mourned over Joaquín's cruel selfishness
and had allowed Alejandro to slip away from him toward the
warmth and understanding of María. María! Don Saturnino raised
his head. If he had not been so blind he would have noticed
then that María was no casual village acquaintance. There had
been a great comradeship between the two children even in the

first days. And what had Rubén said while they were waiting
for Alejandro to go ahead and warn her that they were coming?
The words returned to his mind in wisps of phrases that enlarged
into sentences as he tried to remember: "She is a proper wild-
cat...I thought she was my friend, but she shot at me as well
as the rest...I shouldn't have let the boy go alone. She doesn't
know him well and she'll put a bullet through him." But Alejandro returned for them unwounded, and María, when she
spoke to him, used the familiar "thou" of friendship. So Rubén
was wrong. Alejandro had known María well enough for her to
trust him.

Don Saturnino rose and began to pace the courtyard, his cane
slashing at the violets and nasturtiums in the formal flower beds,
unaware of his actions in his excitement of remembrance. Other
things came to him: Alejandro muttering María's name in his
sleep during the first weeks of exile; Alejandro leafing quickly
through the mail ("Is that an 'a,' Alejandro? How marvelous
to know that that is an 'a' "); Alejandro's disinterest in women;
his eagerness to return to Hidalgo; his constant photography
of familiar foreign scenes ("Behold, Father, here is Europe on
these slips of paper"), to show without doubt to an interested
María. For behind everything was María, with her little house
on the River Road and the door that was locked...what had
Don Nacho said about that lock? "I called on María the other
day, and can you believe it, her door has a fine mechanical lock.
Where did she get it, that pretty one? For there's no such lock
in this valley."

Don Saturnino called loudly for a servant to saddle a horse
for him. He needed to know now the answer to but one question: Why had Alejandro suddenly agreed to marry Evita? For
the decision was made without warning in a letter from Canada.
But wait, why Canada? Why any of those abrupt long journeys
to the States and Europe? Don Saturnino bit his lip in impatience. It was not right that a son should have such secrets from
his father. True, he had never been interested before, but now...
Alejandro was his son, the last Castillo. Unless there was issue
from this marriage with Evita, the proud name that had been a
part of Mexico's history for three hundred years would die out.
Evita was now four years married and still barren. The Cantús
were fertile stock...it could not be her fault. But Alejandro

had stayed away from women in Europe. He had not concerned himself with any girl in the Republic, and then that quick decision to marry Evita ...

Don Saturnino reined in his horse in front of María's door and swung to the ground. He unfastened his cane from the back of the saddle and stared at the door's lock for a long minute before he pounded the cane against the house wall. María opened the door, looked at him with steady dark blue eyes. "Here is your house, Don Saturnino. If you will enter?"

He limped past her and stared about him. Sunlight came in a golden cloud through the window and illuminated the bare, rough furnishings, the single sacred lithograph on the wall with the vigilance lamp burning in front of it. The walls of most houses of this type were plastered with pictures; here there was austerity and a certain beauty. He tapped his cane against the cement floor. "Did Bob Webster put this in for you?" he asked curtly.

She flushed but her voice was steady as she answered, "Yes, but not for the reason you think, Don Saturnino."

"I am quite aware of that." He sat on the three-legged stool, folded his hands over the top of the cane. "He and Alejandro are too great friends for any such nonsense. And Alejandro might have given you a decent chair."

Her face accepted his speech as a patient accepts the decision of a doctor.

"Alejandro told you, then?"

"He told me nothing. His mouth is very secret."

She shrugged, sat on the edge of the cot, waited for more words from him.

He said, "I want the truth, María. All of it."

Her fingers brushed a tendril of hair away from her cheek. "What truth, Don Saturnino? That I am Alejandro's mistress? I think you know that or you wouldn't be here. Have you ... Does ..." She paused, breathed deeply. "Does Evita know?"

"I don't think so. But she must suspect something. She's very unhappy."

María's brows rose in two black crescents. "She is a cruel woman ... cold and cruel. Her unhappiness does not concern me."

Don Saturnino stared at her for a long moment. He felt her

full earthy strength, and her soft warm beauty. "I suppose there is no point in asking you to leave the valley."

She did not answer him. He had not really expected an answer. "María, you love my son very much. I think you have loved him for a long time. How long?"

Her lips softened into a smile. "Since he was ten."

"I see. You know of course that when..." His voice caught as it always caught when mentioning the lost name. "When Joaquín went away, when he died, Alejandro became the last of the Castillo line. It is very important that he should have children—a son to carry on the Castillo name..."

"Please, Don Saturnino." She rose, rubbing her palms against her hips.

He did not pause for her interruption, but continued harshly, "To you and Alejandro it makes no difference now, but later, when he is an old man, he will want his own sons. I understand how it is. Alejandro is very fastidious. Doubtless he feels a deep obligation to you, one that holds him remote from Evita. As you say, you have loved each other for many years, but love is not always the most important thing. Love dies, obligations continue. In time, since there is no legal bond between you, Alejandro will turn away to the more placid life. That is always the history of these affairs. It is difficult, I know, for you to understand these things. You are both very young. But when the hot years are finished, and Alejandro comes to full maturity..."

"He never will!" The words slashed across his words with an almost animal cry of pain. She looked at him, her lids fluttering in an effort to fight tears; then she sat down again on the cot.

Don Saturnino felt a sudden pain in his chest, a breathless sense of warning. "What did you say?"

Her voice was tight in her throat. "What were you saying... you were pounding at me. I have no right to speak. Please, Don Saturnino, please go home and forget you've ever been here. Go home and continue in your placid blind way. It will be much easier for you, and..." Her head twisted from side to side. "No." She faced him for a moment, then rose and went to him, knelt beside him, put her hand on his shoulder. "You know too much now—too much and too little. How you guessed the truth, I don't know. But that's not important. I've wanted Alejandro to tell you the whole truth for a long time, but he loves you too

much. He loves you very much, Don Saturnino. He married
Evita because he loves you. He has kept silent because he loves
you. We could have gone away together long ago ... we would
have been very happy in some strange land beyond these mountains, but we stayed here because he loves you."

"If he loves me so much why has he refused to give me a
grandchild? That was the reason for the marriage." He rubbed
his fingers in the wrinkled space between his brows. "I am an
old and stupid man. Perhaps if I were younger I could understand these things, but ..."

She put her arms around him, held him as though he were a
child. "This is not my secret. In some ways I have no right to
tell it to you. But you should know the truth." And so she told
him the story from the beginning, from the swans in the pool
to the doctor in Canada. Her head dropped against his shoulder.
The words were so muffled he could barely hear her. "He has
never touched Evita. He can't. The throat won't let him. The
only place he is safe and happy is here in this house with me.
As long as he is alive and needs me, I shall not leave." She rose
and went to the table, stared through the window to the line of
western mountains with the fold of hills and the small white
dot that was the Rancho Santo Tomás. "After that, no matter.
After that, valleys or towns or mountains or wide ocean, no
matter."

Don Saturnino pulled himself to his feet with the aid of his
cane. He said dully, in broken words, "I must go home now.
The horse is very tall. If you will help me to mount."

Her strong arms supported him. When he was finally seated
on the horse, he looked down at her, put his hand on her soft
hair. "Our secret, María?"

"Our secret."

"Afterwards ... I think we will need each other afterwards,
little daughter." He jerked the reins and the horse carried him
away from her. Not until he was out of sight did she go in the
house and sink on her knees before the lithograph, dry sobs
shaking her. Finally she rose and shook some copper coins from
the bottom of a vase. As she thrust the money into her pocket,
her fingers encountered Evita's scarf. She smiled wryly. Alejandro had brought her the scarf with a grin for the obvious
planning. Poor Evita, who had no gift but unhappiness. She

thrust the scarf back into the pocket, draped a prayer shawl over her blond hair, and hurried up the road to the church.

Inside, she knelt in prayer for a long time before the image of Saint Ana, mother of the Blessed Virgin and patron saint of marriages. Then she lit three candles: one for Alejandro, one for Don Saturnino, and the third, in pity, for Evita. As she pulled the money from her pocket for the candle offering, the scarf came with it. She quickly replaced it, but a woman was standing behind her in the gloom, a woman who must have seen it. She looked closer and saw that it was Don Nacho's homely daughter, Chela. For a moment the two women examined each other, and María realized with a sudden flash that Chela had not only seen the scarf, but knew what it meant. Then, for the first time, a village woman smiled at her with sympathy and understanding. Instinctively María's hand went out, Chela's strong fingers enclosed it. They said nothing, there was nothing to say. Then María returned to her house, but with a new softness in her for the town she had always hated.

While Don Saturnino was learning the truth from María, Evita was still hunting the scarf. Seeing some of the town women go into Chela's house, she went there for information. A mention of it brought color to Chela's sallow cheeks. She said shyly that a friend had given her such a handkerchief, "with three corners, you understand."

Evita felt the room swim about her. Could Chela be Alejandro's woman? This short-legged, awkward, homely creature? Impossible! Chela was her friend. Chela was ... and then, with a lurch of the heart, she realized that she did not know what Chela was ... Chela, even now entering the room with the scarf in her hands, might very well be the woman to whom Alejandro was so faithful.

Florinda, Xavier's wife, heavy now with child, held up the scarf. It was a three-cornered affair, true, but it was silk, with a splashing yellow and orange batik design. Evita felt the breath spill out of her, and fury pour into the vacancy. How dare Chela gull her so, raise her hopes so high and then toss this absurdity before her? She cried out, "It is hideous ... like an ancient egg broken on the floor!"

Chela's face whitened, then, without warning, she burst into tears. Alma Orona, Florinda Farías, Sarita Calderón turned on Evita like a flock of angry hens protecting their one chick. With an inarticulate gasp of anger, she hurried home, the truth hot in her mind. She might search until she was an old woman, but she would never find the scarf. Because Alejandro knew—had always known. At this very moment he and his woman might be laughing at her over the failure of her simple plan. But there were other ways of finding out the truth. Somewhere there was a clue to the woman. She had found nothing at the ranch house, but in her own home there might be something.

She knew it was useless to look among the photographs in the library. She had gone through the files too many times. But in Alejandro's bedroom—a room she rarely entered—there might be one small forgotten thing to tell her the truth. She lifted shirts and underclothes from their drawers, separated the stacked red handkerchiefs, shook out the piles of white duck trousers which Alejandro wore every evening but Thursdays. She inverted the drawers to see if anything were fastened to the bottom. She looked under the goat skin rugs that were thrown across the red-tiled floor. She peered under the bed and into the closets. Even the extra pair of riding boots, shining with polish in the closet's gloom, were up-ended and shaken. Her hand felt every coat pocket, and finally, inside the pillow case on which he slept, she came across it. It was a picture of María de las Garzas, her long body lengthened as she stretched across the grinding stone to get fresh moistened corn meal out of the pail.

Evita sank down on the side of the bed. María, whose portrait Don Saturnino had hung in the dining room of the Rancho Santo Tomás—María, whom she had discounted long ago—María, the nameless creature from the River Road—María.

She tapped the picture with her long, pointed nail. There was something very familiar about it. The gray pasteboard backing with the ornate scrolls and doves decorating the outer edge... she had seen other photographs like that... many of them.

With an inarticulate cry she leaped to her feet and ran into her own bedroom. Opening a scented box of *limón* wood, she pulled out the contest photograph which she had kept through some perverse desire to see herself as a sullen, selfish creature. Sauceda's flowery signature was on both photographs. The beauty contest—that María had won! Alejandro and his cameras! Alejandro had taken that mysterious snapshot of María, not Bob Webster after all. Evita rose to her feet, her eyes wide and staring into space. What a fool she had been. That contest should have given her the clue she needed... that, and María de las Garzas' insolent beauty. Only a Castillo possession could walk the town with such arrogance. Arrogance fashioned from the sly knowledge that she, a common river wench, could mock the less beautiful, less fortunate Evita Cantú.

Evita took the dagger from the *limón* box. She went about her preparations as calmly and precisely as though everything had been rehearsed. First she changed her high-heeled shoes for rubber-soled oxfords. Then she put on a long skirt that folded about her ankles, and wrapped her head in a *rebozo*. In the deepening dusk whoever she passed would think her a woman from the *Gallineros*. But she did not expect to meet anyone. There was little traffic on the Street of the River at twilight. As for the River Road she had nothing more dangerous to fear than a stray *burro* or cow.

Luckily the kitchen where the cook and the maid were singing plaintive duets was on the other side of the house. She slipped through a side door, ran down the Street of the River and turned the bend between the cliffs to the River Road. In spite of herself she was a little afraid, not of human company, but of ghosts. The dead sweetheart of Juan de Diós, the idiot goatherd, was supposed to walk here in the evenings.

At last the small adobe house of María de las Garzas sprang into view. Cautious as an animal, Evita stopped, and then made her way around to the garden at the back, taking care not to allow a pebble to roll beneath her foot and warn María of her approach, for María had earth strength in her fine tall body.

Evita saw an outdoor fire crackling and snapping in a small, stone-lifted iron stove. Sitting on the ground near it, his back against a huisache tree, a pipe clenched between his teeth, and one knee caught up between his hands, was Alejandro. María was leaning over the stove stirring a great pot of beans, so that the reflected firelight turned her skin from golden cream to bronze. About her hair was knotted the rose-decorated white scarf.

They both saw her at the same time. Alejandro rose slowly

to his feet; María carefully replaced the long wooden spoon in the brown clay bean pot. When Alejandro would have spoken, María stepped between them.

"So," she said in her golden-toned voice, "you have found your way here at last."

"I am not a fool," snapped Evita, her heart beginning to pound so hard that her blouse jerked with its movement.

"Now you know the whole truth," said Alejandro quietly.

Evita's lips curled with derision. "So this is the woman to whom you have been so faithful. This creature without a name ... this river wench!"

"Calling names?" asked María tauntingly. "I thought you were stronger than that."

"Do you want me to thank you for stealing my husband?"

"He was not your husband when he was ten years old. Remember the swans, Alejandro?"

"I remember the coldness of the pool and a lesson in fighting tactics." Their private laughter swirled about them, shutting Evita out.

She clenched her two small hands against her breast. "Why did you marry me, Alejandro? You never meant to be my husband."

Alejandro answered her in his hoarse, polite voice. "For the same reason you married me. It was an affair of family. I told my father I didn't love you. He said love would come after marriage. What was I to answer?"

"You might have told him the truth."

"And have him send María out of the valley?"

"Tell her the real truth," said María suddenly. "We need truth here."

"Very well." Alejandro, eyes steadily on the fire, told her.

When he was finished María said, "His marriage to you was a gift to make his father happy, the only gift he had left to give. And I didn't mind."

"You ... you didn't mind!" Evita could feel unreasoning anger stab through her. "You were happy, weren't you, that Alejandro could be my husband so short a time. You've sat here and laughed together at my efforts to make the world think ours was a happy marriage. You've sat here and laughed at me! At Evita Cantú who could have married any man in the valley. It must have been a very amusing joke."

"Evita," cried Alejandro warningly.

"What did you care about my feelings? You were so sure of yourselves." Her voice rose to a shrill peak. "You didn't even think me important enough to be told the truth! I was nothing but a little gift to please the House of Castillo . . . a thing without importance, without feelings or ambition."

"I offered you your freedom," cried Alejandro. "You wouldn't take it."

"If you offered it to me again, I wouldn't take it." Her head came up, and her eyes blazed with pride. "I am the Vizcondesa de Mogollón. And no river wench shall steal my place from me!" With an animal scream she jumped forward, the dagger in her hand glistening in the firelight.

Alejandro flung María out of the way, caught Evita's wrist, twisted it until her clutching hand relaxed and the knife fell to the ground. Evita beat at him with her hands, kicked out with her feet, turned in his arms as she tried to scratch his face with her long pointed nails.

"Stop this!" he cried. "Stop . . ." his voice ended on a breath of sound. She felt his arms relax, drop from her body as he stumbled back from her . . . heard as from a great distance María's high scream. Through a floating red mist she watched him clutch at his throat, fall to his knees, rock back and forth as terrible choking whispers pushed themselves through his locked teeth. María, sobbing, wrapped Alejandro in her long strong arms. Then something bright and scarlet gushed from his mouth across the amber skin of her forearm. "Do something!" She screamed at Evita. "For the love of God, do something!"

"I don't know . . ." stumbled Evita, terrified. "What shall I do?"

María looked at her sharply. Her tone changed to firm command. "We must get him home. He must not die here."

"Die," repeated Evita, parrot-like, unable to think for herself so that she was like an obeying automaton.

"Can you help me get him home?"

"Home? All the way . . . up the River Road?"

"He can help us. You can walk a little, can't you, Alejandro? Can't you?"

The man's head nodded weakly, as he still struggled for breath.

María dragged him, somehow, to his feet. With his left arm across her shoulder, she supported his full weight.

"Come around to his other side," she gasped to Evita. Like a child, the woman obeyed her. With shrinking fingers she lifted Alejandro's right arm, draped it across her shoulders. It felt heavy as mountain stone. Slowly, step by dragging step, they started up the road. Every few minutes they had to stop and let Alejandro rest. Evita's *rebozo* was wrapped around his neck, the fringed ends pushed into his mouth to stop the bleeding. Time passed, somehow, and distance. Luckily the Street of the River was deserted. Evita was never afterwards able to remember the last part of the journey. They took him in the side door and laid him on his bed. It was María who undressed him while Evita stood helplessly by, trying to focus the situation in her mind. He clung to María as a child clings to its mother. She had to force him to let go of her; then she led Evita into the next room.

"I must leave before anyone sees me. You must tell the world that he was stricken here. Do you understand?"

Evita slowly nodded, unable to take her eyes away from the white scarf around María's hair.

"The moment I am gone, send for the little Doctor. He will know what to do. There is very little he can do. Alejandro is dying."

"Dying," repeated Evita.

"I have no right to ask you, but will you tell me what happens ... at the last?" For the first time the great voice faltered. "You can come during the—funeral. No one would ever know. I'll wait for you on the cliffs where the River Road turns toward El Carmen."

"On the cliffs," repeated Evita slowly. "You are right. No one would ever know."

"I swear to you that afterwards I'll go away. I'll not be seen in the valley again. I swear it by the five wounds of Our Lord."

"I'll come," said Evita stolidly.

Alejandro died twenty minutes later. He did not speak again, but his hand kept feeling weakly inside the pillow case. Evita, realizing what he wanted, slipped a cheap gray-backed photograph into his hand. He laid it against his mouth. He did not know that it was the contest photograph of Evita.

Bob Webster, grim-lipped and silent, went to fetch Don Saturnino, but the old man would not come. "What good to go now?" he whispered. "It is too late. With me, it is always too late."

So Bob returned alone to keep watch with Pepe Gonzalez and Rubén, the candy-maker, beside the body. They said nothing, but they thought Evita strangely calm and brave. She did not cry. She sat in the living room in her black dress and stared into blankness. She noticed vaguely that of all her friends the one person who was not there was Chela. And she was glad, because Chela's eyes were too sharp, her understanding too deep. Evita did not want understanding. She wanted to be left alone to think of a white scarf, her scarf, Alejandro's scarf, María's scarf. A white scarf tied around yellow hair.

Hidalgo men buried Alejandro the next morning. When they came to take his body to the church several women wanted to stay with her. Her mother tried to cling to her, but Evita pushed her away. She kept repeating over and over, "Leave me alone. Please leave me alone."

Father Zacaya said gently, "You are a good daughter of the church. You will not do anything foolish, eh, Evita?"

"No, Father. I simply want to stay here by myself."

The priest nodded and led the mourners out of the room. "Perhaps it is better so," he told them, and as he walked to the church he murmured to Don Nacho, "It is a good custom we have here in Mexico. Women should not go to funerals. It is better that they mourn their dead in peace and in the silence of their own homes."

After the church service, men silently mounted their tall horses, heavy blankets sheathing bodies and faces, broad-brimmed hats pushed forward to the nose. To do Alejandro honor, each rider carried a gun across his knees. Bob Webster rode uncovered and with no gun, his face white and strained.

There were no women on the streets—only men, and the long black coffin strapped to a wagon from the Rancho Santo Tomás. At a low word of command from Pepe Gonzalez, they set their horses in motion, and trees on the Plaza of Independence sent dappled shadows over them. No one spoke. There was no sound at all, save the muted whisper of horses' hooves. Then Rubén took a small clay pipe from his pocket and began to play a mournful melody that had come out of Andalucía in the seventeenth century. As the shrill plaintive notes floated through the still air, Pepe Gonzalez began to sing. Andrés Treviño's high tenor joined, and soon all the men were singing:

> *Where do you go, Alejandro Castillo?*
> *Where do you go, my poor one?*
> *Your horse is wounded,*
> *Your sword is broken,*
> *But your deeds are not forgotten.*
> *For your love there is no ending.*
> *Where do you go, Alejandro Castillo?*
> *Where do you go, my poor one?*

And singing, they passed between the houses and were gone.

Evita waited until the echoing music faded into the distance. Then she draped her head with a black lace prayer shawl and walked across the fields to the cliffs that overhung the River Road. María was crouched on the ground at the cliff's edge, waiting for her. Without preamble, Evita recounted the night's happenings, while she kept her eyes fixed on the white scarf that bound María's hair. After she had finished, there was silence between them, and María began rocking back and forth, holding her body with her folded hands.

"He died so terribly. Why did he have to die like that? Why does God have to punish like that? We've never done anything wrong."

"You sinned against God," muttered Evita.

"I've been punished for it. Do you think I'm never lonely? Do you think I've never envied groups of girls talking and laughing together? After the contest, when the town turned against me, I thought my heart would break."

"That contest was Alejandro's doing. He entered your picture..."

"I know." The golden gong was a muted resonance. "He wanted the town to recognize me...to be aware of the woman it had thrown out. He was like a child with a new toy, fighting the town to keep my picture hanging on the wall. He was so proud of his little joke. So proud—like a child."

"You laughed at the town."

"I had to laugh to keep from washing my face with tears. All my life I've wanted only one thing: someone who would be friendly with me. I was born in the *Gallineros*. Did you know that?"

"No."

"Other children are born there without names. But their mothers marry at last and these children grow up with the others. My mother killed herself."

"That is a sin, too," said Evita stolidly.

"They punished me for it. For that and for being . . . beautiful. They drove me out of the *Gallineros*. I had no place to go but the river bank. I lived in a cave. I ate berries and roots and the fish I could catch in the river. I had to steal my clothes. When I walked in the town men tried to love me."

"Why are you telling me this?" Evita demanded coldly.

"I want you to understand about Alejandro. We met first when he was ten, and I—well, who knows how old I was? There are no years marked in a book for me. But from the beginning we belonged to each other. He taught me to read and write. He taught me about the world beyond the mountains, showed it to me with his pictures. In all my world he was the only soul who loved me."

"You paid him back, didn't you?"

María looked pitifully at Evita. "Don't you understand? He was like a god to me. I worshipped him as I worship the Blessed Infant. He was all my life. We were lovers, yes!" María came to her feet, flung back her head, spoke the words as a proud challenge. "If you think I'm ashamed, you're wrong. I'm proud of it. Prouder than any bride that stands in the church!"

Without conscious thought Evita stepped forward, put her hands against María's chest, pushed with sudden strength. With a thin cry María stumbled backwards, fell out into space, her body turning just before she hit the ground thirty feet below. One arm was flung above her head as though in a vain effort to break the fall. She did not move.

Slowly Evita climbed down from the cliff to the River Road, bent over her and unfastened the white scarf. Then she saw the blue eyes. They were open, and to Evita's feverish imagination they seemed to be filled with the same fierce exultation that María had shown when she was alive. They seemed to say in a resounding golden voice, "Thank you! Thank you! Thank you for sending me to Alejandro!"

With a choked moan, Evita shut the heavy-lashed lids. She fled up the River Road, and she felt as though two ghosts ran beside her, on one side the dead sweetheart of Juan de Diós, on the other the laughing, triumphant María.

She darted into the safety of her living room, slammed shut the door, leaned tremblingly against it. Near her was a table, holding a framed photograph of Alejandro. She spoke loudly so that the ghosts might hear, "In the eyes of the world you belong to me. Nothing can steal you from me now. Do you hear me, Alejandro? At last you are the true husband of Evita Cantú."

Then she pressed her palms against her ears to shut out the mocking golden laughter.

It was Don Timotéo, father of Pepe Gonzalez, who found María. Late that afternoon he was returning from El Carmen, and his horse shied away from the body. He hurriedly fetched Don Ernesto, the *alcalde segundo*, and the official verdict was: "Accidental death, caused by a fall from the cliffs."

Father Zacaya insisted that she be buried in sainted ground. "She was a good daughter of the church." And in this decision, his word was law. Two men from Bob Webster's quarries started to dig the grave. Bob Webster was there, Don Timotéo, Don Ernesto, and the priest. That was all, beside the two gravediggers.

As the spades went into the black earth, the Castillo victoria stopped at the gate, and Don Saturnino came toward them, a tall young man hobbling beside him on crutches.

The old Spanish voice was shaken but clear. "Word has come to me that María de las Garzas is dead."

Don Ernesto raised his shoulders. "The world dies young this day."

"And that you are paying for the burial." The grief-filled eyes examined Bob Webster curiously.

"Yes," Bob answered.

"Why?"

"Because . . ." Bob hesitated. He looked across the valley toward the distant rim of mountains, purple now against the turquoise sky. He wanted to say, Because Alejandro was my friend, and María was his wife. Because, from the moment Alejandro first took me to see her, I've worshipped her. Because I'll always love her. He said, "She was very beautiful."

"Very beautiful," echoed Father Zacaya.

"Too beautiful for common earth," agreed Don Timotéo, pushing his hat to the back of his head to show he spoke with a true mouth.

Don Saturnino turned toward the thin man on crutches. "She saved my life during the Great Revolution. The family Castillo does not forget its debts." And then to the gravediggers. "Bury her on Castillo land, next to Alejandro."

"But, Don Saturnino," protested Don Timotéo, "that will cause a great scandal!"

The man on crutches spoke coldly. "And since when has this valley questioned the actions of the House Castillo?"

"As you say, *patrón*," muttered Don Timotéo, reverting instinctively to the old term of "master."

Father Zacaya looked questioningly at Bob, who silently nodded. So María was put into the earth next to Alejandro. When the service was finished, Don Saturnino, his hand resting on his companion's shoulder, went back to his carriage.

Bob touched Don Timotéo's arm. "I'll buy you a drink, friend."

"I need one," whispered Don Timotéo, staring after the slow-moving victoria. "For I have seen a ghost this night. I would swear by the blue robe of the Blessed Virgin that the man with Don Saturnino was his oldest son, Joaquín, dead these sixteen years!" He crossed himself and kissed his thumb. And later he sacrificed a young kid to the eagle witches, so that the living Christ and the dead old gods would keep him safe from ghosts and other terrors of the night.

The Avenue of Illustrious Men

Though we are all of the same clay, a jug is not a vase.
—Mexican proverb

T HERE WAS GOING TO BE A PLAY!
Abel, the *árabe* tradesman, had posted the notices just that morning, but already the news had spread through the five villages and even into the neighboring valley of the Three Marys. And what a wonderful play it was going to be! The notices read:

A MAGNIFICENT TRAGEDY IN FIVE ACTS

La Cabina del Tío Tom

TICKETS: FIFTY CENTAVOS, TWENTY CENTAVOS, TEN CENTAVOS

BEAUTIFUL SEX ADMITTED FREE

Don Nacho had rented the patio of his house for the entertainment, and two of the actors were already in town, setting up the stage: a simple affair of planks mounted on sawhorses. Doña Fela had graciously donated two of her great wool blankets for the outer curtains, and Doña Mariliria had offered the use of her clothesline on which to drape the curtains. Children on their way to school scurried through the tunnel-like hall and watched the working actors with avid curiosity, for was it not a well known fact that actors—like goatherds—were a race apart? Strange people who spoke written words instead of normal speech, and painted their faces into semblances of what they were not? These two actors were men in their forties and, to the children's disappointed eyes, seemed much like other men, with one exception—they really worked instead of standing around and talking about it.

The tolling bells called the children to their lessons, the girls marching primly into one door, the boys into another. Since the Boy's School was next door to Don Nacho's, the sound of the hammering was still plainly audible, and it needed several raps of Professor Porfirio Diaz Aah's ruler on his desk before books were opened and the boys began to study aloud in their sweet singsong voices.

Professor Porfirio Diaz Aah was a quiet little man of five foot three, delicate of feature and body. He was an outlander from the dank hot jungle country of Michoacán. After he was graduated from the preparatory school, he contracted a nasty cough, from years of too close study in the thick damp air. The doctors warned him that he needed to go to the dry northern mountains if he wanted to escape the dread sickness of the lungs.

The first year he was in Hidalgo, he was a shy and bitterly lonely man. The language of the hot country is not mountain talk. Words changed their meaning. Expressions of simple affection in the South were vile phrases in the North. Usual everyday speech was different. He had to learn a new vocabulary for words like knife, fork, and spoon. The word in Michoacán for cigarette case meant a clothes trunk in Nuevo León. He was a foreigner in his own language. And as he was normally a shy man, this lack of communication thrust him even further into loneliness. The priest and the little Doctor were kind to him, but they were men in their sixties, and he was twenty-six, so that there was a further barrier of age between them. With their help he soon learned the language, but he was still friendless. The villagers were simple folk and he was a man of learning. Even Don Nacho —that great man—took off his hat when the Professor passed. Hidalgo was certain of one thing. A knowledge of books was a true magnificence. And certainly the Professor in charge of the Boy's School was a man of letters. The two women who taught in the Girl's School did not have this learned aura. They were Hidalgo girls who had gone to the Normal School in Monterrey, and since the village had known them from their birth, they were regarded with tranquillity. But the Professor's gentle delicacy impressed the village people, and his quick graceful gestures, so different from the large, full-bodied gestures of the northern men, had in them a quality of aloofness, making him as truly foreign as though he had come from the misty shores of Spain.

The children neither liked him nor disliked him. They had made fun of him at first, but he seemed so unconscious of their humor that the jokes died from undernourishment, and after a while his learning drew from them a grudging respect. To him they looked monstrous—for northern children are bigger than those of the south—and he was terrified by them, but after he had that conversation with Chela, the old maid, he was not afraid of them any more.

Actually Chela was only twenty-five, but in a valley where the normal marrying age is sixteen to eighteen, her twenty-five years were a sorrow to her parents. If the Professor had a quality of aloofness, Chela had the quality of age. At sixteen she looked forty. When Father Zacaya remarked on this with sadness, the little Doctor said sharply, "Nonsense! When she's sixty, she'll still look forty. Let these chickens cackle about her now. They'll weep to resemble her when they are sixty."

But Chela did not know this, and her own appearance was magnified and terrible in her eyes, and she would cry silently in her bed at night. Her legs were too short for her torso, so that her body appeared square. Her shoulders were broad and made her nicely shaped head look smaller than it really was. She had beautiful hair—very glossy and black, but although it was thick, it was so fine that it made only two wisps of braids and never stayed in place, always straggling about her cheeks in untidy locks. Her eyes were green and slanted, tilted upwards at the corners, and her mouth was wide and generous. Her teeth were good, but just uneven enough to call attention to themselves and away from the firm chin and the lovely curve of the throat. The unlined skin had a golden tinge. When she was small those slanted eyes and golden skin often made Don Nacho wonder if some adventurous ancestor of his had run away with a Chinese girl. It never occurred to him that this exotic taint may have come from Doña Mariliria's side of the family.

Village girls liked to walk down the street with Chela because her homeliness made such a pleasant contrast to their own fresh beauty. But after her generation came to the marriage age, Chela drew away from her friends. These girls talked incessantly of nothing but boys. "Did you know that Pepe Gonzalez spoke to me twice on the plaza last night?" "Have you heard that Alejandro Castillo gave Evita Cantú a bracelet on the Day of the Magi?" "When I marry, and my husband dies, I shall close my house and mourn for him just as the Widow mourns for General Valdez."

Such words as these were not Chela's words. No young man stood beneath her window and murmured flowery phrases. No boy in all Hidalgo rolled the eye at her on the plaza, and she privately considered the Widow a rather stupid woman to waste the rest of her life over a man long dead. Doña Fela and Doña Juanita Perez were much more sensible with their contention that life was for the living, and the cemetery for the dead.

Her friends were scandalized, and even Don Nacho fussed at her, when she flatly refused to be in Evita Cantú's wedding. Evita had wanted her as maid of honor, but Chela said stiffly that she was too shy to stand up before so many people, and no arguments would induce her to change her mind. The truth was that Chela had been wandering down a street near Alejandro Castillo one day when María de las Garzas walked past, and she saw the expression in his eyes, the tensing of his body. Chela was extremely sensitive to other people's silence. If he had turned and told her the truth, she would not have known it more surely. But it never occurred to her to go and tell Evita about it. Chela hated gossip. Actually, the affair of Alejandro and María did not affect her as subject for gossip. For Chela lived in a world of her own, with a sense of values all her own. Village morality was not her morality. María de las Garzas lived alone on the River Road because she was too beautiful. Chela Villareal lived alone in Hidalgo because she was not beautiful enough.

When the Professor first came to the village, Chela, sitting in the iron-barred window of her house, would watch him stroll by, and the sensitivity that was in her felt his shyness. The months passed, and Chela, who had never spoken to him and knew nothing of his past, understood him almost as well as he understood himself. She knew what it meant when he paused hesitantly on the corner of the Casino and then turned in the opposite direction instead of entering the Club as he longed to do. She felt his agony of embarrassment when Doña Fela cornered him on the plaza and gave him a lecture about Hidalgo history. One day she saw his expression after a small boy passed him, and in that moment she realized his terror of the children he taught. This unspoken, desperate fear pushed her into deliberate action. For the first time in her life she stepped outside of her own world into the world of another human being, for she pitied this man who could be afraid of a child.

At noon that day, as the Professor crossed the Plaza of Independence to go to Doña Juanita Perez' house, where he lived, Chela, seated on a bench, ball of crochet cotton ready in her hand, tossed it in front of his feet. Naturally he returned it to her. Chela's slanted eyes look up at him with friendliness, "Thank you, señor Professor." Her voice had values in it he had never heard in the voices of other village people. It was warm and intimate, as though she had known him all her life. He dropped the ball into her hand, lifted his hat to her in easy salute, and walked on...but his walk was lighter and quicker than usual, almost as though he were dancing. Chela smiled to herself, gathered her crocheting together, and went home. She knew he knew who she was. Everyone in the five villages knew Don Nacho's homely daughter. That night as she lay in bed, she was grateful for her homeliness. Any other village girl with fawn-like prettiness or delicate beauty, would have terrified him into stiff response, but homely Chela was as comfortable to know as worn leather, or the fragrance of meat stewing in chili on a cold day.

The next time he passed her on the street he tipped his hat to her and smiled. She smiled back, but she looked at him straight and fair. Florinda or Evita or one of the other girls would have quickly lowered her lids in studied shyness. But the Professor did not need flirtatious shyness. He needed friendship. Chela could not have explained to anyone how she knew this. She simply knew, just as she knew that Pepe Gonzalez did not always go to Monterrey when he said he did, or that Porfirio, the carver of wood, did not turn over to his wife all the money he received from the carving of a door or a dower chest. But the adventure-loving Pepe Gonzalez and the money-loving Porfirio were no concern of hers. The Professor, for some reason Chela could not fathom, was.

On the plaza the following Sunday night, as she sat sedately by her father, the Professor came to speak to Don Nacho. Beyond the conventions of greeting he paid her no attention, nor she him. But a smile was there between them, so shy and secret that Don Nacho, whose sole ambition in life was to marry Chela off to a good husband, did not even notice it.

Another week went past. The Professor no longer cut across the plaza to Doña Juanita's house. Instead he followed the sidewalk that passed Don Nacho's house. If Chela were sitting in the window, he tipped his hat, and she bowed her head in greeting. If it were Don Nacho or Doña Mariliria he would stop and speak of the weather or the state of national politics. Now and then he would pause at the window of the Jail and the *Juez Civil*, where Don Nacho had his office, and the two men would talk of many things: the valley crops, the goats that belonged to the mayor of El Carmen, the fighting ability of the cocks of San Juan Iglesias. Don Nacho liked the quiet little man and was glad to see him becoming more friendly. He told his friends about it at the next domino game. "You frighten him," he told them sententiously. He glanced in turn at the priest, the little Doctor, and Don Rosalío. "Religion, a profession, and a long white beard. Ah, yes, you frighten him. But me? What is more simple than a man with a great stomach?" and he roared with laughter at his own mild jest. The three men smiled in sympathy, and the game continued. So far as they were concerned, the Professor was still an outlander. He had done nothing in the past months to bring himself to their attention. As long as he minded his own business and proved himself a good teacher, they need not concern themselves with him. Of course if he bought property in the valley or fell in love with a village girl, that would be different. But they had seen him around the village girls. He was far too shy to start a flirtation. And he was too poor to buy a house. So he slid away from their consciousness, and it was a fine domino game.

The next Sunday night it was a natural thing for the Professor to invite Don Nacho to have a plate of ice-cream at the roped-off stand at one end of the plaza. That Chela happened to be with her father was merely an additional ten centavos. The two men talked, and she silently ate the frozen delicacy made from goat's milk and then watched the men and women parading past to the music of Don Alonso's orchestra. The girls called out to her and she waved her hand at them. She knew they were saying to each other: "There sits poor Chela without sense enough to flirt with the Professor, and he so busy talking to Don Nacho. Not that her flirting would do any good with the great man from beyond the mountains. Poor Chela. Poor Chela." She smiled faintly at her own thoughts. Over the rim of her mind she could hear the Professor talking in bright spurts of sound, and she knew that he was talking so well because she was there. He drank a courage from her and that pleased her.

Don Nacho pulled his great silver watch from his pocket, shook it, peered at it and pursed his lips. It was time for him to go to his domino game. As they rose from the table, Chela said idly that the next afternoon she had to walk out the Mina Road to the house of her aunt, who had promised to show her a new stitch in crochet. "I thought I would go at six in the afternoon, Father. It is not so hot then, with the sun behind the mountains."

Don Nacho, with his mind on a new way to vanquish Don Rosalío, did not pay her any attention. Chela's eyes came slowly up to the Professor's face. She saw an awareness of her meaning in the lift of his brows, the pulling back of the skin across the high cheekbones. Then she lowered her lids and murmuring good night followed her father's great bulk home.

The Boy's School did not let out until five. It seemed a very long day to Chela. Every few minutes she would glance at the position of the sun—her only clock—but it seemed glued against the sky. At last it curved its golden disk toward the western mountains, and she was free to go up the Street of the Sad Young Poet, which lengthened into the Mina Road. Where was the Professor waiting for her? Not too close to the village, surely, for he wanted gossip no more than she—and Hidalgo needed very little to start a fine scandal. It came to her with a sudden sense of shock that she was very close to loving the Professor, closer than she had been to loving any man since Joaquín, the wild one, rode away to fight with Obregón.

As she passed the Castillo grounds, she glanced through the great iron gates to the white-walled, red-tiled house set far back in a grove of lime and orange trees. Chela had been thirteen when Joaquín left, and she remembered him with startling vividness.

She paused and stared with awe at the rich blue sky. Around her were wide fields of desert *yuca* and cactus. In the distance was her aunt's house, but Chela hardly noticed it, for she knew now why men had never meant anything to her. They were not Joaquín Castillo.

She sat down in the dark shadow of a giant maguey and examined this discovery about herself with amazement. Did not she measure every man she saw against that laughing black-haired boy? He had taken her riding on his great black horse, Rocinante. The village had thought that a terrible name for such a magnificent animal. But one day on the plaza when Joaquín had stopped to allow his horse to drink—for in those days there had been a pool where the orchestra platform was now—Chela had patted the horse's nose and chuckled at him.

"Ay," Joaquín called down to her in his beautiful clear voice, "you love horses, little one?"

"Oh, yes, Don Joaquín. And this one has such a funny name."

"Do you like the name, golden skin?"

"But yes, Don Joaquín. Did not Don Quixote call his horse by the same name? And he loved his Rocinante. He thought her without peer in all the world. It says so in the book."

That was when Joaquín had lifted her to the saddlebow. He stared into her homely little face with eyes that seemed to penetrate through the bones of her head to her mind. "Where did you learn such wisdom, little slant-eyes, that you know the reason why I named my horse?"

She shrugged her thin small shoulders and stared back at him —at the arrogant lift of the head, and the large full-lipped mouth. He was not nearly so handsome as his younger brother, but he had something else—a magnetism that drew the eye of every woman.

As a reward for her intuition, he had taken her for a ride at full gallop around the plaza. She clutched at him with her thin, spindly arms and laughed as the wind tore through her fine black hair, tossing it away from her head like a shimmering black cloud. He often took her riding after that.

And then, one night, he put saddle to Rocinante and went away. Perhaps Don Saturnino grieved for him in the white house with the red-tiled roof. Chela certainly grieved for him in her father's house on the Avenue of Illustrious Men.

"Eh," said a voice behind her, "dreaming in the twilight?"

She jerked her head. The image of Joaquín Castillo was still so clear in her mind that for a moment she did not recognize the little Professor.

Embarrassment closed down on his face. "I have shame," he stammered. "I didn't mean to startle you."

Chela forced herself to smile at him. "It was nothing, señor. I have not yet visited the house of my aunt."

"No? But it is late. The sun is already behind the mountains."

Chela rose, shaking the sand from her skirt. "It is too late now. I must return to the village."

"It is better for me to walk with you, with your permission." He twisted his hat between his fingers and stared fiercely at the ground. "The dark comes quickly and it is not safe for you to be alone. I was walking this way. I often take these little walks in the evening." He was blushing. Even the tips of his ears were pink.

"Thank you," she said gravely. "My father will thank you for your kindness. I should never have left the village at so late an hour." She started to walk toward Hidalgo, and he hurried beside her. In his nervousness he seemed to take two steps to every one of hers.

"Your father will not scold you? He must not scold you. It is not right that he should scold you."

She laughed softly. What a funny little man he was. He reminded her of a monkey that Joaquín Castillo once owned as a pet. Ay, what use to think of Joaquín? He had probably been shot in battle, or executed as a prisoner, or killed in some private fight. But living or dead, Joaquín Castillo would never come back to Hidalgo. And even if he did—of what use to Chela Villareal? Was he not the son of Don Saturnino Castillo? It was true that she was daughter to the mayor of the village, but Castillo blood was proud blood. And even if it had not been a question of blood . . . Joaquín would never have tossed her a second glance— not to Chela, the homely one. What man ever looked twice at Chela?

"You are so quiet," said the Professor. "You are angry with me, perhaps?"

"Angry?" Chela had to return from the far reaches of her imagination, and it made her feel stupid. "Why should I be angry with you, señor?"

"I was not taking a walk, señorita. I heard you tell your father that you were coming this way this afternoon. I came to meet you."

"So?" Chela gave him a long slow smile that slid from her lips to her eyes. Poor creature. He was trying so desperately to be friendly, and she was not helping him at all. "I am glad you came. Already it is growing dark. By myself I would have been afraid. I am a great coward."

"But no, señorita, surely not a coward. You have the look of bravery." How earnest his voice was. It lacked the full, clear richness of Joaquín's, but it was pleasant none the less. "I do not think you could be afraid of anyone."

"That is a beautiful compliment, señor. But women are never as brave as men."

"You are thinking of your northern men, señorita. They seem so sure of themselves."

"Are the men from the South less brave?"

"Oh, no, señorita, I didn't mean it that way. It is just that—but then, I think I am not like other men."

"Are you afraid of something?" As he started to speak she added swiftly. "No, don't answer me. It is better not to put such things into words."

For a few minutes they walked the darkening road in silence; then she paused and lifting her head looked at the sky above the western line of mountains. It was heavy gold, streaked with crimson and long fingers of black clouds. "How beautiful it is," she whispered. "Tell me, señor, you are a man of learning. What does it mean, this setting of the sun?"

He cleared his throat, and from some filing card in his memory, stated in precise tones, "It merely means that the upper limb of the sun, because of a change in the earth's atmosphere causing the light rays to appear other than they are, sinks beneath the level of the visual horizon as caused by the diurnal revolution of the earth."

"Dear Mary and all the saints," breathed Chela. "So many big words to explain that?" She waved her hand toward the glowing sky.

"It is a phenomenon easily understood by astronomers," he said stiffly, and once more she saw the secret withdrawal into himself, and the shielded terror that she had noticed when the schoolboy passed him. He thinks I am laughing at him, she thought pityingly. She said aloud, "But it is magnificent, this learning. Always you have the answer to everything. Your students think there is no end to your learning."

"My—students?" His eyes held an appeal. "You mean they—I don't know the word I want," he finished helplessly.

"They admire you so much," she said gently. "Everyone in the village admires you, señor. Only this morning my father was saying that any fool can be a politician. It takes a great man to be a professor."

"I am not very wise," he said humbly.

She shook her head and started to walk again. She did not notice when they passed the house of Don Saturnino.

The village quickly realized the change in the little Professor. He seemed suddenly to have acquired a new surety about himself. Where he had once glided along the walks like a shadow, he now tripped through the streets with a ready smile for everyone. When he wanted to enter the Casino, he did so without hesitation. When he wanted to walk around the plaza with a group of laughing girls, he walked with them—telling them strange stories of stars and moon: that it took fifty years for the light of the Pole Star to touch the earth, and that the rabbit they saw in the moon was no rabbit at all, but volcanic craters. No one believed these amazing tales, and he soon had a reputation for being as great a liar as Don Timotéo Gonzalez, the maker of cheese, but everyone liked him.

Oddly enough, a village that was so quick to catch at a glance and a smile, never noticed that he walked with girls only when Chela was one of the group, and that his stories came pelting only when she was there to hear them. Chela had for so long been the old maid of the village that no one ever associated her with a man.

It was after the *kermés* race, when he defended Hidalgo's honor, that the little professor was made a member of the ruling council. And this was important. For the men on the council were not men to the village, but symbols. Don Nacho represented the people; the priest, religion; the doctor, health; and Don Rosalío, money. To these four had been added learning. Why, it was almost as good as having Don Rómolo Balderas—that great historian—come alive again. And Hidalgo decided that when the Professor died, he would not be allowed to breathe his last in San Juan Iglesias, nor Monterrey, nor far-off Michoacán, but in Hidalgo, as was right and proper.

The months passed, and a year, and a new year came, and it was the cold, rainy month of February. There was never anything to do in February. The orchestra did not play on the plaza. People did not leave their houses unless it was absolutely necessary. The one cold month turned the village into a desolation. The sun stayed behind low gray clouds, and the rain fell continuously in silver sheets. And worst of all, Easter came early this year, which meant that Lent began in February. How terrible a thing to begin Lent without Carnival! But the air was too cold, and heat-softened bones shivered. Not even the dreary prospect of forty days of abstinence from laughter could put people in Carnival mood.

Then came the good news. A group of actors were coming to Hidalgo. They were going to put on a play. They were from the South, where the rainy cold lasts from July to September, and, poor fools, when they bought the northern route, no one told them of the North's dreary February. Now they were trying to reach Monterrey, where they could remain in some comfort until Lent was finished and they could tour again in the bright warmth of April. But travelling costs money, and food costs money, and beds cost money; so they had to stop at villages along the way and put on benefits.

It was a small company of two women and four men, including the manager who played all the leading roles. This year they had Manolo de Fuentes, a new actor with them—but the actor-manager, one Décimo Canales, was not very happy over him. Manolo was not only a better actor, but had far more sex appeal than Canales, which was an impossible combination. This naturally limited the choice of plays, already limited by the demands of Canales' wife, who was the leading lady.

Her favorite script was *Madama X*, in which she played the gaunt, dark heroine, and Canales her lawyer son. But in that play was a trial scene, and in that trial scene was a judge who sat up on a platform where everyone in the audience could see him. Canales wanted Felipe or Gregorio to play the judge. The señora Canales said no. She said that Felipe was too good a prompter to waste on the stage, and as for Gregorio, that old fool, he made faces and blew his nose during her best scenes, and she would not have it. So Manolo played the judge, and was very proper, and did the part so well that the fascinated audience could not take its eyes off him, expecting him to say at any moment, "So you stole a goat, eh? Five pesos or five days."

No, the tragedy of *Madama X* would not do at all. Canales had another play, his own version of *Cradle Song*, in which Gregorio, under strong protest, played the part of a nun (into which was compressed all the lines spoken by about seven nuns in the original manuscript); Carmen Garza, the ingénue, played the young Teresa, the señora Canales the part of Sor Juana, and Canales himself the only good male role, the Doctor. This, of course, left Manolo with the role of Antonio, which he had to play behind a curtain out of sight of the audience, since the scene was a cloistered convent, and a young man was not expected to enter it. Canales, when he first conceived of this play, thought it a wonderful idea. He was really happy during rehearsals. Then, the first night of performance, the catastrophe. The audience could not see Manolo, but it could hear him. And that beautiful voice won more applause than anyone else in the company. *Cradle Song* was definitely a mistake. Canales could not even think of it without groaning. But one momentous day in Saltillo, Canales discovered a Spanish version of *Uncle Tom's Cabin* in his room. As he read it, he visualized himself as Uncle Tom, Gregorio as Simon Legree, the señora Canales as little Eva, Carmen Garza as Eliza, and Manolo—oh beautiful saints in Heaven—as the off-stage barking of the bloodhounds. Surely no audience could take to its heart the barking of a bloodhound. Canales was so elated over this solution of his troubles that he generously allowed Manolo to come on stage a few moments as Eliza's husband during the slave auction scene (conducted by the señora in a mustache and a man's hat and coat). There were no lines to the part, of course, and Manolo would wear black grease-paint, but it was an appearance, and what more could an actor ask? Canales expected some temperament trouble from Manolo, but none evolved. Manolo seemed quite pleased with the part. "I don't like to learn lines," he said. But Canales was not quite content with this explanation.

For the first time he began to wonder just what Manolo was doing in his company. The man had a northern accent, and he was probably trying to get free passage home, but he chose a strange method of doing it. Actors in small stock companies were social outcasts, and only true love of the art drew a man to the profession. Manolo could easily have obtained a job with one of the fine companies that played the big cities. The great clown Pepe Bobo would have been glad to hire his talent. Instead of that he preferred to jog along in this little fifth-rate show. Oh, there was a mystery here, and no doubt of it. It worried Canales. Was ever a man so afflicted with misfortune? Here he was with a route of which he knew absolutely nothing (bought because his wife, a northern woman, was tired of the South), an actor on his hands who was a mystery, and worst of all, the month of February—the cold, dark month of February, followed immediately by an early Lent. He was very miserable. And he was convinced that Manolo was, at least, a murderer using his company for camouflage. The señora Canales thought her husband was crazy for harboring such an idea and said so. She also refused to allow him to discharge Manolo. "If the people pay to see him, why should you care? The important thing is the money in the cashbox, not the murderer in the dressing room."

And so the little troupe continued on its route. The premiere of *Uncle Tom's Cabin* was to be in the principal valley town of Hidalgo. Canales looked at the announcements and smiled happily. He especially liked the line, "Beautiful sex admitted free." It was always good business to let the women in free. They forced the men to come, and most families had three or four men with only one woman. Canales thought it a magnificent idea, forgetting that Manolo had suggested it to him. Manolo had also suggested sending Gregorio and Felipe ahead to build a stage, as the northern villages had no proper halls for a play. If Canales had stopped to think about it, he would have realized that Manolo seemed to know a great deal about the valley people. But he was so happy over his triumph of casting his new play that he paid no attention to Manolo's behavior. So Gregorio and Felipe, with fearful grumbles, arrived in Hidalgo a day ahead of schedule and went to work converting planks and sawhorses into a stage. As they worked, they could hear the children chanting their lessons aloud. The actors banged their hammers and wondered what it would be like to be tied to a village with a family and a little farm perhaps, and no worry over tonight's bed or tomorrow's meal. For a moment they thought it would be very wonderful, and then they realized that such life would never include the nervous pricklings of stage fright, nor the smell of grease paint, nor the sound of beautiful words that followed each other like notes in music, and the two men felt very sorry for the village pople who would never know the beauty and mystery of that strange thing called Theatre.

Professor Porfirio Diaz Aah was worried. The little Doctor had warned him that morning that Doña Fela had taken him under consideration as a possible future son-in-law. He had not had a chance to find Chela and ask her what he should do about it. He did not want to get married. In time, perhaps, after three or four years, it would be nice to have a wife and children. But he was happier than he had ever been before, and he could see no reason for changing his status. Once in a while he would dream of the wife he would someday marry. Years ago he had seen Anita O'Malley on the stage in Mexico City, and here in Hidalgo he had often seen María de las Garzas. So the little Professor visualized for himself a wife with the exotic grace and appeal of the O'Malley, the beauty of María, and the understanding of Chela . . . attributes which the daughters of Doña Fela certainly did not have.

The more he thought of it, the more frightened the little Professor became. He imagined himself as a very small black fly which a plump spider was quietly but inexorably drawing into her web.

He knew there was no use in trying to see Chela until evening. If he stopped by her window at noon, people would conclude that he was courting her, and he wanted no scandal about Chela. She had been much too good for him to repay her in such a fashion. But at six it was a social event to go down and watch the Monterrey-Torreón train puff into the station. Also, the rest of the troupe was arriving, and in the excitement it would be easy enough to signal her away from the crowd.

The day, accompanied by the steady hammering from the patio, passed slowly, but at last it was five, and he was free from school.

The sun, as though aware of the evening's importance, was attempting a pale yellow smile, but the winds whistling down from the mountains were cold. By the time he hurried up the Avenue of Isabella the Catholic to the railroad station two kilometers from town, most of the village seemed to be en route.

When the Professor reached the station, Chela had not yet arrived. He bought a bottle of Topo Chico water, and while he stood there sipping it, the train came puffing around the last curve of track. He saw Doña Fela and Evita Cantú. But where was Chela? Why didn't she—ah, there she was! He hurried towards her. She was standing with Alma, wife of Porfirio, the carver of wood, and Sarita, wife of Pepe Gonzalez. As he passed the group, he tipped his hat to them politely. Only Chela saw the quick upward jerk of his chin. She nodded slightly. As the train came to a slow, grinding halt, she moved away from Alma and Sarita, both too intent on looking for the actors to notice either her or the Professor. She walked swiftly down the narrow village road and took a turning across the open field that brought her to the gates of the cemetery. Inside, among the graves, she sat and waited for him.

He told her his troubles in pelting sentences. What was he to do? Doña Fela, a strong-minded woman... once her mind was made up it was impossible to fight her. Even Don Rosalío was afraid of Doña Fela, and the priest had to pray to that heavenly warrior St. Michael every time he saw her.

"I don't want to marry one daughter or the next. I don't want to marry anyone, señorita."

"No," said Chela slowly, "no, of course not." She sat down on a narrow cement bench and gazed slowly about the walled enclosure. There was a funny little pain in her heart that made breathing difficult.

"But what am I to do, Chelita?"

It was the first time he had ever called her by name, and even now, she knew he did not know he had used it.

After a moment she said, "There is only one protection—one sure protection."

"Of course. But can you think of anyone... anyone at all? The whole day I have thought of girls in this valley, and in the Three Marys, and even those I have met in Monterrey—but there is no one. Can you think of anyone?" He seemed so eager, like a small child asking her for candy. She looked at him through a blur of suspended tears. Was she in love with this man, or was it only her vanity that was hurt? He had no idea, of course, how he was hurting her. A man would never ask such a question of any other woman—only of poor homely Chela, who could never hope to win a man for herself.

"Perhaps," he was saying anxiously, "I could say something about a girl in Michoacán—one who has been waiting for me to establish myself. Do you think they would believe it?"

"Would you—in their place?"

"No," he said miserably. "Already they think I am a teller of tremendous lies, because I speak of things they do not understand. But I have never told them lies, only the truths of science."

"Yes," said Chela, "I know."

"And now that I do want to tell a lie, no one will believe it because of the truths I have spoken." He pulled a handkerchief from his pocket and wiped his forehead and the line beneath his jaw.

The cold wind blew the sound of distant laughter as the village people escorted the actors into town.

"You have always lived in books, señor," she said gently, "and books are very wise. They know the answer to everything. If you looked in your books, perhaps—or even, who knows—in this evening's play . . ."

"But, of course," cried the Professor, beaming at her. "It is not the books that are wise but you, señorita. How stupid I am that I did not think of that myself. All my life I have lived by what is written in books, and now . . ." he flung his hands in a wide, shrugging gesture, "like any stupid fool I forget my best teacher."

He helped her to her feet. She drew her shawl closer around her face and hurried home before Don Nacho missed her. How stupid, she thought wearily, how stupid. I thought he might have come to love me a little, but for him it is only friendliness. And for me, the long lonely years. Ay Joaquín, why did you not take me with you when you left? Joaquín, Joaquín, how lonely I am. Joaquín . . .

Don Nacho's house was in a turmoil of excitement when Chela reached it.

"Where have you been?" cried Doña Mariliria. "I have saved some food for you. Here." She thrust a plate of brown beans and *tortillas* into Chela's hands.

"But it is too early to eat," protested Chela. "I thought . . ."

"Eh, and your father promised those actors the kitchen for a dressing room. There is a hanging blanket to divide the space, that is true, but I say it is not proper for men and women to dress in the same room, even with a blanket between."

"But Mamá . . ."

"Silence. *Vaya*, you talk too much. Always chattering. And half the men in the village are tramping through the hall taking chairs to the patio—and suppose it rains, what then? I asked your father, but he could not answer me. Men are fools!" Doña Mariliria rushed into the patio to supervise the placing of more chairs.

Chela sighed and went into her own room. When Don Nacho had built the house, he had expected to have a large family and so had provided an extra bedroom. But Chela was an only child. Thus, out of all the girls in the village, she was the only one to have a room to herself.

Chela shut the door and threw herself across the bed. She buried her face in a pillow so that no one could hear her, and released the dammed-up tears. "Oh, Joaquín, Joaquín," she sobbed, beating against the pillow with her clenched fist. "Come home! Come home!"

The play was to begin at precisely nine o'clock. Rocking chairs had been placed down front for Doña Fela, Doña Juanita Perez, and—because it was her own patio—Doña Mariliria. To the right of them were armchairs for the priest, the little Doctor, Don Nacho, Don Rosalío, and the Professor. And there was one more chair, a cushioned armchair, grander than the rest, for Don Saturnino. The rest of the patio was filled with straight chairs arranged so as to leave a narrow aisle down the center. Against the back wall were a few benches for those who could pay only a small price.

Gregorio and Felipe had done their work well. The stage was neither broad nor wide, but the playing area was adequate. Two poles stood one at each end, from which was suspended Doña Mariliria's clothesline, with Doña Fela's blankets thrown across it for a curtain. Also from the poles dangled two gasoline lanterns which emitted a brilliant white light. Another lantern hung above the village orchestra, which was clustered at the left end of the stage playing "My Blue Heaven" with intense joy and little melody. Directly in front of the stage, in the exact center, was a straight chair. There was no shell to shield the prompter from view, but the audiences always enjoyed the prompter as much as they did the actors; so no one minded.

Don Nacho noticed with satisfaction that it was a clear night with stars shining. He had burned three candles in the church to San Cristóbal, patron saint of travellers, with the request that there be no rain and to please send more warmth than usual. He did not know who the patron saint of actors was, and he hesitated to ask anyone in the company for fear his ignorance would offend them. But St. Christopher had been most kind. The night was as warm as a night in March, and there was even promise of a moon.

The large-stomached old man stood at his door and beamed as the people entered, for he had always loved plays, and now he was actually having one in his own patio. Pepe Gonzalez and his two good friends, Andrés Treviño and Porfirio, the carver of wood, stood at the door with Don Nacho to keep him company. Porfirio was trying to get the job of bouncer so that he would not have to pay for an entrance ticket. Pepe and Andrés were taking great delight in telling Don Nacho how strong Porfirio was.

"It comes from swinging the hammer," they assured him. "He has wrists of steel, this one. Show Don Nacho your wrists, Porfirio."

Porfirio obediently thrust out his hands.

"See, Don Nacho ... see how strong. One twist and a man's neck breaks—like that." Pepe snapped his long facile fingers.

Don Nacho pretended to examine the wrists. He pursed his lips and thoughtfully blew through them. "But I don't want any man's neck broken tonight, friend Porfirio."

"Perhaps a little crack then," suggested Pepe eagerly. "Just one small crack in the neck."

Don Nacho considered this and then shook his head. He, Pepe, and Andrés were already in secret league to see how much Porfirio would finally pay for the ticket that cost a peso. Alma Orona had already gone into the patio with Pepe's wife, Sarita Calderón, and Andrés' wife, Nena Santos. Now that Alma was inside, she would refuse to leave; so the conspirators knew they were safe in teasing him.

"The actors have their own bouncer," said Don Nacho sadly, with a wink at Pepe. "Did you not see him? That tall young man with the black mustache at whom the women rolled the eye?"

"I saw him," said Andrés, "but he is not so strong as Porfirio."

"He is very strong," sighed Don Nacho, "and actors do not like people who will not pay."

"Then let me take tickets at the door," asked Porfirio quickly. "That is a fine occupation."

The three young men watched Don Nacho shake his head. "But we already have a taker of tickets. It is Don Serapio's nephew Xavier."

"And why should he be chosen over me?" demanded Porfirio, irritated.

"He has very little money, and you know what Florinda is like. If she wants to see a play, there is no peace until she sees it."

"I could sell candy," Porfirio suggested. "Or cold drinks."

"Listen," said Don Nacho, raising his hand. From the patio floated a man's voice calling, "Candy—fine candy of burnt milk, of sweet potato, of cactus heart. Good candy, sweet candy."

"You see?" said Don Nacho. "Rubén is selling his own wares. He, too, wants to see the play."

"But the drinks?" asked Andrés. "Don Dionisio told me he was going to see this play sitting down."

"That's right," said Pepe. "Since he has put up the stand at the station and makes so much money from the tourists, he can now view a play in comfort."

"Well," said Don Nacho with a broad grin, "he is still at the saloon. If you can persuade him, it is agreeable to me."

The three laughed, patted him on the shoulders, shook his hand, and hurried up the street to the Saloon of the Devil's Laughter. Don Nacho grinned in pleased anticipation. The play on the stage was undoubtedly very fine, but the play in the audience would be even better when Alma caught sight of her husband selling soft drinks to pay for a ticket he could well afford. Still smiling, he turned to greet the entering audience. He shook hands with all the men, bowed to all the women, and had time for a small amount of regret that the Widow Valdez's perpetual mourning did not allow her to attend such grand functions as this one. It was a great pity, too, he thought, that none of the family Castillo would be there, for word had just come that Don Saturnino was ailing, and Alejandro, with Tía Magdalena to help him, had been called to his ranch by a sickness among the animals.

Presently to Don Nacho's ears came the sound of running feet, and Porfirio nearly crashed into him. "Behold," he cried, thrusting forward a deep tray on which stood bottles held firmly upright with chicken wire. "I am now a seller of cold drinks."

Pepe and Andrés came puffing behind him, a tin tub of ice and more drinks swinging between them. "This weighs more than I do myself," said Pepe disgustedly, dumping his side of the tub on the sidewalk so that Andrés was forced to release his. "I did not bargain to pay for my ticket and carry your extra bottles, too."

"Now, Pepe..." began Porfirio, who had an instinct for what was coming.

"Don Nacho, do you not think Porfirio should supply me with free drinks?" asked Pepe.

"Of course," said Don Nacho. "And Andrés also."

"No!" cried Porfirio. "The saloon made me pay for every bottle. Whatever is given free, I lose in silver."

"Is that friendship?" cried Pepe, digging a bottle of violently orange-colored liquid from a covering of ice. "I ask you," he added disgustedly, expertly snapping off the metal top with his teeth, "if kind labor should not be repaid with kindness."

"By all means," said Don Nacho. "And I will have a bottle of grape."

"Ten centavos," said Porfirio weakly, watching Pepe transfer the bottle of purple liquid from the tub to Don Nacho's waiting hand.

"But do I not allow you to work here?" asked Don Nacho, wiping the top of the bottle with his palm. "That should be worth ten centavos, eh, Porfirio?"

"At this rate I shall not even have a small profit," wailed Porfirio. "No! Andrés!"

But Andrés was already drinking a bottle of ginger ale.

"You go inside and sell your drinks," said Pepe kindly. "We three will watch your supply for you."

"No, you won't," said Porfirio firmly. "If I leave all of you with that tub, there will be no full bottles left. I know you."

"But you can't sit on the tub and sell drinks, too," pointed out Don Nacho.

"Such a lack of trust in his friends," sighed Pepe, who was hunting in the bucket for another bottle to empty.

Porfirio was almost in tears. He was chained to the tub by these robbers, and yet, to make a profit at all, he had to leave it and go inside to sell the drinks.

Rubén, the maker of candy came to the door. "They have rung the second bell," he said. "In a moment the play will begin."

"Rubén," Porfirio caught the candy vendor by the arm. "I am selling drinks to pay for my ticket. You must help me."

"So?" Rubén's eyes slid over the group by the tub, and a smile caught the corners of his lips. "And how much did you pay for all that fine refreshment?"

"Five pesos," said Pepe. "Five pesos to save fifty centavos admittance. Our Porfirio is truly a man of business."

"But I shall make a profit of at least two pesos," protested Porfirio, "if these bandits do not ruin me."

Pepe pulled a bottle of root beer from under the ice.

"Pepe," moaned Porfirio. "That is the third one."

"Carrying a tub is thirsty business. Have another one, Andrés."

"Well," said Andrés doubtfully, seeing Porfirio's anguished expression. But when Don Nacho took another, his doubts were removed, and he, too, buried his arm in the ice. Porfirio slapped his forehead with the palm of his hand and wailed aloud, "Rubén, help me!"

"But what do you want me to do?"

"Keep these bandits from the tub while I am selling the drinks inside."

"But, Porfirio, I have my own candy to sell . . ."

"Naturally," Porfirio interrupted quickly, "but selling is dry work. When your throat becomes as the desert come out here. To you I will give free bottles. One man drinks two bottles less than three men. That is logic. And while you are drinking I will go inside. It is a good plan." He looked so pleadingly at Rubén that the candy vendor had to turn his head to one side to keep from laughing aloud.

"It is a plan," he admitted. "I think it can be arranged."

Just then the theatre's third bell clanged its warning. Porfirio herded Andrés, Pepe, and Don Nacho through the hall to the patio, calling over his shoulder, "In one little moment I will be with you, Rubén."

The crowded patio was silent with that noisy silence of relaxing bodies. Felipe, the prompter, emerged from the blanket curtains. The orchestra played the applause music. At the last stirring chord, the audience clapped loudly, and Felipe shook his own hands above his head in greeting. When the people quieted down, he said in the full, round tones of an old actor, "To you, ladies, and to you, gentlemen, greetings. This evening you are here to see a play . . . a play of the *Yanquis* across the Río Bravo." There was polite applause and he bowed in answer to it. "As you all know, there are many strange people amongst the *Yanquis*, and some of them are black—not just on face and hands, you understand, but black all over."

There was a murmur of pity and a voice from the back of the patio called out, "Is it some strange disease, friend?"

"No," the prompter shook his head and took another theatrical pause. "They are so by God's hand. But they are good christians, friends, even as ourselves." There was a mutter of incredulity, which quickly died away as Felipe continued his little speech. "Also, it is very cold in the country of the *Yanquis* .. so cold that the rivers turn to solid ice—such ice as is used for the cooling of beer in the saloon."

Porfirio decided that this was his cue, and he immediately burst into an animated sales talk, moving down the aisles and holding out bottles in what he hoped was a tempting manner. The audience, realizing the reason for his selling, burst into enchanted laughter. Alma Orona rose and screamed at him, "You, Porfirio, put away those bottles and sit down like a decent christian."

"Leave him alone, Alma," called Don Nacho. "He is making two pesos profit. He says so himself."

"If you don't drink it all up," retorted Porfirio.

The audience laughed again. Pepe's wife Sarita caught at Alma's wrist. "Sit down, *comadre*. He is enjoying himself, and that is the main thing."

Alma sat down, but she was still talking. "How much did you pay for this privilege?"

"Five pesos."

"Five pesos? Saints in Heaven!"

"But I will make two pesos profit. Don Dionisio said I would."

"That is true, Alma," called Don Dionisio from his seat near the back wall. "If he sells every bottle, it will mean two pesos profit."

"But I can't sell every bottle," yelled Porfirio. "These robbers have already stolen..."

"Stolen!" howled Pepe. "We took them in honest payment for helping to bring them over here. Friends, I ask you, is that not fair?"

"Of a surety," responded the audience in one voice.

"Besides," said Don Nacho, making his way to his own chair down front. "We drank only three or four. What is the difference between a peso seventy-five and two pesos in profit?"

"Nothing, Don Nacho," answered the convulsed audience.

Don Nacho waved his hand at them and sat down. The orchestra, feeling they should contribute to the clamor, played the applause music over again, and there was more clapping. Alma sighed in helpless acceptance, and people began buying the bottles from Porfirio.

In the meantime Felipe, aware that village problems were more important than problems of a play, jumped from the stage and settled himself in the prompter's seat. When the audience was finally quiet, he clapped his hands. The play began.

It was difficult to hear the actors at first because the acoustics were so good in the long narrow patio that Felipe's voice, proceeding at a steady murmur, always just one word ahead of the players, was far louder than that of the señora Canales or of Carmen. At last the señora could stand it no longer. She came to the edge of the stage and told him to lower his voice. "You make so much noise, I can't hear my own."

The orchestra played the applause music. There was a heartfelt clapping. The señora took her rightful bows, and the play continued. The first act was quickly finished, and Porfirio went out to relieve Rubén at the tub.

But the second act, which included the slave auction scene, was so interesting that Rubén kept forgetting to sell his candy. Once in a while he remembered to thrust a handful of candy under someone's nose, and once in a while someone would remember to pay him. But he did not call his wares, and to Canales on the stage, this was the greatest victory, for when even the vendors were silent, that meant the true spell of the theatre was on the audience.

When Eliza was put up for sale, Dorotéo Lozano, the thick-necked, snub-nosed orange farmer from across the river, wanted to join in the bidding. He insisted that his money was as good as that fool's with the whip on the stage. Rubén was trying to keep the man quiet, well aware that Dorotéo had been imbibing too freely of mescal—and Canales gave a warning glance to Manolo, who, his face covered with black grease paint, was standing in the shadows at the back of the stage. Manolo shrugged and started forward, but relaxed as Don Nacho stood up and faced the back of the patio. "You Dorotéo Lozano, sit down and be silent," he ordered.

"But, Don Nacho, she is a pretty girl, and the nights are lonesome on the farm."

There was a shout of laughter from the men, and small scandalized shrieks from the women.

"Sit down!"

"Yes, Don Nacho." Dorotéo collapsed grumblingly onto the hard bench. He rubbed his mouth with the back of his hand and muttered something about wanting a drink, but otherwise he was silent, and the act continued to its close.

During the third act it was Porfirio's turn to go inside. Rubén warned him to gather up the empty bottles, as Don Dionisio always gave a refund on them. Porfirio, in gratitude, gave him an extra bottle of ginger ale—which was not as cold as the rest.

Dorotéo Lozano returned from the saloon as the third act started. He was very angry because Don Dionisio, knowing that all Hidalgo and many people from the surrounding towns, were viewing the play, had locked the saloon doors, and there was no drink to be bought except from Porfirio.

"How about a little *mescalito?*" he asked Porfirio, who shrugged his answer. "Then a small beer, eh?"

"But I have no beer, either. Leave me alone, Dorotéo. I must gather up the empty bottles.

"But I want a beer," insisted Dorotéo. "I am already a little drunk, and I would like a beer to make me drunker."

"Don Ricardo will put you in jail."

"And he with but one arm? And myself the strongest man in the valley? Ho!"

"Leave me alone," insisted Porfirio, "I have work to do."

He shook himself free of the farmer and went inside, but the third act had already begun. When he tried to gather up the empty bottles, people hissed at him. He managed to collect a few before Alma reached out and snapped her fingers under his nose. "Sit down and behave yourself!" Porfirio, who was terrified of her, obediently plopped himself down in the aisle.

Canales was very happy. In spite of the interruptions, the play was going well. No one in the audience understood the story, but the elemental passions involved were clear to them, and the scenes were gliding past with unusual fluidity and ease. There was a man who looked like a *Yanqui* sitting on the third row who followed the Uncle Tom scenes with rapt attention, at times covering his face with his hands, his shoulders shaking with obvious emotion. Ah, it was all very fine. Gregorio, as Simon

Legree, was in full voice, and Canales could hear him being extremely villainous as he attempted to seduce Eliza. When Eliza finally escaped from him the audience went wild with delight, the orchestra trying desperately to keep up with itself and the applause music at the same time.

"All goes well," said Manolo, who had taken off his make-up, and was waiting to bay like a bloodhound for the next act.

"Yes," said Canales. "Listen to me, Manolo. If that fool in the audience makes any more trouble, you stop being a bloodhound and throw him out."

Manolo shrugged and lit a cigarette. Canales eyed him thoughtfully. "You're not afraid of him, are you?"

"No, I'm not afraid of him."

"He's a frontier man, and these frontier men are strong."

"I'm a frontier man myself," said Manolo indolently, "and I, too, am strong."

Canales nodded at him and rang the warning bell for the next act. He half hoped that the village man would prove too strong for Manolo. Not too much, just enough to give the troupe an excuse to go off to Monterrey and leave him, but Canales hastily throttled the wish. He was at heart a kindly man, and in spite of his doubts, he liked the rich-voiced Manolo.

Porfirio told Rubén that he was worried. "I didn't get a chance to pick up many of the empties. Alma made me sit down."

"I have to go in now," said Rubén. "People buy more candy between the acts."

"Do you think any of the bottles will be broken?"

"One or two perhaps," and at Porfirio's moan. "Don't worry. I'll pick some up for you."

"You are a good friend to me, Rubén," said Porfirio gratefully. "I will carve a small bull for the young Gitanillo."

"No bull," answered Rubén sharply. Then he grinned placatingly at Porfirio's crestfallen face. "He thinks too much on bulls now. A little bird, perhaps. That would be very fine."

He went inside to sell his candy. He picked up a few bottles down front, but Doña Fela wanted some candy and it took her so long to make a choice that he did not reach the back until after the third act had started. Eliza was leaping from ice floe to ice floe—purely imaginary spots on the floor—and managing with remarkable agility to stay in the same spot. Canales, on the roof of Don Nacho's kitchen, was slowly emptying a bucket of salt over her head to simulate snow. This was wasted effort, as the audience, never having seen snow, could not understand why salt was raining on her—but the *Yanquis* were peculiar people, and perhaps their country rained salt instead of water. When Manolo began to bay like a bloodhound, the audience shivered with delight. Ay, this was a wonderful play.

At that moment Dorotéo Lozano decided that he had been a martyr long enough. He remembered that the prompter had said there was ice on the stage—the same sort of ice that cooled the beer in the saloon. And if there were ice, perhaps there was also a bottle of beer. He stood up on the bench and yelled at Eliza, "You, woman, sell me a bottle of beer. Take it out of the pretty ice and sell me a bottle of beer. I will give you sixty centavos for it—twenty centavos more than I pay to that robber, Don Dionisio."

There were yells to him to sit down. Don Nacho started to rise in wrath, but Father Zacaya touched his arm. "There is nothing to do now, friend. Dorotéo wants beer, not arguments."

Rubén tried to quiet the farmer, but Dorotéo pushed him out of the way and kept on yelling.

Manolo stopped baying, sighed, carefully took off his coat, and stepped around the corner of the stage. He walked lightly up the aisle, and as he passed Chela, she saw a faint smile at the corners of his lips. Dorotéo, standing on his bench, glared down at the actor. "I want a bottle of beer."

"A matter known to all the world," said Manolo easily. "Will you leave this patio in grace on your legs or in disgrace on your back?"

"I paid twenty centavitos for a ticket, and now you are cheating me. You will give me no beer, and I am a thirsty man."

"Beer," said Manolo, "flows in the rivers of Hidalgo, not on the stage of *Uncle Tom's Cabin.*"

"So," whispered Dorotéo, narrowing his lids. No outlander dared insult his valley. "Beer flows in our rivers, eh? You think everyone here is like me, a drunkard and lazy good-for-nothing? I shall close your mouth on the outside of your teeth." He lashed out and just missed Manolo's chin. The tall actor grasped him by the arm. Dorotéo twisted away from him, hopped down from the bench, and reached for Manolo with a strong bear-like hug.

A circle was hastily cleared for the fighters. Don Ricardo started forward half-heartedly, but stopped at a signal from Don Nacho. A fight was better than a play at any time, and although Dorotéo was the heavier man, Manolo was the smarter. "A good beating tonight and a day of rest in jail tomorrow will be good for Dorotéo Lozano," Don Nacho muttered to Father Zacaya.

Dorotéo gave a bellow of rage as he realized that Manolo had broken free of his strong grasp, and he advanced on the slim young man, his arms flailing the air, his face creased in a ferocious expression he had always found had a terrifying effect on his opponents. But this light-moving enemy merely laughed at him, danced out of his way, and pummeled his head and chest with quick, painful jabs. Dorotéo lowered his head and rushed Manolo, intending to butt him in the stomach. Manolo skipped backwards. The audience howled with delight. Ay, this was a magnificent fight—one to be told to grandchildren. Just then Manolo's left heel came down on an empty bottle lying on its side. He staggered and tried to keep his balance, but a lunge from Dorotéo forced him to swing aside. He fell forward to the hard cement floor of the patio. Realizing his advantage, Dorotéo jumped on him, and the combined weight of the two men was too much for Manolo's left leg, which was twisted under him. There was a sharp crack and a yell of pain from the actor.

The Professor caught the little Doctor's arm. "His leg—see—his leg!"

The two men were standing on chairs, watching the fight across the heads of the audience.

"I see it," muttered the little Doctor. He called loudly, "Stop that fight!" and forced his way through the crowd to the back of the patio.

Pepe, Rubén, and Andrés launched a united attack on Dorotéo, managing to lift him off Manolo, who had fainted from the pain. They swung the farmer high between them, then aimed his thickset body at the pool where Doña Mariliria did her weekly laundry. He howled from the cold bath, and it was a simple matter for Don Ricardo to take charge of him and hustle him off to jail.

The little Doctor finished his examination of Manolo's leg. "Bring one of the shutters from a window," he said, "and four of you men carry him to my house."

The actors, their make-up streaked from rubbing their faces in the excitement, pushed through to him. "He is badly hurt?" cried the señora Canales.

"His leg is broken just below the knee."

Carmen, her black Eliza make-up grotesque on her pretty, vapid face, thrust back her head and wailed. The señora Canales expertly slapped her and explained to the crowd that Carmen had lately decided that she was in love with Manolo. Canales was muttering to Gregorio. He now came up to the little Doctor. "This means, of course, that he cannot go with us to Monterrey?"

The little Doctor sniffed. "He must stay in bed until the bones heal. And then there will be weeks on crutches."

Porfirio, with Bob Webster's help, had taken down a shutter from the kitchen window. Xavier, Pepe, Andrés, and Rubén waited patiently by the semiconscious Manolo until the doctor told them how to move him with the least pain.

The little Doctor gave quick instructions, annoyed because Chela was trying to interrupt him. "Go away, child. This man must be taken care of immediately."

"Please, little Doctor, listen to me. You live two blocks away. To be carried so far with such an injury is a painful thing. Why not put him to bed here?"

"Here?" Everyone stared at her.

"Of course. He can stay in my bedroom. I can sleep in the parlor. And here there would always be someone in the house to look after him. But at your house, little Doctor, there is no one. And you have to be gone so much."

"Chela is right," said Doña Mariliria firmly. "Of course he can stay here."

The Professor had wormed his way through the crowd. He looked at Manolo—at the long graceful body, the good shoulders, the dark face with the thin line of mustache above the full lips. He said suddenly, explosively, "No!"

Eyes swung to his face and he reddened with embarrassment. "I mean—he is a man and a stranger. It is not right to so impose upon the goodness of this house. Bring him to my room. I will take care of him."

"And you gone to the school all day?" Chela's thick brows rose in two crescents. "It is better that he stay here."

"That is true," called out several voices.

Canales felt that it was time for him to say something. "You understand, señorita, we appreciate your kindness, but we are actors. For us our art is our food and our bed." He lifted his hands high, dropped them again. "In fact, we have no money."

"And shall a man who cannot even crawl from our door be thrust out because he has no money?" snapped Doña Mariliria, her lips quivering with anger. "Is this not a christian house? You, Pepe, you, Andrés, yes and the rest of you, carry him into Chela's bedroom."

Pepe, who recognized the voice of authority, signaled to his friends with a jerk of his chin, and they carefully set about the delicate business of moving the hurt actor. In the melee, the Professor caught Chela's arm. "Are you so kind to every pigeon with a broken wing?"

"What is wrong with you?" asked Chela, puzzled. Her mind was on other things than the Professor. With a muttered, "Forgive me," she hurried off to lead the way to her room. The Professor kicked at the floor, and felt Bob Webster's hand on his shoulder. "Let us find Pepe Gonzalez and split a bottle of cognac." The little man blushed that his jealousy could be so easily read, but he was glad to follow Bob out of the house. The rest of the evening the Professor lectured his two friends on the wickedness of actors whose profession it was to please women, especially soft-hearted women like Chela.

But Chela was not thinking of the Professor as she hurried about the house, getting the various basins, hot water, and bandages that the doctor called for. When he wished for plaster of Paris to make a cast, it was Chela who remembered that Don Dionisio, whose hobby was molding little figures and heads from the material, always kept a supply on hand in the saloon. It was Chela who had the nerve to hold Manolo's twitching shoulders while the little Doctor set his leg. It was Chela who got rid of the crowd, and saw to it that the actors had hot coffee and sweet bread before they went off to Doña Juanita Perez' house for the night. An energy seemed to flow through her and out of her as though at last Chela, the homely one, had found her place in life.

The little Doctor gave Manolo a shot of morphine, and then came into the parlor. Don Nacho was a quiet figure in the shadows of the room, but Chela and Doña Mariliria stood in the circle of lamplight near the table. The little Doctor smiled at them. "I'll spend the night with him, but tomorrow, Don Nacho, you must telephone to Monterrey and get a nurse. It would really have been better," he added, "to have taken the poor man to my house."

"No," said Chela, "and we need no nurse. I can take care of him."

"You?" the little Doctor looked at her curiously. "My dear child, this man cannot move from his bed for at least three weeks..."

"Nurses cost money," said Chela. "He has no money. You heard that actor say so."

"But the man needs care, Chela—care that you do not know how to give him."

Chela's slanting eyes narrowed, and a stubborn expression settled about her mouth. "I have taken care of sick ones before."

"And what she cannot do for him, I can," said Doña Mariliria.

The little Doctor sighed and shrugged. "This is agreeable to you, Don Nacho?"

The big-stomached man in the shadows laughed softly. "When these two set the chin there is no arguing. Yes, it is agreeable."

And Manolo slept dreamlessly in Chela's bedroom.

The next morning, before the early train for Monterrey, the actors came to say good-bye to their friend.

"If there is anything we can do," suggested the señora Canales half-heartedly to Doña Mariliria. An actor with a broken leg was a liability to any touring company, and the señora was, above all else, a business woman. Carmen suddenly burst into tears. "I want to see him," she mourned. "I want him to know that I leave my love to comfort him."

Chela heard this from the hallway. She had a tray with a glass of hot milk and some sweet bread. Her head jerked in annoyance as she went into Manolo's room.

He watched Chela curiously as she came to the bed. He had never paid much attention to women. They were creatures of convenience and little more, but he smiled cheerfully at her as he smiled at everyone.

"It seems I lost the fight, señorita."

"Not you, no." She puffed some extra pillows behind his back and placed the tray on his thighs. "Porfirio, I understand, is doing penance in the church."

Manolo grimaced as he moved his weight slightly in the bed. "Is Porfirio the buyer of beer?"

"That was Dorotéo Lozano. He is in jail."

"And Porfirio . . . ?"

"You slipped on an empty bottle of Topo Chico water. Porfirio was the vendor. He should have picked up all the empties." She suddenly laughed at the memory of Porfirio's anguish over the money he had lost the night before, and she told the story of Porfirio's business scheme with the ease of old friendship while Manolo ate his breakfast.

The actor felt this camaraderie and warmed to it. He thought, It is strange. Why did I think she was homely? She has charm, this one. The eyes are extraordinary. That golden skin. And the hair . . . what would it be like, loose of those stupid braids? I wonder who she is. He said, "You are all kindness, señorita. And I don't even know your name."

She looked contemplatively at him for a moment. "My name is Chela. The alcalde of Hidalgo is my father."

"And this is your house?" At her nod he continued. "You were all charity to bring such kindness to a penniless actor."

"It was nothing," said Chela harshly. "The members of your company are outside. They go in to Monterrey this morning. Do you want to see them?"

"Must I?" Manolo opened his eyes wide like a small child who knows he is being bad.

"One of them—the youngest woman—weeps for you. She wants her love to comfort you."

They smiled at each other as though at a secret shared between them. "Carmen changes her love as she does her dress. It means nothing."

Chela walked around the foot of the bed and opened the long shutters at the window. The sunlight poured into the room, and Manolo had a clear view across the Plaza of Independence and the roof of Doña Juanita Perez' rooming house to the mountains that walled the eastern side of the valley. It had been too dark to see them clearly when he arrived last night from Monterrey, and this was his first true glimpse of them.

As she turned from the window, she paused at the expression

on his face. There was a tear-washed brightness in his eyes, and he was staring at the mountains as a hungry man stares at a loaf of bread.

"They are so beautiful, the mountains," he said, half under his breath, and she knew that he had forgotten she was there.

"You like mountains?" she asked gently.

"The mountains of the South are far away and cold. But these are kindly mountains—near at hand and friendly." His voice dropped to a thread of whisper. "To the northern man from home, only the northern mountains can cure the soul sickness. And I have been gone from home too long."

He sank back against his pillows, shutting his eyes. Chela lifted the tray and carefully smoothed the covers over him. At the door she paused for a moment and glanced back at him. Her voice was low, too, but it reached the man on the bed. She said, "Welcome home, Don Joaquín." Then she went out and shut the door.

In the days that followed, Chela spent most of her time with Manolo. In a village where girls seldom spoke alone with young men, it was a strange situation. The town teased her about the actor. A few mischievous souls asked her when Father Zacaya was going to post the banns for her wedding; but no one believed it was anything else but teasing. Was Manolo not a vagabond actor. Was Chela not the homeliest girl in the valley? Ay, it was a grand joke, this teasing, but nothing more.

The little Professor thought differently. He snapped at his pupils. He refused to play dominoes with Don Nacho and the rest. Most of the time he stayed in his room and sulked. When Doña Fela tried to entice him toward her daughters, he was almost rude to her. He took long walks up the Cañon Road, trying to think through his troubles with suitable logic. He read book after book to see if they could provide him with panacea, but books, he found, had a disgusting habit of bringing in outside forces—the god in the machine—to help the hero. And there was no god in the machine for him. Previously he could always go to Chela in his trouble, but now Chela was his trouble. . . . Perhaps she—after all, what had he ever done for her, and she had done so much for him? The next morning he gave the school a holiday and went in to Monterrey to buy her a present.

The city with its narrow paved streets, its taxi horns and street vendor's cries resounding from the building walls, disturbed him. He walked down Morelos Street from the great Central Market to Calle Zaragoza, feeling what he was—a country man out of place in the crowds of hurrying tradesmen, busy housewives shopping for the day, and strolling tourists. He looked in the windows of the *árabe* stores, but every one displayed waxen figures wearing white satin wedding gowns. The book stores had windows filled with bright-jacketed paper-backed novels, but they also showed missals bound in ivory or molded celluloid to be carried by brides at the wedding mass. And most of the tourists who passed him were North Americans obviously on honeymoons. Wherever he looked, the Professor saw all the external details of a happy marriage. He knew at last that he loved Chela. He was truly miserable.

He finally reached a corner building that housed a famous Chinese firm. These windows displayed nothing more romantic than strangely shaped bottles of perfume. The Professor greeted the store with a sigh of relief.

Inside, the light was dim, but not too dim to reveal grotesquely carved figurines, hanging tapestries, robes and tiny slippers of embroidered silk. A quiet walking Chinese clerk came up to him. The Professor spread his hands and explained that he wanted a present for a young lady. Perfume he ruled out at once. He knew that Chela would never accept such an expensive present. A robe or a pair of slippers? No, impossible. Too intimate. Just a small remembrance, please. The clerk patiently drew out object after object: an ivory chess set, a large paper fan, a picture that used hummingbird's feathers in place of paint, an intricate ball-within-ball of ivory filigree. The Professor was not satisfied. These things were not Chela. A large handkerchief? Of silk, perhaps? The clerk brought out a large selection—pink, lavender, gold, crimson—a butterfly profusion.

With an exclamation of delight, the Chinese flicked one from the bottom of the pack. "This one, señor, very fine. Not Chinese, no. From Bali. Colors put on with wax. Many colors. Very beautiful."

The Professor looked at it critically. The dominant note was a clear bright orange. Streaking across it in batik fashion were shades of green and blue and yellow, with black and purple for emphasis. This handkerchief looked like Chela. Her yellow skin was there, her black hair, the green lights in her slanting eyes. And the blue and orange were the flashing changes of her personality.

"That is the one I want," he said.

In Hidalgo that night he walked up and down the block several times before he could muster courage to knock on the door. Doña Mariliria came to greet him.

"Don Nacho is playing dominoes," she began automatically, and then her dim eyes recognized him. "Why, señor Professor! Enter, enter, what a nice surprise. You came to see our invalid, without doubt. He is a fine one. The doctor says that in a few days he can leave his bed and walk on crutches. Is that not magnificent news?" As she chatted, she led the way to Manolo's room, and the Professor was forced to follow her. Over her shoulder he could see Manolo and Chela playing cards, using the side of the bed for a table.

"Why, Professor." Chela hurried across the room to pull up a chair, smiling at him. "How nice of you to come. Eh, Manolo, this is the Professor Porfirio Diaz Aah. He came to us from Michoacán four years ago."

"So short a time," said Doña Mariliria proudly, "but already he is truly one of the village. Indeed, he often plays dominoes with my husband and the rest."

"I have been hearing about those domino games," smiled Manolo, holding out his hand in greeting. "To be a member is, I understand, both honor and accomplishment."

The Professor shook Manolo's hand and then stumbled backwards to the chair. How had he ever allowed himself to come into this room? The man was an actor. What did professors have to do with actors? He looked at Chela, but the single lamp was turned too low for him clearly to see her face. Sensing his embarrassment, she said gently, "We have been playing cards. Manolo has taught me a new game. It is called railroad. One wins and loses very fast."

"Chela wins," grinned Manolo, "and I lose."

Chela, thought the Professor. Manolo—they call each other that so easily. I have known her four years, and between us there is only Professor and Señorita.

"I know little of card games," he said coldly.

"The Professor is a man of books," explained Chela.

"We have been reading books," said Manolo. He lifted a paper-backed novel from the bedside table, and displayed the drawing on the cover. It showed two duelling men in seventeenth-century Spanish dress with a woman cowering in the background. "*The Adventures of Pardeán*. It is in twenty volumes. We are now in volume four."

"It is very exciting," said Chela. "Manolo reads so well. It is like a play." They smiled at each other.

The Professor felt his hands turn cold and dry. There was a searing agony in his chest. He said through stiff lips, "I have little time to read such ..." he paused to allow his condemnation to encircle the room, "... books. I prefer history and biography."

Manolo sighed and relaxed against his pillows. He had done his part. It was now the Professor's turn to be entertaining. Doña Mariliria said something about its being time to prepare Don Nacho's evening coffee, for he would soon be home from the domino game. She went off to the kitchen. There was an uneasy silence, which Chela broke by asking the Professor how he had enjoyed his trip to Monterrey. The Professor replied that cities gave him a headache. There was silence again. Manolo told an amusing story about the Capital, but the Professor was a poor audience and the story lacked brilliance. At last the little man rose to go. Chela went to the door with him.

Now that he had her alone, he found himself with nothing to say. He thrust the handkerchief into her hand, muttered, "I saw this in Monterrey. It was in a store window. I saw it quite by accident, you understand. I thought you might like it." Before she could thank him, he hurried away. He was furious with himself. After all, he was a man of culture and learning. Yet he had allowed Manolo to show him up as a fool. And the present of the handkerchief ... an expensive, foolish gesture. The trip to Monterrey had cost more than he had expected—the train fare, the food—and he had to pay for the meals he missed at Doña Juanita's as well. And what had he gained by it? Nothing but a stupid, miserable evening. Better for him to give up his job and leave Hidalgo. This northern frontier was too cold for him. Once again he felt the sickening nostalgia for the eternal green of Michoacán.

When Chela returned to Manolo's room she opened the tissue-wrapped package. The handkerchief felt soft to her fingers. "Is it not beautiful?" she cried. "Look, Manolo." He had never asked her to call him Manolo, but she had done so because the name Joaquín belonged to the proud Castillos, whereas Manolo de Fuentes was kin to her own people.

"Batik," he said, "and it looks like a good one. This handkerchief cost your friend a nice price, Chela."

"Oh." Chela's face was troubled. "He does not have much money. He should not have been so extravagant."

"He's in love," said Manolo lightly. "There is no such word as extravagance to lovers."

Chela stood very still. "What makes you say that?"

"But it's true, Chela. Any fool could see it." He plumped his pillows and smiled at her. "He doesn't like me."

"No," said Chela quickly, "you are mistaken. Only the other day he was saying there was no girl in all the valley for him to marry. Not even in San Juan Iglesias." Her voice broke slightly on the end of the word.

Manolo stared at her through half-closed eyes. He reached out and wrapped his long Castillo fingers about her wrist. "Do you love him, Chela?"

She started to shake her head. Then she paused, her lower lip caught between her teeth. "I don't know. I don't know, Manolo. I thought I did, but now—I don't know."

"Do you love me, Chela?"

The blood rushed to her cheeks. She tried to pull her hand away, but the fingers held too tightly. "You should not ask me that," she said under her breath.

"Why not? There is nothing wrong in people saying they love each other."

Her body began to tremble as with a chill. With a choked moan, she dropped to her knees and pressed her face against the bed. He heard her voice as through a long tunnel. "Why do you make fun of me?"

He released her wrist and dropped his hand on her head. After a moment, he took out the pins and began to unplait the fine mist of hair. "I thought so," he said. "Your hair should be light and loose around your face. It has been bound too tightly, Chela," but his voice was not referring to her hair.

She looked at him. The tears had left marks on the high cheekbones. "How can you love me? I am the homely Chela. Men do not love homely women."

Manolo grinned impudently at her. "Are you an authority on men, little one—and you with a choice between two of them?" He slid his arm around her and pulled her up to him. "To the devil with the Professor," he said, and kissed her.

Later that night, Chela lay on her hard pallet on the parlor floor and stared into the darkness. She could not understand what was wrong with her. Ever since she was nine years old, she had dreamed of Joaquín Castillo. In those dreams she had changed into a slim lovely creature no man could resist. They wept for her favors, but she refused to look at them. Instead, she stood outside her door and waited for Joaquín to ride past on his great black horse and pull her up to the saddlebow. Now, Joaquín had come home—had come here, to her house—had told her he loved her—had kissed her and asked her to marry him. The fairy tale had come true, but something was wrong. She should have been dancing with joy, and instead she was thinking of the Professor's face in the moonlight as he gave her the handkerchief. Why did the Professor have to spoil her fairy tale? She would not think of him. She would think only of Joaquín—Manolo—strange how Joaquín had changed into Manolo. As she floated on that mysterious river that flows between waking and sleeping, the stories that Manolo had told her of his exile repeated themselves to her.

During the Great Revolution he joined a small group of Obregón's followers. His finer education drew him to the attention of their leader, a peasant general named Suarez from Sonora. Joaquín had stayed with this Suarez through most of the fighting years. Then the general was killed, and after the final victory Joaquín found himself in a Republic that could not make up its mind as to what it really wanted, either politically or economically. He had floated from job to job, working at anything that would feed him, practicing a simple philosophy: if you don't own anything, nothing owns you. He changed his political relationships with agility, managing to stay out of jail most of the time. It was during this period that he changed his name to Manolo de Fuentes, for his Spanish family pride could not visualize the proud Castillo name on a police blotter. And then a friend introduced him to a man who was owner of an acting route that led through Tlaxcala, the holy city of Cholula, and as far south as

Puebla. Manolo asked for a job because there was nothing else in view and he had to eat. He was engaged, and from then on he stayed with the small companies. He memorized easily, he was always travelling, which he liked, and the work involved very little effort.

When he heard through the theatre grapevine that the Canales troupe was going north, he realized that valley men, no matter where they go, must always return to the valley. He had thought for a long time about appearing on the stage in Hidalgo. Villagers have dim eyes for faces, but they remember a gesture of the hand, a way of turning the head. Luckily, one of his vices was reading —anything and everything on which he could lay his hands. And he was bilingual. In a North American newspaper he read an account of an *Uncle Tom's Cabin* revival. Remembering the story, he grinned. Canales' professional jealousy would welcome the opportunity to turn Manolo into a backstage bloodhound. Thus no person of Hidalgo would see him, but he would see all of the old familiar faces, especially his beloved Tía Magdalena, and the baby Alejandro, grown now, somewhere in the audience.

When he had come on stage in the black make-up of Eliza's husband, he had been childishly disappointed to see Don Saturnino's empty chair. Although there was bitter enmity between them, he still retained a son's respect for the proud old man. "It is a part of the Castillo heritage," he later explained to Chela, "to love our ancestors." Neither could he find in the audience Tía Magdalena, nor any man resembling Alejandro.

Then Dorotéo Lozano began his loud interruptions. Forced to go out front, Manolo walked quickly, hoping that time and interest in the fight would prevent recognition. Then came the accident, and the next morning's revelation that Chela knew him.

Chela assured him that she was the only one who had guessed his secret. Doña Mariliria's eyes were dim. Don Nacho, who did not approve of actors, rarely came near the sick room, and then only to thrust his head inside the door, bellow a greeting, and leave. The little Doctor had come to the village long after Joaquín had left. When Chela wanted to announce his return, he said quickly, "No! Joaquín Castillo died in the vertigo of Revolution. This Manolo de Fuentes is a creature without substance, a vagabond actor. What has he to offer the great House Castillo?" So the passage of days brought no killing of the calf for the prodigal.

However, there was one person he insisted on seeing, and one afternoon, after Doña Mariliria had gone to rosary, Chela slipped across the Plaza of Independence to the house of Bob Webster.

When she told Tía Magdalena that the actor wanted to consult her, the old woman was oddly flattered. "Eh," she said, "even an outlander knows that an eagle witch is more powerful than a common doctor who knows only science."

But when she entered Manolo's room she lost her arrogance. For a moment she had paused at the foot of the bed, not believing what her eyes were seeing.

He had stretched out his hand to her. "So, Tía, no word of welcome for me?"

The old woman sighed the name between still lips, "Joaquín."

As she stumbled forward Chela had slipped out of the room and shut the door.

After that Tía came every day, bringing herb soups to give his body strength, and once she had brought a bottle of French cognac. "Don Bob thinks I am drinking it to relieve the pain in my ancient bones. But all my pains are gone, now that you have returned, Joaquín."

As she left the house that afternoon, she took Chela's face between her palms. "You are a good girl, Chelita. Is there any need for me to say, 'Do not bruise the heart on Castillo stone'?"

Remembering the words, Chela turned restlessly on the pallet. If she married Manolo . . . if? When. When she married Manolo . . . no, not when. She could not visualize herself as Manolo's wife. His face kept changing into the Professor's and back again. "Hurry, my darling," she whispered, "or you will be late—late for school—late for the play—late—late . . ." She was asleep.

The following morning Doña Mariliria brought Manolo his breakfast. "Where is Chela?" he asked quickly.

"Eh, lazy one, do you think she lives to wait on you?" The old lady glared at him. She had tried so hard to dislike this actor, but his charm had won her in spite of herself. "The little Doctor says you are to try and walk today. Chela has gone to the house of Rubén, the candy-maker, to borrow the extra crutches of Don Cardito, his father-in-law."

Manolo thrust back the covers and attempted to pull himself out of bed. "I want to put on my clothes."

"Your breakfast first," said Doña Mariliria firmly, giving him a little push that toppled him over sideways. "And you as weak as a new-born rabbit."

At last Chela came with the crutches and a brilliant red dressing gown she had borrowed from Alejandro for the occasion. When Manolo reached out for her, she shook her head. "Please, Manolo, give me time." She smiled tremulously at him. "I have loved you most of my life, I think, but it is difficult to turn away from the dream to life."

Before he could argue with her, the little Doctor entered. The two of them, with Doña Mariliria hovering like a bossing hen in the background, finally transferred the invalid from the bedroom to the patio. Manolo was glad to sink into a large chair, that Chela had hastily filled with cushions, near the laundry pool. "That was a greater journey," he gasped, "than from Vera Cruz to Acapulco."

"One half hour, no more," said the little Doctor firmly.

"An hour," said Manolo, shutting his eyes and lifting his face. "The sun is so good."

"He is as stubborn as a burro," muttered Doña Mariliria affectionately.

The little Doctor winked at Chela. "In half an hour he will be thinking of excuses to take himself back to bed. You will see."

He bustled off, and Doña Mariliria went into the kitchen to prepare chicken *mole* to honor the occasion. Chela drew a small chair close to Manolo's, playing with the tasseled ends of the silk cord that belted the dressing gown.

"Alejandro lent me this magnificence. He said we could keep it as long as you had use for it."

Manolo ran his fingers down the satin lapels. "I used to have one exactly like this in the old days. He must have had it copied."

"He loves you so much. Please, let me tell him."

"No, my slant-eyes. A tearing open of old wounds is no good to anyone. Me, I am the wild one, the misfit. Come, no sadness. Tell me about Alejandro's fine new house."

"There is a columned porch around the patio, and trees with hammocks fastened between them, and a fountain that plays. At night you can turn on lights in the fountain. It is very grand."

"I can never give you a house like that," said Manolo. "For us it will be a wandering from town to town. But we shall have a patio as big as the Republic, with one corner in Quintana Roo, and the other in Sonora. The Río Bravo will be our fountain, and we will sling a hammock between Popo and the Sleeping Lady." *

Chela looked at the palm of her work-roughened hands. "It sounds so very big. I would fit better in a small hut with a pot of flowers at the door."

"You've never left this valley, have you?"

"I went to Monterrey once. And Monterrey is a large city. I didn't like it."

"That is because you were not with me. When you see the sun on the white peak of Orizaba, and the green shadows of Michoacán, you will change your mind."

"Michoacán," repeated Chela thoughtfully. "It is beautiful, that state?"

"The jewel of the Republic," said Manolo enthusiastically, having completely forgotten that the Professor came from there. He went on to tell her of Lake Chalco, where the fishermen dip their butterfly nets; of the rough cobbled streets of ancient Uruapan, and of the jungles where white men rarely penetrate, and interpreters are needed to talk to the secret Indian tribes. It was a new world to Chela—a world of barbaric emerald beauty. To think that all of this was in the memory of the Professor. The delicate little man was changing in her imagination into a strange, mysterious creature whom no northerner could ever understand. She visualized him walking through bird-shadowed jungle paths, meeting an Indian chieftain who knelt in front of him, called him "cacique" and kissed his hand. She saw him wearing shining silver armor, his fingers resting carelessly on a cross-shaped sword hilt, demanding from cowering Indians piles of gold, and the secret of the mysterious jade, never found in Mexican earth, but often seen in pre-conquest jewelry.

"Eh, Chela, dreaming? And with open eyes?" Manolo lifted her hand to his lips.

Chela, with a frightened glance at the kitchen, jerked away from him, and he laughed at her. A strange sound filled the patio. It bounced from the walls and seemed to settle about their heads. "What's that?" gasped Manolo, twisting in his chair and peering about him. "Are there a million bees buzzing near us?"

---

* Popocatépetl (a volcano) and Ixtaccíhuatl (a mountain shaped like a sleeping woman) stand a few miles south of Mexico City.

As Chela laughed the brief tension was broken. She rose and put away her small chair. "It is only the children in the Boy's School studying their lessons."

"But I never heard them before."

"The house walls are thick. You were on the other side."

"The Professor teaches there?"

"Yes," said Chela lightly, "the Professor teaches there. And I think you are a little jealous. Now you must go back to bed."

Without giving him time to argue, she slid the crutches under his arms and helped him, protesting loudly, to his room. But he slid thankfully between the covers, content to lie still and watch the people pass along the sidewalk outside his window. Chela had pointed them out to him, and he knew them now—Doña Fela; Don Genaro, the civil judge; Don Timotéo Gonzalez; and the younger people, Andrés Treviño, Pepe Gonzalez, Porfirio, the carver of wood. He knew Evita, too. But all the time he had been sick he had never seen his father or his younger brother. Once the Castillo victoria had passed by, but only Evita and Doña Fela were in it. And Chela had lifted him high on the pillows so that he could see Bob Webster, Alejandro's greatest friend, chatting to Don Rosalío on the plaza. But none of these people were Castillos. Strange, Manolo thought, how he wanted to see his family —not to talk to them, but just to see them—to see the changes that the years had brought. This curiosity often puzzled him, for he was a man not normally curious. But something had happened to him in Hidalgo. He was in love, of course, but could love work such a miracle in him who had always accepted women so casually? And there had been so many women—in Mexico City, in San Luís Potosí, in Tabasco, in Vera Cruz—tall women, short women, blondes, brunettes, a few with red hair. When he had been a guide in the Capital, there had been North American women—middle-aged tourists who discarded their inhibitions as they acquired their anonymity in this strange, romantic country. His knowledge of English, his dark, flashing charm, had made him popular with them. One evening he was waiting in a hotel for one of them to come down and start a round of the night clubs. A long pier glass was near his chair and he saw himself for a vivid moment not as Manolo de Fuentes, guide, but as Joaquín Castillo, educated in Paris and England. He saw his father and brother sitting at table in the great dining room of the Castillo house with the candle-light gleaming on china and silver brought from Europe when Nuevo León was one of the richest provinces in New Spain, and the men and women who ate at the table wore stiff brocades with lace at throat and wrist. In that moment Manolo saw not only Don Saturnino and Alejandro, but all those other Castillos: his slender, delicate mother; his stern grandfather, and the others he had never known . . . the Castillos who helped finance the ill-fated Maximilian episode; the Castillos who had remained loyal to Spain in the liberating Revolution of 1810; the Castillos who had helped rule in the Palace of the Viceroys; and, before Mexico, the Castillos who had ridden in the armies of the Catholic Isabel to drive the Moors out of Spain.

In all that great line, Manolo was the only one to rebel against the established order of things. Now he saw himself as little better than a male prostitute, trading on his virility and the starved sex of life-grabbing women. He stood up and walked out of the hotel. Twelve hours later he was in Jalisco, working as a common cowboy on a cattle ranch. It took the sun and rain two years to bleach out of him the memory of those nerve-racking moments by the pier glass.

Manolo lifted his head and shook it as though trying to rid himself of a gadfly. What had forced him to remember that closed chapter of his life? Was it his desire for Chela? Strange how, even in the old days, he had preferred her to all the village children. But was it fair for him to marry her, take her away from the valley and her friends, because he could never stay here? When he went away the first time, he had given up any hopes of ever living in Hidalgo again. Yet if the nostalgia were powerful enough to bring him back after sixteen years of exile, what would it do to Chela, who had never known any shelter but the calm security of these mountains? Did he really, deep in his heart, love Chela, or was it only that she symbolized the valley to him? Perhaps it would be better for all of them if he left Chela to the little Professor and went away from Hidalgo alone. But the thought of those lonely years ahead of him frightened him. Where would he find another woman like Chela who would love him without question, who would leave him free to follow his own desires, and, above all, who came from the same valley with the same memories as his own? He slipped into a nightmare-ridden slumber, in which he thought he was trying to climb a wall to reach Chela, a wall that kept changing into the barring arms of Don Saturnino.

During the next few days, Chela moved in her own world. The Professor and Manolo had taken on new aspects to her. Manolo, through his sickness and dependence upon her, had ceased to be the laughing arrogant Joaquín, and was now a child whom she loved very much, but who had to be definitely handled with a strong will. The Professor, once her child, was changed into a strange, mysterious figure, silhouetted against green jungle growth, whose short stature and quick gestures were masks of the shining cacique splendor within. And still she could not decide. The mother quality in her cried for Manolo, but the romantic ego demanded the Professor.

Chela blamed herself for her vacillating. "I must make up my mind," she kept repeating over and over. "I wish I'd never seen either of them. Dear Santa Ana, blessed patron of marriage, help me. When I am with one, I want to be with the other. When Manolo touches me, it is the Professor's hand I want to feel. When the Professor smiles at me as he passes on the street, it is Manolo's face I want to see. Please, Santa Ana, advise me, aid me."

Manolo steadily grew stronger. He handled the crutches with dexterity, and would swing himself back and forth between the patio and the bedroom with a contempt for his broken leg that kept Doña Mariliria fussing at him all day long.

The little Doctor came in to see him, and finding the bedroom empty, passed through the hall to the patio. He paused for a moment, shocked. What was Alejandro doing, wearing a dressing gown and playing cards with Chela? Then the illusion passed, and he recognized Manolo. He rubbed his eyes fretfully. Alejandro's serious illness was too much on his mind, these days. It was making him see visions.

As he moved toward the patio, Manolo bent across the narrow board and kissed Chela's hand. Hmm, thought the little Doctor, these actors! He pursed his lips to give his words importance. "Chela, go to Porfirio's house and fetch me a wooden mallet and a chisel."

"A mallet and . . ." she caught her breath, talking fast to overcome her fear that the doctor had seen Manolo's impudence. "You are going to take off the cast!"

"But naturally. This young rooster is almost well."

Chela rushed to the hall door, where she pivoted on one toe. "We must celebrate today, Manolo. Ay, this is a grand occasion."

When she was gone, the little Doctor looked down at the actor's still face. "What is wrong? For you there is no joy."

Manolo shrugged, a defensive, mocking laughter near the surface of his eyes. "This has been an amusing time. I do not like it to end."

"Actors," said the little Doctor gravely, seating himself in Chela's vacant chair, "do not make good husbands for village girls."

Manolo's mouth twitched. "Is it written in my face then?"

"So." The little Doctor clicked his tongue. "And the village has always thought Chela would never marry."

"She has charm—kindliness—understanding. Why shouldn't she marry?"

The little Doctor lighted a cigarette and gazed over the patio walls at the eastern mountains. "You are an actor," he pointed out again. "In the States, actors, I understand, have a certain social position. But here..." he shrugged. "Outside of the Capital, what is an actor in Mexico?"

"I have talent," said Manolo coldly. "I could act in the Capital if I liked."

"You are how old? Thirty-five, thirty-six? If you have so much talent, why aren't you in the Capital now?"

Manolo's long hand clenched in anger. "What affair is this of yours?"

"I like Chela," said the doctor, looking at Manolo's hand. "Her father is my friend. I am naturally..." he broke off abruptly, reached out and caught Manolo's wrist. "Let me see your hand."

Manolo tried to twist it out of his grasp, but the little Doctor was surprisingly strong. He stared intently at the narrow hand, with the little finger that was as long as the ring finger. "A gypsy in Sonora once told me that good actors always have a long little finger. It's strange. I've never seen a hand like that except in Bob Webster and the family Castillo. The Castillos are the great family of this valley." He sighed deeply. "The son Alejandro has need of acting, poor boy." He released Manolo's wrist and relaxed in his chair. "If the hand means anything, perhaps you can act. But Chela is not for Mexico City. She belongs in Hidalgo."

Manolo was frowning. "Poor Alejandro Castillo. What do you mean by that?"

"Alejandro is not important to this conversation," said the little Doctor with precision. "Men do not look easily at Chela. And these village girls are gentle creatures. The family here has been kind to you. In a few days you will be strong enough to travel."

"You want me to go away—and alone."

"Precisely."

Manolo politely hid a small yawn. "Let us talk of Alejandro Castillo. I find the subject more interesting.

For a brief moment anger flared in the little Doctor's eyes. His voice was very low as he said, "I warn you..."

Chela came running through the hallways. "Porfirio had such a time finding the mallet." She giggled softly. "I think he wanted to charge me rent for the tools, but he had no nerve to ask me. That man and his love of money!" She paused and looked at the stern hard faces. "What is wrong? What has happened?"

"The little Doctor was warning me of something," said Manolo casually. "Just what were you trying to say, Doctor?"

The little Doctor sniffed angrily, but did not answer. Instead, he took the mallet and chisel and began to carefully chip away the plaster cast from the leg. When he had gone, Chela sat down by Manolo.

"What were the two of you saying?"

"He wants me to leave the valley."

"But why?"

"It seems that I might break your heart."

"He did see you kiss my hand. I knew it!"

Manolo was not paying her much attention. "Chela, tell me something—what is wrong with Alejandro?"

"Alejandro?" She looked at him in bewilderment. "I don't..."

"Alejandro. My brother, Alejandro. What is wrong with him?"

"Why, nothing, Manolo. What should be wrong with him?"

"I don't know." He pounded his clenched fists together. "That little man said, 'Poor Alejandro has need of acting.' What did he mean by it?"

"Oh, that." Chela flushed slightly and started pleating her skirt in embarrassment. "It is nothing, Manolo—really. I am surprised that he knows. I thought no one knew."

He leaned forward and forced her to look at him. "What has that old man, my father, done to Alejandro?"

"Nothing, Manolo. Don't excite yourself."

"Will you tell me, for the love of God?" His eyes shone with anger, and his tone was sharp and strange. She had never believed his easy indolence capable of such rage, and it startled her. She drew back from him as he said harshly, "When my mother died, Alejandro was all I had for remembrance. If that old man has hurt him, I'll..." he was silent, but his fingers twisted rapidly against each other.

"I told you. It is nothing to do with your father. I am not even sure that I know, but..." Chela hesitated, and then she told him of seeing Alejandro's expression when María de las Garzas passed.

Manolo bit down on his lower lip. "Alejandro, mixed up in an affair with a common river girl..."

"No," said Chela swiftly, "it's not that at all. You have never seen María. She is..." Chela paused, wondering how to convey the truth. "I can't explain it. The river girl is—but how can any woman describe her? She is beyond any description beautiful... warm as sunlight...all golden sunlight and dark blue sky. As for Evita—you have seen Evita. You know what she is like."

After a pause Manolo said wearily, "Why did Alejandro marry her? Why didn't he pack this river beauty off to Tehuantepec or Yucatán where he is a stranger?"

"The village thinks his marriage to Evita is an affair of the heart. And your father was so pleased."

"But of course—Alejandro worships our father. If it pleased that old man..." Manolo shook his head. "Still, I have a feeling that this scandal was not in the little Doctor's mind. It was something else he meant. But what?"

"I don't know." She was silent, and the clear children's voices sang sweetly about them. Manolo hit the arm of his chair with his fist. "Damn those children! That Professor is making them scream on purpose to annoy me."

"Manolo! You know that's not true."

"These little men—they are quiet and clever. It is the big ones who are stupid. Blundering and stupid. Is Alejandro a big man?"

"Yes," admitted Chela reluctantly. She did not like to see

Manolo so excited. It frightened her—her Indian blood which responded automatically to the dreaded anger of the Spanish overlord. "He is as tall as you, I think. He's the tallest man in the valley. Evita can stand under his arm."

"And this river girl? She is short?"

"No. I have to look up at her when I speak to her."

"Then it is Evita who is the dangerous one. In the Revolution I have seen it. The tall generals won the glory and the short generals won the battles." He began to tremble, and Chela, definitely worried, put him to bed. She wanted to send for the doctor, but Manolo fell so quickly into exhausted sleep that she hated to disturb him.

As she went about her household chores, she puzzled over Manolo. Her fine instinct had deserted her. There was something in him that she could not understand, and this frightened her. She had a feeling that whatever it was—this unknown thing—affected not only Manolo but herself, and in some strange way, the Professor. The little man of letters had not been back to the house since the night he gave her the handkerchief. He no longer walked past her window, but cut across the plaza on his way home. When she swept the sidewalk in the morning, she would see him going into the school. They always bowed to each other, but formally, as people do who often see each other but have never been introduced. He was so much in her mind, but she saw him far less than she had when he first came to the valley. Chela sighed and rubbed her hand across her eyes. If Manolo had never come back to Hidalgo, would she have learned that the Professor loved her? And he did love her, she knew that, but in a silent, hurt way, far different from Manolo's possessive attitude. Manolo took it so much for granted that she would go with him when he left. At intervals she believed it herself, but when she tried to visualize that time, there was a blankness in her imagination. She had read a story once about a man who found a great book in which was written the future of the world, but when he turned to his own name he found only an empty page. That was the way she felt about her own future. And with a childish passion she wished that she were an old woman looking back on her life with all the problems solved.

In the late afternoon Chela slipped through the patio gate into the Street of the Three Crosses. She hesitated for a moment and then hurried up the Street of the Governors to the Church of Our Lady of the Miraculous Tear. In there she would be quiet and safe. No one would bother her. Manolo would be leaving soon, and she had to decide if she would go with him or stay with the Professor. This useless wavering in her mind had to stop. Better never to marry at all than to go with the one and turn into a second Evita from grieving for the other....

María of the River Road was also in the church. They looked at each other without speech. Chela thought, she is so beautiful and I so homely. How strange that we should be sisters in our love for Castillo men. Her hand came out and María grasped it; then María went away, and Chela knelt on an old, scarred *prie-dieu*, its red velvet cushion frayed and worn from the pressure of many knees, and rested her forehead against her clasped hands supported by the high back of the prayer stand. Would all these complexities finally unravel themselves? She was so tired—so tired. She fell asleep.

When she awoke, it was dark. Her body was stiff, and her knees ached with a slow steady pain. For a moment she could not locate herself in space and time. Then she realized where she was, and memory flooded through her. She pulled herself upright and staggered a little as the circulation began to move faster in her legs.

At last she was able to walk a little better, and she went into the street. Several people hurried past her towards the Street of the River. "Eh, Chela," called Sarita Calderón through the darkness, "is it not a terrible thing?"

"What has happened?" Chela caught up with the slow-moving Doña Fela.

"Do you not know, child? Poor Evita. I weep for her." Doña Fela carefully wiped her eyes with a lace-edged handkerchief. Before Chela could say anything, the old woman placidly continued with her news.

Chela drew in a deep, sobbing breath. Her first thought was not of Evita but of Manolo. Pulling her shawl closer about her head, she ran toward her own house. Doña Mariliria, a bowl of hot broth in her hands, was just coming out.

"Don Saturnino wants your father and Bob Webster to take care of all the details. That good old man up there alone in that big house—it isn't right. I wanted Nacho to stay with him, but no! Men never do things in a sensible manner." She clutched the bowl of broth tighter between her thin, transparent fingers. "There is probably no food in Evita's house. People never think of the thing they need most when tragedy strikes. You will have to stay with the actor." This flood of words rushed along on one thin thread of breath. Chela said nothing as her mother scuttled away in the darkness. She shut the heavy, hand-carved street doors and went into Manolo's bedroom. He was sitting in a chair near the lamp, reading a book. As she entered, he looked up and smiled at her.

"There seems to be excitement in the streets. I can hear the people hurrying past. Has another actors' troupe decided to brave the dangers of Porfirio's empty bottles?"

"Manolo." Chela paused for a moment, then walked toward him and put her hand on his arm. It was the first time that she had ever touched him of her own free will. He bent his head and kissed her fingers.

"You look so serious. As though the world had died. Is there gossip about us, perhaps? All villages enjoy gossip. In a few days you need worry no more about it. We will be gone from..."

"Manolo," she repeated, interrupting him. At the pain in her voice his light chatter stopped.

"What is it, Chela? What has happened?"

"I don't know how to tell you."

He glanced toward the window. "All those people hurrying past." His voice tightened. "There's been an accident."

"Yes." Chela in an unconscious gesture, lifted the shawl from her hair and allowed it to fall in deep folds over her shoulders.

"My father. Something has happened to..."

"No, Manolo. Not your father."

Manolo seemed to contract within himself. The book slid unheeded from his knees to the floor. His lips formed the name but there was no sound. She said quickly, "It seems Alejandro had a sickness. No one knew about it but the little Doctor—not even your father."

"What kind of a sickness?"

"A trouble of the throat. He had a hemorrhage this evening."

"Was there much pain?"

"I don't think so. Not at the end."

"So that's what the little Doctor meant. 'Poor Alejandro has need of acting.'" Manolo shut his mouth tightly to still the trembling of his lips. A small pulse beat low in his cheek. "You said he was big and strong. You told me that." It was an accusation.

"I thought he was, Manolo. Everyone thought so. This has been a terrible shock to the village."

"Yes. I feel so sorry for the village." The bitterness in him made an unreasonable anger flare in Chela for a moment. How dare he criticize Hidalgo? Then, with a twisted humor, she realized that Manolo was no outlander but a villager like herself. Surely he had as much right to criticize as she did.

Manolo was saying, "The last time I saw him he was thirteen. He waved good-bye to me from the train that was carrying him to the States to school. And now he is a man—and dead. A man I've never seen." His voice broke. Chela bent over him, but he pushed her away. She moved to the window and closed the long, heavy shutters.

He said, "I want to go to my father."

"But, Manolo, you can't! I'll go and fetch him. He'll come here."

"No. I'll go to him."

"But your leg . . ."

"During the Revolution I crawled five miles through cactus and flowering thorn with a bullet in my thigh. I am the last Castillo now. It is necessary that I go to that old man's hou—" He paused and pulled himself erect, reaching for his crutches. "It is time that I go home."

She knew better than to argue with this determination. "Wait, Manolo. My father has a horse. He keeps it stabled at the blacksmith's. I'll go and get it." She left quickly so that he could not argue with her.

It was very difficult getting him up on the horse. He wanted her to ride with him but she said no. "It is too dark. It is better that I guide the way." She slid her hand through the bridle and turned the horse up the Avenue of Illustrious Men. There were neither stars nor moon. In the excitement of the evening, Don Serapio had forgotten to light the oil lanterns on the Plaza of Independence. The darkness wrapped about them like a cloak, and the silent streets echoed the slow beat of the horse's hoofs.

Chela found the way from memory. She could see nothing. She

felt suspended in space, with only an awareness of Manolo's nearness. He seemed far away from her now—as though he had left her and gone into another world. For the last hour he had not thought of her at all except as a convenience to help him reach his father. She remembered her brief anger at his criticism of the village. And suddenly she knew why she had been angry. She knew, too, what was the strangeness in him that had been alien to her. And in the knowledge all of her problems were settled. She felt a release and a settled security. How wonderful it was to be sure—to know the answer to her difficulty. She remembered her childish wish to be an old woman looking back over life, and she smiled in the darkness. She thought: I am a woman now. This morning I was a girl, but tonight I am grown and a woman. And she remembered with gentleness that other moment when she had ceased to be a child and had become a girl—that moment when Don Nacho had told her that Joaquín Castillo had ridden away on his fine black horse to join the Revolution. Chela's hand slipped from the bridle to the velvety nose of the horse she was leading. She asked aloud, "What became of Rocinante?"

Manolo's voice floated toward her like sound from an invisible source. "She died. They always die—the brave and beautiful."

"Yes," said Chela, and did not think it strange that he should quote this most Spanish of proverbs, which sounded stupid to her New World ears. They reached Don Saturnino's house.

Manolo slid from the horse's back with a low grunt of pain and groped for her shoulder. She did not bother to tether the horse. He would find his way back to the corral, and Manolo had no more need of him this night. She unfastened the crutches from the back of the saddle and slid them under the man's arms. The great iron gates were difficult to manage, and she tore her fingers on the lock. At last they swung open. The two of them stumbled along the avenue walled by lime and orange trees. Chela was afraid that she might guide Manolo into one of the tree trunks, but after a moment she found that he was guiding her, and the knowledge shocked her a little. This ground, so strange to her, was familiar to him with the familiarity that comes from childhood and never leaves the memory. In spite of Don Nacho's great friendship for Don Saturnino, she had never been on the estate.

When they reached the door she instinctively put out her hand to knock, but Manolo had already swung it open. He moved a little ahead of her into the red-tiled hall with the brass lamp flickering palely on the lid of a heavy carved chest. The ceiling was low, white between the great beams of dark wood that criss-crossed its surface. Carved doors led off this hall into other rooms. Chela felt lost, like a small animal trapped in a strange cavern.

Manolo was swinging his long body forward, moving the crutches with certainty toward a door at the back, where light gleamed through the cracks. He opened this door and went into a large room with a great fireplace at one end in which logs of mesquite wood were burning. Chela stared around her with wonder. She had never seen such a room. The ceiling-high windows were covered with heavy drapes of cream brocade that fell in soft pools on the floor, tiled, like the hall, in red. On the white plaster walls were paintings of many men and one woman in strange stiff clothes, but all had the long-fingered Castillo hands. The black wood of the furniture gleamed in the firelight, and the heavy chairs were piled with cushions, as though the velvet and silk were meant to soften the ascetic Spanish carving.

Don Saturnino was sunk in a corner of the long divan, his fine head with its crest of white hair drooped forward against his chest. Manolo, who now, in some mysterious transmutation, was no longer Manolo but Joaquín, sat down beside him and laid his head on the old man's shoulder. There was no start of surprise— no crying out in exclamation and wonder. One Castillo had gone away. Another had come home.

Chela shut the door and went out of the house into the fragrant darkness—the fragrance that comes not from flowers but from the soil, and the labor of green things growing into spring. On impulse she bent and pushed her hand into the earth. She knew now that this house with its low ceilings and heavy furniture was not for her. In her world people laughed and cried as easily as the sun shone or rain fell. In this ordered Castillo pattern, the blood was thin with restraint. That was the true difference between the great families and other people. It was not a matter of having ancestors with more wealth and power. It was a blending of the blood, so that the family itself was more important than any individual. Joaquín, the rebel, was the strongest

Castillo of them all. He had even changed his name so that nothing he did could reflect back upon the family. And he had returned to Hidalgo because the roots of the family were here. She had been angry at his criticism of the village because the family Castillo—first settlers of this valley—were far greater outlanders than the little Doctor, or Abel, the *árabe*, or—she whispered the name gently in her mind—the Professor. The family Castillo owned the land, but they did not belong to it.

The valley possessed the villagers. The mountains punished them with storms but protected them from the world beyond. The earth demanded their bones for fertilizer, but gave back food. And the villagers felt this ownership, and it gave them a sense of security so that they did not have to be afraid of what they thought and felt. But the Castillos saw the mountains as barriers, the earth as a servant. They looked to themselves for their own protection, and so they had to build their own defenses.

Chela moved easily through the darkness, thinking of these things. She even had a moment to feel sorry for Evita. No wonder the girl had been unhappy married to Alejandro. It was true that the Cantús were an old family—they had come to the Sabinas in the first days of the 1810 Revolution—but the Cantús had never been afraid to mix their blood with the villagers. They lacked the superiority of the pure strain. Evita, who could ride into anger or laughter as easily as any valley girl, could not understand the remote Alejandro. As for Joaquín, the wild one, he, too, had set up his barriers. Let him call himself Manolo de Fuentes or Fulano de Tal,* he could never change the truth of his Castilloism.

As Chela reached the Casino corner, she saw a man standing on an upturned box, busy fastening a flickering oil lantern to its pole. She paused to watch him. What a natural thing that it should be the Professor who remembered to light the lanterns on a night of such excitement. She crossed the street. He heard her light footsteps and turned his head. She saw the amber light flicker across his face, darkening the eye sockets and emphasizing the high cheekbones. He saw the exotic mask of her face in the shadows. For a moment, to each other, there were no bodies, only

* The Spanish equivalent of John Doe.

the suspension of faces against the dark cloak of night. Chela timidly extended her hand toward him and the immovable instant was past. He jumped down from the box and came toward her. His palm touched hers. The fingers turned and clasped each other. The lantern swung dangerously in the wind but neither noticed it.

The Street of the Forgotten Angel

December, 1930

I, too, am in the far lost land.
Oh, Sainted Heaven, if I but had wings.
                    —Mexican folk song

B OB TURNED THE BRASS PAPER KNIFE BETWEEN HIS FINGERS. "But surely that is a matter for Don Saturnino or Don Joaquín to decide."

The foreman of the Rancho Santo Tomás shrugged his shoulders. "Don Saturnino sent me to you, Don Bob. He said you were very learned in the matter of horses—as all the world knows."

"All the world also knows that Don Joaquín knows more of horses than anyone in the Sabinas—including the young Xavier."

"As you say, Don Bob," the foreman murmured politely.

Bob flung the brass paper cutter on his desk and pushed back his swivel chair. The foreman's thin, bowlegged body seemed to bisect the large office window, and this double view of the western line of mountains was irritating. He walked to the window and spoke without turning his head. "Don Saturnino is in all matters wise. I will talk with him and then send you a message."

The foreman shifted his weight from one booted foot to the other. He wore tight leather trousers that fastened with straps under the insteps, and a loose tan blouse, the tails brought around and knotted over his stomach. He held his wide-brimmed straw hat in both hands, and he twisted it now, playing with the neck cord. "If your grace will let me know soon? The man to purchase the animals arrives at dawn, and he plans to continue to Monterrey for the Guadalupe dances..." His voice withdrew into silence.

To both men the moment was charged with embarrassment, for Don Saturnino had told them in effect, and through them the valley, that Joaquín lacked both authority and judgment in handling the affairs Castillo.

When Bob remained silent, the foreman made his farewell bow. Bob watched him ride down the mountain trail, then began to pace the narrow office. He hated the situation in which he found himself more and more enmeshed, and yet he understood and sympathized with the proud, grieving old man who lived in isolated grandeur in the white-walled house with the red-tiled roof.

Joaquín, it was true, had come home; had tired of his years of wandering and had returned in time to put on the black suit of mourning for Alejandro and take his place as the young Castillo. But the Sabinas could not accept him easily. From Topo Grande to Mina it was whispered that a man who had run away from his duty once would do it again, and that he was not to be trusted.

Also, there was the laughter in him. Not the kind, sympathetic laughter of Alejandro, but a mocking laughter, making no sound in his mouth, living in his eyes, so that every man to whom he spoke felt somehow faintly ridiculous. It was always there, even when he walked into Sunday mass behind his father, and good christians do not mock the sweet-scented house of God. Only Chela, in all the valley, had a good word to speak for him, and Chela, as was well known, had nursed him when he was ill of the broken leg and doubtless looked upon him as a child to be pitied. And that, of course, was another scandal: that the Castillo had returned to his home, not in dignity, but as an actor, and actors were like beggars, all of them men of little worth.

So Joaquín drank his evening cognac alone in the Casino, and rode alone through Hidalgo streets, with no one to call out a greeting to him, or to wave a friendly hand. The village had watched curiously to see how Bob would react, for Alejandro had been Bob's great friend—and was not surprised when he saw Joaquín as a man without substance. But Bob had a private and stronger reason for disliking the elder Castillo.

Joaquín, without a thought save his own desires, had run away from home and left the full duty of Castillo heir on the shoulders of the too young Alejandro. Because of Joaquín, Alejandro had made that disastrous journey ending in the nerve sickness that finally led to his death. Because of Joaquín, Alejandro had been forced into marriage with Evita. Because of Joaquín, Alejandro's gentle life had ended too soon. Because of Joaquín, María's ripe and golden beauty was enfolded in misty darkness.

At thought of María, Bob shut his eyes and pounded his fist against the desk top in an effort to still the pain that grated through him. Grief enveloped him like a flood raised in little brooks by sudden rain. It flowed over him, and yet there was already an abatement. For nine months his mourning had been a long, sober shower. Now there were new channels eroded in him, and his emotional current was slowly adjusting itself to a new passage. But the process of erosion was still painful.

María, María, María. The name sang itself over and over in his mind. He had loved Yvonne with youth and Candelaria with peace, but to María he had given a devotion that was all the more passionate and deep because he dared not reveal his feeling by expression or gesture. María had belonged entirely to Alejandro, and Alejandro was his friend, his—he twisted the word in his mind—*compadre*.

If I had gone to see María the night Alejandro died, Bob thought again, as he had thought so many times, she would never have thrown herself from the cliff. I could have helped her through her grief. But, María, can't you understand? I dared not come to you. Everyone would have whispered, "His friend is dead. Why is he not here, when his friend is dead?" You were Alejandro's secret. How could I betray his secret?

He picked up a paper weight from the desk, balanced it in his hand, and flung it with a savage movement against the wall. It hit with a snap of sound and fell to the floor. He looked at it a moment, and then sat down at his desk. Bending forward, he pulled open a drawer and took out his bankbook. The balance surprised him a little, as it always did. He could never really convince himself that he was a comparatively wealthy man. Living expenses in the valley were low, and although he had made a few vacation trips to Mexico City, he had never found occasion to spend much money. He had some furniture that Alejandro had bought for him in Paris, some good pictures. His monthly bills for books and phonograph records might be considered extravagant, but outside of these few things he had found no need of money, and so most of his salary had gone into the bank, gaining interest and multiplying itself.

I've enough to live anywhere I want, he thought. I can do what I please, travel where I please. And with Don Saturnino making it so apparent that he prefers me to Joaquín, perhaps it might be better if I leave the valley...

But the thought of leaving frightened him. Here he had found an earth stability. There was magic in the Sabinas that held him as a woman holds a child. And here María was buried. How could he go away and leave her? One part of his mind said these things, while with the other he began to draft a letter to Harper Paschal, superintendent of the cement plant in Monterrey. He took up a pencil and began to write slowly in English, "I've decided that ten years of dynamiting rock from a quarry is nine years too long. Get someone else to pile the rock on the flatcars. I'm quitting, I'm stopping, I'm through..." The lead dived downward in a startled line as a soft Indian voice murmured, "May I speak to the *patrón?*"

Bob glanced upward with an exasperated frown. "What is it, Hilario? I'm busy."

"I know, *patrón*, but..." The man rubbed the back of his hand across his mouth. He was obviously ill at ease, and Bob, who had learned long ago that under their stoic calm the Inditos had the quick sensitivity of children, said resignedly, "You doubtless want money. You understand that you have drawn three months ahead against your salary. To draw more would not be wise."

"Not money, *patrón*," protested the thin singsong. Like most of the quarry men, Hilario wore thonged sandals, gray trousers belted with rope, a pink shirt, and a high-crowned, roll-brimmed straw hat. He was short and stocky, with closely cropped black hair, and a short-nosed, broad-cheeked face too wide for its length. He might have been twenty, he might have been fifty. On the books he was listed as thirty-six. Bob wondered if he himself looked as young or as old as this man who was his own age.

"The flowers that surround the office," Hilario said, "are indeed beautiful, *patrón*. Each year more beautiful, not so?"

"True words," Bob agreed politely. No use to ask the man what he wanted. He would arrive at the subject in his own manner.

"Perhaps it is because the hand that planted them knew the secrets of the earth. A good green hand. It was a man, perhaps?"

"A woman," Bob answered gravely, knowing that Hilario knew as well as he who had planted and tended the bougainvillaea and the profusion of larkspurs, dahlias, iris, and carnations.

"Women," said Hilario with a solemn nod, "are indeed useful creatures. In my place, since the death of my wife, there is no woman. Three sons I have, and a daughter, and no woman to care for them, save the sister of my wife who has seven of her own."

"A sad thing." Bob was wondering about going to Monterrey and seeing Harper about the resignation. I've got to get out of this valley. I've been here too long, ten years too long. That's the line I'll use. There are no arguments against it. He said aloud, "I'm sorry, Hilario, I didn't hear what you said."

"I repeat my very words, *patrón*. Don Anselmo says that with him there are no objections, but the decision must be yours."

Bob shrugged wearily. This little farce of asking for a few days' leave always irritated him. If one of the Inditos wanted a vacation, he went, with or without permission. He would stay as long as the mysterious travel urge remained in him, and then he would return to meekly receive Bob's scolding, without ever comprehending what wrong he had done.

"Very well, Hilario, go to Mina to visit your sister, or Monterrey to visit your aunt, or Torreón to pray in the church. But see that you are back in seven settings of the sun, or there will be black anger in me."

Hilario's eyes rested in blank astonishment on Bob's face. "But I have no sister in Mina, and no aunt in Monterrey. And as for the church in Torreón, it is doubtless a beautiful temple. Your grace is wiser than I, and if you say it is beautiful, then I, too, say so with all my mouth."

"Excellent, we are of one mind." He realized that Hilario wanted to go off on a secret pilgrimage, perhaps to the hidden cave of a powerful medicine man to cleanse himself of some strange tribal sin. It really made no difference where he went. "But remember what I said. In seven days it must be finished. No longer."

"Then the *patrón* gives his permission?"

"Naturally. Leave me now, Hilario, for I have work to do."

Hilario bobbed his cropped head and moved his muscular body to the door with the dignified grace common to the mountain Inditos. "As Don Anselmo has spoken, your grace is indeed a generous man. And tomorrow, the day of our gracious Lady of Guadalupe, my children will light a candle for you in the church."

Bob rose and bowed his thanks. Hilario also bowed. As ceremonious as two Chinese, thought Bob, as the little man trotted away. He is probably my own blood cousin. I wonder what he would say if I told him that? He did not realize he had spoken the last sentence aloud until Joaquín drawled from the doorway, "Told who what?"

Bob sighed and sat down again at his desk. "Enter, Joaquín. Consider the office yours."

"Such politeness," Joaquín murmured, entering with his usual royal air of owning the room and all that it contained.

"I do not feel polite," Bob snapped, resenting the mocking laughter in the black eyes framed by lashes as long as a woman's. "But this seems to be my day for interruptions."

Joaquín shrugged, taking a cigarette from the silver embroidered pocket of his short jacket. Like many Mexicans who loved horses, he was a member of the National Charro Association* and wore his clothes with the grace characteristic of his type. Bob looked at the gray-clad figure and shook his head in pretended admiration.

> *How silver is our charro,* [he quoted]
> *The tight woolen trousers buttoned with silver,*
> *The silver plate to protect the* reata† *fastened on his hip,*
> *His short leather jacket frogged with silver braid,*
> *The red satin tie fringed with silver thread,*
> *The broad-brimmed hat sheathed in felt,*
> *The cupped crown displaying the silver eagle.*
> *And the striped Saltillo blanket*
> *Fastened with silver chains to the cantle.*
> *The pistol butt, hammered by hand from silver,*
> *Carried in a silver holster.*
> *Silver is stamped on his saddle,*
> *And his silver spurs sing silver songs.*
> *Silver, all of silver, is our* charro.

"Very pretty," Joaquín drawled, flinging his gray felt sombrero on the window seat and lounging beside it. "You are very learned in matters *charro*. You know the significance of the hat, perhaps?"

"Naturally. The metal embroidery is the treasure hidden in Mexican earth, the peaked crown represents the mountains, and the broad brim, the plains. Any more questions, teacher?"

Joaquín blew a smoke ring and absently punctured it with his finger. "I have worn mourning nine months. Three is the required period. But for nine months I have worn the black. Unfortunately all the black suits in Spain would not bring Alejandro back again."

---

* A club organized in 1921 to preserve the national dress, dances, and especially excellence in horsemanship. The word *charro*, meaning "man on horseback," is used interchangeably to refer either to the man or to his clothes.

† The saddle rope, of twisted hemp or horsehair, used for lassoing animals, or as a weapon, for it is possible to kill a man with a *reata*.

Bob said nothing. He lifted the bronze paper cutter and began to turn it slowly between his fingers.

"So, you do not approve? Nor does Don Nacho. When he saw me this morning he put his hand over his eyes to shield his sight from—shall I call it my silver elegance?"

"Call it anything you like. Wear anything you like. You are the young Castillo. Who is there in the valley to say what you should or should not wear?"

The bitter tone seemed to amuse Joaquín. "Precisely. Alejandro, I understand, wore only the black dress *charro*, and that only on Thursday nights when he dined in state with my gracious father. But I am not Alejandro."

"No," said Bob slowly, pushing the paper cutter away from him, "you are not Alejandro." He sat back and rested his chin on his clasped hands. "Did you come to the quarry to visit, or on a matter of business?"

Joaquín grinned, his mocking eyes turned to the window. "But how blunt. Where is the famous courtesy of which I have heard so much: the delicate approach, the kindly patience..."

The quick anger flared in Bob as it always did when he heard the beautiful, sarcastic voice that lacked the hoarse friendliness of Alejandro's. "Damn it, Joaquín, I have work to do, and there've been nothing but interruptions this morning. If you want something, please say so. I suppose you've come about the *ranchito* horses."

"So?" The long narrow hand that held the cigarette paused in mid-air. "What about the horses?"

"I told the foreman that I would have to speak to Don Saturnino first. After all, you're the one who has to decide which animals are to be sold and which ones not. The ranch is yours now. At least it has reverted as Alejandro's property to the Castillo estate. And you are presumably in charge of the estate, not me."

Joaquín dropped the cigarette to the floor and ground it to powder with a booted heel. "As I understand your words, my father sent the foreman of the Rancho Santo Tomás to you to judge in the matter of selling some horses?"

"You know that he did."

"But I didn't." Joaquín's eyes were shielded under the sleepy lids. "This is news to me."

"Oh." Bob reddened in embarrassment. "I'm sorry. I thought Don Saturnino told you."

"My father is not given to confidences," Joaquín said dryly. "We keep our distance, he the Montague and I the Capulet. We seldom find conversation amusing." His mouth under the clipped mustache curved into a smile. "But in this matter he is right. You have been here several years. You know the ranch and how Alejandro would judge the horses. As for me, I am an outlander."

"I'm sorry, Joaquín."

"For what? It is not difficult to be an outlander. One has merely to go beyond the mountains. But then you are a true valley man. You have the feel of the valley in you. For you the world is bound by Saddle Mountain and the Prow."

"Not any more," Bob said abruptly. "I'm leaving the valley."

Joaquín lighted another cigarette. "Is it possible? You return to the States?"

"Perhaps. I haven't decided yet."

"I see." He rested his silver-embroidered back against the casement and stared through the window at the sweeping view. The brilliant yellow sunlight warmed the gray rocks and turned them lavender, and a cloud shadow hung over the distant fields. Two Inditos trotted past, long poles, supporting water buckets, balanced on their shoulders, "Very interesting," he drawled. "If I opened the window and shouted to them, 'Good morning, cousin,' I wonder what they would say."

The words were so close to Bob's own silent thoughts of the Inditos that they startled him. "The poor creatures would be offended, naturally. They would think you were laughing at them."

"'The poor creatures,'" Joaquín quoted. "How Spanish you are. All filled with the importance of the pure blood like my esteemed father."

"I didn't mean it that way..."

"Forgive me. I am a stupid person. During the Revolution I learned that an Indito with a gun was very superior to a mestizo or a creole without one. It was a most illuminating experience."

Joaquín was not looking at Bob. His head was still turned toward the valley. Bob gazed at him curiously. In his silver-encrusted gray suit, with the silver-weighted gray sombrero beside him, he looked like a travel poster painted to entice the tourist. He had a theatricality that was as false and yet as real as the theatricality of Mexico itself.

Outside the window, an Indito paused to admire the flowers. Here were the two sides of Mexico's golden coin: the stolid earthen creature, and the quicksilver figure; the reality and the romance, the humility and the arrogance. Then the Indito walked on, and the picture dissolved into the pleasant view of distant mountains.

"That one who stopped," Joaquín was saying, "he lacked the hands. In the old days when I used to come up here before the trumpets of the Revolution sounded, I used to look at their hands. Because it would show, I think, in the hands. They are the mark of the family Castillo." He spread out his own narrow palms, with the little finger almost as long as the third, and gazed at them speculatively. "Have you ever noticed how much alike are all the Castillo hands? The next time you come to the house, look at the ancestral paintings. The faces are different, but the hands are all the same."

Bob extended his own narrow hand. "It means nothing. I have them, and I am certainly not a Castillo."

Joaquín nodded. "I know. I noticed them the day of María's funeral. I have always been very conscious of hands, ever since I read the Fausto diaries when I was nine years old." He settled himself more comfortably on the window seat and grinned reminiscently. "My father had gone to Torreón, and my mother, who was a lovely lady, permitted me to play in the library. It was a secret occasion, for my father was very strict about the books. Hidden at the back of a shelf, I found the Fausto diaries. They were written in that elegant script young gentlemen affected in 1845. In them he told how his elder sister Isabela had been kidnapped by the Huachichil Indians, and in her pride had suicided herself. But my mother and I amused ourselves with the romantic tale that she had not really died, but had married an Indian, and that the real heir to the Castillo land lives, unknown and unknowing, in one of these caves. For by Castillo custom, the inheritance passes through the eldest child, regardless of sex. It was our secret story, for my father would have been very angry to learn that we could imagine that a Castillo would mate with an Indian." He leaned forward and watched three small boys playing leapfrog dangerously near the mesa edge. "After my mother was kil—

after she died, the secret was mine alone. I've never told anyone." He shrugged and relaxed against the casement, and the mockery came back into his eyes. "You are too good a listener. You make me talk too much."

There was a little space of silence. One phrase from Joaquín's speech had captured Bob's attention: "After my mother was killed," for surely the word he had almost said was "killed." What had he meant by that? Everyone in the valley, from Tía Magdalena to Alejandro had always said that Doña Elvira de Castillo had died in childbirth when Alejandro was born. Mysteries again, Bob thought. For a town that fed on gossip, Hidalgo had its roots embedded in mystery. He thought briefly of the Widow Valdez encased in her silent house; of Lolita, wife of the candy-maker, who had once in idle conversation corrected Alejandro's description of a chuch in Madrid, and then quickly, with a frightened glance at her husband, had changed the subject; and Alejandro's widow, Evita, who had begged Don Saturnino to give her enough money to live in Mexico City so that she could escape ghost laughter in her house. So many mysteries, thought Bob, and Joaquín the greatest mystery of all, even more mysterious now that he had opened a gate in the wall of reserve behind which he existed.

"Of course," said Joaquín dreamily, "this Castillo heiress doubt-less suicided herself. She must have been very proud, for the Castillos have the disease of pride. But if she did condescend to mate with an Indito, the child must have been illegitimate, and therefore, under the law, I am the true Castillo. You see how easily one argues oneself out of the improbable?"

"Mexican logic," Bob said lazily, "is always founded on the illogical."

"Precisely. You have the observant mind. But you seek too much to the roots of things. Me, I prefer the unreal. Many nights I have sat at my window and stared down the dark and silent streets of a strange town. Sometimes a lantern would move along through the darkness—nothing else visible, only the lantern—not the hand that carried it, nor the body that propelled it, but the circlet of light only. And it was for this I waited, because the mystery charmed me. Where did it come from, where did it go, this strange man-fashioned—and held—firefly? A shout of greet-ing would give me the answer, but I never shouted. The gleaming phantom was too moth-delicate to be disturbed by knowledge."

The beautiful voice possessed an almost wistful quality. For the first time Bob found himself attracted to this man who was in himself so much like a firefly floating mysteriously in darkness. Then he glanced up and saw Joaquín's eyes, and for a moment hated him with elemental fury, because the eyes belied the words. The eyes with their mocking laughter seemed to say, "You see how easy it is? I can make you like me in spite of your dislike if it pleases me. And because of this I am stronger than you."

Bob rose and said brutally, "It's obvious I'll get no work done today if I stay here; so I'm going back to town. Are you coming with me, or do you prefer to stay here at the quarry and hunt for your cousin?"

Joaquín came to his feet with a dancer's ease. "By all means let us return to town. After all, I came up to fetch you to the magnificence of the jail telephone."

Bob shut the office door and locked it. "What are you talking about?"

"A phone call came for you this morning to the delight of the village, especially as the voice was a woman's—and speaking Spanish. Don Nacho was himself going to come and tell you, but I offered to be the messenger. In my soul is a desire for good works."

Bob quickly saddled his white horse, his mind in a turmoil. "A woman—speaking Spanish?"

"A Tejano Spanish. At the moment Tía Magdalena is doubtless casting spells to protect you from foreign witches."

Bob thought excitedly, a Tejano accent! It can't be, and yet...

Joaquín said lazily, "I like that horse. If my heart were not with the Castillo blacks, I might be tempted to dare the ghost of *El Caballo Blanco*, and ride a white animal also. Did you know that during viceregal days horses were for gentlemen only? The mulatto rode a mule and the Indian a donkey. Only by royal seal was a mestizo allowed to mount a horse."

Bob pulled in the reins so quickly that *El Blanco* reared in protest. "What do you mean by that?" His sharp voice cut the air like a whip.

Joaquín turned a puzzled face toward him. "Nothing. It was only a bit of Mexican folklore, like the proverb: When I am mounted on my horse only God is taller than I. What did you think I meant?"

"I—it was a foolishness that occurred to me."

"You are a strange person," Joaquín commented, spurring his black to trot in rhythm with the white. Since both were lead horses, they had a tendency to pull away from each other, and it was only by excellent horsemanship that both men kept the animals side by side. "Very mysterious."

Bob laughed harshly. "From the mysterious Joaquín Castillo, these are amusing words. Shall we race to the village?"

"A bottle of French cognac to the one who reaches the *Gallineros* first," Joaquín agreed enthusiastically.

Both bent across their pommels, standing almost erect in the long stirrups in the Mexican fashion. Joaquín, with a shout, tossed his hat back so that it dangled between his shoulders by the silver twisted neck cord. With the shout for signal, the two horses leaped forward, black legs and white rebelling against the spurs that urged them down the mountain trail. The descent kept them close together, neither gaining, until they reached the flat valley land, and then Joaquín, with another shout, the battle shout of his house, "St. James and Castillo!" put his hand on his horse's arched neck. It was as though the mercurial spirit of the man passed into the animal, and the two swept beyond Bob to pull to a halt at the cactus-enclosed *Gallineros*. As Bob rode up, Joaquín cried out, his face brilliant with laughter, "Not for all the silver in Mexican earth would I surrender one of my blacks!"

Bob shrugged lightly. "I owe you a bottle of cognac. I should have known better than to wager at all. When I first got this horse the young Xavier warned me, 'Never race him. White horses have the heart but not the endurance.'"

"But in spite of the warning, you raced him. The lady on the telephone must be very lovely."

"If she's the person I think she is, she has a fat chunky body and a too wide mouth. At least she did the last time I saw her."

"And when was that?"

"Ten—no—is it possible, seventeen years ago. You have, perhaps, a proverb for the passage of time?"

"Nothing but the reminder that old houses always leak."

"And that means?"

"The older a man grows, the less wise he is."

"You're trying to say something, Joaquín. What is it?"

"Words, friend, flung on the breeze, signifying nothing. And there is the mayor's office with the telephone encased in its grandeur, like a rare jewel set in a saint's crown."

The telephone was very new to Hidalgo. It had been installed three months before at the suggestion of Joaquín, and the towns-people had not yet become used to the idea of standing in the village and speaking to someone standing in Monterrey. Some of them, including Don Nacho, were privately convinced that it was under the patronage of Grandfather Devil. Since it was in the mayor's office, he treated it with the greatest formality, carefully removing his hat when he looked at it, and always addressing it in the morning when he came to work, for he felt that if he treated the Devil with respect, the Devil would be less inclined to mischief.

When Bob and Joaquín entered the office, they found Don Nacho, Don Genaro, the civil judge, and Don Ricardo sitting and gazing at it.

"It rang," the one-armed policeman explained gravely. "I was sitting in the patio, and it rang."

"Three times," Don Nacho agreed. "So." He gave a solemn imitation of the ringing, and Don Genaro nodded.

"That is true. After the third ring I came and answered it. These two are not so travelled as I. I have been to Monterrey and Torreón. I understand the instrument."

"A woman's voice spoke through it," volunteered Don Ricardo. "It asked for you, Don Bob, in a woman's voice."

Joaquín chuckled deep in his throat. "Luckily I was standing on the plaza and heard the ringing. I came over and joined the amazement. I even spoke to her. She has a good voice...a bit common but with a singer's tone. She gave me the number you were to call. You have the number, Don Nacho?"

The mayor lifted his hat which had been guarding the scribbled sheet of paper as a trap guards a mouse. Ten years before, Bob would have been convulsed with laughter and at the same time angry at this interest in his private affairs. Now he was as serious as the rest. He realized that this event was of importrance, and would provide conversation not only for the village but for the entire valley for the next six months.

He took the paper, examined it, nodded, and turned to the telephone, which was gaudy with golden oak and a long curved mouthpiece. It was fastened to the wall near the window, and as he gave the preliminary ring on the bell handle to attract central's attention in Monterrey, three little boys playing in the street came running to the window bars. One was Pepe Gonzalez' oldest son, the second belonged to Porfirio's brood, and the third was the small Gitanillo.

"Eh, Don Bob," Pepe's son cried shrilly. "Let me talk, let me talk."

"Let me talk," all three screamed in chorus.

"Away from that window!" yelled Don Ricardo, advancing on them with his face twisted in a ferocious scowl. Instead of running away in fright, they tried to clamber higher on the twisted iron bars, but they, with the men, were silent as Bob began talking to a ghost voice across the humming wires.

"It is English he speaks," Porfirio's son said wisely. "I, too, can speak English. I can say, 'Hello, keed.'"

"Hello, keed," shrieked the small Gitanillo. "Hello, keed. Hello, keed. Listen to me. I am speaking English. Hello, keed!"

Bob put his hand over his ear to shut out the sound. That distant woman's voice was claiming his entire attention. Joaquín grinned in sympathy and strolled toward the window. "Silence, little ones," he said reprovingly, "or I will call Tía Magdalena."

The threat of the witch's presence was more effective than Don Ricardo's police authority, and Bob clearly heard the distant voice saying, "I'll expect you tonight, then, at the Terpsícore." There was the click of the receiver, and the wire hum grew louder. He turned to face the four men.

"We will now discuss the matter," Don Nacho said gravely. "This woman, she wants something?"

Bob nodded, pulling at his lower lip. "I have to go in to Monterrey."

"Impossible," Don Genaro said flatly. "Tomorrow is the twelfth of December."

"That is a great truth," agreed Don Nacho. "And Evita Cantú's youngest sister is to represent the blessed Guadalupe."

"That Evita Cantú," sniffed Don Ricardo, "gone off to Mexico when she should be mourning for Alejandro in her father's home. I do not understand it."

"I'm going to be in the cart with the Guadalupe," screamed the small Gitanillo. "With a sombrero and a sarape, and a maguey plant, and my name will be Mexico. Me, behold me, I am going to be in the cart."

"How can you not be here on the day of Guadalupe?" Porfirio's son asked anxiously. "You are always here, Don Bob."

Bob jerked his head. "I'm sorry, but this is a matter of importance. I have to go to Monterrey."

Joaquín pulled a chair toward him and bestrode it like a horse, his folded arms resting on the back. "One must be practical in these matters. Trains from Monterrey arrive here in the evening. Trains for Monterrey arrive here in the morning. Just how are you planning to make this journey?"

"I've thought of that." Bob's forehead creased in a frown. "It means riding my horse. I'll have to start now. With your permission, Don Nacho . . ." He bowed to the mayor, who rose and also bowed.

"We will miss you at tomorrow's celebrations," the fat mayor said wistfully.

Gitanillo struck his small fist against the iron bar and began to sob loudly, "You won't see me, and I will be so beautiful in the cart."

Bob went to the window and knelt in front of the child. "I will bring you a present from Monterrey. A man on a horse, all woven of palm leaf, or perhaps a small bird hammered from tin."

The child's large black eyes were moist with tears. "Alejandro wouldn't have gone. Alejandro would have stayed to see me." He jumped back from the window and ran blindly down the sun-bright street toward his home.

For a moment no one spoke. The other two children, conscious that something they could not understand had happened in the adult world, retreated to the safety of the plaza. The knuckles on Bob's narrow hands whitened as he convulsively clenched his fists. The men did not look at each other. Bob picked up his hat and went into the street. Through the side window they could see him pass the Casino and go around the corner to his own front door, his shoulders stooped, his feet lagging in the dust.

"I do not understand it," said Don Ricardo. "For Don Bob to

desert us on the twelfth of December, and for a woman. The Blessed Guadalupe will not like it. There will be bad luck in the valley this year, and I was planning to plant barley on my new farm across the river. No need to plant it now. The Guadalupe will not let it grow. 'For this,' she will think, 'I am the patron saint of Mexico? Of what value am I if an earth woman can steal a man of such importance, and on the day sacred to me?' No, the beautiful brown Virgin will not like it."

Don Nacho sighed ponderously. "True words. But he would not go if it were not important. He recognizes his duty to the valley."

"What duty?" Joaquín asked sharply. "Is he the great man of the Sabinas? Does he belong to the House Castillo?"

Don Ricardo and Don Genaro moved closer together. They did not like Joaquín gay, and Joaquín angry they liked even less.

Don Nacho folded his hands over his stomach and examined Joaquín with his small black eyes. "You have been gone too long from the valley. Everyone here recognizes Don Bob as a man of importance. Even the small Gitanillo. Even your father."

Joaquín flinched, and a bitter smile twisted his lips. "It is amusing, is it not, that while a Castillo still lives another man comes to take his place in the Sabinas? And when my father dies, what then? For I shall not leave the valley, Don Nacho. Sixteen years I have lived in exile. Now I am home. These are my mountains and my valley. Here I stay."

"A man cannot live alone," Don Nacho pointed out with cruel bluntness.

As though the words were a catapult, Don Ricardo ran out of the office and across the plaza to the priest's Residence. It was a great decision Don Nacho was making, to send a Castillo from the Sabinas. He needed his counselors beside him.

But in the office Don Ricardo's absence was not noticed. Don Genaro's eyes were turning rapidly from Don Nacho's placid immobility to Joaquín's silver and gray splendor. The young Castillo had turned very white under his tan. When he spoke his beautiful voice thinned to a silky tone.

"But I have lived alone. The Revolutionists fought with me, but they gave me no comradeship. My general could neither read nor write. He distrusted all men who could. But he needed me. I made him need me. And afterwards..." he shrugged, the silver embroidery on his coat contracting, "who will offer friendship to a tourist guide, or to a cowboy in Jalisco, especially when the guide refuses to split commissions, and the cowboy would save his horse at the sacrifice of a fine steer? And later I became an actor. And who, outside of actors speak to actors? I am well versed in the art of living alone, Don Nacho."

Before the old man could answer, the priest came quickly through the door, followed by Don Rosalío and the little Doctor, with Don Ricardo hovering in the doorway. Joaquín looked at all of them, the smile on his lips twisted up at one corner and down at the other.

"So, the four wise men to tell me that a Castillo is no longer necessary. I am to abdicate, perhaps? And name my successor? Or will you name him? It seems strange, a *Yanqui* name in the Sabinas. Don Bob Webster. No, it lacks the music of the name Castillo. But then Bob's mother was undoubtedly Mexican. It shows in the shape of the cheekbones, and the long slant of the eyes, and the texture of skin and hair. Perhaps he will agree to take her name. Symbolically it should be very common: Lozano, or Gonzalez, or García. A good strong common name from good strong common stock. No more of lordly Castillo."

"You are drunk, Joaquín." Don Rosalío passed his hand agitatedly over his white beard.

"Naturally. Drunk on family pride... the famous Castillo pride. Have you ever noticed that Bob's hands and mine are very much alike? You have, little Doctor, you mentioned them to me once. Beware of the long narrow hands. They hold pride as a man holds a woman. And Bob is proud. He will not enjoy a report of this little scene. For weeks he has been fighting against it. He knows that my father recognizes his overlordship. Is that a surprise to you, my wise old ones? Ay, yes, this very morning my father said in effect, 'When I die, to you, Don Bob, comes the Castillo estate. Joaquín is but a feather tossed on the wind. Joaquín is without judgment.' If my father were a lover of proverbs like myself he might say, 'I will light a candle to the saint who deserves it.'"

The priest said sorrowfully, "This is a terrible thing that has happened, Joaquín."

"Why? Is the darkness of the hidden cave worse than the brilliance of the open sunlight? For nine months the words that

I am saying have been a foetus in the village womb. The moment of birth has come. And birth is always painful."

"So many words," the little Doctor snapped. "What do they mean?"

Joaquín laughed harshly. "A simple truth that none of you have recognized. Again I give you the proverb, 'Ranch violin, I've caught you a professor,' which means that in necessity, a man's true worth appears."

"And what is your true worth?" Don Rosalío asked, one eyebrow raised in distaste.

"Not mine, Don Rosalío. Bob's. He told me this morning he was leaving the valley. So you see, it is the pretender who abdicates. And he begins by not appearing tomorrow afternoon for the Guadalupe feast."

The little Doctor, Don Rosalío, and the priest stared at Don Nacho, who ponderously nodded. The civil judge said quickly, "He had a telephone call. He says he must go in to Monterrey."

"But how?" Father Zacaya asked blankly. "There are no trains."

"Thank you for reminding me, Father." Joaquín went to the telephone and rang a number. He said over his shoulder, "At least I have the power of my name left to me. That is, I suppose, a consolation." A voice spoke over the wire, and Joaquín gave rapid orders for a special engine and one pullman car to be in Hidalgo that afternoon. "And have it ready in the morning. It must bring someone back to the village." He hung up and rested his forehead for a moment against the curved mouthpiece. "You see, I am generous. He will be back in time to applaud the small Gitanillo, and take his place in Alejandro's shadow beside my father. I will be even more generous. I will remove myself so that the Guadalupe will not be disturbed by my presence. I can afford to be generous. He is going away. He recognizes what you do not: that I am the Castillo. And so ends the Revolution, with no shots fired, and no dead on either side."

He tilted his gray felt sombrero over his left eye, gave the *charro's* characteristic stamp with his foot so that the silver spur lisped delicate sound, made them a deep bow, and, smiling, passed from the office. Once outside, the smile vanished, and a mask of pain clamped down on his face. He could hear Don Nacho say, "You Ricardo, and you, Genaro, this is a private matter and not to be gossiped in the town. Do you understand?"

Accompanied by their murmuring assent, Joaquín crossed the street to the Casino. Pepe Gonzalez and Andrés Treviño were drinking their pre-noon *mescalitos* in the bar. They glanced up and saw him, nodded with politeness but no friendliness, and continued their private conversation. Joaquín went into the deserted patio, stepped on a round tub holding a dwarf orange tree, caught hold of the wall top and pulled himself upward, gave a twist to his body, and dropped down on the other side in front of Tía Magdalena's kitchen door. The wall's yellow lime dust powdered his gray suit, and he absent-mindedly brushed himself off as he removed his hat and went into the kitchen.

Tía was crouched in front of the brasier, blowing on the coals, and paid him no attention as he picked up a bellows and added its air to her efforts. When the coals were redly glowing, she said, "The bellows are quicker, but the wind in my lungs is still strong. Are you hungry?"

"No."

He watched her go to the scoured table and set it with a fork and a glass. She ladled fat red beans from the simmering pot into a soup plate, covered them with chile sauce, and pulled some *tortillas* from the hot ashes, examined them critically, blew the ashes from their paper-thin sides, and put them on a small plate. Then she poured coffee and hot milk into a cup, liberally sweetened it with sugar, and beckoned him to the table.

He said, "I told you I wasn't hungry."

"You're always hungry," she told him tartly. "When you were a little boy you were always whining, 'Tía, I'm hungry.' And I notice that you always come to the kitchen now."

"I come to see you," he said, but he sat down and began to eat. She went back to the brasier and crouched on the floor to watch the coals.

"He's going to Monterrey," she said after a while. "On a horse. And tomorrow the twelfth of December."

"I ordered a special train for him. He'll be back tomorrow."

"He is a good man," she said. "Stupid, like my dead son Gregorio, but a good man. He looks like Gregorio, not so?"

"You've said that every time I've come here. It's all right. I'm glad you work for him."

She rested her face against her bent knees. "You understand,

when I came to work here I did not know you would return to
the Sabinas. In all your letters you never said you were coming
back."

"I should not have returned, Tía. My father is still alive. I
never meant to stay. But sixteen years is a long time, and the
mountains were calling me."

> *How far am I from the land where I was born,* [she quoted]
> *An immense nostalgia invades my memory.*
> *And to find me so far and alone like a vagrant leaf on the*
>   *breeze,*
> *It makes me to cry, it makes me to die, of loneliness.*

"Not only in the song, Tía, but in the heart also."

"Does that old man speak to you at all?" she asked curiously.

"In front of the servants, a great politeness. Alone no. After
that first night of grief, nothing. He has pride."

"And so have you. Too much, I think. If you had less, you
would leave the valley."

"Would you come with me, Tía?"

"Naturally."

"And what of Don Bob?"

She rubbed her veined hand over her bony knee. "Don Bob is
like my Gregorio. He is a sweetness to me. But you are the child
of my heart, Joaquín."

"That is not the thought in your mind, Tía."

"You are like Chela Villareal. You see too clearly."

"Tell me what is in your mind, Tía. I am very humble at
present."

"Humility is good in the young. I will tell you. Don Bob has
a strength in him, an Indian strength. But you are in spirit like
the eagles floating between the crags. They hover without effort;
they dip toward the earth, seldom touching it; and when they
do, it is but to rest a brief moment. They skim over it to snatch
their prey, and then mount again into the air."

He smiled at her. No one save Chela would have recognized
the gentleness in him. "And you are the prey I so poetically
snatch?"

"No, Joaquinito. Even eagles must come to rest on the crags.
They need the security of the stone. I am the stone against which
you may rest." She went to him, took his head in her arms and

pressed it against her thin body. She could feel the grief shaking him, "Eh, my little one," she whispered, "your blessed mother who is now with the saints said to me when she lay dying, 'This new baby belongs to his father, but my Joaquinito will be an orphan now that I am gone.' And I said to her, 'He will be my child, and I his mother.'"

Joaquín's voice, muffled, came to her. "He killed her. I heard the doctor tell him, 'If she has another child, she will die,' and he answered, 'One Castillo heir is not enough. There must be two.' I heard him say it."

"Quiet, my little one," the old woman keened softly. "That is an ancient pain—too ancient for such present grief."

"And he killed Alejandro, too, with his own arrogant power. He drove Alejandro into marriage with that devil of an Evita Cantú. And Alejandro loved him. When he spoke, Alejandro's face would have such a light on it. Even at ten years old, such a light. And now Alejandro is dead and my father killed him, as he killed my mother, with coldness and contempt, and the duty of the Castillo name."

"He is your father," Tía murmured. "Such hatred is not good to hold against your father."

"Is it not?" Joaquín pulled away from her and rested his arms on the table, his face cold and set. "Everything I have ever loved, he has destroyed. Even you he has tried to banish from the valley as he once banished me. And now that I have disobeyed him and come home, he so carefully convinces the Sabinas that I am of little worth. He would rather have Don Bob as the Castillo heir. To Don Bob he is a wise and gracious man. Bob, in the shadow of Alejandro, believes that pretty legend. But I know better. He does not like to see his portrait in my eyes. It is not a pretty portrait."

"Nor in my eyes," said Tía thoughtfully. She laughed suddenly, the sound hoarse and old. "There are always ways to fight, Joaquinito. There are always ways."

"Not for me. Not any more." He walked to the brasier and poked at the glowing coals with a stick of charcoal. "My father has won. Don Nacho and his three friends have just informed me that the Sabinas would be happier for my absence."

"So? And what did you tell them?"

"Pride put the words in my mouth. I had much oratory. I told them they could not drive me out, and they said they would ostracize me. I can pull in my tail like a coward and run away, or ..."

"I will go into the mountains tonight and consult the Sleeping Ones," Tía said thoughtfully. "You will do nothing until you hear from me."

"No, Tía, this is my own ..."

"Quiet." She held up her hand as Bob's voice called from his bedroom at the front of the house.

"Tía, when Don Fidencio brings my horse, have him take it to Don Saturnino's. I have to go up there on a matter of business."

"Don't let him know I'm here," Joaquín whispered.

"Do I ever?" she retorted sharply. She went into the patio, and stood by the tiled lily pool that had replaced the old well.

"What need of a horse, Don Bob? Don Joaquín ordered a special train for you."

"What do you tell me?" Bob came out of his door and stared at her in astonishment.

"Naturally. The village feels the need of you tomorrow. You feel the need of going to Monterrey today. A special train was the only solution."

"But why the devil would Joaquín do a thing like that for me? A special train costs money."

"The disappointment of the village is important to a Castillo."

He tugged restlessly at his hair. "You know, Tía, I don't understand Joaquín."

"Stop pulling your hair. Do you want to grow bald as the carrion vulture? And naturally you do not understand Joaquín. How could you? And his mother twenty years dead when you came to the valley. Go now to Don Saturnino's and let him speak to you of Doña Elvira. It is an interesting story."

When Bob saw her mouth close into a thin line, he knew that she had nothing more to say to him. He shook his head, started to tug at his hair again, saw her narrowed eyes watching him, dropped his hand to his side with an embarrassed snort, and quickly left.

It was a very short distance along the curving Street of the Forgotten Angel to the Castillo gates, and Bob was soon crossing the mosaic courtyard to the front door. A servant opened it, and led him into the library, the thick walls shutting out the sun's warmth so that blazing logs were necessary in the large stone fireplace.

The book-lined walls with portraits of dead Castillos in the separation panels attracted Bob's attention as they always did. He noticed that Alejandro's portrait, done on his last visit to Madrid, had been added to the collection. While Bob waited for Don Saturnino, he examined it. It showed Alejandro in formal court dress with the maltese cross crowned with grama-grass pinned over his left breast—the hereditary decoration of conquest given to the Castillo family by Philip II of Spain—his hand resting on a carved table, behind him dark green velvet drapes. It was very stiff, very Spanish, and utterly unlike the true Alejandro in his dusty riding clothes and red neck-handkerchief. The nervous hands were still, there was no laughter in the brown eyes, the mouth was set and proud. Bob shook his head and turned away, and then he saw it, with its splashing primitive colors and rich illusion of sunlight, hanging isolated from the other portraits near the great stone fireplace. María, thought Bob. María. María.

He heard Don Saturnino's cane tapping on the red-tiled floor, and he turned as the thin, stooped old man came into the room. "You've moved her from the ranch," he said slowly.

The old man nodded. "She was lonely out there," he said childishly, "and this room needs her warmth." He looked around him at the portraits. "All of them stiff and cold—as stiff and cold as death." He shivered and came closer to the fire.

Bob said, "Only two women in all this room of men." He moved over and stared at the portrait of a woman in the low-bosomed dress and Spanish comb with fringed *mantilla* in the fashion of 1840. "Who is this? Alejandro told me once, but I've forgotten."

"Isabela Castillo. She was kidnapped by the Huachichil Indians and committed suicide before my grandfather, her brother, could rescue her. She was the oldest child. If she had lived and married, her grandson would be in this house instead of myself. It is an amusing turn of fate, no? I sometimes speculate on the personality of that unborn child—an amusement perhaps too Spanish for you to understand."

"I know what you mean," Bob said slowly, remembering how many times he had visioned what his own life would have been had his natural father admitted his existence. No Ireland, no

Morocco, and certainly no Mexico. He would never have come to this valley. He would never had encountered the sweet pain of María. His eyes went back to the portrait over the mantel, and her golden beauty flowed into his veins. You were worth it, he thought. You were worth all of it, my beautiful. He knew that Don Saturnino was watching him and he said quickly, "I would like to ask a favor of you. I have never seen a portrait of Alejandro's mother."

A change came into the old man's chiseled face. It turned cold and hard, but when he spoke his voice was polite. "There is only one. It hangs in Joaquín's room. I will have a servant show you, as stairs are difficult for me." He moved to the bell cord with its heavy gold tassel and tugged at it. From the back of the house Bob could hear the faint answering chime.

Don Saturnino lowered himself to the sofa in front of the fire-place. "I am much displeased, my son. Don Nacho sent me word that you are planning to leave the valley."

Bob was no longer conscious of any amazement at this quick circulation of news. "That is true. I have been here ten years. The world calls me."

The old man shook his head. "I do not want you to go."

"But, Don Saturnino . . ."

"I have few years left to me. You are all that remains to me of Alejandro, for there is nothing of Alejandro in Joaquín, but much in you." A servant entered, and Don Saturnino's voice changed to casual indifference. "I should like you to consider my request. Primitivo, conduct Don Bob to Don Joaquín's room to view the portrait of Doña Elvira."

The servant, his white house-clothes a sharp contrast to his brown skin, stepped back on noiseless feet and led Bob up the curving stone hall stairs, the runners hollowed with generations of mounting feet. In the upper hall as they passed Alejandro's closed door, Bob was tempted to stop a moment and open it. The room was shrouded in dust. It was obviously just as Alejandro had left it when he moved into his marriage house. The wide bed of gilded wrought iron brought from Venice stood on its own platform under a canopy of white silk net to ward off mosquitoes; the lacquered highboy from China with its design of scarlet and gold; the feather-soft sofa upholstered in white velvet, with the worn place on one arm where Alejandro's too-long legs had rested; and the continuous frame around the wall filled with photographs that Alejandro had taken in Europe, in the Orient, in the States. The room had a feminine quality about it, although Alejandro had lacked any trace of femininity.

"Tell me," Bob abruptly asked, "before Don Alejandro was born, was this Doña Elvira's room?"

"That is true," the man agreed politely. "The bed was hers, and the sofa. The chest was in a room downstairs. The story is that it was brought from China to Acapulco in the days of the China trade as a present from her father to Doña Isabela Castillo." He added the usual refrain, "That is the story. I do not know it for true."

Bob nodded and gently shut the door. They went on to Joaquín's room. The servant knocked with a sideways glance at Bob. "Don Joaquín seldom comes through the house. He uses the outside stairs." Hearing no answer, he opened the door, and Bob entered.

There was no trace here of feminine occupation. The gaudy brilliance of Joaquín was not reflected in his bedroom. The floor was red tile, the walls and ceiling white. There were no curtains at the deeply recessed windows. The bed was a narrow cot covered with a striped Saltillo blanket, and one thin pillow in a plain case. Near the bookcase was a heavy brown leather chair with a hassock for the feet and a table holding an oil lamp which might have been found in any poor *Gallineros* hut. Bob bent forward to look at the books. Most of them were paper bound. A few were bound in leather. They had all obviously been read a good deal. There were volumes on the care and training of horses, orange tree culture, and goat raising. A few were German and French, the rest, English and Spanish. Bob bit down on his lower lip. The books were suddenly pathetic to him, as though Joaquín had prepared himself for a career that no one would allow him to follow.

The servant said gravely, "The portrait is on that wall, Don Bob."

He turned. It reached from ceiling to floor. In front of it was a very low table holding a bowl of December roses and a gold and blue vigilance lamp in which a wick burned with a flickering flame. Bob was only vaguely aware of these things because the portrait claimed his entire attention. The woman had soft white arms and a long throat emerging from a pink brocaded gown, the train swirling around her pink-shod feet, and near them a sheaf of roses. The face beneath the soft bangs and curls of her dark hair lacked strength, but it was imbued with a delicate shy sweetness, with kindness and sympathy in the dark eyes. Bone molding and mouth cut she had passed on to Alejandro, but the eyes behind the shadow of thick black lashes she had given to Joaquín. She was not a beautiful woman, but she was a lovely lady, and Bob turned away from the portrait with a sense of embarrassment; he felt that he had entered a secret world which belonged entirely to the Castillos, and in which he had no part. He walked slowly down the stairs and into the library.

Don Saturnino was still seated in front of the fireplace. "You have a solemnity, my son."

"She has a quality . . ."

"I know. She was an angel, too delicate for our world." The old man sighed. "She gave this house two sons." His veined hands were crossed on the head of his cane. He rested his chin on them and stared into the fire. "For her that was enough. But it was not enough. There should have been three, for with Alejandro dead who will carry on the Castillo line?"

"Joaquín is still a young man. He will doubtless marry . . ."

"No!" The word was explosive in the quiet room. "No marriage could hold Joaquín. Before the—the Great Revolution, I arranged a suitable marriage for him with one of our Spanish cousins. True, she was not beautiful, but the alliance was most suitable and would have brought the Spanish property into this branch of the family. But Joaquín saw fit to disregard my wishes. He lacked the dutiful spirit of Alejandro. What a pity that Alejandro left no son."

Bob felt a sudden resentment against Don Saturnino. He remembered Evita's cold and selfish face, her shrewish voice. If the Spanish cousin were anything like Evita, Joaquín had been right not to involve himself.

This long room with its portraits pressed in on Bob. For a moment he glimpsed from the corner of his eye the picture of Isabela, who had suicided herself rather than mate with an Indian. They have the pride of kings, he thought. They mate to produce children. Their ethics is based on duty to the family. And Don Saturnino cannot understand that there is no place for a Castillo tradition in this modern world. He and Joaquín are fighting their private revolution and because neither will surrender, Don Saturnino prefers to form an alliance with a foreigner rather than admit defeat. For all his Spanish pride, he is now being truly Mexican. Here is a microcosmic bit of Mexican history being played out in terms of family rather than of nation. By begging me to stay here and help him he is merely repeating the monarchist's appeal to Austria's Maximilian to protect them from the liberal Juarez. And Yucatán's appeal for annexation to the United States as protection against the armies of Santa Ana. Maximilian accepted and was shot for his generosity. Buchanan had sense enough to refuse Yucatán. And if I have any sense, I'll refuse, too.

Bob looked at the old man: at the white hair, the thin face, the grief circles under the eyes, and his heart turned in him. Weakness and age were in Don Saturnino; youth and strength in Joaquín. Bob had to shake himself physically to keep from blurting out, "I'll stay as long as you need me." He said gently, "I must go now. I merely came to tell you that in the matter of the Rancho Santo Tomás . . ."

"Yes, I know. I see it in your eyes. You think the decision should rest with Joaquín."

"He knows more of horses than I, Don Saturnino."

"But you know the ranch, Bob. You know what Alejandro wanted."

Bob felt impelled to say, "But the ranch is Joaquín's now. Alejandro is dead." His own loyalty to Alejandro made him say, "I'll be glad to tell Joaquín the things he should know."

"He will not listen," sighed Don Saturnino. "Joaquín has the stubbornness of his own ignorance. What can an—actor—know of horses?"

"He lived with the Castillo blacks long before he was an actor, Don Saturnino. And now I must really go."

He went to the old man and rested his palm on the bent shoulder. When Don Saturnino extended his hand Bob impulsively kissed it with Alejandro's gesture.

Don Saturnino said slowly, "A third son. You have the Castillo hands. Perhaps it is an omen. You believe in omens, Roberto?"

Hearing his name spoken in Spanish for the first time since his mother's death had a profound effect upon Bob. It was as though at last he had come into his inheritance, as though he had found for himself a fixed position. A sense of security came into him, and he knew that he would never again be sensitive to gibes or insults. This release brought laughter into him, and he said lightly, "I live with omens. Do I not have an eagle witch for a housekeeper?"

Again that expression of repressed hardness veiled the old man's face. "I had forgotten," he said politely, and Bob, remembering the secret feud, confusedly made his farewells and went out of the house.

In the courtyard he paused and looked up at the sky. It held that December blueness with the distant mountains like flakes of gray flint sharp against it. Slowly he became aware of a resonant voice reading aloud. He went around the corner of the house to the side terrace. Joaquín was sitting in the shadow of an oleander bush, the pink flowers drooping around his head, his feet resting on the tiled ledge of the low pool, reading aloud to an intent Gitanillo.

"'For governors of the Plaza, there were chosen the Marqués del Valle de Oaxaca—'"

"That was Hernán Cortés," Gitanillo interrupted excitedly. He was sitting on the edge of the pool, his elbows resting on his knees, his chin on his closed fists, and he was gazing at Joaquín with a delighted interest.

"True," Joaquín agreed politely, and without condescension to Gitanillo's six years, "but in 1618 Oaxaca was the son not the conqueror. 'And,'" he continued reading, "'many counts and captains, to whom were awarded the golden canes of judgeship. Near the gates was erected a magnificent box, richly adorned, to be occupied by the Viceroy and his lady, the Archbishop, and the lords of the Inquisition. For the occasion one hundred bulls were purchased...'"

Bob walked softly away without disturbing them, the music of Joaquín's rich tones floating after him.

When Bob reached the station to go to Monterrey, he found the entire town assembled. A special train was an event such as Hidalgo had never before known, and even Tía Magdalena had condescended to come and view the spectacle. Don Alonso was there with his orchestra, and the musicians were happily playing the *Golondrina*. Pepe Gonzalez was singing the nostalgic words in his pleasant tenor:

> *Where does it so swiftly fly,*
> *The swallow that leaves this place?*
> *Ay, if it should tire,*
> *Hunting a cloak of safety*
> *That it cannot discover.*
> *Close to my couch I shall build a nest*
> *Where it may find refuge.*
> *I, too, am in the far lost land.*
> *Oh, Sainted Heaven, if I but had wings!*

Lined up near the pullman were Hilario, the Indito from the quarry, and his four children. They looked strangely grotesque to Bob until he realized that Hilario's shirt and the children's clothes were all stitched from the same bolt of yellow calico decorated with little pink daisies. They were grinning and bobbing small bows to him, and he gravely returned their salutations.

Most of the people were intent on the train rather than on Bob. Children were swarming over the engine, and Rubén, the candy-maker, Andrés Treviño, and Porfirio were inside the pullman car, sitting in all the seats to test their softness, heedless of the porter's frantic protests that their clothing would stain the beautiful green upholstery.

Bob, who had not been home, recognized the moment he saw her that Tía was angry about something. Her eyes were blazing, her lips were set, and her arms were folded across her thin chest. He wondered what event had called forth her wrath as he walked toward her, and he quickly tried to count over in his mind his own past sins, but he could discover nothing at all except innocence.

"Creature without a heart," Tía snapped in a loud whisper. "And Candelaria weeping in the kitchen."

"Candelaria?" Bob asked blankly. "What's wrong with her? She was all right this morning."

"Such blandness. If you lack affection, you might at least have gratitude. Candelaria is molded from kindness."

Bob ran his fingers dazedly through his hair. "What are you talking about, Tía?"

"Ha! And you as innocent as seven small angels fresh from the fingers of God! Four children! May Grandfather Devil have mercy on you when you go to dance on his tail!"

Before Bob could ask her what she meant, the conductor came up to him, a strained expression on his face. "If you please, señor. If we do not start, these people will leave nothing of the train to take us into Monterrey."

"Yes, of course. Tía, keep your riddles until tomorrow."

"Riddle, is it? And tomorrow the day of the Blessed Guadalupe, and you with such a sin on your conscience."

Bob swung himself up the pullman steps. Rubén, Andrés, and Porfirio embraced him, expressing the fervent hope that he would not be so comfortable that he would forget to descend in Monterrey. They leaped to the ground.

The orchestra, tiring of the *Golondrina*, split into two sections, one half playing a sad ballad of an illegitimate child to whom no one would speak because of his misfortune, and the other half concentrating on "My Blue Heaven." There were squeals from the front as children were brushed off the train, the engineer added his whistle to the bedlam, the wheels started to turn, and people began to shriek farewells, with the admonition to return by three the next afternoon in time for the Guadalupe dances.

Bob grinned through the window and waved his hand, with a special salute for Don Nacho.

Hilario and his four children, still arranged in a straight line, clutched their various sombreros against their pink-dotted yellow stomachs and bowed in quick, regular succession. Tía continued to stand rigidly like a small walnut figure of artistic anger. Bob, with the guilty feeling of the truly innocent, hastily turned to the opposite window. The open fields were rosy in the light of the setting sun. Joaquín, the small Gitanillo on the pommel in front of him, was a gray wax image on a black wax horse. Then Gitanillo glimpsed Bob's face and began enthusiastically to wave one small pink-shirted arm. Joaquín touched his horse's leg with his whip, and the glossy animal bent one knee in a graceful curtsey. Bob waved at them as the train swung around a curve and into a double line of earthen walls, blotting them from view.

The porter sighed with relief and took a pack of cards from his pocket. "If it would amuse you to play *Tresillo*, señor? The conductor plays and also the brakeman. It is two hours to Monterrey," he added suggestively.

Bob shrugged. The conductor and brakeman were summoned, and they settled down to the classic game which, like chess, has its traditional plays and its own maxims.

The conductor intoned one of the proverbs as he shuffled the cards, "He who wins riches can also win poverty."

"Calculate what you say or calculate what you pay," the porter said promptly.

The brakeman shrugged, pursed his lips and thought a moment. At last he produced, "Knowing when to pass is knowing when to play."

They all looked at Bob, who shut his eyes and concentrated intently, for a player was not permitted to repeat a proverb. His memory finally gave him, "The valiant are good warriors, the daring, good card players."

The three train men nodded contentedly, for by the proverb the player is known. *Tresillo* is not a game, it is a passion. Experts will not tolerate the amateur, and only the expert knows the proverbs which are passed like precious jewels from one player to another.

Bob picked up the cards and looked at his hand. The designs had confused him when Pepe Gonzalez first taught him the game ten years before: the rosy cups, the golden coins stamped with a woman's head, the blue daggers, and the pink and green clubs, the king, the man on horseback, and the medieval page. But they were so familiar to him now that an English deck would have looked strange to him.

The stakes were posted, and the game continued with its usual slow thoroughness. He lost more than he won, for these men could really play, and he had no time to worry about Tía's anger over Candelaria and the strange matter of the four children.

Candelaria had always been a quietly closed chapter in his life. All the Sabinas knew that she was his mistress, and he was much admired and she congratulated for his constancy to her. At first he had been in love with her. He found in her a refuge for his bruised spirit. But as time passed, the love changed to affection, and her peaceful quality rested but did not excite him. For a long time he wondered if it were possible for him to love any woman deeply. And then Alejandro introduced him to María. His desire for her was so great that many a night he had fled to Candelaria in a desperate effort to wash the golden wine from his heart. He had never been successful, but Candelaria had become even more of a refuge. He could not conceive of life without her, nor did he ever try. She was as much a part of his existence as Tía's motherly scoldings, and the sweeping valley view from his office window. In his decision to leave the valley, he had not taken into consideration what his life would be like cut off from the two women who had so completely molded his placid existence. And because of this, Tía's anger made little impression on him. The old woman was always becoming indignant over something. It so happened that this time the subject was Candelaria. Bob was not impressed. He played his cards and dropped his money in the betting dish with no thought save for the game and the exciting evening that awaited him.

When the train pulled in to the Monterrey station, he made arrangements for his return to Hidalgo the next morning, and went out to take a taxi. Automobiles were waiting but he preferred a fringed surrey. Cars and traffic made him nervous. He always travelled behind horses when he could.

The driver flicked his long whip and they rattled over the brick-paved narrow streets walled with porchless houses. The man twisted around in his seat. "To the Ancira?" he suggested. "There is a new hotel, the Colonial, very Spanish, but the Ancira has now blue tiles in the lobby and is very grand."

Bob grinned. "Do you think me a tourist, friend? To the Hotel García. And how much commission does the Ancira pay you?"

The driver laughed, and launched into a history of his life. By the time they arrived at the hotel, he had reached his fifteenth year, and was already a hero from saving many lives in the great Monterrey flood of 1909. He trotted after Bob into the green-tiled lobby, and was just starting to fight in the Great Revolution, "I was with Carranza, me," when Bob signed the register. The clerk had been one of Obregón's men; so the driver was not received with pleasantness. They were still arguing as a bellboy took Bob to his room. Bob thoughtfully examined the boy's pleasant face. "You were doubtless too young to fight in the Revolution?"

"My father was a great hero," the boy said enthusiastically. "He was from the South, you understand, and followed Zapata. These frontier men with their grand talk of their generals! With

Zapata there is no need of speech. One has only to speak the name, and all must bow in reverence."

When Bob said nothing the boy added anxiously. "Forgive me, señor. You are a frontier man? I am sure that your general must have been very grand."

Bob laughed and tossed him a peso. "Drink a *mescalito* to the fine memory of the great Zapata."

The boy clicked his tongue with delight and bowed himself out. The grand generals, Bob thought with amusement. How consumed Mexico is with its own history. All its paintings, its sculpture, its literature born from its history. He pulled a new novel from his bag and looked at the title: *The Shade of the Commander*, by Martín Luís Guzmán, and read the first paragraph:

"The cadillac of General Ignacio Aguirre crossed the streetcar tracks on the Avenue of Chapultepec and came to a stop a short distance from the headquarters of the Insurgents ..."

He shut it with a snap and tossed it on the bed. Another story born of the Great Revolution. Guzmán had been one of the Intellectuals who had found themselves trapped between their two commanding geniuses: Zapata in the South and Villa in the North. If I had been in Mexico then, Bob wondered, whom would I have followed? The white-bearded Carranza? The one-armed Obregón? The stone-faced Calles? Or would I have been one of Villa's Golden Men? One thing certain, I would never have belonged to the white-clad soldiers of Zapata. The boy was right. I am a frontier man.

He crossed to the window and stared out at the mountains, for in Monterrey a mountain stands at the end of every street. Four years in the Great War, he reflected, and what had he brought from it? No loyalty to a general, no ripe heroic tales. The Great Revolution should have been his war, and he had missed it. It was Joaquín who crawled through Mexican rocks, not Bob Webster.

He looked down at his narrow hands and smiled faintly to himself. Even their hands were alike. Was that why they could find no comradeship, because they were too much alike? More alike than Joaquín and Alejandro. Or than Alejandro and Bob.

These comparisons brought him to the memory of the woman he was to meet that evening. Would there be any resemblance between them, he wondered. When he looked at her would he see himself reproduced in a woman, or had the years between so changed them that it would be like two strangers meeting?

He considered her and his own reactions to her with curiosity. He felt that he should be pleasantly excited, and yet they had been separated for so long that there was no feeling of tenderness, and certainly none of kinship. What was she like, this woman whom he had last seen as a chubby little girl? He had clipped her pictures from newspapers, but publicity photographs were notoriously bad. Her voice on the telephone had been deep and husky, and Joaquín's comment was correct: it did have a common tone. He was, Bob felt, getting to be as caste conscious as a Castillo. Which returned the circle to Joaquín.

What was he to do about Joaquín? He admitted honestly to himself that at moments he liked Joaquín more than anyone he had ever known, and at others disliked him with equal heartiness. Could their warring personalities ever allow them to live peacefully in the valley that Bob had come to love with a strange and possessive tenderness? And if one of them had to leave, why should it be himself? Everyone in the Sabinas, including Don Saturnino, wanted him to stay and Joaquín to go. But Joaquín's fierce Castillo pride would not permit him to go, and Bob admitted ruefully, he himself was the outlander. The Sabinas was Castillo land, and while Joaquín lived there was no room in the valley for Bob Webster. Now that he was in Monterrey he would call Harper Paschal and settle the matter of his resignation as quarry master. The time to do it was now, before Don Saturnino's influence weakened him.

He walked quickly to the room telephone, and was lifting the receiver as a knock came at the door. The bellboy entered with a small bouquet of flowers and a note.

Bob, much puzzled, stared at the flowers: six roses tied against a flat thorny cactus leaf. He ripped open the note addressed in a strange hand. It was headed: "Dictated by telephone from the township of Hidalgo," and signed with Joaquín's name.

"Dear friend," Bob read, "Candelaria has come to me in tears. She desires most urgently to convey a message to you, and although I assured her that you would be home tomorrow, she insisted that there were reasons why you might prefer to stay away for at least a week. She kept repeating, 'He told the creature seven days,' and weeping loudly between each repetition. Candelaria really wanted to write you a letter, but Tía's book on the art of epistolary composition appears to contain only one illustration for correct correspondence between a man and woman, entitled, 'A Soldier to His Sweetheart Notifying Her That He Has Been Sent to the Fourth Artillery Regiment,'—which, according to Candelaria, does not seem exactly to satisfy her need.

"I offered to write a letter for her, but she preferred the more cryptic language of flowers. 'It is,' she explained, 'an affair of privacy.' And so I am ordering the roses and thorny cactus. In case you do not have a flower dictionary with you, I give you the double translation. Ordinarily roses encased in thorns mean, 'I love you in spite of your cruelty.' But in the flower appointment book, they indicate, 'Meet me by the cactus plant at one o'clock.' As you know Candelaria better than I do, I leave the interpretation to your intelligence.

"Personally, I think she heard you went in to Monterrey to meet a woman. Since the flower for jealousy is the red anemone, I may be wrong. But even in tears, Candelaria is extremely beautiful. If you would agree to stay away the seven days, it would enchant me to import for you from Mexico City a sheaf of almond flowers, which implies, as any flower dictionary will tell you, extreme jubilation. I sign myself your sincere servant, Joaquín Diego Sanchez Castillo Buentello, Vizconde de Mogollón."

Bob crushed the paper into a ball and flung it into the wastepaper basket. Even in jest, he thought, Joaquín cannot resist the subtle barb and the delicate reminder that he is lord of the Sabinas. I'll bet he'd be jubilated if I stayed away for seven days. He'd be hysterical with joy if I stayed away forever.

Unfastening the flower bouquet, he dropped the blossoms from his hotel window. A chair vendor and a beggar woman snatched up the roses and waved them at him with beaming smiles. He glared at them, went into the bathroom, and turned on the shower. He was still so angry with Joaquín while he undressed and bathed and dressed again that there was no room in his mind for the tearful Candelaria.

He ate his dinner in the hotel dining room. It was a family hotel known to tourists, where most of the guests had stayed so often through the years that familiar faces were the rule rather than the exception. The waiters were mostly Spaniards from Catalán, and their clicking speech was a harsh contrast to the soft Mexican singsong. There were few tables, and two men came to sit at Bob's. He knew them slightly. One worked at the Bolivian consulate and, in his spare time, wrote art plays which were never produced. The other was a wigmaker who had once visited Spain, and since then forbore neckties and affected lisping c's and rolled l's in his otherwise completely Mexican speech. He was much coveted by hostesses as a parlor monologist.

The men's unconscious sophistication amused Bob. To him they symbolized Monterrey, that strange city of contrasts, which industry had transformed into a Texas suburb, and which had yet remained so essentially Mexican that it was hated and envied by the entire Republic.

The consular servant told them the story of his new play in vivid detail. It dealt with a man who shot his wife and then rushed from the theatre into the street, shrieking that he was an assassin and imploring the police to arrest him. "The difficulty," he admitted, "is that the novelty would disappear after the first performance. But," he brightened, "what realism, what an unexpected ending. Conceive of it—the entire audience arrested as witnesses to a murder. The thought intrigues me."

"In the real theatre," intoned the wigmaker, "the scenery should belong to the imagination, and the characters be concentrated in one performer. What need have I for anything but a chair and a glass of water to clear my throat? I raise my voice and the world attends me."

He pulled down his vest with a slight tug, carefully placed his feet so that one was drawn back and away from the other, dropped his left hand to his knee, and lifted his right in graceful gesture. After a small cough, he said loudly, "I shall now recite 'The Philosophy of the Libertine.' "

Chatter from the other tables was hushed. People turned and smiled at him, patting their hands in muted applause. Bob lit a cigarette as he prepared to listen, and relaxed in comfortable enjoyment.

The wigmaker began to speak, each word carefully formed in his mouth before escaping from his lips, his hand moving in rhythm to the meter like an orchestra director's batón.

> *What is drink? How can I speak*
> *To the curious amongst you?*
> *I cannot explain, because to life*
> *Drink is the hope of death.*
> *The bees in the flowers*
> *Drink the precious honey,*
> *And the sweet lovers drink light*
> *From each other's glances,*
> *Drink glory from their love ...*

The voice had found its monotone cadence and the sense of the words slipped away from Bob's mind. He found himself wondering if Joaquín, in his actor days, had ever entertained a hotel dining room with didactic verse. But Joaquín would not be contented with such a subject as this. He would prefer the more dramatic "Tearful Laughter" of Juan de Diós Peza, or the lugubrious, "Prayer for a Son Soon to be Executed," speaking the lines in solemn dignity falsified by the satiric laughter in his eyes.

And how Alejandro would have hated every grandiloquent syllable. Strange, Bob mused, Alejandro never cared much for literary Spanish. He knew Shakespeare better than *Don Quixote*, and the exploits of Robin Hood instead of Chucho el Roto's. He felt the same way about art and music, preferring Rousseau to Rivera, and Victor Herbert to Manuel Ponce. Of course his European background had much to do with his taste, but fundamentally Joaquín was much more Mexican than Alejandro. This comparison interested Bob, and it was with a self-conscious start that he realized the wigmaker was approaching the climax of his poem. The voice had deepened until it cascaded with resonant ripples from ceiling and walls, resolving into a rushing stream of words:

> *And if together we imbibe*
> *Without thought for what we were*
> *Nor tears for what we shall be,*
> *Raise your glass to us,*
> *For in that moment, we, too, are alive!*

The wigmaker rose, put his right hand on his heart, and bowed to the applause. He did not smile, and his eyes were closed, because he was an artist accepting his laurels, not an actor begging for reward.

Bob paid his bill while the consular servant made a small speech of appreciation for the poem, made his own small speech in his turn, and went out of the hotel into the busy night traffic of Monterrey, carrying with him a sense of complacency, for he had had a good dinner with pleasant companions, and it did not seem strange to him that what he now enjoyed would have bored him in the old days and forced him back into his private morass of bitterness.

He began to whistle softly under his breath, and winked at a flower girl and some *mariachi* singers who mistook him for a tourist. On the small Plaza Hidalgo, hemmed on three sides by glittering tourist hotels, and on the fourth by the municipal palace, he found his favorite *coche* driver.

After bits of Monterrey gossip, the man said as the horse trotted closer to the Terpsícore gates, "It is said in the city that Hidalgo is not happy with the return of the young Castillo. It is said that he is an individual without dignity or knowledge of valley affairs."

"That is gossip lies!" Bob flared. "The young Castillo has much talent."

He was amazed at his own furious reaction until he realized that Joaquín was, after all, a Sabinas man, and it was not permitted for an outlander to criticize the valley.

The anger was still in him as he paid off the coachman and walked through the deserted club rooms to the garden at the back. As usual, he paused to admire the scene. The thickly planted orange and lemon trees were heavy with fruit and flower. Rosebushes in full bloom formed an aromatic hedge around the tiled dance floor, and glass umbrellas, with spokes of amber and violet, served as shades for the electroliers. At the far end was a fountain, the water playing over cherry and turquoise lights.

Small tables were placed along the platform edge, and Bob made his way to his usual corner, skirting the dancers, who were mostly North Americans from the Colonia Mirador, or tourists. The few Mexicans were either married couples or men.

Bob's waiter appeared with a cup of coffee and a small cognac without waiting for an order. As he poured the steaming coffee he murmured polite joy at seeing Bob once more. "Nine months is a long time, Don Bob, to stay in that village. Or perhaps you have been visiting the City?"

"No. I stayed in Hidalgo."

"Ay, yes. And Don Alejandro so fine a young gentleman, and so young to die. The news is that his brother returned the same night of his death."

Bob shrugged without answering. He took a cigarette from his case and the waiter bent forward to light it.

"The news is also that the Sabinas is not pleased with the brother."

"So I have heard," Bob said dryly.

"The news is not true?"

"Is gossip ever true?"

"No, Don Bob. But we have a bit of news that is true. A new singer. She is magnificent. You will like her."

"I have heard. You will take her a note from me?"

"It is useless, Don Bob. For the young men, her eyes are cold, and her answer is always the same, no!"

Bob grinned and scribbled a note on the back of a menu. "Perhaps this time it will be yes. Take her this."

The waiter held the writing under the table lamp, peered at it, sighed, and said dolefully, "It is in English. I do not understand English."

"The note is to the singer, friend, not to you."

"Yes, Don Bob." The man sighed again, then brightened at the tip, and hurried away.

Bob sipped his coffee and looked about him. At the next table three young Mexicans were drinking beer and watching the dancers with expressionless faces. Beyond them was a group of North Americans. For a moment Bob thought he recognized one of the men, a blond with an oval-shaped head and good shoulders; then he realized that the man was merely a Texan type and let his attention wander to the bandstand.

The music stopped and the dancers returned to their various tables. The trumpeter rose and blew a fanfare. Then a woman's voice, low and husky, began singing from the tree shadows. The musicians played softly, and she came forward into the light. Her body was full and curved under the tight flowered dress. Heavy strands of gold beads hung about her short neck. Her round face lacked molding, but the large black eyes were slumberous under the well marked brows, and the black hair grew to a widow's peak on her forehead. The mouth was too wide, but the lips were full and red, and she moved them very little, allowing the throaty tones to flow from them.

She drips with sex, Bob thought objectively. Strange that I don't resent it, but it's as though I'd never known her.

The waiter came to his table, a puzzled expression in his eyes. "She wants to see you as soon as she finishes singing. I don't understand it, Don Bob."

Bob grinned. "You are too young for such mysteries. Bring me another cognac."

"Yes, Don Bob. And you are wanted on the telephone." He shook his head. "Has Hidalgo air a certain virility, perhaps?"

"I've read a book," Bob assured him solemnly, "on how to be attractive to women." He stepped through an opening in the hedge onto the grass so as not to disturb the singer and went into the house. He decided that it was Joaquín, who was calling him for a joke.

The telephone was in a small booth off the main lobby. He closed the glass door and lifted the receiver, giving his name in a bored voice for Joaquín's benefit.

A man said in English, "This is Harper Paschal. I'm sorry to bother you, Webster, but some friends came in from the States at the last minute. You know how it is. Don't wait for me. I may not get there at all."

Bob frowned. How did Paschal know that he was at the Terpsícore? Had Joaquín taken it upon himself to inform the superintendent that he was thinking of resigning? Bob clenched his narrow hand in suppressed anger.

He said coldly, "I'm sorry, Harper. I'm a bit confused. I didn't know you were to meet me here."

"What's the matter with you? We talked about it at dinner. Hey, which Bob Webster is this?"

"Why..." Bob held the receiver away from his ear, stared at it, and then replaced it. "I'm from Hidalgo. Who the hell did you think it was?"

"I thought it was queer you'd acquired a Mexican accent." Bob blinked at this. He had no idea his English had become tarnished with nine months of speaking nothing but Spanish. Harper was saying rapidly, "I asked for Bob Webster and with you there the waiter made a natural mistake. You shouldn't have such an ordinary name. Would you give the fellow I want a message for me? He's a blond, about your height, in a party with one woman and two other men. They're all from the States."

"Right. Listen, Harper, I want to see you in the morning."

"Important? It's Guadalupe Day. I was counting on some golf at the Country Club."

Bob was silent for so long that Paschal asked sharply, "Bob! Are you still there?"

"Yes, I . . . No, it's not that important. I can write it to you."

They said good-bye, and Bob leaned against the booth wall, staring blankly into nothingness. It had suddenly occurred to him why he had thought he recognized the blond American. We're brothers, he thought dazedly. Half brothers. It was myself I saw in him. Myself and . . .

For the first time in years the vision of the blond man in the swivel armchair saying, "Admit an Indian is a son of mine? Damn it, I'm a white man," no longer knifed him with pain. At the same time, as though it were a speaking film superimposed on another, he could hear Joaquín's bitter, "My father and I keep our distance, he the Montague and I the Capulet . . ."

The marked resemblance between himself and Joaquín was now so strong that he could not ignore it: both of them dominated through their mature years by a hatred of their fathers.

He began to laugh softly to himself, and it was then he realized that the old pain was gone. He opened his hand and looked down at its narrow length. A new lightness came into him, and something of Joaquín's swagger. It made no difference that the blond young man would never know he had a dark-haired brother. He opened the booth door.

In the garden the singer was finished and dancing had begun again. The blond Bob Webster had risen and was waiting for his partner to put out her cigarette when Bob reached them. The two men were of a height, with twin-shaped bodies, but the heads were so different that no one would ever recognize a resemblance between them.

Bob said quietly, "Mr. Webster? I have a message for you from Harper Paschal." As he gave it, he tried to listen objectively to his own voice, and heard with surprise the softening of the vowels and the faintly inflected syllables.

The blond man smiled, his blue eyes crinkling at the corners. "Have a drink with us?"

Bob's hand came up with an instinctive gesture. "Thank you," he said politely, and was confused when the other Bob Webster called a waiter. "Whiskey and soda? Brandy?"

It took a moment for Bob to remember that in the States, "Thank you" meant acceptance, not negation. He knew the singer was waiting for him, but he could not resist this little comedy. How Joaquín would enjoy this situation, he thought, and realized that Alejandro would have considered it bad taste. He shrugged, bowed to the woman, and sat down.

"Did we meet at Paschal's house? There were so many people..."

Bob hesitated for a moment; then, for the first time since his fifteenth birthday, he gave the name on his baptismal certifiate. "Ortega. Roberto Ortega. Your servant."

Webster introduced the others. The woman was married to one of the men. They were all spending the week-end in Monterrey. "I'm from San Antonio," Webster explained, "but I've been living in New York for the past twenty years and this southern vacation is the first chance I've had to get down here since I was a kid."

We're almost the same age, Bob thought. I'm probably about two years older. He sipped his cognac and listened to the group's delighted comments on Mexico's beauty.

"You speak such good English," the woman exclaimed. "Did you go to school in the States?"

"In many places," Bob answered blandly. "In the States, in Ireland, in Morocco, in Paris." It's true, he thought. An Irish jail is an education. A Morocco gambling casino, Yvonne in Paris, the war... they were all my schools.

The woman smiled at him, and the men seemed oddly impressed. He finished his cognac, bowed, murmured polite phrases, and walked quickly away toward the house and the singer's dressing room. The woman's shrill voice followed him, "Wasn't he exciting! And the aristocratic ones hardly ever come to these dancing places. I come down here a lot and I know."

Bob's mouth lifted in its slow sideways smile. Some lines from Alejandro's beloved Shakespeare floated through his mind:

> *Why bastard? wherefore base?*
> *When my dimensions are as well compact,*

My mind as generous, and my shape as true,
As honest madam's issue? ...
Now, gods, stand up for bastards!

Still smiling, he knocked on the dressing room door.

The singer opened it and stared at him with angry eyes. "It took you long enough to come," she said curtly and moved back to allow him to enter the small, stuffy room, the smell of grease paint heavy on the air. She wore a faded wrapper, and her feet were thrust into comfortable carpet slippers. A pot of coffee with two cups stood among the litter on the dressing table. She took a bottle of cognac from a drawer and glanced over her shoulder at him. "With or without coffee?"

"The coffee without the cognac."

Her eyebrows rose in surprised arcs as he relaxed on a straight chair. "You're not much like our father then."

"Your father, Sofía, not mine."

"Still the pride?" Her full lips tilted upwards at one corner.

"No—not pride. Just fact." He took the cup she offered him and looked down at it. "Do you know who's at one of the tables tonight? A blond man sitting in the right corner. Notice him the next time you go out to sing if he's still there."

"I know the one you mean. There's something familiar about him, but I couldn't place him."

"He's Bob Webster."

Her cup jerked in surprise and the hot coffee splashed out on her hand. She automatically wiped it against her hip. "You mean —him? This man's too young."

"Oh, not my honorable father. This is the son. What a charming family group we made: you singing, I at one table, he at another."

"Still bitter, aren't you, Berto?"

The old nickname made him grin. "No, Sofía. In the beginning—yes, I was bitter."

They were both silent. Bob remembered with slow clarity his mother's voice telling him that Ramón Ortega was father to Sofía but not to himself, and of how she had gone to work in the Webster house as a maid and had fallen in love with the blond young Robert Webster. "You are not of worthless blood like that Ortega. Go to your real father. Ask him to help you, to

make a fine gentleman of you. He is so good ... so good!" And
then she had died, and Bob had gone to Robert Webster. His
reception had cut into his pride, even though he knew that in
Texas, that in all the border States, the prejudice against the
border Indito is very strong—the Tejanos, who are neither Mexican nor North American, who speak a patois rather than a
language, who are in their way as illegitimate as Bob was in his.
And because of his wounded pride his only desire had been to
escape from the environment that bred him, to establish himself
as a man of position, as an individual whose blood was a pleasure
rather than a disgrace. So he had run away to Ireland with a
schoolmate, Ned Kelley. Ned came from an immigrant Irish
family which had come to the States after Ned's father was
killed in one of the Rebellions. The two boys had worked their
way across the ocean on a cattle boat, and the warm odor of a
barn still brought vivid recollections of that trip and Ned's
pleasant voice telling tales of Irish heroism against oppression.
Something in the stories fired Bob's imagination. He felt himself
a spiritual brother to the black-browed heroes. But the reality
disappointed him. In 1913, Ireland's battle was too spasmodic. It
lacked co-ordination, and leadership. The raids were individual
outbursts rather than a part of a planned campaign. Ned Kelley
was caught and hanged, and Bob spent a fearful night in a narrow
stone cell.

All of this flashed in pictures across his mind. He saw his
mother's narrow long hand, transparent from illness, on the pink
crocheted coverlet, his grandmother crouched in grief in a corner
of the room. Then came the picture of his father's office, and the
golden-oak swivel chair. Next the cattle boat. And finally Ned
Kelley's expression as he realized he was to be hanged.

Bob drew a deep breath, rose, and carefully put the cup down
on the dressing table. He said, "It used to be my ambition to
walk into that man's house and say, 'Look well at me, my father.
I am your son.' But now—tonight I had a cognac with my brother,
and when he asked me my name, I said, 'Ortega.' "

Sofía shrugged. "You were always a strange one, Berto. The
mother used to say, 'Some day you will be proud of your brother,
Sofía. He will be a great man—a famous man.' And now you are
what? A quarry foreman in a town no one ever heard of, and

me, I am the famous one." She lifted a large scrapbook from the top of her trunk and brought it to him.

He wanted to say to her, "I know about you, Sofía. For many years I have kept clippings of your career." But a feeling of remoteness from her and all that she represented kept him silent.

She flicked the open pages. "Look—papers from Cuba, Argentina, Chile, Colombia, Mexico City. And after this tour I go to Hollywood. They are starting to make films in Spanish out there. They want me to sing."

"I'm glad, Sofía . . . very happy for you."

"Eh, what do you care?" She replaced the book on the trunk with a soft bang. "I am no more your sister than he out there is your brother. Even our Spanish is different. You talk like these frontier men." She lit a cigarette and rested one hip against the dressing table. "Are you proud of me, Berto?"

"Of course, Sofía," he lied politely. "You have made a fine name for yourself."

Her laughter was harsh and without mirth. "In the old days you would not have been so polite. But I could see it in your face when you were looking at my clippings. When I was out there singing, I recognized you. I watched you walk out on my song."

"I was called to the telephone," he explained, embarrassed by the expression in her eyes.

"Perhaps. It doesn't matter. You've turned into a true Mexican. The night-club singer is very amusing to play with but not to have in one's family. Console yourself. We have been strangers for twenty years. We shall be strangers for twenty more. I would not have bothered you this time, but our grandmother left you an inheritance. She died not long after you ran away. I forgot the inheritance until I found the envelope in an old trunk two months ago. I had just signed the Hollywood contract. I was feeling generous. It cost me two hundred dollars to have detectives trace you."

He reddened slightly, took his checkbook from his pocket, and quickly wrote out a check. She held it loosely between her fingers, waving it back and forth to let it dry. "Ten years ago," she said thoughtfully, "this would have been a fortune."

"Ten years ago it was all the money I owned."

She examined him through the smoke of her cigarette and suddenly smiled. "What difference? Times die, like people."

"We have a proverb in the valley: The cactus fruit that has been pecked is the one that knows best about birds."

She nodded, pulled open a drawer of the dressing table, and took out a large envelope, stained and yellow with age, the flap fastened with heavy blobs of sealing wax. "Your inheritance, my brother. There's no money in it. The old woman had to swear that to keep me from tearing it open."

He took it and rose. "Well, Sofía, end of the road?"

"I think so. There is nothing between us." She moved her hand in a gesture of finality.

He nodded and looked at the long narrow hand. "We have the same hands, Sofía. Our mother had them. That is between us."

"No proverbs for that?"

"Only the old one: When you talk, be friends. When you act, be enemies."

"It is a good proverb." She came to him suddenly and laid her palms flat against his chest. "I like you, Berto. For a long time I have hated you because you ran away from us. But the poet has written, 'It is just that man should seek his destiny in the blood of the coming morning.' You see, I have my proverbs, too." She stepped away from him and extended her hand.

He held it for a moment between both of his, and then bowed and kissed the long fingers.

"Yes," she said gravely, "you are very changed, Berto. But I think the proverb of my own invention is best. Times die, Berto. Times die. Good night. Go with God."

He paid his bill, went out through the building and the front garden to the street. At first he started to hail a passing taxi, but decided against it and walked slowly along Balderas Street toward the center of town. He pulled his watch from his pocket and looked at it. The hands pointed to one-fifteen. He thought, it is already Guadalupe Day.

He had reached the Purisima Plaza with the towered Purisima church facing it. On impulse he went up to the big doors and pushed them open. Inside, the darkness was punctuated by votive candles in front of the various shrines, and there was a mist of light over the main altar. People filled the pews, and organ music floated from the choir loft. The priest in his white and gold

robes was intoning the Vexilla Regis for the night adoration.
Incense hung like invisible smoke in the air.

Bob moved quietly down the center aisle and turned to the
left where was hung a large lithograph of Our Blessed Lady of
Guadalupe, the patron saint of Mexico. He lit an adoration taper
and dropped some coins in the candle box. Then he sat down in
a near-by pew, and relaxed to allow the beauty of the service to
filter through him.

The choir boys, their voices sweet and thin, began to sing a
Guadalupe hymn:

> *Oh, María,*
> *Blessed Mother,*
> *Dear consolation of man.*
> *Aid me,*
> *Guide me,*
> *To the celestial land.*

The words sank into him and he sat on, not thinking, little
pictures flashing through his mind of his mother, his grandmother, Sofía as a chubby little girl, his drunken stepfather, his
own father, Ned Kelley, Yvonne, Tommy Eaton—all the people
who had made up his life in that other time, the time that was
now dead. And it was as though they were pictures that belonged
to another person, a person he had once known but now no
longer knew. I'll change my name, he thought, back to Ortega.
The valley will like that. They could never pronounce my
Yanqui name. He put his palm against his face in the pale darkness as though he were meeting a new person, and merging into
that person, and becoming that person. Then he rose and walked
tranquilly back to his hotel.

In his room he sat on the edge of the bed and examined the
envelope Sofía had given him. Written on it in a spidery, beautiful hand, the capital letters shaded on the down strokes, was
the name: Roberto Ortega Menéndez, and a date: July 7, 1913.

Two months after I ran away, he thought, and five months
after Joaquín ran away. He felt a flash of resentment against the
chain of fate that seemed to bind him to the young Castillo, and
he quickly slid his finger under the envelope flap and shook the
contents out on the counterpane. There were eight folded sheets

of paper. One was his own birth certificate. Then there was his mother's marriage license to Ramón Ortega, and her birth certificate. He picked up a letter in the handwriting he recognized as his grandmother's:

"My dear eldest child of my only daughter," he read. "I desire you to read all the other papers before this one." He grinned. How like Tía Magdalena, he thought. Even after death the grandmother has to command. But he obediently put the letter down and lifted the other documents. Three of them were old and fragile, streaked with dirt and already tearing at the folds. He opened them carefully. They were all written by hand in Spanish. The one dated June 12, 1844, was by a priest from the parish of Our Lady of Guadalupe in the City of Monterrey, State of Nuevo León. It said that he had joined in marriage the woman Isabela Castillo and the man Mariano Menéndez, both of the Huachichil tribe from the mountains west of Monterrey. The next, dated March 23, 1845, was written by the same priest, in which he inscribed the baptism of a male infant, Daniel Menéndez Castillo, parents, Mariano Menéndez and Isabela Castillo de Menéndez, a couple wedded in the sight of God, Church, and man. The third paper was a letter signed by Isabela Castillo, with a covering note by the same priest, which read:

"Brought to the deathbed of this woman, Isabela Castillo de Menéndez, I have listened to her confession, and swear that to the best of my knowledge, coming as it does from the lips of a woman soon to face the judgment of God, it is true; and I swear that this knowledge was given to me under the seal of the confessional and is therefore sacred to myself alone."

Bob slowly began to read the letter.

"August 27, 1845. My dear son, Daniel Menéndez Castillo, his child, and the child of his child, greetings. Know then, that on November 8, 1842, my esteemed father, Don Diego Castillo Tejada died, leaving to me, his oldest child, the Castillo properties and wealth, and also the care of my young brother Fausto (may the saints curse his name forever), who was to carry the title of Duque de Huachichil until I married and a son was born to me, at which time the title would pass to my son. All of this was free knowledge, and many men of good family loved me. My brother Fausto, seeing this, grew afraid for his own future, and in his evil arranged with the Huachichil warriors to make a raid upon my carriage and dispose of me, so that the blame would come to them, and the Castillo estate and titles to himself and his heirs forever. For this service he paid the Huachichil warriors the sum of five thousand pesos in gold coin. I was brought to these mountains, and my brother Fausto (may he burn forever in the devil's mouth) was told by the warrior Mariano Menéndez that I, in my Castillo pride, had suicided myself. This was done at my request, for I planned to marry the Indian Mariano Menéndez, and when my son was grown to send him to the house of my brother and demand what was his. My brother Fausto (may he eat his hands in eternal agony) has the Castillo pride of the pure strain within him, even as I have, and this is my revenge: that an Indian shall be true heir to the Castillo title and estate.

"That these facts are true I swear by the Blue Robe of the Blessed Virgin, by the Sacred Ribs of Christ, and by the Castillo name.

"But God has willed for me to die, and so I order you, my son, and through you, your children, to do that for me which I cannot do. I embrace you and give to you the blessing and duty of your signed mother who commands you to obedience. Isabela Castillo de Menéndez."

Bob sat for a long time, the letter dangling from his fingers. Then he examined the remaining paper. It was the marriage certificate of Daniel Menéndez to Jovita Chávez. And now he again picked up his grandmother's letter.

"As you well know, my Berto, in 1871 I married Daniel Menéndez, known on the frontier as *El Caballo Blanco*. Many times when drunk he would tell me the story of his great inheritance and swear that he would never claim it until he could go as a grand señor and not as a begging Indian. For this reason, he said, he became a bandit, so as to gain much gold and jewels. But Daniel was a man of many whims, and he could never save the treasure he robbed, but would spend it on fine clothes, or silver encrusted saddles, or sweet wines, or pretty women. None of this I minded save the women. But in my jealousy I betrayed him, and the barbarians shot him, and I weeping in my house for my sin. And when my child was born, a woman and in poverty, I did not tell her of her inheritance because I prayed to the Blessed Guadalupe that Rosa in her turn would marry and have a fine son and that he should gain much wealth and go back in dignity to claim that which was his. My prayers have been answered. You are Rosa's true son and eldest child, and although your father did not take her in wedlock, the inheritance passes to you through her.

As you know I was stern with your youth, teaching you fine manners and reverence for your grandfather and love for the valley west from Saddle Mountain that is your own. God's blessings be upon you, and the devotion of your signed grandmother who embraces you. Jovita Chávez de Menéndez."

Bob lit a cigarette and smoked it without thinking of it, his eyes following the automatic up-and-down movement of his hand. The voice of Joaquín was a bell in his ears: "It would show, I think, in the hands. They are the mark of the family Castillo... the faces are different, but the hands are all the same."

Bob saw again in his imagination the long narrow hand of his mother on the pink coverlet as she lay dying, Sofía's hands, his own. It was true. They were all the same, the little finger almost as long as the third. The Castillo hands.

His eyes wandered to the bed, and he saw his name written on the envelope. My grandmother inscribed it wrong, he thought dazedly. It should be Roberto Ortega Menéndez y Castillo. That is the way Don Saturnino would write it, for the Castillo name must not be lost. And the title: Vizconde de Mogollón, some day to be Duque de Huachichil. No, that's wrong. Don Saturnino doesn't count. Whether he's alive or dead, it makes no difference. With my grandfather dead, I am the Duque de Huachichil. He tilted his head to one side and began to laugh. What was it that woman said this evening? "And the aristocratic ones hardly ever come to these dancing places." His laughter ripened until it filled the room. He vaguely realized that it had an hysterical edge to it, but he made no effort to fight it. "Now, gods," he cried aloud in English, "stand up for bastards!"

He fell backwards across the bed still laughing. "Damn you, Joaquín," he shouted, "I'm the Castillo! Do you hear me? And the Sabinas is mine! Try to make me leave now, if you can. You're the one to go, not me. The Sabinas is mine!"

He rolled over and buried his face in one of the fat white pillows. María, he thought. María. If you had lived you would have been a duchess, my beautiful, golden María. Oh, María, why did you kill yourself when I loved you so, María? His clenched hand hit against the pillow, and for the first time since her death the channels of his grief were opened, and he began to cry with the desperate heartbreaking sobs of a child in a dark and lonely place.

On the train back to Hidalgo he refused to play *Tresillo*. "There are thoughts in my mind," he explained.

The porter nodded, and said to the conductor and brakeman, "The señor is a man of learning. To such ones thoughts are important."

With many bows they left him alone, and he looked out of the window at the passing landscape. I will tell them this evening, he thought. Do it and be done with it. I wonder if Don Saturnino will be pleased? He implied yesterday that he wished I were his heir. But the Indian blood . . . Does he like me more than he hates Indian blood? Will he agree to stay on in the valley? I want him to stay. Even if I weren't fond of him, for Alejandro's sake I want him to stay. I wonder what I would have done if Alejandro had been still alive. Would I have told them, and taken the valley away from Alejandro? But it is a duty on me from Isabela Castillo. "And so I order you, my son, and through you your children, to do that for me which I cannot do." I don't think Alejandro would have minded, really. He never had a deep affection for the valley. But Joaquín . . . What will Joaquín do? Will he be grateful for his release from valley obligations? If he chooses to stay, will I insist that he leave? Joaquín can be a dangerous enemy, I think. But out of the valley who cares for enemies? Out of the valley, who cares for anything?

He pressed his head against the window glass and watched the desert landscape whirl past, the green cactus, and the brown *yuca* standing with etched sharpness against the yellow ground and the distant gray mountains.

To his surprise the train jolted to a stop not long after passing Abasolo, but before entering the Hidalgo curve. Joaquín, dressed all in brown today, the gold embroidery heavy on hat and jacket, thrust his head in through the door.

"*Hola, joven*," he cried jovially. "For you this is the end of the line."

"What the devil . . ."

"Behold him," Joaquín mocked. "I come to save his life and he

calls on the Devil." He said to the porter. "Fetch the bag of the
señor. Come, Bob, the words will pour out of my mouth once
we are safe in the hills."

He took the bag, and was giving quick instructions to the train-
men to return to Monterrey as Bob stepped from the pullman.
Tethered to a near-by thorn bush were Joaquín's great black
and his own white horse. Joaquín fastened the suitcase to the
back of his saddle while Bob mounted. In a moment the two
men were cantering easily across the fields toward the eastern
mountains.

"What the devil..." Bob began again.

Joaquín shook his head. "A bit monotonous. Remember, a dry
weed needs water, and I fancy myself as a watering pot."

"And I the dry weed, is that it?"

The gold-embroidered shoulders lifted in a quick shrug. "Very
dry, and like to split in two. You are in trouble, friend. Did you
forget that women and hogs cannot be rounded up?"

Bob pulled his horse to a halt. "I've said it twice and I'll say it
again: What the devil are you talking about?"

"Candelaria, friend. One Candelaria Carvajal, a woman of dark
loveliness. You should quote the poet, 'Her beauty was ordained
to be my scaffold.'"

His lips trembling with anger, Bob said through clenched
teeth, "I don't see that Candelaria is any of your affair."

"I know." Joaquín put his arm across the pommel and rested
his weight on it. "But she belongs to my people, Bob. And what
touches them, affects me." His eyes, under the shadow of the hat
brim, were sombre and stern. "Actually I have no authority. The
Castillo power has been dead since the days of the Great Revolution. But there is a quality of the heart—I don't know how to
explain it to you. Let me put it this way: my ancestors for over
three hundred years have ruled this valley. In the beginning they
had the power of life and death. Their word was law. The
viceroy in Mexico City, if he ruled unwisely, had to return to
face a court of inquiry. But up here the Castillos recognized one
God, their own, and one king, themselves. And in spite of revo-
lutions and the breaking away from Spain, and later from Maximilian, the outside world had little to do with the Castillo power
in the Sabinas. The Great Revolution changed all that. It was
time to change. It was not good for one man to say, 'This one

shall be rich and that one poor—this one shall live and that one die.'

"I believed in the Great Revolution and I fought in it. But no matter what socialistic theories breed in my mind, three hundred years of authority breed in my bones. And as long as I have a voice to speak, a gun at my hip, and a *reata* on my saddle, no harm shall come to my people through anyone."

Bob's hand went down to the rope tied loosely on his own saddle. "You accuse me of evil then?"

"You know the answer better than I."

Bob unfastened the rope with hands that were cold and steady. He knotted the slip noose in one end of the tightly twisted length of hemp. Joaquín's *reata* was woven of horse's hair bound with silver. It was heavier, but not so pliable. Bob was silent while Joaquín unfastened the suitcase and dropped it to the ground; then both backed their horses. Their faces were white, their lips set. Joaquín lifted his hand to push his hat back between his shoulders, but when Bob tossed his aside, Joaquín did likewise.

There was a space of fifty feet between them. To each the only reality was the pale compressed face of the other, and they were blind to the sweeping fields, the gray mountains, the arch of blue sky studded with white clouds. The yellow sun poured heat over their heads and shoulders. Some vultures, scenting death, hovered in wide circling turns above them.

They bent across their saddles, the ropes with the extending noose, whistling above their heads. Their heels dug into the flanks of their horses, and they rode at each other at full gallop. The ropes snaked through the air. Horsehair hit Bob's shoulder, hemp Joaquín's saddle, and the animals swept them past to safety. Both reined in tightly, forcing their horses to make a rearing turn. Yellow sand spurted in little clouds around them. Again they dashed towards each other, and again the ropes missed.

On the third pass, Joaquín's noose dropped over Bob's head and fastened around his throat. The horsehair burned like dry ice. He dropped his rope and clutched at the *reata* with both hands to keep from strangling. Joaquín whirled his horse, and the quick pull jerked Bob from the saddle to the ground. The great black dashed forward, and Bob stumbled to his knees, tearing through cactus and thorn bushes. The noose at his throat was tighter than his hand strength. His face twisted with pain, his eyes swam in darkness sparked with red and yellow lights. Loud hammers pounded on his eardrums. Whiteness flared. Silence.

For some reason his lids were too heavy to open, and there was a pain in his throat. He realized vaguely that he had a hand, but he did not know how to move it. Something wet and cool filled his mouth, and trickled past the pain, easing it. Somewhere, far off, a voice was speaking, but the words were a melody of sound and made no sense. Again the wetness flowed into his mouth, and this time his lips reached for what he knew was water. The distant words slid out of melody into comprehension. "Slowly. Slowly." He tried to lift his lids. A faint crack of light fluttered against his eyeballs, and he saw Joaquín, strained and tense, bending over him.

Bob tried to speak, but Joaquín shook his head. "It was the horse. He felt the weight on the rope and turned for the pull. He probably thought you were a calf to be branded."

Bob tried to grin before he remembered that he and Joaquín had just had a rope duel, about something, about... He shut his eyes and tried to concentrate—to push out the pain in his throat and allow thought to come in. "Candelaria," he whispered.

"She's in Hidalgo, Bob."

"Berto," Bob muttered. "Roberto. I'm not..." The Spanish syllables, although liquid and soft, pushed against the pain and enlarged it. He was floating into stillness again. Once more the cantine was tilted against his lips, the water, this time, laced with brandy. The liquid fired his veins and gave him new strength. He gasped, "What were we fighting about?"

Joaquín sighed and sat back on his heels. He lighted a cigarette, slipped it between's Bob's lips, and lit another for himself.

"It's all right to get tired of a woman," he said slowly, "even an Indito woman, but to give her to another man for wife... I understand," he added quickly. "No woman should despise a good husband. So says half the village and most of the quarry women, for Candelaria is too beautiful to have them on her side."

"Too beautiful," Bob repeated, seizing the words and forgetting the speech. "María was too beautiful."

"Not María, Bob. Candelaria. María is dead."

"I know." Bob opened his eyes wide and looked almost pleadingly at the brown and gold figure. "I killed her."

"What?" Joaquín stiffened with surprise.

Bob pulled the words through the pain one by one. "If I had gone to see her that night— She was alone—Alejandro dead—but I wanted no scandal—because of Alejandro." He paused for a deeper breath. "Next morning she—suicide. I could prevent— María." He shut his eyes again.

Joaquín said gently. "She fell from the cliffs, Bob. She didn't suicide herself."

"That's the tale for the village—I know better—she belonged to Alejandro—my beautiful María."

Joaquín rose abruptly, flicked away his cigarette, and walked over to the horses. He ran his hand down the quivering velvety nose of his black. "So that's why my father had her buried next to Alejandro, brought her portrait from the ranch," he said dully. "He knew the truth, but he would not tell me. And I, too, loved Alejandro." He rubbed his cheek against the horse's cheek while Bob pulled himself to a sitting position.

"Do you have more—brandy?"

Joaquín took his silver flask from his hip pocket and brought it to Bob, who tilted it against his mouth. He pulled the back of his hand across his lips. "That tasted good. I've been saying a lot of stuff, I think. My brain doesn't work right."

"No matter. How is your throat?"

"Better. It hurts. You nearly strangled me."

"I'm sorry. I was angry. Tía has been lecturing me on my Castillo duty since last night. But now that I am free of her influence my reason tells me that you are right, of course. Hilario will make Candelaria a good husband."

"Husband?" This brought Bob to his feet in astonishment. "You mean Candelaria wants to get married? But she never— why didn't she tell me about this?"

Joaquín blinked at him. "No, she doesn't want to get married. It's you who want her to marry. Half the village agrees with you, and the other half agrees with Tía Magdalena in thinking you cruel and inhuman. I am supposed to belong to Tía's group. My father naturally belongs to the other half. If Tía warned the village of a flood, my father would say it was merely a gentle stream."

Bob felt lost in this swirl of words. "Slowly, Joaquín, slowly. Begin at the beginning."

"Candelaria came to me in tears yesterday and insisted on sending you the flowers. Did you receive them?"

"Yes, but they didn't make sense."

"And I thought my dictated letter a masterpiece of clarity. No matter. She was crying so desperately I took her to Tía Magdalena, who is, you understand, my secret wisdom. But Tía already knew about it. It seems that an Indito widower with four children, one Hilario Campos, came to you and asked for Candelaria's hand in marriage, her father being agreeable. You consented, but told him they must marry within seven days. And Candelaria, whose life is in your hands, is broken-hearted over your decision."

Bob shut his eyes, opened them, lifted the flask of brandy and took another and longer drink. "I—this makes no sense. Hilario came and asked me something—I wasn't paying any attention—I thought he wanted to take a short vacation—that's why I said seven days. Candelaria wasn't even in my mind."

Joaquín put up his hand to hide a grin. He managed to control his laughter and said solemnly, "But you gave your word. What is done cannot be undone."

"The hell it can't," Bob snapped in English. "If that fool thinks I'll marry Candelaria off to him..."

"Quietly, quietly, friend. A woman and a guitar are dependent on who plays them, and if Hilario is wise he will remember that a wild mare hates the stable, meaning that an unwilling woman is no fit wife."

Bob stumbled toward his horse. "I'll tell Hilario Campos to find him another mother for his four progeny."

"As you say," Joaquín murmured. "The sweetheart of the student is no wife for the professor. But unfortunately, Bob, you gave him your promise."

"I told him he could go on a vacation."

"But he understood it differently. What may be thick chocolate to you is clear water to him."

Bob turned away and sat down, resting his head in his hands. "This—this makes no sense to me." The pain in his throat had abated, but the skin on his neck was raw and tender from the rope's burn. He touched it lightly with his fingers.

Joaquín said, "It makes very good sense, now that you are leaving the valley. You can't take Candelaria with you, and it is only right that you should leave her settled with a good husband. If we present the matter to her and the valley—and Tía Magdalena —in that light, who can complain? Candelaria is a sensible girl. Better a present husband than an absent lover."

"Leaving the valley?" Bob repeated blankly.

"Well, aren't you? That's what you said yesterday you were going to do."

"Leave my valley? These mountains and that sky and this earth? This valley that is so newly mine?"

"So!" Joaquín chuckled and struck his leg with the tip of his silver-wrapped riding crop. "I thought when the time came you would change your mind. And even if you had gone the valley music would have sung in your ears." He lifted his head and on his face there was a look of listening. "The wind plays it in the harps of the *yucas*. And the mountains grind it from their stone organs. The white clouds carry the melody against the counterpoint of deep blue sky; and the flowers: the scarlet cactus blossom, the purple wine cups, the yellow flowering thorn, the gray sage and the white hanacahuita—all of them add their harmonics. It is a great symphony that is played here. One night when I was a guide, I heard it. How it boomed in me, with the added drums of Saddle Mountain and the Prow. It has a siren motif, to call you always home." His beautiful voice slid into silence.

Bob said, after a moment, "So that's why you came back."

"Yes. I never meant to stay. I knew my father didn't want me to stay. Why should he? In his book I was dead. But he was wrong. I lived. It was Alejandro who was dead. And Castillo land needed a Castillo heir."

Bob's hand went to his coat pocket, his palm flat against the bulk of the paper-filled envelope. "Suppose there had been another son. Would you have stayed?"

"No. How could I? I was an exile who had broken his bond." Joaquín rested one booted foot on a flat stone, and swung the crop in a slow arc above the square cut toe. "My father made that very clear when he sent me away before."

"But Alejandro said you ran away."

"A pretty fable. Alejandro's only wisdom was our father's mind. But he was not my wisdom. I would not join the Federal troops and get me a pretty uniform covered with gold medals. He told me I was no true Castillo. It was not proper for one of our House to agree with the Revolutionary party that all men are created equal, and an Indito is as good as a creole. So he told me my name would have the word 'Dead' written after it, and banished me from the Sabinas, and put Alejandro in my place as the young Castillo."

This is the answer to all my questions, Bob thought. Don Saturnino would never accept my Indian blood. Never. At the same time he felt an almost sick relief at the knowledge that Joaquín was not responsible for Alejandro's unhappiness and death. He listened in silence to Joaquín's words.

"Have you ever thought how lucky Alejandro was? He had everything: a great name, great wealth, a beautiful woman, a fine friend..." the crop swung out toward Bob and dropped again, "and all his illusions." He gave a half chuckle deep in his throat. "So lucky—the little Alejandro. I never saw him grown, you know. When I was recovering from the broken leg I used to watch for him from Chela's window, but he never came by. I saw you, and Evita, but never Alejandro or María. Was she really more beautiful than Candelaria?"

"How can I describe her? I loved her. The portrait above the mantelpiece in your house is very good."

"I thought that was just the artist's imagination."

"I have some photographs of her and of Alejandro, too, if you'd like to see them."

"Would you show them to me?" The eagerness in Joaquín's voice startled Bob. "My father destroyed all those in the house, and naturally I could not ask Evita, and she in mourning."

"Of course." Bob rose and tried to brush the dust from his clothes. Joaquín moistened his handkerchief with water from the cantine and offered it to him. "You'd better wash your face."

Bob loosened his collar to free his burned neck from the contact. Joaquín peered at it and clicked his tongue. "How are we going to explain that to Tía Magdalena?"

"I don't know. You're the one with words. You think of a plausible tale."

"Umm...let me see. You scraped it with your razor."

"All the way around my neck? Nonsense."

"I know. A barber burned it with a hot towel."

"Do you think she'll believe that?"

"No. But it sounds very grand. Let us now go and face the eagle witch."

They entered Hidalgo by way of the River Road and trotted up the deserted Street of the Hidden Water. "All the world is waiting for you at the station save Tía and Candelaria, who are mourning in your house. I told them I'd take you off the train," Joaquín explained as they fastened their horses to the hitching rings fastened into the house wall. Bob knocked on the door and Tía opened it. Her eyes moved rapidly over him and ended at his neck.

"Hm!" she said. "It would appear that Joaquín won the duel." Her glance snapped past Bob to the young Castillo. "Shame should be on your head, and you the finest thrower of the noose in the two valleys."

While the two men were looking guiltily at each other, she called sharply, "Candelaria!"

The girl appeared like a shadow, her *rebozo* pulled low over her forehead and covering her nose and mouth.

"Run to Doña Nimfa's and ask her for ten *centavitos* of quince seed ointment."

"Yes, Tía." She slid past Bob without glancing at him, and hurried around the corner of the house.

Tía stamped her foot. "Enter, enter. Is all the world to know you have been fighting?"

"But, Tía, all the world is gone to the sta..."

"Silence, Don Joaquín. And you, Don Bob, I have words to speak to you."

Joaquín said quickly, "It was all a mistake, Tía. He did not heed the words, and thought Hilario was asking for a vacation."

"So?" Tía's brows rose, and then her face crinkled into a smile. "After ten years with me, and still a stupid one." She followed them into the patio.

While Joaquín lounged on the tiled ledge of the lily pool, and Bob stretched out in the hammock, she fetched them a bottle of tequila.

"The French brandy, Tía. I owe Joaquín a bottle, anyway."

"Brandy is for common men. But for warriors, tequila!"

They laughed at her and drank the fiery liquor, Bob grimacing with pain as it slid down his bruised throat.

"In the matter of Candelaria," she said thoughtfully, "explain it again, Don Joaquín."

He did, with much wealth of detail which Bob had not included in his own account. Bob smiled as he listened. He decided that the fight and Joaquín's victory had freed a hidden bitterness in this man who was so like—not quicksilver, not today, in that gold-embroidered brown *charro*, but quickgold. And with the mocking laughter gone from the black eyes he had in him an Alejandro quality of gentleness and pleasure over simple things. But Alejandro, Bob thought, could never have made that speech on valley music. The Sabinas had never owned Alejandro. If María had not lived on the river bank, he would probably have passed his days in Paris, returning only for brief duty visits. No, to Alejandro the valley was a part of his inheritance, but it was not his heritage.

And Bob knew that he himself could never have made that speech. He might have felt it—indeed, he did feel it, but such words demand a deep love and a deeper understanding. To him this valley was home. Here he had found his dignity of being and his place in an ordered society. To him it meant security. But to Joaquín it was—what?

A passage in a travel book he had once read returned to him: "Mexicans have a peculiar quality of patriotism. Other nations regard their country as sacred ground, as do, for example, the English: *'this scept'red isle, this earth of majesty, . . . this other Eden, . . .'* Not so the Mexican. To him his country is at once his mother and his mistress, his child and his wife. His country is a woman, and its symbol is a woman—the brown Virgin of Guadalupe . . ."

Alejandro, Bob mused, had María, and I have the memory of María and the shy placidity of Candelaria. But Joaquín is in love with the Sabinas. How can I take it away from him? For I know what it is to lose the well beloved.

Joaquín's voice broke into his thoughts, "I have a plan regarding this great promise. You, Tía, will sacrifice tonight to the old gods. I will purchase a fine cock for you from the father-in-law of Pepe Gonzalez, that great breeder of magnificent birds—and the signs will say that Candelaria will bring sorrow meal to the house of Hilario."

"Eh," said Tía, "and suppose the sleeping gods prefer Hilario?

He is of the Inditos, and Don Bob with his *Yanqui* name..."

"I meant to tell you," Bob said lazily, "I'm taking my mother's name. After ten years of struggling with Webster I have decided to change to..." He paused. Now is the time to say it, he thought: Ortega Menéndez y Castillo. He saw Joaquín's face, the brilliant eyes at rest after the long months of mockery. His tongue said, "Ortega," and did not go beyond the solitary noun.

"Ay..." Tía sighed with satisfaction. "The Guadalupe will like that. And on her day, too. There will be much planting in the valley this year, for there is no doubt that the crops will be good with the Guadalupe pleased. You, Joaquinito, see that you put in a large field of oats and barley."

"As you say, Tía," he agreed politely. "And you will sacrifice the cock?"

"Naturally. And the old gods, too, will like the name Ortega. Already I can feel their laughter shaking in my bones. You, Candelaria, stop hiding in the hallway."

"Yes, Tía." The girl came toward them, handed Tía the small jar of quince ointment, and crouched beside the hammock. Bob dropped his hand on her soft hair.

"Tía," he said, too contented to move, "Don Joaquín wants to see the contents of the green box in my wardrobe."

The old woman gently kicked the girl with her foot. "Fetch it while I bandage this sore throat."

As the girl came to her feet, the tolling bells dropped a blanket of sound over the village. "The church festival begins," she whispered. "Hilario will be there—and all his children." Her eyes turned with dark agony to Bob's face.

"What of it?" he asked, squirming away from Tía's competent but rough hands. "What is Hilario—and all his children—to you, little one?"

Light burned within the globe of her head. Both hands covered her mouth to quiet the happiness, and when she went into the house to fetch the box, she was no longer a shadow moving but a dancing girl.

Bob opened the green lid, rummaged beneath the photographs, and pulled out the Sofía clippings. As he tore them between his fingers, he thought, you were very right, Sofía. Times die, but new times are also born, and there is a birthing in this patio this afternoon.

He was so intent on the shredded paper that he did not see the relief in Tía's eyes. So, she thought, taking the box from him and handing it to Joaquín, that wicked Sofía is gone from his life at last, and he is no longer in danger of going to a life beyond the mountains.

Joaquín looked at the pictures in silence, holding them so that Candelaria's shy curiosity could also be satisfied. Bob, free of Tía's ministrations, went in to bathe and change his clothes.

Through the bedroom window he could hear Joaquín and Tía speaking. Tía had murmured something about Alejandro, and Joaquín said, "My father loved him, I think, a little at the end."

"Perhaps," Tía sniffed, "but in all his life that old man has loved but three things: Castillo pride, the Castillo name, and the Castillo land."

Joaquín laughed suddenly. "Then he can never deny me as his true son, old woman, for do I not love the same three things?"

Tía laughed with him, and then called out, "Hurry, Don Bob. The festival cannot begin until you and Don Joaquín arrive to lead the entrance procession into the church."

"Just a moment," Bob answered her. He took the dirt-stained envelope from his discarded coat pocket, weighed it in his hand a moment. He was still not certain of his own desires. In his heart he knew that the Sabinas belonged to Joaquín, and yet the hated mockery was too newly gone to be lightly discounted. One more test, but what? Should he wait until they reached the Guadalupe ceremonies, and watch Joaquín's reaction to the beautiful pageant of the black-haired village beauty dressed in the star-dotted blue robe of the brown Virgin, with Gitanillo as Mexico at her feet?

Surely he already knew what Joaquín's reaction would be: a warm delight in the colorful symbolism. No, something more personal was needed to display the truth.

And then, as he looked through the window, he saw Joaquín fling out his hand in a theatrical gesture as he described to Candelaria the Guadalupe procession at the famous shrine outside of Mexico City. That gesture, assured and perfectly in tempo with his words, was strongly reminiscent of the wigmaker's monologue technique.

Bob, delighted with his own cleverness, called, "Joaquín! Say a poem for us."

"Not now, Don Bob," Tía protested. "The Guadalupe dances
..."

"In your own words cannot start until we arrive," he finished
quickly. "And if we are a little late, what matter? I am a sick
man today and must be humored. Recite a poem from your
actor's days, Joaquín."

The dark eyes, sensitive to sarcasm, turned to Bob's face. "But
I never recited poems, Bob."

"Not even 'Lament for a Son Soon to be Executed?'"

The veiled laughter in Bob's voice puzzled the three people in
the patio. Joaquín gave a small shrug. "Such poetry has never
amused me."

"Then do one that does amuse you."

"Don Bob ..." Tía began, but Bob waved her to silence with
his hand.

"I owe you a racing debt of a bottle of French cognac, but
you owe me something for this burn on my throat. And it
pleases me to ask for a poem. I don't know why you are all
staring at me so strangely. I like poetry, especially delivered in a
voice as beautiful as Joaquín's."

"Please the poor stubborn one," Tía sighed. She fitted her old
bones carefully into the softness of the hammock, and Candelaria
crouched beside her.

Joaquín laughed and pushed his hat back so that it dangled between his shoulders. He bent his head while he was choosing the
lines, and the sun drenched his brown shoulders and golden embroidery. At last he said, "These are some verses by Alfonso
Reyes called 'In Praise of My Land.' It is a play of words upon
a folksong."

He paused for a moment, and then the liquid syllables began
to flow in amber tones:

> *Scarlet poppy*
> *In the valley of your birth.*
> *If you are not in love,*
> *Fall in love with me.*
>
> *Here the red carnation is sleeping,*
> *And the jasmine builds a white tower.*
> *But this place is disdained by the thistle,*
> *Forever disdained by the laurel.*

An acolyte burns honey.
It is the orange in flower.
And also the amorous pomegranate—
Wine and blood—ruby and gold,
But it is you, I love,
Scarlet poppy.

At the foot of the leafy fig tree
Is spread a carpet of shade.
Here grow the courtesan roses,
Beloved of the shimmering humming birds,
Beloved of the gossamer butterflies.
But it is you who enchants me
With your opium amphora of dreams
In the valley of your birth.

When the day first appears,
And the hour of sleeping is over,
The locusts begin their singing,
And the air is loud with their music.
Then why, scarlet poppy, so frigid,
Or so pure, or so silent?
Why do you fill me with longing,
If you are not in love?

Are golden stars born of your chalice,
Your cradle of thought and tears?
You need no sonorous chanting.
It is your silence I hear.
I am enveloped within you
As your voiceless harmonics surround me,
Scarlet poppy of my land,
Fall in love with me.

As the deep, resonant tones faded into silence, Candelaria began to weep a little, moved by the lovely sound of words she could but dimly comprehend. Tía's smile was gentle as she stretched out her hand to Joaquín. He bent to kiss it, but Bob, watching the tableau, felt remote and alien. Joaquín's passionate tenderness for the Sabinas was too strong an emotion for Bob to parallel in his own lonely heart, and with the knowledge came the full realization of what he must do.

He went to the fireplace, knelt, and applied a match to the envelope. As he watched it burn he had the strange sensation that Alejandro was kneeling beside him, whispering words that were lost in the crackle of the blackening paper, and yet the words left an echo in his mind. "There are two sides to every coin, the side seen and the side unseen. And now, you, too, hold your great secret in Hidalgo."

Bob smiled at the fantasy, and went quickly into the patio. He said politely, "Shall we go, cousin?"

Joaquín's laughter was fresh and free. "The word is *compadre*, or twin, or even brother, not cousin."

Bob, pleased with his private jest, said firmly, "The word is cousin. I prefer it."

The brown shoulders shrugged. "As you say, stubborn one. Cousin. Another *tequilito* first?"

"Better to drink in the Casino after the festival," Tía said dryly. "And no coming home drunk, either of you, or Don Bob's throat will be swollen larger than his head."

They both grinned at her, linked arms, and walked—Bob, earth-solid and firm, Joaquín, air-light and arrogant—out of the patio.

The two women waited for a decent interval. Then they draped their shawls over their heads, and they, too, went to the church.

The patio, with its tiled pool, its roses in bloom, and its trees in fruit and in flower, was quiet in the golden light.

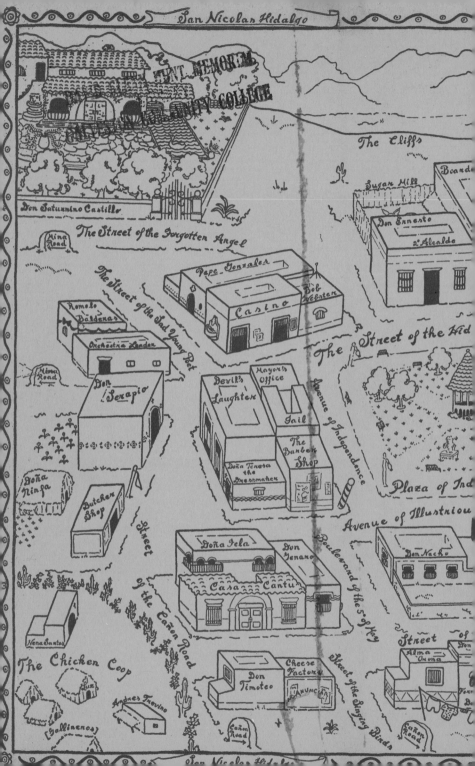